OF
LOVE
AND
LIFE

OF
LOVE
AND
LIFE

Three novels selected and condensed
by Reader's Digest

CONDENSED BOOKS DIVISION

The Reader's Digest Association Limited, London

With the exception of actual personages identified as such, the
characters and incidents in the fictional selections in this volume
are entirely the product of the authors' imaginations and have no
relation to any person or event in real life.

The Reader's Digest Association Limited
11 Westferry Circus, Canary Wharf, London E14 4HE

www.readersdigest.co.uk

ISBN 0-276-42627-4

CONTENTS

PRECIOUS TIME

ERICA JAMES

When Clara Costello and her young son Ned
set off on a round-Britain trip in their camper
van, the plan is to travel when and where the
fancy takes them. But when they arrive at the
small market town of Deaconsbridge, they
find themselves unexpectedly caught up in the
lives of some of the locals. And two people in
particular seem destined to get under Clara's
skin: Gabriel Liberty, a cranky old man who
has alienated his family, and Jonah his
extremely attractive son.

 **CHAPTER ONE**

CLARA COSTELLO'S FRIENDS were all of one opinion: that she was mad. Away with the fairies, crazy, doolally, Harpic, was just a sample of what they had to say about her. And just for the record, Harpic was her favourite: it was their cute way of saying she was clean round the bend.

They had reached this diagnosis six weeks ago, at the end of January, when she had announced she was giving up her job to take to the road in a secondhand camper-van with her four-year-old son.

Louise, her closest friend, had been disappointed that her gallivanting was to be restricted to the shores of Britain. 'You might at least have come up with something a little more adventurous,' she had said.

'That's because you and David are such dreadful snobs and want nothing but the most exotic postcards adorning your kitchen notice board,' Clara had responded good-humouredly.

'And what about Ned? You've only just got him into St Chad's.'

'I don't care. He's only just turned four and he'll learn more doing this than he would stuck in a boring classroom every day. And, anyway, school will be waiting for him in the autumn. If I don't do it now, I'll never do it. This chance will never come round again.'

The car in front braked sharply and Clara did likewise. The carrier bag of good-luck cards and presents she had been given during her farewell lunch slid forward on the passenger seat and dropped to the floor. She left them where they were.

What neither her friends nor her parents knew was that they were all partly to blame for this rush of blood to the head, as Louise had so charmingly referred to Clara's shift of perspective.

It had started in the new year, when Clara's parents had embarked on their trip of a lifetime to Australia to visit her brother Michael, his wife and their newborn baby. Kissing them goodbye at the airport, Clara had felt the sting of being left behind. It wasn't jealousy, more a case of acknowledging that it was too easy to let the glorious opportunities of life slip by without catching hold of them. For as long as she could remember her parents had talked about travelling the world, but it was only now, since her father had retired, that they felt they could justify such an extravagant trip. But what if one of them had fallen ill at the last minute or, heaven forbid, died? What would have been the point in all that waiting?

Pondering this in the busy airport, she had suddenly realised Ned was crying. His tearstained face was pressed against the smeared glass of the window as he tried in vain to see his grandparents for one last time. She held him tightly, wondering how she would ever fill the vast gap in his world created by Nanna and Granda's departure.

The following evening she had gone for dinner at Louise and David's. It was their usual fivesome: David and Louise, Guy and Moira, and herself. At around midnight, the time when Guy was most likely to start philosophising, once he'd progressed from wine to liquer, he had asked, 'If you only had a year left to live, what would you do?'

'I'd buy the house I'd always wanted,' Moira said, 'my dream home, and to hell with the expense.'

'So what's wrong with the one we've just bought?' Guy frowned. 'I thought it *was* your dream house.'

'It doesn't have a conservatory and the garden's too—'

'I know what I'd do,' David interrupted. 'I'd give up work and travel.'

'No, you wouldn't,' smiled Louise, 'you'd be bored to death within a week. You can't even go on a fortnight's holiday without reporting in.'

It was daft, drink-loaded, late-into-the-night talk, no one giving the question the thought it deserved. They were a group of thirty-some-things, with no children (apart from Clara) and no real responsibility to anyone other than themselves. But driving home later, Clara did give it some serious thought, and she knew exactly what she would do if her days were numbered. She would spend her time with Ned.

As a single mother working long hours as a production manager for an international pharmaceutical company, she was all too aware of how little time she had with her son. It was hard to admit, but somewhere along the line she had got her priorities wrong and had ended up squeezing Ned into her busy schedule when and how she could, giving him the tired, worn-out bits of herself rather than the best.

With her parents away, taking care of Ned had become even more of a juggling act. They had looked after Ned for her most days. They adored him and were as much a part of his life as she was. They would pick him up from nursery, drive him to the park where he could play on the swings and ride his bike, then take him home to give him his tea and generally spoil him. But since they had gone to Sydney, Clara had had to persuade Ned that he had to go to a new nursery school where he could stay in the after-school activity club until she came to collect him.

On his first morning his dark eyes had pleaded with her not to leave him. She stooped to kiss him goodbye and saw to her horror that, beneath his shiny fringe, his eyes were filling. 'It'll be OK, Ned,' she said. 'You'll have so much fun that the day will whiz by and before you know where you are I'll be here to take you home.'

He swallowed. 'I want to go home. I want Nanna and Granda.'

'Oh, Ned,' she whispered, 'I wish they were here too.' Then, all businesslike, she tilted up his chin and straightened the knot of his red and grey tie, although it was already perfectly straight.

Two bigger boys cruised by, and gave Ned a contemptuous once-over. One said, 'What's that in your hand?'

He smiled and proudly showed them what he was holding. It was a small plastic mermaid that had belonged to Clara when she was little and had gone everywhere with her. Now it went everywhere with Ned. 'It's old,' he said brightly, 'nearly as old my mummy.'

The boys drew in close for a better look. 'It's a doll,' one sneered. 'Dolls are for girls.' Sniggering, they sauntered away.

'Shall I look after Mermy today for you?' Clara asked, wanting to scoop Ned up and get him out of this place.

He shook his head, and pushed Mermy back into his pocket. With her heart fit to break she watched him square his shoulders ready to brave the day ahead.

That day, she had worried about Ned constantly. She didn't care a jot about the production of the latest infertility drug, nor about the rumours that, once again, Phoenix Pharmaceuticals USA were thinking of selling their UK division in Epsom, Surrey, to a French company. From their offices on the floor above her, Guy and David had emailed her with what was allegedly going on. Both suggested that she brush up on her French.

She left as early as she could and drove like the wind, dreading to find Ned in a crumpled heap of misery.

What she found was a tired-looking little boy sitting on the floor with a group of glassy-eyed children watching a cartoon on television. She was approached by one of his teachers who said she want a 'little word'.

'He's been all right, hasn't he?'

'Oh, he's an absolute delight,' the woman said. 'He's fitted in just fine. But goodness, what a disorganised little boy he is. A head full of clutter. And he never stops talking. But don't worry, I'm sure that between us we'll soon have him licked into shape.' There was laughter in her voice and Clara could see that she wasn't speaking unkindly. Even so, she could have slapped her face. For heaven's sake, he was four years old. What did she expect?

It was while she was driving home, with Ned almost asleep, his hands wrapped around Mermy, that Clara made her decision. It was now or never. She had until September to give Ned what he deserved. She would use the precious time available and give him her undivided attention and, hopefully, a little adventure into the bargain.

Ned was waiting for her when she arrived at St Chad's to take him home. The smile on his face as he raced across the wooden floor to meet her said it all. Just as this had been her last day at work, this had been his last day at school for what, for him, would probably seem like for ever. She picked him up and spun him round. Freedom beckoned.

More than 250 miles away, in Deaconsbridge, a small market town in the Peak District, a man sat brooding on an uncomfortable plastic chair. His name was Gabriel Liberty, and at the age of seventy-nine he believed he had earned the right not to be kept waiting.

He stretched out his stiff legs just as a shrill ring sounded, followed by an even shriller voice announcing that the doctor was ready for patient number sixteen. Gabriel hauled himself out of his chair. 'About time too,' he muttered.

Without bothering to knock, Gabriel entered Dr Cunningham's surgery. 'Humph, not seen you before,' he said, sitting down in front of the fake teak desk. Sitting behind it was a spry little Indian man in shirt-sleeves. His name was Dr Singh, if the engraved plaque in front of him was to be believed. 'What happened to Dr Cunningham?' asked Gabriel.

'He died.'

'Mm, that doesn't surprise me. He never did strike me as a good advertisement for his profession. Always looked overworked and underfed. What got him? Every doctor's weakness, the booze and fags?'

'No. A car crash in Portugal while he was on holiday with his family. Did you not read about it in the local paper?'

'I've no time for local rags. The Portuguese are the worst drivers on earth, aren't they? Mind you, your lot aren't much better. I was in Delhi once, never seen anything like it. Just passing through, are you?'

Dr Singh gave him a thin smile. 'No, I'm here for the duration.'

He turned and stared into his computer screen. 'I see it's some months since you last paid us a visit, Mr Liberty. So how is your arthritis?'

Gabriel waved his distorted large-knuckled hands. 'I'm giving them a rest, decided to ease up on the fiddly work of brain surgery. Truth is, I can't find the brains. Not round here anyway.'

Dr Singh rested his elbows on the desk. 'So what can I help you with?'

'I was wondering when you'd get to the point. It's this . . .'

Lunch wasn't proving as enjoyable as Gabriel had hoped it would be. For a start his usual table was occupied by a couple of day-trippers, and then there had been no steak and kidney pudding on the menu; he'd had to make do with egg and sausage instead. He didn't like having to make do. The day was not going well.

He was sitting in the Mermaid Café overlooking the square where Friday's market was in full flow. As pathetic as it was, coming into Deaconsbridge had become the high spot of his week. He came here every Friday to browse in the bookshop, to pick up the odd item of food—kippers for his supper that evening—and to go to the bank and the post office. And, of course, to have his lunch cooked for him.

He munched a mouthful of sausage and slowly wondered at the tedium of his life. Other than his son, Jonah, who did the bulk of his shopping for him, he rarely saw anyone during the week. And Jonah only ever made a fleeting visit. As for Caspar and Damson, well, if it hadn't been for Val's funeral, he might not have seen them at all these last couple of years.

It was strange, but since the death of his second wife eighteen months ago, he had thought more and more of Anastasia, his first wife. The memory of her had grown sharper as Val's faded. Anastasia had been the mother of his children and had died thirty-four years ago.

He had been away on business in Nigeria when it happened and had missed her death by twelve hours. He had arrived home to be told that he was the widowed father of three children—Anastasia had died giving birth to Jonah. Help was brought in to take care of the children, but nothing was ever the same again. As the years passed, it was clear that the children, in particular the twins, Caspar and Damson, who were growing wilder by the day, needed a mother. So he married Val. It was a union of convenience on both sides: he had needed someone to organise the house and his family so that he could devote himself to the running of Liberty Engineering, and Val had wanted the security that a husband could offer. They never deluded themselves that the arrangement was perfect, but he liked to think that it had worked well for the most part.

His plate had been cleared away and he was ready for his dessert now. He banged his spoon sharply on the table and caught the eye of a waitress. Fellow diners looked his way and he returned their stares disdainfully. The waitress came over with his bowl of apple pie and custard, just as she always did when he summoned her with his spoon.

'Everything all right?' she said.

'No,' he said, 'everything is far from all right. I'm at the wrong table and there was no steak and kidney on the menu.'

'We'll have to see if we can do better next Friday,' she said breezily. 'Tea or coffee?'

'You know I always have tea.'

He spent the rest of the afternoon doing his errands before awarding himself an hour of browsing in the bookshop.

On the way home, Gabriel realised that he had forgotten to call in at the chemist's, so he had turned the Land Rover round and gone back to town. Dr Singh had said it was imperative that he started the antibiotics as soon as possible. He had also said that Gabriel would have to come into the surgery again in a couple of days to have the dressing changed.

'That's a very nasty burn,' the doctor had said, when Gabriel had rolled up his sleeve. 'It's also infected. When and how did you do it?'

'Some time last week. I . . . I was careless with the kettle.'

'And you didn't think to get it seen to?'

'I thought it would heal on its own.'

'Do you live alone, Mr Liberty?'

'What's that got to do with the price of eggs?'

'Push your sleeve right back and let me have a good gander.'

'You know, for a foreigner your English isn't bad.'

'And for a man with a burn the size of a chapatti, you're lucky you're not in hospital. Any family to keep an eye on you?'

'Mind your own business.'

Eventually he drove back to Mermaid House in a foul mood. The approach to it was almost a mile long and the bumpy track made for hard going; it was a tossup whose suspension would give out first: the ancient Land Rover's or Gabriel's. Cursing as each bump jolted his arm, he knew he would rather die than be forced to move. Perched high on Hollow Edge Moor, his home was surrounded by unrivalled scenery.

From the front of the house, Deaconsbridge nestled in the shallow plateau of the valley with its old mill and factory chimneys just visible, but turn to the right, to the south, and you had the swell of the dales of the White Peak. Walk round to the side of the house and, on a clear day, the windswept hulk of Kinder Scout dominated the skyline.

When he let himself in, Gabriel saw that Jonah had been and gone. There were three carrier bags of shopping on the table with a note saying he had put away the perishable items in the fridge and freezer.

Damn the boy! It had become Jonah's habit to call when he knew his father was out.

The nature of Archie Merryman's work meant that he saw more than his fair share of bereavement. A house-clearance job usually meant that he was tidying up the loose ends of someone's life and death, and even after twenty-five years in the business it never failed to touch him. 'You always were a soft beggar,' his mother used to say to him.

He climbed into his van and smiled goodbye to the two women whose father's house he had just cleared. What wouldn't he give to hear a sentence as coherent as that from his mother these days?

He trundled the van slowly down the hill, away from the stone-built farmhouse and its 'For Sale' board. He wondered what he would find at home that evening. Since his mother had moved in with them after her stroke, things between him and Stella had gone from bad to worse. 'Over my dead body,' had been her exact words when he had suggested it, and he hadn't been surprised by her hostility; Stella and his mother had never hit it off. But he had hoped she would come round to the idea. Thankfully she had, and Bessie had moved in last month.

Bessie had had the stroke just before Christmas. It had robbed her of nearly all the strength in her right arm and hand, and her right leg had also taken a beating, which made walking slow and difficult. Making herself understood had been a problem too. Her speech was a lot clearer now, and that was down to weeks of diligent speech therapy, although if she was tired or anxious the words came out slurred or jumbled— 'humble drier' for tumble drier, 'rarehush' for hairbrush.

What saddened him most was that his mother apologised frequently for having become a burden and there was nothing he could do to convince her that she was not. The woman who had brought him up single-handedly and taught him always to see the best in others, would never be a burden to him.

His shop, Second Best, was situated on the corner of Millstone Row and Lower Haye in Deaconsbridge. Positioned just off the market square, it had the bonus of convenient parking to the side where, with Samson's help, Archie unloaded the van. Samson—his real name was Shane—was the extra brawn Archie relied upon for those larger items of furniture he couldn't manage on his own. At six foot two, Archie wasn't small, but Samson dwarfed him. His conversational skills were restricted to a nod and a grunt, but he was a godsend with a wardrobe on his back and a horsehair mattress between his teeth. On the occasions when Samson was on a house-clearance job with Archie, or they were delivering furniture, Comrade Norm—so called because his parents had named him Norman Lenin Jones—kept a part-time eye on the shop.

He said good night to Samson, checked that all was locked and secure, and set off for home—a ten-minute walk across town. The low evening sun brought a soft glow of light to the square. The market traders had gone, leaving behind a vacant cobbled square splattered with squashed fruit and veg and discarded hot-dog wrappers. Over by the war memorial, a blue and white carrier bag was swept along by the breeze until it came to rest at the foot of a litter bin. Archie strolled over and popped it in. Straightening up, he waved to Joe Shelmerdine, who was just locking his bookshop.

Further along was the Deaconsbridge Arms, but Archie rarely showed his face in there. He carried on briskly but slowed when he got to Cross Street: it was one of the steepest roads in the town and it always took him by surprise. He paused to catch his breath, leaning against the painted handrail on which generations of small children had swung upside-down.

He and Stella had wanted children but, sadly, it wasn't to be, and as the years passed they had resigned themselves to being childless. They had moved to Deaconsbridge not long after they had married and had lived in a rented flat until they had enough money to put down a deposit on a three-storey end-of-terrace house in Cross Street. They had been there ever since.

When he reached home he let himself in at the back door and was surprised by how quiet it was. A sixth sense told him something was wrong. He moved fast now, calling his mother's name as he took the stairs two at a time. He burst into what had been the spare room, but which was now her room.

She wasn't there.

He was just about to go into his and Stella's room when he heard her voice. He bent over the balustrade and saw his mother looking up at him from the bottom of the stairs.

'Ser-late,' she said, pointing to her watch.

He put his heart back where it belonged and joined her in the hall. 'Only a little late tonight,' he said. 'I had a busy day. Where were you? Didn't you hear me calling?'

She took his arm for support and led him slowly towards the front room. On the mantelpiece was an envelope with his name on it. He knew without opening it what it would say.

Stella had left him.

 # CHAPTER TWO

IT WAS SUNDAY MORNING and Ned and Clara were being treated to a brunch-party send-off. While Moira helped Ned to the last of the chipolatas and crispy bacon, Clara watched the goings-on outside where Guy and David were putting the finishing touches to Winnie, the three-year-old camper-van that was soon to be Ned and Clara's new home.

When Clara had first seen it, the salesman had explained that its previous owners were a nice couple who had only parted with it because they were upgrading to something bigger. 'I had no idea camper-vans could be so well kitted out,' she had said, as they stepped inside.

'This is actually what we call a motorhome, and quite a modest one at that. You should see what we have at the top end of the market. The Winnebago, now that's what we call deluxe.' He pointed through one of the side windows to a massive buslike vehicle that looked as if it might accommodate at least two touring rock bands.

While Ned carried out his own inspection, the salesman had filled her in on the superior coach-built workmanship, the spacious dinette, the two-burner combination cooker, the tilt-tolerant fridge, the swivel cab seats and the ingenious bathroom that contained a flushable toilet as well as a shower. He left the sleeping arrangements till last, showing her, with a magician's flourish, the double bed over the cab, complete with little ladder, and the two single beds in the dinette area that could also convert to a comfortable double.

It was while they were driving home, after she had written a cheque for the deposit, that the camper-van had been christened. Clara had been thinking of the ridiculous buslike monstrosity and had said scornfully, 'Winnebago. What kind of a name is that?'

'Winnie, Winnie, Bago,' chanted Ned. 'Is that what we're calling our camper-van?' he asked.

'We could shorten it to Winnie,' she said. 'What do you think?'

He considered her suggestion earnestly, then smiled. 'Poo,' he said.

'Oh dear, can you hang on until we get home?'

A grin extended across his face. 'Not that. Winnie-the-*Pooh*.'

Apart from filling Winnie with provisions, clothes, books, toys, games, cassettes, a basic tool kit, and anything else they might need for the next five months, they had also had to pack up other possessions. During their absence, a young professional couple would be renting their house and they were moving in on Monday.

Her friends had been concerned about money. 'I just don't understand how you'll manage,' Moira said.

'I've got a PEP that's just dying to be let loose,' she had said. 'And our needs will be quite modest while we're away. And if the worst comes to the worst we could resort to busking.'

'I wouldn't put it past you.'

'Oh, and since when did I become such a rebel?'

'You've always been a rebel, Clarabelle,' Guy had said. 'You've never been fully in step with the rest of us.'

Though Clara knew that there was an element of truth in what he had said, she was hurt to hear it voiced so openly. Suddenly everyone had an opinion about her.

David said, 'You know jolly well that you're the resourceful one of us. For goodness' sake, you're the only one who knows what to do with a power drill.'

'And you're a natural facilitator,' Guy said. 'A doer who has to do things her way.'

'Are you saying I'm bossy?'

'Well, you do like to be in charge, don't you?'

'Not always!'

'Face it, Clara,' David said, 'you put us all to shame. Just look at what you've achieved single-handedly. You've carved out a great career for yourself, you have—'

'Enough!' she had cried.

Clara was still watching her friends outside when Louise came and joined her at the window. 'Just look at them! Anyone would think you were getting married.'

Decorated with party streamers and shaving foam, Winnie indeed looked like the archetypal honeymoon getaway vehicle.

'You know, it's not too late to change your mind about this hare-brained caper,' Louise said.

'And why would I want to do that?' Clara asked.

'Oh, you know, now that you're finally setting off, the extent of your madness might be dawning on you. Only you're too proud to admit you might have been a little hasty.'

'And you're too proud to admit you're envious of what I'm doing.'

'Me? Jealous of being cooped up in a box on wheels with a chemical loo? You must be joking!'

'Come on, Louise. Admit it! Aren't you just a tiny bit envious that I'm escaping, taking time out so that I can enjoy each day as it comes?'

'No, I'm not. I'm more concerned with living in the real world, not this frothy concoction you've invented for yourself.'

'It feels real enough to me.'

'But it will only be as real as a holiday, which, when it comes to an end, will bring you back to where you started.'

'Maybe it won't. Maybe I'll find my personal Utopia out on the road and never come home.'

'And you can take this as a first official warning. If you stop washing your hair and turn into a New Age hippie, I'll publicly disown you.'

Clara smiled. 'Is that a promise?'

'Oh, come here, and give me a hug. I'm going to miss you. You will write, won't you? I'll need phone calls, too, to keep me going.'

Clara hugged her back. 'I'll miss you too. Of course I'll keep in touch.'

They drew apart. 'And don't you dare quote me,' Louise said, 'but, yes, part of me is jealous of what you're doing. Who wouldn't be?'

Clara embraced her again. 'And that happy thought will be with me every time I clean out the Chemi-loo!'

At last they were ready to go.

'Come on, you intrepid explorers,' David said, lifting Ned down from his shoulders, 'that's enough goodbyes. It's time you were on your way.'

'Glad to know you're eager for us to be gone,' said Clara. She settled Ned into the front passenger seat.

'That's because the sooner you go, the sooner you'll be back.'

'I wouldn't count on it,' Clara said as she hugged everyone and received their unhelpful words of advice with good grace.

Louise moved in to have the last word. 'And don't do anything stupid while you're away. We want you to come back in one piece. OK?'

'This may come as a shock to you, Louise, but that's something I'm keen to do myself.'

An hour into the journey and with Walton-on-Whinge—as she and the gang referred to Walton-on-Wineham where they all lived—well behind her, Ned had fallen asleep. She turned off his story tape and, now that she was used to driving Winnie, she relaxed a little and thought how wonderfully free she felt. She loved the idea of being able to stop at a moment's notice, park up wherever and feel instantly at home. It was this that had appealed to her when the idea had first occurred to her to take Ned travelling. A camper-van would provide a home-from-home environment that would give them a comforting sense of self-sufficiency. And certainly, right now, with Ned at her side, she felt as if she had everything she would ever want in the world.

She switched on the radio. A song came on that she recognised—it was Nancy Griffith singing 'Waiting for Love'—and tugged painfully at her heart. She had first heard it when she was living in America, and it would be forever synonymous with that period in her life.

She had only recently arrived there, single and carefree, looking forward to the challenges of a year-long secondment at Phoenix's headquarters in Wilmington. But it hadn't been quite the career move she had thought it would be. She had returned home before the end of her secondment with a bruised heart and a pregnancy to explain to her friends and family.

Gabriel was up earlier than usual. Last night when he had drawn the curtains the track had fallen down. Dust and bits of plasterwork had showered over him and something had got into his eye. He had tried bathing it with an old eye bath, but it hadn't helped. Now, after a sleepless night, his eye hurt like hell.

He had another rummage in the bathroom cabinet, and right at the back he found an ancient eye patch. The elastic had perished but he tied a knot in it and it held firmly enough round his head. He closed the cabinet door and took a long, hard look at himself in the mirror.

He was presented with an unshaven, grey-haired old man wearing a black eye patch. He smoothed down his thick, uncombed hair and decided he looked no better sideways on. His cheeks had lost their firmness and sagged under the weight of so many lines. His mouth had withered into a rigid downward curve. Dear God, when had he become such an ugly brute?

He walked the creaking length of the balustraded landing and paused, as he did every morning, to look down on the garden. The sun was still low in the eastern sky, but a pale light shone on the sloping lawn, planted sporadically with daffodils. It stretched down to a thick bank of rhododendrons and beyond was Hollow Edge Woods.

When Anastasia had first seen Mermaid House, it had been love at first sight, but she had had her work cut out in convincing him to buy the place. It cost much more than they could afford, and was miles from where Liberty Engineering's factory was situated, but eventually he had given in to her.

It was only when they moved in that they appreciated the state of the place. It dated back to the mid-nineteenth century, and it was a wreck: dry rot and wet rot, Mermaid House had them in spades. Busy with work, he had left Anastasia to deal with the restoration, and she was determined to see the job well done. He had never regretted the purchase. To see her happy was enough. And then Caspar and Damson had arrived. The upheaval in their lives was colossal, but Anastasia took the twins in her stride, claiming that she loved the challenge of two lively children. It was five years before they took the plunge and tried for another child. Then Jonah was born.

And Anastasia died.

Gabriel tightened the belt of his dressing gown and continued along the landing, passing closed doors to dusty rooms he hadn't been inside for months. He took the stairs slowly, finding his one-eyed view gave him a misleading impression of the closeness of the floor.

The kitchen didn't catch the morning sun, and even in the height of summer it was the coldest room in the house. Val had had an Aga installed, but not long after her death it, too, had given up the ghost.

Since then Gabriel had bought himself an electric cooker and one of those portable heaters on wheels with a large gas cylinder inside it. Now, he switched it on—he had to keep clicking the button until eventually a spark ignited the gas and a whoomph of flame shot across the blackened panels. It had been while he was doing this, the other week, that he had burned his arm. He had lied to Dr Singh about the kettle, because he had thought that otherwise it might seem that he couldn't be trusted with a gas fire. Scalding oneself sounded less dangerous, somehow.

It was four days since he had been into Deaconsbridge and had his arm seen to. He hadn't been back to the surgery; he had decided there was no point. He had finished the short course of antibiotics and had changed the dressing himself, swapping the bandages and gauze for a clean handkerchief and securing it with a couple of safety pins. But now he had this wretched eye to deal with. He would give it a day or so, and if there was no improvement, he would go into Deaconsbridge—make his Friday visit on Thursday perhaps.

Gabriel switched on the wireless to listen to the *Today* programme, sweeping aside several days' worth of plates, cups, knives and forks, dirty pots and pans, until at last he had cleared a space around the kettle and toaster. His breakfast made, he added a tot of twelve-year-old Glenlivet to his tea, just a drop to kick-start his day.

He was still sitting at the table when he heard a knock at the door. He pushed his feet into his slippers and shuffled off reluctantly to deal with whoever had come here to bother him. He slid the bolts back, top and bottom, turned the key and opened the door.

'What the hell do you want?' Gabriel growled, when he saw Dr Singh standing before him. 'And don't tell me you were just passing and thought you'd see if I was in.'

'No, Mr Liberty, I wouldn't dream of lying to you. I am here because you didn't return to the surgery for me to check your arm.'

'Very considerate of you, I'm sure. But you've wasted your time in coming here because my arm is better.'

'Perhaps you would be good enough to let me be the judge of that. Now, are we to conduct surgery business on the doorstep, or am I permitted to come in?'

Gabriel showed him through to the kitchen and realised at once that this was a mistake. He could feel Dr Singh's dark eyes appraising the situation, and the mess seemed a hundred times worse. Damn! He pushed up the sleeve on his dressing gown. 'There,' he said, removing the makeshift bandage, 'just as I told you. Practically as good as new.'

Dr Singh gave the handkerchief a disapproving look, but nodded at the improvement in Gabriel's arm. 'You're right, it's healing nicely. But since I'm here I might just as well apply a proper dressing, and while I do that, you can tell me what you've done to your eye.'

'I got something in it last night,' Gabriel said airily. 'It's a bit sore, that's all. There's no need for you to have a gawp at that too.'

But Dr Singh insisted that he be allowed to do his job. 'And how did you come by this?' he asked, when Gabriel had removed the patch.

'A curtain track fell on top of me, if you must know.'

After pulling a small-beamed torch on him, Dr Singh said, 'I don't like the look of it. You need to see a specialist. It's inflamed and you might have damaged the retina.'

'Don't be absurd. I've just got dust in it, that's all. Can't you give me some drops or something?'

'The "something" is a trip to hospital, Mr Liberty. Do you really want to risk going blind in that eye?'

'God! You foreigners make me sick. You come over here, you get yourselves an education at our expense, then start telling us what to do.

Well, you know what you can do with your trip to hospital, don't you?'

'Mr Liberty, listen carefully to what I am about to say. Either you do as I say or I shall inform Social Services that you are incapable of looking after yourself. And, trust me, they will descend upon you faster than you can say Enoch Powell and you will rue the day you ever ignored my advice. So, *old chap*, what's it to be?'

Gabriel's jaw dropped. 'You wouldn't dare.'

'Care to put me to the test?'

'Couldn't we just try the eye drops first?'

'No. Now, if you would be so good as to get dressed, I will drive you to the hospital. I was going there anyway.'

With no class before lunch, Jonah decided to bunk off school. He pulled on his jacket and took the stairs two at a time. At the bottom, and pressed against the lockers in a slobbering, face-washing clinch, he found Tim Allerton wrapped around Shazzie Butler. He gave a discreet little tap on the locker beside them. 'A-hem.' They sprang apart, which wasn't easy, given the tangle of arms and legs.

Assuming a deadpan expression, he said, 'On the basis that by now you've fully explored each other's dental work, perhaps you would be so good as to find your way to whatever lesson you should be attending.'

He strode off, leaving them to wipe themselves down.

Outside in the car park, he opened the rusting door of his J-reg Ford Escort, wondering why he bothered to lock it. Half the kids he taught at Deaconsbridge High—or Dick High, as its inmates referred to it— would have it open without the aid of a key in seconds flat.

He turned right out of the school gates and took the Lower Moor Road towards the centre of town, where he joined the one-way system and drove up towards Hollow Edge Moor. He was going to see his father, and had planned it this way deliberately. With only an hour and a half available to him, he would be able to say what he needed to say then get out. Direct and to the point, that's what he had to be. Above all else he must not flinch at his father's response, which would, of course, be of the ballistic variety.

Jonah always felt a chill run through him when he came home to Mermaid House. A knot of anxiety formed in the pit of his stomach, with a desire to make his visit as short as possible. He tried to kid himself that it was the bleakness of the house that made him feel like this, but he knew it wasn't. It was the memories . . .

Mermaid House was of an unusual, almost whimsical design, with a tower, four wings and a central cobbled courtyard. Jonah parked next to his father's Land Rover in front of what had always been known as the banqueting hall: it boasted original timbers, trusses, and a massive fireplace. He crossed the courtyard to find the back door unlocked. He knocked cursorily and let himself in. He called to his father, and walked through to the rest of the house. He passed the laundry room, noting the piles of unwashed clothes, bedding and towels in front of the washing machine, and kept going until he came to the kitchen. These days, the mess seldom shocked him; it shocked him more that he had grown used to the conditions in which Gabriel was prepared to live.

He called to Gabriel again, and helped himself to an apple from the bowl of fruit he bought religiously every week for his father, and which Gabriel rarely touched, then wandered out into the hall. He stood at the bottom of the stairs and shouted, his voice echoing in the musty emptiness of the high-ceilinged house. There was no answer. Where was he?

Jonah didn't have time to mount a search party. He would have to come back another day. To his shame, he felt relieved as he retraced his steps, knowing that, for now, he wouldn't have to go through with what Caspar had asked him to do.

It was four days since Stella had left him, and while Archie wasn't entirely surprised by her departure, he had been taken aback by the way she had gone about it. It was the coward's way out and he had never thought of Stella in that light.

The note had been blunt and to the point; printed. It seemed that the affair he had thought was over had picked up again and Stella had decided, finally, where her future lay. And it was not with Archie, the man to whom she had been married for twenty-six years.

Indicating right, he pulled off the main road and parked in the hospital car park. He felt angry. It was always Stella who was supposed to feel the loss of not having children. What about him? He had wanted children, too, but no one had thought he was bothered by his and Stella's incompleteness as a couple and no one had thought to ask.

Next to him his mother was struggling with her seat belt. 'Here, love,' he said. 'Let me.' He pressed the red button and released the strap.

She straightened her hat and smiled at him. 'Ready now,' she said.

'Ready.' He smiled back.

She had dressed specially for the occasion—a trip to the speech therapist was a big day out for her. He helped her to take her seat in the hospital waiting room, and could feel the heavy tiredness in her body: the short walk from the car park sapped most of her strength. But it did nothing to dampen her desire to enjoy her big day out. She smiled at the woman opposite, who looked as if she was dressed in her party frock.

The woman didn't respond to the warmth of his mother's smile. Disappointed, Bessie turned to Archie and said, 'Cobbly cow.'

He tried not to laugh, and was still trying to contain himself when it was Bessie's turn to see the young girl who was patiently teaching her to speak again. Though with a phrase as beautiful as 'Cobbly cow'—so much better than 'snobby cow'—he wondered whether it wouldn't be more fun to teach the rest of the world to speak as Bessie did now. He left them to their phonetics and went in search of a cup of tea.

The vending machine was situated in a bright, airy space where pieces of artwork from the local comprehensive were displayed on the stark white walls. As he drank his tea, he started thinking about how he was going to manage Second Best and look after Bessie on his own. She wasn't so bad at the moment, but he could see that in the future she would need a constant eye on her. He crumpled the empty cup, dropped it into the nearest bin, and cursed himself for having taken advantage of Stella in the way that he had. In relying on her to be at home during the afternoons—she only worked mornings—he had felt that he was doing the right thing by his mother. It served him right that Stella had left him. He had given her a gold-plated final straw.

With ten minutes before Bessie would be finished, he went for a stroll and caught sight of a face he recognised. It was that nice Indian doctor from the surgery, the one who was always so good with his mother.

Archie went over to say hello. 'Touting for business, Dr Singh?'

'Ah, Mr Merryman, good to see you. Are you here with your mother?'

'Yes. She's with the speech therapist. It's slow going.'

'Patience, Mr Merryman, she'll get there in the end. Remember what I told you, there's life after a stroke so long as everyone involved pitches in. You just have to keep the faith.'

'I know. Some days she's quite clear, but others I can't make head or tail of what she's saying. So what brings you here?'

'An errand of mercy. And here he comes right now.'

A tall, grizzled man came towards them. A dressing covered one of his eyes but not the scowl that darkened the rest of his face. 'Bloody hours I've been stuck here, and it's all your fault, you interfering little man!'

Not missing a step, Dr Singh was the epitome of politeness. 'Do you know Mr Liberty, Mr Merryman?'

'Er . . . no.' Archie held out his hand. 'Pleased to meet you, Mr Liberty,' he said affably. But when the other man made no attempt to shake it, he said, 'Well, then, I ought to be getting back. Bessie will be wondering where I am.' He turned to go.

Behind him, he heard, 'A bloody waste of time. Nothing that eye drops wouldn't have sorted. Just as I told you.'

When the phone rang, Jonah was standing on the top rung of the stepladder. He knew straight away who it was. Caspar was the only person he knew who could make the telephone ring with menace.

He put the brush between his teeth, picked up the pot of paint, and made his descent. By the time he had found the phone under the dust-sheet by the side of his bed, he could easily picture his brother's tight-lipped face at the other end of the line.

'Liberty Escort Agency, how may I help you?'

'Yeah, very funny, Jonah. Now, perhaps you'd tell me how you got on. What did the old man say?'

'Absolutely nothing.'

'Oh, I know what happened, you didn't see him, did you? You lost your bottle. You always were a coward.' Caspar's voice was hard.

'You could talk to him yourself,' Jonah said. 'It *is* your idea.'

'Look, we've been through this before. These days, you're the only one who can get anything sensible out of him. He'll listen to you.'

Exasperated, Jonah pushed a hand through his hair. 'Actually, I did go to see him this morning, but he wasn't there. Now, if there's nothing else, Caspar, I'm in the middle of decorating, so I'd appreciate it if you would let me get on.'

'Good God, why do you insist on living like a peasant? Get a genuine peasant in to do it for you.'

'Caspar, was there anything else?'

'Yes. Speak to Dad as soon as you can. Every day you botch this up, is another day of . . . well, never mind that, just do it.'

Back on the stepladder, Jonah resumed painting his bedroom ceiling. If ever a child had been born to upset the sibling applecart, it had been him: Caspar and Damson had never let him forget that his birth had precipitated their mother's death. As children they had been cunning and wilful, had taken pleasure in setting him up as the fall guy and enjoying the spectacle of him being punished. He was the perfect stooge, trailing behind in their contemptuous wake, needing their approval, wanting, stupidly, to be just like them: the mysterious, all-powerful twins.

By the age of nine he had wised up and had kept his distance from his brother and sister. But whenever they got the opportunity they played their games with him. They would sneak into his room late at night when he was asleep and steal whatever was precious to him—stamps, comics, books, pocket money. Gradually, he learned to outwit them. He discovered that he was smarter than they were, and by the age of eleven he was spending more time in their father's library than anywhere else. He discovered that trying to gain Gabriel's approval was infinitely more worthwhile than being accepted by Caspar and Damson.

Until then his father had been little more than an occasional visitor in his life, forever away on business, an autocratic figure. But when Jonah showed an interest in the books Gabriel had collected over the years, the two almost connected.

Jealousy had caused the twins to step up their bullying campaign, but they soon found themselves in more trouble than they could have imagined. Late one night Gabriel discovered them in his library, defacing two of his most highly prized first editions. Their plan had backfired. They were grounded for a month, their allowance was stopped and their combined birthday party cancelled. It was then that Val began to question the previous crimes Jonah was supposed to have committed.

If Jonah had a less than generous opinion of his brother and sister, the regard they held each other in could not have been higher. In Caspar's view, Damson could do no wrong. But, as far as Jonah could see, she had spent most of her adult life switching from one good cause to another with intermittent bouts of self-absorption. Of the three, she was the only one to have married. She was also the only one to have divorced twice, and lucratively so. She was currently going through what she called her 'centred space' phase and was living, in peace and harmony, she said, in a commune in Northumberland.

This latest search for her inner self was just another in a long line of explorations from which she would doubtless emerge to plunge back into the hedonistic lifestyle she enjoyed: men, partying, shopping, and whatever else made her think she was happy.

Jonah didn't think she had ever been truly happy.

On the stroke of midnight, Jonah called it a day. It was handy living next door to a church: there was no danger of losing track of the time when the bells rang out every hour. He had moved into Church Cottage last August, when he had come back to the area as head of history at Deaconsbridge High. Before then he had been living in neighbouring Cheshire. He had been ready for a change and had followed his instinct when he had seen the post advertised. It had seemed the right thing to do, given that his father was now on his own in Mermaid House.

And it was the house that was at the bottom of Caspar's insistence that Jonah speak to Gabriel. Caspar could dress it up any way he liked, but Jonah knew his brother too well. Caspar didn't give a damn about their father's welfare: all he was concerned about was getting his hands on the capital that would be released if Mermaid House was sold. Jonah agreed that their father had reached an age when he might be better off living in a property a tenth of the size, but had never found the right time to broach it with Gabriel, not when he knew how insincere and grasping it might sound to their father.

And what his brother didn't know was that Jonah intended to make it clear to his father that if Mermaid House was to be sold, Gabriel should not donate a penny of the proceeds to his children to avoid inheritance tax, which, naturally, was the main thrust of Caspar's argument for selling up now. Caspar would capitalise on a Third World disaster if he thought he could get away with it.

And there were many things Caspar *had* got away with over the years. Just as he had stolen from Jonah as a child, he had continued through adulthood to help himself to anything else which took his fancy. So far Jonah had lost two girlfriends and a fiancée to his brother. Admittedly the loss of the girlfriends had taken place during his teens, but Emily had been another matter altogether, and he wasn't sure that he could ever forgive Caspar for what he had done.

Downstairs in the kitchen, while he washed the paintbrush under the tap and squirted a dose of Fairy Liquid onto the bristles, Jonah wondered if a family as bitterly divided as his could ever be reconciled.

 **CHAPTER THREE**

WITH NED'S HELP, and with the aid of a simple device that turned a white plastic barrel into a mini garden roller, Clara was pushing their fresh-water supply across the dewy grass of the Happy Dell campsite towards Winnie. This was their fourth day on the road, and already Clara and Ned considered themselves old hands at camper-vanning.

Ned loved their new home, especially his bed over the cab. He would lie up there with Mermy and his battalion of cuddly toys, reading to them from his favourite storybooks, and Clara was relieved that, so far, he had shown no sign of missing anything he had left behind. But, as

Louise would have been quick to point out, it was early days yet.

Since leaving home on Sunday they had slowly made their way north. Their first night had been spent at a campsite in Stratford-upon-Avon, where the following day they had immersed themselves in all things Shakespearean and, more to Ned's liking, had visited a museum devoted to teddy bears. From Stratford they had moved on to the West Midlands, taking in Cadbury World and the Museum of Science and Industry in Birmingham. Ned had been as pleased as punch when their guide picked him out from the crowd to press the button to start the steam engine. He was happier still when they left an hour later with a model of it, and he had spent the evening back at Winnie explaining enthusiastically to Clara how it worked.

Until now, they had decided together where to go each day while curled up in bed and flicking through touring books and maps. But their next port of call was to be a surprise for Ned, which Clara hoped he would enjoy.

When they had packed everything neatly away, and had paid the man in the campsite office, they were ready to go.

'Chocks ahoy,' said Ned, as he did each morning when they set off.

She smiled. She had given up telling him it was 'chocks away'. 'Chocks ahoy' sounded just fine to her. The people on the next pitch waved goodbye. They were an interesting couple in their mid-fifties who called themselves 'full-timers'. They lived all year round in their camper-van, which they had personalised by painting Ron's name on the driver's door and Eileen's on the passenger's. Over a glass of wine late last night, they had given Clara their list of the top ten campsites in Britain. They were out of the way, not always listed in the touring guides: it was to one of these that Clara was heading today.

An hour later, and with the M6 behind them, Clara took the B5470 out of Macclesfield and found herself driving through rolling hills of lush green farmland crisscrossed with dry-stone walls. It came as such a surprise that she slowed down to take a better look. It was beautiful, just as Ron and Eileen had said it would be.

But it wasn't the scenery that had drawn Clara to this part of the Peak District, it was what, according to the guidebooks, had also drawn Victorian day-trippers from the neighbouring industrial towns and villages: the chance to see a mermaid. An underground cavern that claimed to have a rock formation that looked just like the real thing. Given Ned's love for Mermy and his desire to meet a real one, this was probably as near as she could get to fulfilling a dream for him.

They drove on, the road becoming steeper, until eventually they reached the summit of a hill. Dropping into a lower gear, Clara took the descent steadily, with extra care on the tight bends.

Their first sighting of Deaconsbridge revealed a small town nestling in the shallow dip of a valley. From a distance it looked a soft shade of industrial grey, with rows of terraced houses tucked into the slope of the hillside. A church with an elegant spire stood self-consciously to one side of the town, surrounded by a cemetery, where the gravestones seemed to flow out into the moorland behind.

With a queue of cars itching to overtake them, they trundled ever nearer, and just as the road began to level, narrow, and guide them to the centre of the town and its one-way system, Ned bounced in his seat and let out a loud, excited cry. 'Look, a mermaid! And there's another. Over there! Mummy, there's lots of them!'

Once Clara had squeezed Winnie into the pay-and-display car park—no mean feat, given how busy the small town was and the lack of space available—she could see that Ned was right. Deaconsbridge was awash with mermaids. Almost every shop front in the market square where they were parked had a sign depicting a mermaid.

Across the square a sign showed a rosy-cheeked mermaid wearing an apron and holding a large wooden spoon. It was an inviting sight. 'Welcome to Deaconsbridge, Ned,' Clara said. 'Ready for some lunch?'

The Mermaid Café was busy, and at first glance Clara thought they would have to try somewhere else. But in the farthest corner, and beneath a large mirror flanked by two prettily stencilled mermaids on the wall, she could see a waitress clearing a table that had been vacated by a couple of intimidating-looking, leather-clad bikers now queuing at the counter to pay their bill. One smiled at Ned, who smiled back.

The waitress continued to add dirty plates to a tray already stacked high with an assortment of crockery, and for a few moments Clara and Ned were forced to stand with the two bikers. The one who had smiled at Ned did so again, this time adding a wink. Then he turned to Clara. 'He's a cute-looking kid,' he said. 'A dead ringer for his mum, or his older sister, perhaps? If you want a worthwhile tip,' he went on, 'we can recommend the chef's special. You can't go wrong with it.'

'Insider knowledge,' said his friend and reached into a small basket of lollipops and gave one to Ned. 'Here, have this on us.'

Ned's face lit up. 'Thank you,' he said.

Clara was about to add her thanks to Ned's, when the waitress came over. 'Sorry to keep you waiting, dear,' she said, 'but these leather joy-boys make so much mess.' She gave the two bikers a broad grin.

The one who had spoken to Clara gave the waitress's red cap a light flick. 'Mum, I've told you before, keep the wisecracks for when we're at home. Do you want me to take that tray into the back for you?'

'No, Robbie, I want you to pay your bill and sling your hook. You're cluttering the place up.'

Thanking the two young men for the lollipop, Clara shepherded Ned towards their table. 'Those men were nice,' said Ned, settling himself into his chair. He propped Mermy against a bowl of sugar.

'They were, weren't they?' she replied. She thought about the one who had treated her to some friendly flattery. He must have been at least ten years her junior. Older sister indeed!

Catching sight of herself in the mirror above Ned's head, she supposed her new haircut made her look younger. She had gone for a radical change in Stratford, deciding that her shoulder-length hair would be a pain to take care of while they were away. In the salon, everyone had agreed that the new style took years off her, that her dark hair now framed her small oval face perfectly and accentuated her brown eyes.

She turned away from the mirror and, with the two bikers still on her mind, asked herself when had been the last time a man had paid her an unexpected compliment? She couldn't remember, and wondered when she had become so unaware of or immune to male charm.

Since Ned had been born, she had had little time or inclination to seek out a boyfriend, and she had known that to embark upon a series of going-nowhere relationships would do her no good. Also, she didn't want to confuse Ned by bringing home a succession of men. And, more importantly, she had a very real fear of accidentally getting pregnant again. Not that she had ever regretted having Ned. She loved him just as much as she would have done had she planned his conception.

They feasted on sausages, beans and chips, followed by the best Bakewell tart Clara had ever tasted. When she commented on this to their waitress—biker-Robbie's mother—she was told, 'I'll tell my sister that, she'll be well pleased. It's an old family recipe.'

'Is this a family business, then?'

'No. It's just a coincidence that we work together. Are you here for the day, or staying longer? The weather's supposed to be breaking by the weekend, so you'd best do your walking sooner rather than later.'

'Is that what everyone does round here—walk?'

'That, and go down the cavern to see the mermaid. To be honest, there's not a lot else to do.'

Ned leaned forward in his seat. 'A mermaid? Is it real?'

The waitress's eyes flickered over Mermy on the table. She sucked in her breath. 'Well, now, it's as real as you want it to be, I suppose. But if you've come to see it, you're too early. It doesn't open for another week. You could always go across to Castleton or down to Buxton. Between them they've got more caverns than they know what to do with.'

'Do they have mermaids?'

'No, it's only us that can boast something as special as that.'

They left the café unsure what to do next. If the Mermaid Cavern wasn't open for another week, should they move on and come back, or stay put and use Deaconsbridge as a base for visiting the surrounding area?

Keeping her options open, Clara decided they would inspect the campsite Ron and Eileen had raved about and take it from there. She put this to Ned as she unlocked Winnie. But now that Ned had heard about the Mermaid Cavern, he clearly didn't want to move on.

She started the engine and reached for the map. Eileen had said the campsite was somewhere off the Hollow Edge Moor road. The road was marked on the map and she manoeuvred Winnie out of the market-square car park and went in search of a pitch for the night.

Nearly an hour had passed before she gave up. 'This is ridiculous,' she said, exasperated. 'We've been up and down this road so many times we're on first-name terms with all the sheep. I'm sure they're laughing at us. I'll go mad if I don't find this wretched campsite. I could also do with going to the loo. I'll just drive down this handy little track and park up.'

Ignoring the 'Private—No Entry' sign, and taking the handy little track, turned out to have been a mistake. It was longer and narrower than Clara had expected and, with dry-stone walls almost touching Winnie's sides, there was no space to turn round. And reversing was not a viable proposition: it was the only trick of driving a camper-van that she hadn't mastered.

Referring to the map again, Clara could see that if she carried on along this road they would eventually come to a belt of trees and a dwelling called Mermaid House. It looked as though the road widened sufficiently by the trees to allow her to turn and drive back to join the main road once more.

Her guesswork proved right and, in the shelter of the trees, she brought Winnie to a halt. 'Time to stretch my legs,' she said, smiling at Ned as she climbed out of her seat to go through to the toilet.

When she came out, Ned said, 'Can we go for a paddle? I can see a bridge over a stream and there might be some fish we could catch.'

'They'll have to be very lazy fish, the type that we can catch with our bare hands.'

He slipped out from his seat. 'It's easy. I saw it on the television. This man had a stick and he watched until the fish came right up to him and then he—'

'Yes, I get your drift,' she interrupted, not wanting the gory details. 'Couldn't we just shake hands with them and invite them in for a fish supper?'

He rolled his eyes. 'Fish don't have hands, Mummy.'

'You sure about that? What about octopuses? I thought they had eight hands.'

'Now you're being silly. Everyone knows they're called testicles.'

She laughed. 'Tentacles, Ned. Come on, let's see if there's a nice bit of smoked salmon just waiting to make our acquaintance.'

Taking a rolled-up towel with them, they approached the bridge and the length of river Ned had spied.

'It'll be cold in there,' Clara said, looking doubtfully at the clear shallow water. 'Wouldn't you rather play Pooh sticks?'

Beside her Ned was sitting on the bank and tugging at his laces. 'We could play that after. Help me, please, Mummy. This one's in a knot.'

The water was icy cold; it made them both gasp and squeal as they slipped off their shoes and dipped in their toes. They rolled up their jeans and bravely went in deeper. Clara held Ned's hand as they waded out, and joined in the game of looking for their supper. 'Do you think there are sharks here, Ned?'

'Ssh!' he whispered. 'I can see something.' He let go of her, bent down to the water, cupped his hands, and made a sudden scooping movement. 'I've caught something!' he cried.

Amazed, she lowered her head to see what he had.

He shrieked with delight and splashed her face. 'Fooled you!'

'Why, you little monkey!'

The water fight was noisy and spectacular, and left them both drenched. Shivering, but laughing, they put on their shoes and went back to Winnie to change into some dry clothes. They were soon warm again, and just as Clara was about to make them a hot drink they heard an engine. Ned stuck his head out of the window of the driver's door.

'It's a car,' he said. 'A green one. It's got two men in it and it's stopped behind us. They're getting out.'

Clara decided it was time to investigate. She stepped outside and didn't like what she saw. Two lads of about the same age as the bikers came towards her. One had a baseball bat and was smacking it against one of his palms. They both looked her over. She swallowed, and moved back a pace to shield Ned, who was still leaning out of the window. 'Get down,' she whispered, 'and don't say a word.' They came in close and, one on either side of her, they pushed her hard against the driver's door: they smelt of sour beer and stale cigarette smoke.

'Please,' she said, 'take what you want and leave us alone.' Outwardly she was doing her best to appear calm, but inwardly she was frantic.

They both laughed, and a coarse, fleshy hand stroked her throat. For a split second she considered bringing her knee up into the youth's groin, but as the hand began to exert more pressure on her windpipe, squeezing it painfully, she heard another man's voice say, 'Take your hands off that woman and get the hell out of here.'

The grip loosened. Twisting her head, Clara saw an elderly man coming towards them. A patch covered one of his eyes and raised to the other was a double-barrelled shotgun. Her legs began to wobble and she hoped to God that the old man knew what he was doing with it.

The gun still held high, he drew nearer. 'And do it before I lose my patience and blast both your heads off! Go on, get out of here!'

The hand dropped from Clara's throat. 'Take it easy, Granddad, don't go giving yourself a heart attack.'

'Less of the lip, you scum. You're on my land and I want you off it. Pronto! Do you understand that, or do I have to spell it out into simple words that louts like you can understand?'

The two lads started backing away. 'Bloody cocky with your words, aren't you, you stupid old git?'

Tightening his finger on the trigger and lowering the shotgun until it was aimed directly at the youth's crotch, the man growled, 'So tell me, just how cocky do *you* feel? Get out of here.'

They fled to their car and, with the gun still trained on them, they turned it round and shot off down the track.

Clara realised she had been holding her breath and let it out now, in a long sigh of relief. Her legs were still shaking. She leaned against the van, steeled herself, then opened the door and reached in for Ned. His face was as white as she felt hers must be. He trembled in her arms and she hugged him to her.

She turned to face the formidable man who had come to their rescue. 'I'm so grateful to you,' she said. 'If you hadn't turned up . . . Well, I'm not sure how I would have got out of that. Thank you very much.'

To her surprise, the man simply stared at her, bristling with disapproval. Then with a loud crack, he broke the gun and shoved the butt under his arm. 'You can save the fawning pleasantries,' he growled. 'I'm not interested. Maybe in future you'll think twice about trespassing on private property, especially somewhere as remote as this. Damn stupid of you to put yourself and the child in danger. Women! Bloody fools, the lot of you!' He turned his back and started to walk away.

Clara was outraged. 'Why, you miserable old bugger!' she burst out angrily. 'Come back here and apologise this instant.'

'What did you call me?'

'You heard. And if I wasn't holding a terrified child I'd call you a lot worse.'

'If that child is terrified, then you have only yourself to blame.'

'Oh, because I'm a woman on my own I'm not allowed to take my son paddling. Is that what you're saying?'

'Paddling in *my* water? I ought to bloody charge you for that.'

'Do that, you old skinflint, and I'll report you to the police for behaving in a threatening manner with a dangerous firearm.'

'I'll wager that wasn't what you were thinking a few moments ago. I bet you've never been so pleased to see a crazy old fool with a gun.'

'If I'd known it would be you, I'd sooner have taken my chances single-handed.'

'The hell you would have!' He guffawed.

They stared at each other. In the silence that followed, Ned lifted his head from Clara's shoulder. 'I need a wee,' he murmured, and started to sob. Then Clara felt wet warmth running down her front.

The grumpy old man lowered his one eye to the puddle forming on the ground at her feet. 'Poor little beggar,' he said gruffly. 'Get him changed and I'll make you some tea.'

Near to tears herself she said, 'I can manage, thank you. I wouldn't want to take up any more of your valuable—'

He silenced her with a fierce one-eyed stare. 'Don't look a gift horse in the mouth, young lady, until you're sure you can really do without it.'

Winnie seemed terribly cramped with the three of them inside it: their guest, as he fumbled around making tea, was too tall and bulky for such a confined space. By the time Clara had calmed Ned, changed their clothes and they were sitting at the little table with their tea, she thought she should introduce herself. An apology seemed appropriate too.

'My name's Clara Costello, and I'm sorry for some of the things I said out there. This is my son, Ned.'

He took off his coat and laid it on the table. 'Well, Miss Costello, the name's Liberty, Mr Liberty, and I never apologise for anything I say.'

In spite of herself, she smiled. 'You know, that doesn't surprise me. Do you often go for an afternoon stroll with a gun?'

'When I feel like shooting something, yes.'

'Well, much as I disagree with the ownership of guns, I'm glad you felt the need to shoot something today.'

'Don't be so bloody patronising. Drink your tea and be quiet. That goes for you too, young man.'

'What's wrong with your eye?' Ned asked.

'And what's wrong with your manners, Mr Nosy Parker?'

Unabashed, Ned carried on, 'You look like a pirate. If you chopped a hand off, you could be Captain Hook.'

This seemed to amuse him. He looked down at the badly swollen fingers that were wrapped round his mug of tea. 'I'll bear that in mind.'

'Come on, Ned,' Clara said, 'drink your tea and leave our guest alone.'

'Do I have to? It's horrible. It's too sweet. Can't I have some blackcurrant juice? Please.'

Sliding out from the seat she was sharing with Ned, Clara went over to the fridge, poured a cup of blackcurrant juice, and reached into a locker for a packet of biscuits.

He was a funny old stick, shabbily dressed in a moth-eaten green pullover with frayed cuffs and the elbows worn through. The points of his shirt collar were also worn and his brown corduroy trousers were scruffy and dirty. She sat opposite him and offered the packet of biscuits. His distorted fingers poked clumsily at the plastic wrapping as he helped himself, and she wondered just how good a shot he would have been if he had fired that wretched gun, now resting against the wardrobe. Thinking that she could take advantage of his local knowledge, she said, 'We're trying to find a campsite for the night. Perhaps you know where it is.' She got to her feet to fetch the map.

'I doubt that very much,' he said, when she returned. 'Camping's hardly my scene.'

'Heavens, are you always this helpful?'

He swallowed the last of his tea. 'You've got me on a good day.'

'Lucky old us.' She put the map down on the table between them and pointed to where Ron and Eileen had said the campsite was. 'It's called Hollow Edge View. I was told it was—'

'It's gone,' he interrupted. 'The owners beggared off down South last winter. Bankrupted themselves. Softies from London. I knew they'd never make a go of it. I told them so too.'

'Wow, and to think they didn't stick around to enjoy more of your warm neighbourliness. What were they thinking of?'

He looked up sharply. 'Nothing wrong in speaking one's mind.'

'Depends on the state of the mind. Can you recommend anywhere else for us to stay?'

'No.'

'Well, then, and since we've clearly exhausted you of your charm, you can leave us to sort ourselves out. I wish I could say it was a pleasure meeting you, *Mr* Liberty.'

Gabriel was smiling to himself as he trudged home across the fields in the late-afternoon sunshine. He hadn't enjoyed himself so much in a long while. It wasn't often he came up against somebody brave enough to cross swords with him, but that spiky, sharp-tongued young woman had made more of a go of it than anyone else ever had.

Back at Mermaid House he let himself in and went through to the gunroom. It was only then, as he stood in front of the locked, glass-fronted cabinet, that he realised he didn't have the gun with him.

Damn and blast! He had left it behind with that girl and her son. A shiver of unease crept over him as he recalled the cartridges he had put into the pocket of his coat, which he had also stupidly left behind. He hoped to God that that little boy had been brought up to understand that guns were a no-go area for children.

He was about to retrace his steps across the fields, to see if the camper-van was still there, when the telephone rang. To his surprise he heard Jonah's voice at the other end of the line. Now what was this about? When was the last time any of his children had phoned him?

It was Ned who spotted them. 'Look, Mummy, Mr Liberty's forgotten his coat and gun. What shall we do?' he asked, anxiously.

'We could either wait and see if Mr Liberty comes back for them, or we could go and find him.' She turned and looked at the map that was still laid out on the table. 'My guess is,' she mused, 'that since he claimed to own this land, our friend Mr Grumpy-Pants Liberty lives here.' She indicated with her finger. 'What do you think?'

'I thought he was funny.'

'I didn't. He was rude to us.'

Ned looking thoughtful. 'He stopped those horrible men from hurting you. And he made us tea because I was frightened.' He lowered his gaze. 'I'm . . . I'm sorry I wet myself.'

At the poignant reminder of what the old devil had done for them, Clara put her arms round her precious son. 'I nearly wet myself too,' she admitted. 'It was scary. And you're right,' she added, 'it's time I learned to be more tolerant of other people's shortcomings.'

After Clara had put the gun inside a wardrobe, they washed up their cups, stored them away and set a course for Mermaid House.

As was to be expected, there was no helpful sign at the end of the track to lead them to where Mr Liberty lived. She juddered over a cattle grid and pressed on. They rattled along for almost half a mile before they set eyes on the most extraordinary sight. Clara whistled. 'Now that's what I call a house.'

Ned was impressed too. 'It's a castle, Mummy!'

There weren't any battlements, but there was a tower built into one of the corners of the house, and it didn't take much imagination to picture a cursing Mr Liberty standing at the window, shotgun in hand, ready to defend his home from the onslaught of double-glazing salesmen.

They came to an archway that led to a central courtyard. Clara parked alongside a battered old Land Rover and turned off the engine. Then she hooked Mr Liberty's coat over her shoulder and picked up the gun. She and Ned got out of the camper-van and walked towards the door. Not finding a bell, Clara rapped loudly with her knuckles.

'Shall I call him?' Ned said, pushing open the letterbox.

'That's probably not a good idea,' Clara said.

But it was too late. Ned was already peering through the gap. 'Ooh,' he exclaimed, 'it's really untidy. There's things everywhere. Oh, I can see Mr Liberty. Hello, Mr Liberty, it's us, you forgot your gun.'

'No need to make such a song and dance about it, young man.'

Bending down, Clara could see that Ned was nose to nose with the formidable one-eyed owner of the house.

'We've brought your coat too,' Ned carried on. 'Your house is nice. It's just like a castle. Can I come in and see it, please? I'll be very good.'

It was time to intervene. 'It's OK, Mr Liberty,' Clara said. 'We're not here to bother you. I'll put your gun and coat here on the step and leave you in peace. Thanks for your help earlier this afternoon. Ned and I really appreciated what you did.' Taking her son's hand, she lowered her voice. 'Come on, Ned, we mustn't make a nuisance of ourselves. Besides, it's getting late and we have to find a campsite.'

The door opened suddenly. 'You're too early.'

'Too early for what?' asked Clara.

'There's only one campsite in this area and it doesn't open for another two weeks.'

She sighed. 'Oh, that's brilliant. Why didn't you tell me that before?'

'Oh, so it's my fault you didn't do sufficient background research before you came here, is it?'

She sighed again. 'Mr Liberty, do you realise just how rude you are? Because if not, let me tell you that I have seldom come across a more cantankerous and mean-spirited man.'

'And I have seldom come across a woman with as much ungracious impudence as you, Miss Costello,' he snarled, 'so I know that if I were to suggest you use one of my fields for the night, it would be a pointless gesture. You would only throw it back in my face.'

Astonished, Clara hesitated. It was getting late, the light had almost gone and she was tired. Also, the incident that afternoon had left her more rattled than she cared to admit. It seemed eminently sensible to be within shouting distance of help.

'Perhaps we could come to some other arrangement,' she said. 'Rather than spoil one of your fields by driving across it, how about we stay right where we are in the courtyard?'

He considered this. 'Just the one night?'

'Just the one night,' she confirmed. 'In fact, we'll be gone first thing in the morning. It will be as though we'd never been here.'

Ned gave one of his most engaging smiles. 'Would you like to have supper with us, Mr Liberty? Oh, Mummy, please say Mr Liberty can have supper with us.'

Oh, well done, Ned, Clara thought. A cosy evening with Mr Misery. Perfect. 'You're more than welcome, Mr Liberty,' she lied, 'but it will be very simple. Pancakes. Nothing fancy, I'm afraid.'

Mr Liberty's enthusiasm for the idea seemed as great as her own. He said, 'Pancakes? I can't stand them. I've got a nice bit of rump steak and a glass of claret I'm looking forward to.' He turned back towards the house, but before he disappeared, he tossed them one last piece of invective. 'And remember, no noise or trouble.'

Gabriel went to bed early that night. He often did. Sleep was a welcome antidote to boredom. He stepped over the mess of plaster and curtains that he hadn't done anything about since he'd pulled the track off the wall two nights ago, and got into bed. He didn't turn out the light straight away, but sat for a while to contemplate his day, a habit of Anastasia's that had rubbed off on him. He wondered how his guests were getting on.

Thinking of the pancakes they must have enjoyed, he thought of his own supper—a lukewarm tin of Heinz tomato soup. He had lied about the rump steak and claret, just as he frequently lied to Jonah about what he ate. Often he didn't eat what Jonah fetched from the shops for him. The fresh fruit, the vegetables, the chicken breasts—it was too much trouble. Cooking for one was bad enough, but eating alone was worse.

So why hadn't he accepted the invitation to join that well-mannered little boy and his mother for supper?

Since Val's death, he had got out of the habit of being sociable, not that he had ever been gregarious. Val had been the driving force when it came to showing one's face at local functions; he had preferred to devote himself to work. But even that had palled as the years went on. And then came the day when, finally, he had had to resign himself to the truth that none of his children was interested in taking over the business he had inherited from his own father. It had been a bitter day indeed when he sold up and retired. He had never forgiven Caspar and Jonah for letting him down. Damson had never really been in the running.

And what had they chosen to do instead? Not much. After dropping out of university, Caspar had thrown himself into a series of get-rich-quick scams that had all turned into financial disasters. He was an idle beggar who thought the world owed him a favour. Currently he was peddling overpriced cars for a living. As for Jonah, the brightest of the bunch, he was wasting what talents he had been given by teaching in a third-rate school and earning buttons. It went without saying, of course, that Damson had never held down a proper job. She had been too pre-occupied with enjoying herself.

So Gabriel had entered the twilight zone of retirement. It hadn't suited him, isolated from the only world he had been interested in—industrial engineering. He had soon realised he had few friends; the people he had mixed with had been business associates in the steel-producing heartlands of Sheffield. And other than his love of books, he had nothing else to occupy him. Then Val had died, and it was easier to retreat further still, to batten down the hatches and let the world go hang.

He knew the house was a mess and that he should do something about it. But where to start? It had got so out of hand that the task now seemed insurmountable. He knew, too, that at times he was offhand and acerbic, but he didn't have the patience to be polite. He had always been direct and to the point—that was how one survived in business. And that was what he had liked about the Costello woman. She had said exactly what she thought. Good for her. She was smart too. He could tell that by her waspish, quick-witted manner. Smiling to himself, he thought of all the names he had been called that day. *A miserable old bugger. An old skinflint. A cantankerous and mean-spirited man.* Not bad for starters.

He switched off the light and wondered what he might be in for tomorrow morning. Then he remembered that his feisty guest had said they would be gone by first thing in the morning. He turned the light back on, reached for his clock and set the alarm for six thirty. Just in case he overslept. It would be a shame to miss out on a parting shot.

 **CHAPTER FOUR**

THAT NIGHT, UNABLE TO SLEEP, Archie stared at the ceiling above his bed. He had received a letter from Stella's solicitors telling him what he already knew, that more than two decades of marriage was to be reduced to *Mrs S. Merryman versus Mr A. F. Merryman*. The letter suggested that the matter could be brought to a swift conclusion as Mrs Merryman was happy to leave her husband's business concerns out of the negotiations, but the house was another matter. As Mrs Merryman had been a party to the original purchase of the property as well as a regular contributor to the mortgage payments, she was entitled to her share of the matrimonial home.

Archie had no argument with that. It was all true. And as much as he wanted to avoid the upheaval of selling the house, he knew he had no choice: he had no other means to pay off Stella.

Still restless, he rolled over onto his left side and tried to relax. But his mind was racing through the years he and Stella had shared. The good times, and the bad times.

Ten minutes later, as sleep continued to elude him, he let out a sigh of defeat. He slipped on his towelling dressing gown and went downstairs quietly, not wanting to disturb his mother.

In the harsh glare of the overhead strip light, he stood in the kitchen, listening to the kettle coming to the boil. The speech therapist at the hospital had said that Bessie was improving, and he hung on to this glimmer of hope, wanting to believe that his mother would make a good, if not full, recovery.

Archie sat at the kitchen table to drink his tea. It occurred to him that maybe he could get Bessie into the shop for a few hours a day. She might like that. Give her small tasks to do, such as polishing some of the small pieces of furniture. If he planned it carefully, there would be any number of little jobs he could find for her to do. But he would have to be subtle about it: his mother was no fool. He would have to make out that she was doing him a big favour, that he needed her help.

He swallowed the last of his tea, rinsed the mug under the tap, put it ready for his breakfast in the morning, and went back upstairs to bed.

As he pulled the duvet over him, life didn't seem so bad after all. He had always believed that for every problem there was a solution. It was just a matter of reasoning it through. Drifting off to sleep, he felt better than he had in days. Maybe things would start to pick up now.

Clara woke to the sound of rain pattering on the roof of the camper-van. Stretching beneath the duvet, she opened her eyes and looked at her watch. It was eight o'clock. Goodness, as late as that. Still, there was no hurry, and as Ned was sleeping soundly, she could savour a rare lie-in. She closed her eyes, listened to the rain, and hoped it wouldn't develop into a full-blown downpour. They had been lucky so far on their trip: this was their first wet day.

She should be keeping a diary. In years to come, when she was slogging away on the treadmill, it would make interesting reading. Well, it wasn't too late to start. She would buy a book in Deaconsbridge and encourage Ned to play his part. He could write his own entries, draw a few pictures, and maybe stick in postcards of where they had stayed.

She sighed contentedly. How pleasant it was to know that one's only concern for the day was to find a washing machine and something to eat, with a little amusement thrown in. Thinking of Ned, Clara rolled onto her side and looked towards his sleeping compartment. There was still no sign of movement from behind the curtain. He must have been shattered last night to sleep so long. It's all the fresh air, she thought. That would meet with her mother's approval. As babies, she and Michael had been put outside in their prams in all weathers. 'Toughened you up nicely,' her mother had said, and she'd tried to do the same with Ned. 'Just airing him,' she claimed, when Clara arrived to collect him after work and found him on the patio with wind buffeting the pram.

'Airing him or freeze-drying him, Mum?'

Though she had made clear her views on how she wanted her son treated, Clara knew that while her back was turned her mother did as she pleased. But so long as Ned thrived Clara couldn't complain. Anyway, she was glad to have parents prepared to help out. Without them, she wouldn't have coped nearly so well.

When she had discovered she was pregnant there had been no dilemma over whether or not to keep the baby. She had loved her unborn child's father, so it had seemed natural to want his baby. But telling her parents that she was pregnant had been one of the hardest things she had ever done. She knew she had let them down.

'Is there really no chance of the father taking on his responsibility?' her mother had asked, stricken.

'No, Mum. He's already married,' she told them. 'I knew all along that he was married. At the time, though, he was separated from his wife.'

They had seized on this glimmer of hope. 'Is he divorced now?' her father asked.

'No. He and his wife are reconciled.'

Her father had picked up on the one aspect of the tale she had tried to gloss over. 'Did you tell him you were pregnant?' he asked.

'No.'

'But, darling, why not? He's the father, he should know,' her mother remonstrated.

'You only think that because you want to believe he'll wave a magic wand over my pregnancy and make it nice and respectable.'

'That's a little hard on us,' her father said.

'But it's true, isn't it?' she said.

'You haven't told us his name,' her mother said, pushing this uncomfortable home truth to one side.

'There's no need to. You won't ever meet him.'

In the end, and once the shock had worn off, her parents made it clear that they would be standing right by her. Their love and solidarity was just what she needed. It still brought a lump to her throat.

Clara slipped out of bed and filled the kettle. After wiping away the condensation that had formed on the window above the cooker, she opened one of the vents in Winnie's roof, by which time the kettle had boiled. She made a pot of tea, then, surprised that the whistling of the kettle hadn't woken Ned, she stepped onto the first rung of the ladder and poked her head through the curtains.

Her heart leapt into her mouth. Ned's bed was empty.

It was every parent's worst nightmare. Cold, debilitating fear consumed her, then panic took hold. She leaned across Ned's rumpled bed and flung back the duvet as though he might be there after all.

Next she stumbled down from the ladder and checked the rest of the van. No sign of him. She stood for a moment to gather her thoughts. Had someone sneaked into the van while she slept and abducted him?

No. Ned must simply have gone for a walk. In the rain?

Without bothering to change out of the oversized T-shirt she had slept in, she pulled on a pair of jeans and pushed her feet into her trainers. She opened the door and stepped outside. The rain was coming down heavier now and splashed against her face as she scanned the courtyard. She made a dash for Mermaid House and hammered wildly on the door. At last, and almost in tears, she heard the familiar, but welcome sound of Mr Liberty cursing. 'Hell's teeth, what's all the rumpus?'

he growled, throwing open the door and staring at her fiercely.

'It's Ned.' She gulped. 'He's missing and I don't know where to start looking for him. Will you help me? Please. I thought you might know—' From behind him a head appeared, followed swiftly by the rest of Ned in his slippers, pyjamas and stripy dressing gown. Clara went weak with relief. He was safe. She pushed past Mr Liberty, knelt on the stone-flagged floor and hugged Ned. But hot on the heels of relief came irrational anger and, to her shame, it was all she could do to stop herself shaking him. 'You know you're not supposed to leave the camper-van on your own,' she said, as calmly as she could. 'I was so worried. I thought something terrible had happened to you.'

'Please don't be cross with me, Mummy,' he said, tremulously. 'Mr Liberty said it would be all right.'

If Clara had felt like shaking Ned, she now felt like punching Mr Liberty. She got to her feet. 'Let me get this straight. This was *your* idea?'

He cleared his throat. 'Saw the little lad peering out of his window and thought he might appreciate some company. Which he did. Isn't that right, young man?'

'What gives you the right to think you can encourage my son to break a rule? What did you think you were doing?'

'Mummy—'

'Ned, please, I'm talking.'

'But, Mummy, Mr Liberty showed me a secret door and the tower. He said there used to be a ghost up there. He told me that—'

'Ahem, possibly not the time, young man,' Mr Liberty murmured. 'Maybe we both ought to be apologising to your mother. She's looking a mite bothered to me.'

Clara flashed him a look of pure fury. 'Bothered? I was out of my mind with worry. I thought—' She stopped as her anger suddenly subsided, and the heart-thumping pain of relief returned. 'I thought you didn't go in for making apologies.'

He looked uncomfortable. 'Miss Costello, I meant you and your boy no harm, and I'm very sorry that I caused you a moment's concern.'

'I'm sorry too, Mummy.' Ned's hand crept into hers. 'Don't be cross,' he added, shooting down any remaining vestiges of anger with one of his heart-melting smiles.

Suddenly she couldn't speak, but Mr Liberty filled in the silence. 'Well, if we're through with the sentiment, can you decide what you want to do next?' Contrition dispensed with, he went on, 'You can either stand here for the rest of the day freezing to death, or you can warm yourself by the fire in the kitchen while I make you some tea.'

Clara decided to accept, and she and Ned followed as Mr Liberty led the way. She was appalled at what she saw. Mess and clutter lay everywhere, piles of junk as far as the eye could see. The house smelt too. She had imagined a comforting, old-fashioned kitchen, not this dingy room, with its grimy walls and flaking paintwork.

'Don't stand on ceremony,' he commanded. 'Sit yourself down.' He scraped one of the heavy chairs away from the long table and put it a few feet short of a gas-fired heater. She crossed the room reluctantly, her shoes sticking to the scummy floor with each step, and sat in front of the meagre source of warmth. Mr Liberty threw a tea towel at Ned. 'Don't stand there idly, young man,' he said. 'Help your mother to dry her hair. We don't want her catching her death, do we?'

A dubious brown crust on the tea towel made her wonder if a mug of tea was such a good idea. Ned tried helpfully to dab at her hair. She ducked out of his reach. 'No, Ned,' she whispered. 'It's dirty.'

'Shall I ask Mr Liberty for a clean one?' he whispered back.

Mr Liberty was rinsing mugs under the tap, and whipped round. 'Complaining again, Miss Costello? And there was me on the verge of offering you something to eat.'

The very idea made Clara want to gag. But, to her horror, Ned said, 'Breakfast would be nice.' He smiled at Mr Liberty.

Clara stepped in fast. 'Why don't I cook us all a fry-up in the van? We've got plenty of eggs and bacon.'

He looked at her shrewdly. 'Are you implying that my house isn't good enough for you? That it's not clean?'

'I'm not implying anything of the kind,' she said. 'I'm telling you straight. The house, what I've seen of it, is a health hazard.'

He flared his nostrils. 'You have quite a nerve, Miss Costello. Are you always so direct with people you hardly know?'

She gave him a conciliatory smile. 'I'm being unusually restrained with you. You should think yourself lucky.'

He gave a short bark of a laugh. 'Ned, m' boy, you have an extraordinary mother, did you know that? And just to prove that I don't harbour any ill feelings, I'm going to take up her offer of a cooked breakfast.'

Inside the camper-van, Gabriel tucked hungrily into his plate of bacon and eggs, relishing every mouthful.

'Would you like some ketchup, Mr Liberty?' asked Ned.

'Ketchup's for *caffs*,' Gabriel replied tersely. 'It's the opium of the common folk.'

'What's opium?'

'He doesn't need to know,' his mother chipped in.

'Why don't I need to know?'

'Yes, Miss Costello, come along now, don't be shy. Surely you have an answer for your naturally inquisitive son. You seem to have an answer for just about everything else.' To his delight, a slightly raised eyebrow indicated that he had scored a point.

'It's a drug made from poppies, Ned,' she said, 'and it's highly addictive. It melts your brain. And before you ask what addictive means, it means that you want it all the time.'

'Like chocolate?'

'Yes. But you want it even more than chocolate.'

'But how does it melt your brain? And if I ate too much chocolate, would my brain melt? Would it pour out through my ears, going gloopy-gloopy-gloop if I shook my head?' He gave them a demonstration, his eyes swivelling.

Gabriel was reminded of Caspar and Damson as small children. They had always been on at him, question after tiresome question. Jonah had been the opposite, hardly opening his mouth. If he wanted to know something he found it out for himself. 'Jonah's an intelligent boy, Gabriel,' Val often said. 'You should do more to encourage him. Show how proud you are of him.' But Jonah had thrown away his potential.

Sighing inwardly and feeling his good humour drain out of him, Gabriel stabbed a piece of toast into the yolk of his second egg. He could remember the stinging blow Jonah had dealt him when he had announced his intention of becoming a teacher.

'Please, Dad,' he had said, 'don't make this any harder for me than it already is. Just hear me out and respect my decision. That's all I ask.'

'And all I've ever asked of you is your respect, loyalty and duty, as my father expected them of me.'

'And maybe your father was wrong to expect so much of you. If he had treated you differently, you might have treated us differently.'

Incensed at the criticism levelled at both himself and his father—a man he had both feared and idolised—Gabriel had done the unthinkable: he had lashed out and struck Jonah, knocking him clean off his feet. In shock he had watched his younger son pick himself up from the floor, then touch the bloodied corner of his mouth. But something more than anger was raging inside Gabriel. He never knew whether Jonah had done it deliberately, but his gaze, as he dusted himself down, moved from Gabriel's face to the portrait of Anastasia above the fireplace. It was as if he was saying, 'And what would she say of your behaviour?' But in a quiet voice, he had said, 'Why can't you trust me to cock up my own life, Dad? Why try to do it for me?'

Not another word passed between them. Not for the rest of that evening, that week or the months that followed. After Jonah had walked out on him that night, Gabriel didn't set eyes on him again for a year.

The sound of an engine jolted Gabriel out of his thoughts. 'Shall I go and see who it is?' asked Ned, opening the top half of the camper-van door so that he could peer out. 'It's a car,' he announced, standing on tiptoe. 'There's someone to see you, Mr Liberty.'

'Top marks, young man,' said Gabriel, recognising the car with annoyance. Didn't the wretched man have the sick and the dying to attend to?

'Shall I invite him in, Mummy?'

'No, Ned, I'm sure Mr Liberty would rather entertain his guest in the comfort of his own home.'

Dr Singh was already knocking on the back door by the time Gabriel made it across the courtyard in the rain. 'You know what your trouble is,' he said to the doctor. 'You've got too much time on your hands. I suppose you want to come in?'

'Good morning to you, Mr Liberty. Yes, entry to your fine house so that we can both get out of this terrible rain would be in both our interests, I suspect.'

'And I suspect you of foul play,' Gabriel said when they were standing in the kitchen, and Dr Singh was requesting a look at his arm. 'You're keeping a close watch on me and I don't like it.'

'Mm . . . It's improving nicely. Eye next. Foul play? In what way?'

'You're biding your time before you start insisting that I do something about getting help around my house. You'll pull another of your blackmail stunts on me if I don't do as you say.'

'Tsk—tsk, Mr Liberty. I can't think what you're referring to. Mm . . . yes, your eye looks much better. But you do need help and I'm determined to make you see that. You're not—'

'I'm not getting any younger,' Gabriel finished for him. 'Blah-di-blah-di-blah. You're just dying to get Social Services onto me, aren't you?'

'A tempting suggestion, and certainly something to consider. As risky as it is, may I wash my hands?' He pulled out a small hand towel from his medical bag, along with a tiny bar of wrapped soap.

'Oh, please, be my guest.'

'Talking of which, would I be correct in thinking you have one?' The doctor looked through the window, out across the courtyard. 'A member of your family, perhaps?'

Family, echoed Gabriel privately. Now there was an idea. But would it work? Surely it had to be worth a try? 'Actually, you're spot on. My daughter's come to stay with me.'

Dr Singh turned off the tap with the tip of his forefinger, picked the small white towel from his shoulder and dried his hands. 'That is wonderful news. So, will your daughter be playing a more active role in your life from now on?'

'Oh, do me the honour of getting to the point. What you're really asking is, am I going to let her help me clean up my act?'

'You put it so well, Mr Liberty.'

'And if that were to happen, would you stop turning up here with spurious excuses to check on my welfare?'

'I might.'

'Well, you stay right there while I go and fetch my daughter for you to meet. You'll soon see that I'm now in good hands.'

Crossing the courtyard, Gabriel had no idea if Miss Costello would play ball, but it had to be worth a try. All he had to do was inveigle her into telling a white lie or two and everyone would be happy.

Clara listened to Mr Liberty's extraordinary proposal. 'Now let me get this straight,' she said, 'you want *me* to pretend to be your daughter?'

He shuffled again. 'I thought I'd just made that abundantly clear.'

'Would it be too much of an imposition to ask why?'

'I might have known you'd make matters difficult. Why can't you just accept what I've asked you to do?'

'Because I like to be presented with all the salient facts before I make up my mind about anything.'

'All right, all right. I need to prove to that annoying quack that I have a loving member of my family clasped to my bosom who is eager to keep a watchful eye over me.'

'And if you can't prove that that is the case?'

'I'll probably have Social Services snooping round here faster than you can say meals on bloody wheels. And they won't leave it there. You've seen the state of the house. Their next move will be to have me rehoused, claiming I'm incapable of taking care of myself.'

'You don't think you're overreacting just a touch? They couldn't do that unless you allowed them to.'

'If it was your freedom in the balance, would you want to risk it?'

'OK,' she said, 'I'll do it. And given that we don't have time to concoct anything elaborate, we'll have to keep our story simple. Agreed?'

He nodded. 'If he asks, I thought you could tell him you were coming to stay indefinitely.'

'And Ned? What do we say about him?'

Mr Liberty hesitated. 'I suppose he'll have to be my grandson.'

At this last remark, and with his hands cupping an enormous bubble, Ned turned from the sink. He beamed and gave the bubble a long, steady blow. It moved slowly from his hands, drifted up towards Mr Liberty and came to rest on his shoulder. Where it burst.

'Let's hope that's not what's going to happen to our story when we meet your Dr Singh,' Clara remarked.

Dr Singh was absorbed in a three-month-old *Daily Telegraph* that was lying on top of a box of old shoes and jam jars when Gabriel and his newly acquired family entered the kitchen.

In a loud, jovial voice, Gabriel said, 'Dr Singh, I'd like you to meet my daughter, Damson, and my grandson, Ned.'

'I'm very pleased to meet you,' the doctor said, coming forward to shake hands. 'But, Mr Liberty, you didn't tell me you were fortunate enough to be a grandfather. And such a fine-looking boy.'

'You're not my priest, I don't have to confess everything to you.'

Dr Singh smiled at Miss Costello. 'Your father is a very unusual man. His sense of humour is not to everyone's taste, I think.'

'Oh, he's a quirky old devil, but that's his charm. Affectionately cur-mudgeonly, is what we say about him. Isn't that right, *Dad?*'

She's enjoying every moment of this, thought Gabriel, with a half-smile. But then, truth to tell, so was he. 'If you say so, *dear.*'

'He tells me that you're coming to stay with him,' Dr Singh said.

'Yes, that's right. I thought I'd take him in hand, tidy the place up a bit, maybe even encourage him to find a housekeeper.'

Dr Singh smiled again. 'I wish you luck in those tasks.' He cast his eyes meaningfully around the kitchen.

'Oh, I think I'm more than up to the task of whipping my rascal of a father into shape. No worries on that score.'

'Well, if you've both finished discussing me as though I were a dimwit,' Gabriel said tersely, 'perhaps you'd be kind enough to show the doctor to the door, *Damson.*'

'Yes, *Dad*, of course.'

Thinking how easily they'd got away with it, Gabriel watched the doctor being lead out of the kitchen. Despite the rain, Miss Costello walked the doctor to his car. Through the window, Gabriel could see that they were deep in conversation.

'Well?' he said, when she came back into the kitchen. 'Did we get away with it?'

'For the time being, yes. You've earned yourself a reprieve until next week. He said he's going to pop in on Monday to make sure your eye has recovered.'

'This is victimisation,' Gabriel roared. 'This is outrageous! I'll—I'll pretend I'm not in. Or, better still, I'll go to the surgery. That'll show the stupid little man.' Then, in a less acerbic tone, 'Why can't people understand that I just want to be left alone? Is that really too much to ask?' He slumped into a chair at the kitchen table.

With her hands resting on Ned's shoulders, Clara observed him from across the room. The poor man made a desolate picture. And for the first time since meeting him, she saw not a growling, teeth-baring tyrant, but an elderly man who wanted to preserve his dignity. It was just that he was going about it in the wrong way.

Why is Mr Liberty so sad?' Ned asked, his voice loud and too clear.

'I'm not sad,' rumbled Mr Liberty. He removed from Ned's hands the magnifying glass he had unearthed from an overflowing shoebox of junk on the table. Ned had been using it to inspect Mermy at close quarters.

'I'm sorry things didn't pan out better with your tenacious doctor,' she said. 'But the only way you're going to get him off your back is to meet him halfway. Clean the place up and prove to him you can fend for yourself. Can't you enlist your real daughter's help?'

Mr Liberty brought the magnifying glass down on the table with a sharp bang. 'Damson doesn't show her face here unless she has to.' His voice was hard, scornful.

'Damson's an unusual name. Was it your idea?'

He shook his head. 'The credit goes to my first wife. She had a fondness for the eccentric.'

Clara realised that this was the first time he had referred to his family. 'Do you have any other children?' she asked.

'A pair of sons who are both two shades of stupid. Caspar is a con man with as much head for business as a watermelon. My other son, Jonah, is a weak-willed idealist.'

'And what terrible crime did he commit to gain such approval?'

'*That*, Miss Costello, is none of your business. And while we're on the subject, why have you started asking me so many questions? I thought you were going.'

'I was simply wondering why you don't ask for their help. And you've given me the answer. You've scared them off, haven't you? But, like you said, it's none of my business so I'll say goodbye. It's been an education.' She held out her hand.

He stared at it hard, rose to his feet, and took it in his large distorted paw. 'Tell me, Miss Costello,' he said slowly, 'you strike me as a woman who enjoys a challenge. Am I right?'

'It has been said of me, yes. Your point being?'

'I'd like to make you an offer. Help rid me of that interfering quack by pretending to be my daughter for a while longer.'

'Are we talking more lies? And perhaps you'd elaborate on what "a while longer" actually means. Another day? Another two days?'

'It depends on how long you think it would take to sort out this mess.' He indicated the kitchen.

Clara was stunned. He couldn't be serious. 'Whoa there, I'm not sure I like where this is going. What on earth makes you think I would be interested in dealing with this little lot? Ned and I are on holiday. Cleaning up after somebody else doesn't feature on our itinerary.'

'But you do owe me a favour.'

'Since when?'

'Since I rescued you from those goons when you were trespassing on my land.'

The breathtaking cheek of the man! 'Oh, nice try,' she said derisively. 'You think you can toss that one in and hold my conscience to ransom. Well, think again, buddy, because you've got me all wrong. Anyway, I've already carried out one favour for you by lying to Dr Singh.'

'If I can't appeal to your good nature, then maybe your purse will be a better option.'

'Sorry, not interested. Try flaunting your money at the Yellow Pages.'

'I don't want strangers in my house. Please, won't you even consider my offer? I'm willing to pay you whatever it takes.'

She held her ground. 'Look, you might be used to bullying people into doing what you want them to do, but you can't do the same with me. And, for your information, I'm not for sale.'

'Come, come, everything is for sale, surely you know that. And just think of the challenge.'

'The answer is still a resounding no.'

It was the most monstrously ludicrous idea Clara had ever heard, and as she and Ned packed up Winnie, she didn't know whether to feel flattered by Mr Liberty's proposal, that he clearly approved of her, or downright insulted that he had thought she might want to waste her holiday cleaning up his mess.

It was a power thing, she suspected. Old Laughing Boy needed someone he could treat as a skivvy. That was what this was about. Well, not this girl. She was nobody's skivvy. No, sirree. And how dare he think she could be bought? She hadn't given up a well-paid job to become a cleaner for that miserable old goat!

 **CHAPTER FIVE**

CLARA'S SEARCH OF DEACONSBRIDGE had revealed that it was a launderette-free zone. It hadn't been a complete waste of time, though. She now had the lie of the land and knew that there was a modest supermarket a short distance from the market square, where they could stock up.

'Ho-hum,' she said to Ned, as they circled the square one last time, the rain coming down and the long wiper blades swishing across the windscreen, 'I guess I'll have to admit defeat. Perhaps the next campsite we stay at will have a machine we can use. Shall we get the shopping done now?'

'Then can we go to the Mermaid Café for lunch?'

'Good thinking, and while we're there, we'll make our plans. We'll look at the map and see if we can find a campsite we like the sound of. Oh, and we must buy a large notebook and some postcards.'

Taking the next left, Clara told Ned about her idea that they should keep a diary. He liked the sound of this. 'Can we buy some new crayons, please?'

She smiled. 'I think the budget will stretch to that. Right, here we are. And, thank the Lord, it's free parking if we're only here for an hour. Life just gets better and better, Ned.'

They dashed through the rain from the van to the front of the super-market, grabbed a trolley and made a start. But with Ned at the helm it was only a matter of time before they crashed into someone or some-thing. He gave the job his entire concentration, but just as they were coming into the home straight they rammed a trolley being pushed by a long-faced man in an expensive suit. Miraculously they arrived at the check-out relatively unscathed and with everything they'd gone in for, except the notebook and crayons.

There were only two check-outs in use, so they joined the one with the smallest queue. To Clara's embarrassment, the long-faced man pulled in behind them. She noticed that his trolley contained a dozen bottles of champagne on special offer. 'Come on,' he muttered irritably after a few minutes. 'What's the holdup?'

The question was directed at nobody in particular, and Clara had no intention of answering it. Instead, she finished loading their shopping onto the conveyor belt, and looked at the woman in front of her. She was in her mid- to late seventies, Clara reckoned, and was wearing the type of felt hat Clara's grandmother used to wear. She looked upset and was glancing from the check-out girl to the purse in her trembling hands. She said something that Clara didn't catch. In response an over-plucked eyebrow hitched itself skywards. 'You what?'

Whatever the older woman had said, it wasn't getting her anywhere, and the girl—a sullen piece of work dressed in a pink and white over-all—rolled her eyes at Clara as if to say, 'Got a right one here.'

'Will you please get a move on?' the suit man demanded from behind Clara. 'I don't have all day to waste.'

Queue rage, thought Clara, with disgust. She left Ned scaling the side of their trolley and went to see if she could help. 'What's the problem?' she asked the check-out girl.

'Search me. The daft old bat's not making any sense.'

Clara turned to the older woman. 'Can I help?'

A pale, anxious face looked at Clara. Trembling hands showed her the purse: it was empty. Oh Lord, thought Clara, now what?

'Oh, this is ridiculous. Will somebody *do* something?'

Clara turned and smiled sweetly at the suit. 'For a start, you could try piping down, mate, and go and join the other queue.'

He stared at her furiously. 'And *you* should try keeping your brat under control. He's stepped on my foot three times.'

She did the adult thing, poked her tongue out at him, then turned back to the woman. 'How much is it?' she asked the girl on the till.

'Three pounds seventeen.' The girl pouted.

'Goodness, a king's ransom.' Digging into her bag, Clara offered her credit card. 'Right, stick it on this and put my shopping through as fast as your fingers can manage it. OK?'

Clara turned to explain the situation to the woman. 'There's no need to worry,' she said. 'I've paid it for you.' But her words seemed to add to the poor woman's anxiety and she started speaking so fast that Clara couldn't understand what she was saying. 'Here,' she said, 'this is your bag of shopping. Will you be all right?'

The head shook again, and the woman said, 'You . . . with me.'

'You want me to come with you?'

A smile of relief and a nod confirmed that she had understood correctly. 'But where to? Do you want me to take you home?'

Clara didn't understand the answer, but after she had bagged up her shopping and paid for it, the three of them left the store. They had run out of time in the car park, so Clara explained to the woman that they would have to drive to wherever it was that she lived. Getting directions was going to prove interesting, though. Then she had the idea of asking the woman to write down her address.

When she gave the woman a piece of paper and a pen, it became evident that her hands lacked the dexterity to hold anything firmly. Nevertheless, after she had made a huge effort, Clara read the word 'stroke'. Ah, so that was it. She asked the woman where she wanted to go. It took a long time, but 'Second Best' and 'Son' appeared.

Following the woman's hand signals, they drove back into the market square, past the bookshop and the Deaconsbridge Arms, then took a side road called Millstone Row and there, on the corner, they saw a shop called Second Best. There was just room to park in front of it. Seeing that her passenger was struggling to release her seat belt, Clara did it for her, then called through to Ned, 'OK, you can get out now.'

They entered the shop, their arrival heralded by a bell. It was jampacked with cupboards, wardrobes, three-piece suites, bookcases, mirrors, ornaments, and any number of chairs—dining chairs, kitchen chairs, garden chairs. Despite the quantity of furniture and knickknacks crammed into the confined space, there was a surprising degree of order to the shop and Vivaldi's 'Four Seasons' was playing on a radio.

'I'll be right with you,' a man's voice told them.

The old woman took a few painfully slow steps through the shop and disappeared behind an old gas cooker.

'Hello, Mum, you back already with Samson? He found you all right, then? What's wrong?'

This was progress, thought Clara. They'd found the son. After a torrent of jumbled words, he appeared with his mother.

Clara explained who she was and what had happened in the supermarket. At the man's side, his mother kept muttering something that sounded like 'Bunny. Blow bunny,' and twice showed him her empty purse. Then she started to cry. Her son put his arm round her. 'Hey, it's OK, Mum, it doesn't matter. You took the wrong purse, that was all. Now, why don't you sit down and I'll make you a cup of tea?'

Having helped her out of her coat, he settled her into a chocolate brown Leatherette sofa. Clara was impressed by his kindness and patience. He was well over six foot tall and struck Clara as very much the gentle giant. She put him somewhere in his mid-fifties.

'Would you excuse me for a minute?' he said to Clara. 'I'll just go and put the kettle on.' In his absence, Clara joined his mother on the sofa. The woman reached out to Clara's arm, squeezed it, and eventually produced, 'Bes-sie. Name . . . Bessie.'

'I'm pleased to meet you, Bessie. My name's Clara. This is my son, Ned.'

The anxious expression gave way to a smile. 'Juggly poy. Juggly pies.'

'Juggly poy?' Clara repeated, hoping for enlightenment.

'She's saying he's a lovely boy, and has lovely eyes.' The son was back. He set a mug of tea on a small table beside his mother. 'I'm Archie Merryman, by the way,' he said, holding out a hand to Clara, 'and I'm extremely grateful to you. My mother had a stroke not so long ago and the words don't always come out as they should.'

'So I understand. I had the idea of getting her to write things down, only I didn't realise it would be so difficult for her.'

'The stroke did its worst down your right side, Mum, didn't it?' he said, turning to his mother to include her in the conversation.

In the silence that followed, Clara looked round to see where Ned was, and located him on the other side of the shop where he was inspecting a commode. 'What's this for, Mummy?' he asked.

'I'll tell you later.' She glanced back at the owner of the shop, who was smiling. 'Children,' she said, with a shrug, 'questions, questions, questions. You don't mind him poking around, do you?'

'Of course not. It's good to see him enjoying himself. He's a grand little chap. Are you here visiting Deaconsbridge?'

'Is it that obvious we're interlopers? I thought we were blending in rather nicely.'

He laughed. 'I've been here more than twenty years, and I still stick out like a sore thumb. But where are my manners? I should have offered you a drink. What can I get you?'

'That's kind, but no thanks. I've promised Ned lunch in the Mermaid Café.' Ned had moved to a coffee table where he'd found a *Star Wars* jigsaw. 'No, don't tip it out, Ned,' she called, seeing him ready to settle in for the afternoon. She stood up to go. 'Goodbye, Bessie, it was lovely meeting you. You take care now, won't you?' Then to Archie Merryman, she said, 'I know it's a cheek, but would it be all right if I left our van outside your shop while we have something to eat? We won't be long.'

'Sure. It's the least I can do for you. Enjoy your lunch.'

The bell tinkled merrily behind them as they left, and as they crossed the road to the market square, Clara thought how nice Archie Merryman was. 'A juggly man,' she said to herself, with a smile.

'It's beginning to feel like home, this place,' Clara said to Ned, when they were sitting at the table they had used yesterday and had been served by the same waitress, whose name was Shirley.

The café was even busier today and it was a while before the waitress brought them their meal. She explained that it was always like this when the weather turned wet. 'It brings the walkers down from the hills and moors in search of something warm to stick their ribs together,' she said. 'It'll be crazy like this for some days.'

'I thought you said the weather was breaking at the weekend. What went wrong with the forecast?'

'I was only out by a couple of days. And any road, we have our own climate round here. We're a law unto ourselves.'

'It means that, like any true Deaconite, she makes it up as she goes along.'

The three turned to see who had spoken.

'Ah, and what would you know about the weather, Archie Merryman? Are those flowers for me by any chance?'

He gave her a wink. 'Another time, Shirley . . .' He turned to Clara. 'Mind if I join you for a couple of seconds? I won't keep you.'

'No, no, of course not. Please, sit down. What's wrong?'

'Nothing. It's just that I forgot to pay you back for my mother's shopping. And . . . and I also wanted to give you these, to say thank you for what you did.' He sat down and handed the flowers across the table.

Clara was touched. 'I don't know what to say except thank you. They're lovely. But there was no need for you to go to all this trouble.'

'I'll have to disagree with you on that point. And this is for you, Ned.' From a carrier bag that Clara hadn't noticed until now, he pulled out the Star Wars jigsaw Ned had been looking at in the shop.

'Ooh, thank you,' he said, kneeling up on his chair for a better look.

'This is very generous of you,' Clara said, 'but really—'

From his shirt pocket he retrieved a roll of money. 'Now, then, how much was my mother's shopping?'

'It was hardly anything. I don't need reimbursing. I was just pleased I was there to help.'

Archie turned to Ned, who was working on a strand of spaghetti. 'Ned, you have a peach of a mother. You take care of her, won't you?'

Clara laughed. 'Please, stop it, you're embarrassing him. To say nothing of what you're doing to me.'

'In that case, I'd better go.' He stood up. 'Are you leaving Deaconsbridge today or will we be lucky enough to see you round town for a few days yet?'

'If I can find a suitable campsite nearby, there's every chance you might see us again. Our plans are fairly flexible.'

'We're going to see the Mermaid Cavern,' Ned piped up. 'And I've got a mermaid of my own. She lives in my pocket. Do you want to see her?'

'A mermaid in your pocket? Now, this I have to see.' He watched as Ned dug around inside his pockets.

'Mummy,' he said, his voice wavering and his face crumpling, 'I can't find Mermy.' His lower lip wobbled. 'I've lost Mermy,' he wailed.

Ned was inconsolable. Clara knew that if she was going to calm her son, she would have to convince him that, no matter what it took, she would find Mermy. With most of the occupants of the crowded café looking sympathetically in their direction, Clara lifted Ned onto her lap. She took a paper napkin from the holder on the table and wiped his eyes. 'It's OK, Ned,' she soothed, 'we'll find her. Don't worry. She probably slipped out of your pocket in the supermarket.'

'Or she might be back at my shop,' Archie said.

Ned peeled himself away from Clara's shoulder. 'Mummy, I think I know where she is.' He sniffed loudly. 'I left her at Mr Liberty's house.'

Clara didn't know whether to be relieved or disappointed. A return visit to Mermaid House and its splenetic owner—just how much fun could a girl cope with? 'Are you sure?'

Another messy sniff and a nod. 'I was playing with her at the table when you were talking to Mr Liberty.'

Clara vaguely remembered Ned inspecting Mermy with a magnifying glass. 'And you haven't seen her since?' she clarified.

'I don't think so.'

'Well, that looks like it's settled,' Archie said. 'Where does this Mr Liberty live, by the way? Will you have far to go?'

'He lives in a castle,' Ned said, wiping his eyes. 'He has a tower and I've been up it. *And* he has a secret passageway.'

'He lives at Mermaid House, near Hollow Edge Moor,' Clara said.

'What will you do?' Archie asked. 'Go up there now and see if the little lad's toy is there, or would you like a hand checking out places closer to home first?'

Touched again by his thoughtfulness, Clara said, 'Ned seems pretty sure that he's left Mermy at Mermaid House, so we'll start our search there. If we draw a blank, we'll come back and have a look at the supermarket. Thanks for the offer of help, though.'

'I'll give the shop a good going-over as well, just in case. If I find it, I'll put it somewhere safe for you. Anyway, I'd better be getting back. Take care now. And thank you again for what you did for Mum.'

It had stopped raining by the time they left the café, and they crossed the square to where they had left Winnie. Through the window of Second Best, Clara could see Archie talking to an enormous young man. As she started the engine, they both turned. In response to Archie's wave, she waved back and pipped the horn.

'Right,' she said to Ned, 'fingers crossed that Mermy is where you think she is.' And fingers crossed, she thought, joining the flow of traffic, that Mr Liberty hasn't done something unspeakable to her. There you go again, she told herself, bad-mouthing a man she scarcely knew. Perhaps she ought to stop and ask herself what had happened to him to make him so unlovable? And why was he deliberately isolating himself from his children?

Having experienced nothing but love and support from her own family, Clara couldn't imagine what it would feel like to be so alone. As for cutting herself off from Ned, she might just as well lop off a limb.

Before she conceived Ned, she had never been one of those naturally maternal women who go all gooey at the merest glimpse of a Mothercare catalogue. And with her not being married, or in any hurry to be so, she had not felt the lack of a baby in her life.

But then she had met Todd Mason Angel and she began to think that marriage might be something she could entertain, maybe even children. Todd was seven years older than her and had a smile that lit up his face and softened the lines around his mouth. He was from Wichita, Kansas, and had worked for Phoenix at their headquarters in Wilmington since graduating from Harvard. He was honest and up-front, and never hid from her the facts about his marriage, which had recently broken down, or the emotional tie he still felt to Gayle who was the mother of the two daughters he adored. Clara had insisted they kept their affair secret at work because she didn't want anyone to accuse her of getting on by sleeping with someone so senior. He had gone along with this, but she had always felt that it was less out of respect to her than because he hoped that one day he would be reconciled with his wife. To put it bluntly, she had known all along that she was playing with fire.

Ironically, the day of reconciliation came twenty-four hours after Clara discovered that she was pregnant. She and Todd had arranged to go away for a long weekend, during which she planned to tell him her news. On the day they were due to set off, he had come into her office and told her that Gayle had phoned him to say that she wanted to give their marriage another try. Though he had tried his best to let Clara down gently, and to conceal his happiness, the thud with which her heart had hit the floor had rocked her world. She knew she could never tell him she was pregnant. She had smiled bravely and said she wished him well, that if there was a chance of his marriage being put back together, he had to take it; he owed it to himself and his children.

'I'll never forget what we've had, Clara,' he had said. 'I've only ever loved two women, and you're one of them. I just hope you don't feel that I've used you, because I haven't. I'm really not that kind of a man.'

With an airy wave of her hand, she had said, 'Go on, get out of here. You've a family to get back to.'

'No hard feelings, then?'

'You know us Brits, stiff upper lip right to the finishing line.'

He had leaned over her desk and kissed her forehead. 'I'm sorry, Clara. I wish we didn't have to end it like this.'

'Hey, it was always going to have to end. We both knew that. And I'm really pleased about you and Gayle. Now, let me get on with some work.' She had wanted him gone from her office. A moment longer, and her resolve would have been shattered.

Some might say that she had behaved heroically, but she saw it differently. Such was her love for Todd that she knew she had to sacrifice her own happiness for his by letting him go.

She had spent the rest of that day going through the motions at work, until eventually she gave up and went home early, claiming she was feeling sick. It was true. She did feel nauseous. For the next two months, her morning sickness was so bad she lost a stone. A month later she returned home.

Louise was the first person she told and, predictably, she was horrified. But no amount of questioning would make Clara reveal who the father was. Much as she loved Louise, Clara knew that she would be sure to tell David, who would tell Guy, and before long, the whole of Phoenix Pharmaceuticals would know that Todd Mason Angel, the company's newly appointed finance director, was the father of Clara Costello's baby.

And every time Clara's mother said that Ned had a smile straight from the angels, she had no idea how close to the truth she was. Todd's could warm the coldest heart and Ned had inherited it. Now, as she drove to Mermaid House, Clara hoped that Ned's face would soon be its normal smiling self when he was reunited with his pride and joy.

When Gabriel looked out of the kitchen window and saw the campervan being driven through the archway, his face broke into a wide, sardonic smile. So she was back, was she? She had a price, after all. Well, now they were in for some fun.

He went to meet them. 'Looks as if you can't keep away from me, Miss Costello,' he said, as she climbed down from the driver's seat. 'But I knew you'd reconsider. So, what figure have you in mind?'

But his words went unanswered as Ned came barrelling up to him. 'Mr Liberty, have you got my mermaid? Is she in the kitchen where I left her on the table?'

And then he understood why they were back: not to help him but to help themselves. 'You'd better go and take a look,' he said to the little boy. 'You know the way.' Ned shot off into the house.

Embarrassed at his mistake, the old man said, 'It seems I've just made a colossal fool of myself, haven't I?'

Clara felt a pang of sadness for him. How hard he made life for himself, she thought. What a contrast he was to Archie Merryman. 'Perhaps only a mild fool of yourself,' she said softly. 'But tell me, just as a matter of interest, when was the last time you bought anybody flowers?'

He raised his one-eyed gaze. 'I beg your pardon?'

'What I'm really getting at is, when was the last time you made a spontaneous gesture of kindness to another person and felt good about it? Because if you did it more often, I'm sure you wouldn't be in the position you are now—bullying a stranger into helping you.'

'Are you saying that if I was nicer you would want to help me?'

'I was talking generally, about you being nice to your fellow man.'

'I'm not interested in talking generally. And as for my fellow man—'

'Look, Mr Liberty, stop being so quarrelsome. Be more gracious and see where it gets you. For instance, instead of blackmailing me this morning by saying I owed you a favour, you should have just asked me politely if I would help you. As it was you got my back up.'

'A man should be allowed to be himself,' he said stubbornly.

'I couldn't agree more, but common courtesy wouldn't go amiss.'

The sound of Ned's voice made them both turn. 'Mummy,' he cried, 'I've found Mermy. She was on the table just where I left her.' He came running towards them, and threw himself against Clara, who scooped him up and hugged him. You see, she wanted to say to Mr Liberty, it doesn't take much to be happy, does it? Then a rather more dangerous thought occurred to her. What effort, what *real* effort on her part, would it take to make Mr Liberty happy? Here she was lecturing him on how to be more gracious, so why wasn't she leading by example?

Because she was on holiday! His problems were not hers. But it would still be a holiday, she argued with herself. And Ned would enjoy himself just as much here as somewhere new. And it would be a week of earning some money as well as landing themselves free parking, and by then the Mermaid Cavern would be open. But it was a decision that couldn't be made in isolation. Still holding Ned she whispered in his ear, 'How do you feel about staying on here for a short while?'

'Will we still go to see the mermaid in the cave?'

'Of course.'

He nodded and smiled.

She lowered Ned to the ground. 'Mr Liberty, I'll do you a deal. I'll give you one week of my precious time, and in return you have to agree to certain conditions, the principal one being that you must promise me you will try to be less disagreeable, so that when Ned and I have gone, you will be enough of a human being to attract further offers of assistance. How does that sound?'

'Sounds to me as though it's a deal heavily weighted in your favour. What are the other conditions?'

She smiled archly. 'We'll sort those out as we go along. For now, though, I need to hook the van up to an electricity supply. For which, I'd like it made clear, you will not be charging me. I also need water and an up-to-date copy of the Yellow Pages.'

'I'm not having any contract cleaners in. I told you that. You do the job, or no one does it.'

'It's a skip I'm after. My guess is you have a lifetime's rubbish lying about this place, and ditching it will be the only way forward.'

'I'm not going to regret this, am I?'

'Let's hope that neither of us does.'

It was raining again as Jonah drove home from school, the light already fading. Other than a stack of essays to mark, he was looking forward to a quiet, uneventful evening. Supper and the pleasure of listening to Mahler's Symphony No. 5 was all he had in mind.

Despite the dreary weather, he was in a relaxed and happy mood. With the exception of a couple of pupils, he was pleased with his GCSE students and had high hopes for them when they sat their exams next term. If he could keep them motivated, he reckoned he could get the best history results Dick High had had in years. It was particularly gratifying to know that within his short time as head of the department, he had turned it round so dramatically. His predecessor had long since lost the plot: he'd grown tired of battling against cuts, damning league tables and hostile Ofsted recommendations.

As he drew near to his cottage, at the top of the narrow road next to the church, the evening he had planned evaporated. Outside his front door, in a flashy blue Maserati, was his brother, Caspar.

61

ERICA JAMES

Jonah parked alongside the cottage, gathered up his briefcase from the back seat of his dilapidated Ford Escort and approached the sports car. He tapped on the window to attract his brother's attention.

The electric window slid down. 'You're getting wet,' Caspar said.

'Could be something to do with the inclement weather. Are you coming in, or are you happy to stay out here showing off your new car to my neighbours?'

Caspar gave him a look of disdain. 'You mean these little shacks are occupied by real people? Heavens, whatever next?'

Jonah let them in and took his brother through to the kitchen. He knew Caspar hated his house, that he found the old weaver's cottage cramped and claustrophobic. Caspar lived alone in a stark loft apartment in Manchester that was a temple of clean lines and minimalism.

He watched his brother prowl uneasily round the tiny, low-ceilinged kitchen. He was dressed in an expensive dark blue suit with a crisp white shirt, a red silk tie and black lace-up shoes. The contrast between the two brothers could not have been greater. Jonah wore baggy corduroy trousers, a loose-fitting shirt and his dark brown hair was thick and wavy, the opposite of Caspar's smooth, well-cut locks.

'I see you still haven't got round to doing anything about the state of this kitchen,' Caspar remarked.

'Actually, Caspar, this *is* done. Are you stopping long enough to warrant me offering you a drink?'

'Depends what you've got.'

'You'll have to be a lot more honey-tongued if you want anything better than instant coffee.'

'What do I have to do for a glass of Chablis? Fawn all over you?'

'No, go out and buy one. I don't have anything here of the ilk that would agree with your sensitive nose and palate.'

Caspar gave him a pitying look. 'Ha, ha, as droll as ever, I see.'

Jonah reached for a bottle of Merlot from the wine rack. He poured two glasses of wine and passed one to Caspar. 'What are you doing here, Caspar?' he asked. 'The phone not good enough for you, these days?'

'I've been sampling the heady delights of Deaconsbridge,' he said, 'in particular, Mainwaring's, the estate agent. It's just as I thought. It's the perfect time to sell Mermaid House. It's now or wait another year, maybe longer, until things pick up again.'

'Anything wrong in doing that?'

Caspar narrowed his grey eyes. 'I told you, Jonah, we need to move on this sooner rather than later. If we let the old man stay put, the house will slide into a total decline.'

62

'And how do you know what state the house is in now? When was the last time you paid Dad a visit?'

Caspar banged his glass down on the table between them. 'That is hardly the point! Why do you always have to be so damn picky?'

Jonah leaned against the sink and considered his brother's outburst. What was the urgency about selling Mermaid House? Had Caspar, yet again, got himself into a financial mess? He decided to push. 'Since you're in the area,' he said, 'why not go and see Dad this evening? If it's money you're short of, he might find it in his heart to bung you a few quid.'

Predictably, Caspar rose to the bait. 'Who the hell said anything about me being short of money? That's an accusation I find vaguely absurd coming from someone who knows nothing about business.'

'It was a logical assumption. You've been on at me to go and see Dad—'

'Yes, and I'd like to know why you haven't.'

'I've been busy. If you must know, I'll be going to see him tomorrow.'

This seemed to mollify Caspar. 'Oh. Right. Good. Well, it's about time too. But mind you be firm with him. Don't give in to his bullying.'

The amusing irony of this instruction stayed with Jonah long after Caspar had left. The essays dealt with, his supper coming along nicely, and Mahler well into his stride, Jonah reflected on his brother's unwelcome visit. He's desperate, he concluded, stirring the pan of mushroom risotto, then adding more stock. Caspar's need for money must be greater than it had ever been. It was a grim prospect.

Caspar's scheming over the years would make humorous reading, if there wasn't always some poor soul who had lost out to his ruthlessness. The most breathtaking example of this had occurred two and a half years ago when Jonah had, unwisely, decided to introduce Emily to his family. He had been putting it off for nearly six months, but now that they were planning to marry, it seemed only right that Val and his father should meet his future wife. Val had insisted on a full Liberty turn-out with everyone spending the weekend at Mermaid House. Damson was in her most recent post-divorce state and Caspar came with his latest girlfriend, a model half his age with a fake tan, whom he ignored for the entire weekend. He was much more interested in Emily.

It was just what Jonah had been terrified of. Until then he had deliberately kept Emily away from Caspar; he had even told her why. She hadn't taken him seriously, though, and had said he was being paranoid. 'It's you I love. Why would I be interested in your brother?'

But that evening during dinner, he had seen Caspar working his charm on Emily, and seen that she was flattered by his attention. He was the perfect dinner-party guest, regaling Emily with stories of Jonah growing up, telling him what a great kid brother he had been.

'You make your childhood sound so idyllic,' Emily had said, 'like something out of *Swallows and Amazons*.'

To have told the truth would have seemed churlish and petty, so Jonah had said, 'It had its moments.'

Caspar had laughed. 'Just listen to him.' Then, 'But what I don't understand, Jonah, is why the long face? For heaven's sake, cheer up.'

While they were getting into bed that night, Emily had said, 'Your brother was right, you did look miserable during dinner. Are you sure you haven't exaggerated the stories you've told me about him?'

'Why would I do that?'

'Because you're jealous of him.'

'*Jealous?* You have to be joking!' He had tried to laugh off her accusation, but she had pursued the subject doggedly.

'You kept looking at him as though you hated him, Jonah. I've never seen you like that before. It's very worrying.'

All he could say was, 'You've never seen me in the bosom of my family before.'

The next day, after breakfast, Caspar had suggested they go for a walk. Emily had reacted as though she had just been invited to fly to Paris for lunch. 'What a wonderful idea, Caspar. A walk is exactly what I need to blow away the cobwebs.'

Caspar and Emily strode on ahead, leaving Jonah to plod along with the sulky model who was getting the message that she was history.

'Is Caspar always like this?' she said, pausing for the umpteenth time to catch her breath as they climbed the gentlest of slopes.

'Always like what?'

'So rude. And why don't you stop what he's doing with your girlfriend? Or are you so stupid you haven't noticed?'

Oh, he'd noticed all right, and if the skinny girl hadn't stopped every few hundred yards, Caspar and Emily wouldn't have got so far ahead. Way off in the distance he could see Caspar standing behind Emily, an arm over her left shoulder as he pointed out landmarks—Kinder Scout, Cracken Edge and Chinley. Then he saw the hand stroke her wind-blown hair. Then Emily turned to face him, her face tilted upwards so that he could kiss her, and Jonah knew it was over.

Leaving Caspar's girlfriend to sort herself out, he took off back to Mermaid House. He packed his things and left without telling Val or his father what he was doing.

That evening, Emily called to tell him what he already knew, that their engagement was off. She told him that she was moving in with Caspar, that she had never known anyone so amazing. 'It was love at first sight,' she went on. 'He's literally swept me off my feet.'

But in less than a month Caspar lost interest in her. She wrote to Jonah saying that she didn't know what had come over her. She even asked if there was any chance of them getting back together.

He never replied to her letter. What was there to say? He had warned her that Caspar liked nothing better than to play games with other people's emotions.

When the dust had finally settled, all Caspar said on the matter was, 'She clearly wasn't in love with you, Jonah. If she had been, I wouldn't have been a temptation for her. Think on the episode as my having done you a favour. You're better off without her. No need to thank me.'

Now, as he tipped his mushroom risotto onto his plate, and poured himself another glass of wine, Jonah wondered if anything, or anyone, could shame Caspar into behaving like a decent human being.

Their breakfast eaten and everything in the camper-van tidied away, Clara was keen to make a start on Mermaid House. Her only concern was keeping Ned occupied while she got down to work. Though he could amuse himself for quite long spells, she wasn't sure how soon it would be before he was bored. The answer was to keep him busy, and having already glimpsed some of the ground-floor rooms, she felt there was enough safe-looking junk lying about the place with which Ned could play for hours.

But first, she and Ned drove into Deaconsbridge and made a return visit to the supermarket where, with a sub from Mr Liberty's wallet, she filled several carrier bags with cleaning products, rubber gloves, cloths, tins of polish, air fresheners, and some rolls of bin bags.

Back at Mermaid House, Clara let Ned run on ahead to knock at the door. It was opened almost immediately, as if her employer had been waiting for her to arrive and clock on.

'Is your eye better now, Mr Liberty?' asked Ned. The patch had gone and without it he looked a little less fierce.

'It's as good as new,' he replied starchily, and stood back to let them in. 'Where will you start? The kitchen?'

'We'll start first with improving labour relations,' Clara said. '*You* will bid *us* a good morning, then *you* will offer to put the kettle on. And while *you* are making *us* some coffee, I will assess the extent of the damage.' She handed him one of the carrier bags. 'There's a jar of instant in there, along with a packet of biscuits.'

He grunted and led them through to the kitchen.

'Ever thought of buying a dishwasher?' she asked, when she saw the piles of dirty crockery still untouched on the draining board.

'A waste of money just for one person.'

'There are some reasonably priced ones on the market, small machines designed for people on their own.'

'Reasonably priced,' he repeated. 'I don't need things to be *reasonably priced*. I have money.'

'Well, try spending it! Or are you hell-bent on leaving it to the family of whom you've spoken so highly?'

He snorted, then reached for a pen and a used envelope. He handed them to Clara. 'Make a list of all the things you think I need.'

'I'll put "new heart" at the top of it, shall I?'

Her first job was to shift most of the junk onto either the table or the floor so that she could get at the worktops to scrub them clean. Once she had done the sink, she tackled the washing-up, then moved on to the cupboards, which were full of things she doubted were ever used.

While Ned helped to empty the lower cupboards of old pans, buckled lids, steamers and fish kettles, Clara called Mr Liberty. He appeared in the doorway and looked aghast at the mess. 'You've made it worse,' he said, as he surveyed the scene.

'Oh, bring on the gratitude, why don't you?' said Clara sharply. 'Now, listen, I need you to decide what you want to keep.'

He shrugged. 'You decide for me.'

She took him at his word, and put together a collection of pans for his cooking needs and instructed Ned to take them over to the sink. He could mess around with soapy water under the guise of washing them.

'What will you do with the others?' asked Mr Liberty.

'Some are fit for the dustbin—which reminds me, that skip I ordered should be here around lunchtime—but the better ones could go to a charity shop. Do you have such a thing in Deaconsbridge?'

'There was one, but when the rents on all the shops in the market square went up, it closed.'

'It seems a shame to ditch them when they're in pretty good nick. Put the kettle on again and I'll have a think.'

With a bucket of hot water dosed liberally with disinfectant, she started to clean inside the cupboards. There was something satisfying about bringing order to chaos, and she was enjoying herself. By the end of the day she would have this kitchen all shipshape and Bristol fashion, or her name wasn't Miss Clara Costello.

Calling herself by her full name made her think about the formal way in which she and Mr Liberty referred to each other. It amused her, and if she wasn't mistaken, it amused him.

Behind her, she could hear Ned talking to Mr Liberty as he spooned coffee into mugs. He was chattering nineteen to the dozen, just like he did at home with Granda, and she realised that as long as Ned had someone to talk to, he would not get bored.

When Mr Liberty handed her a mug of coffee he said, 'You've been working like a Trojan since you got here, why don't you take a break?'

She doffed an imaginary cap. 'Gawd bless you, guv'nor, for taking pity on a humble scullery-maid. I'm touched.'

He held out a hand and helped her to her feet. 'Bring your coffee with you, and I'll give you a guided tour,' he said gruffly.

She tugged off her rubber gloves and, Ned following with the biscuits, Mr Liberty led the way into the vast hall.

'I know the way,' said Ned, and sped off down its gloomy length.

'Where's he taking us?' Clara asked. 'And do you mind?'

'To the library, and it doesn't look as if I have much choice.'

When they caught up with Ned, he was swinging open a heavy door. 'Slow down, partner,' Clara told him.

The library felt cold and damp, but was comparatively tidy, in as much as it contained a few basic items of furniture: two leather armchairs at either side of a stone fireplace, another two in the bay window, a footstool and a lampstand with a dented shade. Two of the walls were lined from floor to ceiling with books. But it was difficult to make out anything in any detail: the curtains were drawn, keeping out the light.

'Do you always have the curtains like this?' she asked.

'Not always.' He went over to the window and gave the burgundy velvet drapes a hefty tug. 'But it stops the light destroying the books.'

So the man had a weak spot. Books above humans, by the looks of things. She changed her mind when light flooded the room and she saw the painting above the fireplace. 'Who's that?' she asked.

Mr Liberty stood beside her. 'My first wife, Anastasia.'

Clara stared at the young woman, her confident gaze and the beguiling gentleness in her expression. The eyes were full of warmth and humour and as dark as her thickly tousled hair. 'She was very beautiful,' she said softly.

He took a noisy swallow of his coffee. 'Yes. And I suppose you're wondering what she saw in someone like me?'

Before she could deny or refute this, Ned called, 'Mummy, come over here. This is where the secret passage is.'

She went to where he was standing, and stared at the rows of leather-bound books that he was pointing to. 'Are you sure?' she asked, playing along with him. 'All I can see is a load of old books.'

His eyes danced with excitement as he glanced at Mr Liberty. 'Shall I show her?' he asked.

Mr Liberty sucked in his breath. 'I don't know, lad. Can she keep a secret? We don't want her blabbing all over the county, do we?'

Ned's face grew solemn. 'Mummy, you won't tell anyone, will you?'

'Hand on heart,' she said, as seriously as she could. 'I promise not to tell a living soul about Mr Liberty's back passage.'

Mr Liberty snorted. But the hint of a smile on his face didn't escape Clara.

Despite the misty rain, the views from the tower were spectacular. They would be even better if the windows were clean, thought Clara, wondering if there would be sufficient time in the coming week to add the tower to her agenda.

Mr Liberty took them down the creaking narrow staircase, along the dark corridor and back into the library. From there he showed them the rest of the ground floor: the dining and drawing rooms, the gunroom, and the laundry room, which was a glory hole with bells on. Piles of yellowing newspapers, boxes filled with empty whisky bottles, dirty clothes and bed linen. 'Machine's not working,' Mr Liberty muttered. 'Do you know what's wrong with it?'

'Haven't a clue. It's too modern and fancy for me. Jonah bought it for me. It's supposed to dry as well as wash. All it does is bang about a lot.'

'I'll take a look at it later,' she said.

He looked at her scornfully. 'You can mend a washing machine?'

'Sure. So long as it's not the electronics, they're usually straightforward enough. Sounds like the drum belt may have worked itself loose.'

'Mummy can mend all sorts of things,' Ned said.

'Is that right?' Mr Liberty said.

'I don't like things to get the better of me,' she responded.

The tour continued upstairs, and mercifully the mess didn't get any worse. As far as she could see, the damage was superficial, but it was the scale that was so awesome.

'This was my second wife's room . . . It was where she died.' Mr Liberty unlocked the door and let them in.

It was a long, oblong room with a view over the garden and the moors beyond. 'Val loved to look across to Kinder Scout,' he said, 'which is why she chose this room. We never shared . . .' He cleared his throat. 'We didn't have that kind of relationship.'

Clara would have liked to pursue this tantalising confidence, but held back. Instead, she said, 'What did she die of? Ned, don't touch!'

They both looked at Ned, who had settled himself on a stool in front of a dressing table. Set out before him was a dusty array of scent atomisers, pots and tubes of cream, lipsticks, powder compacts, necklaces, and bottles of nail varnish.

'It was heart trouble,' Mr Liberty said. 'I should have got rid of this lot, but I couldn't bring myself to do it. Makes me look like a sentimental old fool, doesn't it?'

'Would you like me to sort it out for you?' she asked.

He said, 'There's clothes too.' He indicated two large mahogany wardrobes and a matching pair of chests of drawers.

'Just let me know what you want to keep, and I'll bag it up for you . . . if that's what you'd like.'

Next he showed her the rooms that had belonged to his children. It was at this point, standing in what had been his daughter's room, that Clara realised it was what Mr Liberty didn't say, coupled with the emptiness of some of the rooms, that revealed most about him. She realised, too, that she hadn't seen a single photograph of any of his children. Other than the portrait of the first Mrs Liberty, and the second wife's belongings, there was no record of anyone else having lived there.

As Mr Liberty went on to show them the rest of the ten bedrooms, she began to think it was no wonder he was so miserable. If she had to live in this mausoleum, she too would turn into a crabby old devil. She felt angry with his children. How could they have left him to rot here?

This thought was still with her when Mr Liberty showed her his bedroom. It was almost thirty feet long with a spectacular view over the garden and the moors beyond. She made a mental note to deal with the curtains, which were lying on the floor.

When he made a surprising offer to take Ned off her hands and play a game with him, she returned to the kitchen with renewed determination. She switched on the radio, moved the dial to Classic FM and pulled on her rubber gloves. She turned her attention to the Aga and hoped it wasn't a lost cause. If she could get that running smoothly, it would make all the difference to the dreary atmosphere in the kitchen.

Gabriel passed Ned the pack of cards and told him to shuffle them.

As he jumbled the cards, Ned asked, 'What are we going to play?'

'What can you play?'

'Um . . . Pairs. But we usually use picture cards. Nanna gave them to me for my birthday.'

'Well, let's try it with these. Have you finished messing them up yet?'

'I think so. Shall I spread them out for us?'

'Be my guest.'

Leaning across the dusty table, placing the cards face down, Ned said, 'That's what Granda always says to me. If I ask him if I can play outside, he says, "Be my guest." Nanna and Granda are in Australia,' Ned carried on. 'I have a baby cousin now. Do you think Nanna and Granda will see any kangaroos? Kangaroos are funny. They go *boing, boing, boing*.'

Just as Gabriel was despairing of ever keeping up with such a butter-fly brain, the child got down from his seat and gave an impromptu demonstration of how he thought a kangaroo would bounce around the library of Mermaid House.

'And you'll go *boing* in a moment if you don't get back into your chair. I thought we were playing Pairs.'

Gabriel watched the boy climb up into the leather armchair and resume setting out the cards. He caught the sound of music coming from the kitchen—blast the woman, she'd gone and fiddled with his radio—and his gaze moved from the boy to Anastasia's portrait above the fireplace.

She was very beautiful, had been Miss Costello's words earlier, but they didn't cover half of what Anastasia had meant to him. They had been the best of companions, the best of lovers. She was reassuringly self-sufficient, which suited him. Being so busy with work and travel-ling as much as he did, he had needed to know that she wouldn't be lonely without him. He and Anastasia relished being independent spir-its, but the welcome he received when he came home never left him in any doubt that his wife loved him as passionately as he loved her.

He sensed that, in many ways, Miss Costello was from the same mould as Anastasia. She was a confident young woman who would glide through life on the strength of her own determination. But, while he could appreciate her strengths, he realised he knew little about her.

He realised that he shouldn't, but with his curiosity aroused, and with the means to satisfy it sitting opposite him, he saw no reason not to ask a few questions.

'Finished!' Ned said, sitting back in the large chair and admiring his handiwork. The circular table was now a patchwork of blue and green tartan. 'Shall I go first?'

'As Granda would say, be my guest.'

A short while later, when Ned's pile of successfully matched cards was greater than his own, Gabriel said, 'You're not bad at this. Do you play this a lot at home with your mother?'

'I do now. But not when we were at home. Mummy was too busy then.'

'Oh? Busy with what?'

'Work. She had a very important job. She told lots of people what to do. But she gave up her job to be with me,' Ned said with unashamed pride. 'She said she wanted to give me an adventure I wouldn't forget.'

'And here you are playing cards with an old man who can't remember where the nine of clubs is . . . Aha, got it.'

'You're getting better, Mr Liberty. But I'm still winning.'

'So who looked after you when your mother was busy telling people what to do?'

'Nanna and Granda. And I went to nursery too. Nanna and Granda are in Australia.'

'You said. Do you miss them?'

He nodded. 'Yes. But not so much now.'

'Why's that?'

'Because I see Mummy all the time now.'

'And you prefer that, do you?'

'Ooh, yes. I wish it could be like this for ever and ever.'

'But you'll have to go home some day, won't you?'

'I suppose so.'

'And your mother will have to go back to bossing people about. I can see she'd be good at that.'

'She's not bossy with me.'

'She isn't? You sure?'

'She loves me.'

When he heard the boy express himself so simply and honestly Gabriel was jolted by something he didn't understand. It was a faint stirring of an emotion that was buried deep. 'And what about your father?' he ventured. 'You never speak of him.' As soon as the words were out, he regretted them. The boy looked confused. Gabriel suddenly felt horribly unworthy. Supposing his father was dead?

'There's lunch on offer if anyone's interested,' said a stiff voice.

It was the boy's mother and Gabriel reddened with shame. *Damn!* How long had she been standing there? And how much had she heard?

His guilt was multiplied many times over when he stood in the kitchen and saw the transformation. The surfaces were all cleared and scrubbed to a high sheen and the cupboard doors were so shiny that reflections bounced off them. The floor was no longer sticky underfoot and the windows looked as if the glass had been removed. There was no sign of

grease or burnt-on stains on the cooker, and the rubbish that had covered the table had vanished, and lunch had been set for three. There was
a white embroidered tablecloth he didn't recognise, and in the centre of
the plates of sandwiches and glasses of orange juice, there was a small
vase containing some purple flowers.

'Ned, do you want to go to the loo before we eat?' Clara said. 'It's
down by the laundry room. Be sure to wash your hands. I've put a clean
towel in there.'

Gabriel walked awkwardly over to the Aga, which had also been
given a clean and a polish. 'Miss Costello, I'm truly amazed at what
you've done. Thank you very much.'

She gave him a steely glance and turned off the radio. 'If you want me
to stick to our agreement I'll thank you not to interrogate my son.'

He hung his head. It was a long time since he had felt so ashamed.
'I'm sorry,' he mumbled.

'At least have the decency to look at me when you're apologising.'

'I'm sorry,' he repeated, looking straight at her. 'Shouldn't have done
that to the little lad. Not on at all. Not my business.'

'Good,' she said briskly. 'Should you feel the need to play the part of
grand inquisitor, please just ask *me* what you want to know. OK?'

'Agreed.' Contrite. Meek. These were strange feelings to him, but that
was exactly what he felt. What could he do to make her think better of
him? And when was the last time he had ever been concerned with what
anyone thought of him?

Still beside herself with barely controlled fury over Mr Liberty's scur-
rilous behaviour, Clara was putting the surge of energy to good use.
After lunch she took the grimy curtains she had unhooked from the
kitchen windows outside into the courtyard. She wanted to get the
worst of the dust off before washing them. As she shook the curtains her
anger began to subside. 'Just let him try a stunt like that once more,' she
muttered, 'and I'll be out of here faster than . . . well, faster than anything he's ever seen move!'

Marching through to the laundry room, she threw the curtains onto
the floor. Then, with the contents of the toolbox she had fetched from
Winnie, she started to take the washing machine apart.

To her satisfaction, she had it in working order in no time at all. Not
only that, but she soon had two loads of washing pegged on a line she
had rigged up in the courtyard. While a third load was sloshing around
inside the machine, she went outside to catch her breath. As she stood
in the courtyard, the skip arrived.

'Sorry I'm late,' the man said, when he had lowered it into position and she was signing the form confirming its delivery, 'but it's been one of them days.'

'Tell me about it,' she said, with feeling.

Ned and Mr Liberty came to investigate just as the man was driving away. 'You don't do anything by half do you, Miss Costello?' Mr Liberty said when he surveyed the scene—a large yellow skip and a line of his freshly laundered clothes, including some items he would perhaps rather not have had on show.

'Not if I can help it,' she said. 'Aren't you going to thank me for mending your washing machine?'

'I was just about to. But why aren't you using its drier?'

'No need—not when we can dry your unmentionables for free. Looks to me as if you could do with investing in some new ones.'

He scowled in embarrassment.

Enjoying his discomfort, she said, 'Now, then, as you're both here you can help me ditch some of the rubbish I've collected. First to go will be those boxes of bottles from the laundry room.'

Under her directions, they worked steadily for the next hour and a half, until Mr Liberty suggested he make some tea. 'Got to keep the workers happy,' he said.

 # CHAPTER SIX

THE MOMENT JONAH had driven through the school gates that morning and the exhaust had dropped off onto the tarmac, he knew that it was going to be one of those days.

Now it was three o'clock and he was accompanying Jase O'Dowd to the doctor's surgery in Deaconsbridge. He had been in the staff room, drinking a cup of coffee, when Larry Wilson, the design-technology teacher, poked his head round the door and asked if anyone would mind taking O'Dowd to the vet's to be put down. 'The bloody idiot's tried to chisel off a finger,' he grumbled, when Jonah agreed to forgo his hour of free time.

Jonah found Jase waiting outside the secretary's office. He raised his bandaged hand at Jonah. 'I'm gonna sue,' he said. 'It's not safe making them chisels so friggin' sharp. I'm gonna get a lawyer.'

'A cracking idea, but let's get you stitched up first, shall we?'

Exhaustless, they roared through the school gates, through the town and into the surgery car park, where Jonah switched off the engine and said, 'I'm not doing much for your street cred, am I, Jase?'

'Could've been worse. Could've been old Ma Wilson bringing me here.'

'I was referring to my car.'

They reported to the receptionist, then took a seat in the waiting room.

'How long do you think it will take for this to get better?'

Jonah looked at the bandaged hand on Jase's lap. 'A week or two. Why? Worried it might get in the way of your love life?' He knew that, since Christmas, Jase had been devoting his time to Heidi Conners, an anxious girl who was painfully thin—Jonah suspected she was anorexic.

Jase's face coloured, all the way to his sharp-curled quiff. 'Friggin' hell, sir, you ain't 'alf got a filthy mind! I was thinking of my exams next term and whether or not I'd be able to write.'

Suitably put in his place, and mildly surprised, Jonah apologised. 'I expect it'll be fine by then.' He knew that Jase could now put together a history essay that covered enough salient points to get him a C grade, possibly even a B, but as to his other GCSE subjects, he wasn't so sure.

A shrill bell announced that whoever would be attending to Jase was ready to see him. Expecting a nurse to stitch up Jase's finger, Jonah was surprised to be greeted by a slightly built man, who introduced himself as Dr Singh.

'I've heard of educational cutbacks,' the doctor said, unravelling the bandage from Jase's hand, 'but removal of a pupil's finger is going a step too far in my opinion. Ah, there we are, and what an impressive attempt has been made to slice through this fine finger.'

While Jase studied a poster that advocated a healthy diet of fruit and vegetables, the doctor completed his task with speed and efficiency. His small talk never once dried up as the needle dipped and rose, and a layer of gauze and a bandage were expertly applied. 'I see from your notes that you're up to date with your injections, which means you'll be spared a tetanus jab, so it's not all bad today, is it? Now, tell me, is school as awful as I remember it? Are your teachers, present company excluded, of course, as sadistic as they were in my day?'

Jase shrugged. 'Some of them are, but Mr Liberty's OK.'

Standing at the basin now and ripping off his surgical gloves, the doctor looked at Jonah. 'Forgive my inquisitiveness, but are you by any chance related to Mr Gabriel Liberty of Mermaid House?'

Surprised, Jonah confirmed that Gabriel Liberty was his father.

The doctor sat down at his desk. 'Well, how extraordinary. And isn't life strange? Suddenly the world is full of Libertys. In one week I meet first your father, then your sister, and now you.'

'You've met my sister?' It was news to Jonah that Damson was in Deaconsbridge.

'Oh, yes,' Dr Singh said. 'I met her yesterday, your nephew too. They're staying with your father, didn't you know?'

Jonah gaped. Nephew? Good grief, Damson had had a baby!

The light was fading when Clara remembered to bring in the washing. It was dry enough to be ironed, so she folded it neatly into the laundry basket. She was just adding the last of Mr Liberty's threadbare underpants to the pile, when she heard an almighty racket. The throaty rumble grew louder and nearer. Someone's car was in need of a new exhaust.

She went inside the house to find Mr Liberty. Interrupting a rumbustious game of Snap in the library, she told him he had a visitor. Like her, he assumed it was Dr Singh. She followed a few steps behind him, but stayed out of sight when they reached the kitchen. Peeping round the doorframe, she saw they had leapt to the wrong conclusion. Standing beside the table, and with several carrier bags at his feet, was a tall man in a leather jacket. His collar-length hair was thick and wavy and, as he stared round the kitchen in obvious amazement, his profile and stance reminded Clara of a Renaissance painting.

'Good God, Jonah, what are you doing here?'

He turned. 'It's Friday, Dad, the day I always go shopping for you, and the day we agreed I'd come and see you. What's been going on here? It looks fantastic. Has Damson done this?'

'Damson?' Mr Liberty snorted. 'Damson be damned!'

Having sized up the situation and worked out that this was the youngest of her employer's uncaring darlings made flesh, Clara decided to leave them to it. She turned, but a commanding voice bellowed, 'Oh, no, you don't, Miss Costello. You come right back here and take the credit for all your hard work.'

She stepped into the kitchen. 'I'm in no need of credit,' she said briskly, making her tone hostile. Irrationally she wanted this casual-looking Renaissance man to know that she disapproved of him.

'Miss Costello and I have what one might call an arrangement, Jonah,' Mr Liberty explained. 'For an exorbitant sum of money, she is staying with me for the week to do my bidding.'

'What your father is trying to say, in his clumsy way,' Clara said sharply, 'is that I'm here to tidy up Mermaid House.'

Jonah continued to stare, confused. 'Could someone please explain exactly what's going on?' he said. 'And where's Damson?'

'Hell's bells, what makes you think she's here?'

'I was told she was. Apparently I have a nephew, too.'

Clara exchanged glances with Mr Liberty. She said, 'Have you been talking to a certain Dr Singh?'

'Yes, this afternoon. I was at the surgery and he told me—'

'That your sister was staying here,' interrupted Mr Liberty. He smiled triumphantly at Clara. 'Didn't I say we'd taken him in? Hah!'

But Clara wasn't so triumphant. 'Hang on a moment, hadn't you better check with your son that he didn't blow your little scam out of the water?'

Liberty Junior held up his hands. 'Whatever scam it is that you've got going here, I'm not guilty of trying to spoil it.'

His father needed convincing. 'You sure about that?'

'I played my part beautifully, dumb schmuck, right to the end.'

'Now why doesn't that surprise me?' muttered Clara.

Even by her standards the remark sounded more caustic than she had intended, and Liberty Junior frowned at her. He said to his father, 'Would it be too much to ask why you've gone to the trouble of duping Dr Singh into believing that you have a daughter staying with you?'

A short while later, the shopping put away, a pot of tea made and explanations given, Jonah watched his father leave the kitchen to fetch Miss Costello's son. He was overwhelmed by the shame this acerbic woman had made him feel. He wanted to thank her for what she had done, but he was mortified that a stranger had walked into his father's life and achieved what no member of his own family had even tried to do.

'This must seem odd to you,' he said. 'From the outside looking in, it must appear as though we, his children, don't care.' He hoped she wouldn't judge him too harshly.

She gazed at him severely. Astutely. Assessingly. 'Well, you probably *don't* care. Not enough, anyway.'

'That's not fair,' he said, defensively.

'OK, then,' she said. 'I'll be generous and say you've simply got used to the chaos and squalor in which your father has been living and turned a blind eye to it.'

'Are you always so blunt?'

'Yes.'

'Then that's probably what my father likes about you. Few people ever gain his approval. And just because one is related to a person, it doesn't mean you understand each other. Or even get on.'

She surveyed him steadily, her eyes cool and measuring. Unnerved, he turned away.

Jonah had never seen his father talk to a child before and, intrigued, he watched him with Miss Costello's young son, Ned. He was a sweet-faced boy, who seemed extraordinarily comfortable with Gabriel. He had shiny, dark brown hair, the same colour as his mother's, with dark, alert eyes and an engaging smile. Jonah had no way of knowing if his mother had passed this on to him, too, because he had yet to see her smile. From the disapproving glances she flung at him, Jonah was getting the message that she despised him for not doing more to help his father.

The boy seemed remarkably well behaved for a four-year-old, never once spilling his drink or dropping crumbs. The nearest he got to making a *faux pas* was when he told his mother with his mouth full that Mr Liberty was going to teach him to play draughts the next morning. 'He says I can be white and go first. He's shown me the board, it's very old.'

'Mr Liberty won't teach you anything if you spray everyone with biscuit crumbs, Ned,' his mother reminded him gently.

His lips tightly sealed now, he was chewing extra fast. He swallowed hard and continued excitedly, 'But he says I might not be clever enough to play draughts because I'm so young. Do you think I'm clever enough to play, Mummy?' Suddenly he looked grave, his eyes wide.

'You're as clever as you need to be, Ned,' she said reassuringly. 'No more, no less.'

'Another of your inscrutable replies, Miss Costello. Do you lie awake in bed at night practising them when you can't get to sleep?'

'Not at all, Mr Liberty. I'm naturally inscrutable. Moreover, I never have trouble sleeping. I put it down to having a guilt-free mind.'

Jonah felt strangely isolated. There was a light-hearted repartee going on between this woman and his father that seemed designed to exclude him. Oddly, he felt as though he was playing gooseberry to their . . . extraordinary double act of sparky lovebirds.

He got up and walked over to the window and stared out across the darkening courtyard to where the yellow skip stood and, beyond, to where Miss Costello's camper-van was parked. Hearing his father laughing, an ugly thought occurred to him: he was jealous. Jealous that this stranger could make his father happy and he could not.

He turned round and heard her say, 'Eight o'clock suit you tomorrow morning? I want to finish sorting out the laundry room. Then I'll make a start on getting the dining room into apple-pie order.'

He grunted. 'Eight o'clock? Working part-time already, are you?'

'And you're too full of sweetness. Come on, Ned. Time for some supper and our own more congenial company.'

Ned climbed down from his chair. 'Good night, Mr Liberty,' he said. 'You will teach me that game in the morning, won't you?'

'A promise is a promise, young man. Now, be off with you.'

Both Jonah and his father saw them to the back door and watched them go. When a soft light glowed from the windows of the camper-van, Gabriel shut the door, led the way back into the kitchen and said, 'Right, then, why don't you get to the point as to why you've come here?'

Which Jonah did, but only when his father was searching the cupboards for a bottle of whisky.

'Dad, have you thought that maybe it might be a good time to think about selling Mermaid House?'

The last of the cupboard doors crashed shut and his father turned round, a bottle of single malt in hand. He banged it down on the table, poured himself a large measure and took a long gulp. 'And why would I want to do that?' he asked finally.

'Because you might be more comfortable in something smaller, easier to manage.'

He topped up his glass. 'How small were you thinking? Coffin-sized?'

'Don't be ridiculous, Dad.'

'That's rich! You don't think *you're* being ridiculous by coming round here and suggesting I change my lifestyle to suit your conscience?'

'It's got nothing to do with my conscience.'

'No? Then perhaps it's more to do with lining your pockets. Caspar and Damson's bottomless pockets as well, no doubt. Have they bullied you into coming here tonight?'

'Of course not!'

He gave a contemptuous snort. 'You never did have a talent for lying, Jonah. Unlike your brother. So what line is he taking? Death duties?'

'Whatever Caspar may or may not have in mind, you don't have to go along with it. Look, Dad, I've come here tonight to suggest that it might be in *your* interest to think about moving to a house that would be more convenient for you to live in. What's more, what you choose to do with the proceeds of Mermaid House would be your affair. Personally, I'd rather you used it for your own pleasure, or gave it away to someone a whole lot more deserving than anyone with the name of Liberty.'

'A dog's home, perhaps? Or how about Miss Costello? She strikes me as being an eminently deserving case.'

In spite of himself, Jonah looked up sharply at this. 'It's your money. If you think Miss Costello would benefit from it, then give it to her.' Slipping his jacket on, he added, 'I've said all I came to say, so now I'll go before either of us says anything we'll regret. Good night.'

It wasn't until he was driving home, that he knew he had omitted to say one important thing: that above all else, he cared about his father's welfare and happiness. The old man could never resist fanning the smouldering flames of a difficult conversation into a roaring argument. His comment that Miss Costello was 'eminently deserving' had been a blatant attempt to ignite their heated exchange. Even so, he couldn't help wondering how Caspar would react if he thought there was a chance that the threat might be carried out.

The thought stayed with him for the rest of the evening and the next morning. So when the telephone rang on Saturday afternoon, and Caspar demanded to know the outcome of Jonah's visit to Mermaid House, he couldn't stop himself pursuing what could only be described as a wanton act of malicious stirring. It was petty and foolish, but none-theless he relayed the goings-on at Mermaid House to his brother, labouring the point that their father seemed very taken with the attractive woman who had appeared from nowhere to work for him.

To hear the taut shock in his brother's voice was worth every second of the earbashing to which he was then subjected.

Caspar cancelled his plans for that evening and scooped up his keys from the bowl on the table by the front door. He locked his apartment, took the lift down to the garages on the ground floor and slipped behind the wheel of his Maserati. As he nosed the car into the early-evening traffic he tried to steady his temper by switching on the CD player, at the same time focusing his thoughts on the smoothness of the drive.

It worked. By the time he had picked up the A6 and had driven through Disley, he could feel the knots easing in his neck and shoulders. He knew he shouldn't let things get the better of him, and knew, too, that while Damson was under the thumb of the hippies she lived with up in Northumberland, he could no longer rely on her. But old habits die hard: he still saw her as his rock. As children she had been the more daring and cunning of the two of them. But where was she now when he needed her support and reassurance? The tension was building again in his shoulders as he tried not to think of how much he missed her. It was ages since he had last seen her—Val's funeral probably.

He pressed his foot down on the accelerator and sped on towards Mermaid House and the devious woman who had designs on his father.

The day had gone well for Archie. The shop had been busy from the moment he had opened. A cold northeasterly wind had provided him with a steady flow of day-trippers coming in for a browse.

Alone in the shop now, he was locking up. Just as he was slipping the last of the chains and bolts across the door, the telephone rang. Because Archie was thinking of his mother, he rushed through to the office and snatched up the receiver.

'Is that Mr Merryman at Second Best?' asked a woman.

'Yes, it is. What can I do for you?'

'You might not remember me, but my name is Clara Costello and I—'

'Of course I remember you. How are you? Still enjoying the delights of Deaconsbridge?'

'Yes, but not quite in the way I thought I might. I've got a proposition for you. Have you got a moment?'

'I'm all ears.'

When he'd heard what she had to say, he laughed. 'Well, I think I could manage that. I'll put it in the diary for Monday afternoon, around three o'clock. That soon enough for you?'

'Yes, that'll be fine. Do you need directions?'

'No, thanks. I've a nose on me like a bloodhound.'

After he'd rung off, he reached for the diary to make a note of the appointment.

'Mr Liberty, please don't think you can take advantage of me. I'm really not that sort of a girl.'

Gabriel scowled. 'Miss Costello, I may have lost some of my social skills of late, but as far as I'm aware I believe I only offered to cook you supper. There's not the slightest chance of me wanting to seduce you. As disappointing as that might be to you.'

They were standing in the dining room where she had been hard at work all day. She was polishing a pair of silver candlesticks he hadn't seen in a long while. Without looking at him, or giving him an answer, she said, 'What are you hiding behind your back?'

He cleared his throat. 'Ahem . . . It's a peace offering.'

She turned slowly and he held out a tightly wrapped bunch of red tulips, their petals still closed. She didn't say anything

'You rather rudely asked me the other day when was the last time I had bought anyone flowers. Well, I saw these when I was in Deaconsbridge this afternoon and they made me think of you.' He cleared his throat again. 'I've always thought of a tulip as an efficient-looking flower. Upright and businesslike. In short, purposeful. Like . . . like you.'

Her gaze met his. It was softer than it had been. 'Hush now, Mr Liberty, or you'll have me blushing to the tips of my ears. But you mentioned they were an apology. For what exactly?'

'I just want to say that I've been left with a nasty taste in my mouth after that incident with your son. I had no business prying into your affairs and I wanted you to know just how sorry I am.' His mission completed, he clumsily thrust the flowers at her and turned to flee.

He was nearly at the door when she said, 'That was really quite good, Mr Liberty. Full marks for content, but running off before taking a final bow loses you valuable points when it comes to artistic expression.'

He didn't risk looking at her, kept his face to the door. 'Please don't make fun of me. Not when I'm—'

'Trying to be nice?' she finished for him. 'Now, why don't you come back here and let me thank you properly? That's if you have the nerve.'

It was a challenge he couldn't refuse. But when he stood in front of her again and she raised herself on her toes and softly kissed his cheek, he wondered if he hadn't met his match. 'We'll make a decent human being of you yet, Mr Liberty.' She smiled.

Caught so thoroughly off guard, he couldn't stop himself from lifting a hand to his cheek and touching, with his fingertips, the spot where he could still feel the light pressure of her lips.

Still smiling at him, she said, 'I hope you're not going to withdraw your offer of supper.'

'You should know well enough by now that I'm a man of my word. But don't expect anything other than plain fare. I've got some boil-in-the-bag cod in parsley sauce knocking about in the freezer. Is that good enough for her ladyship and her son?'

'Quite good enough. Talking of Ned, where is he?'

Glad of the diversion, he led her out of the dining room and along the hall. 'I took the liberty—no pun intended—of buying him a little something while I was in Deaconsbridge.'

In the kitchen, Ned was kneeling on a chair, his head bent over the table. When they came in, he looked up. 'Mummy, Mr Liberty bought me a scrapbook and some postcards. I've been drawing a picture of his house. Do you like it?'

Clara stroked the top of Ned's head absently and studied his drawing. 'Ned, it's brilliant. How clever of you to draw the tower so well. But, my goodness, who is that handsome man?'

The boy beamed. 'Mr Liberty.'

Curious, Gabriel drew near to see how he had been depicted. Expecting to see a scowling old man, he saw instead an enormous matchstick man who dwarfed the tower of his house. His massive head was wearing a ridiculously large pair of ears, and stretched between them was a crescent-shaped smile. 'You've forgotten my nose,' he said.

The boy reached for a coloured pencil and gave the matchstick man a pastel pink swirl that obliterated one of his eyes.

'Perfect,' his mother praised him. 'And thank you, Mr Liberty. You couldn't have given Ned a better present. It was very kind of you.'

Twirling the pencil in his hand, the boy said, 'Mr Liberty said he'd help me with some writing tomorrow.'

'But only if you're good,' Gabriel said, crossing the kitchen to the freezer compartment above the fridge. When he had found the cod in parsley sauce, he realised that Miss Costello was standing behind him. 'What's that smirk on your face for?' he asked.

'You wouldn't be going soft on me, would you?'

'Of course not. I'm feathering my own bed. By keeping the boy out of mischief I'm ensuring that you get more work done. I don't want you having an excuse for slacking.'

Clara decided that they would eat their supper in the room she had spent all day cleaning. It had proved a lot less trouble to sort out than the kitchen.

Mr Liberty seemed greatly amused by the splendour of the setting for their simple boil-in-the-bag supper. He had wanted to eat in the kitchen, but Clara had insisted on showing off her efforts, barring anyone entry until she had everything just right.

'Ta-daa!' she chorused, when at last she allowed him and Ned to come in.

She watched his face as he stood for a moment, taking in the scene. Even to her critical eyes the room looked magnificent. Darkness was pressing in, so she had drawn the heavy brocade curtains and lit the room with candles, their flickering flames bouncing soft light off the furniture and panelled walls. There was a look of burnished opulence to the room and copious amounts of fresh air and lavender polish had seen off the musty, depressing smell of neglect.

'It's like Christmas,' Ned said. 'Only bigger.'

Mr Liberty set down the tray of food on the table and made a low bow. 'Another day, another miracle for you, Miss Costello. I applaud you once again.'

Despite the blandness of the meal, it was their most convivial so far— a second bottle of Chablis might have had something to do with that. Ned, who was sitting on two cushions to get him up to the right height, was surprisingly perky for one whose bedtime should have been more than an hour ago.

'What was that?' Clara asked suddenly and cocked her head towards the door.

'What was what?' asked Mr Liberty.

She allowed him to top up her glass. 'I must be spending too much time with you. I'm going mad and hearing things.'

He crashed his glass against hers. 'Here's to you. May you always speak your mind!'

'Just you try and stop me.'

'I suspect I'd need a Panzer tank to stop you doing something you'd put your mind to.'

They were both in mid-laugh when Clara noticed the door open slowly at the far end of the room. She froze. Mr Liberty turned to see what she was looking at. A smartly dressed man had come in. Clara would have recognised him anywhere. It was the long-faced rude man from the supermarket with the trolley full of champagne.

'Hello, Father,' he said, in a pompously creepy voice. 'Do hope I'm not interrupting anything.'

'As a matter of fact you *are* interrupting. What is this? Suddenly everyone's treating my home as if it was Liberty Hall.'

Caspar forced a smile. 'Never underestimate those old jokes, Dad.' He stepped further into the candlelit room. 'Liberty Hall indeed.' His words were directed at his father, but he was more interested in Gabriel's dining companions, in particular the woman: the scheming Miss Costello. Though she was scruffily dressed in khaki trousers and a loose-fitting T-shirt she didn't match up to the pierced, tattooed, New Age scrounger he'd pictured. But appearances could be deceiving.

It was odd, though: the more he looked at her and the child, the more he felt he had come across them before. But where?

'Caspar, are you going to stand there all night gawping at us,' his father barked, 'or are you going to share with us what's brought you here? Or perhaps you were just passing through and thought you'd check up on your dear old pater.'

'Passing through' was exactly the cover Caspar had decided to use, and he slipped seamlessly into his prepared speech, pulling out a chair beside his father. 'As it happens I *am* just passing through. I've been to see baby bro Jonah. I had no idea how concerned he is about you.'

Gabriel snorted. 'Hah! That'll be the day, when any of you worry about me.'

Caspar laughed. 'Come on, Dad, there's no need to take that line. You know jolly well that we all care about you. But where are your manners? Aren't you going to introduce me to your dinner guests?'

'Cut it out, Caspar,' Gabriel said. 'I know exactly why you're here. And it won't do.' Gabriel slapped one of his knobbly hands on the table. The cutlery rattled and the small boy with staring dark eyes jumped and leaned in towards his mother.

'I think it's time we were going, Mr Liberty.'

The scheming minx was on her feet now and staring pointedly at him as she manhandled the child out of his seat and hooked his short legs round her waist.

'There's no need for you to leave, Miss Costello,' his father said. 'In fact, I would rather you stayed.'

'No can do, Mr Liberty. Ned's tired and I need to get him to bed.'

'As you wish, Miss Costello. Good night.'

What was all this? '*As you wish, Miss Costello*' and '*No can do, Mr Liberty*'? What kind of game did they think they were playing?

The door closed behind her. Caspar pushed back his chair and turned to face his father. But Gabriel gained the advantage by creaking to his feet. 'I hope you're satisfied, Caspar,' he glowered down at him, 'because for the first time in a long while I was enjoying myself. As usual, you had to spoil everything. Nothing changes with you, does it?'

Caspar's jaw dropped. Good God, it was worse than he'd thought. The old fool had got it bad. 'I'm not sure what you're getting at, Dad. What exactly did I interrupt here this evening?' He cast his eyes meaningfully over the remnants of the candlelit dinner.

Standing by the fireplace, one clenched fist jammed into his side, the other on the mantel, his father stared at him. Then, inexplicably, he began to laugh. A nasty sneering laugh that started as a low rumble until it grew into a full-blown body-shaker before climaxing in a fit of wheezy coughing. Gasping for breath, Gabriel moved back to the table and took a swig from his wineglass. The situation was bloody hilarious!

Stupid, greedy Caspar thought his father had finally lost his marbles and fallen for the charms of a pretty girl! Ha, ha, ha!

'Are you going to tell me what you were laughing at, Dad?'

Using all his guile, Gabriel kept his face poker straight. 'Caspar, I know this may come as a shock to you. The thing is, I'm fairly well smitten with the lovely Miss Costello. But you must have grasped that. You've seen what a beautiful woman she is. Intelligent. Poised. And utterly charming. Quite a catch for an old thing like me.'

He saw his son stiffen and it was all he could do to stop himself grinning. 'And for some reason that is quite beyond my comprehension, she seems besotted with me. So, what I'm trying to say is, and I know she's much too young for an old duffer like me, but how do you feel about a new stepmother? Your approval matters to me, you know.'

There was little to be gained from telling Caspar to calm down—Jonah had tried that already, only to provoke a louder and more incoherent outburst—so he poured his brother a glass of wine.

Caspar took the glass and tossed back half of its contents in one gulp. To Jonah's relief, it brought his brother to a standstill, and he repeated, more calmly, what he had said on his arrival at Church Cottage. 'This proves beyond all doubt that the old man is losing it.'

'What's happened to cause such a rush of blood to your normally temperate head?' Jonah said. 'I still haven't a clue as to what you're raving on about.'

Caspar's face hardened. 'Look, Jonah, our father is on the verge of marrying for the third time. Do you have any idea where that will leave us? Out in the cold.'

'Who is he thinking of marrying?'

'The gold-digging Miss Mop.'

'But that can't be right.' Jonah was stunned.

Caspar regarded him pityingly. 'Of course it's not! But I'm pleased to see that I'm finally getting through to you. We've got to put a stop to this nonsense . . . Any more of this lighter fuel going?'

Jonah poured the remains of the bottle into Caspar's empty glass. Opening a second, he wondered if the joke he had played on his brother had been trumped by a bigger one from their father.

He leaned against the Rayburn. 'Right, Caspar, tell me exactly what Dad said to you. Try to remember his exact words. Don't exaggerate.'

Caspar rolled his eyes. 'He asked me how I felt about having a new stepmother. He also said that he was smitten by the lovely Miss Costello and that she was equally besotted with him.'

'Did he say anything else?'

'Plenty, most of which makes me cringe to think of it. He even asked if I thought it might be worth his while to see the quack about some Viagra! He's certifiable if you ask me.' He took a long sip of his wine. 'Do you suppose that's a line we could pursue? Put a stop to the marriage by proving he's not in his right senses?'

Having listened to Caspar, Jonah was doubly suspicious that his brother had been duped. Never in a million years could he see their father seeking advice about Viagra. 'Did the object of Dad's affections have anything to say on the matter?'

'No. This all happened after she'd left us alone. They were in the middle of a romantic candlelit dinner when I arrived.'

'And her son?'

'Oh, he was there too.'

'So, a romantic dinner *à trois*, then?'

Caspar looked at him hard. 'She could hardly have left him sitting on the doorstep with a bottle of pop and a bag of crisps.'

Sidestepping, Jonah said, 'I think our best policy is to stay quiet and see how things progress.'

'Oh, that's bloody typical of you, isn't it? Some tart is planning a move on our inheritance and you want to pretend nothing's going on. Don't you care that if Miss Costello becomes the third Mrs Liberty, we can kiss goodbye to Mermaid House?'

'You speak as though you have a right to it,' Jonah said.

Caspar's expression grew tight. 'That's because I do. A share of Mermaid House *is* my birthright. I hardly need point out to you that it's what our mother would have wanted for each of us.'

There was absolutely nothing Jonah could say to this dangerously loaded comment, so he kept quiet and waited for his brother to leave.

The next morning Jonah's curiosity had got the better of him, and after calling in at Kwik-Fit to have a new exhaust pipe fitted he drove out to Mermaid House.

He parked alongside Miss Costello's camper-van and turned off the engine. Through the side window of his car, he looked across the courtyard to see the energetic figure of Miss Costello hurling a cardboard box into the skip. He got out of the car and strolled over, uncomfortably aware that he was trying too hard to put on a casual air.

Seeing him, she said, 'You've got your exhaust fixed then.'

'And Dad's got you hard at work even on a Sunday.'

'Understand this, Master Liberty,' she said. 'It's me who sets the agenda. I decide the hours I work.'

'I don't doubt that for a minute. Here, let me help you.' He expected her to refuse his offer, but she didn't, and between them they added a smelly rolled-up rug to the pile of rubbish. 'Caspar will be furious if he thinks you're chucking away the family heirlooms.' His tone was light, but she didn't say anything. 'I believe you had the pleasure of meeting him last night,' he added.

'I'd had that pleasure already. In the supermarket, in Deaconsbridge. I decided then and there that he was the rudest, most arrogant man I'd ever set eyes on.'

Jonah tried not to smile. 'And did last night alter your opinion?'

She didn't answer him. Instead she said, 'If you're looking for your father, he's in the library.'

He was clearly being dismissed and, baffled, he wondered what he had done to deserve such frostiness. 'Miss Costello, you don't like me very much, do you?'

She paused and looked him straight in the eye. 'Does that bother you?'

He was used to brutal honesty from his family, but not from someone he hardly knew. He decided to fight back. 'If you're going to be my step-mother,' he said mildly, 'don't you think we ought to make more of an effort to get along?'

'Well, what can I say?' she said. 'I suppose you're right. How do you suggest we go about it, young Master Liberty?'

'First you can stop calling me Master Liberty. My name's Jonah. And second, you can be honest with me.'

'Oh, I don't know whether that's a good idea. Families are rarely honest with each other, are they? There's always something we like to keep from each other. By the way, who spilled the beans about your father and me getting hitched?'

'Dad told Caspar last night.'

The conversation wasn't going at all how Jonah had thought it would. But he was determined to get a straight answer to a straight question. 'Miss Costello, please, will you level with me?'

'Don't be so formal. Call me Mother. Or would you prefer Mum?'

'Please,' he tried again, 'a straight answer for a straight question. Are you indulging my father by playing along with another of his games?'

'As I always tell Ned, you must believe what you want to believe.'

'In that case I don't believe a word of what my father has told Caspar. Or that you're a gold-digger as my brother thinks you are.'

She stuck out her chest and placed her hands on her hips provoca-tively. 'Is that because you don't fancy me in the role of stepmother?'

He knew that she was teasing him, but her playful tone and the sight of her breasts showing through her thin T-shirt were an unexpected turn-on.

'I'm afraid that imagining you as my stepmother would take too much suspension of belief.' He lowered his gaze. Exasperated, he said, 'I'm going to see my father?'

As Clara watched Jonah go inside, she almost felt sorry for him. What in the world was the incorrigible old man up to now? He might have had the decency to warn her that she was not only his stand-in daughter but also his fiancée. How would they explain that to Dr Singh?

Whatever his feelings towards her, Jonah couldn't help being impressed by the effect Miss Costello had had on the house. There was a lightness about it that he hadn't felt in years. It was as though, with each room she had touched, the house was being coaxed out of mourning.

Hearing a squeal of laughter, he walked towards the library. He pushed open the door and braced himself for another difficult encounter. But he had miscalculated his father's mood.

'Jonah? Well, I can't say I'm surprised to see you, not when I'm suddenly flavour of the week, but your timing is perfect. Pull up a chair and help me. This cheeky whippersnapper has me on the run.'

After shifting a dusty pile of *National Geographics* from a chair to the floor, Jonah joined them in the bay window where a game of draughts was in progress. The 'cheeky whippersnapper' smiled exuberantly at him. 'I've just taken another of Mr Liberty's pieces,' he said proudly.

'Enough of the boasting, young man. Now, ssh! I need peace and quiet while I think out my next move. What do you advise, Jonah?'

Jonah observed the board, the same board on which he had learned to play both chess and draughts—games his father had always played ruthlessly to win.

'Strikes me that you're in real trouble, Dad,' he said. 'Any move open to you looks risky to me.'

'And since when have I ever been afraid of taking a risk?' Licking his lips, Gabriel nudged one of his few remaining pieces forward. 'There now, you little rascal, pick the bones out of that!'

Lost in the depths of the leather chair opposite, the boy stared hard at the board. Jonah willed Ned to see for himself that with one simple move he could win. A small hand hovered over the left of the board. Jonah felt disappointed. He cleared his throat to attract Ned's attention and looked meaningfully at the other side of the board. Ned's hand moved towards one of his kings, and with a burst of gleeful realisation he claimed the last of Gabriel's pieces. He sat back in his chair and smiled. 'Mr Liberty, I think you've lost.'

Gabriel stared at the board. 'Clearly, I've been too good a teacher. Well done, young man.'

Leaning forward in his chair, Ned said, 'Can we play again?'

'Not now. Maybe after lunch. My poor old brain needs a rest. You run along and tell your mother what a smart lad you are, while I have a chat with my son. I doubt I'll need my brain for that.'

Alone, and expecting his father's mood to change, Jonah started setting out the board ready for another game. He said, 'Do you remember teaching me to play?'

'Like it was yesterday. And talking of yesterday, I imagine that's why you're here, isn't it? Come to get the news straight from the horse's mouth about my approaching marriage, I presume.'

'Why are you doing this, Dad?'

'What? Marrying the delectable Miss Costello? Wouldn't you if you had the opportunity?'

'We're not talking about me, Dad,' Jonah said firmly. 'We're discussing why you're pretending to Caspar that you're marrying the "delectable" Miss Costello, as you describe her. It's another of your games, isn't it?'

'I'll say this for you, Jonah, you're verging on the astute.'

'So why taunt Caspar?'

'Because it was fun! You should have seen him. I thought he was going to pass out with shock. I haven't enjoyed myself so much in years.'

'But is it right to do so at somebody else's expense?'

'What do I care for Caspar's finer feelings? When did he or Damson ever care about mine, eh?'

'Am I not to be included in that condemnation?'

'Carry on with this interrogation and you might well find yourself top of the list!' His father turned abruptly and looked out of the window. 'Damn! It's started raining. I was hoping to take young Ned for a walk later on. Do you want to stay for lunch?'

Jonah couldn't remember the last time his father had made an invitation so spontaneously. Prepared to take whatever was on offer, he said, 'Lunch would be great. Thanks. Do you want me to see to it while you prepare yourself for another whipping at the hands of your protégé?'

Upstairs, Clara was sorting through Val Liberty's belongings. She had wondered who had been responsible for the clutter in the house, and now felt sure she had found the culprit: the second Mrs Liberty had been an inveterate hoarder.

Mr Liberty had given Clara *carte blanche* to get rid of everything. 'None of it's of any use to me, so you might as well ditch the lot.'

Folding yet another thick woollen skirt and adding it to the bag of clothes she had already sorted—there were two piles, one destined for a charity shop and the other for the skip—Clara thought how funny it was that the three of them had slipped into such an unlikely but easy-going routine. Ned was perfectly at home with Mr Liberty, whom she suspected he regarded as a temporary grandfather. Which was fine by her, because, as far as she could see, they were all getting something out of the week. Mr Liberty was getting spring-cleaned, Ned was being entertained, and she was getting paid enough to convince herself that she hadn't been mad in taking on such an extraordinary assignment.

With the rails of the first wardrobe empty now, she stood on a chair to clear out the stuff from the top shelf. She found a battered hatbox hidden beneath a pink candlewick bedspread. It was quite heavy, so she took off the lid and found that it contained a bundle of large notebooks.

She climbed down, sat on the bed, and pulled at the frayed satin ribbon that held them together. Picking one at random, she opened it and saw that it was a diary. She knew she shouldn't but she couldn't stop herself reading the erratic writing that covered the lined pages.

Sunday, September 16

There are times when I hate this dreadful house! I know that sounds overly dramatic, but there it is, that's how I feel today.

The trouble started the moment Caspar and that dim girlfriend of his arrived to celebrate Jonah and Emily's engagement. During dinner I could see what Caspar was up to and knew that no good would come of the weekend. Poor Jonah, he just sat there quietly seething, his mood darkening by the second. 'Do something!' I wanted to shout at him. He just let his brother walk all over him as he always has. He's frightened of him, I know. Frightened of Damson too. And Damson could see what Caspar was up to, and I think that maybe even she was shocked. But she made no attempt to stop him—she's the only one who can rein him in—and in doing nothing, she condoned his behaviour.

By lunchtime today it was all over. Jonah left without saying a word. I watched him from the kitchen window as he drove out of the courtyard—I don't think I've ever seen anyone so angry.

Minutes later, Caspar's girlfriend came hobbling into the house in my borrowed boots. From what I could gather from her colourful language, she and Jonah had seen Caspar kissing Emily, in Jonah's favourite haunt by the rocks. And while she waited for Caspar and Emily to reappear, she phoned for a taxi and packed her bag. When Caspar did deign to show his face, she slapped it hard for him and left. Emily had the grace to look ashamed of what she had done, but Caspar was his normal arrogant self.

During all this commotion, where was Gabriel? Where he always is. Hiding in the library. Why won't he deal with his family? Why does he always leave it to me? I'm tired of it, and often wonder what would become of them all if I was no longer here.

A flurry of footsteps out on the landing had Clara shoving the books back into the hatbox, slapping the lid on it. The door flew open and in came Ned, 'Mummy, guess what? I beat Mr Liberty at draughts.'

'Aren't you the clever one?' She knelt on the floor and hugged him. 'Do you want to help me up here now? Or would that be too boring?'

He shook his head. 'I'll do my scrapbook downstairs with Mr Liberty.' He was already moving towards the door.

'OK, then, but don't make a nuisance of yourself, will you?'

'I won't.'

'Oh, and while you're with Mr Liberty, remind him to bring me up some coffee. It's well past eleven.'

As soon as she was alone again, Clara slipped the lid off the hatbox and reached for another diary. Just a couple of pages, she told herself.

Friday, December 2

Well, he's finally done it. I never thought he would, but he's sold up. And I know he feels terrible about it. He won't say anything, of course, but the whole thing has taken a far greater toll on him than he will ever admit to.

I can see how much it hurts him that none of his children wanted to step into his shoes—he so badly wanted at least one of them to do that. But I can see it from their point of view too: they have their own dreams to follow. Why does he always have to take things so personally?

Again, the sound of footsteps had Clara furtively hiding the diary.

'Dad sent me up with your elevenses and an apology for being late.' It was Jonah with a mug and a plate of ginger nuts. 'How's it going?'

'Slowly.'

'I guess it's easier if you're detached from it. I know I'd struggle to be objective. I did volunteer to do it for Dad, but it was probably too soon for him.' He looked about the room. 'Oh, and if it helps things between us, Dad's told me the engagement was a wind-up for my brother's benefit.'

'Oh, so I don't even get the chance to be jilted at the altar. How disappointing. And to think I was so looking forward to being your wicked stepmother.' Given the room they were in and its contents, Clara wished she hadn't said that. How could she have been so insensitive?

He spoke before she could apologise. 'Not all stepmothers are wicked, you know.'

'I'm sorry.' Wanting to make good the damage, and intrigued by the entries in the diary, she said, 'What was your stepmother like?'

He hesitated, then said, 'To put up with us Libertys, Val was two parts saint and one part sergeant major. On reflection, I think we gave her a terrible time. I don't think she was always very happy.'

'How old were you when she married your father?' she asked.

He moved over to the window. 'A little younger than Ned, and before you ask, no, I can't remember a time before that.'

'Not even your real mother?'

'Not likely, given that it was my birth that killed her.'

Once more Clara wished she could retract her words. 'Oh dear. I'm sorry. I keep putting my foot in it.'

'"Oh dear", indeed. It's quite the party-stopper that line, isn't it?' He was moving again, this time towards the door. 'Lunch is in an hour, so you'd better not scoff too many ginger nuts or you'll upset Chef.'

'And we all know the consequences of annoying your father.'

'Sorry to disappoint you, but it's not my father's culinary delights you're being treated to. Lunch is on me.'

For the next hour, Clara worked doubly fast to make up for the time she had spent reading. But all the while she was sorting through Val Liberty's things she kept wondering what kind of a woman she must have been to take on such a family.

Clara had done many things in her life of which she had later thought better, but this was perhaps the most unworthy. She knew she had no right to do it, but she was hooked. Having begun to see the Liberty family in a new light, she wanted to know more, understand them better. She took the diaries from the hatbox and slipped them into a carrier bag with the intention of reading them in bed that night. She would return them to Mermaid House tomorrow and no one else would be any the wiser. Where was the harm in that?

 **CHAPTER SEVEN**

IN BED THAT NIGHT, long after Ned had fallen asleep, Clara was reading the diaries. As she turned the pages, she was conscious that she was actually stealing the private thoughts of a woman who, if she were alive, would have every right to be furious at Clara's intrusion into her honest record. Clara knew from what she had read that Val had been a fair woman. Yet there were times when she got annoyed with Val's 'understanding'. She longed to shout, 'Stop making excuses for them all!'

The first diary began a month after Val, in her own words, had 'taken on the job of nanny and housekeeper at Mermaid House'. This bleak description of herself seemed to have been prompted by a case of good intentions on her part that had gone disastrously wrong.

I cannot believe what happened today! I'm still shaking with anger and indignation. I have to get my thoughts and shock down on paper—hence this journal.

The trouble started last week when I suggested to Caspar and Damson that the three of us ought to get our heads together and do something about Jonah's birthday. 'How do you know it's his birthday?' Damson had asked. 'Why, is it a secret, darling?' I replied. She didn't say anything and I didn't think it strange until that moment that no one had mentioned the fact that Jonah's fourth birthday was just round the corner. I only found out about it by chance when I had been putting some documents away in Gabriel's desk, and saw a card from the doctor's surgery recommending that Jonah be brought in for his preschool booster. It was then that I saw the date of his birth.

I asked Caspar and Damson why neither of them had thought to tell me when their brother's birthday was. Damson said, 'If you'd wanted to know, you only had to ask.' There was something in her voice that made me want to snap back at her. Restraining myself, I said, 'Well, why don't we arrange a party for him? You'd like that, wouldn't you?'

Eventually it was decided that we would organise a surprise party the following Saturday for Jonah, and that it would coincide with the day their father was returning from his three-week trip to Helsinki. I should have smelt a rat when Caspar and Damson insisted I didn't mention to Gabriel what we were doing, but I was so caught up in my own pride that I was finally forging a link with the twins that I didn't see the warning signs. Oh, if only I had! The pair of them made the invitations and I wrote out the envelopes with the addresses of Jonah's little friends from his nursery school. These were duly posted—or so I thought—by Caspar and Damson.

Meantime, I had forged ahead with the shopping and baking, and last night I worked like a mad thing in the banqueting hall, blowing up balloons, setting out the trestle tables, decorating them with colourful paper tablecloths, plates and cups. And before going to bed I iced the cake I'd made that morning, placing a blue candle at each corner.

Then, this morning, on Caspar and Damson's instructions, I wished Jonah a happy birthday, but kept quiet about the present we had for him—the twins had claimed that it wouldn't be fair to their father for Jonah to open it without him being there to share the moment. I should have thought something was wrong when Jonah didn't pursue the matter. He just looked at the card I had given him. So intent was his scrutiny, it was as though he had never seen anything like it before.

Why, oh why, didn't I suspect? Why didn't I question the fact that in the run-up to his birthday he never once referred to it? In my defence I shall have to put it down to my ignorance of children and their mores. Jonah's quietness is also a factor. Rarely does he speak unless spoken to directly, and even then his words are so reluctantly given one can hardly make them out. 'Speak up!' Gabriel yells at him. 'Stop muttering!' But that only makes it worse, as I often tell him. Jonah needs someone in his life with a gentler manner than his father has.

Just after breakfast, Gabriel phoned to say that his flight was going to be delayed, but he hoped to be home by three, which unbeknown to him, meant he would miss the first hour of the party. By now I was almost as excited as a small child myself, imagining the delight on Gabriel's face when he walked into the middle of his youngest son's party. But by half past three, my excitement left me. Not one child had shown up. Poor Jonah, there he was, standing in the banqueting hall, tearful bewilderment all over his face.

'Looks like no one's going to turn up,' Caspar said.

Jonah went over to the tables, stared hard at the plates of crisps, sandwiches, and jugs of juice. There was such a look on his face. I couldn't fathom it for the life of me. And then we heard the sound of a car. It was Gabriel. The twins rushed out to meet him, but Jonah came and stood next to me. The next thing to happen was Gabriel came marching in. 'What the hell's going on here?' he roared. 'Whose idea was this?' Jonah stepped behind me—dear God, he was actually hiding from his own father! I could feel his small body shaking against my legs.

It breaks my heart to say what happened next, but Gabriel continued to shout, oblivious to the harm he was doing to Jonah. In the end I took hold of Jonah who looked as if he was going to be sick with fright and carried him into the main part of the house. Gabriel followed, the twins at either side of him, and told me I had had no right to do what I had. 'But why?' I demanded—I was close to tears myself now. And then it all came tumbling out. Jonah's birthday was never celebrated because that was the day his mother—Gabriel's first wife—had died. 'So—so why didn't anybody tell me?' I stammered. 'It's not something I care to mention,' Gabriel snapped back at me. 'And what about Jonah,' I pressed—the poor lad was still burying himself in my skirt. 'Doesn't he deserve better than this?' I got no answer, and after Gabriel had stormed off, the twins trailing in his wake, I was left to explain to Jonah that there had been a terrible mix-up. He never said a word. Just stood there holding back the tears. I bent down and hugged him. 'Don't worry, darling, you'll have your party if it's the last thing I do.'

Silently cursing Caspar and Damson's deviousness—my goodness, how that sly pair took me for a fool and manipulated me for their own pleasure!—I knew that from then on I would have my work cut out bringing this family together.

There was a gap of several weeks before Val took up her pen again. It seemed she had won herself, and Jonah, a small but important victory.

An agreement has been reached. Jonah is to be allowed to celebrate his birthday, but on the condition that it's done a week after the official date. According to Gabriel, this will give the memory of his first wife the degree of respect it deserves.

Clara's eyelids were drooping, so she turned out the light reluctantly and her thoughts turned to Jonah and lunch that day, when they had been sitting at the table in the kitchen. She had watched him talking to his father and had realised that what she had previously condemned as his irritating, casual manner was an act. The relaxed body language was there to cover his uneasiness: the reserve between father and son could not have been greater. And reflecting on his inability to do more than the weekly shop for his father, Clara wondered if this was the only way he felt able to help a man he was scared of.

And what of Gabriel Liberty? What heartbreak had he buried beneath that gruff exterior? What bitterness did he still harbour over his children's refusal to carry on the family business?

The next morning Clara woke early, made herself a cup of tea, then slipped back into bed to carry on where she had left off last night. The diary had moved on to November 1973.

Just as I thought life was beginning to settle down, the building bricks of normality, which I have been so carefully arranging, have come tumbling down on me yet again. For the fourth time in as many weeks, Jonah has run away from school. But at least now Gabriel will have to do something. 'He's not happy,' I told Gabriel, when the phone call came. This blatant truth was reinforced by the headmaster when he summoned us to school to discuss the matter.

There we were, in the headmaster's study, to discuss Jonah's fate. Gabriel was of the opinion that Jonah needed to take the rough with the smooth, but I stuck my neck out (I knew I'd never forgive myself if I didn't) and said, 'I have heard nothing here this afternoon to convince me that this is the right environment for a sensitive boy like Jonah.' Once Gabriel had got his furious throat-rattling under control, the headmaster said, 'I whole-heartedly agree with you, Mrs Liberty. Jonah would benefit from a different school.'

Yes, I thought, as we drove home with Jonah ashen-faced in the back of the car, you're washing your hands of a problem child who challenges the whole ethos of your horrible school.

Gabriel can't stomach the notion that he is the father of a problem child. 'There's no shame involved,' I told him, as he gripped the steering wheel. His face was grim and I saw his eyes flicker to the rear-view mirror to look at his son in disgust. Poor Jonah, eight years old, and the weight and guilt of the world on his young, inadequate shoulders.

The sound of creaking from Ned's bed above the cab had Clara snapping the diary shut and sliding it under her mattress. She waited for him to make his way down the short ladder before slipping into bed with her to claim his all-important first hug of the day.

Just in time she remembered what day it was. When he appeared at her side, she said, 'Ooh, Ned, what's that on your nose?'

His hand flew to his face. 'What?' he said, alarmed.

'April Fool!' She laughed. Pulling him into bed with her, she planted a huge kiss on his cheek then blew the fruitiest of raspberries into his warm neck. As he squealed, giggled and wriggled, the strength of her love for him rose within her and she held him tightly, vowing never to make him unhappy as Jonah Liberty had been.

Mermaid House was the most extraordinary place Archie had seen in a long while. 'Well, I'll be blowed,' he said, when he first caught sight of it on the brow of a rise in the landscape. 'What a godforsaken place to live.' He pulled in beside Clara Costello's camper-van, and wondered how many times his modest end-of-terrace could fit into this vast old place. He got out and crossed the shiny wet cobbles of the courtyard but came to a stop when he drew level with the skip. He couldn't resist having a quick shufti. His surreptitious foray was brought to an abrupt end by a none-too-friendly voice saying, 'Who the hell are you and what d'you think you're doing snooping through my belongings?'

Clara had warned Archie what to expect. 'Herr Liberty runs a boot camp up here on the quiet,' she told him, 'but take no notice of his commandant persona. He's a real sweetie when you get to know him.'

Archie stepped forward. 'Archie Merryman's the name. Miss Costello phoned on Saturday about some odds and ends you want to get rid of.'

'Uh, so you're that rag-and-bone man she got in touch with, are you? I suppose you'd better come in. But be sure to wipe your feet.'

Archie did as instructed, then followed him to a large kitchen. The old man went over to an open doorway. 'Miss Costello,' he bellowed, 'your disreputable rag-and-bone man's here.'

A door opened and footsteps sounded.

'Mr Liberty, there is no need to shout. And how many times do I have to tell you, Mr Merryman runs a secondhand shop and he's the least disreputable man I know.' Her voice and footsteps grew louder until finally she came into the kitchen. 'Hello, Archie,' she said, 'the Commandant treating you as rudely as I said he would?'

'Not so badly. How's that lad of yours? Did he find his mermaid?'

'Oh, yes. It was here just as he said it would be—'

'Great Scott! How much longer have I got to put up with this tea-party chatter? I thought there was some business to be transacted.'

Clara winked at Archie and tutted. 'You leave the business to me, Mr Liberty. But talking of tea parties, bung the kettle on, would you? I'm sure Mr Merryman would appreciate a cup of your finest PG Tips.'

Mr Liberty's nostrils flared and Archie speculated as to who was the real commandant here. He fell in step beside Clara as she led him the length of the house. 'I'm afraid none of it is of any great worth,' she said, 'but I've tried to organise everything into two piles: stuff you might be able to sell and stuff that's a little more dubious.'

She pushed open a heavy door and showed him into an enormous drawing room about thirty feet by twenty. Stella would have loved all this, Archie thought suddenly: the grandness of the room, the high ceiling, the massive fireplace. For years she had been on at him to move.

The furniture wasn't up to much though. The room was home to a bamboo table with a cracked glass top, a Chinese wall-hanging, a set of African drums, a lacquered chest, and a cabinet full of jade and ivory.

He began to look at the room more critically, seeing the cracks in the ceiling and the gaping holes in the plasterwork above the moulded skirting boards. Other than Stella, who would want to take this on?

For the first time since Stella had left him he felt angry. Until now he had resigned himself to what had happened: he had failed his wife, so what else could he expect? But now he felt the sting of the implied criticism, the cruel, underhand way in which she had carried on her affair.

Realising that Clara was waiting for him to speak, he shook himself out of his despondency. 'Sorry, what were you saying?'

'That if any of these things are too awful to contemplate, you must . . . Are you OK, Archie? You look a bit bothered.'

He forced himself to smile. 'I'm tired, that's all. Now, then, let's see about this little lot, shall we?' And with a supreme act of will, he focused his attention on the boxes on the floor. Without needing to sift too deeply through them he could see that the assorted junk was mostly saleable and what he couldn't get rid of he'd pass on to a fellow dealer. 'No problem,' he said, 'I'll take the lot. Is that it?'

She pulled a face. 'I'm afraid not. I've got a load more upstairs.'

'I'll say this for you, you're doing a thorough job here.'

'A little too thorough at times.' Mr Liberty was lumbering in with two mugs in his hands. 'Having her around is akin to taking laxatives,' he said to Archie, handing him a mug of tea. 'She sweeps you clean, whether you like it or not.'

'Thank you for sharing that delightful analogy with us, Mr Liberty.' Clara smiled. She took her mug. 'Was there anything else?'

Judging from the twist to his mouth, the old boy had taken his dismissal with pleasure. Strange man, thought Archie. 'What on earth possessed you to take on this colossal task?' he asked Clara.

She laughed. 'A question I've been asking myself several times a day since I started. I'd like to say that it's down to pure altruism, but my friends would claim it's due to my perverse desire to take charge and organise everything around me.'

'Now that's just what I could do with.'

'Oh?'

Something in her tone made him want to unburden himself. Go on, he urged himself, confide in her. She's an outsider. Who would she tell?

Staring at him over the top of her mug of tea, she said, 'It's none of my business, but is it something to do with your mother?'

'Yes and no,' he volunteered. 'Mother is certainly one of my concerns, but . . . well, the thing is, my wife left me recently and I haven't a clue how to deal with it . . .'

'Oh, Archie, I'm so sorry.' She reached out and touched his arm lightly. 'Come and sit down.' She led him across the room to two high-backed armchairs in the bay of the window. 'It must be awful for you. Did you have any idea that this was going to happen?'

'I'd be lying if I said it came as a surprise. Things have been difficult for a while, and what with Mum's stroke and her moving in with us, well . . . let's just say I haven't helped matters.'

'But it must have been a terrible blow.'

'I think it's only now that it's finally hitting home.'

'Do you know where your wife is?'

'She's in Macclesfield with the man who—' He broke off. 'Sorry, it's just that hearing the words out loud makes it seem all the more real. I suppose I've been keeping it to myself so that I haven't had to face up to what I ought to do.' He smiled ruefully. 'I'll agree to the divorce, sell the house and move into something smaller and cheaper. I'll keep Second Best going and somehow look after Mum.'

'That takes care of today. What about tomorrow?'

In spite of his flagging spirits, he laughed, and felt better for it. 'That's just the kind of talk I need.' He drained his mug. 'Now, then, let's get back to work or that man Liberty will be after me.' They both rose to their feet. 'Thanks,' he said, 'thanks a million.'

'What for? I haven't helped you resolve anything. More's the pity.'

'No, but you've listened, and maybe that was all I needed.'

Before he had even opened his eyes Gabriel knew the day would not be a good one. It was Friday morning, Ned and Miss Costello's final day at Mermaid House. He didn't know how it had happened, but somehow during the last week he had got so used to having them around that he was going to miss them when they were gone.

A glance at the clock on the bedside table told him it was a quarter past seven. He pushed back the bedclothes, thumped his feet down on-to the floor, then launched himself stiffly upright. He went over to the window and gave a cautious tug at the curtains. They glided smoothly along the track. Miss Costello had even filled in the gaping holes left by the chunks of plaster that had fallen out. He stood at the window and sighed heavily. Life was going to be dull without them around.

He washed, shaved and dressed in his pristine bathroom, and went downstairs. The kitchen was beautifully warm—another of Miss Costello's miracles. She had had the Aga serviced by a man who knew what he was talking about: turned out all that had been wrong with it was a faulty thermostat. He put the kettle on and went to sit in one of the Windsor chairs she had placed in front of the Aga.

On day one of her assignment to sort out Mermaid House, Miss Costello had taken him at his word and put together a shopping list of things she considered would make his life easier. Then, the day before yesterday, she had dragged him off to the shops. They drove in her camper-van to the retail development on the far side of Deaconsbridge where he hadn't been before. The vast range of electrical appliances on sale in the store was bewildering. But Clara knew exactly what she was looking for and, much to Gabriel's admiration, badgered the young assistant into giving them a ten per cent discount, plus free delivery for that same evening. He had watched in further admiration late that night after she had put Ned to bed when she had got down on her hands and knees and plumbed in the dishwasher. 'Are you deliberately trying to make me feel completely useless?' he had said, passing her a spanner.

'Not at all. You do too good a job of it yourself.'

Eating his toast and marmalade as he sat by the Aga, Gabriel listened to the news on the radio—or, rather, listened to the news on his new all-in-one, all-singing-all-dancing radio-CD-cassette player. It was another of Miss Costello's fine-tunings. The reception and sound quality were certainly better than he was used to from his old radio, but the news was still as tedious. As from tomorrow, when Clara and Ned had gone, the highlight of his day would be answering back at some jumped-up nobody who fancied himself a political smart-aleck.

As her son dipped his spoon in and out of his bowl of Coco-Pops, Clara had the feeling he wasn't looking forward to moving on.

But the same was true for her. While she hadn't fallen in love with the cranky owner of Mermaid House, she had enjoyed seeing him mellow. She'd also enjoyed keeping up the game of formality between them. She always made a point of calling him Mr Liberty to his face, and he still referred to her as Miss Costello, but in her mind he had become Gabriel: a man with a softer side to him than he was used to exposing.

It had been a week of hard slog, but she would leave knowing that she had spent the time doing something positive and worthwhile. She wasn't so sure of how long the benefits of her work would last. If left to his own devices, Gabriel would probably let things slide back to how they had been. But she couldn't do anything about that. Perhaps she could speak to Jonah before she left and impress upon him that his father needed a cleaner, or maybe a housekeeper.

In the back of her mind she heard Louise and the Gang telling her to leave well alone: 'Stop trying to control what isn't your concern.'

Mercifully Caspar had stayed away from Mermaid House, and she hadn't seen Jonah since Sunday. Apparently he had been away on a school history trip to northern France and Belgium. Having read Val's diaries, she could only marvel that any of the Liberty children had survived their childhood. She alternated between being furious with Gabriel for ignoring the needs of his family and feeling desperately sorry for him. Clearly the death of his first wife had left him a broken man with no one to turn to. At various times she had been tempted to ask him more about his past, but the moment never seemed right.

Still, whatever Gabriel and his family had suffered, it was really none of Clara's business and she had no right to pry. Guiltily, she made a mental note to return Val's diaries before she and Ned left.

At Gabriel's insistence they were to have lunch in town at the Mermaid Café. 'It's one o'clock, and I declare you officially out of contract now,' he said, when she appeared in the kitchen, expecting a sandwich—or a 'shambly', as Ned called them. Presenting her with an envelope, he added, 'It's your wages. You'll find I've been more than generous.'

Without opening it, she slipped the envelope into the pocket of her jeans. 'Fair enough, but I insist on driving. I'm not going anywhere in that deathtrap of a Land Rover.'

He put up a show of resistance that got him nowhere, and after she had changed out of her filthy work clothes, they set off.

'Can I have chips, please, Mummy?' Ned called from his rear seat as they turned into the market square. 'And ketchup?'

'It's market day,' Gabriel said. 'You might have trouble parking.'

'Mm . . . and lots of vinegar, please. I like vinegar.'

'There! There's a space. Quick!'

'For goodness' sake, Mr Liberty, calm down! You'll give yourself a heart attack at this rate.'

'No chance. I'm saving that pleasure for when I've over-feasted on a coronary lunchtime special.'

They were met by Shirley and a raised eyebrow when she saw who they had with them. 'We missed you last Friday, Mr Liberty,' she said. 'Thought perhaps you'd taken your business elsewhere?'

'You mean you hoped I had.'

She smiled at Clara. 'Shall I get you some drinks while you choose? How about a nice strawberry milkshake?' This last remark was directed at Ned, who nodded enthusiastically.

It was Ned who brought up the subject of their leaving. Expertly dipping the end of a chip into the pool of ketchup on his plate, he said,

'Will you miss us when we've gone, Mr Liberty? Will you be sad when you're all alone again?'

'That depends, doesn't it?' Gabriel said evasively. 'If I thought I was never going to hear from you again, that *might* make me sad.'

They both looked at Clara. 'You could send Mr Liberty the occasional postcard, Ned,' she said, thinking fast, while hiding her surprise that Gabriel had said something so refreshingly agreeable and tactful. 'That way he'll know what we're up to.'

'But how will we know what Mr Liberty is doing?'

'You won't, lad. No one ever knows what I'm up to. And that's the way I intend to keep it.'

Over pudding—the obligatory apple pie and custard—Gabriel said, 'Do you really have to rush off, Miss Costello? We came to an arrangement a week ago, couldn't we do something similar again?'

'And what about the holiday Ned and I are supposed to be enjoying? We've been here for over a week and we still haven't had so much as a glimpse of what we came to see. We want to see the sights.'

'Then stay on at Mermaid House for a few more days as my guests, and you can do all the day-tripping you want to do in this area.'

She hesitated, and in that instant knew that she had lost the argument. Gabriel leaned in towards her. 'Miss Costello, I would very much like you to stay so that I can repay a little of your kindness.'

'But you've done that already. You've paid me.'

'It's not always about money.'

She smiled. 'Is this the same man who once said everything had a price, that everything was for sale?'

He shifted in his seat. 'Well, maybe I've . . . changed,' he mumbled.

It was difficult for her not to laugh at his discomfort. The poor man had come a long way in just one week. 'Well,' she said, 'just so that we're clear on a few points. If, and I say *if*, we were to stay, there would be no more scrubbing and polishing?'

'I said *as my guests*. Don't you ever listen?'

'Only if I like the sound of what's being suggested.'

'And do you?'

'In parts. But before I commit myself, I have to mull it over with the boss. Ned, what do you think we should do?'

His eager face was answer enough.

At bedtime that night, Clara knew it was important to put the brakes on Ned's excitement. 'We'll be moving on first thing on Monday morning, Ned,' she told him. 'There's so much more to see and do.' He nudged the book she was supposed to be reading to him. He hasn't been listening, she thought, when she eventually turned out his light and gave him one last kiss. He thinks two more days will turn into three, then four, then goodness knows how many.

Later, as she pulled her duvet out of the cupboard beneath the seat, and caught sight of her filthy jeans hanging on the shower door, she remembered that Gabriel had offered her the use of his washing machine before they left. She also remembered the envelope he had given her, which she had stuffed into the pocket of those jeans. Better remove it now before she forgot about it and threw it into the washing machine tomorrow morning. Ripping it open, she extracted a slip of paper on which was written: 'Don't even think about turning this down!' Paperclipped to it was a cheque. When she saw the amount—he had doubled the agreed sum—she shook her head, partly with disbelief, but also with affection. 'Silly old fool,' she murmured. A rush of fondness for him brought tears to her eyes. She was deeply touched.

The next morning, Ned woke first. He got dressed without disturbing Clara, and she only realised he was up and about when he slipped under her duvet for a hug.

'Shall we ask Mr Liberty to come with us today?' he asked.

'Do you think he'd want to? He's probably seen the Mermaid Cavern.'

'But not with us. Shall I go and ask him?'

'How about some breakfast first?' But he was already standing by the door, a hand working at the lock. 'Oh, go on, then.' She gave in. 'But don't be surprised if he shouts at you for disturbing him.'

Yawning, she dragged herself reluctantly out of bed and watched Ned scamper across the courtyard. The back door opened before he reached it and she saw Gabriel staring down at his early-morning caller. She strongly approved of Ned's suggestion and she hoped Gabriel would accept the invitation with good grace: it would be her way of thanking him for his more than generous cheque.

According to the guidebooks, the Mermaid Cavern was often overlooked in favour of the bigger and more commercialised show caves in nearby Castleton. Nonetheless, they agreed that it was of geological and historical interest and worth a visit. But the million-dollar question was: Did the mermaid rock formation really look like a mermaid?

Parking Winnie between another camper-van and a people-carrier containing two panting, slobbering labradors, Clara asked Gabriel if he knew the answer.

'It's so long since I saw it, I can't remember,' he said.

'How long ago? Time for her to have grown taller?'

'It was 1963, if you must know. I came here with Anastasia. We went for a picnic afterwards, but it rained. It came down so hard, so suddenly, we had to shelter under a tree. She joked we would get struck by lightning and that we would both die and go to heaven. I told her I was already in heaven.'

Moved by the unexpected tenderness in his voice, Clara turned slowly to look at him. 'And you've never been back?'

'Wouldn't have been the same.'

They paid for their entrance tickets at a wooden booth and were shepherded through to a dimly lit tunnel where they joined a group about to embark on a tour of what had once been an old lead mine.

Fifteen minutes later, Clara was glad she had bundled Ned up in his warmest clothes: it was bone-numbingly cold. As she listened to the guide and watched the direction of his torch, which he used to indicate points of interest—the stalactites and stalagmites—she thought of the harsh conditions in which those early miners had worked.

The guide led them further into the series of caves, warning them to be careful and to hold on to the rail as they took the steep descent down towards the pool. When they reached the bottom, a boat was waiting for them. They were helped into it and, when all was secure, they moved smoothly through the water. It didn't seem very impressive at first: the ceiling of the cave was still quite low, and though a few lights were fixed into the rock face there wasn't much to see.

But then they turned a corner and there was an 'Aah!' from everyone in the boat. Even Gabriel looked impressed. The roof of the cave soared above their heads, and shimmering lights gave it a serene, cathedral-like quality. People reached for their cameras, including Clara. After they had taken their pictures, the guide took them on further.

They came to a large rock that jutted out into the pool, steered round it and there before them, raised out of the water and subtly illuminated with softly glowing lamps, was the mermaid. There was her tail, the forked end skimming the surface of the pool, and her curvy body reclined gracefully against another rock.

The guide told them how she came to be there. The story went that she had been a real live mermaid who had got lost at sea and had somehow found her way to the cavern. She had liked it so much that she had made it her home and, after wishing that she could stay here for ever, she had been turned to stone to make wishes come true for others.

The guide pointed the beam of his torch at the small raised pool behind the mermaid. 'If you want her to grant you a wish,' he said, 'you have to throw a coin into her pool.'

Clara reached for her bag. 'Go on, Ned,' she said, 'make a wish.'

He took the ten-pence piece from her. 'But what about you, Mummy? Don't you want a go? And, Mr Liberty, you have to make a wish too.'

Gabriel pulled a face. 'I've never heard anything so absurd in all my life. A lot of stuff and nonsense.' But then he smiled and produced a pound coin from his pocket. 'Shall we make it a good one, Ned, eh?'

They waited for the rest of the group to throw their pennies and make their wishes, and then, at last, it was their turn. 'Don't say it out loud,' Ned informed Clara, 'it won't come true if you do.' Four years old and how well-versed he was in these matters.

Clara's wish had been the same as it always was. She wanted Ned to be happy. She glanced at Gabriel's face in the subdued light. There was no knowing what he had wished for.

On Monday morning, as Clara unhooked Winnie from the electrical supply at Mermaid House, Ned was anything *but* happy. He wanted to stay longer. The weekend had passed all too quickly, with most of it spent sightseeing. They had visited Peveril Castle, the plague village at Eyam, Buxton, and another cave—the Blue John Cavern in Castleton. But now they were preparing to leave.

'There's still more to see,' Ned said, pointing to a picture in one of their guidebooks that showed a place in Matlock Bath where they had cable cars to get you up and down the wooded hillside. 'Couldn't we go there today? Oh, please.'

She stopped what she was doing, sat down, and pulled him onto her lap, knowing that if she wasn't careful, she'd have a tearful rebellion on her hands. She flicked through the pages of the book to the next section. 'And look,' she said, 'even more to see.'

He stared at the picture of a traditional steamer crossing Lake Windermere, then at the one showing the Beatrix Potter museum.

'Couldn't we take Mr Liberty with us to see Peter Rabbit? He'd like that, wouldn't he?'

She put an arm round him. 'I'm not sure he's a Beatrix Potter kind of man, Ned. Besides, Winnie is only big enough for the two of us. Imagine having a great big man like Mr Liberty sharing it with us. And I bet he snores as loud as a giant.'

For the first time since getting out of bed that morning, Ned smiled and Clara hugged him close.

With the situation more or less under control, and Ned rounding up his cuddly toy collection, there was a loud thump at the door. 'Time you were going, isn't it?' It was Gabriel. 'Always a mistake to outstay your welcome,' he growled, filling the doorway. 'Remember that, Ned. When it's time to go, you go. No hanging around.'

Clara felt a wave of gratitude towards him for being his usual blunt self, for not making things worse for Ned by giving him a show of treacly affection. 'And a good morning to you, Mr Liberty.'

He stepped inside, looked at his watch. 'It's afternoon, as near as damn it.'

'Mr Liberty, guess where we're going?' Ned chimed in. 'We're going to see Peter Rabbit and some big lakes and mountains. And Mummy says we'll go on a really old boat that has steam coming out of it. And—'

'Sounds much too exhausting to me,' Gabriel interrupted.

'I think we're about done now,' Clara said. 'If you'd like to say goodbye to Mr Liberty you can climb into your seat and strap yourself in.'

Ned put his hands behind his back and screwed a shoe into the floor. Then a little voice mumbled 'Goodbye', and his lower lip wobbled and she knew they were in real trouble. Gabriel got there before her. He bent down to Ned, gently picked him up and carried him outside.

Staying where she was, Clara watched them go. She tried to ignore the large lump in her throat and the tears that were threatening to do their worst. Damn the man, why and how had he got to them both?

Finally they were in their seats with the engine running. Coming round to the driver's side of the van, Gabriel poked his head through the open window. 'You take good care of yourself, won't you?'

'And you take care as well. Don't lose any of those instructions I spent ages writing out for you. The dishwasher will need salt and Rinse-aid adding now and again, and you'll also have to—'

'Yes, yes, yes, Miss Costello. I have your infernal instructions Sellotaped to the inside of the cupboard, just as you insisted.'

'Well, then, nothing more to be said. Apart from thanking you for having us to stay. Ned and I have had a great time. We won't forget you in a hurry, that's for sure.'

'Pah! You'll forget me so fast you won't even remember to send me a postcard.'

'We will remember,' cried Ned. 'We'll send you one every week.'

'Goodbye, Mr Liberty. Despite everything, it's been a pleasure.' His grizzled head was still close to the window and, seizing her chance, she leaned towards him and kissed his bristly cheek.

'What was that for?'

'What do you think, you silly old fool?'

'I never thought I'd say it, Miss Costello, but if I were younger—'

She laughed. 'If you were younger, I wouldn't have dared to kiss you.'

He laughed too, then reached through the window, lifted her right hand off the steering wheel, raised it to his lips, and very gently kissed it. 'I'm going to miss you, you delectable sharp-tongued girl. You've been a breath of fresh air for me. Goodbye now. Drive safely. And if you're ever passing . . .' but his voice trailed away.

Touched, she said, 'We wouldn't dream of not calling in on you if we were in the area. You can take that as a promise. Or maybe a threat!'

Steering Winnie out of the courtyard and tooting the horn, they waved to the solitary figure standing under the archway. As they neared the end of the drive, they saw a car approaching. It was Jonah.

Clara was glad to see him. She suspected Gabriel could do with some company right now. She pulled over so that Jonah could come alongside the van. They wound down their windows at the same time.

Clara said, 'How was it on the Western Front with your school trip?'

'All quiet when we left it. Wet and cold too.'

'Too bad. So, not at school today shaping fertile young minds?'

'No, we've broken up for the Easter holidays. I've come to see if Dad wants some shopping fetching. Where are you off to?'

'The Lake District. You'll be pleased to know I've given up trying to marry your father and swindle him out of his vast fortune. Ned and I are moving on to pastures new, where scheming gold-diggers are given the proper respect they deserve.'

He smiled, not hugely, but enough for her to realise how attractive he was. Yet what struck her most about him, as she took in the curve of his mouth and the way his hazel eyes caught the light, was that his likeness to the painting of his mother was unmistakable. She wondered if Gabriel found it a comfort or a painful reminder of what he had lost.

'Caspar will be relieved to hear the news,' he said good-humouredly.

'I bet he will. Do me a favour, will you? Persevere with your father.'

The smile was gone and his face turned defensive. Annoyed that she seemed to have a knack for rubbing him up the wrong way, she said, 'I might have misjudged you when I first met you, but . . . well, a week with your father and I think I understand things better now.'

But the smile didn't reappear as she had hoped it might. 'I doubt that,' he said, with feeling. 'Thanks for everything you've done for Dad. I'll do my best to carry on where you've left off. That's if he'll let me.'

'I find the shotgun approach usually works. You ram it up his nose and lay out your demands. Nothing to it. Goodbye.'

CHAPTER EIGHT

April 10

Dear Louise and associated rabble,
The hardship continues! Currently languishing beside beautiful Lake Windermere with Mrs Tiggywinkle and chums and getting fat on cream teas. Sorry I still haven't got round to phoning—will try to mend my ways. Do hope you're all behaving yourselves and missing us terribly.
Love from Clara and Ned

April 11

Dear Mr Liberty,
Just to prove we keep our promises, Easter greetings from Dove Cottage, the home of William Wordsworth.
Ned says thank you very much for the money you gave him—that was v. naughty of you, but v. kind. He's used some of it to buy himself a pocket-sized Peter Rabbit.
Take care,
Ned and Miss Costello

P.S. Have you advertised for a cleaner yet?

2 Canal View,
Manchester

April 21

Dear Damson,
What the hell's going on? Why won't you speak to me? Five times I've tried to get you on the phone and on each occasion some Guardian-reading, bean-eating, beardy type has told me it's not convenient. Since when is it not convenient to speak to your brother? Or is this all part of the brainwashing process that's going on up there?
*If I don't here from you soon, I will personally come up there and beat the **** out of that patronising wimp who won't let me speak to you.*
Caspar

Rosewood Manor Healing Centre

April 26

Darling Caspar,
    If you really care about me, don't be silly and drive all the way up here just to take out your frustration on poor Roland. Instead, why don't you write and tell me what's wrong. And please don't deny that there is anything bothering you—as twins, you know I always feel it when something is wrong with you.
    Love and warmest wishes,
    Damson

April 27

Dear Louise and everyone,
    Here we are north of the border! Glasgow is terrific! Moira, you'd love it—more designer shops than you can shake a stick at. Tomorrow we're setting sail for the bonnie banks of Loch Lomond—Rob Roy country.
    It was great to speak to you on the phone last week, Louise—it almost made me miss you!
    Love,
    Clara and Ned

April 28

Dear Mr Liberty,
    Saw this wonderful card of a fierce-looking Scotsman playing the bag-pipes and thought of you! Hope you're taking care of yourself and haven't slipped back into your bad old ways.
    Best wishes,
    Ned and Miss Costello

17 Cross Street,
Deaconsbridge

May 7

Dear Stella,
    Before the solicitors get too carried away with their expensive games, why don't we meet and discuss matters in private, just the two of us? It's the least we owe each other.
    Yours hopefully,
    Archie

2a Carlisle Terrace,
Macclesfield,
Cheshire.

May 12

Dear Archie,
  I could meet you a week next Tuesday after work in Buxton, but only
for a short while. I'll see you at 6.00 by the bandstand.
  Stella

Date: 14/05/01 14.44 GMT Daylight Time

From: ClaraCost@hotmail.com

To: GuyXXX@Phoenix.co.uk

  It had to happen sooner or later; I've found myself in
a cyber café in the middle of Edinburgh emailing you
silly boys. How goes it? Who and what is the latest gossip? Don't hold back on the dirt!

Date: 14/05/01 14.49 GMT Daylight Time

From: GuyXXX@Phoenix.co.uk

To: ClaraCost@hotmail.com

  Hey, Clarabelle, is that really you? This is like old
times. Makes me realise how much I miss your sharply
worded emails! We have it on good authority that the big
chiefs in Wilmington are dispatching a couple of their
smart-alecky types to suss out the takeover — Les
Français Garçons are definitely putting their Francs on
the table, so it's all systems go. And guess who's coming to see us? None other than the big honcho lawyer himself, Fenton Bexley and the finance director, Todd Mason
Angel. Aren't we the lucky ones?
  Didn't you get to know TMA during your stint in
Wilmington? What's he like? Is he likely to drive the
women on the packing line mad with desire? You know what
they were like with the last blue-eyed wonder boy who
crossed the water to see us!
  Fondest etceteras,
  Guy

 **CHAPTER NINE**

IT WAS FIVE WEEKS since Gabriel had received the first of the postcards from Ned and Miss Costello, and he had kept each one they had sent, lining them up carefully along the kitchen windowsill. Every day, around twelve o'clock, when the postman finally got round to making a delivery at Mermaid House, he hung on to the hope that there would be a new addition for his collection.

This morning, as he bent down to gather the scattering of envelopes, he glimpsed a flash of blue sky. The glossy picture showed the busy harbour of Whitby. Gabriel turned over the postcard and smiled. Miss Costello had written it, but Ned had added his own name in his over-sized writing.

Gabriel read it through, then placed it on the windowsill in the kitchen. But, unlike the rest of the postcards, he positioned it so that the writing faced him. And while he made himself an early lunch, he continued to stare at Ned's handiwork, picturing the lad in the camper-van, kneeling up to the narrow table, his fingers gripping the pen and his tongue poking out of the corner of his mouth as he concentrated. The thought of Ned's determination, and the attachment he seemed to have made to an old man he scarcely knew, caused Gabriel to stop chewing his sandwich. His *shambly*.

A few moments passed before he could swallow what was in his mouth. If someone had told him two months ago that he could be so moved, he would have laughed in their face. But every time he thought of Ned, he experienced a tightening in his chest. And if he pictured that moment in April when the boy had tried to say goodbye to him, he felt overwhelmed by sadness so heavy his breath caught. It made him feel as if his heart had just been torpedoed.

Solitude had never bothered Gabriel in the past, but now he wanted none of it. He craved the sound of a small child's excited voice calling to him, the hurried, purposeful footsteps of a young woman, the crisp humorous taunt, the robust mocking smile. But he knew he would never know them again.

Oh, how he missed that little firecracker and her son.

Jonah stayed late at school to do some marking. Instead of going home after he had finished, he drove to Mermaid House. He was concerned about his father. Since the miraculous Miss Costello had moved on, Gabriel had been morose. She had touched his father in a way that few people ever had. Amazingly, she had made him happy.

But what worried Jonah most was that his father's trademark fighting spirit had dwindled to nothing. He had mentioned this to Caspar on the phone, but all his brother had said was, 'Well, it was bound to happen at some time or other. He can't go to his grave snapping and snarling— we'd never get the lid down on him.'

'For pity's sake, Caspar, how can you talk like that? He's our father.'

'He's also a miserable old man who won't listen to a word of common sense, and who, I might add, took malicious pleasure in making me look a fool over that Costello woman.'

Jonah had put his brother out of his misery about their father supposedly marrying for the third time. Caspar's anger had been cataclysmic. 'I thought you might have been relieved,' Jonah had reasoned.

'Relieved he despises me so much that he had to humiliate me in front of a complete stranger? Are you mad?'

Changing tack, Jonah had said, 'So how's business?'

But the ground had opened up beneath him. 'And what the hell do you care about my business?' Caspar had sniped.

'Hey, I'm only asking.'

'Well, don't! Take your snivelling civility and stick it—'

Jonah had ended the conversation by putting the phone down. There was nothing to be gained from talking with his brother when he was in that kind of mood.

It was still light when he arrived at Mermaid House, and he found his father in the gunroom. 'Bloody crows,' he said. 'They've been at the lambs again. Vermin. Should be wiped off the face of the earth. What brings you here? And what's that smell?'

'It's this.' He held up a paper carrier bag. 'Indian take-away. Thought you might fancy a change from your usual beanfeast.'

Gabriel eyed the bag suspiciously. 'You did, did you?'

'It'll need heating up in the oven for a short while. Shall I see to it?'

'Feel free.'

A week had passed since Jonah had last called in, and he was relieved to see that his father was still keeping the place relatively clean and tidy.

'Any luck with finding a cleaner?' he asked, bending down to a cupboard for two plates, then opening the cutlery drawer. He knew that Gabriel had placed an advert in the local paper.

'No. Word's probably gone round that I'm a no-go area. Drink?'

'Thanks. But only a small one. I'll add some water.' Despite his father's look of disapproval, he took the tumbler of whisky over to the sink then added an inch to the glass. He raised his glass. 'Cheers.'

While they ate, Jonah kept up the conversation as well as he could, but it was hard going. His father was even more uncommunicative and morose than usual. For something to say, he told him about a girl at Deaconsbridge High called Sharna, who had been bunking off classes. Jonah had been to visit her and her mother to try to persuade her to return to school.

'Sounds like you're wasting your time there,' Gabriel said, picking at his food. 'If people don't want help, you can't force it on them.'

Jonah looked up from his chicken korma. 'So you think they should be left to dig themselves a deeper hole from which there's no hope of them ever climbing out?'

Gabriel lowered his gaze. 'I didn't say that. You have to wait until people are ready to accept your help. Or ask for it.'

'But not everyone knows how to ask for help.'

'True. But maybe in the end they do.'

Jonah hadn't expected the conversation to take this turn and he steeled himself to ask, 'Dad, who are we really talking about here? Disadvantaged teenagers or . . . or you?'

As soon as the words were out, he regretted them. Gabriel glowered at him, his mouth set so firmly that his lips had all but disappeared. Oh God, he recognised that look. He had seen it a million times and felt the consequences. Why couldn't he have kept quiet?

But when his father spoke his voice was anything but firm. 'I . . . I would have thought that was patently obvious, Jonah.'

It was madness to go any further, but with the thought of Miss Costello's parting words echoing in his head—about the shotgun approach—he felt compelled to force his father, just once, to be honest with him. 'Are you saying what I think you're saying? That you want my help but don't know how to ask for it?'

The heavily loaded question trapped them in a long, silent pause, and they stared at each other across the table. Then, to Jonah's horror, his father's eyes were swimming with tears.

Dad?' Jonah rose from his chair uncertainly. Dear God, what had he done? He moved slowly round the table, every step filling him with alarm and confusion. His father's tears were flowing freely now, his body had slumped forward, his head was in his hands and his breathing was coming in sharp, noisy gulps.

Jonah bent down to him cautiously, and for the first time in his life, he placed a tentative hand on his father's shoulder, expecting it to be pushed away roughly and to be told, 'Don't touch me!'

But there was no rejection. Gabriel turned into him, rested his head against his shoulder, and continued to weep. Words streamed out of him, but Jonah could make no sense of them. It didn't matter, though. For now, comforting his father was all that was needed.

Gabriel woke with a start. There was someone—*something*—in his room! He sat bolt upright. A shadowy figure was coming towards him.

'Dad, are you all right?'

'Jonah?'

'I've brought you a cup of tea. How are you feeling?'

Through dry, gritty eyes Gabriel watched Jonah draw the curtains, letting sunlight spill into the room. He blinked at the brightness. 'Why are you here?' he croaked. His throat felt as if it had been sandblasted and his voice sounded distant, not like it normally did.

Jonah came and sat on the bed. There was an expression on his face that made him look different somehow. Something in the eyes, the mouth too. It was something oddly familiar . . . something that made Gabriel's heart miss a beat and made him, inexplicably, want to cry.

Panic-stricken, he was terrified suddenly that something awful had happened to him while he had slept. He gripped his son's hands and drew a deep, shuddering breath. 'Jonah, has something happened to me? Tell me the truth. Have I had a stroke? I feel different. Strange. Not myself. Am I making sense to you?'

'Dad, calm down, you're fine.'

But the frown on Jonah's face only made him think he was being lied to. 'The truth,' he demanded. 'Tell me why you're here.'

'Don't you remember last night?'

'What about last night?'

The frown deepened. 'We were having supper together, we were talking and . . . Dad, do you really not remember?'

But suddenly Gabriel did have a glimmer of recall. 'You brought an Indian meal . . . we were talking about somebody called Charlene—'

'Sharna. She's one of my pupils.'

He groaned, remembering vaguely that something had caused him to lose control in the kitchen. Appalled, he closed his eyes. He recalled his younger son holding him, and later helping him upstairs to bed. And all the while he was blethering like a lunatic. But even as he felt the debilitating shame of what he had done, he sensed a closeness to Jonah that he couldn't explain. He knew, though, that he could never talk to him about it. He would never be able to find the right words. And there was always the danger that if he tried, he might lose control again. He jerked his eyes open and said, in his firmest voice, 'I think it would be better all round if neither of us referred to last night again.' He saw hesitation in Jonah's face. What was left of his dignity lay in his son's hands and Gabriel willed him to do as he had asked.

'Is that really what you want, Dad?' Jonah asked.

'Yes, it is.'

'You don't think we ought to talk about what happened?'

'No, I don't!'

'OK,' he said soothingly. 'If that's what you want, that's fine by me.'

Relieved, Gabriel sank back into the softness of the pillows. He was home and dry. Jonah passed him his tea and as their eyes met, his son smiled. And suddenly Gabriel wasn't so sure that he *was* home and dry. He knew that smile so well, had loved it. A hot wave of panic flooded him. He wanted to speak, but couldn't. He summoned all his strength, heaved himself out of bed and blundered blindly from the room.

His head spinning, he locked himself into the bathroom and sat on the edge of the bath. He pressed his clenched fists to his eyes and wept as silently as he could. God in heaven, why had it taken him thirty-five years to see just how like his mother Jonah was?

The May sunshine had warmed the wooden bench Archie was sitting on, which helped to relax him a little. He wasn't a jumpy man, but today his nerves were shot to pieces. It was crazy. He was only meeting Stella, for heaven's sake. A woman he'd known for most of his adult life. But perhaps he hadn't ever *really* known her. If he had, surely he wouldn't be sitting here in Buxton, in the Pavilion Gardens, waiting to meet her so they could discuss their divorce.

'Archie?'

He started. 'Stella!' He got to his feet. Was it really her? Surprise must have been stamped all over his face.

Self-consciously she patted her short, flicked-back hair. 'I'm still getting used to it,' she said.

But the dramatic change in hairstyle and colour—from mousy grey to harsh teak—wasn't the only thing that was different. She had lost weight, more than a stone. She had changed the colour of her lipstick too. It was darker. Too red. It gave her teeth a yellowed appearance. 'You're looking great,' he said.

'You too,' she said as they sat down. 'How's your mother?'

'A little better.' No thanks to you, he wanted to say, with an uncharacteristic spurt of malice. Oh, this was no good! They wouldn't get anywhere if he carried on like this. What was done was done. Bitterness wouldn't help either of them.

'So what was it you wanted to discuss?' she asked.

He moistened his lips and launched into what he wanted to say. 'This isn't easy for me, Stella, but I just wanted you to know that I'm sorry.'

She looked at him blankly. 'Sorry?'

'For not being the husband you needed. I let you down and this . . . this awful awkwardness between us seems a heck of a price to pay, especially when you think how happy we once were.'

She continued to stare at him, and in such a way that he wondered if what he'd said hadn't made sense.

'I'm not coming back, Archie,' she said, her tone icy. 'I thought I'd made that perfectly clear. I have a new life now. One that makes me happy. I only came here to make sure you understood that.'

He was stung by her hardness and felt himself shrivel inside. 'Stella, I asked you to meet me so that we could try to make things easier between us. To make our divorce less painful. I thought it would give us the chance to go our different ways with a more positive attitude.'

'I don't believe you. You wanted to drag me here to flaunt your forgiveness at me, to make me feel bad about what I did. You always did want to be the good guy—self-righteous Archie Merryman.' Her voice was tight with recrimination. Suddenly she leapt to her feet. 'There's nothing to be gained from this. I knew it would be a mistake. And look!' She pointed to his left hand accusingly. 'You're still wearing your wedding ring. You haven't accepted anything at all.' Without another word, she wheeled round and marched away.

He was dumbfounded. As he watched her stride away through the strolling holidaymakers, her unfamiliar hair bobbing up and down, Archie thought, If your new life makes you so happy, Stella, why do you look and sound so miserable?

He drove home to Deaconsbridge more confused than when he had set out. What had she meant by him always wanting to be the good guy? Sure, he liked to be liked. Who didn't? It was human nature to want to get on with other people. The belief that there was good in everyone was at his core. Take that Mr Liberty, for instance. He certainly wasn't everyone's cup of tea, but Clara Costello proved his point perfectly. She had seen something worth digging for beneath the layers of prickly rudeness. Why else had she put herself out for him?

To his surprise, by the time he reached home and was locking the car, he no longer felt so sorry for himself. It was Stella his heart went out to. Her bitterness seemed so much greater than his own.

He let himself into the house and went through to the sitting room.

'Hi, Mum,' he said, forcing himself to sound carefree and jolly. He reached for the evening paper, which had slipped onto the floor beside her armchair, and passed it to her. It was then, when she made no move to take it from him, that he realised she had had another stroke.

The doctor, a woman in her early forties with a kindly smile, said there was no need for him to stay at the hospital. 'You might just as well go home and get a decent night's sleep,' she advised.

But Archie said no. 'I wouldn't sleep anyway.'

The doctor nodded. 'I thought you'd say that. But do your best to grab the odd nap. We don't want you conking out on us. You look too useful a chap to lose.'

With the curtain drawn round the bed, Archie sat alone with his mother while she slept. Except it wasn't a true sleep. She was now in a world where he couldn't reach her. He laid a hand on his mother's and hoped she could feel his touch. He wanted to believe that she knew he was there and that she wasn't facing this alone.

That night Clara dreamed she was running through fields of long, dry, swaying grass. Her feet were bare and a warm breeze blew through her hair and in her arms she carried Ned. In the distance, there was a hill, and perched on the hill was a man. He was waving to them. Standing beside her now, Ned clapped his hands. 'Mummy, there's a man waving to us. Is it Mr Liberty?' But as she shielded her eyes from the glare of the sun, she caught Ned by the hand and started running again. 'That's not Mr Liberty,' she cried, 'that's your father.'

She woke violently from the dream, her heart racing. That was twice now she had dreamed of Todd.

Didn't you get to know TMA during your stint in Wilmington?

How innocently Guy had typed those words, never once thinking they would have such an effect on her. How hard it had been to email him back and say casually, 'Oh, I met him once or twice. And yes, you'd better keep him safe from the women on the packing line!'

It was stupid of her, really, but she should have guessed that Todd would be assigned to oversee the buy-out. It was part of his job.

She straightened the duvet and turned onto her side, knowing that sleep would elude her for a while yet. She wished there was someone in whom she could confide. For more than four years she had kept her own counsel and convinced herself that she would never have to deal with Todd again. But now, because she knew Todd would soon be arriving in England, a voice was asking if she had done the right thing in keeping the truth about Ned from him. Would he be angry, if he were to find out about Ned, that he had been denied the right to know his son? That was what worried her most.

Even so, part of her was convinced that it would be better to go on keeping Todd in the dark—what the eye didn't see, the heart couldn't miss. But what if he discovered that Clara Costello had jacked in her job to spend more time with her son? She could imagine the conversation all too well. 'She had a son? When did she marry?' An awkward pause. 'Oh, not married. How old is the child?'

When he had done the sums, would he track down those to whom she had been closest at work, and through them seek her out?

And that was where the need to talk to somebody came in. Should she confess to her friends so that Guy and David could be on their guard against any unfortunate slip of the tongue, and prime them to lie about Ned's age? She knew that to expose them to such a secret wasn't fair. No. Her only hope was to carry on as before and pray that Todd wouldn't ask after her. He hadn't up till now, had he?

They arrived at the Haworth campsite shortly after twelve and decided to have lunch. It was warm enough to sit outside, and while they ate Ned kept his eye on a family a few pitches away. Two small girls were laughing at their father as he danced around like a gorilla with a rubber mallet in his hands; their mother looked on, amused, as she brushed grass off a large plastic ground sheet.

Clara watched Ned closely. What was going through his mind as he took in this ubiquitous family unit? Did he feel he was missing out?

Inevitably Ned had enquired where his father was: the children he mixed with at nursery school seemed to have one, if not two, in their lives—there were plenty of stepfathers on the scene. Clara had been dreading this question. She explained that sometimes adults had to make difficult decisions, and the hardest one she had had to make was to bring him up on her own because his father lived a long way away and wasn't able to be a real father to him. She had waited for him to probe deeper, but the questions didn't come. She didn't fool herself that she could get away so lightly for much longer, though. The older he became, the more enquiring he would grow, and she would have to be more honest with him.

Haworth was beautiful. Surrounded by deserted, unspoilt moors, it was easy to conjure up the brooding sense of melancholy conveyed in Emily Brontë's novel, *Wuthering Heights*. The long walk up to Top Withens, reputedly the ruins of the house that had inspired Emily's novel, almost defeated Ned, and Clara had to carry him for a short while. Afterwards they rewarded themselves with tea in a pretty café in the steep main street of Haworth. Then they had a leisurely snoop through the gift shops and found some beautiful handcrafted wooden toys. Ned picked out a funny little acrobat who swung his brightly painted body when the sides of the toy were squeezed, and Clara bought herself a copy of *Wuthering Heights*.

It was when she was lying in bed that night, having turned out the light, that her thoughts slipped back to Todd, and her anxiety returned. It was a warm night and, with several windows open, she tossed and turned for nearly an hour. Before long, the surge of worry turned into a thumping headache, and she slipped out of bed and opened the locker above the cooker. It was too high for Ned to reach and in it she kept the first-aid kit and the bottle of paracetamol. It wasn't easy to find in the semidarkness. She pushed aside a bulging A4 envelope and her mobile phone, and continued to rummage for the paracetamol, then found something large and bulky that she didn't recognise. With a flash of guilt, she realised what it was: the tied-up bundle of Val Liberty's diaries.

She let out a moan of self-reproach—how many times had she made a mental note not to forget to put them back?—and lifted the notebooks down from the locker. Despite herself, she couldn't resist the pull of Val's words. She found the paracetamol, slipped back into bed, switched on the overhead light and flicked through Val's last diary. Scanning the pages for something of interest, her eyes were drawn to the final entry.

> To whoever is reading this (and it will probably be Jonah, he is the only one who would be interested), all I ask is that you give my diaries to Gabriel when I am dead and ask him to read them. I know he won't sort through my things (just as he didn't with Anastasia), but I do so badly want him to know that in my own way I did love him. There was so much unsaid in our marriage—so much that needed saying—that this is perhaps the only way I will be able to communicate my feelings to a man who has been too hard on his family, but mostly too hard on himself. He wasn't able to offer his children the love and affection they needed, for the simple fact that one can't give what one hasn't got. A broken heart is exactly that—a broken vessel with the love drained out of it.

Though Gabriel might not like what I've said, I want him to know that he has to forgive everyone he thinks has let him down. He needs to forgive himself and be reconciled with the truth that all any of us can ever do is our very inadequate best.

There were tears in Clara's eyes as she closed the book. It wasn't so much the poignancy of the words that touched her but all the blank pages that followed.

She turned out the light and knew that she had no choice but to return the diaries to their owner. And, just as surely, she knew that the task had to be performed in person. There could be no cheating, no sending them anonymously in the post. She had no idea how she was going to explain to Gabriel why she had 'borrowed' them.

 **CHAPTER TEN**

IT WAS JUST AS CASPAR feared: the bank had pulled the rug out from beneath him. They had turned down his request for another thirty days' grace. And with no one else to turn to, it was financial meltdown time.

He threw the letter onto the pile of bills on his desk with contempt and directed his anger at those who could have helped. His accountant for not moving fast enough to save him from bankruptcy; his father for being too stubborn to sell Mermaid House; the bloodsucking man at the Inland Revenue for hounding him so relentlessly; the European Commission for insisting that forecourt prices had to be cut.

Through the glass panel of his office, which looked out onto the showroom, he watched a young man approach a Jaguar XKR and slip into the driver's seat. With his well-cut suit, open-necked shirt, gold watch, deep tan and collar-length hair, he bore all the hallmarks of a vulgar young blood: in other words, a genuine punter.

Caspar waited for one of his salesmen to materialise. Minutes passed, but no one appeared. He was about to go and deal with the man himself, when the telephone on his desk rang. He hesitated, caught between the two. Then he thought, What the hell? The business was sunk.

He sat at his desk with his head lowered, and let the phone ring until the caller gave up.

In the staff room at Dick High, Jonah put down the phone. He had never rung his brother at work before but, then, he had never been so worried about their father.

It was several days now since he had witnessed the unimaginable: Gabriel Liberty crying. Since then he had called at Mermaid House every day, intending to carry on where Miss Costello had left off, but his father had had other ideas. 'What has got into you all of a sudden? Why have you taken it upon yourself to keep pestering me?'

He had wanted to say, 'Because I'm worried about you,' but his courage had failed him: showing concern was tantamount to showing weakness, and that was something no Liberty was ever allowed to do.

Jonah was convinced that his father was depressed. On more than one occasion he had found him standing in the library staring blankly at Anastasia's portrait. He had tried several times to get him out of the house, suggesting they go for a walk. But anything he put forward was thrown back at him with the reply: 'Why can't you just leave me alone?'

Jonah had to face facts. As ever, his presence was adding to his father's discomfort. Or, more accurately, his presence was the cause of his pain. He had considered getting in touch with Dr Singh, but, again, his courage had failed him. The concern that was uppermost in Jonah's mind, and the reason why he had taken the unprecedented step of phoning Caspar at work, was that he felt their father's mental state might deteriorate. Jonah feared that one day he would go out for a walk with one of his guns and never come back. Why he thought Caspar would be of any use, Jonah didn't know. Perhaps turning to his brother just reflected the depth of his concern. In desperation, he even wondered if it would be worth his while to get in touch with Damson.

He sighed deeply, thinking how sad it was that the only person who could lift their father's spirits was not a member of the family but the redoubtable Miss Costello. He found himself wishing he could track her down. He would drag her back to Deaconsbridge and make her wave her magic wand over Mermaid House once more. Admittedly, his altruism was transparently thin. He didn't want Miss Costello back just for his father's benefit. Since her departure from Mermaid House, he had thought of her constantly. He wanted to figure out what had attracted him to her. Had it been her challenging manner? Or the sharpness of her mind and the way she always seemed to be one step ahead of him? He smiled wryly. Or perhaps it had been nothing more than the pose she had struck that day in the courtyard? Was he merely the same as the next man, aroused simply by the thought of a woman's body. What did it matter anyway? She was never coming back.

Yorkshire was behind them now. They had left Haworth early that morning in a blaze of sunshine, taken the A629 south to Halifax, then on to Huddersfield and Holmfirth—*Last of the Summer Wine* country—before crossing the boundary into Derbyshire. If they kept up their current speed, Clara reckoned they were less than an hour from Deaconsbridge. She had thought of ringing Mermaid House to announce their arrival, but Ned had begged her not to: he was desperate to surprise Mr Liberty.

The boy had been overjoyed when she had told him that they would be making a return trip to Mermaid House—though, of course, she hadn't told him the reason behind their visit. Eyes wide with excitement, he had burst out that this was what he had wished for when he'd tossed his coin into the mermaid's pool in the cavern. 'You see, Mummy,' he'd said, hopping from one small foot to the other, 'wishes do come true!'

Gabriel pushed his stockinged feet into his walking boots, slipped a shotgun over the crook of his arm and shut the door after him. He crossed the courtyard and skirted round the front of the house, across the sloping lawn and towards the copse.

His thoughts turned to Jonah and how badly he had treated him—and still did. But it was too late to make amends for the damage he had wreaked. What good would it do to tell Jonah that he was sorry? It wouldn't change anything, not the words, the gestures, the neglect, or the downright cruel way he had excluded and blamed the boy.

If only he had been a better man—a better father—he would have realised that his younger son had never deserved such rough punishment. It hadn't been Jonah who had killed Anastasia: fate had done that. But for all these years, ever since Gabriel had come home in the middle of the night and had been told that his wife was dead, he had needed to lay the blame on someone. It was years before he was able to lay eyes on the child without wishing he had died instead of Anastasia.

Tolerance had been the best he could manage. A thin veneer of tolerance that was often stripped back to reveal his bitterness, and to let his child know what it was to suffer. Oh, how callous he had been.

And what had woken him to the truth? It was the shock of recognising Anastasia's face so clearly in Jonah's. Seeing the two of them so inextricably bound together had made him, for the first time ever, see Jonah for what he really was: his mother's son. He was not, as Gabriel had made him out to be, the malevolent stranger who had walked into his life and wrecked it. He was the son of the woman Gabriel had never stopped loving.

Now, whenever he looked at his son, he saw Anastasia staring back at him. The pain of his guilt went so deep inside him that sometimes Gabriel had to sit down and wait for it to pass. But the one thing he couldn't do was face Jonah and confide in him. He was too ashamed. That was why he continued to rebuff Jonah. Having him around only added to his grief. Because that was what it felt like. Since that appalling night when he had broken down, it was as if he was being forced to grieve for his darling Anastasia all over again.

Plunged further into misery, he pressed on down to the copse where, in the dense shade of trees that were now in full leaf, a blanket of blue-bells shimmered. He'd had enough of the strain of knowing that he would never be released from the shame and the guilt. It was too much for him. He wanted to be with Anastasia. He needed her forgiveness for what he had done.

The weight of the gun pressed heavily on his arm. He shifted it to a more comfortable position and entered the wood. He paused, making up his mind where he wanted to be. As to the rest, he had thought it all out, had prepared himself so that he could at least get this right.

The triumphant entrance Ned had hoped to make was spoilt by Gabriel not answering the door.

'Shall we go inside and find him?' Ned asked. He pressed his forehead to the door and peered in through the letterbox.

Clara tried the handle and stepped inside, Ned at her heels. 'Yes, but we'll only go as far as the kitchen,' she said.

She was surprised to see that, while the kitchen had gathered a few extraneous piles of paperwork, the place was still reasonably clean and orderly. Leaving Ned to call Gabriel, she noticed the postcards lined up along the windowsill. Touched that he had kept them, she went over to look at them, recalling exactly when and where each had been written.

Still not getting any response to his eager cries, Ned joined her at the sink. 'Do you think he's gone for a walk?' he asked.

'I think that's precisely what he's done. Shall we see if we can find him?' She had seen the battered old Land Rover in the courtyard, so it was a safe bet that he hadn't gone far.

They shut the back door and set off towards the copse, which, according to Ned, was where Gabriel liked to go. 'He makes sure the badgers are all right,' he informed Clara.

It was a truly glorious day. The sun shone brightly in a perfect canopy of blue, and the air smelt sweet from the grass beneath their feet. Nearing the copse, Clara was overcome by the most beautiful sight:

bluebells, hundreds of them. She stood for a moment to take it in. It was so tranquil here. So perfect.

'He usually goes this way,' Ned said knowledgeably, pointing towards a leafy path that twisted through the thicket of trees.

They had only taken a few steps into the cool woodland when Clara stood still. She craned her neck. Ned looked up at her. 'What?'

'I thought I heard something.' She smiled. 'It was probably one of Mr Liberty's badgers.'

But within seconds they had stopped again, and she knew she wasn't imagining it. Someone else was in the copse. Remembering that day down by the river when they had first arrived in Deaconsbridge, she held Ned's hand firmly. The sound grew louder and she wasn't sure what it was she could hear. It was a groaning of such guttural rawness it was animal-like. Bravely she carried on, until at last they came to a small clearing and she saw the source of the noise.

It was Gabriel Liberty. He was on his knees, crumpled over the trunk of a fallen tree, and he was shaking violently.

'Stay here, Ned,' she commanded. Confusion written all over his anxious face, he did as she said, and she moved closer to Gabriel who seemed to have no idea that they were there. He didn't react and the racking groans and rasping breath continued. 'Mr Liberty,' she said, 'it's me, Clara—Miss Costello. Are you hurt?'

He turned towards her, his face contorted with abject misery. Disbelieving eyes, brimming with tears, focused on her. It was then that she saw the shotgun cradled in his arms. She prised it out of his shaking hands and placed it on the other side of the tree trunk. Then she got down on her knees and took him in her arms. She held him tightly, hushed him with soothing words, until, finally, he gave one last, shuddering sob, slumped against her and gradually became still.

It took all of her strength to pull him onto his feet and then sit him on the tree trunk. When she had settled him and found a grubby old handkerchief in one of his jacket pockets, she beckoned Ned over.

'Mr Liberty isn't very well, Ned,' she said matter-of-factly. 'Come and sit down and help me make him feel better.'

With one of them sitting on either side of him, the poor man's first coherent words were, 'I—I can't bear you to see me like this.'

'And I can't bear to think of you suffering like this all alone. What's been going on?'

He dropped his chin to his chest. 'It's—it's Jonah . . .'

'Jonah? What's happened to him? Has . . . has there been an accident?'

Gabriel looked at her, confused. 'No,' he murmured, 'it's me. It's what

I've done to him. I'm so dreadfully ashamed. And there's no going back. I know that.' His voice cracked and she felt a tremor run through him.

She took his hands in hers and squeezed them. 'There might not be a pedal for going backwards,' she said, 'but there's always one for going forwards. Do you think with my help you could make it up to the house?'

He raised his red-rimmed eyes to hers. 'Miss Costello, I honestly believe that with your help, I could do almost anything.'

She kissed his cheek, then helped him to his feet. 'Well, before we take on the world, let's start with the short walk home, shall we?'

In Clara's opinion, the best place for Gabriel was bed, but he refused point-blank to do as she said. Just as he had vehemently rejected her suggestion that she ought to ring Jonah or Dr Singh. So she removed his jacket, sat him in the chair next to the Aga, sent Ned upstairs to fetch a blanket—the poor man was shivering despite the warmth of the day.

While Ned was out of the room, Clara knelt in front of him. She rubbed his hands. 'We can't talk now,' she said, 'but later tonight, when Ned's asleep, I want you to tell me what's been going on here. For now, all I can do is dose you with hot, sweet tea and some chocolate cake we brought for you from Haworth.'

'Dear girl, why are you so good to me? I don't deserve such kindness.'

'Ulterior motive. I'm still hoping to get that ring on my finger.'

He laid his hand over hers. 'What made you come back so soon? Did you forget something?'

'In a manner of speaking,' she hedged, 'but we'll talk about that later.'

Ned burst into the kitchen. 'Will this do?'

Clara took the heavy, feather-leaking eiderdown from him with a smile. 'Perfect, Ned. Here, help me to wrap up Mr Liberty.'

They sat with their mugs of tea and plates of cake. Clara let Ned do all the talking: sitting on Gabriel's lap, he told him about their travels, of the castles they had seen, the mountains, the lakes, and the people they had met. Drawing breath, he paused before saying, 'But nowhere was as nice as this. We didn't meet anyone as nice as you, Mr Liberty.'

'I'm delighted to hear it.'

Clara topped up Gabriel's mug with more tea, relieved to hear a glimmer of his old spirit returning.

When the time came for Ned to go to bed, Gabriel said he wanted them to be proper guests and stay the night inside Mermaid House. Apart from his bedroom, Val's old room was the only one Clara had cleaned and sorted, and though she had irrational reservations about using it, she made up the double bed to share with Ned.

When she bent to kiss Ned good night, he hooked his hands round her neck and pulled her closer. 'I'm glad we came back,' he said.

'I'm glad too.' She kissed him again. 'Come on,' she said, 'it's late and you need to get some rest. Enjoy your night's sleep in a proper bed. And no kicking me when I join you later.'

'I promise,' he said drowsily.

Turning out the light, Clara felt the day catching up with her. More tired than she had felt in a long while, she took the stairs slowly, knowing it would be several hours before she would lay her aching head on a pillow. It was now time to get to the bottom of Gabriel's problems.

He was waiting for her in the kitchen. She poured two glasses of whisky, wondering who needed it more. When they were settled beside the Aga, she said, 'So what drove you to think about killing yourself?'

Gabriel flinched. Hearing her put into plain words what he had tried to do filled him with self-loathing. Once again, he had put himself first, prepared to leave his family to clear up the mess. He was nothing but a coward. He took a gulp of his drink. 'Failure,' he said, at last. 'I've been a lousy father and it's only just dawned on me how much harm I've caused.'

'Who do you think you've failed the most?'

'The lot of them. But especially Jonah. I've also failed Anastasia.'

'Not Val?'

He kept his eyes lowered. 'Her too. I never gave her the credit she deserved. She was a good wife and, against all the odds, a good mother.'

A silence settled on the room. Gabriel took a long sip of his drink.

'Tell me about Anastasia,' Clara said softly. 'She was the true love of your life, wasn't she?'

'That phrase doesn't even come close.'

'How did you meet?'

'At a wedding. And let me tell you, she outshone the bride by a long stretch. She was the most beautiful girl present—the most beautiful I had ever seen.' He cleared his throat, shifted in his seat. 'She dazzled me from the moment she spoke. She was so genuinely warm-hearted. So full of joy. She had this wonderful ability to make me feel special. Corny I know, but the truth. She had that same effect on me even when we were married. We could be at a party, separated by a roomful of tedious people whom I had no desire to talk to, and our eyes would meet, and it would be as if we were alone.'

'You're lucky to have experienced that depth of love. Few people do.'

'It didn't feel lucky to have so much one minute, then have it snatched away the next.' His tone was bitter. 'Sorry, back to wallowing in self-pity again.'

She waved aside his apology. 'Did you ever allow yourself to grieve for Anastasia when she died? And I don't just mean going through the motions of accepting well-meant platitudes and attending a funeral. I mean, did you let yourself howl? Did you give in to the pain and let it render you helpless?'

Fiddling with his glass, he said, 'You know the answer to that, or you wouldn't be asking.'

'But today you put yourself beyond caring, didn't you? Today you did openly grieve for her, and for everything that has happened since.'

He nodded. 'And I know what you're going to ask me next. You want to know what precipitated all this baring of the soul and the realisation that I've let Anastasia down, quite apart from what I've done to Jonah.'

'Forgive me for splitting hairs, but you've known that all along. It's why you've suddenly acknowledged it that needs explaining.'

Swirling the last of his drink round, then downing it in one, he said, 'I see, as ever, that you have your gloves off and are sparing me nothing.'

'Business as usual. So what was the catalyst?'

'You, my dear.'

'*Me?* But how? Why?'

'You and Ned made me feel better about life,' he said simply. 'You made me realise what I'd been missing out on.' He swallowed, suddenly frightened that his emotions were in danger of sliding out of control again. He was being so honest it hurt. As if understanding, she reached for the bottle of Glenmorangie on the table and refilled his glass. When she had sat down again, he said, 'In a nutshell, you cared.'

As ever, she said just the right thing. 'I might have known you'd try to lay the blame on me.'

He managed a small smile.

'So how did you get from seeing life as a more worthwhile proposition to viewing Jonah differently?'

'After you and Ned had left I realised how lonely I was.'

'And you shared this with Jonah?'

'No. Oh, I wanted to, but have you any idea how hard it is to admit that you're lonely?'

'You've just done it with me.'

'That's because you're . . . you're different. You're a girl of unique charm and sensibility.'

She raised her glass to him. 'Still up to speed with the schmaltz, I see. But back to Jonah. What changed between the two of you?'

'I . . . I stopped blaming him for his mother's death.' Keeping his voice as steady as he could, he explained about the night he had broken down in front of Jonah, how a connection had been made between them, but which he had found impossible to acknowledge or discuss. 'And it was all because I suddenly saw the likeness between Jonah and his mother.'

'And you'd never seen it before?'

'It sounds absurd, doesn't it? But no. Not consciously.' With a deep sigh of regret, he added, 'What does any of it matter? Jonah will never forgive me for what I've done.' He stared at her miserably.

She met his gaze with a shake of her head. 'You know jolly well, just as I do, that Jonah is one of the most compassionate people alive, and that he'll forgive you at the drop of a hat. What you're scared of is how that will make you feel. That all this time his love and forgiveness were there for the asking, but you were such a heel you chose to ignore it.'

'You don't think it's too late for reparation, then?'

She looked at him sternly. 'No, I don't. And, what's more, the sooner you do it, the better. Because then you'll realise that Jonah was one of the many gifts Anastasia left you. Perhaps the best gift of all.'

'But how will he react when I tell him that all these years I blamed him for her death?'

'You don't think he's always known that? Come on, it's time to be brave. Jonah's a big boy, he can take whatever you throw at him.'

He took a moment to absorb this idea. Finally he said, 'And what about Damson and Caspar? What do I say to them?'

She rubbed her eyes and yawned. 'If you don't mind, I'd rather leave those two until tomorrow. For now I need to go to bed. I'm shattered.'

'Yes, of course. You must be tired after your long drive.'

After they had locked up and turned out the lights, they climbed the stairs together. When they reached the top, Clara said, 'I might not be as old as you, or have gone through as much, but my guess is there's no easy way to cope with grief or guilt. You have to plough headlong through it, take whatever it chucks at you, good or bad.'

'You sound as if you're talking from experience.'

'This might come as a shock to you, but you don't have a monopoly on self-reproach. Most of us scourge ourselves from time to time with a little bit of soul-searching.'

'Even you?'

'Oh, yes. Even me.'

He walked her to Val's old room, and as she pushed open the door, causing a shaft of soft light to spill from the landing across the carpet to the bed where the cause of her own soul-searching slept, she suddenly felt emotional and overwrought. She was tired, she told herself firmly. Nothing that a good night's sleep wouldn't cure.

But she slept fitfully, tossing and turning in the large creaking bed. One minute hot, the next, freezing cold, all the while crashing from one bizarre dream sequence to another.

She woke to find the other side of the bed empty and her head thumping. She was drenched in sweat but icy cold. Her eyes were sore, her throat felt dry, raw and lumpy, and her chest was tight. She had only experienced full-blown flu once, but she suspected she was in for a second taste of it. Determined to prove herself wrong, that it was only a cold, she launched herself out of bed. A hot shower was all she needed. She was halfway across the room when the door opened and Ned came in. He was dressed in the clothes he'd worn yesterday, and a few paces behind him was Gabriel with a breakfast tray. He took one look at her, and said, 'Good Lord, what've you been up to? You look dreadful.'

'I feel dreadful,' she croaked.

She was immediately chivvied back into bed. Gabriel fetched some paracetamol from the bathroom and she washed the pills down with the mug of strong tea on the breakfast tray. She couldn't face the toast and marmalade he had made for her, though, and within minutes her head and eyelids were drooping and she was aware of a door shutting quietly.

When she surfaced again she needed to go to the loo.

Rallying her aching body, she made her way to the bathroom. When she had traversed the landing and had locked the door after her, she had the second shock of her day. Damn! Her period had started. She groaned, recalling that she didn't have any of those wonder items tucked away in Winnie that would enable her to swim, roller-skate and skydive to her heart's desire. She groaned again. There was nothing else for it: she would have to drive into Deaconsbridge. With chattering teeth she unlocked the door, pulled it open, then jumped back, startled. Looking for all the world like a welcoming committee, Ned and Gabriel were waiting for her.

'We heard a noise and came to check on you,' Gabriel said. 'No need to ask how you're feeling. You look ready to drop. Back to bed with you.'

She wrapped her arms around her shivering body. 'Er . . . actually I need to go into Deaconsbridge.'

'Yes, my dear, and I need to marry Lucrezia Borgia. But before I send out the wedding invitations, you must go back to bed.'

'No, really. You don't understand, I *have* to go shopping.' But even as she was speaking, she was being taken by the arm and steered towards the bedroom. She was back in bed before she knew it. Sitting next to her, Ned said, 'Mummy, are you very sick?'

She forced a smile. 'Just a little. But I'll be fine. Honestly.'

Gabriel passed her the mug of tea he had brought up. She took it gratefully, then remembered about her need to go shopping. She knew, though, that in her current state, driving would be a monumental challenge. Yet the thought of asking Gabriel to buy her such personal items seemed far more daunting.

Down in the kitchen, Gabriel cringed at what he had been asked to do. Though he had been married twice and had raised a daughter, 'intimate womanly matters' had been an accepted no-go area of secrecy and mystery. Now, though, he was expected to walk bold as brass into the chemist in town and hunt through the shelves for . . . for . . .

He ran his hand through his hair and shuddered. He couldn't bring himself to say the words, not even inside his head. Worse still, he had no idea what the wretched things looked like.

And yet he had to do it. Miss Costello—the wondrous Clara who had shown him such kindness—was upstairs in bed relying on him. This was no time to be embarrassed. 'What's that you're saying, Ned?'

'The telephone's ringing, Mr Liberty, can't you hear it?'

'Oh, so it is.' He crossed the kitchen, went out into the hall and picked up the receiver, glad of the diversion.

'Hello, Dad, it's me, Jonah. I'm just nipping into the supermarket and I wondered if you needed anything.'

Thank God for Jonah, thought Gabriel, five minutes later, when he had explained that the Costellos were staying with him again and had offloaded the task that had been thrust upon him.

Jonah was still smiling to himself as he worked his way methodically round the supermarket. He didn't know what amused him more: his father's excruciating embarrassment, or the fact that Miss Costello was back, albeit under the weather with flu and 'female malaise'.

Arriving at Mermaid House, he parked alongside the Costello camper-van. He opened the boot of his car and lifted out two carrier bags. One contained everyday bits and bobs for his father, and the other everything necessary to get the patient on the road to recovery.

His father met him at the door. 'Did you get everything?'

'Everything,' Jonah reassured him, and stepped into the kitchen. 'Hi, Ned. Nice to see you again. How're you doing? Hope you're not going to come down with flu. You ought to be careful too, Dad.'

Ned got down from the chair by the Aga where he had been reading a book, and came over. 'Have you brought some medicine to make Mummy better?'

'That's right, lots of medicine. We'll soon have her well enough to chase you round the garden.' He passed one of the bags to Gabriel. 'Do you want to take it up?'

His father's face coloured. 'Er . . . no, I was just about to start cooking some supper. You do it.'

'OK, but why don't you hang fire on the cooking and let me do that?'

He realised when he was climbing the stairs that he hadn't asked his father which bedroom had been turned into a sick room. But the sound of coughing directed him towards Val's old room. He knocked on the partially open door. A croaky voice answered, 'It's OK, I'm as decent as I'll ever be, you can come in. Oh, it's you.'

'You sound disappointed.'

'I haven't the strength to be disappointed. You can come closer, if you want. I promise not to breathe over you. What have you got there?'

He handed her the plastic bag then sat in the chair next to the bed. 'I was going shopping anyway and Dad enlisted my help.'

Despite her discomfort, she smiled knowingly. 'Your poor father,' she said hoarsely, 'I've never seen anyone dissolve into such a heap of toe-curling embarrassment.'

Jonah smiled too. 'Not his scene, I'm afraid.' Lowering his eyes to the plastic bag, he said, 'I've tried to cover every eventuality, but if I've forgotten something or got the wrong thing, just say, and I'll make another trip. The supermarket stays open until eight tonight.'

She rummaged through the bag. He could see the relief in her face. 'Good heavens,' she said hoarsely, 'I'm looking at a small chemist's shop. You're a real life-saver, Master Liberty. You've thought of everything.' She coughed, then reached for a tissue and blew her nose.

He rose quickly to his feet. 'Shall I bring up a drink so you can take the painkillers?'

'Tea would be great.'

She was back in bed when he knocked on the door again. She took the mug from him and said, 'Maybe this is the moment to say that you can call me Clara, seeing as we've been so intimately thrown together.'

'I'll call you Clara if you stop calling me Master Liberty. It's Jonah.'

'Agreed. So where did you pick up such a wonderful understanding of female needs? How come you're not so bashful?'

'No big deal. My last girlfriend suffered badly every month. She found yoga helped. Shall I pop out the pills for you?'

She nodded, then settled back into the pillows and sipped her tea. 'You're too much, Jonah, you really are.' She sighed. 'Emily was a fool to let a saint in human form slip through her fingers.'

He put the tablets into her outstretched hand. 'How did you know her name was Emily?'

'Your father must have told me,' she said.

It seemed unlikely that his father would have discussed something as personal as his younger son's love life, but Jonah let it go. She started to cough again, her shoulders jerking violently.

He emptied some of the contents of the bag onto the dressing table behind him, lining up the packets of Lemsip, throat lozenges, vitamin supplements, and the tissues. He caught her eye in the mirror as she watched what he was doing. 'Well, I'll leave you to it then,' he said. 'And don't worry about Ned. Dad and I will take good care of him.'

He was across the room and standing by the door when she said, 'Thank you for the tea, Jonah, and for everything else. Give yourself a gold star and go straight to the top of the class.'

'I guess it's the least I can do, given the amount you did here for Dad.'

'You need to talk to him, Jonah. There's something he needs to say. Help him to seize the moment. He's not brave enough to do it on his own.'

Puzzled, Jonah went downstairs. He could hear his father's voice in the kitchen. He stood in the doorway, taking in the scene. By the Aga, sitting on Gabriel's lap, Ned was enthralled by the story that was being read to him with relish and enthusiasm. How perfect they looked together. It seemed a shame to disturb them.

The vote was carried by a unanimous show of hands that Jonah should cook cheese and ham omelettes and Ned's favourite vegetable, sweetcorn. He was a happy and remarkably trusting little boy, who appeared to take everything in his stride. It was only when he started to yawn, and Gabriel announced that it was his bedtime and that he ought not to share a bed with his mother that night, that he became anxious. 'But where will I sleep? In Winnie on my own? What if I have a bad dream?'

Jonah stepped in quickly. 'You could have my old room if you like. It's next door to your mother's. Let's go and have a look at it, shall we?'

It was a dreary sight in the dim light cast from the low-wattage bulb hanging from the ceiling rose. But when the bed was made up with a clean sheet and Ned's own pillow and stripy blue and white duvet, he seemed happy enough with the arrangements.

He asked if he could see if his mother was awake to give him a goodnight kiss.

'OK, but be sure to be very quiet, just in case she's asleep.' Jonah waited for him outside the door, not wanting to intrude. Seconds later, Ned appeared, disappointed.

'She is asleep. But I climbed onto the bed anyway and gave her a kiss.'

As he walked Ned to his bedroom, Jonah was surprised when the youngster slipped a small hand into his and said, 'Will you tell me a bedtime story, please?' A winning, toothy smile appeared on his face.

He was hard to resist, so after Ned had settled himself beneath the duvet, Jonah sat on the edge of the bed and started his tale: a jumbled-up version of *The Selfish Giant*. Deciding that there were too many deaths in it for a four-year-old, he improvised and gave the tale a different spin so that everyone lived happily ever after.

His eyes glazed with sleep, Ned said, 'Why didn't the giant like the children who came to play in his garden?'

'Because he thought they were noisy and might spoil his garden.'

'But they didn't, did they? They made it nice for him.'

'And he was jolly lucky to realise that before it was too late,' said a gruff voice at the door. Jonah turned round. How long had his father been standing there? He came into the room. 'Do I get a good-night kiss from my favourite house guest, then?'

Jonah patted Ned's shoulder. 'I'll leave you to it. Good night.'

'Will you be here tomorrow?'

'I'm at school during the day, but maybe I'll pop in and see you in the evening. Sleep well.'

Driving home later that night, Jonah brought his car to a sudden stop. In a swift, decisive movement, he switched off the engine, got out and went and leaned against the dry-stone wall alongside which he had parked. His hands were shaking. It was shock.

What had just passed between him and his father had gone well beyond anything he had thought might come of a heart-to-heart chat. To hear his father asking him for his forgiveness had been unbearably painful, the culmination of a lifetime of confused guilt and regret. A lifetime of wondering how things might have been for his father, and for his brother and sister, if he had never been born . . . if their mother had lived.

'*Forgive me, Jonah. Please.*' He had never thought to hear those words. Never imagined a moment when his father would lay a hand on his shoulder and say that he was sorry. Almost too choked to speak, he had mumbled something about it being OK, that there was nothing to forgive. That it was all in the past.

'It'll never be in the past,' his father had said, 'not until I know you forgive me. I know I've done everything wrong, but I want to change all that now. It's not too late, is it?'

A shake of the head was as much as he could manage. 'It's OK, Dad.

Really. I've never held anything against you. I knew it was all down to circumstances.'

It was then that his father had told him about going down into the copse with one of his shotguns. 'No, Jonah,' he'd said, 'don't look at me like that. I don't deserve your sympathy. Not one ounce of it. I've been a damned silly fool. I can't promise to change over night, but I want you to know that I do care about you. I care very much.'

An awkward silence then followed when neither of them spoke. Not until Jonah said, 'It's getting late. I ought to go.'

They parted at the back door with a warm handshake, as though they were two people who had just met for the first time and had decided they quite liked each other.

Turning from the dry-stone wall, Jonah got back into his car and drove home.

 **CHAPTER ELEVEN**

WHEN THE TELEPHONE RANG again, Caspar could have knocked whoever it was to the ground. He was sick of the phone ringing constantly. Word had soon gone round that he was on his uppers and the vultures had gathered. Friends, they called themselves, well-wishing friends who were concerned about the rumours they had heard.

To hell with that! They just wanted to gloat.

He poured himself another glass of wine from the second bottle he'd opened that evening, staggered to his feet, and grabbed the cordless phone. 'Whoever you are, why don't you take a one-way trip to hell.'

'Mr Liberty?'

'Sorry, did I make that too complicated for you to understand?'

'Mr Liberty, this is Roland Hall. You might recall that we have spoken before.'

'Too right I remember. You're the patronising wimp who wouldn't let me speak to my sister. What do you want?'

'I'm calling to say that I think you should come and visit her.'

'Why? What's going on? And why isn't Damson saying this to me?'

A pause. 'Damson doesn't know I'm making this call.'

'Is that how you operate, then, sneaking behind your punters' backs, tittle-tattling to friends and relatives?'

There was another pause. 'Your sister is ill and I think you should come to see her.'

Clara opened her eyes, wanting to believe that she would feel better today. But she didn't. She felt worse. Her joints seemed to have tightened while she slept and they ached horribly. Her chest ached from prolonged bouts of coughing and her head throbbed.

She eased herself into a sitting position and reached for the box of tissues, then took a sip from the glass of water someone had thoughtfully left for her and forced down a couple of painkillers.

From downstairs, she could hear voices: one high, one low. She glanced at her watch on the bedside table and saw that it was half past nine. This was no good, she had to get herself moving. She swung her legs out of bed, her mind set on having an invigorating shower.

But when she reached the bathroom, it was as much as she could do to brush her teeth and use the loo. Then she shuffled back to bed and pulled the duvet over her. A knock at the door interrupted a coughing fit. 'Come in, if you dare,' she rasped.

'How's the patient?' asked Gabriel.

'Are you feeling better, Mummy?'

'Sorry,' she said, 'but I think I'm worse.'

'I'll send for Dr Singh,' said Gabriel. 'It's about time Sonny Jim did something worthwhile round here.'

The doctor called later that afternoon. But it wasn't the much-maligned Dr Singh, it was a locum: a diminutive young man with nervous blue eyes. He checked her over, diagnosed flu, wrote out a prescription, and advised her to drink plenty of fluids.

'As if we hadn't thought of that,' Gabriel growled, when he'd shown the doctor out and Clara told him what he had said.

'Sorry to be such a nuisance,' she said.

He sat on the end of the bed with Ned. 'Can't be helped. Just glad that you're here with me and not stuck on a campsite in the middle of nowhere. Do you feel like eating anything yet?'

She shook her head, then wished she hadn't. She closed her eyes, waiting for her brain to stop spinning inside her skull, and at once felt herself drifting on a tide of sleep. In the distance she heard Gabriel say, 'Make haste, young Ned, we need to get your mother's prescription made up before the shops close for the day.'

The room went quiet and sleep claimed her fully. She sank into a dream that held her in an endless loop of knocking nails into the hull of a boat to stop the sea flooding in. She roused herself out of the dream, only to slip straight into another. She was dreaming of Jonah. He was carrying a large vase of flowers. 'Put them in the cupboard with the rest,' she told him, 'but don't try eating them. They'll make you shrink.' He gazed at her quizzically. She giggled, thinking how gorgeously fresh-faced and kissable he looked. 'Well, Master Liberty, I'll wager you've broken a few hearts in your time, you being such a romantic cutie.' He came closer, still tilting his head, and still looking adorable.

A slow smile appeared on his face. 'You're not mixing your medication, are you?' he asked.

She grinned back at him, but then began to feel that something was wrong with the dream. It was too real. Raising herself into a sitting position, she dragged her sluggish brain into a more alert state and registered that he was assessing her a little too intently for her liking.

'Did I just say something silly?' she asked.

'Very silly. But it's my fault, I shouldn't have disturbed you.'

She cringed. 'Sorry about that. I keep having these awful dreams that don't make any sense. I thought I was still dreaming when you came in.'

'Ah, well, that would explain the "romantic cutie" bit,' he said playfully. 'These flowers are for you, by the way. Where would you like them? And no worries about me eating them, I'm not hungry.'

She groaned. 'Oh, go right ahead, why don't you? Make fun of a girl when she's too weak to defend herself. If you put them on the window-ledge, the breeze will waft the scent in my direction. And thank you, they're beautiful.' She watched him put the vase on the ledge.

He settled in the chair next to her and stretched out his legs in front of him. 'Where are Dad and Ned?' he asked.

'The last I heard they were going into Deaconsbridge to get my prescription made up.'

'You've seen a doctor?'

'Yes. Your father insisted on calling one out. A boy not much older than Ned diagnosed I had flu.'

He smiled. 'My father's very fond of you, isn't he?'

'This may surprise you, but I'm quite fond of the old devil myself.' She coughed, then coughed again, and once she'd started, she couldn't stop. As she struggled to catch her breath, he stood up and rubbed her back. Within seconds the spluttering convulsion passed and she flopped exhausted against the pillows. 'Sorry about that,' she wheezed.

'Can I get you anything?'

'A new body would be nice, but I'll make do with some cough mixture and a cup of tea, if it's not too much trouble.'

'Your wish is my command. You see to the cough mixture and I'll organise the tea.'

He soon returned with a tray on which he'd placed two mugs of tea, a segmented orange, and a plate of chocolate biscuits. 'Vitamin C and something to give you energy.'

He made himself comfortable in the chair again, and said, 'I thought you might like to know that I took your advice last night.'

She dunked a biscuit in her tea. 'I'm having trouble remembering my name, never mind what I said last night. What did you do?'

'I got Dad to talk to me.'

She looked at him blankly. 'Did *I* tell you to do that?'

'Yes. You told me to seize the moment.'

She thought about this. 'I think I may have been delirious when I said that. Was it good advice?'

He nodded. 'Excellent advice. I have a lot to thank you for.' He ran a hand through his thick wavy hair. 'Dad told me about you finding him in the copse.' For a long moment his words, and what they implied, hung between them. 'I feel I've let him down,' he continued, 'that he reached such an awful point and—'

'Don't, Jonah. There's been enough self-recrimination in this family. You tried your best with someone who wasn't ready to be helped. Just be glad that the two of you are reconciled. And remember, it wasn't your fault that he kept his feelings under house arrest all that time.'

He smiled and passed her another biscuit. 'Yes, ma'am.'

She waved the plate away.

'Feeling tired again?'

'Yes.'

'Anything I can get you before you slip away on another of your hallucinogenic trips?'

She thought about this. 'Actually, yes, there is. I need some clean things to wear. Take Ned with you to the van when he gets back and he'll show you where everything's kept. The keys are in my handbag.'

'Is that all?'

'Mm . . . something to read would be good. Though not the copy of *Wuthering Heights* in the rack above the table. Pick me something else. Something light and comforting.'

'Something romantic?'

She closed her eyes, all her energy now spent. 'No. A nice gory murder would suit me better.'

Caspar's day wasn't going as smoothly as he had wanted it to. A snarl-up on the motorway had added an extra hour and a half to his journey, and it had taken him for ever to find Rosewood Manor.

The house was as he had visualised it: Victorian and unrelentingly grim. It had probably been used as a school, or even a remand home, at some time; it had that institutionalised look about it. Ugly and over-extended, it was a solid mass of brickwork with staring windows. Caspar thought of the elegant flat in Bath that Damson had given up in favour of this remote, heartless monstrosity. What had she been think-ing of when she came here at this time last year?

He parked the car as near to the front door as he could and, with rain pelting down on him, bolted across the gravel towards the shelter offered by the porch and yanked on the metal bell pull. Getting no response, he thumped on the door and waited.

Predictably it was some time before someone deigned to open the door. A scrawny, barefooted individual with a shiny bald head stood before Caspar, placed his palms together, and bowed from the middle. 'Welcome to Rosewood Manor Healing Centre. My name is Jed, how may I help you?'

'Oh, save it for someone who cares. I've had the devil of a day so don't waste any more of my time. I'm Damson's brother, so take me to your leader and then do me the kindness of scarpering.'

Not a flicker passed across the man's face. He bowed again, stepped aside to let Caspar in, then shut the door silently. Caspar was shown into a large room that had probably been built as an impressive drawing room for some Victorian industrialist. A circle of assorted chairs domi-nated the oblong space; the floor was bare, and the walls had been painted an insipid shade of mint-green.

'Mr Liberty?'

'Yes.'

Caspar recognised good-quality clothes when he saw them, and striding across the room, his hand outstretched, was a man of about his own age and height who clearly took pride in his appearance. He was wearing cream chinos and a Ralph Lauren striped shirt. With mounting satisfaction, Caspar knew that he was face to face with the devious brain behind this whole scam. 'And you are?'

'Roland Hall. It's good to meet you at last.'

Caspar ignored the outstretched hand. 'Damson. Where is she?'

'Yes, of course, I quite understand your eagerness to see her. But per-haps a drink first? How was your journey?'

The fraudulent act of smooth charm incensed Caspar. 'My sister's welfare is the only reason I'm here, so let's dispense with the small talk.'

The man's expression remained impassive. 'As you wish. But I feel it only right that I should warn you that your sister—'

Caspar held up a hand. 'I'm not interested in what you have to say about Damson. The half-baked dropouts you're used to dealing with might be taken in by your cool, calm and collected manner, but I'm not. I know a man on the make when I see one.'

He was almost disappointed that Hall's response was restricted to a noncommittal nod. 'I'll take you upstairs,' was all he said. He led the way out to the entrance hall and up the stairs.

They came to a room at the furthest end of a long, thin corridor and Hall knocked softly on the door. 'Damson, it's me, Roland. I've brought someone to see you.'

As they entered the room, it was impossible to know who was more shocked: Damson at the sight of Caspar, or Caspar because he couldn't believe the devastating change in his sister.

Shock rendered him immobile. He stood staring at the woman sitting in the bay window. For a moment, he almost convinced himself that this was some cheap trick on Hall's part. Where's my sister? he wanted to shout. What have you done with her? Who is this bone-thin woman with hollow cheeks and gruesomely short hair? But the words that came out were, 'My God, Damson, what have these charlatans done to you?' Then he was across the room, kneeling on the floor in front of her, clasping her cold hands in his.

Caspar wasn't aware of Hall leaving them, but when he raised his eyes to Damson's pale face, he saw that they were alone.

'Oh, darling Caspar, why have you come? I didn't want you to see me like this.' She kissed him tenderly.

Still holding her hands he moved to sit in the chair beside her. 'I don't understand what's going on, Damson. I got a call saying you were ill, that I ought to come and see you. Not for one second did I think it was anything serious. Why didn't you ring me yourself?'

She sighed. 'It's complicated.'

'Please don't fob me off. Give me the truth. Tell me what's wrong. I mean, you're . . . you're in a wheelchair. Have you been in an accident?'

She shook her head. 'No accident, Caspar. Truth is, I'm dying.'

The shock of her words winded him and he gasped. She placed a hand on his arm. 'Too much honesty hurts, doesn't it, darling?'

'But—but you can't be! Not you. Anyone but *you*!'

'Oh, Caspar, didn't you know? It happens to the best of us. And who knows, this might be something I get right.'

He simply couldn't accept what he was hearing. She was being much too cavalier and flippant. 'It's this place. They've done something to you. If I get you away, you'll be well again.'

'Please calm down, Caspar. This is just why I didn't want you to see me. I have ovarian cancer and I'm in the final stages. I have weeks to live rather than months. Though, personally, I think it might be less.'

He collapsed onto the chair. 'No! This can't be happening. Damson, you have to listen to me, you have to fight this.'

'No, it's you who has to listen. I've been ill for some time. In fact, that's why I came here. I met Roland in Bath at a party, a month after I was diagnosed with cancer. He told me about Rosewood Manor and I thought it would be the ideal place for me to live out my remaining days. I needed somewhere to rest. Somewhere I could resolve things. And before you say anything else about Roland, he didn't know I was ill when we met. I kept it from him . . . from everyone.' She paused to take a small shallow breath. 'You see, Caspar, I knew I wouldn't have the courage to cope with all that chemotherapy—the nausea, the tiredness. Nor did I want to be constantly in and out of hospital, treated like an experiment. So I decided to let nature take its course. It's for the best.'

Clutching at straws, Caspar said, 'So if you haven't tried conventional medicine, how do you know it won't work for you now?'

She smiled at him wanly. 'Roland made me see a doctor earlier this year when he realised that something was wrong. After agreeing to see the local man, I saw several specialists who all said the same, that the cancer was so advanced nothing could be done.

Tears filled Caspar's eyes and he knew real despair. He began to cry. Oh, God in heaven, he was losing the only person who had ever meant anything to him. Damson was the only person he had truly loved.

It was now Saturday and Clara's third day of being confined to quarters. Seeing her so incapacitated made Gabriel realise that she wasn't invincible after all, and that having her here at Mermaid House, where he could look after her, he was repaying a little of her kindness.

He was glad, though, that he had Jonah to share the load, in more ways than one. Since Thursday night, when he and Jonah had talked, he had come to know the truth of Clara's words: Jonah was indeed a gift from Anastasia. His forgiveness had been instant.

The sound of laughter broke into his thoughts and he turned to look out of the library window. Ned and Jonah were in the garden playing football; the little boy was chasing Jonah, who was heading for a pair of makeshift goalposts—two upturned flowerpots.

Suddenly they caught sight of him and waved. Gabriel waved back, then pointed at his watch, indicating that it was time for lunch.

Time was something he had wasted too much of since his retirement and Val's death—he had wantonly frittered it away. Well, not now. What he had left, he would make good use of. But to make things right there was something else he must do. He had reconciled himself with Jonah, and now he had to do the same with Caspar and Damson.

'When were you going to tell me, Damson?' The question had been on Caspar's lips since yesterday afternoon, when his sister had told him she was dying. But until now, he hadn't had the nerve to ask it.

They were lying together on her bed, her head turned towards him. It was years since they had lain like this, although as children they had done it all the time, cutting themselves off from the rest of the world.

'I hadn't thought that far,' she said. 'Cowardice, I'm afraid.'

'You were never a coward.'

'We both were, Caspar.'

He raised himself so that he was leaning on his elbow and looking down into her face.

'Don't look at me like that, darling, not when you know I'm speaking the truth. Help me to sit up, and let me tell you what I've learned while I've been here.'

Caspar slid off the bed and went round to his sister's side. He lifted her frail body gently so that her shoulders were against the pillows.

Last night, he had listened in horror to her acceptance that her life would soon be over. She had told him that she had everything arranged. When the time came, she planned to go into a hospice: she wanted the minimum of fuss. 'Just this once, Caspar, I shall behave myself. I intend to go gently into the night.' He had wanted to go on talking, but she hadn't had the strength and had fallen asleep. He had tucked a blanket round her, and then sat in the growing shadows.

When darkness had fallen, he had gone in search of Roland Hall.

'How is she?' Hall had asked, when Caspar tracked him down.

The man's mild tone had infuriated him. 'Oh, she's fine! Bloody marvellous for a woman who's dying! Why the hell didn't you tell me?'

'You must believe me when I say it wasn't what I wanted, but she made me promise not to. I had to respect her wishes.'

'So why disrespect her wishes and phone me to say I should come?'

'I thought it was time.'

He'd grabbed Hall by the shoulders. 'And who do you think you are making all these decisions? God Almighty?'

Still Hall didn't react. His calmness made Caspar let go of him. 'I'll sue you. You've wilfully let my sister go beyond help. You've as good as murdered her.'

'I can assure you, I've done no such thing. I only ever wanted the best for Damson. Perhaps when you're calmer, we'll talk more. For now, you must be hungry. I'll send something up on a tray for you both.'

Caspar had gone back upstairs to Damson. She was still sleeping. There was a knock at the door and a red-haired girl with a large tray stepped in. She placed it on the low table in front of Damson's wheel-chair, then left without a word. Caspar lifted the stainless-steel domes from the plates and saw that for Damson there was a bowl of vegetable soup, and for him, poached salmon with a baked potato and a green salad. He woke Damson, and after she had shaken off her drowsiness, and swallowed a handful of tablets, they ate.

'You must stay the night,' she said. 'I'll get Roland to organise a bed for you. There's a room next door that's free.'

He was too dazed to argue with her. Under no other circumstances could he have imagined spending a night at Rosewood Manor, but the world had found a new axis on which to spin and everything was slid-ing out of his grasp. Nothing felt real any more.

Now, nearly twenty-four hours later, the situation didn't feel any more real to Caspar. But he was beginning to resign himself to it. He had to accept that, before long, his sister would be dead. He listened now to what she had to say.

'We need to discuss your future, Caspar,' she began.

'It's hardly important to me now, Damson.'

She seemed not to hear him. 'Did you know that when there's not much future left, the past magnifies itself and becomes much clearer?' She didn't wait for an answer, but continued, 'We need to talk about Mermaid House, about Dad and Jonah. I want you to promise me some-thing. It won't be easy, but take it as a woman's dying wish.'

He swallowed hard. As if sensing his pain, she touched his cheek. 'No hiding or running, Caspar. We're beyond that now. Remember when we used to say, "It's the two of us against the world"?'

He nodded jerkily, remembering the first time she had ever uttered those words. It had been the night their mother died. He had crept into Damson's room. 'I can't sleep,' he had whispered. Without a word she had pulled back the bedclothes and let him in. She had cradled him in her arms, already assuming the role of protector. 'It's just you and me now, Caspar,' she had said, 'you and me against the world.' They had fallen asleep, and the following morning, with their lives changed irrevocably, and unable to penetrate the wall that had sprung up around their father, they knew they could rely on no one but themselves.

'Caspar, are you listening to me?'

'I'm sorry, what did you say?'

'I was saying we got it wrong. We shouldn't have isolated ourselves as we did, or been cruel to Jonah and Val. We treated them despicably.'

Caspar felt his body tauten. He didn't want to think about Jonah or Val, the woman who had dared to try to replace their mother.

A knock made them look up. The door opened and Hall poked his head round it. 'Damson, the nurse is here. OK if I show her up?'

'Of course, Roland. Caspar, would you mind leaving me now, please? Why don't you go for a walk? It's such a lovely day.'

But Caspar didn't go for a walk. He shut himself in the room he had been given last night and he lay on the bed. He stared up at the ceiling rose, tracing the circular pattern of leaves with his eyes. He remembered doing the same as a young child in the summer months, when his bedroom was still light and he couldn't sleep. He could recall one particular occasion, before their mother died: Anastasia had come in to kiss him good night before going out to a party. Dressed in an elegant evening dress, she had kissed his cheek and let him twist her lovely long hair around his fingers. Then Dad had come in and kissed him too. How happy he had felt, so loved, so safe.

As Caspar drifted off to sleep now, he was back in his old bed in Mermaid House. He was covered with a blanket of love . . . It reminded him that Damson hadn't been the only person he had truly loved. Before everything had gone wrong, he had loved his parents.

Jonah took Clara's supper in to her. She was sitting up in bed reading, which he took to be a positive sign.

'On a scale of one to ten, how are you feeling?' he asked.

She lowered the book. 'Around four,' she said, 'bordering on five.'

'That's good. I hope you're well enough to eat this.' He placed the tray on her lap. 'Scrambled eggs with smoked salmon and a glass of orange juice. I trust everything's to Madam's liking.' He shook out a white linen napkin with a flourish and offered it to her.

She smiled. 'I could get used to this.'

He passed her a knife and fork. 'Eat it while it's hot.'

'Yes, Teacher.'

'That's "sir" to you. Are you in the mood for some company?'

'Company would be fine. The house is quiet, where is everyone?'

'Dad's taken Ned to the stream. They've gone fishing.'

He positioned a chair in front of the open window and sat down. 'How's the book going? Decided who the murderer is yet?'

'Two chapters to go and I think I have it in the bag.'

He smiled. 'Do you want me to fetch another book for you?'

'Please. Also, if you could bring me my mobile, I'd be grateful. Though to be honest, I think it's high time I pulled myself together. I feel guilty about you and your father having to amuse Ned.'

'Well, don't. Dad and I are quite happy to look after him. He's a great kid. I'm used to teenagers, so a four-year-old is a novelty.'

'I'm not sure I like my son being described as a novelty, but I'll let you off if you tell me about the school where you work.'

When he saw she was genuinely interested, he talked at length about the pupils at Dick High, his frustration with some of the other teachers, and his hopes for the school.

She smiled. 'You're a real heart-on-your-sleeve crusader, aren't you?'

'I don't see it like that. And please don't make me out to be a naïve idealist. I'm not. I'm a determined, hard-working optimist.' He smiled. 'So what about you, then? Tell me about the job you gave up to become a happy wanderer.'

It was the first conversation they had shared without his father as the focus, and because Jonah was curious to know more about Clara, he listened attentively to her husky voice. When she had finished, he said, with a touch of irony, 'And you don't miss all that? The money, the power, and the kudos of being a corporate high-flier?'

'I'd hardly describe myself as a high-flier, but there are bits I miss, mostly the camaraderie with some of the people I was close to.'

'It must have been hard to juggle a demanding career with bringing a child up on your own.'

'I've been extremely fortunate,' she said. 'My parents have been wonderful and helped out selflessly with Ned.'

'And Ned's father, where—where does he fit in?'

She looked up sharply. 'Nowhere.'

'I'm sorry,' he said hurriedly. 'I had no right to ask that.' He got to his feet and took the tray from her. 'Ready for pudding now?'

'No, thank you,' she said. 'I'm full. That was more than enough. It was delicious too. Thank you.'

'Sure I can't tempt you with a strawberry meringue bought fresh from the baker this morning?'

She hesitated. 'Well . . .'

'One meringue it is. Tea?'

'Need you ask?'

While he was downstairs in the kitchen, Clara relaxed and stared through the window. She was tired of being in bed, which was why Jonah had become such a comfort, she supposed. She was sorry that she had just been so curt with him when she liked him so much. He had reminded her of Todd's imminent visit to England, and it occurred to her that Jonah, a good listener, might be just the person with whom she could discuss the problem.

She waited for him to reappear. When he did, she said, 'Jonah, would you mind me using you as a sounding board?'

'I've been used for far worse things, believe me.'

She sank her teeth into the meringue he'd just given her. 'Mm . . . heavenly,' she murmured. 'Now, what I'm about to tell you, you must promise never to discuss with anyone else.'

'You asked me earlier about Ned's father. I'm sorry I was a bit short with you, but, back home, people know better than to press me on who he is.'

'Does that make me incredibly brave, or very foolish?'

She smiled. 'Neither.' Then she plunged in, and told him about her relationship with Todd and its consequences, ending with, 'So, what I want to know is, how would you feel if you were in Todd's shoes, if a secret like that had been kept from you?'

Jonah rubbed a hand over his jaw. He tried to imagine how he would feel if Emily, whom he had loved and wanted to marry, turned up now with a child and announced that it was his. Shock would come first. Then anger that he had been kept in ignorance of something so important. But next would come acceptance, and delight that he was a father.

Looking steadily at Clara, he said, 'If I were in Todd's shoes I would want to know the truth. No matter how complicated it might make my life. Does that help?'

She nodded. 'I think it's the conclusion I'd reached too, but I needed someone else to confirm it for me. Thanks.'

Later, when his father and Ned had arrived back from their fishing expedition, Jonah remembered Clara had asked him to fetch her mobile phone. He had the key already in his pocket, so he went out to the camper-van, thinking, as he turned the key in the lock, that when Clara was feeling better, he would invite her to have dinner with him.

He let himself into the van, and realised she hadn't given him any clue where her phone would be. He began hunting through the racks and overhead lockers. He found lots of maps and colouring books that belonged to Ned, but no phone. There was one last cupboard, the one above the cooker. He opened it and peered inside. Moving aside a first-aid kit he found the mobile and was about to let the door click shut when something caught his eye. He did a double take, thinking he must be imagining things.

But he wasn't. He'd know those notebooks anywhere. He had seen Val with them hundreds of times. What on earth were they doing here in Clara's camper-van?

He sank down on the bench seat behind him, untied the ribbon and opened one of the books. He read the first page, the second, the third, and kept going, turning the pages and absorbing every painful word his stepmother had written. But with every instalment he took in, he was conscious that Clara had been there before him.

So that was how she knew about Emily! Furious, he slapped the diaries together, tied them up, and wondered at her nerve.

 **CHAPTER TWELVE**

BY THE TIME CLARA was feeling better, May had slipped into June and summer had arrived. The weather was glorious, sunny and warm. Although Clara's temperature was normal now, and the racking cough little more than an occasional annoyance, she was still under orders, from Gabriel and Jonah, to take it easy.

Now she was in the library doing some of her new tapestry. Sitting in the window, where the sun shone warmly through the glass, she could hear the trill of birdsong. Other than this, there was no other sound to be heard. Gabriel had taken Ned into Deaconsbridge to post some letters and to buy some cheese and ham and a loaf of bread for lunch.

There had been no sign of Jonah for days now. The last time she had seen him was when she had told him about Ned's father. She missed his company. It had been nice having somebody of her own age to talk to.

She put down her tapestry and looked out of the window. Who did she think she was kidding? Her enjoyment of Jonah's company went deeper than that. She had liked having an attractive man around—she hadn't experienced that in quite a while.

And Jonah was, to use a Louise-ism, borderline gorgeous. He was patient and attentive with a sensitivity that one rarely came across in a man. Beneath it, though, she sensed a strong will and spirit. How else could he have survived his childhood and hung on to his sanity? So why had he disappeared? It was so unfair, just as she was feeling better and looking less like a bag lady, he was nowhere to be seen.

Archie let the door of the estate agent's office close slowly behind him. He had agreed to sell his home or, more correctly, his and Stella's home. It was practically a done deal, with no reason why contracts couldn't be exchanged within two months. Except he wasn't eager to sell. It was his *home* and he was parting with it reluctantly.

He crossed the busy market square to go and view what might well become his new home, albeit a temporary one. It was a small, unfurnished flat above Joe Shelmerdine's bookshop, which he let on a strictly short-term basis. 'It's not very big,' Joe warned Archie now, as he handed him the key, 'and it needs a lick of paint too.'

The entrance to the flat was via a gloomy alley at the side of the shop. Archie put the key in the lock and climbed the narrow stairs, determined to like what he found at the top.

A lick of paint was an optimistic understatement. The walls of the sitting room were covered in dirty marks, and there were holes where picture hooks had once been. However, he told himself, as he stood in the middle of the room, it wasn't a bad size, and there was a working fireplace, which would make it nice and cosy in the winter.

It would do, he decided, until he had made some real decisions about what he was going to do permanently. Really, when all was said and done, compared to others, he was a lucky man. What's more, Shirley from the Mermaid Café had offered to lend a hand with curtains and the like, stuff he was useless with. When he had a bit more time on his hands, he must do something about thanking her for all her kindness.

He stood at the window and stared down at the crowded market square. Now that it was June, and visitors were pouring in, the place had a jolly, prosperous air. He watched a dusty old Land Rover reverse into a parking space that looked perilously small. As the driver got out, Archie recognised the tall, slightly stooping figure: it was the Commandant from Mermaid House. He watched as the man went round to the passenger door to let someone out. It was young Ned, Clara Costello's boy.

After taking one last look around the flat, he locked the door and returned the key. 'I'll have it, Joe,' he said. 'OK if I come back later to tie up the loose ends?'

'Any time you want.'

Out on the street, Archie saw the Commandant with Ned again. They were crossing the road in the direction of the post office. Archie caught up with them as the Commandant was lifting Ned so that he could slip some letters inside the postbox. When Ned saw him, he said, 'Look, Mr Liberty, it's Archie.'

'Archie who?'

Archie smiled to himself. Trust the Commandant not to remember him. 'Hello there, Ned.'

'Ah, yes, I remember you now. You came to the house a couple of times, didn't you?'

'That's right.'

'Mummy thinks we're only here to post some letters and buy some bread,' Ned said importantly, 'but we're going to have a cake and a milk-shake in the café as well.'

'Well, aren't you the scallywag? And how is your mother?'

'She's been very ill with flu and Mr Liberty has been looking after her. Do you want to come and have a cake with us?'

Archie laughed. 'I'd love to, but I've got to get back to the shop. Will you give your mother my best wishes when you get home?'

Ned nodded, then said, 'Do you have anything in your shop that Mummy might like? I want to buy her a present.'

'I'll have to think about that. You go and see Shirley in the café, and I'll see what I can find for you. How does that sound?'

As Archie walked back to Second Best, his mood was lighter. He had been miserable at having to accept the offer on his house. Now things didn't seem so bad: he'd found himself a cheap flat that would tide him over until he'd sorted himself out. If there was one thing he'd learned recently, it was that you never knew what was around the corner.

Half an hour later the irony of those words was brought home to him. The hospital phoned to say that his mother had just died.

With the house still empty, and confident that she would be alone for some time yet, Clara decided to be brave. Well, brave-ish.

She tapped in Guy's work number. It was time to see what he knew about the latest goings-on at Phoenix—specifically if the corporate wonder-boys were over from the States yet.

'Clarabelle!' he said, when he heard her voice, 'How's it going?'

She pictured him leaning back in his chair with his feet up on his desk. 'I'm fine. Well, not that fine, I'm recovering from flu.'

'Poor you—but that explains why your voice is husky and sounds so dead sexy. So where are you now? Outer Mongolia?'

'We're back in the Peak District. It's a long story, but do you remember we stayed with an eccentric man in a place called Mermaid House?'

'Yes.'

'Well, we're with him again. He's been fantastic and taken care of Ned while I've been flat on my back with—'

'Clarabelle, please, you're shocking me. I've told you before, your private life is your own. So how's Ned? Missing us all, I hope.'

'Of course he is. He's grown. He's already gone through two pairs of shoes. My mother would claim it's all the fresh air he's getting.'

'She might be right. Hey, and before I forget, you were right about that Todd Mason Angel dude, the women on the packing line have been drooling over him ever since he arrived.'

Clara tightened her grip on the small mobile phone. 'You always did say I was a good judge of character,' she said lightly.

'What's even more galling is that he's a nice bloke into the bargain.'

'You've met him?'

'Don't sound so surprised, of course we have. David invited him home for a typically English barbecue. The rain never stopped, and the poor bloke thought we were mad when we put the brollies up and carried on as though nothing was wrong.'

Clara couldn't believe what she was hearing. Her friends were socialising with Ned's father!

'Oh, and I mustn't forget,' Guy carried on blithely, 'when he realised you were a close friend of ours, he sent his best wishes. I have to say, it strikes me that you were holding back on us. We're all getting the impression that you knew him a lot better than you've been letting on.'

He laughed and Clara wondered if he was fishing. 'So what else have you been up to with your new-found chum?'

'Not a lot. In a way, we all feel sorry for him. He's obviously homesick. He got some photographs out of his wallet during the barbecue, showed us pictures of his wife and daughters, even phoned home while he was with us. A true family man, I guess.'

Clara couldn't take another word. She took a deep breath and threw herself into the abyss. 'The thing is, Todd is Ned's father.'

There was a stunned silence. Then, 'Gee whiz, girl, does he know? I mean, does Todd know about Ned?'

'No. I never let on that I was pregnant.'

Another silence. Until: 'But, Clara, he's seen pictures of you and Ned!'

It was her turn to fall silent.

Guy said, 'It was late and we'd all had a bit to drink. Well, *we* had, he hadn't, he's practically teetotal, but, oh, Clara, don't be cross, we were in the kitchen and he was looking at the collection of photos David and Louise have on the wall, you know that montage Louise made.'

Clara knew it well. There was a large picture of her with Ned slap-bang in the middle of it. She had an arm around him while he puffed his cheeks with air ready to blow out the four candles on his birthday cake. 'Go on, Guy, tell me the worst. He asked who the boy was, didn't he? And then he counted up the candles, I'll bet?'

'He did.' Guy's voice was miserable.

'Oh, well, that would do it. Did he say anything?'

'I can't remember. It was one of those crazy moments when we were all doing something. Moira was making the coffee, and David and I were sorting out the dishwasher and making our usual hash of it. We weren't taking much notice of him to be honest.'

'So it was Louise who was talking to him?'

'Yes.'

'Then I have to speak to her.'

'I think she's away on a course in London. But she's at home in the evenings. I don't understand why you didn't tell us.'

'I . . . I couldn't. I thought the fewer people who knew, the less danger there was of Todd ever finding out.'

'You don't think he had a right to know?'

'Come on, Guy, you said it yourself, he's a family man. I couldn't rock the boat for him.'

'He's not that committed if he had a fling with you.'

'It wasn't a fling.' She explained that when she had met Todd he had thought his marriage was over.

'So what will you do?'

'I think I have to tell him, but I'm frightened of the consequences. I don't want to do anything that might jeopardise his marriage.'

'And what about you? Do you still have feelings for him?'

'How sweetly put, Guy. But if you're asking am I still in love with him, the answer is no.'

'Are you sure? Or is this why there's been no one since?'

'Don't give up the day job, Guy, you'd make a hopeless agony aunt. You're wrong on all counts. Look, I'm going to have to go, I can hear a car—it must be Ned coming back with Mr Liberty.'

'OK, but before you go, what do we do if Todd starts interrogating us?'

'For now, tell him the truth. That I'm in the Peak District, but you don't know where. Don't let on to him that we've had this conversation. Play it as dumb as you can.'

'You mean, play it like a man, don't you?' The wry laughter in his voice lifted Clara and she said a hurried goodbye, just as Ned ambled in, his face downcast. He came over to where she was sitting, climbed up onto her lap and said, 'I wanted to buy you a present but I couldn't. Because when we went to Archie's shop it was closed. His mummy had died and he wasn't there.'

Although Clara had met Bessie Merryman only once—and Gabriel not at all—lunch was a sombre affair. They both admitted that the faintest association with death tended to make one re-evaluate what was important.

It made Clara realise that the sooner she talked to Todd about Ned, the happier she would feel. She also sensed that now wasn't the right time to hand over Val's diaries, not when Mr Liberty was so downcast.

Across the table Gabriel was thinking about the letters he had posted that morning to Caspar and Damson. He had written late last night, asking his elder children to come and see him: he had something important to discuss with them.

That night, when Ned was fast asleep and Gabriel had also gone to bed, Clara phoned Louise at home. 'Have you heard the news?' she asked, without preamble. 'Has Guy been beating those tom-toms?'

'He has. But I'd guessed already, Clara. Whenever your name came up, I noticed that Todd showed a little too much control over his reaction. Then when I saw his face while he was looking at the photos of you and Ned, the penny dropped and I knew for sure. He went so pale I thought he was going to faint. You could have confided in me, you know. I feel quite hurt that you didn't trust me.'

'I'm sorry, it's just that once a secret is shared, it has a ripple effect that's impossible to contain. Forgive me, please?'

'Done already. So what happens next? Guy says you're going to come clean with Todd about Ned. Are you really?'

'Yes, I am. I have to.'

'I think you're right. The day was always going to come when you would have to be straight with Ned. You might just as well bite the bullet now. I'm assuming you want to do it face to face and not over the phone.'

'You assume correctly.'

'So, tell me about you and the lovely Todd Mason Angel. I must say, I'm pretty envious—he's very attractive. It explains why you haven't looked at another man since.'

'Not you too! I had enough of that from Guy this afternoon. And for your information I *have* looked at another man with lustful thoughts—

quite recently too.' Immediately Clara regretted that. 'Strike that from the record,' she said. 'I never said it.'

'Not on your life. If there's a man up there and you have the hots for him, I need to know all about him. Give.'

Clara squirmed. 'There's absolutely nothing to tell.'

'Thank you, but in view of how close to the chest you play it, I'll be the judge of that. Who is he and what's his name?'

'Louise, this goes no further than you. Do you hear me?'

'Loud and clear. Come on, I'm all agog. What's he like?'

'Um . . . tall, dark and handsome.'

'Oh, please, spare me the cliché!'

'But it's true. He is tall, he is dark and he is handsome. His name's Jonah and he's a history teacher and he's the same age as me.' She told Louise how sweet he'd been while she'd been ill in bed.

'Hot diggity, the man's a gem!'

'I think you could be right.'

'And talking of *bed*, is he a *lurve* machine between the sheets?'

'I wouldn't know.'

'What, no nooky? None at all?' Louise sounded incredulous.

Clara laughed. 'Certainly not. He doesn't even know I like him. Jonah and I are just good friends.'

'Mm, but let's not forget those lustful thoughts you have for him, eh?'

Having made the fatal error of getting herself drawn into the conversation, Clara knew it was going to take real effort on her part to end it: Louise would be reluctant to let go of this one. She realised, too, having heard herself openly discuss Jonah, that he was the first man, since Todd, who made her feel that he might be worth taking a risk for.

On the landing, just the other side of Clara's door, and having been downstairs to make himself a drink, Gabriel considered what he'd overheard. Now, who'd have thought it? The lovely Clara carrying a torch for Jonah. Taking care where he placed his slippered feet on the wooden floorboards, he crept back to his bedroom. By jingo, he hoped that Jonah had the sense to see what was right under his nose.

Sitting at the kitchen table, the last of Val's diaries now read, Jonah stared at his stepmother's final entry and wished that her life had been happier. She had deserved better than she had received from the Liberty family. She had tried so hard to make everything better for them. And what had they given her? Nothing but trouble, heartache and bitterness.

He poured the last of the wine into his glass, then went and stood at the back door that opened onto the garden. Staring into the darkness, he considered the reasons behind his own anger, which had increased with each page of Val's diaries. It was bad enough that Clara had read them, but it was worse that she had kept it from him. From his father too. Draining his glass, and feeling he had been taken for a fool, he decided he would go to Mermaid House tomorrow morning and confront her. It would be interesting to see how she would justify her actions.

While she was hanging out a basket of washing in the warm sunshine, Clara congratulated herself on feeling better than ever that morning. She felt so good she was even humming a little tune, slightly off key. She stopped, though, when she heard a car approaching. It was Jonah. In view of what she had admitted to Louise on the phone last night, she felt awkward suddenly at the prospect of talking to him.

She watched him shut his car door and walk towards her.

'Hi,' she said, 'long time no see. We've missed you.'

'I've been busy. How are you feeling?'

'Much better, thanks to you and your father cosseting me and—'

'Good,' he cut in. 'Are you up to a walk?'

Something in his unfamiliar clipped tone jarred, and it occurred to her that maybe he was nervous. Was it possible that he had reached the same conclusion about her as she had about him? 'I should think so. I'll go and get Ned.'

'I thought we could go on our own.'

She bent down to pick up the empty washing basket and allowed herself a small smile that had a hint of *Yesss!* tucked into it. It was to be a romantic stroll, just the two of them. 'OK, then, I'm game. Shall we go inside and see if your father will agree to look after Ned?'

'Quite all right by me,' Gabriel said, putting an arm round Ned and ruffling his hair. 'You go off and enjoy yourselves. Ned and I will be fine, won't we, lad?'

After she had swapped her slip-on shoes for a pair of trainers, they set off in an easterly direction across the fields, and soon Mermaid House was far behind them. They were alone, surrounded by a patchwork of lush green slopes. In the distance sheep bleated and overhead she heard the call of a bird she didn't recognise.

'What's that, Jonah?' she asked.

'It's a skylark,' he responded, without interest. Puzzled at his terseness, she decided that he was one of those people who preferred to take his nature walks in peace and quiet.

They walked on, the path rising steeply, the sun warm on their backs.

153

They crossed a tumbling stream, and in front of them, Clara saw a gathering of large rocks. Jonah said, 'I expect you're tired. Let's sit here.'

Glad of the opportunity to catch her breath, she chose a comfortable-looking stone on which to sit, one that was large enough to accommodate the two of them. But he remained standing, his back to her, staring at the view. A soft breeze blew at his hair, rippled his shirt, and Clara had to fight back the urge to reach out and touch him. Irrationally, she wanted him to turn and kiss her.

'I used to come up here on my own when I was a child,' he said, turning slowly to face her. 'In fact, it's one of my favourite places, where I like to come and think.'

His expression was serious and made her want to touch him even more. *Kiss me*, she willed him. *One divinely long-drawn-out kiss and I'll never trouble you again. How about it?*

'But you know that, don't you?'

She stared at his sexy mouth, not listening to his words, but taking in the soft curve of his lips and how they might feel pressed against hers.

'Like you know that this is where my brother clinched matters with Emily. Just as you know all about my family.'

Suddenly she saw that the beguiling softness was gone from his mouth, and a feeling of dread swept through her. 'Jonah, what is it?' But she knew what was wrong. Knew it with painful clarity.

He stared down at her, his eyes dark and hard. 'I'm talking about Val's diaries. I found them among your things in your camper-van when I was looking for your mobile.'

There was no point in denying it. 'I—I was going to put them back,' she confessed, accepting that while she had to give him the truth, it would not lessen the seriousness of her crime. She lowered her gaze. 'I'm sorry. It was awful of me, I know. It was when I was sorting through Val's things. I started reading them and was fascinated by what she—'

'You took them and read them,' he said sharply. 'Despite their intensely private nature, you felt you had a right to read them. Val never intended a stranger to read them. A lying stranger at that. They were meant for my father. No one else.' His voice was cold and stinging, utterly condemning. 'What gave you the right to do that?'

'It was wrong of me,' she murmured, 'and I'm sorry. But it was why I came back to Mermaid House. I forgot I still had them, and when I'd got to the end, when I read Val's last entry, I knew I had to give them to your father . . . I've been waiting for the right moment.'

'Perhaps it would have been better if you hadn't come back.'

She let this last comment sink in, then realised she couldn't let it go and, with her humiliation and meekness subsiding, she said, 'If I hadn't come back when I did, your father might have gone through with what he'd intended to do down in the copse.'

He swung round. 'If you're going to take that line of argument I could say that if you had never come here in the first place my father would never have got so depressed.'

Clara was getting angry. She didn't like illogical arguments, and this one was heading that way. 'Oh, please, enough of the self-righteous fest, Jonah! If it wasn't for me, you and your father would still be carrying on like a couple of bickering children.' She saw she'd hit home.

'Don't you dare denigrate what my father and I have been through in so offhand a manner!' he thundered.

She leaped to her feet, stood just inches from him. 'What bothers you most about me reading those diaries? Could it be something to do with the fact that I know more about you than any other living person? That I know your weaknesses as well as your strengths. That you've never stood up to your brother because, deep down, you're scared of him. Oh, I think it's all of that and more, but what probably irks you most is what we both know, that if you had kicked Caspar into touch years ago, you would have married the woman you loved and be standing with her here. Instead you're stuck with me, a "lying stranger". Which begs the question, who do you despise more? Me or yourself?'

For a moment she thought she had gone too far. His face turned white and his eyes took on a wild, shining darkness. His body was taut with barely concealed rage. 'I'm sorry,' she said. 'I shouldn't have—' But she got no further. He stepped in close, pulled her to him and kissed her. She resisted at first, unnerved by the rough suddenness of what he was doing, but then the desire she'd felt for him earlier came flooding back and she relaxed into him and let herself be kissed. His arms held her tightly and she pressed her hands into his shoulders, wanting to feel the warmth and strength of his body through the soft fabric of his shirt, wanting to absorb every bit of him.

But, annoyingly, the need to cough got the better of her desire. 'I'm sorry,' she said, releasing herself from his embrace. 'I hope I'm no longer infectious.'

He waited for her to finish coughing, then circling her waist with his hands, drew her gently back to him. 'What you said a moment ago about Emily, you're wrong. I'd much rather be standing here with you.' He smiled hesitantly, his handsome face now devoid of all animosity. 'May I kiss you again but without the threat of world war breaking out? And when I've done that, it might be a good idea for us to talk.'

 **CHAPTER THIRTEEN**

DAMSON'S MAIL WAS USUALLY brought up to her by one of Roland Hall's acolytes, but this morning Caspar decided he would check her pigeonhole himself. It was Monday and he had been at Rosewood Manor for over a week. While the place and its creepy inhabitants continued to get on his nerves, its isolated location and day-to-day routine made him focus on what was important. Being with Damson was all that mattered now. The rest of the world could go hang, as far as he was concerned.

When he'd arrived, he had been worried sick about the loss of his business—the money he owed, and the humiliation. But stuck here in the middle of nowhere, he was experiencing a strange, unexpected sense of freedom. It was as if he was in exile, buffered from the raging storm the Inland Revenue and his creditors had whipped up, and he felt absurdly safe.

It was weird and he had told Damson about it, just as he had told her everything since his arrival. Damson had made no comment, but had asked if he would do something for her. They were sitting in a secluded spot in the garden and the afternoon sun was shining down from a clear sky. 'What is it?' he had asked.

'I want you to accept that what we did as children, and continued to do as adults, was wrong.' Her voice was faint and he had to strain to catch her words. 'We held Jonah responsible for taking our mother away, and for making Dad so unhappy. But we both know the truth.' She paused, as if stocking up on air and energy. 'We both held onto that anger in the misguided hope that it would protect us from the pain. But, Caspar, it caused us so much more. It still is, for you, isn't it?' Covering his hand with hers, she had held his gaze. 'We turned ourselves into victims, when really we're survivors. Remember that, Caspar. And here's a little Rosewood Manor truism that I want you to think about. For every sixty seconds of anger you experience, you deny yourself a minute of happiness.' From nowhere a smile appeared on her face, and suddenly the real Damson was there beside him, the beautiful, bright-eyed twin sister who meant everything to him.

There was just one letter in Damson's pigeonhole and Caspar

instantly recognised the handwriting on the envelope. Climbing the stairs he felt that his haven was under attack. The outside world was never far away, no matter how much he kidded himself.

Damson was sitting in her wheelchair by the window when he tapped on her door and stepped inside. She was combing her cropped hair. He held out the letter to her. She hesitated, then said, 'You open it for me, darling.' It was almost as if she had been expecting it.

'You don't seem surprised. Does he write to you often?'

'No, but I was expecting this one. The pieces are all coming together, just as they should. Just at the right time.'

'You're getting too cryptic for me.' He slit open the envelope. There was just one sheet of paper.

Damson sank back into her chair. 'Read it to me. Please. And read it nicely.'

He caught a hint of a smile. 'Nicely does it, then,' he said.

'Dear Damson,

Just lately I have been forced into thinking a lot about the past and I'm ashamed to say it's been a painful process and made all the worse by knowing that I put you and Caspar through a hell of a time. I know you will probably regard this letter with cynicism, and I can hardly blame you for that, but, please, I would very much like to see you again. Caspar too. I have written to him in the hope that the pair of you might be prepared to forgive a stupid, selfish old man who should have known better. It would mean everything to me if you would get in touch.

Regards, Your Father.'

Caspar lowered the letter and looked at his sister. Her eyes were shut, her head tilted back against the chair. He reached out and touched her. 'Damson?'

She opened her eyes and took the letter from him, then stared at it, tears filling her eyes. 'I said the pieces were coming together, didn't I? It's the way forward, Caspar. If the future is going to mean anything for you, you must do as he asks.'

'What about you?'

She held the letter to her chest. 'This is enough for my future. He'll understand.'

Caspar left her sleeping peacefully. He went downstairs, and sat in the garden where yesterday he and Damson had chatted. On the other side of a wall he could hear a group of inmates arguing the toss about the best way to deal with slugs—jars of homemade beer was held up as the ideal solution. 'Take a bloody great spade to them!' he yelled at the brick wall. 'Smash their stupid brainless bodies in!'

The voices went quiet.

'For once I'm in agreement with you.'

Caspar turned his head sharply and saw that Roland Hall had crept up on him.

'Oh, it's you. What do you want?'

Hall sat down. 'I want to talk to you about Damson,' he said. 'It's been your sister's intention to move into the local hospice when she feels she can't cope with the pain any more. I think that time is drawing near.'

'You want to be rid of her now, do you?' Caspar muttered savagely. 'She's become a nuisance, is that it?'

Hall's expression was impassive. 'It's what she wanted, Caspar.'

Exasperated, he dragged a hand over his face. 'Tell me, Hall, what the hell did you do before you took up scamming deluded fools. You're so bloody inscrutable. What were you—an MI5 interrogator?'

'Actually, I was a monk.'

Caspar laughed nastily. 'A monk? Oh, that's a good one. But, don't tell me, the celibate life proved too much of a challenge for you?'

'I had no problem with the vow of chastity. It was the other monks I found difficult to live with. There was no escaping them and their in-built prejudice about right and wrong.'

'So what's different about this place?'

Hall sat back. 'I'm not saying it's perfect here—community life can never be that. But no one at Rosewood Manor is forced to be what they're not. So long as one isn't harming another person, one can be oneself here, without fear of being judged. It's why your sister has enjoyed being with us.'

Caspar took this as a criticism of his sister. 'Damson has never been frightened of anyone, or anything.'

Hall looked at him hard. 'That really isn't true, Caspar, and it's time you realised it. Damson was terrified of herself and what she was capable of inflicting on her mind and body. She came to us crippled by fear and regret. She'd had two abortions by the age of twenty-two and she never forgave herself. It's haunted her for most of her life.'

'No! That can't be true. I don't believe you. She would have told me.'

'She never wanted you to know. She told me you idolised her and saw her as perfect. She hated knowing that she wasn't, hated knowing that she had let you down.'

'But she didn't!' cried Caspar. 'She hasn't let me down. She could never do that. Not ever.' He tried to take in what Hall had told him. He was mortified that he had added to Damson's problems. Unable to speak, he got to his feet and left Hall sitting on the bench alone. He went back inside the house. He needed to be with Damson. Needed to apologise to her.

She had been selfless in her support of him and, like a spoilt child, he had greedily accepted her unconditional love. By putting her on a pedestal, he had imposed restrictions on what she could do with her own life. He was allowed to change and make mistakes, but she wasn't. She was his sister, but he had treated her as a mother.

She was sitting by the window where he had left her no more than half an hour ago. He crossed the room silently. There was so much he had to say to her. More than anything, he wanted Damson to know that she would always be perfect in his eyes, no matter what.

But when he knelt beside her, took their father's letter that was still on her lap and laid it on the table, he saw he was too late.

Damson was dead.

He held her in his arms and wept. 'Oh, Damson,' he groaned, 'I'm so sorry for what I did to you. I didn't realise.'

Jonah was seeing Clara that evening. His father would baby-sit Ned, and instead of taking Clara to a restaurant, Jonah had offered to make dinner at his cottage. 'Having already sampled your cooking and enjoyed it, I'll take the risk,' she had said. What surprised him most about the evening ahead was not that Clara had agreed to see him, but that his father was so keen for them to enjoy themselves. 'Don't you worry about me, Jonah,' he had said. 'You go ahead and have a little fun. It's high time you did. Ned and I will have a grand old time of it.'

Clara's first impression of Church Cottage was that she liked it. She could see why Jonah had bought it: it was him down to the ground, from the cosy proportions of the rooms to the eclectic taste in décor and furniture.

'I thought we could eat outside, if it's warm enough for you,' he said. 'Come through to the kitchen and I'll pour you a drink.'

The kitchen smelt heavenly, and she said so.

'Thai fish cakes. Wine?' He held up a bottle of white for her approval.

'That's fine. Anything I can do?'

He passed her a glass. 'No, it's all done. I'm quite organised for a mere man, don't you think?'

'Young Master Liberty, you wouldn't be casting your net in search of a compliment, would you?'

'Credit me with more sense than to do that.' He chinked his glass against hers. 'Cheers.'

They ate on the small terraced area just off the kitchen. It was still light, and just above a pretty lilac tree, a cloud of gnats danced in the warm evening air. The view from where they were sitting was stunning. 'This is lovely,' she said. 'You've created yourself a proper home here, haven't you?'

'It's going to take something very special to make me want to leave. It suits me perfectly. But what about you? What's *chez* Costello like?'

'Oh, executively smart—four beds, two baths, double garage. Not very imaginative, I'm afraid.'

He smiled. 'But eminently practical, like its owner?'

'Eminently practical. I wanted something that would fend for itself and leave me free to enjoy my weekends with Ned. Though I suppose you're the opposite. I bet after a tough week at school you like nothing more than to get stuck into some house-restoration therapy.'

'Something like that. My next-door neighbours keep dropping hints that they might be putting their house on the market. If so, I'm hoping I might get first refusal. Knocking the two together would make a great conversion. I'd love to get my teeth into a project like that.'

'Here's to knocking through, then.' She raised her glass. 'You're a man of many talents, Jonah.'

'If you say so.'

They continued eating in contemplative silence, until Jonah said, 'Clara, it's none of my business, but have you decided what you're going to do about Ned's father?'

'Yes. I'm going home to see him before he returns to America.'

'When will you leave?'

'In a couple of days.'

'Have you told Dad?'

She shook her head. 'Not yet. I only decided this afternoon.'

'He's going to miss you when you've gone.'

'It works both ways. I'll miss him.' She wanted to add, 'and I'll miss you,' but her nerve failed her. Instead, she said, 'And goodness knows how Ned will take it. He loves being here. Mermaid House has become a second home for him.'

Another silence grew between them. Finally, Jonah said, 'Is there any chance you'll come back? You know you'll always be welcome.'

She knew what he was really asking and she knew she had to be straight with him. 'Each day as it comes, Jonah. I need to keep the plans to a minimum. That's what I've learned from this trip. Nothing works out quite the way one thinks or hopes it will.'

'Would it be pushing things to ask you to keep in touch? Just as friends, perhaps?'

She stretched out her hand across the table and made contact with his. 'I think I'd like it to be more than that. But first I need to settle things with Todd.'

'I understand,' he said. Dispirited, he had the feeling that maybe this was the end between them. He could tell from the way she spoke about this Todd character that he'd meant a lot to her. And who knew what the outcome might be of their meeting up again?

The shrill ringing of the telephone made them both jump. 'That's probably Dad checking up on me, making sure I'm behaving myself and not besmirching your good name.'

She laughed. 'Tell him we're being very respectable.'

He answered the phone in the kitchen, but the smile was wiped off his face when he heard Caspar's distraught voice and what he had to say.

'How can this be? It's against nature for a parent to outlive his children.'

Gabriel's voice was thick with bewildered grief. 'Three women. All gone! Tell me why. Just tell me why.' He thumped his fist on the table, sent an empty coffee mug flying and hung his head. While Clara picked up the pieces from the floor, Jonah went to his father.

It had been a long night with only a few hours of sleep for any of them. After he had received the call from his brother, Jonah and Clara had driven straight over to Mermaid House to break the news. Gabriel had been sitting alone in the library, enjoying a glass of whisky and reading. He saw from their faces that something was wrong.

Once the words were out, he had looked at Jonah as if he hadn't understood. Within seconds, though, his eyes had filled and his hands had started to shake. Clara had made them all tea, and while she was in the kitchen, Jonah had pulled up a footstool beside his father, taken his trembling hands and held them firmly. Gabriel had suddenly looked old and confused.

Now, at six o'clock in the morning, as Ned slept peacefully upstairs, Jonah and his father were setting out on the car journey to Northumberland.

Gabriel was too dazed to say goodbye to Clara, but Jonah stood with her for a moment. Jonah knew that she and Ned wouldn't be at Mermaid House when he returned. 'I'm not sure when we'll be back,' he said, 'but when are you going?'

'Tomorrow morning. Take care, won't you?' she said, hugging him.

He squeezed her hard, then pulled away. 'You take care as well. If you want to ring, or drop me a line, you know where I am.'

'I will. And please, explain everything to your father for me. I feel bad that I won't be here to help, but—'

He silenced her with a feather-light kiss, held her gently, pressed his cheek against hers, then got into the driver's seat of the car.

Clara took Ned to the Mermaid Café for breakfast. There was a lot she had to tell Ned: why Gabriel had gone away with Jonah so unexpectedly, but more importantly why they were leaving. She hated lying to Ned, but she could hardly tell him that they were going home so she could arrange to meet his father. Instead, she told Ned that she was feeling homesick and wanted to see her friends.

He listened to what she told him while he munched on a piece of fried bread. 'Does this mean we're going home for ever?' he said firmly. 'No more Winnie?'

She sipped her tea. 'Not at all. We still have two and a half months left before we have to part with Winnie. When I've seen Louise and the Gang, we'll be off on another adventure.'

'Back here?' The change of expression on his face was so rapid, so telling, that Clara didn't know what to say. There was a danger that if they came back to Deaconsbridge, they might never leave. There was so much about the place she had grown to love, from the beautiful countryside, to the pretty market square, and the friendly people who lived here. There was also the small matter of their involvement with the Liberty family. And there was Jonah. With his understated charm and thoughtful kindness, he had tempted her to wonder what it might be like to be in a relationship with him.

'You look lost in thought. Where were you? Lying on a tropical beach having coconut oil rubbed in somewhere unmentionable?'

Clara smiled and passed her empty plate to Shirley, who had arrived to clear their table. 'Not even close.'

'Oh, well, how about a teacake?'

'Ned? Can you manage anything else?'

Ned puffed out his cheeks. 'No, thank you. I'm very full.'

Passing him a lollipop from her apron pocket, Shirley said, 'You're the politest little boy I know.' Then, in a more serious tone, she said to Clara, 'Have you heard about Archie's mother?'

'Yes, I have. How's he getting on? They were very close, weren't they?'

'Cut up something rotten but, like he always does, he's putting a brave face on it. It was the same when that stuck-up, grabby wife of his left him. It was ages before he let on that she'd gone. If you want my opinion, he's better off without her.' She paused to let a customer squeeze past, then continued, 'The funeral's the day after tomorrow. I thought I'd go along. Moral support and all that. Did you know he's sold his house? He's moving into the square, above Joe's bookshop. I thought I'd get him a house-warming present. Something small. Just a token.'

Goodness, thought Clara, when Shirley left them to serve a middle-aged couple dressed in shorts and walking boots, what a lot Shirley has to say about Archie. And how highly she regards him.

Clara paid for their meal and they left the café. Standing on the step outside, Clara felt a pang of sadness: Ned and she had probably eaten at the Mermaid Café for the last time. 'Shall we go and see Archie?' she said forcing brightness into her voice.

The bell tinkled as she pushed open the door of Second Best. There was no one about, so she called Archie's name. 'Hello there,' Archie said brightly, 'and what a sight for sore eyes you two are.'

'How's things, Archie? I heard about Bessie.'

'Oh. Not brilliant. Funeral's the day after tomorrow.'

She nodded sympathetically. 'I know, Shirley's just told me. I'm so sorry, Archie.' He seemed lost for words, so she said, 'Shirley also said you were moving into the square. It's all change for you, isn't it?'

'It's probably for the best. Nothing like a shake-up. Fancy a brew? I was just about to make one.'

'That would be nice. Thank you.'

Turning to Ned, Archie said, 'Have a good old forage in that box over there. If you're lucky, you might find a couple of jigsaws.'

Clara went through to the back of the shop with Archie, to a tiny kitchen area where there was only just room for the two of them. He filled the kettle at the sink where a bowl of mugs lay waiting to be washed. 'Sorry about the mess,' he said, catching her glance. 'It's always the same, the moment I leave Samson in charge . . .' His voice trailed off. 'Hang on a minute, that sounds like the door.'

By the time he had joined her again, she had made their tea and given the kitchen a blitz.

'Here, there was no need for that.'

She smiled and flicked the tea towel at him. 'Drink your tea and be quiet, Archie Merryman.'

Leaning against the sink, he relaxed visibly. 'That's what I like about you, you always cheer me up. So what's new at Mermaid House? Apart from you having had flu. Did Mr Liberty take good care of you? I bet he terrorised you into getting well, didn't he?'

'I've told you before, he's a poppet.' She went on to explain about his daughter. 'I think her death has hit him very hard.'

'Oh, the poor man. To have lost two wives and now a daughter.' He delved into his pocket for a handkerchief. 'Life, eh? If we had any idea how tough it would be we'd give it up as a bad job.'

Clara's heart went out to him. What he needed was a great big hug.

She was still hugging him when a crisp voice said, 'If I'm interrupting, I'll come back later. Or maybe it would be better if I didn't bother.'

Neither of them had heard the shop bell and they sprang apart, which made an innocent embrace seem altogether more furtive.

'Stella, what are you doing here?' Archie's voice shook with alarm.

'I heard about your mother and came to offer my condolences.' The brittle formality of her words was as flinty as the look she gave Clara, which left no one in any doubt of what she thought had been going on.

Clara decided to make a tactful exit. She didn't like the look of Stella. Too much make-up. Too much jewellery. Picking up her bag to go, she said, 'I'll leave you to it, Archie. Excuse me, please,' she added, when Stella made no attempt to let her pass.

'And you are?'

'Clara is a friend of mine, Stella,' Archie said gamely, 'but I think you gave up the right to know who I mix with the day you left me. Thanks for the condolences. Was there anything else?'

Good for you, Clara applauded him silently. And, even better, the horrible woman took the hint and departed as quickly as she had arrived, slamming the door behind her.

Archie looked anxious. 'Do you think I was too hard on her?'

Clara smiled. 'Given the circumstances, you played it just right.'

He laughed. 'And just think, she now imagines that her boring soon-to-be-ex-husband is capable of pulling a woman as young as you.' He laughed so hard the tears rolled down his cheeks. 'What a joke!'

His mirth didn't ring out with pure happiness though. There was a strained false note to it that Clara knew echoed the emptiness of his new life. Watching him wipe his eyes with the back of his hands, she said, 'Archie, how's your social life these days?'

He shrugged. 'About as good as an agoraphobic hermit's. Why?'

'In that case, I think it's time you did something about it.' She smiled. 'Why don't you ask Shirley out? I've a feeling she's quite fond of you.'

He rubbed his jaw, unconvinced. 'You think she'd say yes? I mean . . . well, we've been friends for a long time but this would be different.'

'Oh, come on, Archie, try listening to me. The woman's mad about you.' Clara wasn't sure that this was strictly true but, hey, what the heck?

Shirley wouldn't have gone on and on about Archie in the way she had, if she wasn't just a little bit sweet on him.

They stayed with Archie until Ned had chosen three jigsaw puzzles—having tried them all out—and Clara had explained that they would be leaving the next day.

Archie gave her a hug goodbye. 'You're a regular Mary Poppins, you are. Not got an umbrella with a parrot's head on it, have you?'

She was almost out of the door, when she was struck by what she thought was her second great idea of the day. She turned back. 'I know this is a lot to ask of you, Archie, but I don't suppose you'd do me a favour, would you?'

'For you, anything. Just name it.' But when Archie had waved them goodbye, he wasn't so sure he would be able to carry out her request. Unlike Clara Costello, he wasn't a miracle worker.

Before leaving the next day, and with Ned's help, Clara prepared Mermaid House for the days ahead. Intuition told her that Jonah would suggest that Caspar stay with their father while their sister's funeral was organised. Caspar had been adamant on the phone with Jonah the other night that Damson was to be buried in the churchyard in Deacons-bridge, where their mother was buried.

She changed the sheets on the beds and made up a bed for Caspar in his old room. She put some flowers from the garden on the table in the kitchen, and left a note for Gabriel saying that she had been to the supermarket and had stocked up on easy-cook meals for them. She also promised him that she would be in touch soon. Lastly, she added a post-script: *This is obviously a time for you and your family to be alone. But I want you to know that I'll be thinking of you often.*

She wrote a separate note for Jonah, put it into an envelope, and stuck it down. That was definitely not for Gabriel's eyes.

She locked the door, slipped the key through the letterbox, and turned her back on Mermaid House, wondering whether she would ever see it again.

The silence in the car lay over the three of them like a shroud. On the back seat, his father slept, and in the front, next to Jonah, Caspar was sitting with his head resting against the window. His eyes were closed but Jonah knew he wasn't asleep.

Never before had Jonah seen such a change in a person. Normally fastidious about his appearance Caspar was unshaven, his hair unkempt, his clothes rumpled, and his face sallow and ravaged through lack of sleep. His grief was so tangible it shocked Jonah almost more than the death of their sister.

When they had arrived at Rosewood Manor, Roland Hall had been waiting for them. Jonah had approved of him instantly, grateful for his quiet, reflective manner. He had taken them to Caspar. He was in Damson's room, sorting through the few belongings she had brought with her to Rosewood Manor. Quietly shutting the door behind him, Roland had left them alone. For what seemed forever, they had stood in awkward silence not knowing what to do.

Seeing a framed photograph by the side of the bed, Jonah went over to it. It was of Damson and Caspar when they were teenagers. Dressed in matching velvet flared trousers and cheesecloth shirts, they looked wildly attractive and were undeniably brother and sister.

'Please don't touch it,' Caspar murmured from the other side of the bed. In his hands he held a silk scarf, which he was twisting around his fingers. 'Don't touch anything.'

Jonah and Gabriel exchanged glances. 'So what can we do to help?' their father asked gruffly.

Caspar stared at him blankly. 'Nothing. Absolutely nothing. I don't know why you've come. I didn't ask you to.'

'We're here because we care.'

The blank stare swivelled round to Jonah. 'Well, as you can see, your care has come too late.' There was a trace of blame in his tone.

Gabriel moved slowly across the room and gently removed the scarf from Caspar's whitening fingers. 'I know how you feel, son. Believe me, I do. I lost someone who meant the world to me. But don't make the same mistake that I did. Let people help you.'

Jonah had never admired or loved his father more than he did then. What courage had it taken him to lay down the past and reach out to Caspar in the way that he had?

Raising his head, Caspar looked his father in the eye. Then, from his back pocket, he slowly pulled out a piece of paper. 'The letter you wrote to her . . . I . . .' He swallowed. 'I read it to her yesterday morning . . . She said it came just at the right time.'

Gabriel closed his eyes. 'Too late,' he groaned. 'Too bloody late. I should have done it years ago.' His body sagged. Jonah shot across the room and, with Caspar's help, manoeuvred him into the nearest chair. Gabriel sobbed openly. 'My poor girl,' he wailed. 'What have I done?'

'What have we all done?' murmured Caspar.

There had been a lot to organise, and with Caspar and Gabriel in no fit state to do it, Jonah had dealt with everything. Damson's body had already been taken to a chapel of rest by a local firm of undertakers, who were delivering it to Deaconsbridge for the funeral later that week. There was endless paperwork and phone calls to get through, but with Roland Hall's help, Jonah got it all done. Roland wanted to attend the funeral, so he offered to drive Caspar's car down to Deaconsbridge.

Jonah and Roland had stayed up late, talking long into the night. Jonah was glad of the opportunity to talk to someone who seemed to have understood his sister better than anyone. 'Does everyone here get such special treatment?' he had asked.

Roland took it in his stride. 'Damson was special to me.'

'You loved her?'

'Not in the physical sense, if that's what you mean. I didn't exploit her like so many had before. She needed someone to love her for what she was. Battle scars and all. We were friends. Close spiritual friends.' He looked away, lost in his own thoughts. Jonah realised that this man, who had taken Damson under his wing and given her unconditional love, which she had had from no one else, was grieving privately for her.

They arrived home to find Mermaid House empty, just as Jonah had known it would be. He had told his father in the car on the way up to Northumberland that Clara and Ned would be gone when they returned. He had explained the reasons why, and Gabriel had said, 'She once told me that we all scourge ourselves from time to time with a bit of soul-searching. Obviously, she knew what she was talking about. I hope the boy's father behaves decently.'

It was strange being home. Strange because, though it felt familiar and welcoming, it no longer felt like home. Which was an absurd reaction, Clara decided. They hadn't been away for that long.

But it was great to see Louise and the Gang again. When she had phoned Louise to ask if she and Ned could stay with her and David, she had been met with, 'Oh, so you're bored with being cooped up in a camper-van, are you? No danger of me being proved right, is there?'

'Rule number one for us travelling folk, we grab the chance of free facilities whenever and however we can.'

'You're nothing but a freeloading parasite,' Louise had laughed.

They had arrived at David and Louise's last night. Guy and Moira were there too, and they'd stayed up late with several bottles of wine and an Indian takeaway.

It was now Thursday morning and Louise had managed to get the day off work, so that she could indulge in a marathon gossiping session with Clara. She had devised a simple but guaranteed way to keep Ned amused. He had been denied access to a television since March, so he was putty in her hands when she switched on the telly. Sitting cross-legged on the floor with a tube of Pringles and a pile of videos he was hypnotised.

'I don't approve of you brainwashing my son,' said Clara, when they retreated to the kitchen and Louise put a large cafetière of coffee on the table, with two mugs and a jug of milk.

'Now don't come over the perfect Goody-Two-Shoes mother with me,' said Louise. 'Let me have you all to myself, just this once. I said it last night, and I'll say it again, you look fantastic. Better than I've seen you in years. You're glowing with so much good health I almost hate you. I love the hair too. Makes you look years younger.'

'You should have seen me two weeks ago when I had flu—I looked like death on legs.'

Louise smiled. 'So bring on the lovely Jonah who took such great care of you. Give me a proper run-down on him.'

Clara reached for the cafetière, pushed the plunger down, then poured their coffee. 'Honestly, there really isn't much more to tell.'

'But you think you could go the distance with him?'

'I think I could, but I'm not sure that it's worth the trouble of trying. My life is here, and his is there. Why invest valuable time and effort, not to say emotion, in something that has no future?'

'You don't know that, not for sure. You wouldn't be hedging your bets, by any chance, would you?'

'Meaning?'

'Meaning Mr Todd Mason Angel. Don't forget I've met him. He's smart and extremely easy on the eye, just your kind of man, I'd say.'

Clara frowned. 'I admit he *was* my kind of man,' she said thought-fully, 'which is why I fell in love with him in the first place. But I certainly haven't come back here to meet him under the delusion that we'll magically pick up where we left off. I'm not that stupid.'

'But how would you react if he suggested you did do exactly that?'

Clara was saved from answering the question by the telephone. It was David calling to say that the first part of her plan had been put into place. Todd had accepted an invitation to meet for a drink after work. Except it wouldn't be a drink with Guy and David as he thought.

Ned didn't bat an eyelid when Clara said she had to go out that evening. He was too busy showing Louise his scrapbook and telling her all about Mr Liberty and the amazing house he lived in. Clara kissed the top of his head, gave her friend a grateful smile, and slipped away.

Louise had kindly loaned her the use of her BMW, and with the soft top down she drove to the Kingfisher Arms.

It was a lovely summer's evening, and the car park at the front of the pub was almost full. David had told her that Todd was driving a bronze-coloured Lexus. She saw it straight away and her heart began to pound.

Inside the pub, she scanned the bar, but drew a blank. She ordered a glass of fizzy water and took it out to the garden, where she flipped down her sunglasses and surveyed the tables of drinkers. She eliminated them one by one. Then she saw him. He was sideways on to her, dressed in his work clothes—a lightweight suit and pale blue shirt. He looked well, and just as handsome as she had remembered him.

She began the long walk across the garden, shaking so much that she was spilling her drink. She was almost upon him when he turned. For a moment he looked as if he had seen a ghost: his mouth dropped open and he simply stared. Then disbelief propelled him to his feet. 'Clara?'

She raised her sunglasses, as though it might convince him it really was her, that she was no ghost. 'Hello, Todd. Mind if I join you?'

There was so much they had to say but neither knew where to start, other than with a polite exchange.

'I like your hair. It suits you.'

'Thank you.'

'I hear you've been away, travelling.'

'Yes. Life on the open road. How are you getting on with the French?'

'Fine. We should be done by next week. The shares will really hit . . . Oh, hell, Clara, this is no good. Talk to me properly. Tell me how you really are. Tell me about Ned . . . about our son.'

Our son. Suddenly she felt as if all the strength had been ripped out of her. All this time Ned had been *her* son. Now, just like that, he was to be shared. To her horror, she began to cry. But didn't know why. She felt Todd's arms around her and she leaned into him, remembering how good he had always felt. How good it had been between them.

Through blinding tears, she felt him pulling her up, then leading her away. He took her down towards the river, to the shade and privacy of the willow trees that arched over the water.

'I'm sorry.' She gulped and sniffled. 'I had no idea I was going to react like that. It's just—'

He held her tightly. 'How do you think I feel? When I found out about Ned I nearly went crazy. I've been out of my mind, not knowing what I should do. Oh, Clara, why didn't you tell me?'

She pulled away from him. 'You know the answer to that. I didn't want to ruin everything for you. I knew how much your wife and children meant to you, and the day I discovered I was pregnant, you told me you and Gayle were getting back together.'

'Oh, my God, you knew then.' He took his glasses off and passed his hand over his eyes. 'If only I'd known.'

'It wouldn't have worked, Todd. Ned and I would have got in the way of what you really wanted . . . Gayle and your girls.'

She could tell from the look in his eyes and his silence that she had been right. 'Let's go back,' she said. 'I don't know about you, but I'm in need of a real burn-the-back-off-your-throat drink.'

Their table was still free, and after Todd had fetched two glasses of Jack Daniel's, she said, 'It's important that you understand I expect nothing from you. I made the decision to have Ned and he's my responsibility.'

'Now hold on a minute, Clara. I hear what you're saying, but I can no more turn my back on Ned than I could disown my children back home. Don't I have a say in anything to do with him?'

Clara felt a knot of panic tighten in her stomach. She looked at Todd warily. 'What are you proposing to do?' she asked. 'Tell your wife?'

He lowered his gaze and played with his glass. She knew she'd hit him below the belt. 'I'm sorry,' she said, 'that was uncalled-for.'

'It's a perfectly valid question, though, and one for which I don't have a ready answer. It's what I've thought of ever since I guessed who the boy with the neat smile was in the photographs your friends showed me.'

She relaxed a little and said, 'It's your smile.'

He shook his head. 'That's great. Just wonderful. My daughters look like Gayle, but the child I've never seen takes after me.'

They sipped their drinks. 'You haven't married, then?'

'No, Todd. Probably something to do with not having the time or energy to bag myself a good'un.'

'It can't have been easy bringing up a child on your own.'

'Everyone says that to me, but it's been OK. Mum and Dad have been great. My friends too.'

As if sensing he was treading on thin ice, he said, 'So what made you trade in Phoenix for an RV? I would never have had you down as doing something as off the chart as that.'

'It was Ned,' she said. 'I wanted to spend more time with him before he starts school in September. It was now or never.'

'So what kind of school have you got in mind for him?'

Again, she felt herself tense with possessive defensiveness. 'A dreadful school, of course.'

He looked at her, puzzled. 'What is it, Clara? I'm getting the feeling I'm saying all the wrong things.'

She drained her glass. 'Forget it. It's me. I can't handle this. I thought I could. But the truth is, I'm not sure I want to share Ned with you. I've done everything for him, made all decisions, sat up all the nights—'

He laid a firm hand on her arm and stopped her. 'You did all that because you chose to do it, Clara. Don't sit there throwing hurtful accusations at me. While you were doing all those things, I never even knew Ned existed. So don't try to make me feel guilty. You're angry with me, I can see that. And I can't blame you. But please, don't think I don't care about Ned now. I do. I have no idea how to resolve things, but I promise you, I'll do my best by him. Which doesn't mean I'm about to wade in like an FBI agent and take him from you.' He gave a small smile and said, 'You can put down your weapons now.'

She relented and smiled too. 'So, when do you want to meet your son?'

 # CHAPTER FOURTEEN

THE BACK DOOR SLAMMED so violently that the windows rattled. Caspar was leaving the house to go for another of his long walks. Since they had arrived back from Northumberland, he had done a lot of walking, always alone and always for hours at a time.

They had buried Damson yesterday. It had been an exhausting, emotionally draining day and, not knowing how Caspar was going to survive it, Gabriel had concentrated on keeping people away from his son: their words of sympathy, no matter how well meant, were not what he needed. Once the service was over, they had walked next door to Jonah's house where he had laid on a modest buffet of sandwiches and drinks. While Jonah and Roland had poured drinks and chatted politely with the guests, Gabriel had grabbed a plate of sandwiches and taken Caspar back to the churchyard. 'Your brother has it all in hand,' he'd said, 'let's have some time on our own.' They had sat on a wooden bench in the warm sun, just yards away from Damson's grave. To the right of this was her mother's grave, and further along, her stepmother's.

'Is this supposed to help?' asked Caspar, his gaze on his sister's grave.

Putting the plate of sandwiches on the bench between them, Gabriel produced a dented silver hip flask from his suit-jacket pocket. He passed it to Caspar. 'Can it make it any worse?'

Loosening his tie, Caspar took a swig of the brandy, then another. 'No. You're right. Wherever I am, I'll always feel the awful loss of her.'

'Better to accept the truth of that than spend the rest of your life running from it.'

'Is that what you did with Mum?'

'I never stopped running. It's why I buggered up things with you three children so spectacularly. I turned away from you, left you to cope with something you weren't able to deal with. It's only now that I've come to realise the harm I caused through my selfishness. Heartbreak rots our integrity, Caspar, remember that.' He cleared his throat. 'My biggest regret is that I didn't have a chance to apologise to Damson. Are you going to drink that flask dry?'

Caspar passed it back to him.

'I think Damson was ahead of you, had worked it out for herself. She was always the smarter one of the two of us. One of the last things she said to me was that we're survivors, not victims.'

Gabriel pondered on this. 'From what Jonah's told me, Roland Hall played a crucial part in her life towards the end.'

'Are you saying I didn't?'

At once Gabriel felt Caspar's body turn rigid on the seat next to him. 'No, I'm not,' he said emphatically, keen to avoid upsetting his son. 'I'm saying, you, me, Jonah, we weren't the people she needed at that time.'

'So what's brought on all this understanding, Dad? Bit of a change of tune, isn't it?'

Gabriel ignored the dismissive tone, and after a swig of brandy, he said, 'I came very close to killing myself last month.'

'You? But why? How?'

'I suddenly understood how much I hated being alone and the reasons why I was alone. Having reached that conclusion, I went down to the copse with a shotgun, all ready to blast my stupid head off.'

Caspar looked horror-stricken. 'What happened?'

'You mean, what went wrong? I didn't have it in me when push came to shove. Oh, I meant to do it, I really did. But there I was, bawling my eyes out, the gun shoved up under my chin, when an angel of mercy appeared from nowhere.' He smiled. 'It was Miss Costello.'

Caspar looked confused. 'But I thought she'd left weeks ago.'

'She did, but she came back that day. Was it fate, or just good timing?' He shrugged. 'Who knows?'

The sound of knocking jolted Gabriel out of his reverie. He was expecting Jonah—it was the weekend—but Jonah never knocked twice. He knocked once then let himself in.

He opened the back door and was momentarily nonplussed. It was Clara Costello's junk-dealer friend, Archie Merryman.

They stared at one another warily.

'I was sorry to hear about your daughter—'

'I was sorry to hear about your mother—' they said simultaneously.

Clutching a carrier bag, Archie hoped that he could live up to Clara's expectations of him. She had asked him to visit the Commandant with a view to keeping an eye on the old boy. 'I've brought you this,' he said, dipping his hand into the bag and pulling out a bottle of whisky. 'Just by way of saying I reckon I know what you're going through.'

Gabriel stared at the bottle. He thought of a letter Clara had written, in which she had asked him to keep an eye on Archie Merryman. 'I know you like to think of yourself as an unsociable crosspatch,' she had written, 'but underneath it all, I know you're the sweetest man alive who won't think twice about doing this one small thing for me.'

He took the offered bottle and said, 'Mr Merryman, it's a little early, but how do you feel about a pre-lunch snifter?'

'Please, it's Archie, and thank you, a drink would slip down a treat. Especially after the week I've had. Though yours can't have been much better.'

'You're not wrong there. Not wrong at all.'

'For once it looks as if we'll get through an entire barbecue without a drop of rain.'

Clara passed Guy a glass of wine and agreed with him absently.

'Oh, come on, Clara,' he said, 'lose the long face. It'll be OK. Anyone would think Ned was being put through some kind of test.'

'You're not still worrying, are you?' Louise said to Clara.

'Of course I am! Wouldn't you be, if your child was meeting his father for the first time?' Though Ned was at the bottom of the garden playing football with David and well out of earshot, Clara kept her voice low.

'The important thing is that Ned doesn't have a clue what's going on,' Guy said, equally circumspect. 'As far as he's concerned, Todd is just another of his mother's many friends.'

Clara knew that what Guy was saying was right. But, oh, she just wished this day could be over. It had seemed so reasonable when Louise and David had offered to invite Todd to lunch so that he could meet Ned in a relaxed setting. But now she was regretting the whole idea.

They had discussed this important day on the phone several times and had even met up again for a drink last night. He was as concerned as she was that Ned was not put through any emotional upset.

Determined to safeguard Ned, Clara had laid down the ground rules straight away. She had told Todd that until he had decided whether he was going to tell his wife about Ned and therefore offer a real, open commitment, he could not reveal who he was. It was harsh, but it was Ned's feelings that mattered, not hers, not Todd's. Yet she wasn't without sympathy for Todd. She knew he was up against the worst dilemma he would probably ever have to face. But that was *his* problem. She was a hard-headed realist, if nothing else.

She had said this to Jonah on the phone late last night—she had phoned him several times.

'Nothing wrong in being hard-headed or a realist,' he'd said.

'Did I say there was?'

'No, but something in your tone suggested you were defending yourself.'

'Goodness, you're being mighty forward all of a sudden.'

He'd laughed. 'Only because I know I'm out of slapping range.'

After he'd brought her up to date with how his brother and father were getting on, he'd said, 'It's a pity you're not here, it's a beautiful night.' He hadn't said he was missing her, but the implication was there.

Todd arrived exactly on time. One look at his face as he stepped out of his car and she knew he was as nervous as she was. It made her feel better, took away some of her edginess. Which couldn't be said of her friends.

They tried too hard to show that they were relaxed with the situation. Louise and Moira laughed too loudly at Todd's jokes, and Guy took the bottles of Californian wine he'd brought with such expansive gratitude that anyone would have thought he had been presented with the Holy Grail.

And while they tried to hide their awkwardness, a piercing squeal came up from the bottom of the garden. Seconds later, Ned came running towards them, his dark hair shiny in the bright sunlight, bouncing with each step he took. His face was a huge grin of delight. 'Mummy, Mummy, I beat Uncle David. Ten goals to five!'

'Ned,' she said, 'this is an old friend of mine. He lives in America and his name is Todd. Have you got enough puff to say hello to him?'

Ned looked up at him and smiled confidently. 'Hello, Mr Todd. Do you like playing football?'

It was such an emotionally charged moment that everyone suddenly found something to do—the barbecue needed lighting, the salads had to be dressed, and a bottle of wine opened. Clara watched Todd's face as he hunkered down to be on eye level with Ned. 'Hi,' he said, 'I'm more of a baseball fan, but I'll give football a shot if you'll teach me.'

Ned grinned. 'I'm very good. Jonah taught me when Mummy was ill in bed. He showed me how to tackle. Do you want to see?'

Todd glanced up at Clara and her heart twisted as she saw both sadness and joy in his face. 'Would you mind?' he asked.

She smiled. 'Not at all.'

They were three very important words, she thought later that evening when Todd had left for his hotel, and she was kissing Ned good night.

'Todd was nice,' Ned said. 'Will he come and see us again?'

'I don't know. He's very busy at the moment and then he has to go home to America.'

She pushed the hair out of his eyes, and was about to get up from the bed, when he said, 'Mummy, what do you think Mr Liberty is doing right now?'

'Probably wondering what you're doing right now.'

He seemed pleased by this thought. 'Can we go back to Mermaid House to see him?'

'Don't you like being here?'

'Mm . . . it is nice, but I miss Mr Liberty.' His lower lip wobbled.

'Oh, Ned.' She lifted him out of bed and sat him on her lap. She cuddled his warm body against hers, but the tears had taken hold of him and there seemed no way to comfort him.

Eventually Clara settled him by promising that they would ring Mr Liberty tomorrow morning. When she joined her friends downstairs, she sensed they had something to say to her: they had formed themselves into what looked suspiciously like a deputation.

Guy patted the seat next to him on the sofa. 'Clarabelle, for once in your life you're going to take the advice of your friends.'

'And please don't take this the wrong way,' Louise said, 'but quite frankly you've outstayed your welcome.'

'Yes,' agreed David, handing round cups of coffee. 'So you can pack your things and go. We've had enough.'

'More than enough,' said Guy. 'If I have to hear one more word about Ned's superhuman friend, Mr Gabriel Liberty, I think I'll go mad.'

'And as for the wonderful Jonah Liberty,' said Moira, 'well, please, is any man that perfect?'

Clara stared at them. 'What's going on? What are you up to?'

175

'Get real, sister,' laughed Guy. 'You and Ned have done nothing but go on about Deaconsbridge. And if you hadn't come back here to see Todd, you'd still be up there in the Peak District, wouldn't you?'

Clara nodded. 'Possibly.'

'No possibly about it!' said Louise. 'Now, what's stopping you from taking off tomorrow and seeing how the land lies?'

'But why would I want to do that?'

Nobody answered her. They just stared at her hard.

'Look, the truth is, it has crossed my mind to do as you're suggesting, but I'm worried if Ned and I do go back we might not want to leave.'

'I'm sorry, call me a dumb old bloke,' said David, 'but what's the danger in that? You've found somewhere you like, where you've made friends, and where there's even the chance of you getting off with a real live man. Explain the problem.'

'Are you trying to get rid of me?'

'Yes!' they all shouted together.

'But if Ned and I go back, and we find that we want to stay, what then?'

David sighed as if she was being particularly dense. 'You'll get a job, get Ned into school and find yourself somewhere to live.'

'And if it doesn't work?'

'You come back here,' Guy said. 'But what would be worse, doing that, or knowing you were too much of a coward to try it?'

'You sneaky dog, Guy Morrell. Nobody gets away with accusing me of cowardice.' Smiling she thumped him with a cushion. 'But be serious for a minute. Do you really think I should go back for the rest of the summer and see how it pans out?'

'All you have to do is ask yourself, what have you got to lose?'

With her fondness for having everything organised, and every conceivable contingency catered for, Clara spent the following week planning. At no time did she let on to Ned what she was doing.

There was one important phone call she had to make, to her parents. 'I just wanted to know how you would feel if Ned and I weren't here when you came back from Australia,' she said to her mother.

Her mother went very quiet and said, 'Whatever decision you make, you know we'll go along with it.'

'You're the best, Mum.'

'I know. Now, explain what you're up to.'

After Clara had outlined her plans, her mother wished her luck and asked if Ned was around for her to speak to.

'I'll go and get him, but don't mention anything I've just told you. I want it to be a surprise for him.'

The night before she planned to drive north with Ned, she met up with Todd one last time. His work was almost finished at Phoenix and he was due to fly home in two days. They sat in the garden of the Kingfisher Arms once more, but Clara didn't press him for details about the future.

'I want to thank you for being so understanding,' he said, 'and for letting me see Ned. I'm more grateful than I can say.'

'But I have so much more to be grateful for,' she said. 'I have Ned. He means the world to me.'

'I know he does. I can also see how much you mean to him. He's a wonderful boy, you've done a fine job of raising him. I'm just shame-faced I haven't been there for you both when I should have been.'

There was an awkward moment when he brought up the question of financial support. 'I'd feel a whole lot better if you'd take this, Clara.' He handed her a cheque. Without looking at it she passed it back to him.

'And I'd feel a lot worse taking it. When you know exactly what you want to do about Ned, then we'll discuss money. Not before.'

'Fair enough,' he said. Then looking embarrassed, he added, 'By the way, what . . . what did you put on the birth certificate?'

She smiled. 'What do you think? Your name, of course.'

He swallowed. 'You always did play it dead straight, Clara. Thank you for doing that.'

 **CHAPTER FIFTEEN**

STANDING IN FRONT of the mirror, Gabriel straightened his tie and admired his new blazer. He was glad now that he had asked Caspar to take him shopping for some new clothes, and even more so that he had taken his son's advice and chosen the single-breasted rather than double. Next he turned his attention to his hair. Again, Caspar had intervened and pushed him to have it cut dramatically shorter than he wanted. Grudgingly Gabriel admitted that it was a great improvement. It made him look younger, distinguished—with a dash of jauntiness. He tilted his chin up and mentally declared himself a handsome devil.

Enough preening. Time was of the essence. He still had lots to do. Ned and Clara would soon be here. He paused on the landing outside Val's old room, then went in. With Archie's help, he had had it spruced up for Clara. Shirley had been a help too. Funny, that—he'd only ever talked to her in the café when he was ordering lunch, but she had been ready to lend a hand when he had mentioned the party he wanted to give. 'You'll be needing food,' she'd said. 'Want any help with that?'

'I don't want anything fancy.'

'You mean you don't want anything expensive, you old skinflint.'

She and Archie were somewhere downstairs. It was only a small party he was throwing, but he didn't know how he would have organised everything if they hadn't offered to help. Under the guise of clearing out yet more junk from the house, he'd seen quite a lot of Archie, had found him an agreeable man, and he was pleased, if not a little amused, that he and Shirley were getting on so well. He knew that it wasn't good to be on one's own too much. Having people around made things bearable.

And that was what he had wished for, that day at the Mermaid Cavern. He had tossed his coin into the pool and wished that he would have the pleasure of seeing Ned and his mother again. Because when they were around, life was infinitely better.

Downstairs, he found the kitchen empty. An appetising smell was coming from the oven, but apart from that, there was no sign of any activity. Shirley had been coming to Mermaid House for just over a week now to keep the place in order, and the arrangement was working well. The rooms that mattered were as neat as a pin. He had no complaints at all.

The only gripe he had was that Dr Singh wasn't around to see how smoothly he now had his life ticking over. He'd heard through Shirley that he had moved up to Blackburn. Or was it Bury? Anyway, wherever he had beggared off to, doubtless he was poking his nose into some other poor devil's affairs. Though Gabriel was aware that if Dr Singh hadn't been such a nuisance, he might never have formed the friendship he now had with Ned and Clara. Or be reconciled with Jonah and Caspar. Caspar was currently dividing his time between Manchester and Mermaid House, and though it was hard work having Caspar around, Gabriel didn't want him to be on his own. The more time they spent together, the more alike Gabriel realised they were.

Gabriel took it as an encouraging sign that Caspar had agreed to join the party today. He had expected his son to turn down the invitation.

Jonah was the only person who didn't know what was going on—he had been deliberately misled into believing that Clara was arriving tomorrow. Revelling in all the skulduggery, Gabriel had phoned Jonah and told him to get here when school was finished because there was something important they needed to discuss. Which was partly true, there *were* things he needed to say this afternoon. Things he should have said and done a long time ago.

It was reading Val's diaries that had clinched it for him. Jonah had given the notebooks to him last week, saying Clara had found them when she had been sorting out Val's room. They had made for difficult reading, and it saddened him to know that Val had felt such an outsider at Mermaid House. What moved him most, though, was her determination to try to understand a family that had, in her words, 'had its heart ripped out of it.'

After he had finished arranging the flowers on Damson's grave, Caspar straightened up. Checking his watch, he saw that he would have to leave soon. He wasn't in the mood to be sociable, but he had made his sister a promise, and he would do his damnedest to keep it. He had let her down when she was alive, he would not do the same now she was dead. So a party it was.

He turned and walked away, back down the gravel path and out onto the road where his car was parked in front of Jonah's house.

He was now the not-so-proud owner of a second-hand Rover. The Maserati had been sold, and his beautiful loft apartment was on the market. The bank, the creditors, the taxman, they were all feasting greedily on his remains, but he didn't give a monkey's. It was gone. Another chapter in his life dealt with.

Ironically his father, after refusing to help him, had changed his mind the other day and offered to bail him out when he discovered the mess he was in, but Caspar had rejected the offer. Pride had made him sensitive to pity. Besides, Damson had left him her flat in Bath with a sizeable amount of money. He planned to move down there and start afresh. A new beginning was what he needed. And, thanks to his sister, he had been given the opportunity to do just that.

Damson's will had been clear on two points in particular, that (a) she had been of a sound mind when she had written it, and (b) Caspar was to be the main beneficiary of her estate and that he was to agree to her instructions that Rosewood Manor was to receive a modest annuity from a trust fund she had set up.

He had no problem with this. He might not like Hall and all he stood for, but he would always respect Damson's wishes.

Darling Damson. How dull his world was going to be without her.

Ned was so excited, he was in danger of bouncing out of his seat. If he hadn't been strapped in, he very nearly would have when Clara swerved to avoid a large pothole. They juddered on, and suddenly Mermaid House appeared over the brow of the hill.

Saying goodbye to her friends this time round had been tough, because in her heart she knew she wanted to give Deaconsbridge her best shot: she wanted to stay there and really make it work. Other than the brief sojourn in the States and her time at college, she had never lived away from where she had grown up, she hadn't felt the need to break away. But now she did. And tied into this was the realisation that she wanted to discover what else she was capable of doing. Unless she allowed herself this chance to find out what other talents she had, she would always regret it. She had never liked the expression 'down-shifter', but in essence that was probably what she was opting for. A simple life that would enable her to spend more time with Ned had to be more enriching than the hectic one she had tried before.

But she wasn't without a back-up plan. Gabriel Liberty's part in all of this was crucial. In letting her and Ned stay at Mermaid House for the rest of the summer, he was giving her the luxury of time and space to reflect on her next move. For now, she had only vague glimpses of the future. If she let her imagination break free, she pictured herself running a bed and breakfast. OK, she might be deluding herself that she could scrape a living from it, but the big plus was that she saw herself being happy. Ned, too.

And she would be the biggest liar that had ever walked the planet, if she didn't admit to wanting Jonah to be a part of that happiness. Just to see if he fitted into her life. And if she and Ned could fit into his.

She pulled into the courtyard, and before she had yanked on the hand-brake, Ned was out of his seat. She watched him hurtle across the cobbles and pound on the door with his small fists.

When Clara caught up with him, it was all noise and laughter in the kitchen. Archie was there, and so was Shirley, her face flushed from the heat. With Ned held aloft, Gabriel came towards her. He stooped to kiss her cheek. 'Welcome back. You're late.'

'Well, well, well. And who might this handsomely rakish stranger be with the smart haircut and snazzy blazer? Where's the scruffy Mr Liberty I know and love?'

'But, Mummy, it is Mr Liberty! Look, it's him!'

She smiled. 'I know, Ned. I'm only teasing.'

'Ah, I see the first of the honoured guests have arrived.'

They all turned. It was Caspar. Brandishing a bottle of champagne, he said, 'A contribution towards the merriment.' He put it on the table and held out his hand towards Clara. 'We didn't ever really introduce ourselves properly, did we? Caspar Liberty, the family ne'er-do-well.'

Clara shook hands with him, seeing him as other women might: handsome, charming but, above all else, dangerous. For a lot of women that might be his appeal. But he held no attraction for her.

'We need to hide your van,' Gabriel said, some minutes later, when the kerfuffle of their arrival had died down.

'I'll help you bring your stuff in if you like,' offered Archie.

They went outside together, and after Clara had put Winnie out of sight, and was passing Ned's bag to Archie, she said, 'How have you been since I last saw you? You look much better.'

'Thanks, love, I'm feeling great, on top of things again. And you were right about Shirley.'

'No kidding?'

He smiled shyly. 'And I've moved into what she calls my bachelor flat. Funny thing is, I needn't have moved. Bessie left me her house over in Derby and the money it'll fetch could have been used to pay off Stella.'

She touched his arm. 'For what it's worth, I think you did the right thing in moving. Leave the memories behind.'

'Oh, aye, I don't regret selling up. It was the best thing I could have done. Now I've got a bit of spare cash to enjoy myself. I'm thinking of taking a holiday. Do a bit of travelling.'

'Good for you. Hey, I don't suppose I could interest you in a camper-van, could I? Generous rates for friends.'

He laughed. 'Oh, that sounds dangerous. I might do a Clara Costello—find somewhere I like and never come back.'

She wagged a finger at him. 'Not dangerous, Archie. Adventurous. Living life to the full. That's what you must do from now on. Just think of the fun you and Shirley could have in a camper-van.'

Jonah wondered what his father wanted to see him about. He had sounded serious on the phone and he hoped it wasn't bad news.

He drove into the courtyard and parked alongside his father's Land Rover. He knocked on the back door, then entered. 'Dad,' he called, 'it's me, Jonah.' There was no reply.

Passing the gunroom, he caught the smell of cooking. He pushed open the kitchen door, but stopped dead in his tracks. 'Clara! What are you doing here? I thought you were arriving tomorrow.'

She put down the tea towel she'd been using to dry some plates. 'I could go away and come back in the morning if you'd prefer?'

'Don't even think about it!' He moved forward, was all set to put his arms around her and kiss her, when he held back. 'Are we alone?' he asked. He glanced over her shoulder towards the hall. 'Or are we likely to be interrupted by a curious son and a jealous father?'

'We're alone. And you have full permission to make the most of it.'

He did. Afterwards, he said, 'It's so good to see you again. When did you change your mind about when you'd be coming?'

'Oh, days ago.'

'But you never said anything. We spoke on the phone last night and—'

'The plot thickens, Master Liberty.' Grinning, she took his hands in hers. 'I think it's time you came with me. But you have to promise to close your eyes.'

Puzzled, he did as she said and allowed her to lead him outside. He knew they were crossing the courtyard, but all too soon he became disorientated and didn't know where they were heading. He heard a door creak and she told him there were two steps in front of him. He lifted a foot exaggeratedly. Then the other.

'You can open your eyes now.'

He was in the banqueting hall. It had been thoroughly cleaned, was almost unrecognisable. There were candles everywhere, and balloons and streamers. A long, thin table ran the length of the room, laden with food. There was a square cake in the middle of it all and it had . . . small blue candles on it. And then it dawned on him. It was a party. A birthday party.

His father came towards him with a glass of champagne. 'Happy birthday, Jonah.'

'But . . . it's not until next week.'

His father shook his head. 'This is your proper birthday. This was the day you were born, and from now on, this is when we celebrate that fact.'

Still recovering from the surprise of seeing Clara, Jonah now had this second shock to deal with. To anyone else it might have seemed an act of madness to accept what his father had laid down all those years ago, but it had never bothered him. All families had their foibles, and Jonah had simply gone along with Gabriel's wishes. But it touched him deeply to know that his father now cared enough to rewrite the rule book. He took the glass from Gabriel's outstretched hand. 'I don't know what to say,' he murmured. 'I'm overwhelmed.'

Gabriel turned to the rest of the room. 'Well, in that case, how about we all have a crack at it for him?'

With his arm round Shirley's waist, Archie raised his glass. 'Here's to new beginnings and making the most of what time we have.'

'Hear, hear!' said Shirley, chinking her glass against his.

'Or, how about here's to Clara not discovering that Jonah's gay?'

'*Caspar!*'

'Only joking, Dad. Here's to it, brother, may you always look older and uglier than me. May the heavens always rain on you and the sun shine its rays on me.'

Smiling, Jonah turned to Clara who now had Ned resting on her hip. 'And do you have any words of wisdom?'

'I think I'm with Archie on this one. It's got to be, "To new beginnings".'

They sat in the gathering darkness on the stone bench beneath the library window. The air was warm and still, and way off in the distance, a dog was barking. Archie and Shirley had gone home, Ned was in bed, and Gabriel and Caspar were in the kitchen tidying up.

Clara leaned into Jonah and he rested an arm around her shoulder. 'A good birthday?' she asked.

'The best.' He picked up her hand, raised it to his lips and kissed it tenderly. 'Clara, this might seem a strange question, but why do you and my father still call one another by your surnames?'

'Because it's all part of the act we put on for one another's benefit. It's a sign of affection between us. A code, I suppose. A game that only the two of us are in on. Sorry if that excludes you.'

'Don't apologise. I think it's nice. You realise, don't you, that it's going to be a strange old courtship, trying to win the heart of a woman who lives with my father? Heaven help me if I don't get you home on time.'

She laughed. 'Only you would call it a courtship.'

He laughed too. 'What would you prefer I called it?'

She thought about this. 'Mm . . . after giving it my fullest considera-tion, I think courtship will do just fine. Despite outward appearances, I'm a straightforward old-fashioned girl, who needs to take things slowly.'

'Just my kind of girl, then.'

'I bet that's not what you thought when you first met me.'

'That's true. If I remember rightly it was fear at first sight. I thought, Here's a woman who could more than punch her weight.'

'No better basis for a long and lasting relationship.'

Smiling, he turned his head towards her. 'Dare I ask permission for an extremely long and lingering birthday kiss?'

'Permission granted.'

Having said good night to Caspar, who had decided to head back to Manchester, Gabriel stood in the darkness at the library window. With a glass of whisky in his hand, he gazed at the silhouetted figures on the bench outside.

He raised his glass to them both. 'Happy birthday, Jonah. By God, you've earned it. And to you, Miss Clara Costello. I may have lost my daughter, but I have the feeling I might be lucky and have the gift of another.'

He turned and looked up at Anastasia's portrait, conscious that she had waited a long time for this moment. 'We got there in the end, my darling girl. It took a while, but I think we got there.'

Raising his glass once more, he said, 'To you, my dearest Anastasia. To Val, and to Damson . . . In my clumsy inadequate way, I loved you all.'

ERICA JAMES

'I love to travel, and to set off on a trip around Britain as Clara does would be wonderful,' says Erica James, talking about the central character in *Precious Time*. 'Just to go where the wind blows. How many of us take the time to do that or have the nerve to strike out?'

When it comes to researching places in which to set her novels Erica James does just that—she gets in her car with a pile of maps, her camera and notebook, and just drives around until she finds somewhere suitable. Her search for a market town on which to base Deaconsbridge led her from her home in Cheshire, where she has set most of her novels, into the Peak District. It was during this trip that she came across the man who inspired the character of Gabriel Liberty. 'I was sitting in a café, just watching the other customers and trying to get a feel for the place, when an elderly man suddenly started banging his spoon on the table and continued until the waitress served him his pudding. I had my lunch and then had to drink several pots of tea because I was so fascinated by him.'

She first started writing back in 1989, when a job change for her then husband meant the family moved to Belgium. Up until then she had been running her own knitting business, but she felt that it was time to do something different. Living in a foreign country, however, she found that her options were limited. 'I love reading and naively thought, well if I can read a book why can't I write one? And so I set myself a New Year's resolution to write a novel and I did it. That was my apprenticeship and I learned through instinct, really, how to structure a novel, how to set the pace and so on. No one has ever seen that book and no one ever will—it's definitely bottom drawer stuff.'

Precious Time is the author's seventh novel and looks set to enjoy the same success that all her earlier novels have achieved. Her first, *A Breath of Fresh Air*, got off to a tremendous start when it was selected for W. H. Smith's Fresh Talent promotion and the book rapidly made the best-seller lists. For Erica James this was somewhat miraculous timing, as she and her husband were separating and she needed to get a job to support her two young sons, Edward and Samuel. 'My agent calls it a fairy tale,' she says. 'I am very grounded, but at that time my feet were barely skimming the surface. The book's success was so exciting.'

She now writes a book a year, and this tight schedule means that when she's two-thirds of the way through a novel she's already planning the next one. 'So as soon as I send the manuscript off to my publisher I'm out in my car with my notebook, ready to go!'

Sally Cummings

Something Wild

Linda Davies

꽃

Sarah Jensen is strikingly beautiful,
fiercely independent, and tough as steel—
a woman who has fought to become the
best in the ruthless world of investment
banking and has risked her life working
undercover for MI6. But when she meets
rock star John Redford in the wilds of
Wyoming, Sarah knows she has met her
greatest challenge. As she turns her back
on her feelings for him, she has yet to
discover that he has given her a most
precious gift. It seems that Sarah has not
seen the last of John Redford.

꽃

CHAPTER ONE

BUFFALO RIVER VALLEY, WYOMING

THE WIND BLEW the scent of terror into the horse's flaring nostrils and he began to dance and skip beneath his rider. She shortened her reins, just enough to let him know she was there, but not enough to provoke him further. Here in the wilderness, his instinct was infinitely better tuned than hers. He was not spooked by leaf shadows dancing on the rugged path, nor by the pulsing roar of the wind in the silver birch. The river in spate interested him, but warranted no more than a few cautious glances. She could feel his panic now, his flanks trembling, and she shared it. She attempted to fight it, tried to be the calm one, to offer quietude, but failed. Trying to divine the source of her mount's fear, she looked around, but the valley appeared unchanged. Then she heard it, coming from behind, a wild and throbbing sound—and knew it was the drumbeats of flight.

'Easy there, easy now, quiet boy, it's all right.' But it wasn't. A horse burst into view, galloping out of control. A rider clung desperately to its back, stirrups lost, reins flailing. The horse was going full pelt, heading for the trees half a mile away. There the rider would have no hope. He'd be flung off, hit a tree, break his back, snap his neck. Sarah reacted automatically. She squeezed her knees.

'Come on!' The horse leapt forward, off the broken path, onto the grass of the valley. Sarah guided him in the hope that he would intercept the other horse before the forest. If he could get there in time. She squeezed harder. 'Come on, boy. *Faster.*'

Exhilarated now, he responded; Sarah felt his exhilaration. She was clear of the other horse, but she was coming from an oblique angle. The horses began to converge. She could see the other rider's face now. White with horror. She felt the horse quicken beneath her, saw the other horse respond. Jesus—they were racing! If she didn't stop them both, she *and* her fellow rider would be pulped in the forest.

The horses came closer, faster, closer still. Sarah fought her horse now, yanking on the left rein, pulling him in, battling his compulsion to run. Ten yards, eight, seven, six. She saw the terror in the other rider.

'Hang on, brace yourself!' she screamed. Five yards, four, three, two. With one hand, she gripped her reins and the pommel, with the other she reached out for the flailing reins of the runaway. She leaned out more, legs gripping her horse like a vice. Please God, get the reins. The forest getting closer. One last lunge. She had them.

Now she hauled back, feet jammed in the stirrups, reining back for all she was worth. She felt her horse bunch under her, abruptly shortening his stride. The other horse still tried to keep his speed. She fought being pulled from her saddle. She gave a bit of rein, then yanked back as violently as she could. The other horse bridled, bunched. Sarah inched in another handful of reins. Yanked it. Both horses tried to fight. She fought back. '*Easy now, easy now, whoaaa, whoooaaa.*'

Slowly, slowly, they began to come under her control. The forest loomed. Sarah pulled them to the right. They began to curve. The forest thirty yards away. '*Easy now, easy.*' And finally they slowed, putting the brakes on voluntarily, dust flying. Till they stopped.

Sarah drove away from the ranch where she had hired her horse. Clouds of dust billowed after her. She had escorted the silent horseman back to the ranch where he was staying. The bolter, as she called him in her mind, had said nothing all the way home. He was clearly in shock, which wasn't surprising. He'd nearly lost his life. Sarah had told a worried ranch hand what had happened, and suggested he call a doctor.

As she drove, the tendrils of trauma curled round her heart. The shadow of violent death had fallen over her again. This time, she'd outridden it—just—saved someone else's life, and narrowly avoided losing hers. How many times did death have to stalk her before it claimed her? She had survived so far, in a life strewn with bodies. Her parents, killed in a car crash when Sarah was seven years old. Her best friend, Mosami. Her lover, Dante Scarpirato. Death had recently tried its best to take her brother, too, and now he lay encased in plaster in his hospital bed, waiting for her visit. Alex Jensen had been climbing Grand

Teton in Wyoming when he'd fallen on a rock face. Some widget that should have broken his fall failed to do so. He dropped 100 feet before slamming into the rock outcrop that pulverised his body. Sarah thought of Alex as she'd first seen him, when she arrived after flying from London to his bedside. The bandages round his head seeped blood, his eyelids flickered but stayed shut. He had been unconscious for forty-three hours.

Sarah stared at her fingers, splayed on the steering wheel of her four-wheel drive. They were white and trembling. She pulled off the road and sat for a while, resting her head on the steering wheel until she felt some measure of calm return to her, then set off again.

Alex was reading a book, his face set into its habitual mien of curiosity. Although half of his body was immobilised by plaster, the energy emanating from him was tangible. Even the doctors had admitted that the young man's life force was exceptionally strong.

Sarah gazed at him with eyes full of love as he lay there, the livid gash that gouged his left cheek almost healed. If he hadn't survived, Sarah wasn't sure she would have been able to go on. Orphaned as young children, their sibling bond went deeper than normal.

At that moment, Alex looked up. 'Hello there?'

'Hello, Al.' Sarah planted a large kiss on her brother's cheek.

'You all right?' Alex was looking at her askance. She never could hide anything from him.

Sarah sat down on the edge of his bed and told him about the bolter. Alex listened with horror. 'And I thought *I* was the crazy one. You could have been killed, Sare.'

'That's rich, coming from you.'

Alex looked sheepish. 'Someone's got to be responsible for what's left of this family.'

Sarah tried to force the spectre of loss from her mind. 'Anyway, how's it all going? Doctors say anything?'

Alex looked suddenly pleased. 'Had a good check today. Arms should come off in the next few days, leg in a week.'

Sarah scratched at his plaster casts. 'That's great.'

'But I'll have to have extensive physio.' An awkward look crossed his face.

'What?'

'Nothing bad, don't worry. There's a place back home, in the country— a rehabilitation place. Apparently it's brilliant, best in Europe . . . costs a fortune, Sarah.'

'Nothing is more important than your full recovery.'

Hope flared in his eyes. 'Two months there, then home, and regular sessions of physio. They say in nine months I could walk. Normally.'

Sarah dropped her head to hide her tears.

'That's fantastic, Alex. That's the best news I've *ever* had.'

He took her hand. 'Sare, it's too much. You'll have no change from a million dollars. It's not fair to you.'

She shook her hand free. 'You're my flesh and blood. You're all that's left of our family. You think I care about money next to that? I've got a million. It's not as if I don't work. I'll get more when we go home.'

'I know how important money is to you. How you build up your security. You won't get a million back in a hurry.'

'Maybe I'll start playing the markets again. Anyway, I won't starve, Al—and you will go to this place back home, so let's drop it.'

Sarah drove back to Spring Creek. She'd been there two and a half months, since the day after the hospital's call, and still the view blew her away. Her cabin was on a hill, 7,500 feet up, in Jackson Hole, Wyoming. Below it the valley curled in a huge bowl, fertile, green and lush, and beyond that the Teton Range towered up, craggy and snowcapped, framing the horizon as far as she could see. It was so peaceful here.

Locking the door of her cabin, she poured herself a glass of whisky and debated dinner. First she needed a shower. She smelt of horse and sweat, and couldn't wait to get the dust off her skin.

She had just emerged, swathed in towels, when she heard a knocking at the door. She pulled the towel tighter round her and opened the door.

A stranger stood before her, his face partially obscured by a cowboy hat. He said nothing, just looked at her. Sarah felt a sudden flash of fear, quickly followed by anger. She stuck her hands on her hips.

'Yes?' she demanded.

The man smiled. 'I came to say thank you.' His voice was low, utterly self-possessed. 'For saving the life of my friend.'

'Oh, that,' said Sarah, as if she did it every day. 'Well, what else could I do?' A cold blast of wind made her shiver. She hugged the towel round her and rubbed her arms. She expected the man to take the hint and excuse himself, but he just stood there, looking at her. For a while, they both remained motionless. Then Sarah turned, walked back into the cabin, knowing the man would follow.

'I'm going to put something on,' she said.

He just nodded.

Her fingers fumbled as she tried to do up her cardigan. She pulled on jeans, forced her feet into cowboy boots, and walked back to him. He was standing by the picture window in the main room.

'Like a drink?'

He turned slowly towards her. 'Whatever you're having.' That low voice, the way he said it, turned her blood to smoke. She went into the kitchen, poured out two large whiskies, walked back to him and offered him the glass. He took it, drained half in one go.

'So,' said Sarah, back to her hands-on-hips stance, 'who are you?'

That prompted a laugh. 'Does it matter who I am?'

Sarah shrugged. 'You can take off that blasted hat anyway.'

He did as instructed, eyes on hers. Now she could see his hard, planed features, the scintillating grey eyes the colour of rock, the cold mouth.

'Ah,' she said. 'I see.'

She lay in bed, restless. Her mind turned over, devouring the image of the stranger. She knew the facts, anyone within reach of a radio, a newspaper or a television did. John Redford was one of the reigning gods in the pantheon of rock. He'd sold over 100 million albums in his twenty-year career, and he was still only forty. Christened the hard man of rock by the press, he shunned the high-octane world he dominated for the lure of his ranch in Wyoming and working his horses. His songs were part of her life. She had laughed to them, cried to them, made love to them. He had played her emotions like the master he was. He wrote all his own songs, from the heart. He laid bare his emotions in his songs, but the press always made much of the enigma of the man, accessible and totally inaccessible at once. He did no interviews.

John Redford was a conservationist who fought to keep factories open as keenly as he opposed opening new ones if they would plunder the environment around them. But he wasn't some reformed would-be saint. There were stories of bacchanalian excess. He appeared to be supremely indifferent to his public image, did what he wanted, and was lauded anyway. But always there was a slight wariness in the adulation, as if at any moment the lion might turn and devour his admirers.

He was dangerous all right. That had been obvious from the second he stood outside her door. The danger was part of the most powerful charisma Sarah had ever encountered. Redford was a perilous journey, one that she had no intention of taking.

She'd known her share of dangerous men, taken one of them into her heart. Now he was dead, and she was responsible. Dante Scarpirato had been her boss at the InterContinental Bank in the City of London. Her remit, in a complicated assignment worked out by MI6 and the Bank of England, had been to investigate Scarpirato, who was suspected of masterminding a massive insider-trading operation in the foreign exchange markets. She had no qualifications for such a job, save her abilities as a foreign exchange trader, her beauty, and her appetite for risk, which is what MI6 and the Bank of England had counted on. And she had not let them down. She and Dante became lovers and Sarah discovered that he was innocent. What neither MI6 nor the Bank of England had told her was that the Mafia were involved in the insider trading, and Sarah, unknowingly, had stirred up that nest of vipers. Dante and her best friend, Mosami Masimoto, were murdered for what the Mafia suspected they knew. Sarah had survived only by doing a deal with the Mafia, and with the hitwoman sent after her. The ultimate trade: their freedom for her life.

She had seen her share of danger, and there was something in Redford's eyes that stirred some memory of it in her. But then what did it matter? She would never see him again.

Dusty again after another day's riding, Sarah drove back from the hospital. At the cabin she showered, and found herself vacillating over what to put on. Most of the clothes she had were in serious need of washing. She settled on a pair of not too dirty jeans. The only top that was halfway clean was a vest. She pulled it on. Her bra straps showed. She pulled off the bra. Her nipples showed. Too bad.

Pouring herself a whisky, she sat down in the main room with the latest Elizabeth George detective story. She must have lost herself in the plot, for the knocking on the door made her sit up with a jolt. Her blood racing, she padded across the room and opened the door. She had known it would be him. He stood there before her in his jeans, sheepskin jacket and cowboy hat. Six foot tall, weathered face, muscled thighs, one leg slightly cocked, half-smile playing on his lips.

She smiled in return. 'You'd better come in.'

He gave the slightest nod, followed her in. She walked to the kitchen, fired up the kettle, poured two camomile teas. Neither of them spoke. Sarah went back to the main room, handed Redford his tea, and sat down in the armchair. Redford chose the sofa.

'Your friend ask you to come again?' she enquired.

'He didn't ask yesterday.'

'So why did you come?'

'Curiosity. You did something very brave. You weren't frightened?'

'Terrified.'

'Why'd you do it?'

'I didn't think about it. Your friend would have been mashed to pieces in the trees. Who is he?'

'Strone Cawdor, my manager. So,' continued Redford, 'what's your story. Why are you here, in a log cabin four thousand miles from home?'

'What makes you think you know where my home is?'

'You think I don't recognise that expensive London accent?'

Sarah laughed, then turned to look at the mountains, cast red by the setting sun. 'My brother was out here climbing. He had an accident.'

'What happened?' Redford's voice was suddenly gentle; his eyes, resting on hers, were full of compassion.

Sarah went to the kitchen, returned with two whiskies. She half drained hers before she resumed speaking. 'He was climbing Grand Teton, two and a half months ago. He fell.' Her voice faltered but she pushed on. 'He was airlifted to hospital with multiple fractures, his face torn open. Oh Jesus.' She hid her face in her hands. Redford watched her, waiting for her to recover.

'He was unconscious for forty-three hours. It was touch and go for a while.' She looked up. 'But he's a tough cookie. He survived and now they think he just might recover fully.' She gave a brave, weary smile. 'What brings you here?' she asked.

'I was born here. I come back whenever I can.'

'Escape,' mused Sarah.

'Exactly. Gets a bit tiring, living on the road.'

'What, all that adulation, adrenaline, performance highs, worshipping crowds, the dollars pouring in. Yeah, it's a tough life.'

'Yeah, a real breeze,' replied Redford with heavy sarcasm.

'So what's so tough?' asked Sarah, goading him.

'Long story. One I'm not in the mood for, and you'd not be receptive to, if I'm reading you right.'

Sarah had the grace to smile.

'And what d'you do back home?' asked Redford. 'Ten weeks is a long time to be away. Isn't there a husband, a boyfriend, a job, calling you back?'

'No husband. No boyfriend.'

'Why not?'

'That's my long story.'

'I'm not in a hurry.'

Sarah sighed, half of her relishing the unspoken understanding that seemed to be developing, the other half reminding her that, however familiar his face might be, he was a stranger.

'There are men for love, men for sex, men for games, and companions. Fate has thrown plenty of the last three my way, but it's been stingy with the men for love.' She smiled. 'Anyway, you just need one, don't you, one great love of your life.'

'And you haven't met him?'

'No, I haven't. What about you?'

'I'm single. I have loved but I haven't met the one great love. I wish I could believe she existed.'

'You sing about her.'

'I fantasise, I dream about her. Then I wake up.'

'You're not that cynical, John Redford.'

He finished his whisky. 'Aren't I?'

Sarah walked up to him, tried to take his glass from him. He held on. She looked at close range into his eyes, at once hard and dazzling, all too aware of his own power, but harbouring, too, a hint of uncertainty.

'No,' she said, keeping her gaze unflinchingly on his. 'You're not.'

He released the glass. She refilled it and hers.

'So where're you staying?' she asked.

'My little ranch. Just down the road.'

Sarah gave him a wry smile. 'Little? Yeah, I'll bet.'

'Not big enough for my purposes anyway.'

'Which are?'

'Space, freedom. Thousands of acres for the grizzlies to roam.'

'So buy more land.'

'Not quite that easy. The prices are crazy.'

'I wouldn't have thought that'd be an issue for you.'

Redford gave a wry grin. 'Yeah, all rock stars are loaded. You'd be surprised what we're left with after the record company, agent, manager, accountants and lawyers have had their fill. You have any idea what a nice ranch with a view of the Tetons goes for?'

'Tell me.'

'One was sold a few months ago, two hundred acres, just down the valley. Twenty-five million dollars.'

'That's insane. How come land's so expensive here?'

'It's the playground of the rich, summer and winter. It's incredibly beautiful, and less than three per cent of the land is available to buy; the rest of it's all public, protected lands.'

'You should do a securitisation,' said Sarah. 'Flog off your catalogue of hits to some bored institutional investors looking for something sexy to drop into their portfolios. Look at Bowie. If he could raise fifty-five million dollars, you could probably raise a hundred mill.'

Redford looked unimpressed. 'You think so?' he said.

'Back home there's a bank called Goldsteins International. They're the best finance house there is. If you're ever in London, ask for a meeting with the chairman, James Savage.'

'Maybe I'll do that.'

Sarah got to her feet. Her mention of Goldsteins brought home the reality of life. He was a rock star. She was a banker-cum-private investigator. Goldsteins employed her as a freelance, in both capacities, one acting as a superb cover for the other. After Dante and Mosami had been killed, Sarah had quit InterContinental Bank, and fled to the Himalayas to join Alex for one year, before returning to the UK. Stranded back in London, she'd joined Kroll Associates, the world's best private investigators, and learned her new trade, then quit to set up on her own. Goldsteins were her best, now practically her only client. They paid well, well enough for her to work only half the year, and to pick and choose her assignments. All that would soon end, she thought, visualising the size of Alex's bill. She would have to work solidly for a long time to reclaim her financial independence. Some contrast, she thought, glancing at the man opposite her. *Out of your league,* said her silent voice.

'Will you excuse me,' she said. 'I have to eat then hit the sack. I've got a very early start tomorrow.'

Redford looked surprised. 'Not going back to England?'

'No. I leave when my brother does. I'm going riding, deep into the wilderness, three nights camping.'

'*Alone?*'

'Me, three horses, three mules, a guide and a muleteer.'

'Take a *guitar*? What're you, darn crazy?'

Sarah stared at the man in the cowboy hat, her guide-to-be for the next four days. Sarah felt her temper quickening, but decided to hold her tongue.

'Bad enough you call me last thing, tell me there's gonna be one more; now this strummer friend a yours wants to pack a *guitar*. What else he want, a ten-piece band?'

Sarah had had enough. 'Look, do you want our business or not?'

The cowboy grinned abruptly. 'Guess I rightly do.'

Redford appeared a minute later, just as the guide was gearing up for another verbal assault.

'Hi,' said Redford, extending his hand. 'Sorry to keep you waiting.'

'Hm,' replied the cowboy, disconcerted by Redford's charm. 'You been out this way before? You look kinda familiar.'

'Was born here, on the banks of the Snake River, just south of Moran.'

'Don't say. Who was your ma? Still here?'

'We moved away,' answered Redford flatly. 'So, we going?'

The guide looked unsettled again, thrown by Redford's sudden shift of mood. 'Yep,' he said. 'Can you ride, strummer?'

'Just give me something sane,' said Redford.

'Got just the horse for you, name a Tony. You're going on his twin, Wes,' the guide said to Sarah. 'Sweeter horses you won't get.' The cowboy headed across the corral.

'Sounds good,' said Sarah.

'You got a name?' asked the cowboy, approaching Redford leading a piebald horse, just a touch over fifteen hands high.

'John. You?'

'I'm Dave.' He motioned at a wiry younger man in his early twenties who was crooning to the mules as he loaded them up. 'This here's Ash.'

Ash turned round, shook Sarah's and Redford's hands and turned white as he paid attention for the first time to Redford's face. 'Mighty pleased,' he managed to mutter.

They set out along the banks of the Buffalo River, brown and turgid with snow melt as spring advanced up the mountainsides. The horses picked their way delicately over the rough-hewn path, upwards through groves of silver birch, Douglas firs and lodgepole pines. The air carried the smell of the pine, baking in the hot sun, pure and potent like incense. They were always within earshot of water, trickling, gushing, roaring rivers, and cascades, pooling streams where the horses would dip their soft muzzles and drink.

As they rode into the bowl of a glacier-sculpted plateau, Sarah was amazed by the size of the brilliant blue sky, enormous above them. The meadows to either side of their rocky path were strewn with a profusion of blue and gold wild flowers. Bare stems of branch were budding all around them. Spring came to the high wilderness in mid-June. Sarah gazed at the summits of the distant Tetons and wondered if spring ever reached their snowbound mass. A lake glittered, radiant turquoise, brimful with snow melt; everywhere Sarah looked was potent with beauty, with life and death and renewal.

Redford rode up beside her.

'It's gorgeous, isn't it?' she said.

'Most beautiful place in the world,' he agreed.

They turned onto a winding track along the side of the valley wall. Suddenly the procession stopped as Dave pointed silently to a moose, standing about twenty feet away. The moose regarded them with limpid brown eyes, wary but unafraid. His head was huge and ungainly, but his long, floppy ears were soft velvet and, as he slowly moved away, his legs moved elegantly over the rough ground with the grace of a dancer.

'What an amazing creature,' Sarah said to Redford. 'Ugly and beautiful all in one.'

'Aren't we all,' said Redford. 'Apart from you. You're just beautiful.'

'You must have said that a thousand times,' replied Sarah, unsettled.

'Maybe, but I didn't always mean it.'

For a moment their mutual gaze lingered. Sarah was the first to look away. It still didn't seem real, Redford being here. When she'd told him what she was planning last night, he just asked, as if it were the simplest thing in the world, 'Can I come along?' And she'd answered, just as simply, 'Yes.'

The day passed in a rhythmic dream of hoofbeats and beauty. They found the perfect place to camp high up in a copse of fir trees, overlooking a valley. Dave and Ash tethered, fed and watered the horses and the mules, then pitched tents. Two only. Sarah approached them.

'Need any help with the third tent?'

'Ain't no third tent,' replied Dave. 'You're sharing with the strummer, ain't you?' He caught Sarah's look and grinned. 'Put it this way—it's either him, me or Ash. Take your pick.'

Redford watched Sarah's face closely. She walked away in silence.

'Hey! Before you go,' shouted Dave, 'give me anything scented or edible you might have on you. Toothpaste, face cream, mints, mouthwash, anything with the remotest whiff of sweetness on it. Bears love it. We gotta string it all up fifteen foot from the ground. We don't want to attract grizzlies into camp when we're sleeping.'

They ate a cowboy's dinner, cooked on a campfire: steaks, baked potatoes and salad. They washed it down with beers chilled in a brook. Then John Redford brought out his guitar.

'You do requests?' asked Dave.

'Sure,' smiled Redford. 'What'll it be?'

'Well,' said Dave, 'since it's kind of a starry, starry night, how 'bout that one? Know it?'

Redford nodded, took his guitar in his arms, held it close, like a lover, thought Sarah. She watched him stretch his fingers over the instrument's wooden body, caressing it as he began to pluck the quivering strings.

And then he sang.

When the last chords faded into the valley, he kept his eyes on Sarah. He had seen her rapture, and here, sitting on a lonely mountainside, the intimacy was profound. A slow clapping broke the moment and they both turned to Dave.

'You sure can play some. Beautiful, if yer don't mind my sayin'.'

Ash disappeared into his tent and returned with a pen. He took off his hat and approached Redford. 'Would you autograph my hat fer me?'

Redford took the hat and pen. 'It'd be my pleasure.' He signed. Ash beamed like it was Christmas Day. 'Wait till I show my girlfriend. She'd never believe me if I said I sat out here 'n' listened to a private concert by John Redford.'

'John Redford?' Dave turned white. 'You're *John Redford*? Dang it all to hell. You might have told me.' Now his face turned red.

The singer smiled and gave an elegant shrug.

'Dang it all. Well, how about you play us another song. If I'd known it was you, I'd never have kicked up such a darn fuss.'

'No reason you should know. What'd you like me to play?'

'Well, that song a yours—"Something Wild". I always loved that.'

Redford took up the guitar. Again Sarah was transfixed by the sensuality of his touch. He sat cross-legged on the ground, mug of coffee by his side, guitar cradled in his lap, his hair gold in the setting sun.

> 'You come to me like a hurricane, with storm in your eyes.
> There is earth, wind and fire in your touch,
> You blow me away.
> There are no rules for you.
> You're something wild.

> 'What broke you down? What furnace hardened you?
> Where did you come from, my lovely one?
> You've burned down all my defences,
> And left me hooked
> On something wild.'

For a while, no one moved, as if unwilling to let go of the song.

'That was for you, Sarah,' said Redford, his voice soft. She wondered if she had really heard him. He was a sorcerer, casting a spell on her with the beauty of his song, his voicing of their dreams. Now another voice rose up through the gathering darkness, the long, rising howl of a solitary wolf. As his voice died away, another howl travelled to them across the valley, from the distant slope.

'Two alpha males,' said Dave. 'One owns the valley, he's letting the other know to keep his distance.'

Sarah went to her tent, the wolf howls following her as she slipped into her sleeping-bag and zipped it up. She lay, listening to their wild cries, and to the mules and horses shifting and snuffling as they slept.

When Redford came in some time later, she was turned on her side, feigning sleep. She heard him unzip his sleeping-bag, then zip it up again. She wondered if he could hear the beating of her heart. She didn't know how long she lay there, bidding sleep to rescue her, but it must have done, for the next thing she was aware of was waking suddenly. A sharp, sudden noise had disturbed her. Outside, the mules suddenly started braying and the horses snorting.

'What's going on?' Sarah whispered.

'I'm not sure.' Redford extricated himself from his sleeping-bag.

'Stay in your tent,' came Dave's voice, from close by. 'Get into the middle and stay there. *Do it.*' His voice was urgent. 'There's a grizzly out here. It's all right. We'll deal with him.'

'Oh shit,' said Sarah, eyes blazing with fear.

'These guys know what they're doing,' Redford told her. 'C'mon, let's get closer.'

Sarah shuffled her sleeping-bag into the centre of the tent. She could feel Redford's warmth as he moved his next to hers. The mules kept up their braying. Between their fearful outbursts, Sarah and Redford could hear a calm voice speaking. Suddenly they heard footsteps, not human ones, heavy and purposeful. The footsteps came to a halt outside their tent. Sarah felt fear course through her body, every sinew urging her to flee. As if reading her mind, Redford gripped her hand. There was a loud snuffle, and then a great rending sound as their tent was ripped open. Sarah and Redford looked up and saw the giant head of a grizzly bear.

Sarah just stared at it, saw the long snout, the dark eyes looking into hers. Jesus Christ, where *were* Dave and Ash?

'Easy, boy, easy there,' Redford spoke beside her. 'It's all right, we mean you no harm, we've got no food for you. Easy, boy, easy now. You can go now, it's all right.' As Redford kept up his gentle murmur, Sarah saw something flicker in the creature's eyes. It seemed poised for some kind of action. She heard a gun cock; still Redford's voice spoke, calm, sinuous, gentle, and as he spoke, the great black head above him let out a huge vaporous breath, then moved slowly away.

Sarah let out her own breath in a low hiss. 'We could have been killed.'

'But we weren't, were we?' replied Redford, calm still. 'He was just curious, that's all. He meant us no harm.'

'You two all right?' Dave's head appeared above them.

'We're fine,' replied Redford. 'Thanks.'

'We're not bloody fine,' said Sarah. Her voice was shaking.

'Don't rightly think any of us is fine,' nodded Dave, 'but we're alive and we're uninjured. Ash's keeping watch. The mules'll let us know if he comes back. You two'd best get some sleep. I'm afraid there's not much we can do about the tent tonight, but you can have ours, if you like.'

'No, that's OK,' said Redford. 'Thanks anyway.'

Sarah lay back in her sleeping-bag, the night sky arched above her.

'You gonna be all right?' asked Redford.

'I feel a bit shaken up. I just can't believe I saw a grizzly, eyeball to eyeball practically, and survived! He was fantastic, wasn't he?'

'Magnificent.'

'You charmed him,' she joked. 'I thought for one moment he was going to get right in here with you.'

Redford laughed. 'So did I.'

'It's hard to believe there's civilisation back there, that we just slipped from one life to the other.'

'What do you prefer?' asked Redford.

'Something wild,' replied Sarah. 'Every time.'

'What about me?' asked John Redford, taking Sarah's hand. 'Am I wild enough for you?'

Sarah left her hand in his. Her skin shimmered under his touch. He traced his fingers over hers in feather strokes, so light, so inflaming.

'You are too wild,' she said in a low voice. 'You're like a grizzly. I'd rather see you from a safe distance.'

Redford smiled. 'You mean it's too close in this tent, in the wilderness, with the stars gazing down on us, the wind singing in the trees, just the two of us. Too close for a beautiful woman who's an island.'

'I enjoy being an island. I don't like anyone to come ashore. And you're trouble, John Redford. I didn't choose you.'

'No, you didn't. Fate threw us together.'

His fingers caressed her hand. Still their eyes held, while her mind said *run*. As she said this, silently, like a plea to some greater force to save her, she picked up his free hand. Her fingers traced the fingers she had watched pluck the strings of his guitar. We're all alone, she thought. This is one of those moments in time, complete in itself, when everything is perfect. Just one night, Sarah promised herself. One perfect night, and nothing more.

She kissed his wrist, she licked the warm flesh, taking his taste into her. They moved slowly, finding each other, finding their fit, lip to lip, breast to chest, his thigh between her legs, starlight gleaming in their smiling eyes. They laid down the weapons of their own, unending battles, abandoned their solitude and made love all night. They slept as dawn crept over the towering mountains and woke as the sun kissed their tent, lying in one another's arms, breathing the same sweet air.

Sarah faced down the matron of the hospital, a friend made during her long hours of vigil. 'Is he ready to leave, or isn't he?' she demanded.

'He can leave, sure he can. Not ideal though. Should have another two weeks. What's happened, girl? We done something to upset you?'

'You've done nothing. Nothing's happened. I just want to go home with Alex. If it's safe for him to travel, I'd like to fly out tomorrow.'

The matron gave an almighty sigh. 'All right, girl. Have it your way.'

Sarah knew she had to leave. She refused to have her heart broken by John Redford, and that would surely happen if she stayed. He had marked her already, with their one perfect night. *Run now, quit while you're ahead.* It wasn't just the trader in her speaking, it was the woman who had gone on alone when those she loved had been torn from her. Redford must have had thousands of nights like the last one. He would be inured to them, could walk on easily. She was too raw to be spared so lightly. She had no choice but to go.

The next morning, through a cloudless sky, the plane lifted off, soaring high above the Tetons, carrying Alex and Sarah home, carrying Sarah away from John Redford, who sat alone in his ranch, waiting for a woman who had said nothing about leaving him. Sarah gazed out of the window, feeling her fear lift with every mile she put between them. She was not ready for love, didn't want it, would *not* dance to its tune.

CHAPTER TWO

CARLYLE SQUARE, LONDON, EIGHTEEN MONTHS LATER

SARAH WOKE TO LAUGHTER as the sun sloped in through the window of her four-storey house in Chelsea. She lay in bed for a few moments, listening in bliss before slipping from the sheets and padding through to the next room. She gazed down as a fusillade of smiles greeted her.

'Have you any idea how gorgeous you are, my sweetheart? Have you?' She bent down and kissed the satin skin, almost swooning with pleasure at his scent, his eyes. She reached out her arms. 'Want to come to Mama, do you?' Her son giggled and she picked him up. 'Did you sleep well— did you, my love child?'

Sarah changed his nappy and took him through to her bedroom, where she breastfed him. She put him back in the cot to play and took a quick shower. Afterwards, she dressed in jeans, jersey and trainers, picked up Georgie and headed down two floors to the basement kitchen.

She loved this room. Sunlight streamed in through the east-facing French windows that opened onto her small garden. Adjoining the kitchen was the family room, with deep sofas, bookcases, a huge television and a Bang & Olufsen CD player, which had been cutting edge five years ago, when Sarah was still pulling in nearly half a million pounds a year as one of London's top foreign exchange traders. She laid the baby down on the kitchen carpet with a selection of toys, and put Lauryn Hill, one of Georgie's favourites, on to play.

Breastfeeding gave her a ravenous appetite, so she cut five huge slabs of organic brown bread, toasted it well, smothered it in butter and jam. She deposited Georgie in his high chair, cooked up some porridge for him, added a mashed banana and set to feeding him and herself.

A herd of stampeding wildebeest sounded on the stairs, heralding Alex's arrival. Sarah smiled. That he could walk down the stairs, let alone run, was a small miracle.

Her brother appeared with a swirl of energy and well-being. 'Hi, Sare.' He headed for Georgie. 'How are you, you little rascal? Did you give your mother a good sleep?'

'Not bad,' replied Sarah. 'Up just once last night. No need for you to get up now, with us larks.' The clock on the wall showed six thirty.

'I smelt toast, didn't I,' Alex said with a grin. He was off in a week, for his first expedition since the accident, and Sarah knew he was trying to spend as much time with her and Georgie as possible before he left.

He was a wonderful uncle. He would have been up half the night with Georgie if Sarah had let him. He had driven her to hospital when her contractions started, and he and their beloved Uncle Jacob were the first people to see Georgie. Both had fallen passionately in love with him. Her baby was lucky, Sarah told herself. He had two besotted uncles, and that surely made up for the lack of a father. Her thoughts turned involuntarily, as they so often did, to Redford. Where was he? What was he doing? Did some strange stirring ever waken his consciousness to the existence of someone who shared half his blood, half his genes? Sarah felt the old yearning, that to her discomfort had never gone, but still burned in her.

After breakfast, Alex headed for Sarah's study, spread with his route maps for his next trek in Peru. For Sarah and Georgie, it was walktime. Sarah got her baby ready, and together they headed out in the late summer sunshine. Sarah pushed the pram through streets both familiar and fresh. She and Alex had only just returned to London, after nine months in a rented cottage in the Dorset countryside. Sooner or later she would bump into someone she knew, and her secret would be out. But so far only Alex, Jacob, and her cleaning lady Mrs V, knew of Georgie's existence. She gazed down at the child.

'You are my little secret, aren't you, my love child? I suppose I'll have to share you with the world one day soon, but just for now, it's the two of us, no one else.' Georgie gurgled.

Sarah walked in the haven of Battersea Park for an hour in the warm sun, before heading home. Alex had gone off for his workout when they returned. He exercised six days a week, relentlessly trying to regain his fitness and strength. Alex maintained he was ready to trek the high mountains again. The doctors had cautiously given their assent, although they warned that another fall on his shattered leg, still held together by pins, and he might have to kiss goodbye to trekking for ever. But Alex would always live life to the full. Like his sister, if risk stood between him and what he wanted, he simply leapt.

Sarah settled herself in the kitchen armchair, and took Georgie to her breast for his after-lunch feed. She had just put him to bed for a nap when the doorbell went.

'Shit, who's this?' she whispered, creeping from the room so as not to wake Georgie. She headed down the stairs and pulled open the door.

'Eva Cunningham!' she exclaimed.

'Bad time?'

Sarah shook herself. 'What? Yes—no, sorry.' She pulled her hair off her face. 'I thought you were somewhere in the South Pacific.'

'We got home a week ago,' said Eva. 'Are you going to invite me in?'

Eva came inside and headed towards the kitchen, their usual haunt.

'No, it's a real mess down there,' Sarah said hurriedly. 'Let's stay up here. What'll you have? Coffee?'

'That'd be great.'

Sarah headed downstairs to the kitchen, leaving her friend ensconced in the toy-free drawing room on the ground floor. A few minutes later, she returned with coffee for Eva, camomile tea for herself.

Eva studied Sarah suspiciously. 'So what's up? You look different.'

'Tell me about the South Pacific,' said Sarah, fingers snaking into her pocket to check the baby listener was on. 'How could you possibly bear to leave it?'

'Well,' Eva said wryly, 'Andrew gave up his job, followed me out there, and we lived there on and off for two years. He was beginning to go stir crazy, and so we've come back to start up an investigations firm—

corporate checks, individual checks—you know the kind of thing.'

'The same stuff you and I used to do for Kroll?'

'Exactly. You still working for them?'

'Uh-uh.' Sarah shook her head. 'I set up on my own, freelance, working for Goldsteins mainly, but I've had a sabbatical for a while now.'

'So what're you doing? How do you pay the metaphorical rent?'

Before Sarah could answer, sleepy cries rose from the baby listener in her jeans pocket. Eva's eyes opened wide.

'Excuse me, but I think your jeans are crying.'

Sarah got to her feet, face bare of concealment. She went upstairs to Georgie, picked him up and carried him downstairs.

'Bloody Nora, Sarah. You're a mother!'

Sarah grinned, turning sideways on so that Georgie and Eva could see eye to eye. 'This is Georgie. Georgie, this is Eva.'

'Hell, Sarah. I'm not much of a maternal type as you know, but he's *beautiful*,' said Eva softly.

Her friend beamed. 'He is, isn't he? The most beautiful thing I ever saw. He's the love of my life, the most precious thing on earth.'

'Wow, you've got it bad,' Eva commented. 'I'd never have thought it of you, of all people.'

Sarah sat down with Georgie in her lap. 'I really would die for him. You hear people saying that and you think, how over the top, but it's true. Maternal protectiveness is the most powerful force on the planet.'

'I can well believe it,' said Eva, sitting down opposite them. 'So, where's his father? I didn't know you'd settled down.'

'I haven't. I left him before I even knew I was pregnant.'

'Did you tell him after?'

Sarah shook her head. 'Hardly anyone knows.'

'That explains all the secrecy when I arrived. I thought you had a lover downstairs.'

Sarah grinned. 'I haven't had a lover for so long, I've almost forgotten what it feels like. It's a long way from my current list of fantasies. If it's a choice between sleep and sex, sleep'll win every time.'

'Can I ask you what made you go ahead and have your baby?'

Sarah kissed her son's downy head. 'I was terrified when I found out I was pregnant, but I gave myself time to feel through the terror, and you know, it was as if this little being was speaking to me. I felt his presence, he was living inside me. I fell in love with him even then. And after what happened to my own family . . . the chance to start a family of my own—how could I not go with that?'

Eva nodded. 'Has it been hard?'

Tears came spontaneously to Sarah's eyes. 'The hardest thing I've ever done. The exhaustion is something you wouldn't believe, and you cannot get up and walk away. This little thing depends on you absolutely. There's no going back to the old life. But I wouldn't change a thing. There is nothing like the look of love in his little eyes, when he sees my face; there is nothing like holding him, and feeding him, and the moment when he was born and they handed him to me . . . well, words can't describe it.' Sarah gave Eva a radiant smile.

This was a language Eva couldn't speak, but the strength of Sarah's love for her child moved her.

'One last question,' said Eva.

Sarah guessed what it might be, felt the dread at its coming.

'Am I allowed to ask who his father is?'

Sarah smiled and shook her head. 'He's the most charismatic, totally sexy, gorgeous man I ever clapped eyes on.'

'So why walk out on him?'

'For all those reasons. I told myself I wasn't going to be a slave to love.'

'Do you think you'll ever see him again?' asked Eva.

Sarah shook her head. 'I doubt it. Our paths crossed once in a lifetime. It would be too much to expect them to cross again.'

The telephone rang the moment Eva had left. Sarah rushed in and picked it up, Georgie cradled in one arm.

'Sarah, James Savage.'

'Gosh. Hi, James, how are you?'

Georgie gurgled.

'What was that?' asked Savage.

'The radio,' said Sarah. 'Hang on a sec, let me go and turn it off.' She took Georgie next door, put him on the floor and placated his immediate outburst of tears with his favourite toy, a yellow bunny. She hurried back to the phone. 'Sorry, James.'

'So, would you like some work? I know you said your sabbatical should be over around now.'

Sarah felt her whole body gripped with panic. She wasn't ready to work. That world was so alien to her now. She didn't want to leave Georgie. But she needed the money. After bailing Alex out she was hard up anyway, but now she had a child to support. She had no choice but to go back to work. She took a deep breath.

'All right. I'll do it.'

'Don't you want to know what it is?' asked Savage, surprised.

'Just tell me where to be and when.' She didn't have the luxury to choose what was interesting, to reject anything she didn't fancy.

'My office. Tomorrow at eleven.'

How disconcertingly our outlook can change, reflected Sarah. Work had always been a kind of passion for her, loved and hated, a necessary therapy, and a distraction. Now it was a way to pay the bills, and no more. She had a reason to exist now; she didn't need to justify her existence by competing in the workplace.

The soft closing of the door stirred her as Alex breezed in.

'Hi there.' He picked up Georgie and cuddled his nephew boisterously. 'Am I knackered. Think I'll have a shower and a lie-down.' He rested his eyes on Sarah and his light-hearted smile faded. 'What's up?'

Sarah pulled her hair back off her face. 'James Savage just called. He wants me to go into Goldsteins tomorrow. Got some kind of job for me.'

'Ah.' Understanding flooded Alex's face.

'I'm still breastfeeding,' said Sarah. 'I've never been away from Georgie for more than a couple of hours. How's he going to cope? How'm I going to cope with some bloody meeting in the City? I've scarcely spoken about anything more taxing than which brand of nappies to buy for the past eight months.'

Alex smiled. 'You're not that bad.'

'And who's going to look after Georgie? You have to go to the gym.'

'I could miss it for one day, for goodness' sake.'

Sarah shook her head. 'Maybe I'll ring Jacob,' she said. Georgie and Jacob loved each other to bits. 'It's probably just a one-off anyway. When Savage catches on to my atrophied brain he's bound to send me packing before you can say cut your losses.'

Sarah awoke the next morning gripped by panic. What would she wear? She was still twenty pounds over her normal weight. What would she say? She'd become completely uninterested in anything other than Georgie. She had no idea what was going on in the world at large, let alone in the markets.

In the old days, she could have bluffed her way, but her confidence had flown. She began to pace around and chant, 'You're bright, you have a Cambridge degree, you've earned millions of pounds in your life, you've outsmarted some seriously dodgy characters, *you can do anything.*' It didn't work. She lacked even the ability to convince herself.

When Jacob arrived at nine, Sarah was still in her nightgown, hair and eyes wild. Georgie picked up his mother's panic and cried heartily.

'Hello, Georgie. Hello there! Helloooo, Georgie.' Jacob gave him huge smiles, soon returned by Georgie, who bestowed his ultimate approval by straining away from Sarah towards his great-uncle. 'Come to your Uncle Jacob, come on then.'

Sarah handed him over. Jacob hugged Georgie to him, allowing Georgie to play with his white moustache. 'You go and get yourself ready, sweetie.'

'I don't think I can do this. It's too soon—I'm not ready.'

'Steady there, sweetie, easy now. You'll be fine. You've faced much bigger challenges than this in your time.'

'Have I? I can't remember. Anyway, that was the old me, she's gone.'

'No, she hasn't. She's always there, just waiting for an outing. Give her a chance. Go to that meeting and sock it to them.'

They were all there waiting for her, watching her walk into their midst. At the head of the table sat James Savage, chief executive of Goldsteins. He leaned back, arms folded behind his head of silver hair, resplendent in a razor-sharp, navy pinstripe suit. He smiled. He enjoyed Sarah; she produced results but, more than that, he savoured her unpredictability. Savage, who fancied himself a renegade beneath the pinstripes, felt an immediate affinity. Felt more than that, if he was honest.

He eyed her quickly. She had put on weight, was wearing a baggy pair of trousers and a loose tunic top with clumpy flat shoes. Her skin was in high colour, her cheeks glowing. She looked incredibly voluptuous, the curve of her breasts all too visible through the thin fabric of her tunic. Sarah Jensen was a walking incitement to lust. Today she seemed a little tired, preoccupied, but she was smiling determinedly. How she kept that touch of grace, Savage couldn't fathom. He knew only part of her story, and that bit alone would have clouded the sunniest of souls. But the only hint of the tragedies she had suffered, the battles she had fought, showed in the lines round her eyes, which were too deep for one so young. She couldn't have been more than thirty.

Dick Breden, a private investigator used by Savage for broader investigations than Sarah conducted, welcomed her with a somewhat ambivalent smile. He tended to view Sarah as a rival, but on the other hand, his work and Sarah's was more complementary than competitive. Besides, her blithe, devil-may-care attitude tended to diffuse any rivalry. He got to his feet, elegantly uncoiling, and stood to attention with a soldier's formality. Ten years after leaving the army, he still had a lean, muscled body.

Zaha Zamaroh, the head of the trading floor, summa cum laude, Harvard, brain like a mainframe computer, body of a Rubens nude, Iranian princess by birth, stayed in her seat, legs crossed, black hosiery gleaming. She unashamedly looked Sarah up and down, checking out the wardrobe and the woman, as she did every time they met, looking for a chink, and, judging by her triumphant look, finding it. Zamaroh was perfectly turned out as always, her outrageously curvaceous body swathed in a tangerine-coloured Chanel suit, her raven hair fluid and shiny. Zamaroh was a big, glossy black panther, sinuous, brilliant and powerful. To her, Sarah was sport, good sport because she enjoyed a fight and fought well.

They sat round a polished board table, while a secretary poured coffee from a silver pot. Savage drained his espresso then clinked the cup back in its saucer. The telephone beside him gave a chirp. He picked up the receiver and listened impassively. 'Show him in.'

Sarah drank her mineral water, looking up as the father of her child walked into the room.

She wanted to choke. She struggled to keep the water in her mouth, finally managed to swallow it with a gulp. *Keep calm, keep calm. Breathe, girl, deep, slowly.* She could feel her breasts leaking milk into the cotton-wool pads with which she'd lined her bra; oh God, not even her body was subject to her control. She searched for enough self-possession to gaze ahead levelly, as if she had never met this man, never made the sweetest, most passionate love with him.

Redford took a seat, face cold, as if he too were in shock.

She could hear Savage going ahead with the introductions. 'And this is Sarah Jensen, another trader who's also on the team,' Savage was saying. When Redford turned to her, it seemed to Sarah that he gave her just a glimpse of emotions battened down. In return she gave him the curtest nod. Redford hardened his eyes again, as if to say, So this is the way it will be.

'Hello, Sarah. It's a pleasure.'

She nodded, unable to speak.

'You're on time, and you're alone,' said Savage, summoning a smile.

'And why shouldn't I be? Look, can we cut this rock-star shit?' Redford said irritably. 'I'm a normal businessman, like the rest of your clients. My product happens to have a lot of baggage with it, but only in people's minds. Drop the baggage, life gets simpler.'

'Is your music just a product to you?' asked Zamaroh with surprise.

'Of course it's not,' replied Redford with quick disdain. 'Music's the biggest part of my life, but I also see it from a business perspective.'

'But not when you write your songs?' continued Zamaroh.

'No, not then,' he admitted. 'I couldn't give a damn at that point about how many discs I'm gonna sell. All I care about then is getting across the emotion that I'm feeling, taking people with me.'

Like the Pied Piper, thought Sarah, leading the children away. It was a nasty image, and she rebuked herself as she looked into the features of Georgie's father. Her son's face was writ so large and clear in John Redford's that it was almost too much to bear.

Sarah found her voice. 'Can we get you a coffee?'

'Yes, of course. Do excuse my manners,' Savage was saying, to Sarah's vast relief. 'Coffee, tea, mineral water?'

'A mineral water would be great. No ice, slice of lemon.'

Savage blinked, pushed a button on an ornamental cockerel and Fred the butler appeared, resplendent in a tailcoat. He took their orders, then disappeared like a wraith moving silently on the plush carpet.

Everything in this room whispers *money, position, privilege*, thought Sarah. Savage, Zamaroh and Breden, and she herself, she supposed, all looked refined, tempered. The air-conditioned office with its hermetically sealed double glazing seemed a million miles away from the bloody business of making money. The pinstriped elegance and refinements of butlers were a disguise, a relic of the days when making money was hidden behind locked doors. Just a few floors down, the trading floor thrashed and writhed.

'Would you like to see the trading floor?' Sarah found herself asking Redford. 'The guts of this place. Deals being cut, money being made and lost, emotions running riot? . . .'

'Yeah. I'd like that,' answered Redford, eyes lingering on Sarah's.

Savage looked on with worry; Zamaroh glared. Sarah had just publicly smashed the unwritten rule. Don't show clients the abattoir, where they are the carcasses on which the traders feed. But Zamaroh didn't see in Redford what Sarah knew was there—the raw ambition, burning still in a man at the peak of his profession. She could see that the plush carpeting and butler switched him off, that the only way they would win him as a client would be to show him that they too could be raw, that they too were hungry, even though they appeared fat and self-satisfied.

Leaving the boardroom, they all headed for the lift. Redford stood alongside Savage, with his back to Sarah as they cruised down three floors. Redford wore black woollen trousers and a tight-fitting fine woollen jersey. Sarah could see the cleft of his backbone, and the musculature that swelled to either side. She remembered tracing those contours with her fingers, then with her tongue. She recalled the smell of him, the taste of him. The doors to the lift drifted open and Savage strode out. Redford stood back, allowing Zamaroh and Sarah to exit before him. Sarah kept her eyes straight ahead and moved past him, so close she could almost touch him. She walked towards the entrance to the trading floor, conscious of his eyes on her.

The roar was the first thing to hit them, the raised voices of 500 traders, the electronic beeping of phones, the shouts of anger, of triumph, snatches of conversations: *'I'll take a ton at forty-nine twenty.' 'You bastard, you screwed me on the Entox deal.' 'Yeeeeeaaaas! I'm ten miles up and cruising.'*

Redford turned to Sarah. 'This is where you worked?'

'For seven long years,' she answered. 'With breaks here and there.'

'And are you good?'

'What do you think?' She saw the amusement flare in his eyes before he quickly pushed it down and resumed his poker face.

Back in the boardroom, Redford took the initiative.

'So,' he said, 'securitisation. Tell me how it works.'

'First of all,' said Zamaroh, 'tell us exactly what you want. How did you come to hear of Goldsteins?'

Sarah and Redford looked at each other. She feared that everything would be detected in the gaze which passed between them.

'I'll take over here,' rasped a voice from the doorway. A man in his early fifties stood leaning against the doorjamb, with one hip thrust forward, in a pose half-casual, half-aggressive. The man was lean, jeans-clad, with a leather jacket slung over his shoulder. He had short, thick grey hair which covered only the sides of his head; the centre was a shiny desert. His nose was long and full, his lips thick. It was the man on the runaway horse. Sarah blessed his timing, cursed his arrival. Now her masquerade *would* be blown.

'Can I help you?' Savage got to his feet.

'I'm Strone Cawdor, John Redford's manager,' he announced with a self-congratulatory smirk.

'You're late,' said Savage.

Cawdor looked surprised. 'Late?' he asked, as if the concept were irrelevant. 'Well, I'm here now, aren't I? So let's get started.'

Sarah checked Redford to see how he was taking this. The rock star was watching Cawdor with patience and a tinge of amusement.

Savage performed the introductions. When it came to Sarah's turn, it seemed that Cawdor didn't recognise her. Admittedly it had been a year and a half ago; when it happened, he had been in shock, she had worn a cowboy hat. That was just fine by her.

'We've checked your credentials,' stated Cawdor, taking a seat beside his star, 'and so far, you've got a good rep.' Zamaroh snorted. Cawdor turned to stare at her. 'You're part of a beauty parade,' continued

Cawdor with relish. 'We'll be speaking to other banks as well as your-selves, so,' he took off his gold watch and put it on the table, 'tell me why we should come to Goldsteins.'

Before any of the Goldsteins team could react, Redford spoke.

'Goldsteins has my business,' Redford said evenly, staring at Sarah.

'Say again?' demanded Cawdor.

Redford shrugged and said nothing more. As an elegant display of who held the power, it was flawless.

Cawdor took a deep breath. He turned from Redford as if the rock star did not exist. 'Right then. We got twenty platinum albums—that means each has sold in excess of one million copies,' he added with a patronising smile. 'But total album sales are some way north of one hun-dred million. John's had seven consecutive number-one albums in the States, four simultaneously with the UK. He accounts for three per cent of all the singles, albums and tapes sold annually throughout the whole world. He is *it*. He's at the very apex of his profession and poised to stay there for years. We want the benefit of all that now, up-front. A bond issue, securitisation, the whole works.'

He sat back. Interesting, thought Sarah. She guessed that in his usual dealings with the record company, with lawyers and accountants, he was used to being the one with the power, but if there was to be a suc-cessful deal here, it would be on Goldsteins' terms.

Savage spoke. 'Let us tell you both a little about what we could do for you, and about what we would need from you. Then we'll see if we're compatible.' He gave Cawdor a brief, cold smile.

Cawdor laughed in disbelief. 'Compatible?' he said with derision. 'What are you—an escort agency? It's not like we're gonna go to bed together.'

Redford glanced at Sarah. They held one another's eyes.

'On the contrary,' said the chief executive. 'If we decide to do business together, we become very close partners. We need to find out as much as we can about each other now, take a view on whether or not it will work. For both our sakes,' said Savage emphatically.

Redford took his eyes off Sarah. 'Tell us what you propose, ask us what you need. We'll try to help.' He flicked a glance at Cawdor.

'May I?' asked Zamaroh. Savage gave the faintest nod.

'What we would do is this. Collect all the data on your sales and run projections on likely sales on the existing back catalogue over the next seven to ten years. We would need to know what percentage of cover price goes to you. We work out from that what level of interest burden your income could support, then we calculate from that the principal sum you could raise. We have to decide how you would repay the principal sum in, say, ten years. To see what would work best, we'd have to take a view on the quality of your earnings, how volatile they have been, how volatile they could be.' Zamaroh paused. 'We have to be sure that you will do nothing over the period of the bond issue to harm your reputation and your earnings.'

'Like what?' asked Redford.

'Any crimes which might outrage your record-buying public,' filled in Sarah. 'Drugs wouldn't be a big issue, if they didn't get in the way of songwriting and performing. The same goes for alcohol, but crimes against the person, that's a different matter. Look at what happened to Michael Jackson's sales after the allegations against him.'

'Are you suggesting—' Cawdor began to bluster.

'I'm not suggesting anything,' snapped Sarah. 'I'm trying to explain something as explicitly as I can. I know you're trying to do your job, but none of us is here to impugn your client, so why don't you stop acting like a rabid Rottweiler.' Redford watched Sarah, patently trying to conceal his smile. Cawdor stared long and hard at her.

'You are one hell of a piece of work,' he said to Sarah. He seemed to ponder something for a while before turning his attention back to Zamaroh. 'All right,' he said more calmly, 'it just so happens that my client is totally above board, but why get uptight about all this crap?'

'Let's say something *did* happen that made the public stop buying his records,' replied Zamaroh. 'There wouldn't be enough income to repay the bondholders. You'd be in default, and if you had undertaken a personal guarantee of any or all the proceeds of the bond issue you could end up bankrupt.'

'It'd never happen,' said Cawdor.

'Maybe not,' replied Zamaroh, 'but it *could* happen, that's the point. What we have to assess is the *likelihood* of it happening, the *risk* of it happening, then we *price* and *structure* the issue according to that risk. The lower the risk, the lower the interest rate, the more money you can raise. The people who'd buy the bonds are sophisticated institutions. They make minute calculations of risk and return, but they also know that if Goldsteins are representing a client the deal is good.'

Savage spoke up. 'That's what the Goldsteins name buys you, but we have to ensure that our reputation isn't in jeopardy. So, if you do decide to go ahead with us, we have to do what we call "due diligence". We have to check you out. So you have to be prepared to go down that road if you appoint us.'

'We've got nothing to hide,' Cawdor said. He gazed round the table, then got to his feet. 'Anything else you want to know, John, seeing as you appointed these people?' he asked.

Sarah glanced at Redford. He smiled at her, nodded to Savage, Zamaroh and Breden, and walked from the room. Cawdor followed him out. He paused at the door.

'We'll be back in one week.'

'Why the hell did you take him down to the floor?' yelled Zamaroh.

'What?' asked Sarah, subsiding slowly into shock, now that Redford had gone.

'Shut up, Zaha,' said Savage. 'It switched Redford on, we all saw that.'

'Now everyone knows he was here, they'll guess it's about securitisation,' she retorted.

'It doesn't really matter, does it?' replied Savage. 'Fact is, he's awarded Goldsteins the deal.'

'But can we keep it?' Zamaroh demanded. 'How do I control things now after Sarah's little sideshow?'

'Oh, for God's sake stop bitching,' snapped Sarah, emerging suddenly from her reverie. 'I took him down there because he was bored stupid in the boardroom and I thought the floor would appeal to him. He's visceral and he loved it.'

'It *was* a great idea,' said Breden, with rare appreciation.

'Thank you,' replied Sarah.

'We have one week to become experts on rock securitisation,' said Savage, all business now. 'We missed the Bowie deal and we're supposed to be the pre-eminent investment bank in the world, a market leader, not a follower. We can't afford to be out of the marketplace. This will be a high-profile deal. It's sexy. It's different. We'll get coverage where we never got it before. Goldsteins' name will be spread around the globe. We're going to win this deal with a signature as well as Redford's word.'

'I thought the two were synonymous,' said Sarah.

'So did I,' spat Savage. 'What you don't know is that over the past six weeks we've lost four deals we thought we'd won, worth fifteen million in fees. Some bastard in Goldsteins is handing *our* deals to the opposition. We will not let that happen again.' Savage paused, letting his words grow heavy with threat in the silence.

'The only people to know about this deal until it's signed and sealed will be those of us in this room. So, if there is a leak, I'll know it's one of you three. Sarah, work out if Redford's back catalogue can be securitised, and if so, do a preliminary deal structure, and proposal. You have one week.'

Sarah felt like she'd been punched in the stomach.

'Why Sarah?' Zamaroh demanded. 'I've got ten people on the floor who could do that. They work full time in the markets, they're infinitely more plugged in than a freelance.' Zamaroh glared at Savage.

'I'm not trusting another bastard downstairs until we find and fire the Leaker,' replied Savage. 'I am not prepared to lose this deal.'

'You're assuming I'm happy to do the work,' said Sarah.

'Why wouldn't you be?'

Oh God, You have *no* idea. 'Like Zaha said, I'm a freelance.'

'You can outperform full-timers in half a day if you decide you want to.'

'So make me want to,' said Sarah.

Savage stood up. He glanced at Breden and Zamaroh. 'Excuse us.'

He led Sarah into his private bathroom. She sat on the marble counter, cooling her hands on the cold stone. Savage closed the door.

'Thousand a day plus expenses.'

'You and I both know that's peanuts.'

'So what ludicrously astronomical sum will you find acceptable?'

'Three and a half, plus expenses.'

'You're pricing yourself out of business. Don't you want this work?'

No, she felt like screaming. *I do not want your bloody work. I want to get home to feed my baby and never enter this godforsaken place again.*

'It's a market, James, like any other. Take it or leave it.'

'Hell, you've hardened up. I don't know what's come over you, Sarah. You're different.'

She smiled.

'All right. Three and a half plus expenses.'

Shit, shit, shit, shit, shit. She'd never thought he'd go for it.

'Don't look so miserable,' Savage said in disbelief. 'Anyone would think I'd just consigned you to slave labour.'

'No, just to prison.'

Savage gave her a look of total incomprehension and led the way back to the boardroom.

'All right, here's my game plan,' he told the assembled company. 'Sarah will do the initial structuring and research work. Have it ready in a presentation package in a week. I want to hook Redford and his manager on our preliminary proposal, get them to sign a mandate letter as soon as possible. Once the mandate letter is signed, or we find our Leaker, whichever is sooner,' he turned to Zamaroh, 'we can get your people onto the deal.'

Without back-up, it would be an awesome amount of work to complete in a week. She'd have to work practically all day and night, she'd have to find someone to look after Georgie. She felt tears burn her eyes.

'Zaha, you direct Sarah in this,' continued Savage, 'but not over the phone. Meet in person in the office, or outside it. Ensure there's nothing on paper anywhere in Goldsteins about this deal, that no one overhears a word.'

'What happens when news of Redford's visit spreads?' Breden asked.

'The Leaker probably knows already,' replied Savage gravely.

'Exactly,' said Zamaroh. 'Taking him down to the floor was idiocy.'

'Oh, shut up!' shouted Sarah. 'Don't you think his visit would have been broadcast anyway? How many people will have seen him on his way up here? Doormen, anyone passing through Reception, anyone in the lift. You think people're going to stay shtum?'

Sarah and Zamaroh glowered silently at each other.

'Make a virtue out of the gossip,' suggested Breden.

'How?' asked Savage, interested.

'Set a trap to catch a thief. This deal will be the biggest rock-star securitisation yet. Every investment bank in the City'd kill to get their hands on it. If our Leaker is being paid to deliver, his price will go sky-high on this one. We could use this deal to flush him out. Give Sarah an office on the floor, use her involvement as bait. Hide a movement-activated camera in her office, bug the phones, have sound-activated voice recorders. Let's go nuclear on the bastard.'

Savage smiled. '*Great* idea.'

Sarah felt a wave of despair. Everything was moving way out of control here. The wretched Leaker had given her more work than she'd ever be able to handle. 'I don't like it,' she said.

'God Almighty. What do I have to do to convince you?' asked Savage.

'I don't think you can. I'd be working virtually twenty-four hours a day and those days are long gone. I've got a life.'

'Well, put it on hold.' Savage passed Sarah a note. It said: *£5,000 a day. Final offer.*

Sarah wrote back: *Plus fifty bonus if I find your Leaker.*

Savage read her note. 'You are beyond belief.' He scrunched the note up, put it in his pocket and turned to Breden. 'Dick, you work with Sarah on the mechanics.' Breden inclined his head graciously.

Sarah felt a momentary warmth as she thought of all the money that would soon be pouring into her bank account, before falling back into silent hysteria at the wave of work about to engulf her.

'Zaha, you give Sarah and Dick any suspicions you have,' added Savage. 'Watch your people like a hawk when news of Redford's visit goes out.'

Zaha smiled. 'Have no fear.'

Sarah felt as if they had all thrown a huge net over the trading floor and its 500 occupants. Like the rest of them, she was trapped by it. She was to be hunter and captive.

She could stand it no more. She was desperate to get home. Georgie was due his prenap breastfeed half an hour ago. 'I've got to go,' she told them all, then rushed from the room, slamming the door behind her.

Savage, Zamaroh and Breden gazed after her in surprise.

Sarah raced home in a taxi. A flustered-looking Jacob was holding a screaming Georgie, rocking him frantically to the strains of Lauryn Hill.

'How'd it go, sweetie?' he asked, struggling to be heard.

'It was a nightmare,' said Sarah, taking Georgie and immediately hitching up her top.

She settled with him into her rocking chair and began to feed him. Silence fell like a benediction. For five minutes Sarah just sat with Georgie, gently stroking his hair, both of them recovering themselves. Jacob busied himself getting lunch together. By the time Sarah had put Georgie to bed, Jacob had pasta and fresh tomato and basil sauce ready. Sarah sat down wearily.

'So?' asked Jacob. 'What happened?'

Sarah gulped down some water. 'They want me to work on not one, but two assignments.' She felt herself faltering. How the hell was she going to hide the role of Redford in her life from Jacob? Only Alex knew. No one else would ever know.

'And?' Jacob waited patiently.

'They've got a Leaker, someone drip-feeding details of deals they've almost won to the competition. I'm supposed to find the culprit.'

'Tricky, but not impossible for you. What else?'

Sarah took a minute to empty her plate. She got up to load it into the dishwasher, speaking with her back to Jacob.

'There's this rock star, someone called John Redford . . .' There, she'd said his name. 'He wants to do a bond issue, securitising his back catalogue. I'm supposed to do all the research, come up with a preliminary structure and present it in a week.'

'Oh, sweetie,' said Jacob. 'That's a *lot* of work.'

She came back to the table and slumped into her seat.

'I know. How can I do it? I'd have to stop feeding Georgie. I'd have no time to be with him, take care of him. I wouldn't see him.' Tears burned in her eyes. 'Savage trapped me. I asked for so much money I thought he'd have to throw me out, but he hired me instead.' She got up. 'Forget it. I can't do it,' she decided suddenly. 'I can't leave Georgie, and anyway, there's no one to take care of him.'

Jacob cleared his throat. 'That's not strictly true.'

'What's not strictly true?' Alex poked his head round the door. He headed for the pasta cooling in the saucepan. 'Am I ravenous,' he said.

Jacob smiled. 'It's not true that Sarah has no one to look after Georgie.'

'Absolutely. We can look after him, can't we?' he said to Jacob. 'We'd love it, you know that,' he told his sister. 'You got the work with Goldsteins?'

She grimaced. 'Too much,' she answered bleakly. 'Savage wants me to work on two assignments.'

'With a rock star,' said Jacob, impressed.

'Which one?' asked Alex casually, eyes on Sarah.

'I've never heard of him, of course,' said Jacob. 'Redburn. John Redburn, isn't it?'

'Close enough,' answered Sarah, bending down to scratch her ankle. When she looked back up, her brother's eyes were on her with concern.

When Jacob left fifteen minutes later, Alex went and quietly sat next to Sarah on the sofa. 'You OK, Sare?'

She looked at her brother gloomily. 'No. I'm in shock.'

'You had no idea he'd be there?'

'Absolutely none.'

'What did Savage and co. make of it all?'

'Nothing,' answered Sarah. 'We pretended we didn't know each other.'

Alex pulled a disbelieving face. 'So why's he here?'

'He wants to securitise his back catalogue.'

'Why now? Why Goldsteins?'

'I don't know.' Sarah raked her hair off her face. 'I mentioned to him, back in Wyoming, that he ought to do a securitisation and gave him Savage's name. God, you don't think he can know anything about Georgie, do you?' she asked suddenly.

'How could he?' Alex answered gently.

'I don't know. It's just my nightmare—that he'll somehow find out, and come and try to take him away.'

'He couldn't do that, Sare, even if he found out, which he won't.' A frown crossed his face.

'What?' asked Sarah quickly.

'Well, this assignment might bring him too close for comfort.'

Sarah shook her head. 'I'm going to do this bloody work for Savage, but that's it. I'll keep the mother of all Berlin Walls between me and Redford. He won't get to me. What happened happened. It's in the past.'

219

CHAPTER THREE

VERA VERNON HAD for many years attempted to impose order on Sarah's house, cleaning, ironing, shopping, dispensing advice as she went. As a mother of seven children, it was hardly a leap to chief bottle-making teacher.

'All right, now watch me.' Mrs V poured eight careful ounces of freshly boiled and cooled Evian water into a sterilised bottle, then doled out eight level measuring spoonfuls of formula milk into the bottle. She secured the top, gave it a violent shake, and put it in the fridge. She handed Jacob the next bottle. 'Now it's your turn.'

Sarah watched, holding Georgie in her arms as he tried to grab all the paraphernalia.

Mrs V turned to Sarah. 'Not exactly the best way to start weaning him, is it? Several feeds in one go. You'll suffer for it, the both of you, him with withdrawal, you with all those flippin' hormones flying around. Not to mention your boobs'll feel like Zeppelins.' She smiled. 'But don't you worry, luv. You'll survive, the both of you. Go'n get yourself ready now. Give me your boy.'

Sarah hesitated.

'Come on now. More you linger, worse it'll be.'

Sarah relinquished a screaming Georgie with a gut-lacerating stab and ran upstairs. She pulled on a navy woollen suit. The skirt refused to do up. She turned the zip to the back, hid the gaping gap under her jacket. Pulled on high navy slingbacks and slid her finger into Jacob's huge ruby ring, her talisman. She passed Georgie's room as she tiptoed down the stairs and stopped. Jacob and Georgie were both lying on the floor giggling, oblivious to her look. She gasped in misery, hurried on and out of the door.

She got to Tatsuyo, a Japanese restaurant in Broadgate Circle, fifteen minutes late, but she was still the first to arrive. She felt hot, sweaty and unkempt. Get a grip, she told herself. Walk like a queen and you will be one. She was shown to a table for two downstairs. Sarah ordered a green tea and tried to cast herself into work mode.

Zaha Zamaroh stalked in, twenty-three minutes late. As the waiter was seating her, she reeled off her order without the benefit of a menu. Only then did she acknowledge Sarah.

'I'm in a hurry. You know what you want?'

Sarah leaned back in her chair with an amused smile. 'Hello, Zaha.' She glanced up at the waiter. 'Could I have a menu, please?'

He returned two minutes later, menu in hand. Sarah took another two minutes to study it and make her order, calm and poised under the missiles of Zamaroh's eyes.

'Since Goldsteins is paying me by the day, perhaps we might start,' said Sarah.

'Why don't we?' replied Zamaroh, as if picking up a gauntlet.

The waiters brought their lunch on a tray: miso soup, sashimi and a seaweed salad for them both.

'I'd like an inconspicuous office,' said Sarah, taking a sip of the soup, 'but not too inconspicuous. Let's make it look as if you're trying to hide me, but I've got to be bait, too. Our boy's a tricky bastard I reckon, keen on head games.'

'How so?'

'What he or she is doing is a betrayal, and I'll bet they're getting one hell of a kick out of it. They think they're smart, so let's make it *just* diffi-cult enough to flatter their ego. I want to give them a real red herring. Let's set up a phantom deal and call it "Gravadlax". Perhaps they'll think it's going to be a takeover of Volvo. People always choose a code name which their subconscious links to the name they're trying to conceal, so Gravadlax'll point him in a certain direction, make it easier to track if anyone starts doing something unusual with any Swedish corporates.' Sarah could see the beginning of a predatory gleam in Zamaroh's eyes.

'I want to occupy the office as soon as possible,' she went on. 'Breden will have to get his people in there tomorrow first thing, to do a sweep of my office and yours, and all the conference rooms. If they find bugs, I want them left there; we'll use them in our favour to talk about Gravadlax. I want a good PC, big, strong and fast, twenty-one inch—'

'You talking man or machine here?' interjected Zamaroh.

Sarah burst out laughing at Zamaroh's unexpected shot of humour.

'I wish. So that's a twenty-one-inch *screen*. My computer speaks to no one in Goldsteins. I don't want any other PCs eavesdropping on mine. You and I will have to meet outside the office to talk about Redford.'

'How do I describe you when people ask?'

'Just say I'm doing freelance work. That should tantalise our Leaker. I'm going to get Breden to bug my office and yours with sound and vision so we can check if anyone tries to go through our papers after hours.'

'That is an unacceptable invasion of my privacy,' declaimed Zamaroh.

'Look, it's just for a week or two, until we catch our thief. It's not as if we have much choice. You can't afford to lose any more deals, Zaha.'

'Don't remind me.' Zamaroh grimaced. 'Is there anything else?'

'Yes, there is. Who do you think it might be?'

Sarah had forgotten quite how visceral the trading floor was; the winning and the losing, the measurement of people in terms of pounds sterling, the gamesmanship, the *Schadenfreude*. And most of all, the envy.

It was a catwalk she sauntered down to her borrowed office. She knew it was not just her looks that attracted attention. Any new person drew unconcealed scrutiny, but Sarah was already acknowledged as one of the top traders in the City in recent years. Let them talk, she thought, watching the buzz through her glass walls.

Her mind lurched back to Georgie, as it did about every ninety seconds. Perhaps he'd be fretting without her, objecting to the formula milk. She looked longingly at her phone. Her call would be taped. And if the office were bugged, there was no point in using her mobile. If there was a problem, Jacob'd call her. Yet she could rationalise all day for all the comfort it brought her.

Karen, Zamaroh's secretary, knocked on her door. 'Zaha wanted me to give you these.'

Personnel files, Zamaroh's suspects. 'Thanks.'

She began to plough her way through the reams of paper. After an hour she'd finished them. She made her way to Zamaroh's office.

'Thanks for the files,' said Sarah. 'Tell me why you suspect these two.'

Zamaroh let out a dramatic sigh. 'I have no hard evidence. Just a feeling, just the look in their eyes when I talk to them. You must understand that,' she added with uncharacteristic respect. 'You and your fabled instincts.'

Sarah smiled. 'I'd like to see them, please.'

'Follow me.'

Zamaroh strode to the floor, with Sarah at her side. Zamaroh discreetly pointed out her suspects to Sarah. There was Petra Johnson, government bond sales person, selling Gilts and Treasuries into Europe—the most boring job on the trading floor as far as Sarah was concerned. Sarah recalled her file. PJ, as she was known on the floor, was thirty-five, with a degree in history from Bristol, minor league boarding school, salary last year £75,000, bonus £100,000. Next of kin listed as her father, Julian. PJ was blonde, expensively so, made up, smart clothes veering towards tarty. The brilliance of her hair clashed with the red tones in her face. She was a woman in a hurry. She talked fast, as she got up to consult another trader on a price, and, when she didn't like the price, lost her cool fast. Sarah bet she spent fast. She was single, boyfriendless as far as Zamaroh knew.

Then there was Jeremy St James, known as Jezza. Thirty-one, Eton and Oxford. Salary last year £200,000, bonus £1 million. Next of kin blank. He was flash, ambitious, loud, a little too well dressed. He was Eton-made-good on the trading floor. As he switched between phones he alternated between cut-glass vowels and down and dirty with the barrow boys. Sarah guessed he was whoever he wanted to be, with whoever mattered to him. He was clearly a crowd-pleaser, but Sarah doubted that anyone sought him out as a friend or confidant. He did not exactly have 'trust me' writ large on his face, but the trading-floor persona was often a screen, protecting something finer. It also just as often hid emptiness.

Sarah returned to her office and pondered the suspects. Both chosen by Zamaroh on nothing stronger than instinct, a latent dissatisfaction with them, or else perhaps just pure dislike. Zamaroh was not, in Sarah's eyes, a good judge of character. She was too caught up in her own rage to be sensitive to other beings. She rated them on the basis of the profits they made for her and Goldsteins. Peripherals such as personalities, private lives, hopes and traumas did not register. Zamaroh's take on them was just Sarah's starting point. It was time to talk.

Jezza traded foreign exchange on a proprietary basis, using Goldsteins' own capital. Sarah had done exactly the same at ICB, so that gave her a natural way in. She planned to amble by for a casual chat about the markets, but Jezza beat her to it.

'Sarah Jensen, queen of the FX markets. Don't say you've joined our humble ranks.' He stood in the doorway, lanky frame propped against the jamb, eyes full of mockery and mischief.

Sarah eyed him carefully. 'Let's just say I'm on loan from the real world.'

'Oh puhlease.' He strode forward and stuck out a hand. 'I'm Jeremy St James.'

Sarah shook his hand. St James's handshake was cool, at odds with his smiling face.

'I trade prop FX,' he said, swagger in his voice. The proprietary traders were at the top of the trading-floor food chain. He might just have announced he had a twelve-inch penis. 'You still follow the markets?'

'Sporadically.'

'Follow Cable?'

'A bit.'

'Wanna take a punt?'

'Depends what it is.'

'It's one sixty-four sixty-five now. Close up or down today?'

'What's the stakes?'

Jezza pondered that, a slow smile forming. 'A bottle of vintage Krug. Tonight, at Corney and Barrow.'

Sarah had never been unduly interested in the daily movements of any index, regarding them as erratic, drunken staggers. She preferred to gamble on monthly trends, where some underlying logic came into play, and as for delaying her return to Georgie . . .

'It's gonna close down,' she said, with genuine indifference.

Jezza came back at five. 'Get out your wallet.'

'Just a sec.' Sarah called up her screen, checked the closing prices and burst out laughing. 'You lying bastard.'

He grinned. 'Always worth a try.'

She made a quick call to Jacob on her mobile from the loo. 'How's it going?' she asked urgently.

'Fine, sweetie, don't you worry.'

'Bottles OK?'

'Drunk every last drop. He's been grand.'

'Good.' Sarah felt a wave of relief mixed in with another, less clear emotion. 'He's not missing me, then?'

'Course he's missing you, love. Pining, but not pining too much, OK?'

Sarah took a deep breath. 'Look, I won't be home for a few hours. Can you manage?'

'I'll manage fine. You just do what you have to. We'll be here.'

She hurried out to meet Jezza.

They squeezed through the gathering crowds at Corney and Barrow to take pole position at a corner table. Jezza peeled off to the bar. Sarah scanned the room. Edgy traders coming down after a tough day, hard drinking, heavy smoking. Four years ago, she'd have been at it with the best of them. Now she was counting the minutes till she got home.

Jezza deposited a magnum of vintage Krug on the table.

'Lord above, you don't expect me to drink that, do you?'

'What have you got to stay sober for? You're not trading for us, are you?'

Sarah smiled. 'Research.'

'Aw, come *onnnnn*. Think I'm stupid?' He began to wrestle with the cork.

'I thought they did that for you at the bar,' observed Sarah.

'Always pop my own cherry, darlin'.'

The cork flew out of his hand and ricocheted off the ceiling, coming down to land on a neighbouring table. Sarah wondered again what the hell she was doing there.

St James quickly filled two glasses to just below overflowing.

'To winning,' he said, clinking his glass against Sarah's.

'To winning,' she replied, miming a sip.

'I like your ring,' said St James, eyeing Sarah's ruby. 'From a lover?'

'From my uncle, actually.' Not her real uncle, but Jacob had forever been an honorary uncle.

'Got a lover?'

'Have you?'

'Aw, how d'you even begin to start counting, darlin'?'

'A harem of eager ladies—ah, I see.'

'A harem of ladies.' Jezza warmed to the idea.

You're gay, said a voice in Sarah's head. Why don't you just come out? Because his life would be made hell on a trading floor where conformity was king, where minorities, of whatever type, were sport.

By skipping to the loo twice, emptying her glass into the basin each time, Sarah disposed of two glasses of champagne, while Jezza drank four. He appeared unaffected.

'So, tell me, who's who on the floor?'

Jezza smiled. 'Well, the biggest of the big swingers just has to be *moi*. D'you know how much I made for Goldsteins last year?'

'Tell me.'

'Fifteen mill.' He drained his glass.

'Not bad. And this year?' she asked, plunging the knife in.

His head snapped back. 'Who's counting? It's only September.'

Zamaroh had told Sarah that St James was £8 million down, close to out. Zamaroh was giving him one more month to begin the turnaround, but Sarah doubted he would make it. His bluster was too desperate, his eyes too full of fear. When a trader lost his nerve, he was dead meat in the City's sea of sharks.

'So it is,' said Sarah gently. 'So who's the second-biggest swinger?'

Jezza went through a roll call, down through the pecking order, cruising on gossip. Then Petra Johnson's name cropped up.

'She has to be on the way out,' said Jezza. 'Used to be good. All she thinks of now is catching a rich idiot and retiring.'

Sarah stirred herself. 'Couldn't she just retire on her own savings?'

'Fast living, babe. Taste for the good things.'

'Like what?'

'Good flat, right address, real jewels, right friends, good holidays—'

225

'I get the picture.'

'Where d'you live?'

'Carlyle Square.'

'Flat,' announced St James.

'House,' corrected Sarah.

'Jeez. You must have been good.'

'I was. I know the pressures. I feel sorry for PJ.'

'Don't be. She knows what she's doing. The flat, the clothes, the lifestyle, the frightful friends, all an investment, isn't it? She's not going to meet Mr Fifty Mill in Tesco's, picking up her ready meals.'

'I never realised it was such hard work,' reflected Sarah.

'It isn't, is it, for the likes of you?' This was said with just a hint of bitterness which the bluster couldn't disguise. 'Golden girls, stride into life like you own it, you and Zamaroh. Everything comes easy, doesn't it?' The drink talking at last.

'Yeah, right, and you've got it hard.'

The eyes narrowed. 'You've got no idea.'

'So tell me.'

A quick flash of hatred and Jezza lumbered to his feet. 'Aw piss off, why don't you.' He wove through the crowds, and made his way out.

Sarah searched for a taxi on London Wall, puzzled by Jezza's violent mood swing. Once safely ensconced in a black cab, she wished she could affix a police siren to the roof and speed home through the traffic. She felt as if she hadn't seen Georgie in a month. She craved her baby.

Once reunited with Georgie, she released Jacob with profuse thanks, fed her son, put him to bed, and made one quick telephone call.

'Freddie? It's Sarah Jensen. I know, it's been a very long time. Feels like a lifetime. Look, I've got something urgent. Can we meet tomorrow?'

Jacob arrived at nine the next morning with a huge casserole dish.

'Lunch and dinner. No time to take care of a baby and cook something decent, at least not while I'm still a learner driver.'

Sarah smiled and took a whiff of coq au vin. 'Oh, Jacob, you're a star.'

'Put that in the fridge, and go and get yourself dressed,' he said, swapping the casserole dish for Georgie.

Sarah kissed them goodbye, wondering if the parting from Georgie would get any easier. She got to her office at ten fifteen, just as Zamaroh was swinging by. The Iranian's eyes flared with predatory glee.

'Ah—we have arrived. Good afternoon. No time to waste.' She hissed on the S, just like a snake. An anaconda, thought Sarah.

'As it happens, Zaha, I've been up since five thirty, when I rather imagine you were slumbering in your lair.' Sarah gave her a sweet smile. 'Now, if you'll excuse me . . .' She turned pointedly to the open files on her desk. She felt Zamaroh's eyes on her long after the Iranian had headed back to her own domain, felt her sizing up the navy suit, worn for the second day running. Now she'd have to shop on top of everything else, wasting precious time and money. And all because she had to look the part, feel secure in her body armour. She'd always taken her beauty, her previously perfect figure for granted. Now that both were challenged by childbirth and exhaustion, they suddenly mattered.

She turned on her computer and started to surf the Net, trawling all the information she could on rock-star securitisations, then she logged onto Lexus-Nexus and read through over 100 press cuttings. Savage was right. Rock meets finance *was* sexy. The press couldn't get enough of it: *The Real Price of Fame—celebrity bonds are designed to turn hot talent into a great investment, but will Wall Street bite? Rock solid investment? Forget about the Footsie, consult the pop charts instead. Stars unearth rock of gold. Heavy metal becomes new currency.* The headline writers did their worst. The interest was huge. Sarah could see Savage's vision: Goldsteins' name writ large where it had never been before. *If* they won the deal. *If* the Leaker didn't wreck it for them.

It was twelve fifteen when she finally took a break. She rubbed her eyes and gazed out over the floor. It was braying with the usual cacophony of voices—human, computer and telephone—and seething with exhilaration, despair, greed, envy, terror. So easy to get hooked on the buzz, to have to search harder for the ultimate kick, but the Leaker still seemed to Sarah to be someone motivated by revenge, not by kicks for their own sake.

She timed her next move carefully. As PJ hurried across the floor, heading for the double doors, Sarah followed at a distance. Sure enough, PJ disappeared into the Ladies. Sarah went in after her. As they washed their hands at adjacent basins, Sarah caught PJ's eye in the mirror and waited for the other woman to speak.

'You've just joined us?' asked PJ.

'Yes,' answered Sarah, drying her hands. 'Yesterday.'

'How's it going?'

'Oh, early days are always a trial, aren't they? You know, figuring out the lie of the land, who you can trust, who to avoid, who's nice, who's psychotic.'

PJ laughed. 'The answer to *that* one is about half the floor. Do you have your own office, or are you attached to a desk?'

'Research.'

'Ah. Which area?'

'New products.'

'Any in particular? I mean, you must have *some* area of expertise.'
Hm, the first dagger thrown.

'What's yours?' asked Sarah.

'Governments.'

'Ah.' What the hell could she find to say to that? 'Enjoy it?'

PJ barked out an incredulous laugh. 'Yeah, I just love it, don't I?'

'So why d'you do it then?'

'Why d'you think? You find a better way to pay the rent, you tell me.'
PJ wheeled on her high heels and ricocheted out.

On impulse, at lunchtime Sarah headed into a men's outfitters. She
fingered through the suits until she found three she liked. Then she
picked out six shirts, two each in white, pale blue and pink, and piled
them on the suits. A salesman approached.

Sarah pointed to her pile. 'I'd like to try these, please.'

There was a surprised cough. 'I'm sorry, madam?'

'You heard me. I'm a lactating mother with a figure shot to pieces and
I thought these would be just the ticket. May I try them?'

If the man's eyes grew any wider, they'd roll back in their sockets,
thought Sarah, stifling her grin.

She walked out with three suits and six shirts; all fitted her perfectly.

Back in her office, Sarah was trawling through more background info
on securitisations, when Jezza popped his head round the door. She hit
screen switch and swimming fishes came up on her monitor.

'Hi.' He shifted from one foot to another, reading her for clues, trying
to suss how to play her. She let him sweat.

'Boy, am I hung over,' he said, propelling himself into a chair opposite
Sarah. 'Don't normally drink that much. Was I a bit boisterous? Can't
remember.'

Like hell, thought Sarah.

'How about some dinner tonight?'

'Sorry, Jezza. I'm busy.'

'Tomorrow, then.'

'Busy too.'

Jezza leaned half across the desk. 'Day after, then?'

Did this man never give up? 'Can we play it by ear?'

'Yeah, suppose we could. I get booked up early though.'

'Then I'll just have to take my chances.'

Sarah left at six. Georgie was asleep when she got home and the
house was quiet. Sarah hurried upstairs to the baby's room to take a

peek at him. He was lying on his back, arms thrown out, mouth relaxed, breathing softly. His rosy lips formed the most perfect cupid's bow. His long, dark eyelashes fluttered against his silken skin. Sarah felt her heart glow. She thought of his father, recalled the sensual beauty of his face. Georgie was his too, thought Sarah, with a pang of possessiveness.

After changing into jeans and a white shirt, she tiptoed downstairs to Jacob. Alex had gone out.

'How was it?' she asked, pouring him a glass of red wine.

He took the glass with a smile. 'Good. He was a little angel. He's such a good boy. I tell you, though, I don't know how these single mothers do it. Mrs V came in for a few hours today and I practically jumped up and kissed her.'

'Steady on. But seriously, you're not getting too tired, are you?'

'I'd be a liar if I said I wasn't absolutely cream-crackered, sweetie, but it's a long time since I've felt so satisfied. I adore that boy. Spending time with him is a privilege.'

'Oh, Jacob. I really don't know how to thank you.'

Jacob laid out two plates of steaming coq au vin and Sarah fell upon hers as if she hadn't seen food for a week.

'This is delicious.'

She finished it quickly and got to her feet. 'I should be back in under two hours,' she said to Jacob. 'When you go to bed, just park the listener in the doorway. I'll pick it up when I get back.' They'd decided it would be easier for all of them if Jacob slept over in the spare room for a while.

'Who are you off to see then?' he asked.

'My man in a dirty mac.'

'Ah, one of those.'

She hurried to her safe, took out £1,500 in cash, rolled the notes into two fat sausages, secured them with an elastic band and stuffed each one into her socks. She took a file from her briefcase, shoved it into a carrier bag, and headed out.

It was eight thirty; the summer streets were alive with people dining and drinking in the pavement cafés spilling out onto the King's Road. Sarah caught a cab to Camden, and headed for the Rat and Parrot.

Freddie was seated at his favourite table, nursing a pint of bitter.

Sarah made for the bar, ordered a Virgin Mary, and went to join her friend. He smiled. 'Hello, dearie. Good to see you after all this time.'

She smiled back. 'Good to see you, too, Freddie.'

'What have you been up to? Haven't seen you in an eternity.'

'Oh, this and that,' she answered.

'You look well on it, whatever it is.'

'Thanks. You're a gent.' Freddie Skelton, the charmer, senior partner at Spinnacres, the leading City law firm, was so smooth, with his velvety camp voice, and well-groomed hair, evenly dark, brushed back.

'Sorry to drag you out,' she said.

'If anyone has to drag me out, I'd rather it was you. What can I do for you this time?'

Sarah took the file from her plastic bag. 'Two names. They work at Goldsteins. These are details from their personnel files. I want the works on them, a.s.a.p. Credit-card, bank, telephone statements.'

'It'll cost you, if you want it yesterday.'

'I do.' Sarah bent down and extracted the sausages of money from her socks. She palmed them to Freddie under the table. 'There's fifteen hundred. Let me know if it's not enough.'

'I will. I'll ring you tomorrow, dearie. Count on it.'

Sarah made it to Goldsteins by nine thirty. She was tucking into her second breakfast when Savage's secretary knocked on her door.

'Fed-Ex for you.'

'Thanks, Evangeline.'

Sarah slit open the package. It contained all the financial statements on John Redford.

Redford had written twenty-two albums and over 500 individual songs. Each album sold more than the last. Altogether, he'd sold 108 million albums. He'd done ten sell-out world tours, grossing $120 million. Total merchandising receipts were $80 million. Each year he seemed to earn over $1 million in performance income, the fee payable to him each time one of his records was played on the radio. He'd made a total of $8 million from licensing his songs to appear in television ads. The man's achievement was phenomenal. This man who had sung for her in the wilderness, and given her a child.

Sarah got to her feet, suddenly dizzy. She turned from her desk and gazed out of the window at the City skyline.

It was impossible to handle this as if it were just another assignment. However hard she tried, Redford kept intruding, her son kept intruding. Everything blurred together—love, secrets, longing, the memory of desire. Any hope of objectivity was a myth. Savage would fire her if he ever comprehended the truth.

She sat back down. She felt like a voyeur, flicking through the business life of the father of her child. Redford's actual income was difficult to discern. He seemed to pay out deductions at every turn, to managers, agents, promoters, accountants, lawyers, his record company. After all his payouts, his gross income was in the region of $23 million a year.

God, this stuff would have been great ammunition in another mother's hands, someone who might want to claim maintenance. A combination of pride, possessiveness and her habitual secrecy meant Sarah would never do that. She could and would support Georgie herself. But, despite herself, she felt a quick pang as she learned of the true extent of Redford's earning power. A few million from him, and she'd never have to work again.

She studied the papers for a while longer before locking them in her desk, then going to the loo. She left the dummy Gravadlax papers on her desk, a strand of hair stuck to them to test for molestation, but when she returned the hair was in place, the papers untouched.

After three hours, she managed to put the numbers into some kind of order. She paused for a brief lunch, then opened up her laptop and began to build a picture of Redford Inc, history and future.

Playing with numbers in this way still gave her a real kick. Financial structuring was indulging the art of the possible, fortunetelling with a computer chip and a brain. Sarah's excitement grew as she filled pages with calculations.

Her telephone rang.

'Sarah. Evangeline. Could you drop by James's office, please?'

She found Zamaroh and Breden in attendance in Savage's office. Breden was telling Savage and Zamaroh about the bugging.

'All the offices we tested were clean,' he revealed. 'What I'd like to do now is bring forward our monthly sweep. Better to do it at a random time, anyway.'

'Fine,' said Savage. 'You surprised the offices were clean?'

'Not really,' replied Breden. 'I think we're dealing with a sophisticated individual, someone who knows we'd be debugging offices. Bugging's such an obvious way of extracting information. *Too* obvious.'

'Yes, our Leaker is doing this chiefly for kicks,' observed Sarah. 'I'll bet you a case of good red wine that's his motivation. Bugging's too impersonal. No real theft or betrayal there, in his eyes.'

'And what makes you so sure of this?' challenged Zamaroh.

'Profiling,' responded Sarah simply, 'and instinct.'

'You have anything concrete?' asked Savage.

'Not yet.'

'What about my suspects?' asked Zamaroh, in the voice of a queen asking about her prisoners.

'Nothing to report yet.'

'Tell us about securitisation,' said Savage.

'Arse,' said Sarah.

'I beg your pardon?'

'RSS,' she replied slowly. 'Rock Star Securitisation. The bonds, known as Bowie bonds, because he was the first rock star to be securitised, are typically issued for a ten- to fifteen-year period, on a Single A rating, but paying one to two per cent more than comparable Single A corporate bonds. Often there's some form of guarantee from the music publisher, but if the quality of earnings from the rock star is good enough, you don't need guarantees.

'Bowie's deal was backed by royalties on his albums. What gave Bowie an edge was that he owned the songwriting, publishing and recording rights to his music, so he got royalty streams from all three. Often artists just own the recording rights.

'I believe John Redford owns all three rights, like Bowie, and that makes him an excellent candidate. He's put out twenty-two albums, and has sales of over four million CDs a year on average. There are a whole load of technical issues, like proving he owns the copyright to his work, but assuming they can all be got round, Redford should be the perfect candidate for an RSS.'

'Yield?' barked Zamaroh.

'Say around four hundred and fifty basis points over base, to give a current yield to maturity of around nine per cent. On that sort of rate, given Redford's apparent annual income of around twelve million dollars, he ought to be able to raise a hundred million or thereabouts with a coverage ratio of one point three three. Tight, but doable.'

Savage, Zamaroh and Breden were stunned into collective silence. Even Sarah was impressed by herself. Maybe my mind hasn't completely atrophied, she thought.

'Fees?' asked Zamaroh, recovering.

'We could probably charge an arrangement fee of around five per cent, clear a cool five million, arrange the biggest rock-syndication deal yet, and emerge as market leader.'

'Sounds pretty sexy to me,' said Savage, smiling at Sarah. 'You seem rather keen on Mr Redford.'

'It's a good deal,' answered Sarah, fearing her cheeks were colouring.

'Why does he want to do it?' asked Zamaroh, inadvertently saving Sarah. 'That's what I want to know.'

'An RSS means the rock star is essentially borrowing money and paying it back out of future royalties,' Sarah replied. 'It's much better than getting the record company to pay him an advance on future royalties, because the rock star gets more money up-front, plus he receives a higher royalty rate from the record company, which doesn't now have to pay him an advance. Second, the money received up-front is viewed as a loan. The interest on the loan is tax-deductible, so the rock star can actually reduce his tax burden. Third, the rock star retains ownership of the catalogue that generated the royalties. If the royalties are greater than expected, the bonds get paid off early, so the rock star gets all the upside.'

'Who are the buyers?' asked Zamaroh.

'Insurance companies, normally. The Pru bought all the Bowie bonds, the whole issue. That's attractive to someone like Bowie; it means only one institutional investor gets to pore over all his confidential stuff. It's something I think we should seriously consider ourselves if we want to win the deal.'

'What, eat a hundred million dollars' worth of Redford bonds?' demanded Zamaroh.

'That'd be a big position to carry,' answered Savage, 'but if the numbers back it up, and if we have to buy the deal to win it, we do it.'

Jacob had set off to Golders Green for a night of poker, Alex was in Sarah's study pursuing his love affair with maps, and Georgie was sitting on Sarah's lap, playing with her hair, when the doorbell rang.

Sarah peered through the peephole and relaxed when she saw it was a motorcycle courier. She took the package, tore open the thick envelope and saw bundles of bank, credit-card and telephone statements. Freddie had moved fast, as promised. Freddie Skelton had one of the best little black books of dodgy, subornable contacts; better still, post the Data Protection Act, when investigators and litigators became a bit more nervous about obtaining such information, he had a wholesaler who could do his dirty work for him. Whoever that mystery man was, he had done a great job.

Sarah settled down with a sleepy Georgie in the rocking chair and started with PJ. Petra was twelve grand overdrawn and had a gold Visa card that sucked the cash from her current account. Monthly spending on her card averaged four grand over the past year. Sarah ran through her spending. The woman shopped at Harvey Nichols, sometimes once a week, then she drank, expensively, at Harvey Nich's fifth-floor wine bar, a pick-up joint if ever there were one, thought Sarah. PJ ate at Vong, Momo's, and Alberto's in South Kensington.

Sarah turned to Jezza's credit cards. Eight grand a month split between Visa and Amex. Oswald Boateng suits, three grand, dinners at the Ivy, three hundred quid, drinks at the Met Bar, five hundred quid— the man was quite an entertainer. The only oddity was the more prosaic regular meals at an Indian restaurant off the Brompton Road. Sarah jumped as the telephone rang. Dropping the papers on the floor and cursing, she reached out for the phone. 'Hello!'

'Good evening, Sarah. Dick Breden.'

Sarah looked at the phone with horror, praying Georgie would keep his peace. She picked up the remote and switched on the television to distract him.

'Hi, Dick, how're you doing?'

'I've got some info on our people. I wondered if I could come round now and discuss it with you?'

'Can we do it tomorrow?'

Georgie let out a happy gurgle as a favourite advertisement came on the television. Sarah coughed heavily, trying to drown the sound.

'You all right?' asked Breden.

'I'm fine, thanks, Dick. Where shall we meet? In the office?'

'I'm trying to stay out of the office for a few days.'

'I can meet you in Oriel—you know, Sloane Square?'

'Breakfast? Seven thirty?'

No chance, thought Sarah. She'd be breastfeeding. 'I'm busy till nine thirty.'

Breden had the good grace not to ask why. 'See you there.'

Sarah had had a rough night. Georgie had woken not his usual once, but three times. She arrived at Oriel twelve minutes late, feeling weak and haggard. She'd put on one of her new suits, teeming it with high navy, sequinned mules which, she hoped, drew the attention away from her face.

'Hi, Dick. Sorry I'm late.'

He nodded, letting it ride. 'Can I get you a coffee?'

'Camomile tea, please, and four pieces of toast with honey.'

When the food arrived, Sarah polished off all four pieces of toast, scarcely drawing breath.

'You miss dinner?' asked Breden.

'No, just hungry.' She reached down into her bag and pulled out her growing files on the suspects.

Breden flicked through the papers and looked up. 'You've been busy. Any preliminary thoughts?'

Sarah drained her tea. 'Jeremy St James, alias Jezza. Expensive tastes, generous entertainer, an image to maintain, flew high, now he's about to crash. He's desperate. Possibly has a problem with alcohol, latent homosexual, in denial and that makes him vulnerable. Pent-up anger, swings from that to remorse and guilt.' She told Breden about her drinking session with him. 'As I expected, he avoided me the day before yesterday, then finally plucked up courage to breeze into my office, play it all down, wait for me to give him absolution. Then he asks me out. Problems with intimacy, commitment, likes to live life on the fly, buzz here, buzz there, never settle. Like most traders, low boredom threshold.'

'Fancy him?'

'As our Leaker? He fits the profile all right. Needs the money, fears being fired, so selling information, wounding Goldsteins in the process, all that satisfies him. Leaking makes the Leaker feel one up and Jezza's a real status freak. Likes to think he's number one on the floor.'

Breden chuckled. 'I imagine Queen Zaha would have a few words to say to that. How d'you rate PJ?'

'She's bitter, angry, running out of time and money. High spending, overdrawn. She's got motive, and I get the feeling she's a nasty piece of work. She could definitely get a kick out of betrayal. Trouble is, if I analysed the whole floor, I'd come up with a hundred people with motive and the right profile. Trading floors attract selfish, avaricious, loud, competitive people. They also foster feelings of injustice. No one reckons that the biggest hitters deserve what they earn and everyone thinks they're underpaid by comparison. Trying to find our Leaker's going to be like looking for the proverbial needle.' She sighed.

'You want me to have some of my people take a look at the phone records?' asked Breden.

She jumped at it. Poring over the phone records would be back-breakingly boring, time-consuming work. 'Oh, yes, *please*. I would *love* it. So, what've you come up with?'

'First off, the floor's clean. We did a wide sweep. No bugs anywhere.'

'Hm. So it has to be someone with close access. But that still rules in five hundred people on the floor,' said Sarah.

'It does, but we're watching them. Zamaroh's office is now wired for sound and vision, as is yours.'

'Oh joy. I won't be able to pick my nose in peace. I pity the poor bugger who's got to monitor the tapes.'

'I would say it'd be quite a perk in your office.'

Sarah laughed. 'Anything on our gang of two?' she asked.

'A little bit of background. Jezza lives in a rambling house at the bad end of the Fulham Road. Has a taste for antiques. Er, he drives an Aston Martin.' The minutest flicker of discomfort crossed Breden's features.

Sarah burst out laughing. 'Younger model than yours? Bigger, faster?'

Breden gave her an acid smile.

'PJ is boyfriendless as of about seven weeks ago, smarting by the sound of it. Minor aristo, lots of family dosh. She'd been with the guy three years, probably feels three invested years have gone to waste. She's thirty-five, unmarried, a tad bitter I'd imagine. Basement flat in the Little Boltons. Drives a BMW convertible. I'll tell you more tomorrow. I'm on night shift tonight, watching her.'

Sarah returned home to her office and spent most of the day working on the securitisation proposal. The meeting with Redford was the next day, and she wasn't close to finished. Working from home was infinitely preferable to trekking into the City. She could see Georgie every hour or so, but there was torture in that too, just five minutes of him while she and he craved more. She interrupted herself to feed him his night feed, and to feed herself, then, leaving Georgie with Jacob and Alex, she worked on, finally finishing at three in the morning.

As if by empathy, Georgie let her sleep undisturbed until seven. At eight Jacob took him from her. She was excited and disturbed by the prospect of meeting John Redford again. She tried to convince herself the sick feeling in her stomach came from nerves about presenting her proposal. Perhaps one-tenth of it did.

She picked out her new dark grey pinstripe suit, and a pale pink shirt. She squirted two generous blasts of Fracas behind her ears. A pair of diamond stud earrings followed, and then her lucky ruby ring. She checked herself in the mirror, wondered what John Redford would think, and instantly reprimanded herself for caring.

She arrived five minutes late for the meeting. Savage, Breden and Zamaroh were waiting in the boardroom.

'You're late,' said Zamaroh pointedly.

'I know. I was shagging my boyfriend and it took a while to get cleaned up afterwards.' Sarah flashed a smile. 'You know how it is.'

Savage and Breden guffawed with laughter. Zamaroh, out of the bank, would have laughed too, but here every line was a competition, and she wouldn't acknowledge Sarah's victory.

A discreet cough sounded.

'May I come in?' John Redford stood in the doorway, beside Savage's secretary, Evangeline. He looked tired, but fit. Sarah's eyes were drawn to his sensual lips, curved now into a gentle smile of amusement.

Savage rose to his feet. 'Mr Redford, delighted.'

Redford shook his hand. 'It's John.'

'John,' said Savage, as if trying it out. 'You remember Zaha Zamaroh, Dick Breden, and Sarah Jensen?'

Redford acknowledged them all with a polite smile. The look he gave Sarah suggested that he had heard her quip.

Sarah felt her cheeks flushing red. God, what a great start.

'Nice suit,' said Redford, a teasing look still in his eyes.

Sarah gave him a thin smile, not keen to encourage bantering. Trying to pretend she'd never met this man was agonising. She could only hope that Redford would continue to collude in the pretence. His teasing suggested otherwise.

'Sarah?' Savage's voice cut through her reverie. She dragged herself back to attention. 'You will present our proposal.'

Sarah looked up brightly. 'Of course. Shall we wait for Mr Cawdor?'

'He's not coming.'

'You're not having any representation?' asked Sarah in disbelief.

Redford shook his head. 'Nope. Don't worry, Sarah. I'm a big boy. I won't be lured off the straight and narrow by you. Anyways, I'll give all your stuff to my lawyers later.' His eyes smiled at her, his voice was languorous. He was gorgeous and infuriating in equal measure. She was conscious of Savage, Breden and Zamaroh focusing on the exchange. She could only hope that they'd put his teasing intimacy down to rock-starry immunity to the normal social laws.

She pushed the document she had so carefully worked on into the night across the desk to Redford.

'Right,' she said firmly, nodding at the document. 'To paraphrase what's in there: as we currently understand, your numbers would support an issue of around a hundred million dollars. You could probably secure a Single A rating. That means you could borrow at a cost of around nine and a half per cent. We would charge a fee of around five per cent on that, and—'

'What the hell d'you do for that?' interrupted Redford.

Sarah smiled. 'Other banks will charge around the same. Lesser banks might cut the fee, but your deal might suffer. What we do for the money is this. We start off by giving you an engagement letter which we both sign. In this, Goldsteins International undertakes to, one, securitise a specified part of your catalogue—that is, issue bonds backed by the income stream on that part of your catalogue—two, obtain a rating, and three, place the issue.'

'How long's it all take?' asked Redford with a frown.

'Typically, a one-hundred-and-fifty-day engagement, although that can vary. There's normally thirty days for due diligence, verifying your income streams and convincing ourselves that they're all kosher. Then there's thirty days to size, price and structure the deal. Then there's another thirty days to write the document and to write the investor book, basically a sales document telling everyone why they'd be incredibly lucky to get their hands on a Redford bond. Then there's thirty days for closing, that's when everyone gets hysterical and threatens to call the whole thing off. And we normally factor in another thirty days for contingencies on the "what can go wrong will go wrong" basis. All the while, the rating agencies are working on your rating, we're doing a copyright search to check all your records really are yours, we're checking Lexus-Nexus to confirm you're not a criminal, we're getting a tax opinion and a bankruptcy opinion. If you survive all that, then we launch the issue to great plaudits and huge institutional appetite, and you go home to Wyoming a hundred million dollars richer, minus all the fees of course.'

Redford smiled, and Sarah could see in his eyes that he was thinking of their tent in the wilderness.

'Very impressive,' he said, eyes still on her.

'That's what Goldsteins International can do for you,' said Zamaroh, in hard-sell mode, also seeking to remind Redford, noted Sarah, that this was about team Goldsteins, not about Sarah Jensen, at whom Redford was still smiling. Sarah smiled back, allowing herself just the smallest lapse. She'd done well in her presentation, she could feel Savage beaming beside her, and this was her reward: five seconds of Sarah the woman, responding to Redford the man.

'So,' said Savage, 'do you have any questions?'

Redford's eyes became distant once more. 'Nope, not at this stage.' He got to his feet, slipping the presentation file under his arm.

'Where will you be, if we need to contact you?' asked Savage.

'Back in the States,' answered Redford. 'I'm on tour.'

'You broke your tour to come here?' asked Breden.

'I had a few days off. Besides, it's worth flying to London for a hundred million dollars, wouldn't you say?'

'I would,' replied Breden, 'and excuse me if I'm being impertinent, but why you in person? You could have sent any one of a legion of advisers.'

Sarah shifted awkwardly in her seat. This was becoming dangerous.

'That's why people like me get in trouble,' said Redford. 'They leave everything to advisers, then they wonder why they've been screwed.'

Breden nodded. 'But you could have gone to our offices in New York.'

Redford cocked his head slightly and scrutinised Dick Breden. 'Where're you coming from, here? I don't get you.'

Breden shrugged. 'I'm curious. I like to know why people do things.'

SOMETHING WILD

'Go ask my shrink.' Redford walked to the door. 'I'll be in touch.'

'What on earth got into you?' Zamaroh demanded of Breden, the moment the door swung shut. 'Quizzing him like he was a convict?'

'That's my job. Something doesn't ring true,' replied Breden. 'I'm not sure what it is, I just know it's big.'

'Like what?' asked Zamaroh contemptuously. 'It's nothing to a rock star to get on a plane. Don't be so provincial, for God's sake.'

Breden turned his gaze upon Sarah. 'What do you think?' he asked.

'He's a rock star,' she replied, 'and I'd say they operate on different rules to the rest of us. We should factor that in before we judge anything as odd.'

Breden pondered her answer, before giving a musing 'hm'.

'I think it went rather well,' said Savage, on his own trajectory. 'You mugged up pretty well, Sarah. I think we might just have a deal here, so we need to establish if there is any reason why we might not want to add John Redford to our illustrious list of clients. Redford is a rock star, he's supposed to be bad. I need to know just how bad he is. There's acceptably bad, and there's smearing shit all over our name and reputation bad. Dick, you think there's something fishy. Follow it up.'

Oh no, the best private investigator in London hunting out Redford's skeletons. Sarah was still reeling from this when Savage turned to her. 'You work on this together with Dick.'

'I'm sorry?' She tried desperately hard not to understand what Savage was asking her.

'What's the big deal? Good God, woman, you look like I just asked you to walk through fire. This is part of the work, going forward. You will get on with it if you want your rather hefty fees to continue.' He turned to Breden. 'You do the broad brush stuff. Background, where and how he grew up, what he's done since, financial arrangements, embarrassments, hobbies, homes, the works.' He turned back to Sarah. 'If in a week's time, I'm happy with all the preliminaries, and we have a deal, you delve into the man's soul, find out what's there, what he loves, what he hates, what he can't live without, what, if anything, he'd kill for. You rattle him and his cage until the skeletons come tumbling out.'

'And how do I manage that?' Sarah struggled to say.

'You'll find a way.'

Sarah spent a blissful but poignant weekend with Georgie, Jacob and Alex. Her brother was flying off to Peru, and they all tried to make the most of his last few hours in London for more than two months. They walked the baby in the autumn sunshine and lay with him on the grass

239

in Carlyle Square Gardens. On Sunday, Alex checked the last of his packing and shared an emotional goodbye with his sister, nephew and uncle.

Sarah took his face in her hands and kissed his forehead. 'Good luck, Al, and keep safe, eh? Promise me.'

'I will, don't worry about me. You keep yourself safe, in every way.'

She took his meaning loud and clear and smiled with a reassurance she didn't completely feel. 'I will. Don't you worry about *me*.'

Sarah felt sorrow mixed with pride as the taxi bore Alex off for an adventure they had all doubted he would ever be well enough to take.

That Sunday night, after she had put Georgie to bed, Jacob set off for Golders Green and a night of independence. Sarah heated up the meat loaf he had left her, then sought the refuge of sleep. Georgie was sleeping better now, leaving her undisturbed with the dreams and fears which always seemed to ambush her under cover of darkness.

Monday morning saw Jacob reinstalled as a baby sitter and Sarah back in Goldsteins on the Leaker quest. Perhaps if she did find the culprit, she could take her fifty grand bonus and refuse the Redford assignment. Dreaming of it, she ran into PJ again in the Ladies, this time by accident. PJ was applying mascara.

'Hi,' said Sarah lightly. 'How're you doing?'

'Shit, actually,' PJ replied, with surprising candour. 'My boyfriend dumped me a few weeks ago.'

'Ah,' said Sarah. 'That is shitty.'

'You might know him,' said PJ, turning to face Sarah. 'Giovanni di Castiglio.' PJ spoke the name with contempt, and longing.

Sarah shook her head. 'Why should I have known him?'

'You live in Carlyle Square, yeah?'

'Yeah, I do.' *God*, news travelled fast here.

'So does he. Number eighteen.'

'Opposite side of the square,' answered Sarah. 'Amazing how you can live so close to people and have no idea who they might be. Or what they might be up to.'

'Not if you keep your eyes open,' replied PJ, with a hint of a smile.

Sarah cocked her head. 'Meaning?'

'Well, as it happens, I live down the road from our chief executive.'

'*Do* you?' asked Sarah with interest. 'And?'

'Let's just say I've observed that Mrs Savage has something of a penchant for afternoon tea. Particularly on Wednesdays.'

'You mean afternoon delight?' guessed Sarah.

PJ smirked. 'You said it, not me.' She dropped her mascara into her make-up bag and snapped shut the clasp.

'Just as a matter of interest,' mused Sarah, 'how would you know?'

PJ gave her a dismissive look. 'You never taken a sickie?'

The day passed and PJ's comments faded. Sarah was extra vigilant in her search for the Leaker, but got nowhere. Tuesday and Wednesday came and went and neither she, nor the cameras, delivered the Leaker. Savage and Zamaroh grew increasingly nervous and irritable. On Thursday, short of inspiration, sick of office politics, Sarah decided to stay at home. The sun was shining, the garden square was radiant, and she felt like having a day lounging on the grass with Georgie.

Her mobile stayed silent until just before lunchtime. She grabbed it up, before it could wake Georgie, sleeping on a blanket.

'Yeah?'

'Sarah? James here. Great news. John Redford has signed.'

'That's fantastic,' replied Sarah with wildly mixed feelings. 'The biggest rock-star syndication yet. We've beaten the Leaker.'

'I hope so.'

'Got a good contract with Redford?'

'Pretty good. Fourteen pages which boil down to Goldsteins undertaking to structure, price and lead a bond issue backed by the catalogue of his hits. He, in turn, has warranted that he knows of no prior incident, encumbrance or claim which could threaten the viability of the deal,' recited Savage.

'Has he?'

'I sincerely doubt there are any dark secrets lurking there. Breden's turned up nothing so far.'

'You've decided he's kosher?'

'Enough to sign a mandate letter and certificate of undertaking. If we, or you, find anything along the way we don't like, then that becomes a condition adverse and we pull the deal. It'd be embarrassing, but not disastrous. What *would* be a disaster is to miss something and have it come out while we're launching the issue, or during the life of the bond. Especially if we decide to hold it all ourselves.'

'Will you?'

'That depends partly on what you came up with.'

'That's what worries me, James. There's too much riding on this. I'm almost guaranteed to fail. Rock stars aren't exactly my field of expertise.'

'Reading people is your expertise.'

'I don't know, James. The man's got to be a real pro at protecting his private life. Nearly twenty years at the top and he's probably had his privacy violated so many times he's become an expert at concealment. It's so easy to get it wrong.'

'Come on, Sarah. You're always saying to give you something interesting, something sexy.'

'This is so hot someone could get burned.'

'You've never cared about that in the past. The riskier the better as far as you were concerned, if I remember rightly.'

'Maybe I've lost my appetite for risks. I don't want the job, James. Can't you just accept that? Dick'll do it fine.'

'Dick won't be able to get the access you will.'

'He'll find a way. He always does.'

'Not as good a way as I've got for you.'

'What d'you mean?' Sarah asked, suspicion and panic mounting.

'You go on tour with him for two weeks.'

'I do *what*?'

'I told him and his manager that you'd need to spend many hours going over the business in general, and picking apart all his contracts, to assure Goldsteins that there were no liens there shouldn't be. They said fine, but they are in the middle of a world tour. I left it with them, made it pretty clear they would need to find the time. Cawdor rang back, said you were invited to join them for a two-week leg.'

Sarah couldn't speak.

'New York, London, Paris and Venice with one of the sexiest men on the planet, or so I'm told, and five thousand pounds a day. What more could you want?'

Chapter Four

ONE HOUR LATER, Sarah and Georgie arrived in Golders Green. Sarah carried a sleepy Georgie from the car. Jacob's garden welcomed them with scent of honeysuckle. He was at the door to meet them.

Sarah looked with love into his face. This man had been a surrogate father to her and her brother. When Sarah and Alex's parents were killed, the children were brought back to London by Sarah's father's sister, Isla. They came to this place, Rotherwick Road, in north London, and Jacob was their next-door neighbour. Isla was kind, but too caught up in her work to give the children the attention they needed. Jacob provided warm meals and kind hands to tend their bloodied knees and broken hearts.

His wife had died the year before, and Sarah and Alex's arrival gave him something new to live for. The children's hearts never did heal, but they learned to love again. Jacob was their love, their friend, their mentor, their security.

Jacob had been Sarah's salvation. She couldn't imagine life without him. She feared the loss of Jacob more than her own death. He was seventy-eight, still sprightly, but every new sign of his ageing rent her with pain. She kissed his cheek.

'Hello, sweetie.' He turned to Georgie, who was waking up rapidly, fuelled with excitement by Jacob and his new surroundings. 'Hello, my beautiful boy.' He kissed Georgie's forehead, and the baby squirmed and giggled. 'Come on in.'

He led Sarah and Georgie into his house and Sarah felt once again the balm that had saved her childhood. There were roses on the kitchen table, a chicken baking in the oven, and a bottle of red Burgundy breathing on the sideboard. Jacob took out two of his giant glasses.

'Like one?'

'Love one.'

She put Georgie on a mat on the floor with a selection of toys and took a seat at the table.

'So where're you off to then?' asked Jacob, handing her a glass.

Sarah took a mouthful of wine. 'Is it that obvious?'

'You ring up and announce that you're coming round. You're fizzing with excitement, and trepidation, trying to act cool. I can practically see a phantom suitcase by your side. So what is it? Trip with some new boyfriend?'

'No new boyfriend,' said Sarah. 'I'm going to New York. On tour with the rock star for two weeks.'

'What? That Redfern fella?' Jacob sat down opposite Sarah.

'Redford.'

'And what're you supposed to do with him?'

'Check him out. Shake him till his skeletons come rattling out. If there are no nasty ones, Goldsteins do this deal; if there are, we pull out.'

Jacob got up and doled out chicken and roast potatoes. He didn't speak until they both had steaming plates before them.

'What about Georgie? Two weeks is a long time.'

'I know. I'll try to come back for a few nights, but it'll still be horrible.'

'So why do you want to go?'

Because part of her had loved John Redford from that first passionate night in the wilderness, loved him all the more for being the father of her beloved child.

'Because I feel I have to, Jacob.'

The old man gave her a long, probing look. 'I know I can't tell you what to do with yourself, but for my sake and your son's, look after yourself, sweetie, and I'll take care of your son.'

Sarah felt a sickening mixture of elation and agony. She would leave her baby for two weeks, to be with a man. The lover and the mother rose up in her, in clamouring, denouncing opposition.

Sarah made her way through the thronging airport at JFK, immigration, customs, baggage claim, out onto the chill forecourt where the taxis lumbered up and sped away. Pulling her coat tight around her, she waited her turn. The sun hung bright in the sky, making her squint. It always seemed to be sunny in New York. Each time she arrived, she had been welcomed by radiant sun, summer or winter.

Sarah's turn came. She dumped her luggage in the boot, sat back on the cracked plastic seats of the cab, and smiled to herself, thinking of Georgie. That morning, Sarah had breastfed Georgie for the last time. The finality of it left her utterly bereft. She feared he would no longer be her baby in quite the same way.

After she'd finished feeding him, she took her son in her arms, held his head to her lips, breathed him in.

'I have to go away, my love. But I'll be back. I'll think of you all the time. I'll send you love all the time, I'll . . .' she faltered as tears threatened to overwhelm her. She would not cry in front of him, frighten him with her sorrow. She fought for composure, and when she had found it she held her child away from her so that she could see his eyes. 'I love you, my sweetheart. Mama loves you.'

She brushed tears away now as the taxi pulled up at the SoHo Grand, a strange, red-brick, very modern hotel, almost like an unimaginative apartment complex in Marylebone. This impression was immediately dispelled as Sarah walked into the ground-floor foyer, with its brickwork, industrial metal and glass stairway, watched over by a pair of bronze dogs.

She padded up the stairs to the first-floor reception area and waited to be checked in. Leather pouffes and well-padded sofas marked the lounging area to the right of Reception. Lavish palms with blunt-cut leaves cast Far Eastern shadows. Sarah felt as if she had stepped back into the Jazz Age.

The receptionist straightened when Sarah announced her name and handed over her passport to check in. She was immediately escorted to her room. Correction, into her penthouse suite.

Sarah dumped her handbag and walked excitedly through a huge sitting room to a French door opening onto the biggest roof terrace she had ever seen. She let herself out, gasping as the chill autumn wind whipped around her. Manhattan stretched before her, midtown straight ahead, the East River to her right. A wooden sunlounger lay next to an arrangement of mini firs and decorative cabbages.

She let herself back into her suite. The bedroom was deliciously cosy and snug, with another wonderful sun-drenched view. Wouldn't this be great, if only she didn't have to work! The realisation brought her down with a bump. No such thing as a free lunch, she mouthed to herself, as she finally acknowledged the glowing message light on the telephone.

There were four messages, all from Strone Cawdor, asking her to call him. Take a laxative, she thought crudely, hanging up. She quickly grabbed up her bag and coat and quit the balm of the hotel for a bit of street New York. She loved this city. The energy, the anonymity, the possibility that lay behind every secret smile and tinted window.

She returned to the hotel in time for an exaggeratedly late lunch. Back upstairs, she took out her electronic key and let herself into her suite. She paused on the threshold, senses screaming. Something was wrong. She felt a presence.

'At fucking last. Where the hell have you been?'

Strone Cawdor sauntered out of the bathroom. He walked rudely past Sarah and sat down with his back to her. 'Didn't you get my messages? I left four.'

'Get out of my room,' she said, her voice low. She stood completely still, her face devoid of emotion.

Strone forced out a laugh. 'Did you say *your* room? Two thousand dollars a night, with my signature on your bill, did you say *your room*?'

Sarah picked up a phone. She tapped out three numbers. 'Security? Yes, you can help. There's a man in my—'

'Shut the fuck up!' screamed Strone. He slammed his fist on the phone, cutting the connection. 'Stupid bitch. If the press got hold of this . . .'

'Better get out, then.'

Strone made a stabbing motion at Sarah with his index finger, then rushed from the room. She slammed the door behind him, then leaned back against it, breathing hard, shaking. The doorbell rang. She peered through the peephole: Security. She opened the door and two men rushed in.

'You had an intruder, ma'am?' asked one, eyes scanning the room, while the other crossed it in three long strides.

'It was a misunderstanding,' Sarah found herself saying.

She managed to convince the Security men that she was fine, the victim of nothing more than an error of judgment. Just as she closed the door on them, the phone rang.

'Sarah?'

Her heart jumped. 'Yes?'

'It's John. I'm sorry about what happened. Can I come and see you?'

Redford was wearing faded sweat pants and a white T-shirt. His hair was unwashed, combed only by his fingers. There was a sheen of sweat glistening on his face. Sarah could almost taste him.

'Sorry about the gear.' He gestured to his outfit, walking into Sarah's suite. 'I just came from the gym.'

Sarah remembered every inch of his body, knew it was worked to perfection. She tried to push the memory from her mind.

'Look, Sarah, I'm really, really sorry about Strone.'

'He thought that because you might be paying Goldsteins a fee, he owns everyone who works for them . . .' She paused, her temper still blazing, but checked.

'He's a hothead,' said Redford quietly, 'but he's got a good heart. Problem is, way we live, it's easy to lose touch. He needs a reality-check. We all do. We've been on tour over a year now, and the pressure gets to you.' He saw Sarah looking at her suitcase. 'You're not thinking of running again?'

'Absolutely I am. If this is the way it starts out.'

'Come on, Sarah. Give him a second chance. Please. Everyone makes mistakes. He's actually a nice guy under the bluster. You've got to have a lot of front to do what he does. There's so many people trying to rip me off, he has to play the hard man. He has to be in control the whole time.'

'Yeah well, not of me. I don't see why I should suffer him.'

'All right. How 'bout this deal's important to me?'

'Why's that?' she asked softly.

'You *know* why.'

They stared at each other, searching one another's eyes, for one brief moment dropping their act. Redford's question was all too visible. *Why did you walk out on me?* Sarah turned away and went to the window.

Redford came up behind her. 'How can I make this right?'

Sarah turned to face him. '*I'll* sort it out. I'll get his pass key and I'll pay for my own suite. If he tries to get in here again, I'll ring the press.'

Redford smiled. 'All right, you've got a deal. But look, there's no need for you to pick up the tab. These rooms cost a shitload of money.'

'I'm not an impoverished banker, John. I work only out of choice, not necessity,' she lied. 'I long ago earned myself the luxury of working only when I choose. Strone had better treat me with kid gloves from now on. No one owns me—got it? If I stay, it's for Goldsteins' sake, and because this deal's important to you.'

'So you will stay?'

'For now.'

Sarah pulled back her hair from her face and paced. Redford watched her and waited. She paused by the sofa, gripping its back, keeping it as a barrier between them.

'Can I ask you a question?'

'Yeah, sure.'

'Does Strone know we know each other—*knew* each other?' A blush spread over her cheeks.

Redford shook his head. 'No, he doesn't.'

Sarah felt relieved. She flicked a glance at him. He was watching her.

'I'm assuming Goldsteins don't know either,' he said softly.

'No,' replied Sarah. 'They don't.'

'Well, no point telling them now, is there?'

Sarah met his eye, grateful. 'No, there's not.'

'Good. I'm glad we sorted that out.'

Sarah felt adrift. Redford's intuiting what she needed and giving it to her so elegantly that she was spared any appearance of having shown her hand, disarmed her. She didn't want him to be so reasonable, or so generous.

'Look, I've got to clear my mind, calm down.'

He took the hint, raised a hand in farewell. 'I'm gone.'

Sarah watched the door closing behind him. Why did he have to be so damned sensitive? He was a rock star, for God's sake. He was supposed to be a selfish egomaniac. He must want this deal very badly, she thought bad-temperedly, to be so nice to her.

The bell rang five minutes later. A bellboy handed over a room key, and an envelope. Sarah bent the plastic key double and threw it in the bin, then tore open the envelope. *Dear Sarah, Would you like to start the information process? We can meet you at five thirty in my suite, if that suits you. Strone.* The uncharacteristically conciliatory tone was probably as close to an apology as Strone could come. Sarah picked up the phone.

Strone answered with a bored-sounding, 'Yeah?'

'I'll see you in twenty minutes.'

247

They sat round a glass and steel table. John Redford had changed into faded black jeans and a black polo-neck jersey.

Strone looked over at her. He had swung between relieved and edgy since she had walked in. She wondered what Redford had said to him.

'Would you like something to drink?' he asked her.

'Espresso would be nice, and a bottle of still water.'

He dialled room service and recited their orders. Redford had still mineral water, room-temperature, with lemon.

'How un-American,' observed Sarah. 'Americans normally have lashings of ice.'

'Freezes your digestion.'

'Into healthy living?'

'Aren't you? You look like you are.'

'I like to mix it up a little,' said Sarah. 'Stops me becoming obsessive.'

'Are you obsessive?' asked Redford with interest. 'About what?'

'Details,' said Sarah with a smile. 'Shall we start?'

Redford leaned back in his chair, giving Sarah a faint grin, as if to say, round one to you.

'How do we do this?' asked Strone.

'It's like a tango,' said Sarah. 'Only I'm the man. I lead and you follow.'

'Lead on.' Strone gave her a slow smile.

Sarah turned to Redford, adopting her impersonal banker persona.

'I need to know who you are, who buys your records, for how much and where. I need to clarify your figures, sales, royalties, any and all deductions down the line. Some of this I've seen, but I need a deeper explanation. I'll need to know all about all your contractual professional relationships, bank accounts, assets, homes, cars, shareholdings, why you need the money. I need to know what your plans are for the next ten years, professionally, personally, if it's relevant. I'll write a worst-case scenario, a mid- or most-likely-case scenario, and a best-case scenario. I need to know if there's anyone who might make claims against you, claiming *they* wrote or co-wrote your songs, or claiming anything else that might give them rights over Redford Inc.'

'Wow.' Redford raked his fingers through his hair.

'I know it's not pleasant,' she said, 'but I'm not doing this for fun, or from curiosity. I'm doing this because Goldsteins have a duty of care to provide all the relevant information. This isn't personal.'

'It's personal to me,' said Redford.

'I know, and I'll try to be as sensitive as I can.'

'Isn't there another way, a less intrusive way?' asked Strone.

'Not if you want this deal to work,' replied Sarah. 'The investors down the line will require this information and they will go through all the minutiae with a fine-tooth comb until they're satisfied. Believe me, there's no other way.'

'All right. I don't like it, but I'll buy it,' said Strone. He turned to Redford. 'Yeah?'

'Yeah.'

Then he turned back to Sarah. 'John Redford started writing songs when he was fourteen. His grandmother taught him piano; he sang and accompanied himself.'

Sarah suddenly had an image of a lonely child singing out his dreams.

'Ah, you don't want the nostalgia,' said Strone, utterly misreading Sarah's faraway look. 'Let's stick to the numbers, then. John Redford has made a series of deals with record companies over the years, getting better and bigger all the time. But let me tell you where all the money goes before the last bit trickles down to the artist.'

He bent over and pulled a CD and a calculator from his briefcase. He banged the CD on the table. 'Start off with the price you pay if you walk into, say, W. H. Smith. £14.99. Take off £2.62 for VAT, that leaves you with £12.37,' he said, rapidly tapping out calculations. 'About £3.72 of that goes to Smiths. That leaves £8.65. Ten per cent of that, 86 pence, goes to the music publisher and songwriter, both of whom, happily, is John, leaving £7.79. John gets a twenty per cent royalty, that's £1.56. Let's say he sells a million copies of the CD—that's a total royalty of, let's say, one and a half million pounds to John. But out of that comes what's called the "free goods factor", a rip-off supposed to cover the CDs the record company gives away free to promote the album; that takes fifteen per cent, or £234,000. Then he has to pay another rip-off deduction to the record company: a *reserve* takes another twenty per cent, or £265,200, leaving John with £1,060,800, plus his publishing royalty, which would equate to £860,000, giving him £1,920,800. His agent takes five per cent, that's £96,040. Then I take ten per cent as his manager and business manager, that's £182,476. Then the record company deducts the recording costs, which would be around £200,000, and fifty per cent of the video production costs of £50,000. Legal, accounting and other business costs take around another £200,000. That leaves John Redford, superstar, with £1,192,284 net on a gross sale of £14,990,000.'

Sarah took out her own calculator and tapped out the sums. 'Which amounts to only seven point nine per cent. That's outrageous!'

Strone smiled. 'And *that's* before tax.'

'The penniless rock star,' said Sarah wryly.

'Course, John sells throughout the world. One million per album's just his UK take, so he has the volume to bring in the big bucks, but it makes the point.'

Sarah nodded. 'Presumably the tours bring in a lot of money?'

'Now they do,' replied Strone. 'When we wind up this tour, we estimate 3.4 million people will have come to fifty-nine John Redford concerts. With an average ticket price of forty pounds, that grosses 136 million pounds. From that, the deductions run as follows.' Strone recited all the facts and figures from memory.

'Could you get copies of all the back-up information, all the sources of those figures you've just quoted me, to Goldsteins in London?'

Strone looked uneasy.

'Is there a problem?' asked Sarah.

'There're over forty different companies for different tax jurisdictions.'

'We're used to paper mountains,' Sarah said breezily. 'If you could have someone supply me with the summary you've just given me, I can start to play around more with the structuring.'

'You do that stuff?' asked Strone.

'What do you think I do?'

'Ask difficult questions.'

'I do that too. That's stage one. The structuring's stage two.'

'Don't think me rude,' said Redford, 'I'm just curious. How did you get into all this? What qualifications do you have?'

'A double first from Cambridge in mathematics and philosophy; eight years in the City. Will that do?'

'You don't look like a mathematician,' said Strone.

'Jesus,' said Sarah, 'and I thought the City was sexist.'

Redford was glaring at Strone.

'Do you think I'm some wide-eyed innocent who has come along for a bit of PR?' Sarah asked. 'That you could flash a smart hotel suite at me, give me a backstage pass, a few good dinners and I'd go home and say, "Hey, guys, had a great time, we've got to do this deal"? I'm sorry, but it doesn't work like that with me.' Sarah got to her feet.

Redford stood up too. 'Hey, calm down. Don't you think you're over-reacting a little here?'

'Are you so used to sleeping with groupies you can't get your mind round the concept of a woman with brains?' Sarah asked coldly.

Redford stared at her in anger. 'That's a trashy stereotype.'

'Exactly,' said Sarah. 'Get the point. See how you like it.' She walked to the door.'

Back in her suite, Sarah cursed herself. She sat down heavily on the bed, head in hands. How could she lose her temper so easily? What had happened to her poker-player's sang-froid? She got up and stumbled to the bathroom, where she splashed her face with cold water, then she rang Jacob.

'How's everything?'

'Hello, sweetie. Everything's just fine. So far so good.'

'I miss him so much it hurts,' she said. 'Give him a huge hug and kiss from Mama, will you?'

'I will. Now, tell me. How are things your end?'

'Horrible. I want to come home.'

'Aw, sweetie. Look, you don't have to stay. You can always walk away.'

'Yeah, in theory.'

'In practice. Why don't we toss for it?'

Sarah giggled. Jacob could almost always joke her out of a mood.

'Got a quid in my hand. Heads you stay, and you shut up and like it. Tails you quit. Ready?'

'As ever.'

Sarah heard a coin slapped down on a table.

'Heads,' said Jacob sadly. 'You stay.'

There was a knock at the door.

'Hang on a sec, Jacob.' She headed warily for the door.

John Redford stood on the threshold. 'Am I interrupting?'

Sarah spun round. 'Come in,' she said over her shoulder. She picked up the phone in the sitting room. 'Sorry, Jacob, gotta go. *I'll* toss next time.' She hung up and stood observing Redford with a critical eye.

'You'll toss a coin?' he asked. 'What for?'

'To decide whether I stay or whether I go,' she answered with provocative nonchalance.

'You make decisions on the fall of a coin?'

'I'm a gambler. Don't take it personally.'

'Dammit, Sarah, I do take it personally. This isn't a game to me.' Redford paced across the room, staring at the carpet. 'So you're off?'

'I'm staying, actually. I suppose I really ought to see you in concert tomorrow night.'

Redford took a deep breath, reining in his anger. 'What I'd come to say was, let's try and get off to a better start. Will you come out to dinner with me tonight?'

Redford's black Range Rover dropped them somewhere on the Upper West Side. As they walked into the restaurant together, faces turned, eyes tracked their progress like radar. Poses were struck, envy like

251

missiles launched at Sarah. The couple took their seats in a booth at the back of the room, well hidden from onlookers by a lavish arrangement of pussy willow.

'Jesus,' breathed Sarah. 'This happens all the time?'

Redford nodded.

'How d'you stand it?'

'I hate it, but it goes with the territory.'

Sarah shook her head. 'If looks could kill, I really would be dead. I don't think I've ever been the subject of such envy.'

'Some women love it.'

'I'm not some women. Don't take this the wrong way, but reflected glory isn't my thing.'

Redford laughed. 'I only wish more women felt like you.' Just then, a woman sashayed past, ostentatiously flipping a business card onto their table. Redford ignored it.

Sarah picked it up and read aloud the written message. '"Call me for the fuck of the century." *What?* That a common occurrence?' she asked.

'You wouldn't believe just how common.'

'You know what it feels like to be a woman then.'

'To be a very beautiful woman, maybe, with more propositions than you could handle in a hundred lifetimes. Isn't that how it is for you?'

'Not quite.' Sarah fiddled with her watch, growing wary.

'Please don't get all offended,' Redford said with feeling, 'but you're one of the most beautiful women I've ever seen.'

Sarah looked at him in disbelief. 'I'm two stone overweight, I have permanent black bags under my eyes, and my skin looks like second-hand tinfoil.'

The lights were dim, a candle flickered on the table between them, Sarah's skin glowed peaches and cream. Her feline eyes shone, the curve of her cheekbone and the fullness of her lips gave her a voluptuousness that threatened to spill over. Her tousled hair fell down her back.

'You're looking in the wrong mirror,' said Redford softly.

Sarah smiled. 'Why do you go out at all if you get all this attention?'

'Should I order room service for the rest of my life? I thought you might like to go out, sort of neutral territory, so that we could talk, like normal people. Not rock stars and bankers.'

'Sounds good to me,' replied Sarah, appalled by the prospect.

'What will you drink?'

'Some red wine would be lovely.'

Redford scanned the list. He suggested a 1983 St Julien.

The wine waiter brought the bottle. When he'd disappeared, Sarah and Redford sipped for a while in silence as if collecting themselves.

'I'm sorry about today,' said Redford. 'Strone was an asshole, going into your room, but the rest of the stuff, I don't get it. I'm thinking you're a little bit sensitive?'

'Of course I'm bloody sensitive, but that doesn't get you two off the hook. You both acted as if you could say what you wanted, with no need for consideration. I was trying to tell you I wouldn't put up with two weeks of that.'

A profound weariness seemed to settle over Redford.

'What's wrong?' asked Sarah, puzzled. 'What have I said?'

Redford gave a weak smile. 'Something that no one else has said for a very long time.'

'Meaning?'

'Meaning that no one speaks straight to me, no one tells me where to get off, because they all want something from me. They take the shit so they'll get the goodies. So you dish out more shit 'cos you know you're being taken for a ride, and next thing you know, it's normal and all relationships are like that. You start forgetting how it should be.'

'Other people *must* talk to you like I do.'

'I wish they did. You're a major pain in the ass, but you're a good pain.'

Sarah laughed.

'How come you manage it?'

'Well, I suppose you said it yourself. I don't want anything from you.'

'Nothing?' asked Redford, slowly.

'What might I want?' asked Sarah, wariness mixing with the thrill of it all.

'Heck, I don't know. Jewellery, money, an apartment, a scalp.'

Sarah chuckled. 'I've got jewellery, I have a beautiful house, I have money, enough to enjoy life, not so much that I don't have a purpose. As for your scalp . . . Don't even joke about it. I should warn you, my mother had some Indian blood. She was about one-fifth Cheyenne.'

Redford looked at her, head on one side. 'I see it now, your colouring, your high cheekbones, that long, glossy hair. Mm. I had better be careful, hadn't I? How'd she get to Britain?'

'She didn't. She was American, from New Orleans.'

'Now *that's* a great city.'

'It is. I lived there till I was eight.'

'What then?'

'My brother and I moved to London.'

Redford looked puzzled. 'Your mother? Your father?'

Sarah looked into her wineglass. 'They were dead.'
'Oh, Sarah, I'm sorry.' He took a gulp of water. 'How?'
'Car crash.'
He turned pale, like he'd seen a spectre.
'What is it?' asked Sarah, alarmed.
'My mother was killed in a car wreck. When I was twelve.'
'Oh, John.'
'Might as well have killed my father too. He hung on for four years, then blew his brains out with the rabbit gun.'
Sarah reached out and grasped Redford's hand.
He turned his eyes to hers. The pain in them lacerated her, a broken mirror of her own torment. For a long while neither of them spoke.

Sarah woke late. She lay in bed for a while, going over the evening before. She was horrified by Redford's loss, for his own sake, and because it somehow united them even more.
She pushed herself out of bed with a groan. She thought about her boy, and felt herself almost implode with longing. She shook her head, took a long shower, dressed and refocused herself on business. She rang Strone at ten. He sounded abstracted.
'When shall we get together?' Sarah asked.
'No can do today, sorry.'
'Oh,' said Sarah, pausing. 'Why's that?'
'It's concert day, Sarah. Do you have any idea of what's involved?'
'None whatsoever. But I'd love to find out,' she said with genuine enthusiasm. 'Perhaps I could shadow you for the day.'
Strone laughed. 'All right. Why don't you come early to the Beacon with me, see the stage and the set-up, sound check and all that jazz. I'll pick you up at six. How's that sound?'
'Like a deal.'

At six thirty Sarah and Strone arrived at the Beacon Theatre on the Upper West Side. Redford's picture, a study of an enigmatic gaze, watched them as they entered. Strone nodded to a black-clad, sharp-eyed security man.
'Everything OK?'
'Yeah. No hassles.'
'Good.' Strone swept on. Sarah slowed and gazed around her. The Beacon was a rococo paradise with scrolling, gilt, a mural of a neo-classical utopia, a balustrade, and stained glass. Sarah quickened her steps to catch up with Strone as he walked backstage. About forty men

and women hurried purposefully back and forth across the stage, tending to a series of wires and electronic boxes. Many wore headpieces with small microphones into which they whispered almost constantly. At Strone's appearance, the busyness turned to frenzy. Strone stood still like a centurion watching his troops prepare for battle.

'Tonight's show'll be a miniature of a normal John Redford set,' Strone explained to Sarah. 'He's done five shows at Madison Square Garden over the last two weeks. Twenty thousand seats a shot. Tonight's his goodbye-to-New-York gig. Intimate, you know. Real. Two thousand people. It's—'

Strone fell silent. Sarah followed his eyes to a woman with long blonde hair and high black boots who was approaching purposefully.

'Hello, Zena,' he said wearily.

'Don't *hello Zena* me. Don't you even speak to me. You promised me Ray would get a hike three weeks ago, and what do I see in his payslip? Diddly squat. You know he plays bass like an angel. He *carries* the show. Jake got a rise and he can hardly strum.'

'Zena, Zena, Zena. No one doubts how good Ray is. We all know he's a genius. That's why he plays for a genius.'

Zena opened her mouth and looked as if she were going to lunge at Strone. The manager raised his hand in a pacifying gesture. 'Now just calm down. I do what I can. I'm subject to all sorts of constraints. I—'

'Oh bullshit. You do what you want to do, you're the all-powerful Strone.' Her voice leached sarcasm. 'Mr Potent, don't we all know it.'

Strone's voice dropped an octave. 'Now you're overstepping the mark. I'm busy. Please leave us. You're just a sad little groupie who got lucky. Now disappear and do what you do best. Quit hassling me.'

The blonde's eyes filled with tears of rage. 'You bastard.' She spat her words at Strone before turning on her high heels and running off.

'Stupid bitch,' said Strone.

'That happen a lot?' asked Sarah, still reeling from the viciousness of the exchange.

'All the time. You wouldn't believe the pecking order here. Jake, the lead guitar, gets a rise. Stupid prick blabs about it. So now Ray wants one, and if I give him one, all the other musicians, and their groupie girlfriends'll come clamouring.'

'You don't seem to have a very high opinion of the people in this business,' observed Sarah.

Strone gave her an appraising look. 'For the most part, they're either bastards or fools. 'Scuse me a sec, honey.'

Sarah mooched about, hands in pockets, trying to look as if she belonged in this world. Driven by hunger pangs she headed for the catering cart and bought a hot dog. She leaned against a huge metal trunk and tucked in.

'So who are you then?' asked a friendly voice.

Sarah turned and studied her interrogator. He was a man in his forties, with long wavy hair and brown, amused eyes.

'Who are *you*?' she countered.

'I'm Ray Waters.'

'Ah.' Sarah took a flying guess. 'John Redford's bass guitarist.'

'The one and only. And you're his latest tottie.'

Sarah thought she must have misheard. 'Excuse me?'

'Tottie. T. O. T. T. I. E.'

'My God,' said Sarah. 'You're surprisingly literate for an arsehole.'

Strone reappeared silently at Sarah's shoulder. 'I see you're getting acquainted.'

Sarah jumped. 'You nearly gave me a heart attack.'

'That's his style,' said Ray. 'In-tim-id-ation. Makes him feel the big man.' He turned to Strone. 'Zena told me about your run-in. I don't appreciate you badmouthing my woman.'

'Perhaps you ought to watch your own mouth then,' said Sarah.

'Where's the fun in that, Tottie?' He grinned and walked off.

'Is that how I'm seen, as John's tottie?' Sarah asked incredulously.

'Think about it,' said Strone. 'You're on the same floor of the same hotel. And you have no other reason to be travelling with him that they know of. Seeing as the deal's confidential, tottie's a pretty good cover for you. Don't knock it.'

'I do knock it,' she said with irritation.

'Many women would leap at that position, real or imagined.'

'Many must fulfil it, I would have thought.'

Strone gave her a hard stare. 'Well, I'd say that was John's business, wouldn't you?'

Sarah shrugged. 'Why's it such a big deal to stay in the same hotel as him, and why specifically the same floor?'

'None of the entourage are allowed to stay in the same hotel. Just me.'

'Doesn't he get on with the band?'

'He's not close to them, no. He does his thing, they do theirs. They come together on the night and it works. Offstage the chemistry's different. He doesn't want to see them weaving and screaming down the hallway towards him at one in the morning.'

Sarah smiled. 'Having met Ray and Zena I can well understand that. But why break a rule and put me in the same hotel?'

Strone shrugged. 'Beats me.' He studied Sarah for a moment. 'He's a man of mystery, isn't he, our John.'

Sarah had to get out from under Strone's gaze. She made her excuses and headed off to the Ladies. She thought about what it was to be John Redford. All those people on the payroll, all the gear, all the preparation. How did Redford cope with the responsibility of it all? Behind the circus atmosphere, the apparently free-living roadies, were wives, children and mortgages. Under the stardust and greasepaint lurked bills and the spectre of unemployment. Redford Inc was a one-man show. There was no substitute if he turned in sick, if he didn't feel like going on. He was trapped in something much greater—the Show—and it had to go on, repeated in a hundred different cities over eighteen months of a marathon world tour. All the leaving and arriving, the rootlessness, the entourage in one hotel, the star apart in another. No wonder the atmosphere was isolating, nihilistic. There was no long-term consequence to anything; hit town, move on. Like a raiding party.

Sarah shook herself, tried to free herself from something that felt almost sinister.

The strobe lights scanned the auditorium like weapons of war. The crowd smelt of sweat, perfume long evaporated with excitement. Their eyes flickered back and forth to the stage as the hour approached. Sarah could feel their anticipation, verging on hunger, a craving for the man himself.

The crowd hushed as three black backing singers in short, tight, sequinned dresses undulated onto the stage and took up their places.

John Redford walked onstage, the crowd surged to their feet, roaring and screaming. Adrenaline pumped through Sarah. Redford wore jeans and a white T-shirt with cowboy boots. His face was radiant, wild. He raised his hand and a chord of music rose from backstage. His band came on and took up position at drums, keyboards, lead guitar, bass guitar, alto sax, tenor sax, trumpet and violin. When the roar of the crowd finally faded, Redford stepped into the spotlight and began to sing 'Come to Me', with a rock beat, whipping up the crowd.

Redford sang, roared, ran across the stage. There was something intensely sexual about the way he played the guitar. It hung at groin level, and the movements of his fingers plucking the strings conjured memories and fantasies. From her seat in the front row, Sarah could see sweat running down his face. She remembered how it tasted.

For the first time Redford looked at the crowd. His eyes ranged over the sea of faces. She felt herself yearning for his glance. She was so close,

257

perhaps ten feet away from him, but whether by accident or design, his eyes did not alight on her.

'Good evening,' he said with a complicit smile, voice low, seemingly utterly confident. The crowd roared back.

'It's great to be here, somewhere intimate, like the Beacon. Means you can see me, but you know what?' The crowd roared back, taking up the game. 'It means I can see *you*,' replied Redford, 'and not only that, but I can hear you too.' He smiled, gently parodying. '"He looks good, looks younger. What's he had done?" Or, "Can he really do it for seven hours?" Well, lemme tell you, I've given up tantric sex,' he announced. 'I now do tantric shopping. Shop for seven hours and never buy anything.' The crowd erupted into laughter.

This was where passion met the business of rock. Redford was the performer, the artist; striding the stage like a colossus, giving out what the audience so desperately craved.

He sang three more rock songs, fast paced and furious. What Sarah hadn't expected was how all the individual instruments and performers lived within the whole; live, all the instruments found their own voices and onstage, all the performers achieved a kind of nobility. But Redford still stood above them, undisputed King. Sarah wondered about the long road to his superstardom, the days when he was establishing himself, about the self-belief and the doubts, about how a boy with his history of pain could have cobbled himself together enough to hold a stage.

The set was suddenly plunged into darkness. When the sole spotlight came back on, Redford stood centre stage, alone with his acoustic guitar. He launched into the first of his ballads, 'How'. He moved slowly, dancing by himself, his voice low as he sang. 'How could I do what I did? How could I kill our love?' Sarah felt his pain, wondered who he was singing for.

She watched those closest to her, saw faces stripped of their defences, screens where emotions flickered unhindered, undefended. 'How can I win you back? How I'm going to love you this time, just give me one chance.' It was a seduction, slow and masterful and knowing. Every chord a caress, every word a kiss.

Sarah rarely went to concerts, perhaps because there was something in her that she feared was over-susceptible to a mass seduction. But she, as much as anyone, had a longing for oblivion, to be held in the arms of someone who understood, who sang out her pain, who drew it out and turned it into something beautiful. She could see that the hunger of the crowd was for meaning. John Redford showed them their souls, he showed them their hearts, he ennobled their emotions.

At that moment, Redford looked directly at her. She tried to look away but couldn't. His eyes held her in a current of sexual energy, pure and electrifying. He began to sing 'One Perfect Night'.

> 'One perfect night you came my way,
> With your uncertain smile,
> You stopped awhile in your wild flight,
> And you spent it with me.

> 'You smiled on me, you kissed my face,
> You let nature go her way,
> And you left without a trace,
> Leaving me with nothing but the memory,
> Of one perfect night.'

Sarah's face burned. He *had* to have been singing about their one perfect night. Every nuance of his words conjured up the memory of their night together.

She jumped as someone tapped her on the shoulder. Strone stood beside her. 'Come with me,' he mouthed.

Security men made way for them as they walked to the side of the arena, up a flight of stairs to the stage itself. Backstage, they stood watching until Redford finally walked offstage after a heroic two-and-a-half-hour performance. She gazed at the space he had filled, feeling exhilarated and drained, too. Strone's hand gently touched her shoulder.

"You see it now, don't you?' he asked. 'What he's all about. It's all right. We've all been there. First time I saw John in concert he brought me to tears. I signed him up that same night.'

Sarah turned to him, her eyes shining. 'Did you? When was that?'

'Long story. C'mon. I'll buy you dinner and tell you all about it.'

Sarah sat opposite Strone. She drank exquisite red wine for the second night in a row. Tonight there was a welcome anonymity to dinner. No one paid them any attention.

'Don't you have to go to John?' she asked Strone. 'He can't be alone after that.' She stopped herself with a brief, awkward smile. 'I suppose he's not alone. He's probably got fifty thousand lovers to choose from.'

Strone laughed. 'Don't go believing that old cliché. John's grown out of that. Normally does a load of meet 'n' greet. Record company execs, friends, journos, but not tonight. He did this show just for him, for the fun of playing in a small venue. So tonight he comes down alone. Meditates. Does his yoga and breathing, and goes to bed. Alone.'

'It seems so lonely,' she said, heart soaring involuntarily, 'after performing like that, singing your heart and soul out for all those people, then you go back to an anonymous hotel room, alone.'

'It *is* lonely. Why d'you think I love the guy? Why d'you think I'm here now, alone too in the relationship sense?'

'You love him?' asked Sarah with surprise.

'Course I love him. I found him when he was a boy—sixteen years old. I've seen it all. His ups and downs, his ambition, his courage. I've seen his talent, raw and wild. We've been there for each other through it all,' continued Strone. 'I see the glory and the worship and I see the pain and the loneliness and the sacrifice.'

'What sacrifice?' asked Sarah.

'The whole totally insane roller-coaster ride called rock and roll,' answered Strone. 'It drives you absolutely nuts sometimes.'

'So why do it?' asked Sarah. 'Why doesn't John just retire?'

Strone laughed. 'You saw him up there. Can you imagine what it feels like, to be the performer? The kick, the power, the high. That's the sweetest drug you'll ever take.'

'Tell me exactly how you met him,' Sarah asked, biting into steak.

Strone took a long sip of wine and his eyes became wistful. Sarah marvelled at the transformation in him. Redford's performance had exposed another side to Strone; perhaps he felt freer to show it because he could see how Sarah had responded to his star.

'It was twenty-two years ago. I had been an accountant for five years and I couldn't stand it any more. So I thought I'd try to use accounting to get me into music. I kind of had this dream that I would find a star and manage him. One day I quit my job in New Jersey and set out for the Wild West. After about a year I shipped up in Wyoming, in Jackson. I was nearly out of cash, so I was sleeping in barns. One night I went to a bar and I saw this boy, weaving through the tables, carrying a guitar, on his way to the stage. He just had something. He was young and beautiful and he had this wildness, but a great pathos in his eyes, as if he understood the world, aged sixteen. And then he opened his mouth.' Strone smiled. 'I literally got shivers up and down my spine. I knew he was *it*. I approached him afterwards, used practically my last dollar to buy him a drink.'

'What happened then?'

'I told him I could make him a star. He asked who the hell I was, where did I come from? What was I doing in Jackson? I took a risk and told him I was dossing in barns. He burst out laughing, said that was good. Anyway, he must have seen something in me too, 'cos I scribbled a contract on the back of a napkin and he signed it.'

'Impulsive,' mused Sarah.

'Yeah, but you've got to understand, no one had told him he was good at anything, and he had nothing in Jackson, no reason to stay.'

'His parents were both dead,' said Sarah.

'He told you?'

Sarah nodded.

Strone gave her a sharp look. 'He doesn't normally talk about it.'

Sarah shrugged. 'Yeah, well. So then you went to Melody, Music, Entertainment.'

He nodded. 'John sang and played guitar for the MD. I insisted he see him in person, no demo tape. He had to see John himself.'

'How did you manage that? You were an unknown ex-accountant with an unknown teenager.'

'I was very persuasive.' He smiled. 'I *always* get what I want.'

'Yeah, right. Don't tell me, you're immortal too.'

'There's only one goddess here,' he responded.

'Not me,' said Sarah. 'I lost my illusions of immortality long ago.'

Strone smiled. 'Who would miss you, if you went? That's what we should all be asking ourselves.'

Sarah thought of Georgie and to her dismay, her eyes filled with tears.

'Hey, I'm sorry,' Strone said.

Sarah brushed away her tears. 'It's OK, I'm just a bit over-emotional.'

Strone gave her a gentle smile. 'Not quite the tough cookie you come across as, huh? Whoever you love that much is a lucky guy.'

Sarah turned away. This was getting too close. Redford, via his concert, had opened her up, and she was frightened what might be visible.

CHAPTER FIVE

ROOM SERVICE WOKE SARAH with breakfast at six o'clock. Bleary-eyed, she pulled on a towelling robe, let them in and signed the bill.

She rubbed her eyes, poured a coffee, and rang Jacob. Everything was fine. Sarah spoke for five minutes then hung up. She bit her lip, staring unseeing out of the window at the Manhattan skyline. Then she made herself sit down and start work on Redford's financial papers. She managed an hour, then she rang Savage.

'What've you got?' he asked.

'On the bad side, nothing. On the good, he is an *incredible* performer. His concert last night was amazing—two thousand people spellbound. What have you got for me?'

'Breden came up with drugs,' replied Savage. 'A long habit, apparently. Cleaned up three years ago. Unstable background. Mother killed in car crash, father committed suicide several years later. Blew his brains out. Redford found the body.'

'Oh no.' For an instant Sarah was blinded by the image of her parents, dead, slumped in the front of their car. Sarah knew Redford's pain, knew there never would be any getting over it. No amount of drugs, adulation or adrenaline would ever be enough.

'You think he's clean?' Savage asked.

'Looks incredibly healthy. I'd be very surprised if he were using. I'll keep an eye out. Is it a problem with you?'

'I don't think so. He's a rock star, drugs are par for the course, and he appears to be off them now.'

There was a knock at the door.

'Er, look, someone at the door. Gotta go, James.' She hung up and hurried across the room. A bellboy waited with an envelope.

'For Sarah Jensen. Urgent,' he said, handing it over. Sarah ripped open the envelope. A single piece of paper floated out. It bore seven simple, typewritten words:

To Sarah Jensen. Carry on and die.

She sank down on the sofa. Her heart beat fast and she felt nauseous. Who the hell was responsible? Some loony, warning her off. Off what? Off her investigation? But no one outside Goldsteins knew of it, except Jacob, and he would never have told anyone about her true mission.

It couldn't be Redford. If Redford was trying to cover something up, warning Sarah off would merely act as a signal to dig deeper. Anyway, he needed the deal, and he needed Sarah on side.

She stared at the note. Perhaps it *was* from a deranged fan who'd seen her and Redford together, who thought she was Redford's tottie. All of Redford's crew must have seen her yesterday at the Beacon. It could have been any one of them, or a jealous groupie. Could it even have been Strone himself, warning her off his star? Extremely unlikely. It didn't seem in keeping with what she was slowly learning about the manager's personality. And as Redford's manager, Strone would get ten per cent of the proceeds of the bond issue.

Maybe it was the Leaker. After all, members of the trading team flew in and out of New York every few weeks. Perhaps her trap had been made known to him. Shit, it could be anyone.

She thought of Strone's words, 'Who would miss you, if you went?' and suppressed a shiver.

Sarah was settling her bill with the hotel cashier when John Redford suddenly materialised silently behind her.

Whipping round, she glared at him. Standing beside her, hands wedged in the pockets of a worn leather jacket, he was suddenly human again, the godlike performer left behind on the stage.

'Don't *do* that!' she hissed. 'You nearly gave me a heart attack. What is it with you and Strone? He did the same to me yesterday.'

Redford smiled.

A small, curious crowd of hotel guests was gathering. Sarah nodded in their direction. 'Shall we?'

'Shall we what?' Redford asked mischievously.

'Get the hell out of here,' Sarah said crossly.

The limousine waited outside. Strone was already seated, talking on his mobile. He nodded at Sarah.

'Forward or back?' asked Redford, indicating the seats.

'Why, forward, please,' replied Sarah archly to his courtesy. 'I hate going backwards.'

'Ah. Control freak.'

'Says who?'

'Says any right-minded psychiatrist.'

'And what do *you* know about psychiatrists?'

'Well now, I don't want to give away any advantages, do I?'

Sarah smiled and filed that one away. Part of her was struck again by the absurdity of her situation, sitting in a limo with the father of her child, getting to know him.

'You were amazing last night.'

'Thank you.' He seemed genuinely gratified by her praise.

'It was an incredible feeling, watching you. The music just seemed to flow through us. I felt almost suspended in it, a sea of sound and feeling.'

Redford nodded thoughtfully.

'How does it feel,' asked Sarah, 'to be at the centre of all that?'

Redford smiled and his eyes became sensual and contemplative. 'It's the biggest high there is.' His eyes hardened. 'But the coming down is hell.'

'How do you come down?'

His eyes flickered on hers and away, and that was all she got for an answer. As he reached forward to a cabinet and took out a bottle of Evian, Sarah noticed the bandage on his right hand.

'What happened to you?' she asked, nodding at his hand. Redford looked vaguely embarrassed.

'I hit a wall,' he said, almost in a whisper.

'Why in God's name would you do that?' exclaimed Sarah.

Strone suddenly clicked off his mobile phone and switched on to their conversation. 'Hey, ease up, would you,' he said with feeling.

'I was only asking,' said Sarah, looking from Strone to Redford. 'In my book it's a pretty strange thing to do, to hit a wall.'

Strone leaned towards her. 'Yeah, well, you've never had the pressure of coming down after a concert. You've never had all that stored-up adrenaline coursing round your body with nowhere to go.'

Sarah raised her hands in surrender. 'I'm sorry. Forget I ever said anything.' Redford was watching her with troubled eyes. She turned to the window, trying and failing to push the image of Redford slamming his fist into a wall, with all that implied about his stability, from her mind.

Redford sat next to Sarah on the plane to Paris. Strone sat two seats behind them, seemingly preoccupied with a million details for the European leg of the tour. Redford said little. To Sarah he seemed desperately tired, but wired at the same time.

'Do you enjoy touring?' Sarah asked abruptly. 'It seems a difficult way to live.'

Redford looked at her with quick interest. 'It is, I hate it.'

'Do you? Not the performing?'

'Nah, I love that, but like I said, it's a dangerous drug. It's like corruption. You can feel it licking at your soul.'

'Why corruption?'

'Because there's an awesome power you can abuse if you're not careful. You can take your audience any emotional place you want. It's like brainwashing. You've got to keep it pure. If you do it with an evil soul, you can fill their minds with poison, hatred, anger.'

'You filled my mind with joy and melancholy. And passion,' she added quietly.

Redford looked long and hard at Sarah. She fought to keep her equanimity under such an all-seeing gaze.

'That's what I sing about,' he answered slowly. 'That's what I do. But you see what I mean, you see how it could turn bad?'

'Yes, I see. But why should it?' Sarah felt herself searching and coming close to touching something hidden in Redford's soul. 'I could throw myself off a mountain, but just because I could, doesn't mean I will.'

'But the thought might enter your head and once it's there, what do you do?'

'Climb down quickly,' replied Sarah. She paused a while before asking carefully, 'Is that what the bandaged hand is all about?'

Redford looked away. 'It's about frustration, about feeling trapped.'

'You'd like to quit,' Sarah said in sudden comprehension.

Redford looked appalled, as if Sarah had spoken blasphemy.

'It's not heresy to me,' she said, replying to his thoughts. 'You've made it, you've been at the top for twenty years. Why not give it up?'

'It's not as simple as that. I love to perform, I love to write music.'

'Love hate,' commented Sarah.

'Exactly.'

'Sooner or later one wins, or you snap from the tension.'

A shadow flitted across Redford's face.

'Is that why you want the bond issue? You want to get out now, before anything happens?' Sarah knew she was in danger of pushing too hard, but she could sense some kind of revelation and she just had to get to it.

'Anything happens? Like what?' asked Redford tautly.

'I don't know. Nervous breakdown?'

'Had one of those. You get over it,' he said tartly.

'Drug addiction?'

'Had drug problems. Used to be so drugged up I wouldn't know what I was doing, but those days are long gone. Got over that too.'

'Sex addiction?' tried Sarah with a smile.

'I'm a monk. I'm celibate. These days. I've had the groupie thing. It wore off a long time ago.' His eyes probed hers angrily.

'There's sex without groupies,' observed Sarah, now completely confused as to where the personal finished and the professional started.

'Yeah, well meeting and keeping the right woman seems to be a problem for me.' He gave Sarah an acid look.

'Money addiction?' They were playing a game now, and both knew it.

'Why do you do what you do?' asked Redford. 'You seem to be just a tad conflicted by it yourself.'

'I am. But it's nice to be good at something, to get paid for it.'

'You said you can pick and choose, that you're not an impoverished merchant banker.'

'I'm not impoverished, but I still need the money.'

'Why? What for?'

Because I want to give your son the best that I can, she thought.

Sarah smiled. 'It's called "fuck you" money. Freedom money.'

'I'm familiar with the concept. No ambition, beyond that?'

Sarah pondered. 'Yes, once upon a time. I wanted success and I got what I thought I wanted.'

'And it wasn't enough?'

'It was good, a hell of a lot better than failure and impoverishment.'

'So what was the problem?'

'Does there have to be a problem?'

'It's in your eyes, Sarah.'

'We were talking about you,' she said.

'We've talked enough for now. I'm tired,' said Redford, a flash of the rock star in his eyes before he closed them and reclined his seat.

A black Mercedes bore them to the Hôtel Costes on rue St-Honoré, round the corner from the Place Vendôme. Rock music pumped at them as they walked into the dark, ornate foyer. Sarah got an impression of palms, incense, tasselled lights, red velvet brocade and a dazzling court-yard, lit by the sun, peopled by Grecian statues, gods looking down while their subjects played.

Strone stayed at Reception, apparently renegotiating their room rates. With great ceremony, Sarah and Redford were led to their rooms.

Sarah's suite had its own flower-strewn balcony with roses, clematis and wisteria. She stood there, gazing out over the rooftops in delight. Her bed was a four-poster, hung with rich tapestries. Her bathroom was tiled ornately, with gold taps and a luxuriously long and deep bath. The heady smell of incense lingered, exotic and suggestive. She took a long, lazy shower, dried herself off and pulled on a crocheted silk dress. The fabric was like a caress against her bare skin. There was a light *rat tat tat* at her door.

'Room service,' said a melodic voice. 'Came to ask if you might like some dinner.'

'That's rather forward of room service,' said Sarah, opening the door with a smile. Redford stood before her in jeans, white T-shirt and bare feet. Sarah felt her heart constrict. She'd like to kiss him now, just push him down on the hotel carpet and get on with it.

'My suite, just down the hall. There's a table set up on the balcony.'

Sarah must have looked dubious, for Redford grinned and reassured her. 'The whole of Paris will hear if you scream.'

'Am I in danger then?'

'Only if you want to be.'

Sarah turned away. 'Give me a second.'

In the bathroom she brushed her hair and sprayed on some scent.

She stared at herself in the mirror. Her eyes betrayed her excitement. She was breathing deeply, her chest rising and falling sharply, her cleavage visible in the V of her neckline. She rejoined Redford.

'Lead the way.'

They stood side by side on the terrace, watching the sun set over the rooftops.

'Not bad, is it?' said Redford. 'For the little boy from Wyoming.'

'Not bad at all for the little girl from New Orleans,' agreed Sarah.

'It's so much sexier, New Orleans,' said Redford. 'Down and dirty and exotic.'

'Yeah, but Wyoming is good and pure and beautiful.'

At that moment something flashed in the near distance. Sarah glanced towards the light, but Redford didn't seem to have noticed anything. He was studying Sarah. Sarah rubbed her arms.

'I'm hungry,' she said.

He smiled at her. 'Then we must eat.'

The table was set with the finest silver and crystal. They ate asparagus, and drank a crisp white wine so smooth that Sarah almost swooned. In the last flush of sunset, the lights of Paris came on. Soon the moon rose and shone down on them. It was one of those evenings that survive in the memory, an offering from the gods.

'Tell me about yourself, Sarah Jensen.'

'I'm not good at self-revelation.'

'I'll bet. No one who hides things wants to let them go.'

'And I hide things?' asked Sarah.

'We both know you do.'

'So do you.'

'I don't deny it.'

'So what do we do then?' asked Sarah.

'How about a trade? A question for a question. I ask you, you ask me. No limits. The only condition is truth.'

'How do I trust you? It'd be easy to lie.'

'Would it? Do you lie well?'

'That's your call, isn't it?'

'Mmm. Well then, Sarah. Shall we? Do or die.'

This is crazy, she thought, like a game of Russian roulette. They both had too many secrets. Her only hope was that hers were too well hidden for him to even sense the relevant questions.

'Three questions, no more no less,' said Sarah.

Redford reached out his hand. 'Deal.'

Sarah shook. 'I start. Why d'you need the money from the bond issue?'

'So I can quit, *if* I want to. Gives me the choice.' He took a drink of water. 'What thing has hurt you the most?'

'That's easy. The death of my parents. And you?'

'The same. What are you afraid of?' he asked.

'Ah.' Sarah slowed down. 'Violence to those I love. What are *you* afraid of?'

'A random killer. Walking out of this hotel tomorrow morning in the sunshine, heading off to some bistro for a *café au lait* and some loony tune blowing it all away. Another John Lennon.'

'Are you expecting something like that?'

'My turn,' he said quietly. 'What excites you?'

'Speed. Racing down a ski slope at full pelt, fast cars, fast boats, fast horses, body-surfing a huge wave. Being a little out of control.'

He smiled, as if at a private thought.

'What makes you happy?' asked Sarah.

'Riding my horses in Wyoming. Hiking in the Tetons, camping under the stars.' His eyes rested on hers. 'What makes you happy?'

'Living.'

He studied her. 'Have you come so close to death, have you lost so many people?'

'That's two questions and it's my turn. What excites you?'

'Performing.' He gave Sarah an ambiguous smile.

Sarah had a sense that they should stop now. They'd gone beyond the three questions they'd agreed upon. She hadn't had to lie to him.

'All right,' she said. 'Last question. Make it count.'

He took a long drink of water, leaned across the table and looked into her eyes, giving her no room for escape. 'Why did you run out on me?'

Bright sunshine gleamed against the white courtyard when Sarah went down to breakfast. She took refuge in the rococo dining room, amid the deep velvet sofas and dark corners. A waiter brought her a *café américain* while she scanned the menu. She chose fried eggs and bacon, then sat back to gaze around her, tuning in and out of the fractured conversations of neighbouring tables.

When Sarah's breakfast arrived, she snapped out of her reverie, noticing for the first time that she was attracting more than her usual share of attention—a mixture of interest, admiration and envy. She could imagine the whispers. John Redford was staying, and this woman was the consort of the rock star. She was on display and she loathed it.

She quickly finished her food, then headed for her room. The phone was ringing when she entered.

'Sarah, it's James.' Savage sounded angry.

'What is it?'

'Wake up,' he demanded. 'You sound half asleep.'

'Why don't you tell me who bit you in the arse and why.'

'Someone called Roddy Clark, a City journo creep on *The Word*.'

'Ah. So what's he said?'

'That we're acting for Redford, securitising his back catalogue, that a deal is imminent. I'm surprised he didn't name terms.'

'Shit!'

'Quite.'

'Could you have it faxed through, please?'

'On its way.'

'How'd he find out?'

'That's the question, isn't it? *I* don't know. D'you think Strone or Redford might have said something?'

'Redford wouldn't waste his time, but he might have let something slip inadvertently. Strone is quite capable of it. Let me speak to him.'

'A.s.a.p., and read him the riot act if he has blabbed. Politely.'

'Could it be the Leaker?' asked Sarah.

'Could be, but not his style, is it, to speak to the press?'

'Not so far it isn't. Keep the cameras running. We have to get to the bottom of this.'

'We are. Got anything for me?'

'Nothing tangible as yet. Just hints, spectres in the mist. I'll wait until I've got something more real before I start worrying you about it.'

'Nothing bad, is it? Nothing that would threaten the deal?'

'Not so far.'

'What are you not telling me?'

'Look, James, so far there's no evidence of anything horrific, OK? I'm getting to know the guy. What I'm finding out are the kind of lurgies we all have, the hopes and fears and weaknesses. There's a hell of a lot that's private which isn't relevant to this deal. I'm not going to share that.'

'Don't play God. If you know something bad, you tell us.'

'If it threatens the deal, James, I will tell you.'

'I'll decide if it threatens the deal, not you. I want you back here tomorrow, Sarah.'

And before she could retaliate, Savage hung up.

Sarah slammed down the receiver and strode across the room. A note was stuck under the door. She paused uneasily and looked at it:

Will you never learn? Time's running out, bitch. Back off or die.

I will not react, she thought. I will not be poisoned by some loony tune.

She reached for the phone and tried to ring Redford. The operator told her that all his calls were on hold. Sarah rang Strone.

'Strone, it's Sarah. I need to speak to John.'

'No can do. It's show day.'

'It's important.'

'Nothing's as important as show day. Speak to *me*,' said Strone.

'No. It's something personal. Won't he have five minutes somewhere? I need to tell him something.'

'He does his yoga for hours. His breathing. He centres himself. You charging in there will uncentre him, so you will not have access.'

Strone spoke in an aggressive tone that would normally have sent Sarah off the deep end but Strone was right. The last thing Redford needed to hear about, if he was trying to get centred, was his worst fear, his loony tune, even if he or she was stalking not him, but Sarah.

'Right,' said Sarah. 'I need to talk to you anyway. Now.'

'Come on, Sarah. You a slow learner or something? It's concert day.'

'Five minutes. Right now.' Sarah slammed down the phone, shaking.

'Who the hell do you think you are?' Strone barged his way in.

It couldn't be him, she thought, watching him pass. He'd be too clever to make a mistake like that, to betray himself by his words, even if he did have a motive, which she couldn't possibly see, given the $10 million he'd get if the deal closed. She turned to face him.

'Please excuse my temper. It's contagious. I've just been bawled out by James Savage.' She stalked over to the fax machine and swiped up a one-page fax which she thrust at him. 'Know anything about this?'

He read the article in *The Word*.

'You didn't by any chance speak to Roddy Clark, the journo, did you?'

Strone began to look awkward.

'You did,' said Sarah.

'What's the problem?'

'Confidentiality. The whole methodology of running a deal. There is no ad libbing, no casual chats with the press, or anyone else outside of the designated people who absolutely have to know what's going on, or else your deal goes belly-up. First of all, there are a whole load of laws that govern the way investment business is carried out, and we have to respect them. Second, there's the right way and there's the wrong way to present this deal to potential takers. Investors are wary creatures. They like everything to run smoothly, to follow a preset pattern. Any divergence from the norm is cause for concern. There's a very strict choreography to this. You don't go bumbling onto the financial stage and rewrite it, any more than I would go crashing onto Redford's stage and try to sing with him.'

Strone listened in silence. 'All right,' he said stiffly, 'I won't speak to the press again. Satisfied?'

'Satisfied,' said Sarah. 'But just so's I know, who made contact with whom?'

'The guy rang me out of the blue, said he'd heard that we were gonna securitise the back catalogue, that Goldsteins were running the deal. I said yeah, that was correct, we were gonna do the biggest bond issue a rock star has ever done—'

'Shit,' groaned Sarah. 'We don't know how big the deal's going to be yet. It's totally premature to go round stating sizes. This isn't a case of mine's bigger than yours. You go for something too big and you'll have a flop, get it?'

Strone smirked.

'It's not a joke when it happens to you,' said Sarah.

'Does it happen to you a lot? I imagine you'd terrify most men.'

Sarah moved forward till she was in Strone's face. 'Listen, buster, it's gonna happen to you, and to your star, big time, if you don't start engaging your brain and tying a knot in your ego.'

'You know you have one hell of a temper.' Strone headed for the door. 'You coming to the concert tonight?'

'Wouldn't miss it for the world.'

Sarah changed into a long skirt, slit to the thigh, and a white cotton T-shirt. She threw a lavender-coloured pashmina shawl round her shoulders and was about to head out to the concert when she noticed another envelope stuck under her door. She yanked open the door, eyes raking the corridor, but there was no sign of anyone. She ripped the envelope open. A photograph fell out. Sarah and Redford were standing on his balcony. Her face was bisected by a red slash, gummy to the touch: blood or lipstick. She shuddered, terrified and enraged. The note read:

If you won't stay away from Redford, you must pay. Get ready to die.

She stared at it and then at the photograph. She could ignore their message of hostility no longer. She wasn't ready to leave Redford, he was unfinished business, and always would be, but her love of Georgie pulled her home. To abandon him was unthinkable. She *had* to take the stalker seriously.

She thought back to last night and Redford's final question. She had considered her answer long and hard, before she said simply: *Because I had to*. Before she could weaken, she had left him.

Later in bed, she had dreamed, awake, of how it might have been to make love again with this man, the father of her child, to slip into his mind, to feel his golden skin, to feel the power and the thrill of him.

She stared at the note. You are filled with hate, she thought, and you would destroy me. I will watch you tonight, John Redford, she decided, and tomorrow I will leave you.

She sat in a private box in Parc des Princes listening to the roar of the crowd. Strone had disappeared. She was glad. She didn't want his eyes on her as she looked upon Redford for the last time.

As she watched him run onto the stage, she could see his smile, could feel the thrill he both loved and dreaded as the crowd took him into their hearts. She watched him move, all loose-limbed and sinuous, and she listened to him sing 'Come To Me'.

> 'Walk away now, or come to me,
> Turn your face, or kiss me,
> Button your coat, or let it fall,
> Come to me and let me love you,
> Let it begin, let me look at you,
> And see you, let me kiss you,
> And taste you, let me love you,
> With all of me, every sinew, every breath,
> Every heartbeat . . .'

He sang his way into her mind, into her blood. She wanted to hear his voice talking just for her. She wanted to see him open to her and she wanted to feel his need. She wanted that first, knowing touch, and she yearned to yield in response. She craved this man with a ferocity that frightened her. She vowed to herself she would have him again, to love, to possess and to be possessed by him. One more perfect night, but not now, not under these circumstances, when she was his entrapper, sent to unpick his soul and find his faults and his skeletons.

Sarah sat alone on a wooden chair on her terrace, looking out over the silent rooftops. She couldn't have slept and she hadn't tried to. She decided to sit out here in the dark, with the smell of incense wafting over her skin like a caress, and watch the night turn to dawn.

There was a knock at the door. Silently she rose and padded across the room.

'Who's there?' she whispered.

'It's John.'

Her heart gave a leap and beat faster. Her mouth turned dry.

Slowly, she swung open the door. He looked spent, ravished almost, as if he had relived all the pain and loss he sang about with every word, as if every chord plucked him from any safe place he might try to run to.

'I was sitting on my terrace, just watching the night,' she said. 'Will you sit with me?'

He smiled and followed her out onto the balcony. He pulled up a chair and sat next to her.

'Are you thirsty?' Sarah asked.

'I could drink a river. I downed all the Evian in my suite.'

'Here, let me get you some.' She got to her feet and returned with four little bottles. She watched Redford drink three of them.

'Your performance,' she said, reaching out to touch his wrist, 'was one of the most beautiful things I've ever seen. It was too beautiful to sleep on. I just wanted to sit up all night and watch the dawn.'

'Can I keep you company? All night, until morning?'

She looked at him, long and lingeringly. She was unable to look away. He kept his eyes on hers, leaned across and touched her face. He traced his fingers over her eyelids, down her cheeks, over her lips. All her resolutions fell away. She leaned towards him and kissed his mouth.

His kiss was as she remembered, only more passionate. He pulled her to her feet, led her gently to her bed. He lay beside her, his fingers moving over her body with increasing heat. He pulled up her skirt, stroked the bare skin of her thigh. She pushed against him, pulled him on top of her, opened her legs until she felt him pressing against her. When he made love to her, she gave herself to him in complete surrender.

Afterwards they lay in one another's arms, together in silence and love. There was too much to say to know where to start, so they said nothing, neither of them wanting to break the spell. Sarah must have fallen asleep finally, because she woke to see Redford standing before her, grim-faced. Her eyes travelled to the photograph and the note clenched in his hand.

'Ah.'

'Is that all you can say?' His voice was tight with the effort at self-control. 'Were you going to tell me?'

She got out of bed, pulled on her towelling robe and curled up in an armchair. 'I tried to yesterday morning. Strone said you weren't to be disturbed. What's going on, John? It's happening to you, too, isn't it?'

He sank down on the bed. 'For the last six weeks. I've had a note almost every day, different words, but always the same meaning: 'enjoy it while it lasts, ashes to ashes, dust to dust'.

'It's a jealous woman. that's pretty obvious. Any idea who it might be?'

Redford shook his head. 'Could be anyone. How many notes have you had?'

'Three. One in New York, then one yesterday morning, then another with the photograph, just before I left for the concert.'

'Have you told Goldsteins?'

'Not yet. I will have to.'

'What happens to the deal if you tell them?'

'I just don't know.' She tried to still the turmoil in her mind. 'Maybe they can be persuaded that the stalker is incidental to the deal, but it'll be a tough sell. They won't want the kind of publicity that could go with a stalker, if it got out.' She paused for a moment. 'I take it you haven't gone to the police?'

He shook his head, as if the idea were impossible. 'It would leak out, the media'd go mad with the story, and I'd become a stalker magnet.'

'There must be a way of investigating it discreetly,' said Sarah. 'Look, I have to fly back to London today. I have to tell Goldsteins. I could ask them, they'll know people. They could help you, I'm sure.'

'Not my style. Look, Sarah, is there any way you can *not* tell Goldsteins? I don't want to stir up a hornet's nest. I'd rather just get out, go home to Wyoming.'

'Be driven out, you mean? You can't let this person rule your life.' Sarah got to her feet in frustration and paced around.

'I'm not. It's time to get out, anyway. Quit at the top.'

'The stalker's the real reason, isn't she?' Sarah said, suddenly inspired. '*That's* why you want the bond issue—to escape her. That's also why you don't want me to tell Goldsteins about her, because you're worried they'll pull the deal and block your escape.'

She saw confirmation in his eyes. 'But why d'you need the bond issue to escape?' she asked, mystified. 'I know we've gone over this before, but I can't quite believe you don't have enough dosh to quit now.'

'Part of it's my fault. I pissed away a lot in my twenties—drugs and excess of all kinds. Motorboats I'd give away, parties with everything on tap. I had it all and did it all.'

'And now you're punishing yourself. You're allowing a stalker to make one of the biggest decisions of your career for you. What is it, some kind of quid pro quo? I was guilty of excess, now I must pay?'

'Sarah, it's not that simple. I'm tired of being me, the public me, and yes, I'll admit it, I'm frightened. Hate like that, it gets to you.'

'It's got to me and it's only been going on for a few days. You don't think she could be an ex-girlfriend?'

Redford looked startled. 'None of them hates me, far as I know. Not enough to follow me round on tour typing out notes.'

'Whoever she is, she's obsessive, determined, and out of her mind.'

Redford got up and took hold of Sarah's hand in his. 'I'm sorry. I'm forgetting you in all this. Are you frightened?'

'Of course I am, and I hate it. I hate the whole idea of being stalked. Like your nightmare, you walk into the sunshine, right into the sights of some mad sniper. Bang bang, you're dead.'

Chapter Six

SARAH GOT THE FIRST FLIGHT back to London and headed straight for Carlyle Square. Jacob had brought Georgie home and was waiting on the doorstep when Sarah's cab drew up, with the baby in his arms. She rushed up to them.

'Oh, Georgie, Jacob. My passions. How are you both?'

Jacob grinned. The baby giggled with joy when he saw his mother, reaching out his arms to her. She took him, buried her face in his neck, breathed him in, kissed him over and over.

'How's it all been?'

'Fine, sweetie. He's such a good baby, so easy and loving. We've had a good time, him 'n' me.'

'Oh, Jacob. Thanks so much for all this. I couldn't do it without you.'

The old man smiled shyly, his eyes glowing with pleasure, and Sarah realised that her baby had rejuvenated him. 'Any time. Now, how's it going your end? You look well,' he observed, suspiciously.

'Do I?' she said airily. 'Can't think why. Didn't get much sleep—what with the early flight,' she added quickly.

Sarah stayed for an hour, then got a taxi to Goldsteins.

Jezza was loitering inside her temporary office. Sarah forced a smile. 'Hi, Jezza. What's up?'

'Just wondering where you'd been. Not seen you for a while.'

'Yeah, well. Research, flying here, there, you know how it is.'

'No, I don't,' he said, taking a seat. 'Tell me.'

'I can't. Got a meeting with Savage and I'm eight minutes late.'

Jezza got lazily to his feet. 'My God, we can't have that, can we?' He scratched his nose thoughtfully. 'It's not everyone on the floor who has access to old Savage features. You might want to watch yourself.'

Sarah stiffened. 'What's that supposed to mean?' she asked sharply.

'Let's put it this way,' he said in a stagily confessional voice. 'I don't think all's exactly cosy on the domestic front.'

'Meaning?'

'I think Mrs Savage might be playing away. I saw her one day. I was taking a sickie, saw her in the street with a toy boy.'

God, sickies seemed to be endemic on the trading floor. She remembered PJ's comments about Fiona Savage, the suggestion of afternoon delight. She felt moved to defend her, for her husband's sake, if nothing else. 'Oh come on. He was probably her son.'

'In that case I'd say she had an unhealthily physical relationship with her son, because she was breathing into his ear.'

She felt a wave of distaste. 'Why are you telling me this?'

'For God's sake, Sarah, wise up! Savage is probably looking for consolation. And who better than some new babe on his payroll?'

Sarah glared at Jezza with outrage.

'Get out of my way, you tosspot. I've wasted enough time on you.'

She stormed past and headed for the back stairs, trying to shake the feeling of sleaze that always lay beneath the surface on the trading floor.

'Sarah, Dick, Zaha,' James Savage nodded to them all as he walked in, the king to his court. He poured himself a cup of espresso and drank it back like a snifter, then joined them round the table.

'Still nothing on the Leaker?' he snapped at Breden.

Breden shook his head. 'Very elusive. The investigation's going nowhere fast. I know we're missing something, some key.'

Savage turned to Sarah. 'Do you have anything?'

'I do.' She felt the air quicken around her. 'First of all, it was Strone Cawdor who spoke to Roddy Clark, the journo on *The Word*.'

'Stupid tosser,' spat Savage.

'Strone said Clark rang him, and I've no reason to disbelieve him, so the real question is, who the hell put Clark onto the scent?'

'You did,' answered Zamaroh smugly.

Sarah gazed at her with the look of wary disbelief you give a psycho weaving down the street towards you shouting insanities.

'I'm *sorry?*'

'You and your little stunt, taking Redford down to the trading floor. Might as well have taken out an ad in *The Times*.'

Sarah smiled sweetly. 'The point is, Zaha, that talking to journos is strictly off limits. You must have failed to make that clear to your people downstairs, because one of them sure as hell tipped Roddy Clark off.'

Zamaroh gazed at Sarah with a gleam in her eye. 'So, how do you propose finding out who that person is? That's the kind of thing you're paid for, isn't it?'

'Oh, shut up bitching, will you both,' said Savage. He shook his head. 'How are you going to follow this up, Sarah?'

'We keep digging around.' Sarah turned to Dick. 'D'you think we should get a profile on Clark?'

'I think we should. Your dirty raincoat, or mine?'

'Mine, I think,' replied Sarah with a smile.

'Well, get bloody going on it then,' said Savage with an outsider's pique. 'You're both being paid enough.' He got to his feet.

'Hold on a second,' said Sarah. Savage focused down on her. Sarah raised her eyes to meet Savage's. 'Redford's being stalked.'

There was a collective intake of breath.

'It's been going on for the last six weeks. Wherever he goes, the stalker follows, sending him threatening letters. "Enjoy it while it lasts. Ashes to ashes, dust to dust". The kind of stuff that lunatics get off on. He has no idea who it is.'

'Shit!' said Zamaroh.

'Bugger,' said Savage. 'What the hell do we do about this?'

'And do *you* have any idea who it might be?' asked Breden, the only one to remain cool.

'I think it's a jealous woman.'

'Why? How can you know that?' he asked.

'Because I'm being stalked too.'

Savage commenced an hour-long interrogation of Sarah on every last salient detail of the stalking.

'What I still don't understand,' said Savage with thinly disguised impatience, 'is why *you* are being stalked?'

'I don't know,' snapped Sarah. 'Ask the bloody stalker.'

'Stalker, Leaker, we're plagued by fruit-cakes,' observed Zamaroh.

'Make a guess,' persisted Savage, shooting Zamaroh a scowl.

Sarah gave a theatrical sigh. 'All right. Two theories. One is, she thinks Redford and I have a thing going. The only hole in the theory is why be jealous of me if she hates Redford as she seems to?'

'Love hate?' offered Zamaroh. 'The thin line and all that?'

'Could be,' said Sarah. 'The second theory is that someone knows my real purpose and doesn't want me to discover something which might threaten the deal. But that doesn't make sense either, because the threats would only make me want to dig deeper to find out what's being hidden. And, anyway, who knows my real purpose?'

'Is there anyone who would benefit from the deal being pulled?' asked Breden.

'I can't think of anyone, unless they bore us a grudge. Maybe the band don't want the deal done. There's one guy, Ray Waters, seems like a real jerk.' Sarah paused to think. 'No, the stalker's too vehement, too intimate. I'm sure it has to be a woman.'

Savage narrowed his eyes at Sarah. 'You're not getting too close to Redford, are you?'

'What's that supposed to mean?'

'Well, you know,' Savage squirmed awkwardly. 'Going native.'

Sarah glared at him. 'I'm spending as much time as I can with him, to find out as much as I can about him. That's why it might appear to a deranged stalker that something is going on.'

'And is it?' persisted Savage.

'No, it isn't,' said Sarah quietly and, she hoped, calmly.

'So what do we do now?' he asked. 'This has really thrown a spanner in the works.'

Sarah got to her feet. 'I'm going home.'

'What do you mean?' Savage stared at her.

'We can't take this any further right now, and I've got things to do. A life. I have one. I know it's unfashionable in these circles, but so be it.' Sarah walked from the room and headed home.

She bolted into the back of a taxi feeling as if she were beginning to fragment. There were too many pieces in her life and the effort of holding them all together was fraying her. She forced herself to concentrate, and rang Freddie Skelton on her mobile. The lawyer was in a meeting, but Sarah hooked him out on a plea of urgency.

'Sarah, hi.'

'Hi, Freddie. Sorry to do this to you.'

'Aren't you always, dearie. So what's so wonderfully urgent this time?'

'Nice little thumbnail sketch.' She lowered her voice and intoned just two words: 'Roddy Clark.'

'Ah,' said Skelton.

'You know who I mean?'

'The scribbler.'

'The very same.'

'Cost no object then?'

'Let's start with a basic quick and dirty and take it from there.'

Skelton smiled. 'I'd be delighted.'

'Oh, my sweet, oh, my love.' She hugged Georgie, lips against his soft plump cheek. She held him at arm's length to study him. He reached out to her face. God, he looked so like his father.

'So, how'd the meeting go?' asked Jacob.

'I don't know,' answered Sarah. 'There was all this stuff going on. Right now I don't want to think about it. I'll just take Georgie out for a walk,' she said, before Jacob got into the swing of his inquisition.

She returned two hours later, fed Georgie and put him to bed. She was just boiling the kettle to make some tea when the phone rang. Jacob got it.

'Someone called John,' he said, with a quick look of disapproval. He took over the tea, suddenly making the whole process as ritualistic and time-consuming as if he were a Japanese geisha.

'How are you, gorgeous?' asked Redford.

Sarah smiled. 'I'm fine, Mr Redford, how are you?'

'My, aren't we formal today. Can't talk?'

'That's it.'

'Ah, well maybe I should do the talking, tell you how completely luscious and—'

'Is that a fact,' interrupted Sarah, glancing round at Jacob. He looked up from his tea ceremony and strove to give her an innocent smile.

Georgie chose that moment to let out a wailing sob that the baby listener broadcast into the kitchen.

'What was that?' asked Redford.

'My uncle just stepped on my kitten's tail,' said Sarah, quickly turning down the baby listener as Jacob crept up to check on Georgie.

'Look,' said Redford, serious now, 'I thought you should know. Another note came. A fax, this time, sent from London, from Kall Kwik, whoever they are. It says that I should tell you to stay away from me, that if you don't, Georgie and Jacob will die.'

Somehow she managed to speak. 'I have to go.'

'Who are Georgie and Jacob?'

'Please. I have to go.' She hung up.

She had never felt a rage like this before. If the stalker had wanted to engage her, she had her full attention now. She had unleashed the full force of Sarah's maternal instinct coupled with her orphan's love for

Jacob. A line from one of Kipling's poems shot through her mind. 'The female of the species is more deadly than the male, engined for survival.' Too right. She would kill without blinking to protect her loved ones. How could the stalker *possibly* know about Georgie and Jacob?

With an awful clarity the answer came to Sarah. She must have followed her, all the way from Paris to Carlyle Square, watched her on the doorstep, heard her call out to her child and to her uncle.

Sarah prowled back and forth in the kitchen, trying to breathe in calm, to think clearly what she had to do. She would not have her life and Georgie's and Jacob's contaminated by fear.

She called Eva Cunningham.

'Eva, Sarah. There's something I need to discuss with you, urgently. Could you come round? Oh, and Eva, pretend it's just run-of-the-mill business, would you?'

Eva appeared fifteen minutes later. Sarah let her in.

'Hello, Eva,' Jacob said warmly. 'How are you?'

'Hi, Jacob. I'm well, thank you. How're you doing?'

'Holding up. Not too bad. Fancy a cup of tea?'

'Love one, but I'm afraid your niece wants to pick my brain about something, and since she's going to have to pay through the nose for it, I'd better closet myself away in her office and give her her money's worth.'

'Double, double, toil and trouble . . .' he said with a grin. 'I'll be up in a minute with your brew.'

Jacob deposited a large teapot, two mugs and a selection of biscuits on a table, close to where they sat, to copious thanks. As he was leaving, he said to Sarah, 'Georgie's sleeping, so I'm just off to the shops to stock up.' He blew the women a kiss and disappeared quietly.

Eva turned to Sarah with a look of sharp interest. 'So what's up?'

Sarah gazed back at her friend, her eyes heavy with intent. 'I have to go away tomorrow morning, for two nights. I need to have invisible twenty-four-hour-a-day protection on Georgie and Jacob.'

Eva blew out a long breath. 'What's going on?'

Sarah told Eva about the stalker, and the threats.

'Shit,' said Eva, after she'd listened for half an hour. 'For God's sake be careful.'

Sarah hesitated. 'You can do it then, the full-time cover?'

Eva shrugged. 'What choice do I have?'

'I'd better ring Savage,' said Sarah, 'before you get onto your people.' She was put through to the chief executive.

'I've been thinking, and I've decided we're in danger of overplaying the stalker thing,' she said. 'Every rock star gets threatening letters by the bagful. I don't think we should let one nutter get in the way of our deal. I'll fly out to Venice tomorrow morning.'

His response was galvanic and a furious argument ensued.

'Under no circumstances will you carry on,' said Savage. 'I've been thinking about the whole thing, too, since you waltzed out this morning. Look what happened to John Lennon. To George Harrison.'

'Don't worry, James. I'll behave appropriately to the level of threat I perceive.'

'You could get your head blown off. Haven't you seen enough death?' asked Savage, almost losing control.

'Believe me, James, I will do everything in my power to stay alive.'

'All right, Sarah, I don't have the time or the energy to fight you. My wife's on the other line—I have to go. Do what you insist you must, just don't expect me to weep at your funeral.'

Sarah put the phone down wearily. 'I'm going,' she told Eva.

'So I gather. I'd better start getting people mobilised.' Eva got to her feet. Sarah's phone rang as she did so. Savage's voice rose up from the answering machine, morose and maudlin. 'Sarah? Are you there?'

Sarah snatched up the receiver. 'I'm here.'

'Look, I didn't mean what I said. I'm sorry. I . . . I . . .'

Sarah saved him. 'It's all right, James. Don't give it another thought. I'm not going to die. You don't have to make your peace with me. We'll still be at each other's throats for years to come.'

He laughed. 'Thanks, Sarah. I'm glad there'll be some constancy in my life.'

'What d'you mean?'

'Sorry, Sarah, Fiona's still on the other line.'

'Do you mind if I have a look round your house?' asked Eva as Sarah hung up.

'Go ahead.'

Sarah watched Eva slink from the room. Eva wouldn't be checking the interior design, thought Sarah, half wryly, half bitterly. She'd be seeking out the weak spots in the house. Unease crept into her stomach. She got up and paced around her study, mind working furiously. She replayed her conversations with Savage. Savage's wife on the phone. PJ's comment about Savage's wife having a busy teatime agenda. Jezza's comment about the toy boy. Her fabled instincts were screaming.

She sought out Eva. 'I need a favour,' said Sarah quickly. 'Now. Just for an hour until Jacob gets home, can you watch over Georgie? He'll be sleeping anyway.'

Eva raised her eyebrows.

'Can you do all your phoning here?' continued Sarah.

'Don't worry. I always take my little black book with me. That's not what worries me.'

'Georgie? Don't worry about him. If he does wake up before Jacob's back, just give him a kiss and a cuddle, change his nappy and play with him. You'll be fine.'

Then Sarah rushed off. Fifteen minutes later, slouched down in her old BMW, in a quiet street close to Holland Park, Sarah was in position. She didn't know how long she'd have to wait, just that if she waited long enough, she was sure she'd have her answer.

Half an hour later, a man walked up the street and stopped in front of number 43. He ran quickly up a flight of stairs to the front door. He rang the bell, glancing around as he waited. A few moments later, Sarah saw the door open, caught a glimpse of a blonde head, then the man disappeared. She sat grimly in her car until, almost to the hour, the man re-emerged.

She eased from her car, closed the door quietly, and followed the man. His hair was unruffled, his immaculate City suit uncreased, his grin, as he stopped to cross the road, sickeningly self-congratulatory. Through the streets Sarah shadowed him as he stopped to buy a copy of the *Evening Standard* and then made his way toward the lifts.

When the first train pulled into the platform, he took his seat, and sat, concealed from Sarah by his newspaper. She placed herself out of his line of sight. He got out in the City, at Bank station. She followed him up the steps and out into Threadneedle Street, past the Bank of England. He turned into Throgmorton Street. Sarah hurried, gaining on him. When he moved to turn into the portalled doors of Uriah's, one of the most successful of the City investment banks, and winner of the three deals Goldsteins had recently lost, Sarah, all smiles, touched his shoulder.

'It's Mark, isn't it?'

The man swung round. Young, lean face and body, around thirty. Black hair, blue eyes, cold but amused. He eyed Sarah up and down before answering.

'No, it's not Mark,' he answered slowly, appraisingly.

'You must have a brother, a twin,' said Sarah coyly.

'I'm sorry to disappoint you,' he said smoothly, 'but I don't have a brother, and I'm not Mark.'

'Who are you then?' she asked, teasingly.

'I'm Richard Deane. And you are?'

Sarah leaned close to his face. 'That's for you to find out. Meet me here, on the steps, tonight at eight.' Before he could answer, she had wheeled round and walked away.

Sarah sat in Savage's office, waiting for him to return from a meeting. He looked surprised to see her when he arrived ten minutes later.

'Sarah, hello. What is it?'

'I think I've found your Leaker.'

'Who is it?' he asked quickly.

'I'm sorry, James. There's no easy way to say this. It's your wife.'

He didn't protest. There was no outrage, just shame. Savage hung his head. For a long time he didn't speak. Finally he turned to Sarah.

'You're sure? There's no mistake?'

'Just circumstantial proof, James. Judge for yourself.'

'All right then. Spit it out.'

She wasn't going to subject Savage to the fears of the contagion of trading-floor gossip. 'Well, it started with something you said, about constancy. You hinted things were difficult with your wife, and suddenly the profile fitted; disaffected wife, tries to hurt her husband and get her revenge on him. I went to your house, on a hunch, sat opposite in my car and waited. I hadn't expected to get a result so quickly, but after half an hour, she had a visitor, a man. He stayed for an hour. I followed him to the City, to Uriah's. I staged an encounter with him. His name's Richard Deane. I rang Uriah's switchboard, asked for his title. He's a director in capital markets. He's on the team that won all the mandates that were stolen from Goldsteins.'

Savage put his hands to his face. He rubbed violently at his eyes then turned to face Sarah. Rage began to burn through his shock.

'That's the last time I'll mention the Leaker,' Sarah said. 'Not Breden, not Zamaroh, no one will know of this.'

'I'd like to kill the bastard,' whispered Savage.

'In case you're interested,' Sarah said casually, 'I told him I'd meet him outside Uriah's tonight at eight. I won't be anywhere near there, of course, but if you were to take one look at him, you'd see he's not worth your trouble.'

She knew Savage would want to look over his rival, and she also knew, from the appraising look in his eyes, that Deane would be there.

Sarah got home at eight. She walked into a happy scene of devastation in the kitchen. Georgie was sitting on the floor, surrounded by the entire contents of one large storage cupboard. Opposite him sat Eva Cunningham, a desperate expression on her face.

Sarah burst out laughing. She negotiated the minefield of saucepans and scooped up Georgie in her arms.

'What's so bloody funny?' demanded Eva, hands on hips.

'You,' answered Sarah. 'I've never seen you look anything other than one hundred per cent self-possessed. Where's Jacob?'

'He left a message. He said he'd run into one of his mates and was going to have a half pint or two with him.'

'Sorry, Eva. He wasn't to know you'd be stranded here. Was it all OK?'

'I managed—don't ask me how,' replied Eva. 'Believe you me, I'm bloody glad you turned up when you did.'

Sarah kissed Georgie's cheek. 'Listen, a million thanks for this. How'd you get on with your preparations?'

'I'm getting there. Most of it's set up, the rest will be by tomorrow morning. Don't you worry.'

Sarah fed Georgie, bathed him and put him to bed. Jacob came back from a heavy session of reminiscences, and he and Sarah sat up chatting.

The night passed too quickly. Sarah had just finished breakfast when the doorbell rang. It was Eva again, this time with an overnight bag.

'Will you be my white knight for a few days?' she asked, convincingly. 'The hot-water heater broke down last night. Andrew's away, and the bloody plumber won't be here till tomorrow.' She shrugged. 'You know me and my creature comforts.'

Jacob had appeared in the hall in time to hear the bulk of Eva's story.

'Course you can stay,' he said with a smile of delight. 'We'd be delighted, me and Georgie.'

Eva smiled. 'But not your niece?'

'She's off, isn't she? Venice, no less.'

'Lunchtime,' said Sarah. 'I won't be back for a couple of days.' She took Eva's bag. 'Come on, you can stay in Alex's room.'

Lunchtime came and the taxi waited outside. Sarah held Georgie, trying not to cry. Jacob watched her, compassion etched on his face.

'I love you, my sweetheart.' She kissed her son's downy cheek and handed him to Jacob. 'I love you too,' she said. 'I'll be home soon.' She kissed them both one more time, and prayed that her words were true

Eva escorted Sarah to the taxi.

'Take care of them,' said Sarah, her voice faltering.

Eva squeezed her hand. 'I'll guard them with my life.'

Sarah sat in Garfunkel's coffee bar in Heathrow's Terminal One, sipping a cappuccino, wondering what the hell she was doing there. She thought of Georgie, at home with Jacob, smiling his smiles, playing his little games. All she wanted was to be with him. But Sarah knew that since the stalker bitch had prowled into her life, threatening her and Jacob, threatening Georgie, there was no refuge in denial. They couldn't hide at home, and any outing with her son would be polluted by fear, and would be courting a very real risk. So she would go to Venice, let this thing play itself out, help it along a little.

They flew over the body of the Alps. Blue ridges stretched out like waves on a stormy sea until they blended with the endless sky. Mists shrouded unseen valleys, lakes of mercury ice lay cold and serene beneath Sarah's sombre gaze.

On arrival, Sarah walked through the airport and out to where the water taxis waited, cherrywood gleaming in the sun. Taking the proffered hand of one Venetian taxi driver, she stepped lightly off the dock and down the steps into his boat.

She gripped the side rail as the boat skimmed along the lagoon, furrowing the water into banks of spume. Tripods of ancient wood flanked their passage, like flames along a grand avenue. They roared past a tiny island with terracotta-coloured buildings, cypress trees and palms.

Anticipation quickened in Sarah. She had never been to Venice. She'd been saving it up for the man of her dreams. Now she went to join the man who might play that role in her dreams. John Redford isn't him, she told herself, before her mind could begin its games. He's far from it. The man of her dreams was not a rock star, was not public property, would be hers, and hers alone.

But, oh God, this was the perfect place. The boat slowed, and entered what felt like the inner portals of the city. The beauty of it hit her like a fist. There was nothing slowly captivating about the outrageous beauty of St Mark's Square from the lagoon. The grandeur, the symmetry, the setting, all magnified the power of the Basilica, of the Doge's Palace. The boat eased along the Grand Canal, under the gaze of the palazzos, drew level with the landing dock at the Hotel Principe, flanked by striped red and black poles, protruding from the water to a height of eight feet. Sarah paid off the river taxi, and carried her small case up the steps and onto the terrace of the hotel. She checked in, then returned to the terrace, where she ordered a whisky sour and sat at an ornate white metal table in the afternoon sun, sipping and gazing out across the canal.

She couldn't quite believe she was really here. She felt as if she had entered a living painting. Venice was thrilling and exciting on some visceral level. Maybe it was the water, lapping the buildings with a lover's tongue; she had always loved water. Suddenly she felt eyes on her and whirled round, but there was no one.

It was a perfectly nice hotel, she thought, as the bellboy led her to her room, but not one she would have expected John Redford to stay in. She was still pondering Redford's choice when the man himself stole up.

'How did you know I was here? You got your spies out for me?' she asked.

He smiled. 'Everywhere.' The smile left his eyes. 'I wasn't sure I'd see you again.'

She drew him into her room and closed the door.

'Well, put it this way, I won't allow the stalker bitch to rule my life.'

Redford watched her with concern. 'Can't you just pretend she doesn't exist? I don't want her to cast a shadow over us.'

'Denial.'

'Is that so bad? I'll bet you deny things too.'

'All the time,' she gave a wry smile, 'but then I'm not the model of how to live your life.'

'Seem to be doing all right to me. Come on, let's deny the bitch and go and explore.'

They walked from the hotel and turned left on Lista di Spagna, heading towards one of the few bridges that spanned the Grand Canal. They crossed the bridge, along with throngs of tourists and busy Venetians heading home, stopping halfway across to gaze around. Redford had a baseball cap pulled low over his forehead and so far no one seemed to recognise him.

Darkness was falling as they left the Grand Canal and detoured down a myriad of side streets. The canals that crisscrossed their way were now slick, inky black, reflecting lights as if touched by an Impressionist's paintbrush. As they snaked round the narrow streets, Sarah heard snatches of song, and then, as they neared the singer, a long, parleyed lament. They stopped atop a bridge to listen. Redford slipped his arm round Sarah and drew her to him.

Arms around each other, Sarah and Redford walked on. They crossed the Rialto Bridge. A flurry of boats scurried by and Sarah trailed her hand along the white marble balustrade of the bridge. It felt incredibly smooth, caressed to fineness by centuries of touch. It made her think of Redford's skin, silk over the hard stone of his muscles. Her eyes met his. She turned away, eyes finding refuge in the palazzos, uplit, mysterious and regal in the night.

'I wonder who lives there now,' she mused. 'It must have been quite something to have been one of the noblemen who built these palaces.'

'Would you like to have lived then?' asked Redford.

'Oh no,' said Sarah, shaking her head. 'I'm very happy where I am.'

She wanted no more to travel in time than in place if it meant leaving Georgie. She felt the warmth of his father's arm pulling her close. What would it be like? she wondered, to have them all together, to see Redford's face when he looked at his son. She smashed the dream, reprimanding herself. He would be appalled. Or, worse, what if he wanted Georgie—what if he tried to take him from her? Redford must have felt the current of her thoughts. He turned to her. 'You OK?'

'Yeah, yeah,' she said, freeing herself, ostensibly to push her hair back from her face. 'It's just that stalker bitch. She's getting to me.'

He took her arm. 'Come on. Let's try to put her out of our minds.'

They walked along the Riva degli Schiavoni and turned into the Danieli. In the bar, the lights were soft, red brocade hung on the walls, a pianist played slow, lascivious jazz, and they ordered caipirinas—a mix of Brazilian cane-sugar rum and fresh lime juice. It would have been so easy to yield to the mood, to allow what should have been inevitable to happen, but in her mind she saw the notes with their terrifying lettering, she saw Georgie's face, she imagined a hooded stalker in pursuit, crooked, deformed by evil like the villains of fairy tales.

They moved onto the rooftop restaurant and dined on the terrace, gazing out over Venice by night.

Sarah's eyes settled upon a dome, which glowed like skin in the moonlight, adorned by balustrades and finely carved statuary.

'God, that's beautiful.'

'Santa Maria della Salute,' replied Redford. 'The Venetians' favourite church. Completed in 1682 as a thank you to the Virgin for saving them from the plague, after, incidentally, half of them had been wiped out.'

'You cynic, John Redford.'

'You think so?'

'I don't really. I think you're a desperate romantic.'

He laughed. 'Yeah, maybe. And what about you, the elusive Sarah Jensen? Who does she believe will rescue her?'

She thought of the stalker, she thought of Georgie and Jacob. 'Myself,' she said firmly.

They returned to the hotel at midnight. The air shimmered between them. Sarah longed to spend the night in his arms. She could see the yearning in his eyes.

'I have to go.'

He veiled the hurt that showed only briefly, looked at her a while before speaking, then he leaned across and kissed her.

'Good night, then.'

She kissed him back, then pulled away before heat seared her whole body and she was lost.

Breathing hard, she let herself into her suite. As she had hoped, and feared, a note was awaiting her under the door.

Your life is on its way out. Then your son. Begin counting. Ten . . .

Rage almost blinded her. She stormed back and forth in her room, eyes burning ahead. What did she have—ten hours, ten days, ten minutes? She pulled on combats, her black rubber-soled lace-up boots and a dark parka, and, before even a drop of her rage dissipated, let herself out of her room.

She left her key with Reception and walked out onto the street.

Trying to escape the throngs still coursing down the busy concourse, she turned right, and walked down Calle della Misericordia. The street was so narrow she could almost span the blood-red walls with outstretched arms. The wash of sound from Lista di Spagna soon ebbed away. All she could hear was the gentle pad of her boots on the moon-washed streets. She wanted to stop and turn round, but forced herself to continue the masquerade, meandering slowly as if simply out enjoying the night air.

She stopped, pretended to blow her nose. Behind her came the faintest suggestion of footsteps, then nothing, as if they had stopped. *Walk on, do not even think about looking back.* The night sky was bitumen black ahead of her. There were streetlights dotted here and there, but all they served to do was highlight the darkness.

When Sarah emerged from the narrow confines of these streets, relief swept over her as she rejoined a world of lights, people and open vistas. The footsteps she'd heard were probably nothing more than a late diner returning home. The lights of Lista di Spagna beckoned her, but before she could give into the temptation to go back to the hotel. She forced herself right onto the Calle Vergola. Surrounded by darkness and silence once more, she turned left into an unmarked street, up to a green door. Just before the door there was a recess in the wall, and Sarah instinctively made for it. Now she could definitely hear the sound of footsteps. She froze as the footsteps approached, slowing down as they grew closer. Then a shadow pooled onto the green door, rising like a miasma before her eyes, until the body behind it came into view. Terror flooded through her. She leapt from her hiding place, stifling her scream.

A voice screamed back at her. Black hair tumbled in her fists; nails scrabbled at her face. Their bodies crashed to the ground. Sarah forced herself on top, swung a punch at the face, saw the nose explode with blood, and the woman screamed and writhed. Sarah held her.

'OK, you bitch. Give me one good reason not to break your neck.'

The woman spat in her face. In one smooth movement, Sarah dragged the woman to her feet and slammed her into the wall.

'You threatened me, you sick bitch.' She fought for breath as rage swamped her. 'I should kill you for that.'

The woman went limp and dropped to the ground with a moan. She curled into a foetal position and began to cry.

Sarah felt an unexpected jolt of pity as the soft sobbing continued, plaintive, bereft. 'Come on, stop that, get up.'

The woman turned to stare up at Sarah. She looked to be in her late thirties, skinny, sparrow-like. The remnants of beauty showed in the fragile face, crumpled with tears.

'I'm going to take you back to my hotel. Find out what the hell this is all about.' The woman looked at her with terrified eyes, but said nothing, just allowed herself to be helped down the street.

In her hotel room, Sarah sat the woman in a deep armchair and went to get cold water and two facecloths from the bathroom. After wiping away the blood, she handed over the clean facecloth, wrung out in water.

'Here, hold this against your nose,' she said roughly. 'It should stop bleeding soon.' The woman took it. Fear, sorrow and a kind of madness showed in her eyes, and she started to sob again.

Sarah sank back on her bed, trembling with delayed shock. This wasn't how it was supposed to be. In her mind, she would catch the stalker, vent her fury, beat her half-senseless. Now, sitting before her, this woman looked pathetic, a threat to no one.

She hardened herself, got up and began to pace the room.

'What's your name?'

The sobbing eased. 'Carla. Carla Parton.' The accent was American, with the soft lilt of the South.

Sarah stopped in front of the woman, bent over her. 'Why were you following me? Why did you threaten me and my family?'

Carla's face collapsed again as she began to sob, great, heaving convulsions as if she were giving birth to some unspeakable pain. Sarah watched until the crying abated to a series of dry gulps.

'Talk to me,' said Sarah, handing over a glass of brandy.

Carla took a drink and began to speak.

'It all started thirty years ago, when my folks 'n' I moved to Wyoming. That was when I first met John Redford. We were at the same school, same class. Lord, he was beautiful, and so hurt you could see it oozing out of him. It was just after his mamma died. We all fell in love with him, me 'n' all the other girls. Anyways, he wouldn't let any of us close to him, just went on his own way, riding his horse, playing his guitar. I used to give him my whole packed lunch 'cos he never had any. John was kept in the same grade two years running, and we sorta lost touch, until fifteen years later. I was working as a waitress in New York.

'One evening, I see the posters. John Redford's performing live at Madison Square Garden. I was working, but I thought I might just catch the end of the show, so I got off my shift early, didn't even take the time to change out of my uniform, and hared on down there. But the concert was over. I was so disappointed, I burst into tears. I told Security I was an old friend of John's and they let me in backstage.

'I found his room and knocked. He said to come in, but when I went in, he was behind some kind of screen; I could hear him moving about. So I sat down, waited, and I felt eyes on me, you know. And I began to get frightened. Something wasn't right. I was just about to get up and go, when the lights went off. He grabbed me, pushed me from the chair, and got on top of me.' Her voice faltered; she rubbed tears from her eyes. 'I tried to force him off. I tried to hit him. He pinned me down.' Her eyes locked onto Sarah's. 'He told me if I made a sound, he'd kill me. Then he raped me.'

Sarah looked back, struggling to stay steady.

'Finally he walked out. I heard voices outside, then someone came in. He tied me up, pulled some kind of scarf over my eyes, and gagged me. Then he picked me up, literally carried me out, down loads of stairs, and pushed me into a car. He punched me so hard in the face I passed out. A construction worker found me next mornin', lying in some back-street up in Harlem. He took me to hospital. I had ten ribs broken, broken nose, broken jaw, and I got pneumonia. I was in hospital for six weeks. Then I discovered I was pregnant. Anyways, I terminated it.' Her voice died.

'Did you go to the police?'

'They came to me in the hospital. I told 'em nothing. I wanted my nightmare to be over.'

'So what happened?'

'Well, I had to get plastic surgery. I had four operations over eighteen months. My insurance company paid for all the treatment. Got four million dollars for my face—not bad, huh?' She attempted a smile that nearly broke Sarah's heart. Sarah got to her feet and returned with a bottle of brandy. She filled up their glasses.

'That was fifteen years ago. What did you do in all that time?'

'Therapy for three years. Really sorted me, you know. I met a man and I married him. We were happy for six years. Then we tried for a baby.' The tears started to roll. 'Nothing happened. You see—' her voice broke, 'the termination had left me scarred. I'll never have a child.'

Sarah couldn't hold herself in any longer. Tears rained down her face.

Carla went on. 'When they told me that, I broke down. I told my husband about the rape.' Her eyes found Sarah's. 'You know what he did? He left me.'

Sarah nodded, as everything became clear. 'So you decided it was time to make John Redford, and anyone he looked like having a relationship with, pay,' she said grimly.

'Wouldn't you?'

Sarah knew the power of revenge. She said, 'Go to bed—sleep in mine.' Carla followed her meekly, all rage spent.

'What're you going to do?'

'I'm going to get my head straight. Just try to get some rest.' Sarah sat and watched Carla until she saw that sleep had her in its grip.

How could John Redford have done this, the man who made such tender, passionate love, who sang such heart-rending songs? Sarah's memory of Redford had been destroyed. She remembered his fears of corrupting the audience. The bandaged hand he had slammed into a wall with uncontained rage.

She took her key, and marched up to his door. Heedless of the other guests, she knocked as hard as she could. When Redford appeared, Sarah pushed past him into his suite.

'What the hell's going on?' He followed her, uncomprehending.

She turned upon him. 'Don't speak to me, you bastard. Just listen.' He took two steps towards Sarah, before her words stopped him. 'Are you going to hit me now? Or is rape still your style?'

It was as if she had struck him a blow. 'What are you talking about?'

'Oh, please. Don't come the innocent with me.'

'I'm not coming anything. I don't know what you're talking about.'

'Let me tell you then,' said Sarah, pacing the room, eyes never leaving Redford's face. She watched while Redford picked his way to a chair and sat down as if his whole body was wracked.

'I know who your stalker is, you bastard. Her name is Carla Parton. She was at school with you. She grew up and went to New York. One day she sees that John Redford's in town, her old schoolfriend, so she turns up at the end of the concert. The security guards point her in the direction of your dressing room. So she goes in. You're behind a screen, so she sits down to wait. Then you kill the lights, and rape her. Then you leave her, and get one of your henchmen to clean up. He knocks her out and chucks her from his speeding car like a bag of garbage.'

Redford looked away.

'Watch me, you bastard. She had ten broken ribs, a broken nose and a broken jaw. Oh, and by the by, you'd made her pregnant with your child, which she aborted. And years later, when she tries to have a child with her husband, she discovers that the abortion fatally scarred her, that she will never have children. So her husband leaves her.'

She walked slowly up to Redford's chair. 'How could you do this?' she whispered.

He made no excuses. He didn't speak; he just stared out into space, utter desolation in every feature.

Sarah went back to her room, and later, when Carla stirred, she sat on the bed beside her and took her hand.

'Do you want to get this thing out of your system once and for all?' she asked.

Carla looked up at her with clouded eyes. 'How?'

'I told Redford everything you told me. Go and see him now.'

Carla forced herself up. Sarah saw to her shame that the other woman's nose was bruised and swollen. 'Let me get myself straight,' she said quietly.

A short while later, Sarah knocked on Redford's door again. He opened it, grey-faced.

'Will you see Carla now? You can do that at least.'

He nodded and Carla skirted round the door, which closed behind her. Sarah leaned against the wall and waited. Half an hour later Carla opened the door and called her in.

Redford sat slumped in an armchair. He looked utterly alone and lost. Carla was smiling with a kind of unstable relief.

'I'm going home today,' she told Sarah. 'There'll be no more stalking. It's not worth it. Part of me will always hate this man. But when I look at him now, he's the little boy I used to know again, not that monster who raped me.' Carla turned to look at Redford. 'Knowledge is your punishment. I won't stalk you, but I'll stalk your dreams.'

Carla walked defiantly from the room. Redford watched her go, then dropped his head in his hands.

When he looked up at Sarah there was anger in his eyes. 'Just answer me this. Where do you get off being judge and executioner? Have you never messed up? Have you never done anything terrible in your whole perfect life?'

'I don't get off. I'm sickened. I wouldn't call my life, or the way I've led it, perfect,' said Sarah. 'And I've done my share of terrible things. I sicken myself too, so don't feel lonely.'

'That's my epitaph, is it? I sicken you?'

'You sicken yourself, that's the real point, isn't it?'

'The real point is, I don't know what to think,' said Redford softly.

'Let me help you then. You should feel guilt, and remorse. Don't try to say Carla was making it up. No one could simulate her emotions.'

She needed to hear his contrition, to salvage something from him to show that he understood the enormity of what he had done.

Wearily he looked at her. 'I might have done it. I might not have done it. The awful thing is, I don't know. There were whole nights, and days, when I was so out of it on coke and booze I wasn't sure what I was doing. I managed to perform onstage, I made records, that's the only tangible legacy of about ten years of my life.'

'Surely you would remember a rape, for God's sake.'

Redford shook his head. 'No, I wouldn't. I had blackouts, periods sometimes for a night and a day when I couldn't remember a thing. I would wake up in strange places and have no memory of how I got there. So, yes, I could have raped her. God knows, I hope to high heaven I didn't. But I remember hearing backstage talk, after one of the New York concerts, years ago, about some woman who was bundled out into a car and dumped somewhere. A piece of trash, she was called. Causing trouble. So it could have been me. That poor girl. If I am responsible, I'd do anything to take it back, but I can't.'

'So, do something that is in your power,' Sarah said gently.

'Like what?'

'Give five million to help out battered women and children.'

'It's not that simple. I already give away a lot of money. It doesn't buy me absolution.'

'Stop thinking of yourself. This isn't about *your* absolution. Only God can do that for you. This is about helping someone else. Call it making amends. You could do a hell of a lot of good with five mill.'

'I don't have five mill in loose change.'

'You soon will. If the bond issue goes ahead you'll have a hundred.'

'How can it go ahead now, with you knowing what you know? You clearly assume I did it. Goldsteins would drop me in a second, and don't think I haven't worked out that you're some kind of spy for them.'

'What if I keep silent?' asked Sarah, falling, with horror, into a trap of her own making.

'What, lie to Goldsteins?'

293

Sarah thought of Carla, thought of all the Carlas who lived with their abusers, shackled to a life of violence. Five million could buy these women a haven, a passport to a new life.

'If I lie,' replied Sarah slowly, 'will you give five million to a charity for battered women?'

'This is beginning to sound like blackmail.'

'It's a way to right your wrongs. Take it or leave it.' Sarah turned away, affecting the trader's indifference, her heart raging all the while with hope of what she could do. But another voice whispered in her mind, What if Redford was lying? What if he *had* raped before, and since? Her connivance in his guilt might sentence more women to violation.

His voice broke through her hopes and fears.

'All right, Sarah. You've got your deal.'

Chapter Seven

REDFORD WAS PERFORMING tonight on the mainland, several miles from Venice, in an open-air concert at Jésolo. Sarah had always intended to be there, but now she couldn't get away fast enough. She caught the first available flight back to London. Just before she boarded in Venice, she rang Jacob and told him she was on her way.

As her plane pierced the leaden skies, she attempted to summon up a sense of relief, that she had found the stalker, and that she was now escaping Redford. But her spirit remained as heavy as the sky.

A few hours later, Georgie and Jacob welcomed her home with love, Eva with relief and fatigue.

After a prolonged cuddle and play session with Georgie, Sarah contrived some time alone with Eva in her study.

'All clear,' said Eva, before Sarah could ask. 'Neither I, nor any of my team, picked up anything remotely suspicious. How'd it go in Venice?'

'I don't think the stalker'll be a problem any more.'

'Something's a problem though,' observed Eva.

'Yeah, it is, but this one I can do nothing about,' replied Sarah sadly.

Eva got to her feet, knowing not to push further. 'I'd better go. I told Jacob my water heater's been fixed.'

Sarah saw Eva to the door. After that she carried Georgie down to the kitchen, where she brewed up some extra strong coffee and tried to summon the necessary resolution for her meeting with Goldsteins.

James Savage looked limp with grief. He was drinking bitter espressos one after the other. They seemed to elevate his grief to anger.

'Still alive?' he barked at Sarah.

'So far,' she answered evenly.

'What news of the stalker?'

'No news. Seems to have gone silent.'

'That's strange,' answered Breden. 'He/she's made contact in every other location over the past few weeks, no?'

'Yes,' answered Sarah, 'but nothing in Venice.' She kept her eyes blank. 'Maybe she had to go back to work, or ran out of money. It'll be interesting to see if either Redford or I get a note here.'

Breden looked at Sarah long after she had finished speaking. She attempted to appear nonchalant under his scrutiny, wondering if that was the right approach.

'You got anything, Dick?' she said.

'Nothing dodgy. No more drug problems. Lives a simple life in his place in Wyoming when he's not touring. Lonely guy. No known girlfriend. Does a lot of yoga, rides his horses, gives a lot of money to charity.'

'Does he? How much?'

'Over thirty million dollars.'

'Jesus!' Sarah swallowed, trying to compose herself. 'How's the deal going?' she asked Zamaroh.

'The numbers look great. I'm confident we can raise the full monty.'

'A hundred?' asked Sarah.

Zamaroh nodded. 'We want to take the whole lot.'

'We're *thinking* of taking the whole lot,' corrected Savage.

'It's low risk, Single A, but yielding two hundred basis points above comparable Single As. We've got to take it all,' insisted Zamaroh.

'We've *got* to do nothing,' snapped Savage.

Sarah watched Zamaroh. Her temper was beginning to bubble.

'We cannot sit on the fence, James, however much you happen to like that particular position. Do I have to wait till hell freezes over?'

'Not that long,' said Savage. 'Just till I'm confident that Sarah has nothing nasty hidden.'

'Me?' asked Sarah. 'What are you talking about?'

'Your stalker,' responded Savage, deceptively casual, 'and any other little matters that might not have come to light yet.' His eyes were upon her, dulled by grief, but still sharp. Breden watched Sarah as he spoke.

It was make-your-mind-up time. Lie, or tell the truth. Sarah saw Carla's broken dreams, saw, too, havens for perhaps thousands of women. *It's not for you to play God. Do your job, tell the truth*, said her rational voice. Goldsteins could see $100 million sliding rapidly into the red if Redford had committed not just the one rape, or if Carla's story came out. She paused before answering with a light smile.

'There are no "other little matters", James. The stalker's not ideal, but we can't pull a deal for something so intangible. I'd go for it.'

Zamaroh grinned with delight. Breden looked on with his customary mask of polite interest. Savage seemed to be retreating from the debate.

'Fine.' He waved his hand. 'We'll take it all. You deal with it, Zaha.' He pushed himself up from the table and walked out of the room. Then he paused midway and wheeled round to Sarah.

'Sarah, I need to go over something with you,' he said, nodding at the door. Sarah got to her feet and followed him into his office. Savage closed the door behind them.

'I took your advice,' he said with a gleam in his eye.

'With respect to what?' asked Sarah with a smile.

'That little shit, Richard Deane.'

'What did you do?' asked Sarah.

The chief executive grinned. 'I had my driver go via Uriah's, eight o'clock that night you told me. Deane was there, primping and preening himself, cocky bastard. Anyway . . . I got out of the car, walked up to him and gave him a whacking great punch.'

Sarah burst out laughing, horrified and thrilled at the same time.

'Good for you!' she exclaimed. 'What happened then?'

'He staggered back, sat on the steps, blood all over his shirt. I gave him a look, turned and walked back to my car and drove off.'

Sarah visualised the scene. 'Well done.'

Savage's smile faded. 'Yeah, well, we take our victories where we can.'

Sarah wanted to ask if Fiona had broken off the affair, but feared she had heard the answer in Savage's voice.

Sarah awoke swathed in the luxury of her own duvet. She pulled on sweat pants and a T-shirt and went in to Georgie. She changed and fed him, then carried him across the King's Road to buy the papers.

The sun was shining brightly and the air was crystalline after a heavy overnight rainfall. Up on her roof terrace, she settled Georgie in his mobile playpen beside her and spread out her papers on the wooden trestle table in the splendour of the autumn sun.

The Redford retinue, she read, were moving to London on a wave of plaudits. She practically choked on the PR. 'Redford's tours are magical experiences where an angel swoops down to entertain us for a few golden hours,' said *The Times*. The *Sun's* verdict was more earthy: 'Sex on legs is back!'

Sarah yearned for Redford, as he had been, before she knew the truth about him; and with her new knowledge, she despised him. He had done something vile. She was not good at giving people second chances, but she fought to now. This man was her son's father, even if he didn't know it, and despite her rage, part of her loved him still.

She turned back to the papers and, as if in a vain attempt to exorcise the man from her mind, she tore out the pages with the Redford coverage and dropped them onto the ground. She wanted no more part in the deal. To hear Redford's name, to have to lie and cover up his true character, was more than she thought she would be able to do. But she needed the money, and so did all the women Redford was going to help if she lied for him.

She reached out for her coffee cup and flicked through the rest of the papers, pausing as an article caught her eye: 'A rapist who appears to have struck in at least ten US cities over the past four months now seems to have moved to Europe. Interpol and local police, helped by the FBI, are now investigating rapes in Paris and Venice which may have been committed by the same man.'

There followed a list of the US cities in which the serial rapist had struck. Sarah got up slowly and deliberately, as if unsure that her body would obey her commands, and went to her study. She fished out a sheet of paper from her desk and returned to the terrace. She looked from the piece of paper to the article and back again, then she jumped to her feet, knocking over her cup of coffee. She rocked back and forth on her heels, hugging her arms around her, making a low keening sound. The coffee dripped from the table and pooled on the floor. Georgie watched the flow approaching him and screamed.

The doorbell rang. Sarah picked up her baby and soothed him as she carried him downstairs. 'It's all right, darling. Mama got a shock, that's all. Doesn't matter, doesn't matter.' Her mind elsewhere, unthinking, she threw open the door.

Dick Breden stood there. His customary half-smile vanished as he took in Sarah and Georgie. She glared at him, furious that he had seen the secret she had tried so hard to hide.

Breden looked from her to the child in her arms. 'Your baby?'

'Yes. My son.'

'He's beautiful. Why didn't you tell us?'

'He's my private joy, and anyway, it's none of your business.'

Breden gazed steadily at her, trying to read the secrets in her eyes. 'Something's happened. May I help?'

She shook her head violently. 'Help by going.'

'Can I come back later? We need to talk.'

'About what? About Georgie? He's got nothing to do with anything.'

'Look, you needn't worry that I'll say anything about your baby to anyone, because I won't.'

'Thank you,' said Sarah. 'I would really appreciate that.'

Breden looked at her gently. 'No problem. But we still need to talk. Name a time, I'll come back.'

'All right, eight o'clock tonight.'

'See you then,' said Breden.

Sarah closed the door on him, walked into the hall and leaned back against the wall, Georgie in her arms. She glanced at her watch. It was eleven o'clock. She'd got nine hours to decide what the hell she was going to do. She put Georgie in his pram and headed for Battersea Park.

She walked beneath the red cedars; she strolled around the zoo. Twelve rapes, all committed in the cities where John Redford had toured and, she was willing to bet, at the same time as the Redford entourage had hit town. Who knows how many other women had kept their own vows of silence. She had got it wrong, she had been blinded by dreams of what $5 million could do. And, far worse, she had been blinded by her desire *not* to see. She had wanted to believe that it had been a one-off, an aberration, and that he deserved another chance. What now?

Breden arrived promptly at eight. Sarah greeted him, wearing khaki combats and a clinging brown T-shirt. She had piled her hair on top of her head. Wisps escaped and framed her face. She wore no make-up, just a flash of heady scent that smelt of jasmine on a hot night. Her skin was pale, but her eyes were resolute.

She led Breden up the stairs and out onto her verdant terrace.

As Breden sat down, she studied him. She knew he was forty-five, but he looked less than forty. He had the bearing, colour and musculature of someone who worked out a lot. He moved freely and powerfully, no macho swaggering.

'Would you like a drink?'

'Please. Vodka.'

Sarah returned with a bottle of whisky, a bottle of vodka, an ice bucket and two glasses. She took a seat opposite Breden and poured their drinks. Breden said nothing. He didn't ask her about Georgie, and she respected him the more for his silence. In fact, it seemed to her that she saw a gentleness in his eyes that hadn't been there before.

'I think I may have made an awful mistake,' Sarah said finally. 'I lied about the stalker. I set a trap in Venice, caught her, confronted her.' She told Breden that story. He listened in silence, sipping his vodka. Then she showed him the article in *The Times*. 'I have a horrible feeling Redford's the serial rapist.'

Breden took a while to respond. 'So what's your dilemma?'

'Part of me can't believe it—refuses to believe it. Why would he need to rape someone? He's got so many women hurling themselves at him.'

'Rape is not about sex, is it? It's more about power. Maybe he needs resistance, a fight, to make it feel a proper conquest.'

'How totally sick.'

Breden nodded. 'You said it. But why tell *me* all this?'

'Because I want you to help me find out if it is him. And if it is, we throw him to the wolves.'

'And if it isn't?'

'We keep his secret, the deal goes ahead.'

'And how do I help?'

'You use your sources in the police, Interpol, FBI. You get all the details of the rapes, why the cops think the cases are linked, the exact time they were committed. I'll check on Redford's movements. If he was performing or was at a dinner somewhere public, he's in the clear.'

'What about Savage?'

'There's no need for him to know about this until we have our answer. We can't be sure that the Leaker wouldn't get onto it.'

'Who is the Leaker? I've a feeling you know more than you're telling about that, too.'

'Don't ask me. I can't tell you. Please, it's not relevant.'

'Does Savage know?'

'Yes, he knows.'

Breden nodded. 'All right, I'll let it go. For now. But as for going off on some clandestine investigation, if Savage finds out he'll throw a fit. He's my biggest client—I can't afford to lose him. And the other thing that bothers me is the feeling that there's so much that's being covered up.'

Sarah gazed across the table. 'What can I say? I have my reasons, none of which are to harm anyone. Just the opposite.'

'OK. Just give *me* one good reason why I should get involved.'

'I'm asking for your trust, and for your help, Dick. That's the best reason I can give.'

The doorbell rang the next morning at ten. Sarah was sitting at her desk while Jacob drank tea in the kitchen and Georgie napped. She hurried downstairs and opened the door. A motorcycle messenger thrust an envelope at her.

She returned to her study and ripped open the envelope. An information snapshot of Roddy Clark tumbled out—phone records, bank statements, a brief biography. He lived in Campden Hill Square, was born in 1968, educated at the Dragon School, then Eton, then Oxford. Staff writer on *The Word*, made meteoric progress to news editor at twenty-nine, then became a general reporter, always on the trail of scandal. On the trail of Goldsteins, Sarah mused. She began to scan the phone records when her own phone rang.

She grabbed it, irritated. 'Yes?'

'Hi, it's Strone. I got some more financials and stuff for you. Want to come and go over them?'

She groaned. *Oh God no, anything but.*

'Where are you?' she asked.

'The Portobello Hotel.'

'All right. See you in half an hour.'

The Portobello was in one of Notting Hill's elegant streets, a place of white stucco, with an air of order and quiet well-being. Sarah asked for Strone Cawdor and was sent up to his room. She sucked in her breath when Redford answered the door.

'Er, sorry,' said Sarah. 'They must have sent me to the wrong room. I'm here to see Strone.'

'This is his room,' said Redford coldly. 'He just had to step out to see someone. Be back in five minutes. He didn't tell me *you* were coming.'

'Yeah, well, that puts us both at an equal disadvantage, doesn't it?'

'So this is the way it's going to be, huh?'

Sarah crossed to the window. She didn't want to look at him, didn't want him to see the questions in her mind.

Redford walked up to the window and stood beside Sarah. She wheeled round to face him. 'How do I know how anything's going to be? All I know is, it's all fucked up.'

They stood, braced, questions flaring in their angry eyes.

Strone walked into the room. 'Am I interrupting?'

Sarah and Redford stepped apart.

'Hello, Strone,' said Sarah wearily.

Strone ignored this and turned to Redford. 'The ins—' he cut himself short. 'The geezer who saw you yesterday's here again. Downstairs.'

Redford tensed suddenly. 'He can wait.'

Strone shook his head. 'Says he'll see you *now*. Busy man and all that.'

'Fuck it!' Redford marched out without saying goodbye.

'What's up with you two? Had a lovers' tiff?'

'What? You know, you really have an over-fetid imagination.'

'Do I now? I also know John Redford. I know that he's fallen in love with someone, and that someone has done something to hurt him very badly,' replied Strone, his voice unexpectedly gentle. Sarah turned away from him, tears burning her eyes.

'When's it all gonna happen then?' asked Strone, casting her a lifeline. 'I must have biked round half a ton of paper, and still your Zamaroh woman asks for more.'

'All these deals are paper nightmares,' said Sarah, turning to him, grateful to be back on the solid ground of numbers. 'I'd imagine we're getting quite close to closing,' she said. 'The next consideration then is market conditions. You've got to launch your boat on a favourable tide.'

'I want this deal done quickly, do you understand?'

'You'll get the deal when it's ready, not a moment before. Do *you* understand? Now what are these papers you've got for me?'

Strone handed her a sheaf of documents. 'Shall we go over them?'

'I'll ring you if I have a problem with them,' replied Sarah.

Sarah returned to an empty house. Georgie and Jacob must have gone out for a walk. God, wouldn't that be nice. Ditch all the crap waiting for her and piss off into the autumn sunshine. Dejectedly she shut herself in her study. She picked over Roddy Clark's credit-card statements. The man was a dandy: tailors in London, tailors in Windsor, where all Etonians were outfitted as boys. Touchingly loyal. Then Sarah began to feel the hot wire of a connection burning in her brain. School, loyal, schoolboy, Eton . . . Bingo! She jumped up. Eton. *Jezza.*

Fingers fumbling with excitement she pulled out the Jezza file, quickly flicked through it. Born 1968. She compared the phone records with Clark's, running her finger down the numbers dialled. There was Clark's number, rung by Jezza on September 23, two days before Clark wrote the article on Goldsteins and Redford. She checked back over nine months. The two men had spoken just two other times. Not regularly enough for the call on the 23rd to be mere coincidence. Sarah smiled. *Gotcha, you bastard.*

Sarah caught a cab to the City. She convened a meeting with Savage, Zamaroh and Breden for an hour's time, but first she met Zaha on her own.

The head of the trading floor was coiled in her seat, talking into her telephone headset when Sarah arrived. The Iranian removed her headset with a frown.

'Sarah. What can I do for you?'

'Strone gave me these this morning,' Sarah said. She put the paperwork down on the table and eyed her evenly. 'And I have reasonably strong evidence as to who leaked the Redford deal to Roddy Clark,' she said. 'Jeremy St James.'

Zamaroh jumped to her feet. 'I knew it—I just knew it! The bastard!'

'Just a sec there, Zaha. Have a look at the evidence first.' Sarah showed Zamaroh the telephone records, explained the Eton connection. 'It's circumstantial, not proof,' she warned.

Zamaroh turned on her. 'You want proof?'

Sarah nodded dubiously.

'Get St James in here.'

'Get him yourself,' said Sarah, walking back to her own office. She wanted no part of what she feared was coming. It took only about a minute. From her office, she heard Zamaroh's voice, starting quietly enough, punctuated by Jezza's lower tones. These interruptions just seemed to inflame Zamaroh, for her voice rose and Sarah couldn't help but hear her words.

'You betrayed me, you betrayed the whole floor. Why? Just tell me *why*! I gave you everything. You flourished under me, I brought you on. I gave you the chance. I bailed you out when you fucked up, and for the past eight months you've been existing here on *my* say-so. Why? *Just tell me!*' she screamed. The trading floor had fallen strangely silent. Jezza's humiliation had become a public hanging.

There was a long silence, then Jezza's voice, dripping desperation. 'I wanted to give Roddy something. I wanted to sound plugged in, like I was part of the decision-making process here, not just another slave at the coalface.' There was another long silence. Sarah could almost feel Jezza willing Zamaroh to give him another chance.

'Get out, you little shit.' Zamaroh's voice again. 'Security? It's Miss Zamaroh here. There's someone up here I'd like you to escort from the premises, please.'

Sarah saw St James walking from Zamaroh's office, head bowed, utterly humiliated. Then two security men appeared.

'All right, sir,' said one of them. 'Like to come with us?'

'Give me five minutes, would you?' he hissed.

Zamaroh walked up behind him. 'You know the rules. Out now.'

She nodded to the security men who pulled Jezza from his desk. His gaze roved around desperately over the rapidly assembling throng.

'Oh, for God's sake let him walk freely!' shouted Sarah, walking from her office. 'He's not some bloody murderer.'

The security guards looked embarrassed. Zamaroh turned and walked away, as if bored by the spectacle. The spectators waited.

'And get back to work, you bunch of bloody piranhas,' said Sarah, before returning to her office, sickened.

The next day Sarah resolved to push Goldsteins, Redford, Carla, and the entire outside world from her mind. Jacob had gone home to Rotherwick Road. It was ten in the morning, and Sarah had been up with Georgie since five thirty. He was now blissfully sleeping off his ultra-early start. She'd woken with her whole body aching and she desperately needed to do ten minutes of yoga. She flicked through her CDs and chose Gloria Estefan. Gloria sang of hopes and dreams, of better days and nights full of love. Sarah turned up the volume, and sang along as she fell into her routine. Just as she was finishing, the intercom rang.

Dick Breden was on her doorstep. So much for escape.

'Whatever it is will have to wait till I've eaten. I've got low blood sugar and I'll be ruined if I don't eat right now,' said Sarah.

'Fair enough. I don't want to constitute ruination.'

Sarah glanced round her kitchen. She decided she needed pancakes. 'You hungry?'

'Depends what you're offering.'

'Pancakes.'

'Then I'm definitely hungry.'

Only after Sarah had made eight and consumed four pancakes topped with brown sugar and lemon did she decide she could hear Breden's news.

'All right, tell me.'

Breden took a folded sheet of paper from his pocket.

'Here's a list of the approximate times the rapes were carried out.'

He put the paper on the table. Sarah scanned it, then collected the tour itinerary from her study. The conclusion screamed up at her. All the rapes took place during Redford's stay.

'Did you get a description?'

'I did. Thirty to forty. Five elevenish, fit, hard body. He wore a black hood that was stuck to his skin so it couldn't be pulled off. Several women tried and got nowhere.'

Sarah raked her hair back off her face. 'Redford must be five ten, fit, lean body. He would have to wear a mask. Everyone knows his face.'

'Slow down, Sarah. The rapist doesn't have to be Redford. It could be any one of the people he's got on tour with him.'

'It could also be Redford. Says here all these rapes are committed after midnight and before nine in the morning. He was well finished performing by then. He's wired for hours after a concert. He has big problems coming down. I know Redford fears it, he's told me as much. After his last New York show, he appeared with a bandage on his fist, said he'd smashed it into a wall. Maybe he rapes to burn up all his adrenaline after a concert.'

Breden consulted his notes. 'What was the date of the last New York concert?'

Sarah told him.

Breden grimaced. 'There was a rape in the early hours of the next morning.'

Sarah buried her face in her hands, trying to block out all knowledge.

'Were you with him at all late at night?' asked Breden.

'I was,' Sarah replied with a heavy voice, 'but not in Paris and Venice on the nights of the rapes. Got anything else?' she asked quickly.

'There's a pattern to the rapes. They were all committed in sleazy parts of town, and all the women were waitresses or cooks at late-night cafés. He picked 'em off when they finished work, all after midnight, followed them some way, then pounced.'

A low moan issued from Sarah. 'I didn't tell you. Carla Parton was a waitress. She turned up at Redford's concert after her shift. He raped her in her waitress's outfit. It must have started some kind of fetish.'

Breden blew out a long breath. 'It's not looking good for him.'

For a while they stared at each other in silence.

'So what now?' Breden finally asked.

A plan began to form slowly in Sarah's mind. 'I could be the waitress. I could be the bait. You could organise back-up. Our rapist takes the bait, jumps me, you jump *him*. Bingo!'

Breden's response was deceptively mild. 'It's never quite that simple. And how are you proposing to trap him?'

Sarah smiled. 'We follow him. I'll get myself a wig. I'll wear a short skirt, high heels—'

'And he won't be able to resist,' offered Breden.

'That's the plan,' said Sarah. 'You got a better one?'

'Nope, but I don't go a bundle on this one. Too much could go wrong. For the trap to work, I'd have to hang back out of sight. He could do a lot of damage before I get to him.'

'Were they hurt, the women he raped?' Sarah asked.

'If they resisted, yes. Anything from black eyes to fractured jaw, a punctured lung, busted ribs, broken wrist. Guy enjoys violence.'

Sarah swallowed. 'Does he carry any weapons?'

'He hasn't used any so far, but he might carry one all the same. Rape can escalate into murder, Sarah. The police reckon the guy's beginning to decompensate. The rapes are increasing in frequency. The rapist needs more of the same to get his old kick. Soon rape might not be enough for him. Have you ever experienced violence?'

'Being bait for the rapist doesn't faze me,' she insisted.

'There must be a better way. You seem too ready to throw yourself into the firing line. I don't get it. Seems almost personal to me.'

'It is,' said Sarah, mixing truth with a lie. 'I decided to play God. I was wrong. Now I've got to try to make it right.'

'What about your son? If something goes wrong, you're not the only one affected.'

'Nothing's going to happen,' said Sarah through clenched teeth. 'Look, I've got the best survival mechanism there is. I love that boy more than the whole world, I want to stay alive to love him. All those stories about mothers lifting lorries to save their children, that's the power of mother love.' She also had to know if the father of her child was a serial rapist.

Breden looked away, hiding the sorrow in his eyes.

'So help me,' demanded Sarah, sensing his fears for her. 'Help me defend myself. Teach me some tips to fight him off.'

He suddenly looked resigned. 'Oh, all right. If you must, we'll plan it like a military campaign.'

Sarah was in the kitchen with Georgie when the intercom rang on Saturday morning. She was still in her nightie; her hair was wild and unbrushed. Georgie looked quite happy and he was not yet crawling very far, so she left him and headed upstairs for the door. She threw it open and there was John Redford. He was standing, backlit by the sun, in jeans and a leather jacket, and despite everything, he took her breath away.

'John.'

He looked at her in silence. After a few moments he turned and picked up from behind him a gardenia plant, radiant with white scented flowers.

He held it as if to carry it in for her. She reached out, took it from him, then glanced involuntarily over her shoulder, as if Georgie might suddenly have made his way up the stairs to meet his father.

Redford followed her gaze. Sarah could feel him taking in the tumble of her hair, her sleepy eyes, drawing the inevitable, and wrong conclusion. He gave her a sad smile.

'I'll be on my way, then.'

'Look, it's chaos inside,' said Sarah hurriedly. 'I'd invite you in, I just—'

'No need to explain,' he said. 'I won't intrude.' He turned to go.

'Wait, John. Let's get together later, do something simple, just walk and talk.' She still couldn't believe he was the serial rapist.

Redford paused, indecision flickering in his normally resolute gaze.

'As it happens, I was planning just that for this evening. A long walk, maybe stop at a bar, find some music. We can walk together,' Redford said, half as a question.

'What time?'

'Ten o'clock?'

Sarah gulped. 'I'll come to the Portobello.'

She rang Jacob.

'Hello, sweetie. Everything all right?'

'Everything's fine.' She paused. 'I was just wondering . . .'

'What time would you like me?' he asked, a smile in his voice.

She tried to reach Breden all day. Where the hell was he when she needed him? At nine she gave up, leaving a long message explaining her evening as her insurance policy. She'd just have to go with Redford, take her chances.

Why was she going? To salvage something from the wreck of a relationship, or to hasten its demise? She was no wiser as the time came for her to leave. Her thoughts were clouded, she knew, by her overwhelming wish that Georgie's father were not a rapist.

She dressed for comfort and for speed. She wore her black combats and trainers, with a white T-shirt and a black leather jacket into which she had crammed her money, mobile phone and a can of Mace.

She looked in on Georgie, kissed Jacob goodbye.

'Take care, girl, whatever you're up to.'

'More snooping,' she said with a miserable frown.

'When will this be over?' asked Jacob.

'As soon as I'm paid,' replied Sarah hopefully.

She set off for the King's Road and hailed a taxi. Sinking back into the seat, she suddenly wondered how Redford had found her address. *Deal list*, she realised with a curse. On any deal, the major participants are given a list of one another's home phone numbers and addresses. Jesus, it had been close this morning. She could so easily have answered the door with Georgie in her arms. She didn't want him within a million miles of her child. That wasn't entirely true, she knew that. In one of her waking dreams, she showed her son to his father, bursting with pride at the miracle she had grown inside her.

Sarah shuddered, trying to grab back a piece of reality. Guilty of the serial rapes or not, Redford would always be guilty of the terrible attack on Carla, and part of Sarah could never forgive him.

She arrived at the Portobello at ten, went up to Redford's room and knocked. The door swung open. He stood barefoot, a half-smile on his face. 'Hi. Come on in.'

She stuck her hands in her pockets, sidled past him.

'Thanks for the gardenia,' she said over her shoulder. 'It's filled the whole drawing room with the most delicious scent.'

'Good. I was walking along the King's Road, went into the Chelsea Gardener, some place like that, saw it and thought of you.'

Sarah smiled. 'I'm glad it wasn't a cactus.'

'Wasn't my first choice,' said Redford, 'but they were all out of Venus's flytraps.'

'Ha, ha.'

Every word closed the distance between them by an inch.

'So, you ready for a walk?' asked Redford, still grinning.

'Seems to be a theme, your walking.'

'It is. Every city I choose some place that appeals to me, and take a walk. Walking around, you own a place. Always did it—took off by myself, in the day, late at night, see the city as a native does.'

'All this walking around in cities . . . wouldn't you get mobbed?'

'Uh-uh. Mostly I wear a wig, even a bit of make-up occasionally. Don't get recognised, by and large.'

Sarah felt her heart chill. She bent down, pretended to tie her laces, waited until she felt the shock had crept from her face before she straightened up.

'So, where're we going?' she asked.

'Somewhere in the East End. I like all the tiny streets around Smithfield Market, the all-night cafés. I think there might be a few clubs somewhere round there. We could go and get a drink, listen to a band. D'you know the Spitalfields area?' asked Redford.

'Not really.'

'Then allow me to be your guide.'

'Sounds fine, but what about your disguise?'

'Wait there.'

Redford disappeared into the bathroom, giving Sarah time to study an enlarged *A–Z* of London which was on the sofa, checking for the nearest police stations. A sound made her look up. Redford had approached silently and was standing over her—at least, she presumed it was Redford. This man had a mousy brown mop, where Redford's hair was sleek and dark. This man had pouches to the sides of his mouth, where Redford's skin was smooth. This man had brown eyes, where Redford had grey.

'How on earth did you do that?'

'Wig's obvious, contact lenses're obvious, dental pads not so. I've got two lots of pads taped to my gums, gives me a nice jowly look, just like an English gentleman.'

Sarah laughed, despite herself. 'Not like any of the English gentlemen I hang out with.'

They took a taxi to the City. 'I like to start in the heart of riches, move through, back to the rough places.'

'Like a reverse journey through your life.'

'Yeah, kind of.'

Like one of his songs, thought Sarah, recalling his song about the orphan's lonely walk through life.

> 'I want to go back before the start of the game,
> Get back what I had of old.
> I've searched the whole world
> Looking for what I had . . .'

Sarah's heart went out to him. She knew too well that routeless search. The only sane way was to seek out another path. That path had been given to her. That path was Georgie. Her spell of compassion was broken. She was no longer the orphan, but the mother of a child. Inside her jacket pocket her hand clenched round a can of Mace.

They walked through the canyons of the temples of Mammon, empty now of human traffic. Sarah looked round. Who would hear her scream in these abandoned streets? The City was a ghost town during the weekend. Was that Redford's design? She glanced across at him. He looked back steadily at her, his gaze filled with unspoken questions.

The East End came to life as they turned into Brick Lane, and Sarah felt herself relax. The air was rich with the sweet, acrid tang of curry, the street lamps were a glorious Pakistani rococo. They turned down Hanbury Street, reeled into the sudden roar of traffic on Commercial Street, regained peace on Lamb Street. Sarah suppressed a sudden shudder as the words came unbidden into her mind: *Like a lamb to the slaughter*. She was glad when they saw the portals of the old Spitalfields Market, for cries of life rang from the ancient arches.

Inside, on fields of Astroturf, a series of games of five-a-side football were taking place.

They moved past restaurants lit with orange-burning oil lamps spilling out customers replete with good food, plentiful wine, and abundant conversation. Sarah felt more conscious than ever of the gulf between her and Redford. There was so much she couldn't say to him and, no doubt, he too had his secrets. What they might be, she didn't want to think. So they walked on, alone in their silence.

They walked deeper down Lamb Street, passed Spitalfields Crypt, turned into Fournier Street. Sarah gazed up at the elegant façades of a row of Georgian houses.

'This is where the Huguenots came when they fled France,' said Redford suddenly. 'They were master weavers and dyers, they made damasks, brocades and silks, and they used their new-found wealth to build these houses.'

'I'm impressed,' said Sarah.

'Guidebooks are a wonderful thing,' he grinned.

As they rejoined Brick Lane, a low haunting cry issued from the mosque on the corner of Fournier Street, a muezzin calling the faithful to late prayer. The sound followed them like a wraith. Sarah stopped abruptly before the window of a Metropolitan Police Station. The glass was covered with posters. MURDER. *Can you help*? Or SERIOUS SEXUAL ASSAULT. *Did you witness anything*? It was a grim reminder of the nature of the area in which they now walked. Redford led her into a narrow side street.

'Yes, this is it,' he said softly, almost to himself. Sarah was about to ask him what he meant when her eye was caught by a black Landcruiser approaching at speed. She flattened herself against the wall. There was no pavement here, and the road was so narrow there was scarcely room for the Landcruiser, let alone pedestrians. With a squeal of rubber on tarmac, the car slowed, passed them at a crawl. The windows were blacked out, heightening Sarah's sense that she was being watched by hostile forces inside. With a sudden roar of acceleration, the car was gone, and they were left alone once more in silence. Sarah glanced around uneasily.

'Did you know Jack the Ripper's first known victim was found close by here, off Whitechapel Road?' asked Redford, turning to Sarah.

'Christ! Let's get out of here.' Sarah hoped her voice came out level. Show no fear. Her fingers snaked round her can of Mace.

Redford stopped. Sarah braced herself.

'Hey, you all right?' asked Redford, reaching out to touch Sarah's arm.

'Did you hear that?' she asked, stepping back, looking around.

'What?'

'Footsteps,' answered Sarah, seeking any imagined diversion.

'You spooked?' asked Redford.

'Of course I'm bloody spooked. You bring me out here, and start talking about Jack the Ripper.'

Redford looked hard into Sarah's face, as if searching her for the truth. For those moments neither of them moved and Sarah could imagine that anything was possible, so charged were his eyes.

'Let's go. I'll take you to where you can find a taxi.'

'What's wrong?'

He turned round. 'What's wrong?' he snapped. 'Don't pretend. You don't trust me, do you? What d'you think I'm going to do to you? Rape you? I can see it in your eyes. The dark, lonely streets—something I thought romantic, you think sinister. Trouble is, everything I do will be sinister. You've got me tarred and all you see is black.'

Sarah didn't answer. Redford spoke the truth.

Redford started a slow walk. 'Come on, let's get a taxi.'

'I'm sorry it turned out like this, John.'

'Not half as sorry as I am.'

Relieved to be once more in her familiar world, Sarah paid off the taxi driver and was walking up the steps to her front door when the slam of a car door made her pause. She wheeled round. Dick Breden crossed the street and came at her.

'What the *hell* were you thinking?'

'Shh,' said Sarah. 'Don't shout.'

'What? Are you worried I'll wake your baby? Your little baby's lucky to have a mother, even if that mother is as irresponsible and thoughtless as you.'

Sarah's hand came out like a flick knife. The air cracked as she slapped Breden's cheek. Tears streamed down her face.

'Don't you even think that. This is hard enough without someone who doesn't have the faintest idea what he's on about sticking his bloody oar in. You're right—I *was* stupid. I shouldn't have done it, don't you think I know that? But I'm home now.'

Sobbing, she burst into her house. She leaned against the wall for a few moments, until slowly she got herself under control again.

Breden stood behind her in the hall, his anger washed away by her tears. He stood waiting for her while she walked upstairs.

Georgie was fast asleep, arms thrown out to his sides in confident

310

abandon. Sarah peeped through the open door of the next bedroom and saw Jacob breathing the slow, rhythmic cadence of deep sleep.

Sarah led the way downstairs to the kitchen. Breden followed her. She swiped a bottle of whisky off a shelf and poured out two quadruples.

'Who looks after your baby when you're not here?' asked Breden.

'My Uncle Jacob looks after Georgie. I'd trust him with my life. I'm a good mother. I do the best I can. It's not easy. It's full of conflicts. You do something, you get sucked into the consequences. I have to do lots of things I don't want to but I have my reasons. *My* reasons, get it?'

'All right, I'm sorry. I was frightened for you. What happened tonight?' asked Breden.

She relayed the night's events to him as he listened in taut silence.

'You shouldn't put yourself in that position if you don't think you can carry it off.'

'I thought I could. I could normally get away with it.'

'Not with Redford. He gets through to you. It's as if the two of you are bound together somehow.'

'I empathise with his past,' said Sarah quickly. 'We're both orphans. You don't get much more of a bond than that.'

'That empathy makes you vulnerable. He empathises with you too. He cares about you. It matters to him deeply what you think. If he's innocent, you're really putting him through the wringer. If he's guilty, you're lucky you got off so lightly.'

'Why? After all, it's not the rapist's modus operandi to attack people he knows. Or at least we're assuming that.'

'If he is guilty, you're getting much too close for comfort. Now he knows he's lost your good opinion. And you're the only other person alive, apart from Carla, who knows about the rape. Just you and she stand between him and his good name and a hundred million dollars. If he *is* guilty, killing you begins to look like a better and better option.'

'So why didn't he try?' asked Sarah, suppressing a shudder.

'Perhaps your ruse about hearing footsteps put him off.'

'Pretty thin ruse.'

'And he could, of course, be innocent.'

'But the whole walk, the empty streets, late at night, the disguise, it *sounds* so like the rapist.'

'It does,' replied Breden. 'And I got two new lots of info today which deeply trouble me. Firstly, I was in Lyons until this evening, at Interpol HQ. I've a friend there, high up.'

Sarah felt a pulse of excitement. 'What did you find out?'

'Details. The guy's right-handed. Smells of lemons, wears rubber gloves, uses a condom to prevent collection of DNA. The mask covers his hair, he makes sure the minimum traces get from him to his victims.'

'What traces have they picked up?'

'Clothing, taxicab seats. Nothing else.'

'He never speaks?'

'No. Completely silent.'

'Incredible control.'

'Of himself. Of his victims. Apparently, he is utterly convincing, totally terrifying. His eyes are "merciless, cold, evil"—I quote. Until after it's over, then he looks desolate.'

'The silence—that's another thing that points to Redford. The man with the golden voice, known to millions.'

'The rapist is obsessed that no detail will give him away.'

'He's like a chess player,' said Sarah. 'Planning every last detail.'

'Or a musician. Writing music is a mathematical skill.'

'Oh, Jesus, it all points to him. Is there no other detail? Nothing we could get him on?'

'My friend thinks the violence isn't just to control his victim, it's rage that his smoothly orchestrated campaign is being resisted. The guy's a control freak.'

'That's half of London.'

Breden gave a grim smile. 'True. The guy usually wears a jacket, sometimes leather, sometimes denim, jeans, trainers. Typical urban uniform.'

Sarah stared into space in frustration.

'One thing my friend says mirrors my own personal feeling.'

Sarah looked up, startled by Breden's tone.

'A year ago, the rapes were perhaps one every three weeks. Now it's down to one a week. The guy is definitely getting more dangerous by the day. With each rape, he has less to lose. The next step will be getting smaller and smaller in his mind.'

'And what step is that?' asked Sarah dully.

'Murder.'

'Oh great.' She lapsed into silence. 'What's the second thing you came up with today?'

'Redford's bank account. I've had people going over all the accounts we have access to with a fine-tooth comb. Yesterday a cheque was presented to his bank, made payable to one Carla Parton, for one million dollars.'

'Oh no,' said Sarah, groaning with agony. 'I can't believe it.'

'Do you want to go on with this?' asked Breden.

She looked up at him, taking a while to focus on his concerned features. 'I don't know. I suppose if we know that he's guilty, we might just as well hand him over to the police right now.'

'We don't know he's guilty yet, Sarah. All we have so far is circumstantial evidence. We've no concrete proof.'

'Apart from Carla's word.'

'True, but that was for one rape, not a series. If we went to the police, they'd have to mount some sort of sting operation, try to trap him to get the evidence they need. What we have just won't cut it, Sarah.'

Her face took on a grim resolution. 'Then we continue. We sting him.'

Breden nodded slowly. 'What's the chances of getting close to him tomorrow?' he asked.

'Extremely slim. We didn't exactly part on good terms, and anyway, he always goes into a kind of purdah on concert day. Sees no one.'

'I wanted you to swipe him with a tag, just a tiny sticker that gives off a pulse. Makes it easier to tail him.'

'Even if I could get close, he'd certainly change after the concert.'

'Could you see him after the concert?'

'I suppose I could ask Strone for a backstage pass. Then I could congratulate him on the concert, try to clear the air.'

'Tomorrow's not just concert day, Sarah. Late tomorrow night, or early next morning, is Rape Day. We're counting down. You can step out at any moment, but if you're going to do it, I need to start the clock now.'

Sarah looked out into the night for a long time, then she turned to Breden. 'Start counting.'

Dick Breden lived in Battersea, just over the Albert Bridge, in the penthouse of a glass, metal and concrete block six storeys high. At any other time, Sarah would have indulged her curiosity and wandered around this ascetic temple to minimalism, but analysing Breden, the man he appeared to be, versus the man he was, would have to wait. John Redford and the trap became Sarah's focal point. First she had to keep Savage and Zamaroh at bay. They both spent two hours trading calls with Zamaroh and Savage. Both had to maintain it was impossible for them to come into the office that morning. Both received severe flak. Savage and Zamaroh complained vehemently that neither of their top security people were available.

'Could have done without that,' said Breden. 'Now let's get to work.'

Breden's drawing room was perfect. Huge and bare, save sofas and a glass table, which he pushed to the windows. He explained what he was going to do, then in three easy strides, he moved in and threw Sarah across the room. She did her best to roll on the mattress he'd pulled from his bed, but came up bruised and hurting.

'All right?' asked Breden, concerned.

'I'll live.'

'I'm going to show you something that'll help you put him down—three quick moves you can practise on me.'

Breden drilled Sarah for an hour.

'Only use the moves if you have no choice,' cautioned Breden, 'and then use them with extreme aggression. I've got eight men assembled for the back-up team,' he went on. 'This is what we're going to do.'

'What's all this going to cost?' asked Sarah, when Breden had finished recounting his plan. 'It'll cost a fortune.'

'It will, I'm afraid,' he nodded. 'I'm not going to charge you anything, but I'll have to pay the other guys. It depends what happens, how long the whole thing takes, but you won't get much change from four grand.'

Sarah grimaced. 'Hopefully Savage'll pay me soon.'

Breden left at lunchtime to mastermind the operation from his office. Sarah stayed at his flat. She couldn't go home. Jacob and Georgie would pick up her nerves, and they'd distract her. She felt a new ruthlessness come over her, for their sake, and for that of the women who had been violated.

She rang Strone. 'Hi, it's Sarah. Look, could I have a backstage pass for tonight?'

Strone promised to leave one at Reception in the Portobello. Sarah hung up and paced around Breden's flat, trying to lose the tension in her. She forced herself to eat a large lunch of pasta from his well-stocked kitchen, knowing that she needed to store away as much energy as possible. Extreme stress always exhausted her and after lunch she took herself off to the guest bedroom to try to steal a couple of hours' sleep.

She woke in the midst of a nightmare, more exhausted. The alarm clock showed six o'clock. Shit, she'd slept far longer than she'd meant to. She stood under a hot shower for five minutes then, adrenaline switching through her body, she dressed and took a taxi home.

Jacob was bathing Georgie. She ducked her head round the corner of the door, blew kisses at them both.

'Hello, you gorgeous little beast, and you lovely big old thing. Can't stop. I'll be back late, Jacob, so don't wait up.'

The old man looked up at her with questioning eyes. Sarah was all too aware that he knew she was concealing something. She kissed his cheek, stroked her baby's head. 'Got to go.'

Seeking sanctuary in her bedroom, she closed the door behind her, and sank back against it, sipping at the idea of abandoning it all.

She wanted to hate Redford, or at least rise above him to the plateau of indifference, but still she felt the tumult of love for him, and when she remembered their lovemaking she felt herself burn. She was in thrall to him, tormented by love and doubts, her passionate love for her son cementing something that should have been eroded long ago by suspicion. If he was innocent, she had the chance to make it right. If he was guilty, she could be rid of him, and retreat to a life over which she had control, just her and Georgie.

She moved away from the door and paused before her wardrobe. Part of her wanted to dress as if she were attending her own funeral, a final fling, a last dazzling dance. She picked out a red and salmon-coloured silk and velvet dress—long, figure-hugging, low-cut—and some high, red, strappy sandals. She applied full make-up and surveyed herself in the mirror—one final glance—then set off without a goodbye.

CHAPTER EIGHT

SARAH SAT ALONE in her VIP box at Wembley Arena, looking down at the stage. She bit at her nails, and waited for Redford to appear.

John Redford stalked onto the stage like the pro he was. Blue denim, the loose-limbed walk, fluid and powerful and infinitely sexy. She shuddered. He launched into the first of a whole string of rocking anthems. His voice, so rich and powerful, vibrated through her. She could see him working the crowd into its inevitable frenzy, but before the audience lost control, he switched to a ballad, a new song, just him and his guitar, no backing. The spotlight shone on him alone; he looked into the crowd, and she could have sworn he was looking directly at her.

'One dark night,
One sin, without redemption,
Body and soul broken
Time bomb set.

'I see only suspicion
In your eyes,
You are my judge
And you'd hang me out to dry.

'What do I have to do to say sorry?
Aren't we all allowed just one mistake?
God only knows I'd give everything I own.
To take it back, but not even God can do that.

'Is there another road
We can go down?
Or have we come to
The end?'

The audience stayed silent after the last chords of the song had died with the echoes of Redford's voice. Then the applause started, a small wave that grew into an ocean.

Redford took his bow. 'Thank you. That was my "Song for Sarah".'

John Redford sat alone in his dressing room. Sarah entered with a knock.

'Hello, Sarah.' There was peace in his eyes, as if he had come to some kind of personal exorcism.

'Your song was beautiful.'

'Thank you. A bit out of date now, but what the hell, it's a nice tune.'

Sarah looked at him in puzzlement. 'What d'you mean?'

He shook his head. 'Doesn't matter.' He shrugged. 'Strone said you wanted to see me,' continued Redford. 'Why?'

'To say goodbye,' said Sarah.

'Ah.'

'And to wish you luck.' She opened her arms. He looked at her for a few moments, his face unreadable, before he stood up and went to her. She had the electronic tag on the tip of her index finger; she pressed it to the underside of the collar of his denim shirt as Redford hugged her.

'Goodbye, Sarah. You know, I had hopes for us.'

Sarah hugged him hard, kissed his cheek, and left before he saw the tears teeming down her cheeks.

Sarah found Breden's van parked exactly where he'd said it would be. She took great comfort from this. Breden would run his side like clockwork. The rear door opened as she approached. Awkward in her tight dress and high heels, she clambered in. Breden's eyes widened.

'You look beautiful.'

'Thank you.'

'Why so desolate?'

'I just said goodbye to Redford. I put the tag on him while he was

hugging me. He wrote and sang a song for me, Dick, asking my forgiveness, asking if it was the end. It frightened me. He was acting as if he'd
made his mind up about something.'

'About what?'

'I don't know.' She hesitated, unwilling to voice her fears. 'It was like
he'd come to his own end.'

'Maybe we should forget this whole thing. You can back out even
now, Sarah.'

'No, I can't. Let's see it through.'

Breden gave Sarah an outfit that a waitress might wear, a short white
starched coat. She wore it with beige tights and her own high heels. A
make-up artist worked on her face and hair. When he had finished,
Sarah, under a blonde wig, was transformed into a trampy vamp.

Breden studied her. He nodded at the make-up artist. 'Good job.'

The man nodded at them, then opened the rear door of the van and
jumped out.

'I hope we don't have to wait long,' said Sarah as the door slammed
shut.

Breden looked at her. 'That's the worst bit, the waiting.'

Suddenly, there was a tapping on the darkened window separating
the back of the van from the front. Breden slid it back.

'On the move,' said a voice from the front seat. Sarah caught a
glimpse of dark curly hair, tanned skin. 'Moving steadily, walking, probably heading for his car.' Breden peered through the gap at a monitor.
Sarah saw a small white dot pulsing, and moving north. Breden checked
a tiny earpiece in his ear, and spoke into a small mike attached to his
shirt collar. 'Good. Stay ready.'

'How many vehicles have we got?' asked Sarah.

'Four including this one, two men in each.'

The white dot stopped.

'About to move?' asked Breden into his mouthpiece. 'I'm guessing he's
just got into his car.'

The dot suddenly began to move again, faster now, going south this
time. 'Strap yourself in,' Breden said to Sarah. 'He's coming towards us.
Number two will take him, repeat, number two will take him. Three,
get behind me, four, try to get ahead of him.' As the dot came closer, the
curly-haired man started up the engine, got into gear, and slid out into
the traffic.

'Anyone got visual?' asked Breden. 'Number four? Good. What's his
vehicle? Got a driver? Anyone else with him?' He listened then turned to
face Sarah.

'He's in a Range Rover, blacked-out windows. There seem to be two of them in there, he's probably got a driver. My guys can't see Redford, but he's in there.'

'A driver would complicate things,' said Sarah.

'My guess is the driver'll drop him off and he'll walk.'

'He loves to walk the city at night,' said Sarah. 'He could go miles.'

'Then we'll have to be ready to do the same.' Breden spoke into his mike. 'Be ready to devehicle. Target might go on a long ramble.'

They drove along Harrow Road, heading southeast onto the Westway, at speed. Sarah listened to Breden crooning into his mike.

'Number four, slip back, number two, take up advance position.' Marylebone, Euston, King's Cross. Nice and seedy. She saw the hookers eyeing their car. The white dot stopped. They stopped.

'Number two, got visual?' asked Breden. He listened intently. 'Passenger two, go after him on foot. Car two, stay with his car. All passengers, devehicle, follow on foot. Drivers three and four, move forward at intervals, don't let him get more than a quarter of a mile from you.'

Breden turned to Sarah. 'He's on foot.'

'What happens now?'

'You and I follow by car. My guess is, he'll walk until he finds somewhere suitable, then he'll go into hiding. It's when he stops moving we have to be ready.'

Sarah nodded, her stomach sick. They parked, waited. The dot moved on, along Pentonville Road. Breden listened to his earpiece.

'There's two of them,' he said to Sarah. 'Redford and another guy—at least, they think it's Redford. He's wearing a leather jacket with the collar turned up, and a baseball cap.' Breden turned alert again, listening to his earpiece. 'He's turned onto City Road. There's still two of them.'

'Any idea who the other guy is?' asked Sarah.

'Around six foot, medium build, white, baseball cap, baggy jacket, trainers.'

Sarah shook her head. 'Don't know him.'

The dot moved on relentlessly, down Great Eastern Street. Redford had been walking for over forty minutes now.

'He's heading for Spitalfields,' said Sarah in horror. 'Maybe last night was just a recce.'

Sarah and Breden stared at the flashing dot, as its bearer turned into Grey Eagle Street. Then it stopped.

'Who's got visual?' Breden asked sharply. 'Number two, what's happening?' He turned back to Sarah. 'Redford and his friend have gone into a bar.' He took Sarah's hand. 'You ready for this?'

She nodded. He handed her an earpiece, and fixed a microphone to her collar. 'I'm number five, you're number one. All working?'

Sarah pushed in her earpiece, spoke and listened. 'This is number one. You all hear me?'

A chorus of voices answered 'Yes'.

'Don't speak to him until I get to you. I don't want him recognising your voice and bolting.'

'Silent as the grave,' said Sarah, managing a smile.

Breden suddenly hugged her. 'Good luck.'

Sarah hugged him back. 'Thanks.' She thought he was bound to feel her heart pounding, as if it had doubled in size.

'You call for me, I'll be there in a sprint. Keep up a running commentary, keep your mouth as immobile as you can.'

The van parked on Grey Eagle Street, a long, empty corridor of urban decay. Sarah and Breden slipped out. It was 1.00am. The streetlights glowed orange; falling rain cast a miasma round the light. The bar was called the Fallen Angel. Breden led Sarah in the back entrance.

A man with a ponytail blocked their way. 'What's your game?' he asked, hard-voiced.

'Who am I talking to?' asked Breden.

'I'm the soddin' owner. Who the fuck are *you*?'

'Police,' replied Breden. He produced a laminated police pass, stating that he was Detective Inspector Dick Evans of the Metropolitan Police. The owner studied it.

'What d'you want?'

'We want to use your premises for surveillance. We'd like to wait somewhere quiet then, we're not sure when, we'll need to have my constable here,' he nodded at Sarah, 'show her face in the bar, just for a minute. We'll want you to speak to her, say, "Good night", act as if she's your new, temporary short-order cook, just covering for one night.'

The man raised his eyebrows. 'Why should I?'

'Never needed any favours?'

'Don't we all.'

'Well, let's call it earning some credit, then.'

The owner nodded slowly, as if weighing up his different options. 'You owe me then.'

'I owe you. But only if you do what I say.'

'Better come to my office.'

'Just the constable,' said Breden. 'I'll hang around out here.'

'Please yourself.'

Sarah followed the owner into the Fallen Angel.

The place reeked of smoke, piss and fried onions. A jukebox played rock, something by Bon Jovi: 'You Give Love a Bad Name'. Yeah, right, thought Sarah. The owner led her up some rickety back stairs. The man took a key from his pocket and unlocked his office. He gestured to Sarah to go in.

'Thanks.' She took a seat on a battered sofa.

'So what happens now?' he asked.

'You wait for the detective inspector's instructions.'

The man walked out wordlessly. Sarah bolted the door behind him, then slumped back into the sofa. The voices chattered away in her ear.

'Number three here,' said a soft Irish brogue. 'I'm with number four, in the bar. We've got visual. Two men at the bar, one of them is the one tagged, but he's not Redford.'

'*What?*' Breden's voice rasped into her ear.

'Hang on,' cried Sarah. 'What's he look like?'

'Five ten, eleven maybe, dark wavy hair, brown eyes.'

'Jowly?'

'Yeah. He's heavy round the mouth, I'd say jowly.'

'That's Redford,' whispered Sarah. 'It's his disguise, just like last night. Different wig, that's all. What's the other guy look like?'

'Same height as Redford. Baseball cap, straggly blond hair, smoking.'

'Know him?' asked Breden.

'Nope,' replied Sarah. 'What're they drinking?'

'The blond straggly one's drinking a short, looks like whisky,' said number three. 'Other one's drinking something white and fizzy, could be water, could be lemonade. Eating crisps. Looks ravenous.'

'Redford's always thirsty and starving after a concert,' said Sarah.

'Has to be him,' said Breden. 'Unless he gave his denim shirt away.'

'Yeah, that's likely, isn't it?' said Sarah sarcastically. 'And gave it to someone who came to exactly the same place he did the night before? No,' she muttered. 'It's Redford. I'm sure of it.'

The voices lapsed into silence. Sarah lay back, her breathing shallow. Perhaps nothing would happen. Perhaps Redford would get in the car and go home. She jumped when number three's soft Irish brogue spoke into her ear.

'Unidentified man is off to the Gents. I think they're gonna move soon.'

'Right,' came Breden's voice. 'Number one, be ready. I'm going in.'

Sarah flinched. She heard footsteps, then Breden speaking to the owner. 'I'm going to go and get my constable. Here's fifty quid. Give it to her, say thanks for helping out, all low key, don't overdo it.'

'Not my style,' replied the man laconically.

Sarah heard footsteps, then a knock on the door.

'Open up, it's me.'

She opened the door to Breden.

'Off you go. Good luck.'

She nodded, her throat dry, then walked down the stairs to the hall-way where the owner was waiting. Her whole body trembled, and sweat coursed down her back.

The owner strode into the bar. Sarah held the door, peeking round the edge. The owner walked up to the till, counted out five tens and handed them over to Sarah.

'Fifty quid for a short-order cook. Bloody rip-off merchant.'

'Oh, spare me,' said Sarah, in somebody else's voice. The two men pulling on their jackets at the bar swung round to follow the voice. Sarah looked for just long enough to register Redford's eyes on hers, before glancing away, as if shy, or just flirtatious. She mumbled goodbye to the owner and walked to the door. Then she set off slowly.

'Walking north up Grey Eagle Street,' she whispered to the surveil-lance team. God, it was bleak. The cracking tarmac was strewn with litter. High concrete walls, corrugated iron tinted nuclear-orange by the pall of the streetlights. Tumble-down flats, long since evacuated. Sarah moved on quickly.

'They're leaving the bar,' said number three. She resisted the urge to turn round. 'They're watching you, number one,' said a different voice in her ear. She walked on, slow on her high heels. 'They're talking, look-ing round. Wait, a car's coming up, looks like a minicab. Car's stopped, target's approaching, talking to the driver. He's getting in. Red Volvo estate. Reg number CST 45P. Target's car's pulling away.'

'Numbers two, three and four, take up pursuit of car. Repeat, take up pursuit of car,' commanded Breden. 'Number one. Keep walking.'

Sarah braced herself as she heard the car approach. 'Car approaching me, he's accelerating,' she glanced at the car, saw Redford looking out, straight at her. Christ, did he recognise her? 'He's passing, turning right fifty yards ahead of me,' she continued, relief and confusion sweeping over her.

'Number four, get ahead of target,' said Breden. 'Number three, take up the rear, stay out of sight.'

'What happens now?' asked Sarah.

'Go left into Quaker Street,' replied Breden, 'then take another left into Commercial Street. Walk down to the junction with Hanbury Street. I'll be there waiting for you.'

What a way to spend the night! Now that the drama was over and the danger had passed, Sarah felt an overwhelming weariness, as well as confusion. What had gone wrong? Why had Redford gone off?

She turned into Quaker Street. Away from the noise of the traffic on Commercial Street, the silence descended like fog. She could hear her own footsteps, but no one, she realised, would hear her scream. She didn't think it was possible for the urban landscape to get worse. An empty road ran alongside a railway siding. High wire-netting prevented any vandalism, or perhaps it was to foil any suicides on the track. An empty car park lay strewn with rubbish; dim lights from station arches across the track cast a pall over pockmarked concrete. Desolate yards full of scrap were illuminated briefly as a red BMW roared past, pulsing with music. For a moment she feared the car would slam on its brakes and stop, but it carried on as if oblivious to her. She walked on, now totally alone.

Something made her stop, a strange, squishing sound. She listened, her heart suddenly pounding. It was the sound of footsteps, of trainers on the wet street, getting closer. She began to move, faster in her high heels. The junction with Commercial Street was a mere fifty yards away now. She had an overwhelming urge to run. *Stay calm, Redford's gone*, she told herself. She was nearly at the junction, just another twenty yards, when suddenly there was a rush of sound behind her. She wheeled round; a man was running at her at full pelt.

A scream ripped from her. '*Nooooooo!*' She began to run.

Breden's voice, 'Where are you, number one? What's happening?'

'Help me! Help me! I'm on—' She slipped, her ankle turned and buckled and she crashed to the ground.

She screamed in pain and terror and tried to get to her feet. She was nearly there when the man caught up with her, and flung himself down on top of her. She felt her head slam into the rough ground. The man grabbed her wrists. A wave of nausea flooded her and bright beads of red flashed before her eyes. Desperately fighting to remain conscious, through the haze of red she saw the man looming over her. He wore a black hood, with slits for his eyes. He smelt of lemons. He said not a word, as he stared at her.

The predator knelt over her, crushing her wrists against the ground. She could taste blood in her mouth. She must have bitten her lip when she hit the ground. Dimly, she heard traffic; it seemed to be far away, as if it belonged to a different world. As it did. A world where there was no violence, where there was only goodness. Where there was Georgie.

As she pictured Georgie she felt a surge of strength and heaved with all her might to loosen the man's grip. He responded by punching her in the face. Her head snapped back against the road again, and she felt herself beginning to lose consciousness. Oh no, oh God no, this can't be happening. She fought against it. *Georgie, my baby, Georgie, I love you. Nothing will happen to Mama.* She tried to remember what Breden had taught her.

She tried again to fight off the man. The response was another blow to her head. Oh God, any more of this and she wouldn't be able to hold on. Where the fuck was Breden? The man began to drag Sarah towards the railway siding. Her calves scraped the rough ground. She could feel the blood begin to run as the skin seared off. 'Help me. HELP ME!' she screamed into the mike, but no one came. Each moment stretched into an infinity of terror. *Oh Georgie, I can't let this happen . . .*

Rage flooded her. She bent her knees up, till she got both feet under the man's ribs, and then she lunged at him with all her force. He grunted and fell back. She struggled up. The man leapt to his feet, swinging his fists. One caught Sarah another blow to the side of the head.

She was just conscious of punching his face, of taking blows herself which rocked her, of one almighty punch, of falling backwards. She had unleashed a torrent of violence. She remembered Breden telling her that the more his victims resisted, the more the rapist punished them. She didn't think it was possible to feel more fear, but suddenly her fear seemed to flare like a fire out of control when another pair of arms grabbed her from behind. She screamed in abject terror.

'Sarah, Sarah, it's all right, it's me. It's Dick. It's all right, I've got you.'

The masked man spun round and lurched away. Breden very gently and quickly laid Sarah on the ground, and ran after him. '*Catch him. Please God, catch him,*' Sarah whispered, before a great black wave flooded over her and she thought no more.

Linoleum floors, police milling around, low voices talking.

'Possibly severe head injury, concussion, lost a lot of blood.'

'Doctor's on his way. He'll be here within five minutes.'

Then her full consciousness came back. She sat up and vomited.

Hands went around her, steadied her, held her head.

'Easy there. It's all right. Cough it up, that's right, that's better,' murmured a voice. At that another jag of pain, and up came the vomit again.

'It's all right, Sarah.' Someone took her hand. 'You'll be fine.'

She looked up, trying to focus, and dimly made out the face of Dick Breden. 'What happened?' Then, more urgently, 'Did you catch him?'

'I caught him.'

'Who is it, who is it? Tell me.'

'I don't know. The police won't let me see him. He won't say who he is and there's apparently no ID on him.'

Another voice, a man bending over her.

'I'm Detective Inspector Harding, Miss Jensen. Do you think you're able to take a look at him?'

She saw Breden looking from her to the inspector with doubtful eyes.

'Where's that bloody doctor?' demanded Breden to the air.

'We'll have her examined as soon as he gets here,' the inspector promised. He bent forward towards Sarah. 'You up to looking at this man?'

Sarah wiped her mouth. 'Yes, I want to see him.'

The inspector led her along a narrow corridor. Dick Breden walked beside her, one arm round her, holding her up. They descended a flight of stairs and paused. The inspector turned to Sarah. 'You ready for this?'

She nodded.

He led them round a corner. A group of cells lined the wall. They stopped before the first one. A man sat on the floor, with his back to them.

'Get up, you bastard,' said Harding. 'There's someone here to see you.'

The man slowly got up, and turned to face them. It was Strone.

CHAPTER NINE

IT WAS GONE FOUR by the time Sarah left the police station. The doctor had dressed her grazed calves. The cut to her head was superficial. The doctor had put in two stitches but, more seriously, he diagnosed bad concussion, and wished to admit her to hospital for observation. Sarah, however, insisted on going home. She had to see her son. The doctor and Breden relented, only when Sarah promised that there would be someone to watch over her. Jacob, as always.

A uniformed constable drove her home. Breden had to stay in the station, explaining himself to a DI screaming about entrapment. Strone had been locked up. She shuddered uncontrollably at what had nearly happened to her, at the thought of what had happened to all the victims who did not have a surveillance team ready to bail them out.

She had always kidded herself that she was invincible. Now she would never look at the world in the same way again.

The constable saw her to her door. Sarah tiptoed upstairs to her son's room. The landing light was on, casting a faint glow upon the sleeping infant's features. She crouched down beside him, gazing at him through the bars of his cot, watching his tiny chest rise and fall under the blankets, and weeping silently.

Jacob was waiting for her at her bedroom door. He looked old and frail, wrapped in his tattered tartan bathrobe, white stubble grazing his chin, hair unkempt, fear in his eyes.

'Oh my God. Oh Lord above. What happened to you? What happened to you?' he wailed, fingers brushing the swollen contours of her face. 'God in His heaven, I'll kill the bastard who did this.'

The ringing of the alarm hit her head like a percussion of hammers. She stumbled to her feet, rushed for the bathroom, and threw up in the basin. Concussion, shock, painkillers and exhaustion made a toxic cocktail. She raised her head, splashed water over her skin, flinched, peered through swollen eyes at the havoc wrought upon her face. She gently touched the black eye, the swollen lips, the grazed cheek. Fifteen minutes in the shower and she felt marginally less like death. She dried herself hurriedly, pulled on clean clothes. It was nine. Georgie had long since woken, been given his breakfast by Jacob, and was already into the first of his morning naps.

Jacob was in the kitchen, drinking tea. His eyes as he took her in spoke of his hurt. Her pain was magnified a hundred times in his heart and soul. That he could not bear it for her, that she had not shared her plots and plans with him, given him the chance to help her, was a wound that would heal far more slowly than Sarah's battered face.

'How're you feeling?' he asked stiffly.

'All the better for seeing you and my baby,' she answered.

'Yes, well. Lucky you are to be seeing anything if you . . .'

'I know. I'm stupid, irresponsible—'

'I was out of my mind with worry. I still don't understand why you put yourself at risk like that.'

Sarah went to him and took his hand. 'Jacob, I've told you everything I can. Please, let it go. I have my reasons: allow me those. I'm a big girl. I don't choose to have secrets from you for a whim. Please, trust me.'

He dropped his hand from hers and got to his feet. 'I'm going to make you some breakfast, sweetie.'

It was ten fifteen by the time Sarah knocked at John Redford's door.

She held on to the doorpost, almost crippled by exhaustion. Redford opened the door, dazed by sleep, eyes barely open.

'Sarah. Come in.' He brushed his hair from his eyes. He was wearing the hotel bathrobe. Sarah saw again the little boy, the strange innocence. He didn't know. No one had told him yet.

The sitting room was in darkness. Heavy curtains kept out the light. Redford sank into an armchair. Sarah took a seat opposite on the sofa.

'I've got some bad news,' she said softly. 'It's about Strone. We believe he's guilty of over twenty rapes, in South America, North America, the Far East, now Europe.'

'What?' Redford jolted awake. '*Who* believes?'

She stood up, switched on the lights and turned to Redford.

'Shit! What happened to you?' He got up and went to her. He traced his fingers over the livid bruises colouring Sarah's face.

She flinched and pushed him away. 'This serial rapist has raped in almost every place that you did a show, always in the early morning after a performance,' she said, her eyes never leaving his. 'When I heard about Carla, and then learned about the serial rapist, I thought it might be you. I and my team studied the rapist's modus operandi, and decided to set a trap, with me as bait. I tagged your shirt with a surveillance beeper. I and a back-up team trailed you to the Fallen Angel. I was the woman in the blonde wig and the waitress outfit. That's the type the rapist always went for. I left the club the same time as you. You went off in a red Volvo; I thought the danger had passed. I took a walk round the block. Someone came after me.' Her voice began to tremble. 'He jumped me, I tried to fight back, so he hit me. He must have hit me six times before my back-up team arrived, chased him, caught him. It was Strone.'

Redford sank his face into his hands. 'Dear God, Sarah, I'm sorry. I'm sorry you went through that.' Redford began to pace. 'I can't take this in. He told me he just wanted to walk. He always does, in every city—that's what got *me* into it. And when we went out together, he thought it was a blast to put on a disguise too. I thought maybe it was whores he was after, never pushed that much.' He stopped before Sarah and squatted in front of her. '"Back-up team, surveillance tags". Who the hell *are* you? I said once you were a spy for Goldsteins. That's all you are, isn't it? The numbers stuff was just a ruse to spy on me.'

'It wasn't just a ruse, but part of it was, yeah, sure. Someone had to check for skeletons in your closet.'

'How could you do this? To me, to you, to us?'

'Oh, John. Don't do this, please. I can't deal with it now.'

'Answer me, Sarah. You can't walk in here, dump what you've been doing for the past months on me and expect me to sit here like some patsy and just nod. This is real life, not some financial game, with me as a pawn. Is that why you slept with me? Just doing your job?'

Sarah slapped his face. Redford rubbed his reddening skin, looking almost pleased he'd elicited some passion from Sarah.

'What do you think?' she said.

'How do I know *what* to think? You lied to me from the first.'

'Not in Wyoming,' she said softly. 'And after that, over here, I did everything I could *not* to sleep with you. When I did it had nothing to do with the job, believe me.'

Redford gave a bitter laugh. 'Belief's a pretty scarce commodity round here. You believed I was a serial rapist.'

'I was wrong, but you raped once; it didn't look good for you.'

Redford dragged his hand through his hair. 'The police have been to see me. A detective inspector.'

Sarah looked up sharply.

'Wanted to see me about a Miss Carla Parton,' said Redford. 'Alias Jenni White, alias D. D. Simmonds.'

Sarah felt her knees wobble. She sat on the sofa.

'Carla Parton, sometime resident of various psychiatric wards where she was treated for psychotic behaviour, is wanted across five states in connection with stalking, blackmail and extortion,' intoned Redford. 'A certain rock star, I'm not at liberty to say who, challenged her when she accused him of raping her when he was in a drugged-out haze. He called in the cops, his security people kept Miss White on the premises. Cops printed her, and the prints came up with a rap sheet long as her legs. She's tried it on three other performers before me. All three paid up, compensated her for fucking up her life. She picked her victims so cleverly, just enough possibility of guilt.'

Sarah dropped her face into her hands. She sat there, her breath hot against the backs of her fingers. She had wanted to believe Carla, had wanted to judge Redford, to see the worst, all so that she could be free of him, could break the love that bound her to him, could keep her son from him. She had seen everything through the distortion of her own love and need. Then another thought struck her.

'Maybe Carla was telling the truth the first time. Raped but by Strone. She never saw who she claimed raped her after your concert. Whoever was in the room was hidden behind a screen. She just assumed it had to be you, since it was your dressing room.'

'Strone always has his own room too, to chill out in, to *mastermind operations*, as he puts it,' said Redford tightly.

'She was dressed in her waitress uniform. All the women we think were raped by Strone wore waitress uniforms. If she were raped by Strone, then maybe it dislodged something in her brain and she thought all the other rock stars she blackmailed had really raped her too.'

'Maybe. Whatever,' said Redford. 'She fooled me. I paid her a million dollars,' he added in a tone of self-disgust.'

Sarah paced around Redford's room, her mind a maelstrom.

Sarah decided not to tell him she already knew. 'Why didn't you tell me?'

Redford gave a derisive laugh. 'It was too late, wasn't it, Sarah? You'd already made up your mind about me.'

Sarah began to weep. She got to her feet and ran from the room.

She caught a taxi on Kensington Park Road and headed for Goldsteins. James Savage was the next person to be faced. Just as the taxi was approaching Liverpool Street, her mobile rang. It was Breden.

'I just spoke to the Old Bill. Strone's confessed.'

The shock rendered Sarah silent for a while. 'Confessed? I never thought he would.'

'Confessed a few hours ago. It all came tumbling out apparently.'

Sarah's mind raced. 'Did he say anything about Carla?'

'He did. Apparently she was the first one.'

'That was so long ago! How many times must he have raped in the meantime?' The horror of it all threatened to engulf her.

'You stopped him, Sarah,' said Breden. 'Your courage stopped him.'

'Yeah, well, I'll need some more of it now. I'm just going to see Savage and tell him everything.'

'Good luck,' said Breden.

'Do you want me to keep you out of it? He'll be mad as hell with you.'

'He will be, but no, don't worry. The truth'll come out sooner or later. I'll just brace myself for a rocket.'

When Evangeline saw Sarah's face, and heard her grim request to see her boss immediately, she interrupted Savage halfway through a meeting with a new prospective client.

'What in heaven's name happened to you?' he said.

'Can we sit down?' asked Sarah, suddenly reeling from another onslaught of nausea. Savage led her into his office and sat her down.

'Evangeline,' he called. 'Bring a glass of water, would you.'

Sarah gently sipped the water and began to gather herself.

'Just tell me,' Savage whispered with concerned eyes, 'who did this.'

'It's a long story. I'd better start at the beginning,' said Sarah.

'Bloody hell,' said Savage, getting to his feet as she came to the end. 'You could have got yourself killed. Why did you do all this?'

Sarah bit her lip. Her heart trembled as she tried to separate what she would and would not tell Savage.

'I had my reasons.'

'What reasons? What could possibly justify all this?'

'The stalker. She threatened my uncle, and my child,' said Sarah in a dull voice.

Savage paused. He looked at Sarah with renewed shock. 'Your child?'

'I have a nine-month-old son. She wrote that she would kill Georgie.' Tears began to spill down Sarah's face.

Savage blew out a heavy breath. 'I always knew you were holding back on something. Bloody hell, Sarah, I can hardly think straight. You've really run amok this time.'

'Have I?' asked Sarah, anger building. 'You wanted me to drag the bloody skeletons out of every cupboard, and I've done that. I found your Leaker, I found out that Redford was being stalked, I found the stalker. Now your precious deal is safe. It'll be messy with a prosecution of Strone, but Redford's innocence is what counts.'

'You think I should go along with this deal now?' Savage asked incredulously.

'Why the hell not? If you don't, everything I've done, all the risks I've taken, will have been in vain.'

Savage drew in a number of deep breaths.

He sat down behind his desk and brought out a chequebook. He tore out a cheque, filled it in and handed it to Sarah.

'Here you are. I can't say you don't deserve this, but I wish to high heaven you hadn't taken all the risks you did.'

'There *was* no risk-free way of doing this, James. You must know that. You'd just rather not know too much about our methods, but you still push for the results.'

'Maybe you're right.'

Sarah pocketed the cheque. 'Thank you, James. And the deal?' She thought about Redford and his dreams of retiring. 'Will you go ahead?'

Savage took a while to answer. 'I'll have to think about it. It's so damn messy. Externally, the press'll be all over us, and internally, I'll have Zamaroh to contend with. How the hell do I explain any of this to her? She'll be like a walking volcano.'

'Do it, James,' said Sarah. 'It's the right thing to do.'

Sarah hailed a taxi and slumped in the seat. Her mind went back to her meeting with Redford, to his revelation of Carla's blackmail, and Breden's subsequent news of Strone's confession. How had she got it all so wrong? The personal and the professional blurred until she could see nothing but her own ineptitude, her own guilt. She had loved John Redford. Why was she so frightened of her own motives in loving him? She didn't want fame. Money, maybe. But she would never have chosen someone with a face recognised around the globe. She loved the man, but the rock star frightened her, and so she destroyed him in her mind, killed their love.

She got home, face red with tears, took Georgie from a surprised Jacob.

'What's happened now?'

'I've been an idiot,' she gasped. 'I've messed up so badly, you wouldn't believe. I've—' The ringing of the buzzer drowned out her words. 'Oh, who the bloody hell is *that*?' She strode down the hall and flung open the door. John Redford stood on the threshold. Sarah let out an anguished cry. She turned her body away from him, trying unsuccessfully to shield Georgie from his gaze.

'Who the devil are you?' demanded Jacob, appearing at Sarah's shoulder. 'Shall I get rid of him?' he asked Sarah, squaring up.

Redford's incredulous eyes flitted from Georgie's face to hers.

'No. No need for that.' She spoke heavily to Redford. 'You'd better come in.'

Sarah sat on the sofa and hugged Georgie to her. Redford stood opposite her. Jacob hovered uncertainly in the doorway.

'How old is he?' asked Redford, his normally smooth voice shaken.

'Nine and a bit months,' answered Sarah. She could see Redford doing the calculations.

'Do I need to ask you anything else?' he said slowly.

Sarah had never felt so utterly open, so defenceless. 'No,' she said, her voice a whisper. 'You don't.'

Redford buried his head in his hands. 'Why didn't you tell me? How could you keep him from me?'

She stared into his face and saw, blazing in his eyes, the same ferocity she had seen in Wyoming. Then it was passion, now anger, but through the anger, just a trace of something good showed.

'Oh dear God,' said Jacob. '*You're* Georgie's father?'

Both he and Redford looked to Sarah to confirm the truth they saw all too clearly in the baby's grey eyes.

Sarah turned to Redford, 'Yes. You're Georgie's father.'

CHAPTER TEN

The following year

The Word, June 7

Goldsteins International launched the largest 'Bowie Bond' the industry has seen when they securitised the back catalogue of rock legend John Redford. Goldsteins raised $110 million for Redford. The bonds, rated Single A by Moody's, were taken up by ten institutional investors. Redford does not seem to have suffered adversely from the scandal surrounding his former manager Strone Cawdor, sentenced last week to twenty-two years in prison for serial rape.

Sarah put down the newspaper, bent over Georgie and kissed his cheek.

'D'you want to come out for a bit of fresh air before we bath you and put you to bed?' she asked.

He shook his head violently and enunciated a perfect and definitive 'No!' before turning back to his puzzle.

Sarah smiled. 'OK, my angel. I'll just be five minutes.' She glanced around the room, making sure everything was as baby-safe as it could be, then she walked out onto the balcony and breathed in the bracing air. Summer had come suddenly to the mountains and brought with it a feeling of euphoria.

Each day, the snow that had coated the Tetons like a thick cape just two weeks ago, unravelled a little bit further. Now it just covered the deepest crevices. The sun was beginning to set, casting the rock terracotta red, leaving the identical image, upside-down, shimmering in the lake. Sarah walked down the wooden steps from the balcony, out onto the thickly growing grass. She strolled the twenty yards to the lake and climbed up upon a mossy rock. There she lifted her face to the sun, catching the last of the day's warmth before it dropped like a meteor behind the towering horizon of stone.

She could see down the valley to the plains beyond, with the mountains framing her view to left and right. She saw a moose pick its way delicately from a clump of trees and head towards another. It stopped halfway across. Its ears flicked back and forth, then it turned its head in the opposite direction and seemed to be looking hard at something. It took Sarah a while to spot the source of its interest. Then, slowly, she picked out a moving dot, which grew into a horse mounted by a tall rider in a cowboy hat. The horse was the same terracotta red as the sun-burnished mountains, its carriage elegant and sure-footed as it cantered gently towards her. The moose watched its approach with grave interest, before slowly high-stepping away into the trees.

Sarah climbed down from her rock and walked back to the cabin. She gathered Georgie up into her arms and went outside with him. The horse now slow-trotted towards them. Ten yards away, the rider slipped from the saddle, hooked his reins round the pommel, and walked towards them with arms outstretched. Georgie wriggled in his mother's arms until she put him down on the ground. He toddled towards the smiling man, and said one word, over and over again.

'Dada.'

LINDA DAVIES

Linda Davies read Politics, Philosophy and Economics at Oxford University before joining an American Bank in their mergers and acquisitions department. 'In 1985 the City was a great challenge,' she told me, 'because there were not too many women working there at that time. And I love a challenge! But after seven gruelling years, working ludicrously long hours, dressed in prissy designer suits, watching your back every day, I decided it was time to quit.' Over those years Linda had made a lot of money and had managed to shy away from the peer pressure to spend it. 'I had saved up my "running away money",' she says with a smile, 'and so I discarded those detested designer work suits and locked myself away in my flat in Chelsea to pursue my dream—writing fiction.'

The result was her first novel, *Nest of Vipers*, which heralded the appearance of her fictional heroine Sarah Jensen. 'Once I have created a strong female character, I like to develop her in future books, which is why Sarah has reappeared in *Something Wild*. The trouble is that since writing *Nest of Vipers*, I have married, and am now the mother of two sons, three-year-old Hughie and Tommy, aged nine months. My life has moved on and I found it difficult to fully empathise with Sarah. So, I thought, yes, I know, I will give her a child and the man of her dreams, and now we are back on the same wavelength.'

Linda Davies believes whole-heartedly that research is essential if her novels are to be successful. 'I feel that if I give my readers beautiful locations, it helps them escape, plus I get to research some wonderful places.' For *Something Wild*, Linda visited Wyoming, New York, Paris, Venice and, in sinister contrast, walked the Jack the Ripper streets of the East End of London. 'I always take my husband Rupert with me when I'm on a research trip,' Linda explains, with a smile. 'For his wonderful company and observations, but also because he acts as my bodyguard. In both Venice and the East End we were walking the streets long past midnight and I would never had had the courage—or the stupidity—to do so alone.' In fact, the most frightening part of her research happened when they were in Wyoming. 'Like Sarah and Redford, Rupert and I went out into the wilderness on horseback, camping under the stars with just a guide for company. It was heaven, so incredibly beautiful. But one night we had a visitor—a grizzly bear wandered into camp and swiped our tent as he passed through, looking for food. The claw marks were all too visible, but luckily we were not in it at the time!'

Linda Davies is currently hard at work on her next novel, in which Sarah Jensen and John Redford will feature once again. 'Will their love survive as they settle down to a life together?' I asked her. 'You will just have to wait and see,' Linda replied, enigmatically.

Jane Eastgate

JUDI HENDRICKS

Bread Alone

When she married him, David was the
perfect husband, everything Wyn had
dreamed about. But, caught on the
treadmill of trying to be the perfect
company wife, Wyn is devastated to
discover that David is doing some
entertaining of his own . . .
In the wake of his betrayal, Wyn flees
from sun-baked California to rain-
drenched Seattle, where she discovers her
true vocation: baking bread. And in
rebuilding her life, she learns to be
hopeful about the future and the promise
it holds.

One

LOS ANGELES, 1988

THE BEEPING SMOKE DETECTOR wakes me. No, wait. The smoke detector
buzzes. When I sit up, the room is wavy, an image in a funhouse mirror.
The alarm clock? I turn my head too quickly. It's the old Apache torture.
Strips of wet rawhide, tied tight, left to dry.

I swing my legs over the edge of the bed, blink my swollen eyes. My
mouth feels like the fluff trap in the clothes dryer. I'm wearing a half-slip
and the ivory silk blouse I had on last night. An empty bottle of Puligny-
Montrachet sits on the night table. What did I do with the glass?

I stand up, unsteady. Walk downstairs. Into the kitchen. The bread
machine. How can such a small machine make such a big noise? I hit
the button. The beeping stops and the lid swings open, releasing a cloud
of scent. I wheel round and vomit into the sink. I turn on the water,
rinse my mouth, gripping the cold counter. Then I remember. David.

I lift out the still-warm loaf, set it on the maple butcher's block, a perfect brown cube of bread.

The employment agency is a busy office in a glass and steel building that
has breathtaking views of Interstate 405, still bumper to bumper at
10.30. Applicants crowd the waiting area—mostly women who appear
to be ten years younger than me. The place has a sense of purpose
worthy of the War Rooms you see in a Second World War movie.
Everyone's on the phone or tapping a keyboard or striding resolutely
down the hall.

The only exception is the young woman at the front desk. 'Can I help
you?' she says with a smile.

337

'I have an appointment with Lauren at eleven o'clock. I know I'm early, but . . .'

'That's OK.' She hands me a clipboard with several forms attached to it. 'If you'll just fill these out we can get started with your tests.'

Tests? Oh shit. I sink down onto a chair, my head still twanging, in spite of two aspirins. One thing at a time. Name: *Justine Wynter Franklin.* Maybe I shouldn't use my married name. I try to erase *Franklin* but the eraser is old and brittle and just makes smudges. I scratch a line through it, print MORRISON. Now it looks like I'm not sure.

Address. Telephone. I nail those two. Date of birth. Social Security number. Type of work desired. I put down *Office.* Too vague? Skills. I stare at the blank space and it seems to grow larger, defying me to fill it.

Well, I can still recite François Villon's '*l'Epitaphe*'. Or discuss the effects of the Industrial Revolution on the English novel. Let's see . . . I can make perfect rice with no water left in the bottom of the pot and I have a strong crosscourt backhand. A long time ago I knew how to type, but even then my speed was nothing to brag about.

'Justine Franklin?'

Startled, I look up.

'Hi, I'm Lauren Randall.' The woman standing in front of me, show-ing me her perfect teeth, is obviously very much at home in this world. Fortyish, handsome rather than pretty, wearing a beige silk dress.

When I get up to shake her outstretched hand, the clipboard clatters to the floor. Face burning, I scoop it up, ignoring the stares, follow her down the hall and into her office. She takes the clipboard from me. 'Let's see what we've got. What kind of work are you looking for?'

'General office: filing, answering the phone . . .'

'Have you worked as a receptionist?'

'Well—'

'How many lines have you handled? Have you used a Rolm System?' She ignores my silence. 'I'm sorry. I guess I came roaring out before you had a chance to finish the application. I'll just make some notes and then we can give you the typing test.'

'There's no point in giving me a typing test. I haven't typed anything in five years.'

'That's OK.' She waves a hand breezily. 'It's like riding a bicycle. It comes back to you with a little practice.' She looks at the blank spaces under the 'Experience' heading. 'Are you currently employed, Justine?'

'Wynter. I go by my middle name.'

'Sorry. Wynter, why don't you just tell me what your experience is?'

Deep breath. 'Three years teaching in high school,' I say. 'One year real-estate sales . . .' She's looking at me expectantly, waiting for me to get to the meat and potatoes. 'And I've worked on committees. Cedars-Sinai, the Philharmonic . . .'

'Why on earth do you want to do general office? You'd make more money teaching or going back to selling real estate.'

'I can't sell real estate because I was horrible at it. And I hated teaching.' I grip the arms of the chair with damp fingers.

She sits back slowly, sizes me up. Another wealthy Hancock Park honey whose meal ticket got cancelled. Inside, she's probably laughing her butt off. 'I don't mean to startle you, Wynter,' she says quietly, 'but I hate this job. Sometimes we have to do things we hate.'

I'm on my feet, not knowing how I got there. 'Thanks for the advice.' I walk out of her office, past the receptionist, out of the building.

I sit in the parking lot in the red Mazda RX-7 that was my birthday present three years ago. *Bitch. What the hell do you know about anything?* Why am I even worrying about a job? David and I will sit down tonight and work this out. He's tired, stressed to the max. He'll probably walk in the door with roses or something, say he's sorry.

I turn the key in the ignition. I don't need a job. Especially not one of their piddly indentured-servant office jobs.

My car smells good. Whatever the detailers use on the leather seats perpetuates that new-car smell. It was a typical David gift. The morning of my birthday when I came downstairs, there was a small package sitting next to my orange juice. I thought it was jewellery. Nestled in folds of white satin was a black key. My RX-7 was sitting in the drive, top down, even though the sky was threatening rain. We got a couple of miles up into the hills before it opened up and poured.

It's past noon and I haven't eaten anything. I pull into the first In 'n' Out Burger I come to, order something at the drive-through window, barely seeing what it is. Back on the freeway, up the coast. For the first time I notice what a gorgeous day it is. On my left the blue Pacific, dotted with whitecaps, replicates the blue sky with scattered wispy clouds. On my right the earth-toned bluffs of Malibu still blaze with colour—scarlet bougainvillea, orange and yellow nasturtiums, purple lantana.

Memories of blissfully empty summer days urge me into the turn lane for Zuma Beach. I pull into the nearly empty lot and I stare at the glassy curls of the breakers while The Supremes wonder 'Where Did Our Love Go?' and I wonder when. OK. Lately, there hasn't been a lot of tenderness or laughter or even shared objectives. But does that mean it's over? The first bite of cheeseburger hits my stomach like a rock in an empty swimming pool. I stuff the rest of it into the bag with the cold fries.

Out of the car, slip off my pumps, slither out of my pantihose. Walk across the sun-warmed asphalt into the cold, wet sand. The salty wind whips my hair across my face, makes my eyes water. I walk north, stepping over strands of seaweed, broken shells, half of a crab swarming with flies. I've read that when you become aware of your own impending death, your first reaction is likely to be: 'I can't die. I have tickets to the opera next week.' Now all I can think of is how disappointed my mother will be. She always adored David.

In her version of the story, he was the Handsome Prince who rescued me—not from a dragon, but from something even worse: a boring existence as a high-school teacher who rarely dated, and who spent vacations going on trips with other single women. David installed me in a house in Hancock Park, gave me a red sports car, beautiful clothes, expensive jewellery. All I had to do was to look good, give clever parties, be available sexually when he wanted me. It wasn't a lot to ask.

OK, it's true that I hated teaching. And it's also true that my social life revolved mostly around my women friends. This is not to say that I didn't date. My mother certainly doesn't know everything.

In my experience, a man's good qualities—like warmth, honesty, generosity—are inversely proportional to his physical attractiveness. In spite of this, or maybe because of it, I am drawn to tall, blond, good-looking men like the proverbial moth to the flame. This, as my best friend CM is quick to point out, may be due to the fact that my father, whom I adored and who died when I was seventeen, was the tallest, blondest, fairest of them all. He was also the last of the good guys.

It's been almost fifteen years since he died, but I can still walk into the den at my mother's house and expect to see him in his leather chair, a manhattan in a glass on the side table. He liked them dry with a twist of lemon. My mother had a fit when he taught me how to make them.

He taught me everything. To love books. To ride a horse English-style, when all my friends rode Western. He bought me a car with a gear lever when all my friends had automatic. He taught me to watch the still, August Tahoe skies, to look for the shooting stars to make wishes.

Most men I've known simply haven't measured up.

Not until the night of my friend Paula's twenty-third birthday party. I remember her grabbing me the minute I walked in.

'There's someone you've *got* to meet.'

I threw my jacket on the hat rack next to the hall closet. 'Why?'

'He's tall. Taller than you.'

'So was Frankenstein's monster.'

'This one's not Frankenstein's monster. Come on. You can thank me later.'

She dragged me over to the makeshift bar in the living room where the *ne plus ultra* of tall, blond and good-looking was opening a beer.

'Wyn, Dave. Dave, Wyn. Bye.' She disappeared into the kitchen. I wanted to crawl under the rug, but Dave smiled and shook my hand, apologised for his hand being cold. His eyes were wide-open blue, the colour of the ocean in July. Then he said, 'It's David, not Dave, by the way. And you're Lynn?'

'Wyn. Like Wynter.'

In those days, most guys would invariably say something like, 'Wynter? I hope that doesn't mean you're cold.' And then they'd laugh like idiots. But David smiled and said, 'What a beautiful name. I bet your father picked it.'

That rocked me back on my heels a little.

I poured myself a glass of Chardonnay and asked him where he worked. Even I had heard of Janison, Markham & Petroff, JMP, a very hip ad agency in Beverly Hills.

'Oh, so you're the guy who convinces people with bad credit to buy useless garbage they don't need and can't afford?'

He looked down modestly at his Italian loafers. 'Not exactly. I just sell our services to other companies.' He paused. 'But in my own small way, I help make it possible for the creative types to sell useless garbage to sheeplike consumers with bad credit. What do you do?'

'I teach literature to kids who can't read.'

'Sounds like a thankless job.'

'It has its benefits. Summers off. All the burnt coffee you can drink.'

'You must be pretty dedicated.'

'I'm dedicated to eating regularly.'

He looked thoughtful. 'Well, you could always—'

'Wynter! Oh my God, I don't believe this!' Mary Beth Cole, whom I hadn't seen since graduation—and with good reason—was pushing her way through a knot of people in the hall. She fell on me as if we were twins separated at birth, then without missing a beat, tossed her dyed-red hair back and held out her hand to David. 'Mary Cole,' she smiled.

I noticed him noticing the plunging front of her black halter top while she gave me a look of horror. 'I heard you were teaching high school. Please tell me it's a lie. I'm working as a location scout for a production company called Feldspar. Pay's for shit, but I *adore* it.'

I didn't have the energy to defend myself, knowing she didn't give a rat's ass anyway, and when she and David started swapping business cards, it seemed like a good time to disappear.

That night, like so many others, I ended up in the kitchen, drinking wine and gossiping with three or four friends. After a while the birthday girl appeared, shaking her head. 'What the hell are you doing in here?' she said to me. 'Why aren't you out there lining up the rest of your life? You don't find them like Dave on every corner, you know.'

I took a sip of Chardonnay. 'It's David, not Dave, you know.'

She expelled a loud, exasperated breath, picked up a new bottle of wine and went back to the party.

By 10.30, I could no longer stifle the successive yawns. I went to say good night to Paula. In the hall I collided with David.

'You ran away before I could get your last name. Wyn . . .'

'Morrison,' I said. I couldn't believe he remembered my first name.

He told me again that his name was David (not Dave) Franklin.

'It was nice meeting you, David. But I really do need to leave.' I grabbed my jacket.

'Do you need a ride home?'

'I live upstairs.'

The heart-stopping smile. 'Why don't I walk you home?'

I looked at him, suddenly annoyed. 'Is it a Y-chromosome thing, the way men are only interested when you're ignoring them?'

'Does that mean you won't have dinner with me?'

'I have a standing rule. I don't date men who are prettier than I am.' I turned and let myself out of the door.

I was halfway up the stairs before the first twinge of regret nipped at me. For a brief interval, I stood in front of my own door and considered going back to the party. What excuse could I possibly use? In the end I gave a mental shrug, unlocked my door, and crawled into bed with my little TV.

The next day, Sunday, was one of those Raymond Chandler-esque days that LA gets in the fall. Dry, hot and crackly with a strong Santa Ana wind that makes fire-fighters nervous.

CM was somewhere in Baja with her latest flame, and I thought about going to a movie by myself, but it didn't seem worth the effort. I was hungry but I didn't feel like cooking, and I sure as hell didn't feel like grading the thirty-seven vocabulary tests languishing in my briefcase.

I decided to make bread. It always makes me feel better—or at least more grounded.

I popped the plastic lid off the container that held the *chef*, the starter, and inhaled the familiar, pleasantly musty smell of a living yeast culture.

This *chef* had started as a small piece of dough that I brought back from the bakery in Toulouse where I did a work/study programme the summer after my sophomore year at University of California. By this time, the original French yeasts had intermarried with the LA locals to the point that the dynasty was seriously compromised, but I still liked to think there was a little bit of France in every loaf.

I scooped a cup of the *chef* into a bowl, stirred in a cup of water and a cup of flour, and left it to its orgy of feeding and reproducing. By tonight it would be *levain*, the leaven. I had just put the flour canister back in the pantry when the doorbell rang. I figured it was Paula, dropping by for a post-party analysis. I went to open the door.

Richard Nixon stood on the landing, holding a brown pizza box that reeked divinely of garlic. Or someone wearing a Richard Nixon mask. A pinprick of fear tickled the back of my neck. PIZZA SHACK PSYCHO KILLER CLAIMS SECOND VICTIM IN WESTWOOD. Then I noticed the Italian loafers.

'I think this takes care of the pretty problem, but I can't eat with it on,' he said.

Against my will, I laughed.

'Garlic. No anchovies. I hope you're hungry.'

How did he know that flowers wouldn't work? When I stepped back to let him in, I could have sworn I saw my life spinning away from me like the out-of-control space capsule in *2001*.

We sat on the couch and he set the pizza box on the coffee table, pulled off the mask, running a hand through his hair to make sure it was adorably tousled. As he did it, he gave me a sheepish grin. 'I think we got off on the wrong foot last night,' he said.

A fairly generous assessment of my rudeness.

'I wanted to apologise if I offended you somehow.'

Unreal. How was I going to describe this scene to CM? I didn't know what else to say, so I asked him if he wanted a beer.

He considered, then said, 'Do you have any wine?'

After browsing my collection of four bottles, he opened a Ravenswood Zinfandel. I got two plates and showed him where my mismatched crystal was hidden. He sniffed the air in the kitchen.

'What's that smell?'

'Starter. For bread.' There are certain people to whom I avoid trying to explain the concepts of *chef* and *levain*.

'It smells great. Yeasty.'

'That's probably because it is.' It came out sharper than I intended.

'Would you rather I just went away?'

My gracelessness made me blush. 'It's not that. I just don't know what's going on here, and when I'm uncomfortable, I get . . . edgy.'

'Do I make you uncomfortable?'

'Well . . . yes.'

Back on the couch, I cut the pizza and served it, stringing cheese everywhere. 'Why are you uncomfortable? I mean . . . we were having this really interesting conversation last night, and I turned round and you were gone. Then, when I found you again, you walked out and shut the door in my face. Did I do something totally disgusting?'

'No, it's not that. It's just—' Sitting in the friendly light of my south-facing window, munching on a really good pizza and drinking the soft, round wine, my apprehension was difficult to explain. I looked at him sideways. 'Why are you here?'

'Because I liked you.'

'Why? You don't know the first thing about me.'

'I know you're very . . . attractive.'

I shot him a warning look.

'Well, maybe not in the purely conventional sense, but you do have a certain . . . I don't know. You remind me of a summer camp counsellor. You know, sort of outdoorsy. Clean.'

I continued to stare at him.

'You make me laugh. And you have an attitude.'

'Let me see if I have this right. I remind you of a funny camp counsellor with an attitude. And this appeals to you?'

He nodded, as if this was quite the usual thing to say to a woman. 'You just seem so different from most of the women I know.'

'You mean most of those beautiful, polished, wildly successful and sophisticated women you know.'

He almost blushed, but not quite. 'You're not giving me a lot of encouragement,' he said. 'Are you seeing someone?'

'Not at the moment. Are you?'

'No,' he said.

'Why not?' It was totally not my style to conduct an interrogation, but I couldn't stop myself.

'I've been busy. I work a lot. What about you?'

'I'm picky.'

His laugh was spontaneous. 'I noticed that right out of the gate.'

'So suddenly you're not busy and you want to spend time with me?'

'If I meet your exacting specifications, yes. Is that so outrageous?'

'It's not that . . .'

He leaned forward slightly, resting his elbows on his knees. His face was perfect. 'You keep saying it's not that. So what is it?'

'I don't know what it is.'

He aimed his most potent smile directly at me. 'Neither do I. Don't you think we should find out?'

WE DID FIND OUT.

We found out that we both liked classical music. Even opera. That we both liked scary movies and we both shut our eyes at the bloody parts. We both loved French food and good wine.

I learned that David was a man who actually enjoyed shopping. He didn't seem to mind when I beat him at tennis and he liked it that I wasn't always fixing my make-up.

Like me, he was an only child, but there the similarities ended. His parents, Martin and Estelle, had retired to Monterey, and he talked about them in a remote way, telling me more about their careers—Martin had been a political science professor and Estelle an education consultant—than about them. He listened to my rose-coloured stories about my father with scepticism and envy.

One evening at a bistro in Santa Monica, I got his take on other matters domestic as well—and, more surprisingly, my own. David had just finished ordering wine, when a young couple with a toddler and a very new baby came in and were seated at the table next to us.

David's glance fell on them briefly, and we resumed our conversation about a new exhibit of black and white photography at Los Angeles County Museum of Art. When the waiter returned with our wine, and before corkscrew met cork, David had picked up my jacket and indicated a table on the other side of the room. The woman, now holding the squirming toddler on her lap, looked slightly apologetic, but David bestowed a winning smile on them as we followed the waiter away.

'Allergic to children?' I asked.

'I just know what's going to happen,' he said. We touched our glasses together and, as if on cue, the toddler across the room started to wail. 'I've tried imagining myself as a father,' he continued. 'Somehow I can't see it. Maybe later. After I've done everything I really want to do.'

That moment was a modest epiphany for me. I realised that I had never tried imagining myself as a mother, the whole motherhood scenario just didn't sound even remotely interesting to me.

I set down my glass. The unasked question hung in the air. I shrugged lightly. 'Quite honestly, I've never given it a lot of thought.'

His expression most closely resembled relief.

But the thing that clinched the deal as far as I was concerned, was his attitude towards sex. I never felt like I was being manoeuvred or rushed. I'd always found sex to be a hit-and-miss proposition—mostly miss. I always enjoyed the preliminaries a lot more than the culmination, and I'd about decided that was probably just the way it was, although some of my friends went on like it was something special.

I'd also found how completely it could ruin a relationship, because once you'd slept with a guy, he expected that every date would end in bed. Sometimes you'd try being 'just friends', but that never worked once the magic line had been crossed, and you ended up not seeing him again.

I was reluctant even to start down that road, and David seemed to sense that. Maybe even to understand it. I allowed myself to think that he might be different.

Still, I couldn't imagine that this was serious. It was an odd, though not unpleasant sensation for me—going places with a man who turned every woman's head. As fall turned to winter the relationship hummed along, but didn't seem to be humming along towards anything specific. I came full circle and began to worry about why David wasn't trying to sleep with me. He was a great kisser, but it never went beyond that. Then one night he took me to dinner at Beau Rivage, a wildly romantic little restaurant clinging to the edge of a cliff in Malibu. We drank champagne and stared out at the black velvet ocean, dotted with occasional twinkles of light from passing boats. The steady stream of conversation we'd kept up for the past six weeks seemed to have abruptly run dry.

Afterwards he drove his black T-bird slowly down the dark Pacific Coast Highway, while I huddled into my jacket, certain beyond all doubt that this was the end. He'd just taken me to this wonderful place to soften the blow. Now he was going to tell me it was over.

We pulled up the suicidally precarious drive of his little house in the Hollywood Hills. When he pulled the key from the ignition, I turned my face to the window, making no move to get out of the car. 'Don't be a wimp, just say it,' I said. 'Then you can take me home.'

'What are you talking about?'

'That it's over, of course. Look, I won't make a scene. Just tell me you don't want to see me any more, and you can take me home. I'll live.'

His laugh broke the silence. 'Is that what you think?'

Without waiting for an answer he got out, came round and opened my door. I let him take my hand and tug me gently out of the seat.

'I don't know what's going on,' I said. 'And when—'

'I know. When you don't know what's going on, you get edgy. Come on. Let's be edgy inside where it's warm.'

I'd been to his house a few times, but always in daylight. It struck me as cold and sort of temporary looking, in spite of the artsy black and white photographs on the walls and caramel-coloured leather sofa.

At night it looked completely different. Strategically placed lamps glowed, giving the rooms shape and depth. A fire was already laid in the fireplace, an Oscar Peterson tape cued up. All carefully planned. He was seducing me. I was amused and touched and exquisitely flattered.

If his lovemaking lacked spontaneity, he more than compensated with intensity. I'd never before had such attention given to every square inch of my body.

At some point that night it began to rain. Gently at first, then increasing in volume till I thought the hill would liquefy and send the whole house sledging down onto Sunset Boulevard, with the two of us inside. Finally, towards dawn, the skies relented and we fell asleep, exhausted.

In the morning I discovered that his ocean-blue eyes were grey. He saw me staring and smiled.

'Contact lenses,' he said, pulling me over on top of him.

Ten days later, on my twenty-fourth birthday, he asked me to marry him. I was nearly as astonished and grateful as my mother was.

After we were married, I had one spectacular year of selling real estate—spectacularly bad. Then David pointed out to me that taxwise, it was better if I didn't work. And I would have more time to do the things he wanted me to do. I didn't need much persuading.

What he wanted me to do was easy enough. I was to be the Executive Wife, the charming hostess, the source of contacts. He gave me books to read, subscriptions to the *Wall Street Journal*, Sunday *New York Times*, *Los Angeles Magazine*. He made sure I read his copies of *Ad Age*. He told me in great detail what was happening at work, which clients he thought they might lose, who they were pitching.

We gave parties, went to parties, dinners, benefits, gallery openings, plays. I served on committees for the Philharmonic, Cedars-Sinai Hospital, Sierra Club. And in my spare time, I did lunch with my 'friends', mostly women with husbands that David might want to know.

I soon realised that when he told me he'd been too busy working to have a relationship, he wasn't kidding. He seemed to thrive on all the activity, but I was exhausted, and uneasy about cultivating friends based on their potential to help us economically. However, in the too few, too brief times when we could relax by ourselves, he made it all seem OK.

And for a while, it was.

One morning when I woke up with a sore throat and a body that felt like the doormat for a herd of buffalo, I lay in bed, drifting in and out of consciousness, like you do when you're sick, and I thought in shards and crumbs about my life. I realised with a jolt that I'd been married for five years. That I hadn't seen my best friend in months and I couldn't remember when I'd last spoken to my mother.

Or baked a loaf of bread. My *chef*, which I'd carried home on the plane from France and nurtured and used for six years, had long since expired because I'd forgotten to feed it. The thought of my faithful little yeasts starving to death and drowning in their own acid wastes had depressed me so that I'd cried for days. Scared the shit out of David. He was ready to bundle me off to a Beverly Hills shrink, but I refused to go, having developed a deep distrust of the species after my father died.

Out of desperation, I think, he came home one night with a bread machine. From the start, he loved the thing, loved the whole concept of it. Loved the way you just dumped all the ingredients in, set the timer and presto—fresh, hot bread overnight. I refused to use the machine, so he began to play with it. He got in the routine of making bread—if you could call it that—every night. But in the mornings he was often in such a hurry to go to work that he'd rush off before it was ready.

By then he was being mentioned as the likely Director of Marketing and there began to be even more meetings, weekend gatherings, sometimes including spouses. These things were boring beyond all imagining; I didn't handle them well. We'd fight about it while we were getting dressed, driving there in the car. Then we'd have to go in to cocktails and dinner and pretend everything was fine.

And nothing was actually wrong. Things were going to get better. Just as soon as he became Director of Marketing. We'd have more time. We'd go away for more long weekends and long talks. We'd find it again.

In the movies, the music changes, the menacing cello tremolo lets you know that it's time for The Bad Thing to happen. I've always thought it unfair that real life doesn't come with that sort of soundtrack. Advance notice would be nice.

So I came home one Friday afternoon from a meeting of the Hancock

Park Green Spaces Association to find a gold Lexus parked behind David's black Mercedes in our drive. Before I could even get to the porch, the front door opened and out stepped Kelley Hamlin, one of JMP's account managers. I'd talked to her briefly a couple times at office social functions, but I'd heard from some of the other women on the management side that she was brilliant. Driven. She was also beautiful.

'Hello, Wyn.' She smiled at me, flicked her blonde hair back over her shoulder. David stood behind her, a file folder in his hand. 'Thanks for dropping this off, Kelley.'

The faintest little *ping* sounded somewhere in my brain, so quiet that I almost missed it. I looked at him, and he looked right back at me, smiled into my eyes. But there was no exchange. It was like looking at someone who was wearing those mirrored sunglasses.

After a quiet and seemingly endless dinner, I was reading the new *Los Angeles Magazine* in the den, and David came in, sat down next to me on the black leather couch.

That in itself was a guaranteed attention-grabber, because lately we'd been simply two people who found themselves asleep in the same bed every now and then.

He sat on the edge of the seat, smiled almost shyly, then he said, 'Wyn, I can't do this any more.'

'Do what?' The wrong thing to say. It elicited his hurt/disappointed look. 'I can't keep pretending everything is fine.'

'I know everything's not fine. You're working much too hard and—'

'Yes, I *have* been busy. But it's not just that.'

An image flared. David rolling over in our bed next to someone. Indistinct, no more than a shape under the covers. The scene evaporated instantly, but it left a white shadow, the way a match flame leaves a ghost of itself on your eye.

We looked at each other for a minute before I went for broke.

'Are you seeing someone?'

He frowned. 'Seeing someone? You mean like a shrink?'

'No. I mean like a woman. Is there something you want to tell me?'

'Of course not,' he said. 'I mean, yes, there's something I want to tell you, but it has nothing to do with a woman.'

But he didn't look at me.

'I've just been really unhappy. I'm not even sure why, except I feel confined, like I can't move. Sometimes during the day I'm sitting there in my office and I feel like I can't breathe.'

I started to touch his face, but he intercepted my hand and placed it in my lap. I said, 'Maybe you should go see Dr Geary and—'

'I just had a complete physical. There's nothing wrong with me.'

'Then what is it?'

He blinked. 'It's my whole goddamned life. The house, the job . . .' He paused, but only for a second, before plunging on. 'Us.'

I felt a lurching sickness in my stomach. 'I thought this was what you wanted. I mean—'

'So did I.' His eyes had lost their clarity, become like flat blue stone. 'I don't know if JMP is where I belong. Whether I should try a bigger agency. Or even a completely different—Maybe there's something else, somewhere else I haven't even thought of yet.'

While he catalogued possible causes of his malaise, I had to stifle the impulse to reach over and trace the line of his dark eyebrows, his perfectly straight nose, the plane of his cheek. 'David, believe me, I understand. You're working too hard. The money's not important to me, honestly. I want you to do whatever makes you happy. I don't need—'

'You're not listening to me.' His voice took on a too-familiar edge of impatience. 'What I'm trying to tell you is that I need a complete break from the whole . . .' His hands opened, then closed into fists. 'I need to be completely independent. Of you.'

A somewhat belated flash of insight. This wasn't about us, it was about him. What he wanted. What he didn't want.

He said, 'I've wanted to tell you, but I didn't know exactly how to explain it. You don't deal well with unvarnished truth.'

Sudden tears pooled in my eyes and overflowed. He handed me the pressed white-linen square he just happened to have in his pocket.

'David, the unvarnished truth is I love you. Don't you—'

'It's not that I don't love you.' The words sliced cleanly through the mush of my sentiment. 'I just think it was a mistake to get married. Like we did. So quickly. I don't think we really knew each other.'

Sound concerned, but not hysterical. 'If that's how you've been feeling, why didn't you say something before now?'

He looked pained. 'I shouldn't have to tell you that we're miserable. Don't you even known when you're unhappy?'

'So what are you saying, that you want a—'

'No.' Too quickly. Then, 'I don't know. Maybe we both just need some time alone, some space.'

'David, I don't need any more time alone. That's all I have right now.'

He seemed not to hear. 'Maybe you should move out for a while. I saw a great condo the other day. Not far away. We could still see each other.'

A tiny prickle of anger started at the back of my throat. He'd been looking at condos for me?

'If you're the one who needs some space, why don't you get a condo?'

He straightened, his gaze over my head someplace. 'Because it's my house,' he said.

He slept in the guest room. We hadn't made love in months anyway, but sleeping by myself in the king-sized bed without even the shape of his body nearby was cataclysmic.

The weekend was interminable. He spent most of it at the office. Or at least that's what he said. On Sunday afternoon I dialled his extension, listened to it ring six, seven times, till voice mail picked up. It didn't mean he wasn't there. He could have been in the men's room, the kitchen, a conference room. He could have been on another line. I knew if I asked him, that's what he'd say. 'I was talking to Hank.' Or Tom. Or Grady.

Obeying some ageless instinct, I took a long bubble bath. I put on a classic black skirt and ivory silk blouse that he always liked. I stared at the face in the mirror, somewhat reassured that the woman reflected there still looked pretty good. *You're in your prime*, I told her.

I had my mother to thank for the dark eyes and good skin. The straight nose and wide mouth came from my father. My hair was the problem. Why couldn't I have inherited my mother's hair, dark and shiny like an artist's brush? Or my father's—thick, blond and straight? Instead I got hair like my father's mother and sister—light reddish-brown, thick and curly, completely unmanageable. I battled it now, smoothing the kinks out with a hot comb.

I chilled a bottle of his favourite Puligny-Montrachet. I put on the music he liked—the Brandenburg Concertos. And I waited.

I was sitting on the bed with a book and a glass of wine, doing more drinking than reading, when he appeared at about 11.30.

'Are you hungry? There's some soup.'

He smiled politely. 'No, thanks. A couple of us were working on a pitch. We sent out for Chinese.' He eyed the bottle on the night table disapprovingly. 'Don't you think—'

But before he could finish, I refilled my glass with childish defiance. He headed for the bathroom and I tossed aside the book, listening to the water running in the bathroom. When he came out, the sweet, clean smell of him wrung my heart. 'David . . .'

He turned, but not all the way round to face me. Like he was on his way to something important and I was detaining him. 'Wyn, please. Don't make it any harder than it has to be.'

'We could go to counselling.' I rolled the hem of the sheet between my fingers. 'Do you know how long it's been since we made love?'

He exhaled through his nose. 'Things at the office are crazy. I've got so much on my mind I can hardly sleep, and then I come home and you expect me to perform like a trained seal—'

'I don't expect anything.' My voice cracked annoyingly. 'I just miss how it used to be.'

'Haven't you thought about anything I said on Friday?'

'I'm going to look for a job tomorrow.'

A frosty smile of approval. 'Good idea.'

'But I'm not moving out of this house.'

The smile vanished. He opened his mouth to say something, then closed it, setting his jaw. He turned and walked out of the room.

I drank some more wine and pondered the realities of returning to the work force. When I stood up to take off my skirt, my knees wobbled under me. I sat down heavily, dissolving against the pillows.

Time to get ready for bed. I wanted to lay out the suit and shoes for my interview tomorrow. But my head felt large. Unwieldy. I'd close my eyes. Just for a minute.

CM HAD ACCEPTED a choreographer's fellowship position with a dance company in Seattle over a year ago, and we haven't seen each other since. But whenever we talk on the phone, it feels like we're picking up right where we left off only a day or two ago. She's the one person I want to talk to now, but before I can call her, she calls me on Monday night. At the sound of her voice, my seething emotions attain critical mass and I start to bawl.

'Wyn?'

I blow my nose and keep blotting the tears that refuse to abate.

'What's going on down there?'

'I don't know. David is . . . We're . . . I think we're splitting up.'

As I'm pouring my heart out, I suddenly realise she's laughing. Surprise stops my tears in their tracks. 'I'm sorry, baby. I'm not laughing at you. It's just that I was calling to tell you Neal moved out.' Now I'm laughing too, albeit a bit hysterically. 'I think we should fall back and regroup,' she says. 'Why don't you get your ass on a plane and come up here for a nice long visit?'

The following Saturday, one of those blue and gold September afternoons, finds me on an Alaska Airlines flight heading for Seattle.

I scan the crowded terminal for CM. She's easy to spot, with her mass of auburn hair a good four inches above most other heads, but she's already seen me.

'Wyn!' She runs up and gives me a big hug. 'You look way too good for someone who's just been dumped.'

Actually, she's the one who looks great. But then she always does. CM—or Christine Mayle to the rest of the world—is not classically beautiful. But at just under six feet tall, with creamy skin, green eyes and long auburn hair, she doesn't look like very many other women. Her taste in clothing is, frankly, weird—handmade this, ethnic that, strange colour combinations. But somehow it all looks good when she puts it on, and she carries herself like the dancer that she is—striding rather than walking. I always expect her to break into a jêté.

Her apartment is on the fifth floor of an old brownstone building, and it's very CM. Two bay windows frame sweeping views of Mount Rainier and the ocean. No water pressure, but tons of ambiance.

'I'm sorry I don't have a guest room.' We settle ourselves on her couch. 'This thing is a hide-a-bed. I think it's pretty comfortable.'

I kick off my shoes, pull my knees up, resting my chin on them. 'Tell me about Neal. I'm so embarrassed. I just dumped all my toxic waste on you when you called. I didn't even ask about him.'

'We made it to eighteen months, three weeks, three days. That's our new personal best.' She shrugs philosophically. 'But it was going downhill for a while before he left. I think it started when he lost out on a teaching job. He got in this downward spiral where he couldn't work. Then he started dropping hints about how it was my fault—'

'Your fault?'

'Yeah, you know. Like I pressured him to move up here when he really should have stayed in LA and worked.'

'You know he'll come back. He always does.' It's about the best I can do in terms of comforting.

'I don't think so.' She breathes a weary sigh. 'It was . . .'

Instead of finishing the sentence, she goes to the kitchen, comes back with a bottle of champagne and two juice glasses. After a solemn toast to the Amazons, our high-school nickname, she says, 'What do you think's going on with David?'

I set down my glass. 'I honestly don't know. It hasn't been good for a long time. I guess I was trying to avoid it, just hold it together till things magically got better.'

'Did he say why he's so unhappy?'

'He said he felt trapped—not by me. It's marriage in general. And he might want to change jobs. He doesn't want his options limited. I think for the first time in his life, he's looking for self-realisation.'

'Sounds more like he's looking to screw around,' she says.

'Thanks, Mayle.'

'Sorry. That was a dumb thing to say. It's just that I never knew David to have a philosophical thought in his pretty head.'

'He isn't stupid.' My voice sounds stiff and hollow inside my head.

'If he'd dump you, how bright can he be?' she says, indignantly.

I don't say anything.

'Come on, hate his guts. You'll feel better.'

I take another sip of champagne and study her bare feet, curled over the edge of the couch. God. Even her feet are beautiful.

'You know any lawyers?' she asks.

My stomach turns over. 'We're not talking about the big D. Yet. Maybe if I just give him some space . . .'

She lets it hang there for a minute, and then says, 'Well, if it does come to that, you should call my friend Jill Trimble. In Silver Lake. She divorced Roy a couple years ago. Took his ass to the cleaner's.'

'Could we talk about something else?'

She leans over to hug me. 'I'm sorry, baby. It just makes me furious that he'd do this to you.'

The sofa bed is like every other sofa bed in the world—lumpy and saggy. I dream strange, exhausting dreams about swimming or drowning, wake up, roll around, drift back to sleep, into another dream. Finally at 8.00am I get up, pull on my sweats and sit in one of the bay windows, stare at the fog hovering over the water. I picture David sitting on the flagstone patio with the *New York Times* and his coffee.

CM wanders out, yawning. She looks at the rumpled bed. 'You didn't sleep, did you?'

'I was a little restless. I'm just having weird dreams at the moment.'

'Liar. You can sleep with me.' She dismisses my protest. 'I've got a queen-sized bed. It'll be fine. Besides, since we're having such a bad time with men, maybe we should become born-again lesbians.'

She insists on going out for breakfast. 'There's a great little bakery just down the hill. We can have a brisk walk, get coffee and scones and read the paper. I have to go to a meeting this afternoon at the studio, so you're on your own till dinner.'

'You have meetings on Sunday?'

'Not usually. Right now we're working out an itinerary for a series of master classes in schools back east, so things are a little crazed.'

It's nine o'clock by the time we leave the building. I should have realised that her idea of a brisk walk downhill is my idea of a forced march.

Half an hour later, we arrive at the block of squat, brick buildings that includes the McGraw Street Bakery. CM points at a vacant table near the open French doors. 'Better grab that. I'll get the food.'

I drop gratefully into a chair, looking around me. The place is laid out shotgun style; from the front you can see behind the counter to the serving station, past the backs of the big black ovens, straight through to the back door. The café part is full of mismatched tables and chairs with bright cushions, artworks of wildly divergent styles, and plants. But it's the smell of the place that grabs me. Not just the food, but the space itself—old brick and sun on freshly mown grass.

When I was growing up, my family always vacationed at Lake Tahoe, in the High Sierra. We rented the same cabin every year—two weeks in the summer, a week at Christmas. On Saturday mornings my father and I would drive over to Truckee, a little town with a high concentration of Basque sheep-herding families. There was a bakery there called Javier's and we always tried to get there just as the huge round loaves were coming out of the oven. I could never get enough of the smell of that place—the bread, the strong coffee, the creaking, splintered wood floors—or the feel of the loaf, warm in my lap on the drive home.

The McGraw Street Bakery has some of that same flavour about it.

CM sets down two mochas and an earthenware plate with two scones. 'Don't thank me, just leave a big tip.'

One bite of the scone makes me smile—golden-brown and crisp on the outside, meltingly tender inside and not overly sweet, with just enough chewy currants to provide counterpoint. Funny how the tiniest perfection can make you believe everything's going to be all right.

When CM parks herself in the other chair and crosses one long leg over the other, every male in the place is checking her out. It's always like that, no matter where we go.

It's funny. Most women would kill to look like CM. They think if they were only beautiful, all their relationship woes would be over. They'd probably be surprised to find out that CM has just as much trouble with men as they do. Sure they stare at her, but a lot of them are too intimidated to do anything beyond that. Her looks scare off a lot of nice guys, and her in-your-face independence takes care of the others.

And then there's Neal. He keeps breaking up with her and coming back. Does that mean he really loves her? Or that he enjoys emotional upheaval? Or is he into the power trip of making her cry over him?

Oblivious to the testosterone wafting our way, she takes a long sip of her mocha, and her eyes close in contentment. She sets down the cup and says, 'You know you'd be better off without him.'

My head falls back. 'Don't. I came up here to decompress.'

'You came up here because you wanted me to talk some sense into you.'

'No, I didn't. I just want to float for a while.'

'If you ask me, you've been doing that for the last seven years.'

'I didn't ask you.'

'Wyn, can you honestly say you've been happy? There you are tooling around LA in your sports car and giving dinners for people you loathe. Is this really what you want to do with your life?'

'What do you want me to do?' I say crossly. 'Become a medical missionary in Zimbabwe?'

'I want you to do whatever makes you happy. Are you happy?'

'I love David and—'

'Why? What is it about him that you love?'

'Mayle, I love him because I love him. You can't break it down into components. I know you can't stand him, but—'

'Never mind how I feel about him. In fact, forget him for the moment. Is your life making you happy?'

'How many people are really happy?' I'm shredding my napkin.

She leans forward, grips the edge of the table. 'Answer the fucking question. Are you happy?'

'How should I know? Stop badgering me.'

She leans back in her chair. 'I rest my case.'

'Are *you* happy?'

'Yes.'

'Even though Neal's gone?'

'That makes me sad. I miss him. I like getting laid regularly. But for the vast majority of the time, I'm happy with my life.'

Every morning on her way to the studio, CM drops me off at the bakery. I have coffee, read the paper, eavesdrop on the conversations floating around me, watch the women who work there. Pretty soon, they know who I am, and I know most of their names and what they do.

There's Ellen, one of the owners, with eyes the colour of espresso and short dark hair. She wears long dresses with black Doc Martens and wire-rimmed glasses that keep sliding down her nose while she's waiting on people, and she must know every single person within a ten-block radius. She asks about their husbands, wives, kids, pets—always by name. She'll talk local politics with anybody who shows the slightest inclination, and she's a fount of neighbourhood gossip.

A punked-out kid named Cody is the espresso barmaid. She's got blue hair and a nose ring, wears lots of eye make-up and dresses all in black. From her conversation with the other women, I gather that she just graduated from high school and is in career limbo. She works at the bakery in the mornings, dabbles in a few art classes late in the day, does the club scene at night. I wonder when she sleeps.

Diane is the resident cake baker and Ellen's business partner. She's a Meg Ryan blonde, tall and skinny with that coltish grace that's all elbows and collarbone. She usually rolls in around nine o'clock to start baking the cakes for tomorrow and decorating the ones for today. I love to watch her designs take shape. She does wedding cakes with real flowers. She does birthday cakes with buttercream roses and daisies and ivy, fruits, animals or toys. She probably could have been a sculptor, but when I tell her that, she just laughs and says she likes being a baker because she can eat her mistakes.

On the way back to the apartment, I have a sudden urge to ward off the loneliness goblins by baking bread, so I stop by Thriftway for supplies.

You don't really need a recipe to make bread. It's mostly about proportions—one packet of yeast to six or seven cups of flour, two cups water and a tablespoon of salt—and Jean-Marc, the dark-eyed *maître boulanger* I worked for that summer in Toulouse, used to say that bread may not always turn out the way you intend it to, but it always turns out. Just the same, it's been so long since I've done this, that I use the recipe on the back of the flour bag as a jumping-off point.

PLAIN OLD BREAD

1 Tbsp (1 packet) active dry yeast
$2\frac{1}{4}$ Cups warm water
1 Tbsp sugar
6–7 Cups unbleached white flour
1 Tbsp salt

Most recipes want you to use a whole envelope of yeast. This means the first rising will take only about an hour and the second maybe forty-five minutes to an hour—particularly if you put it in a warm place, which is what they usually suggest. That works fine. If that's the kind of bread you want. Grocery store bread: white—a brilliantly unreal white—with the texture of a damp sponge.

It wasn't until I went to France that I tasted bread that wasn't full of additives and air. It was like a religious conversion for me. In fact it's kind of like sex—one of those things that everyone tells you how great it is, but which is actually pretty uninspiring until you have it one time the way Nature intended it to be.

So, the first thing I do is cut the yeast in half. You don't want the dough to set a new land-speed record. What you want is a long, slow rise to build the kind of texture and flavour that make people think you paid $5.95 for this loaf at a gourmet bakery.

I combine the yeast with the water in a large china bowl, stir in the sugar and let it sit for a few minutes while I measure the flour into another bowl. Then I stir in the flour with a big spoon. When it clumps together and pulls away from the sides of the bowl, I turn it out on the counter and knead it for ten minutes, adding just enough flour to keep it moving. Then I knead in the salt. Dead last. Because salt strengthens the gluten and makes the dough fight you.

When it's smooth and elastic enough to spring back when I poke it, I oil a big bowl, slosh the dough around in it, making sure the entire surface is oiled. Then I put a damp towel over it and set it as far away from the stove as I can, on CM's dining-room table.

With half the yeast, it'll take twice as long to rise, so I pour myself a glass of Sauvignon Blanc and start scraping dough off the counter.

The scent of yeast hanging in the air reminds me of my *levain* and the day that David came to my apartment with the Nixon mask and a pizza. The sharpness of the longing I feel takes me somewhat by surprise. I want to touch his face, smell him, feel his body against me.

I'd settle for talking to him. I'll call the house. He won't be home, but I can leave a message on the machine. Maybe he's lonely too, and he's embarrassed to call me after all the things he said. This way, he'll have the excuse of returning my call to save his fragile ego.

CM has one of those duck telephones that quacks instead of ringing. She calls him Dorian. I punch in our phone number on his belly. I'm expecting four rings followed by the recording, but after two rings there's a click. He's home.

'Hello.' A woman's voice. I open my mouth but nothing comes out. Unless I'm very much mistaken, it's Kelley Hamlin's voice. 'Hello-o. This is the Franklin res—' There's a rustling noise and then a ringing crash as the phone hits the floor. Then David's voice. 'Hello.'

Dorian and I exchange a meaningful glance.

'Hello? This is David Franklin.'

I gently replace the duck in his cradle.

Five minutes later Dorian's quacking his brains out, but I let the machine pick up. 'Wyn, it's me. Pick up if you're there.' Pause. 'Wyn, I know you're there.' Pause. 'Kelley and I are just working on some client files. Pick up the phone.' Pause. 'Shit.'

The line goes dead.

I think I'm going to cry. Then I picture David's face if he could hear his call being announced by Dorian Duck, and I laugh first, then cry.

When CM comes through the door at about 6.30, I'm working my way through a 1.5 litre bottle of red wine.

'And which occasion are we celebrating tonight?' she says.

I hold my glass up to the chandelier and squint through the ruby light. 'Chapter Two. The phone call. In which our unsuspecting heroine calls the handsome prince at the castle, and the milkmaid answers.'

'I see.' She purses her mouth. 'And what did the milkmaid say?'

'Hello.' I pour a glass of wine for her. 'That was about all she had time for before the prince yanked the phone away and it crashed to the floor.'

She drinks some wine before taking her coat off and draping it over the nearest chair. 'And what did he say?'

A rather drunken giggle bubbles out of me. 'I didn't talk to him. But he told Dorian they were working on some files. Wouldn't you think an advertising prince could come up with a more original lie?'

She sighs. 'Oh, baby. I'm really sorry.'

Thursday morning my eyes are glued shut with dried tears. After I rip them open, I see that my tongue is still purple from wine. Unfortunately, I remember most of the evening. Crying and laughing, drinking and walking to a diner because neither of us could drive. Poor CM had to get up and go to work today.

At least I had sense enough to put my dough in the fridge so it wouldn't over-rise and fall flat. I take it out and set it on the stove to come to room temperature, while I shower and dress and clean the apartment for therapy.

By noon it's workable, so, in David's honour, I shape it into two of the oval loaves the French call *bâtards*. I give my little bastards a two-hour rise, spritz them with water for a crackly crust, and pop them into a 425° F oven for thirty minutes.

I've read somewhere that the smell of baking bread is an antidote to depression. It's true. By the time the bread is cooling on the counter, I'm starting to revive. I feel good enough to take a walk. And I feel the need of something chocolate. I know the McGraw Street Bakery closes at two so they can do wholesale baking, but I grab one of the warm loaves and put it in a paper grocery bag to bribe my way in.

Instead of baking, Ellen and Diane are sitting at one of the tables with coffee cups and stacks of paper. When I bang on the door, they look up and smile, but Ellen points at her watch. I unsheathe my secret weapon. I can tell they're wavering. I hold it up to my face and inhale deeply, close my eyes, smile. In a second, Ellen's unlocking the door.

'You made this?' She touches it gently. 'Ooh, it's still warm.'

'Not so fast. This isn't a gift. It's a barter. I need chocolate.'

Diane laughs, rocking back in her chair. 'Have we got a deal for you!'

In less time than it takes to load a bread machine, I'm sitting at the table eating a piece of moist, dense chocolate cake that is sitting on a pool of espresso caramel sauce.

'Is this sourdough?' Ellen's tearing into my loaf, examining it lovingly.

'Nope. It's just bread.'

'It tastes more . . .' She gropes for a description. 'What's the secret? Not that we could change the way Linda makes bread.'

'Who's Linda?'

Ellen sighs. 'Our bread baker. She's very set in her ways.'

'So get someone else.'

She waves her hand as if she were shooing mosquitoes. 'It's not that easy. She came with the place and . . . I'm just a wimp, I guess. Besides, she's not that far from retirement. It's easier just to wait her out.'

'But where did you learn to do this?' Diane's eyes are speculative. 'Are you a baker?'

'Well, I did work in a bakery once. Sort of. One summer when I was at UCLA, I did a work/study programme at a *boulangerie* in France.'

'What an incredible experience,' Ellen says.

'At first I just washed the equipment. But eventually Jean-Marc, the *boulanger*, started letting me shape loaves and rolls and croissants—stuff he figured I couldn't possible screw up.'

'Jean-Marc, huh?' Diane gives me a sly smile. 'Was he gorgeous?'

'But of course. He was French.'

Saturday morning, CM drags me out of bed at seven o'clock and down to Pike Place Market. By the time we get there, they've started the market day without us. At Starbucks we stand in line for extra foam, no-fat lattes, sipping as we stroll through the North Arcade past stalls of handmade jewellery and clothing, paintings and pottery, honey and olives and nuts, flowers and fresh vegetables from local growers.

We watch the countermen at Pike Place Fish toss their merchandise back and forth through the air, and listen while two guys dressed like lumberjacks in jeans, flannel shirts and work boots, debate the merits of cod vs. halibut for fish and chips.

By 11.15, we're casing lunch places. We end up at DuJour, a little self-serve café on 1st Street, where we carry our trays to a table by the window wall that looks out over the market to Elliott Bay.

'OK, I give up. Does every place in this town have a view?'

She takes a piece of sourdough bread and tears it, handing half to me. 'You should think about moving up here.'

I don't say anything.

'I mean if you and David . . .'

I shake my head. 'I'm a California girl.'

She flicks crumbs off her fingers impatiently. 'Just because you were born there doesn't mean you have to die there.'

'I'm just not the adventurous type.'

She nails me with a look. 'You used to be,' she says.

Monday morning I'm reducing a cappuccino hazelnut scone to crumbs and working on my second latte when Ellen says, 'Can I ask you a silly question? Are you by any chance looking for a job?'

'A job?'

She laughs. 'Yeah. You know, a repetitive task for which someone gives you money. Here's the deal. Diane and I really loved that bread you made. We were sort of thinking you could work with Linda and let her teach you the technical stuff—I mean the logistics of making bread in quantity—and then when she retires—You have any interest?'

Her enthusiasm is almost contagious. 'It sounds great,' I say gently. 'Except I don't live here.'

'Well, you could always move.' Her voice goes up at the end, like a question.

I avoid her gaze by opening the Lifestyle section of the paper, folding it back, positioning it carefully on the table. 'I'm in marital limbo at the moment,' I say. 'I'm going back to LA tomorrow.'

I left a message on the answering machine last night, giving David my flight number and arrival time. Not that I'm expecting him to meet me. But just in case, I give the gate a quick scan. Feeling sad and self-indulgent, I throw my bag in the back seat of a cab.

Traffic's heavy for midday, and the air is warm and brown. The driver, a thin-faced guy with yellow skin and dirty brown hair, subjects me to a story about his abusive parents and working his way through junior college, and I can't help suspecting I'm being hit up for a big tip.

My RX-7 sits alone in the drive like some neglected orphan. No client file parties today. Having deduced from my lack of response that I'm not a nice, guilt-ridden rich lady, the driver doesn't bother turning round; he just holds out his hand and says 'Twenty-six eighty.'

I paw through the notes compartment in my wallet. 'All I've got's a twenty. Wait here and I'll get the rest.' I shoulder my bag and start up the walk, only marginally aware of something in the deep shade on the front porch. As I draw under the portico, I see my camera, a portable phone, one of the TVs. My God, I've stumbled onto a robbery in progress. Somebody's in my house bringing our stuff out to load it up. Then I notice the boxes of books and piles of clothes with shoes thrown on top. My breath turns to ice in my throat.

'No.' Then louder to convince myself, 'No way.'

Pushing the boxes aside, I reach the shiny black door. My key fits into the lock but won't turn. This isn't happening. I pound on the door until my hands are stinging hot—stupid, because he isn't here. I imagine windows opening up and down the street, all the neighbours watching my eviction. David wouldn't do this. You can't just throw someone out.

The taxi's horn reminds me that the guy's waiting to be paid. Now what? I set down my bag and walk as nonchalantly as possible out to where he sits, drumming his fingers on the outside mirror.

I give him my most charming smile. 'I seem to have grabbed the wrong key, so I can't get in my house right now. Do you take plastic?'

'No plastic.' His dark eyes narrow.

'Well, I have twenty bucks. I can give you a cheque for the rest.'

He sighs. 'I could call the cops, you know. I've done it before.'

'Go ahead, if you want to sit here and wait for them to show up. Maybe they'll kick in the door for six dollars and eighty cents.'

'Shit. Give me the fucking twenty.' He snatches it out of my hand, throws the cab into gear and peels off, leaving part of his tyres on the road. I walk back up to the porch, still trying to arrive at a different interpretation of the still life sitting there.

The lamp from the den—the only thing in the house I ever bought without consulting David—sits precariously on one step. He hated it.

The lamp looks fragile, but when I pick it up, it's surprisingly heavy. The weight of it in my hand merges with the sight of my belongings strewn around the porch like trash, to ignite a sudden fury in my brain.

I give a roundhouse wind-up and heave the lamp straight into the front window. The plate glass explodes, and the security system starts making that obnoxious noise. My mouth opens in silent, nervous laughter.

While I'm loading the rest of my belongings into my car, the armed response patrol appears at the kerb. The guy opens the car door and calls out, 'Hi, Mrs Franklin. We got an alarm on one of your sensors.'

'Yes, I know. It's nothing. I accidentally threw a lamp through the window.' I smile at him.

'We . . . uh . . . should probably get that sensor turned off. Cops'll be showing up any minute,' he says.

'Good idea. The neighbours are probably going nuts.' I get in my car.

He scratches the back of his neck. 'Mrs . . . Uh . . . Franklin, could you maybe unlock the door?'

'I'm really sorry . . . Ted,' I read off his name badge. 'I just can't right now.' I put the car in reverse and ease out with him walking alongside.

Ted's arms open wide in a gesture of helplessness. 'What should I do?'

I turn and smile at him. 'I don't give a rat's ass.'

Top down, loaded to the gunwales with suitcases, bags, boxes, television, I look straight out of *The Beverly Hillbillies*. I cruise down the street in the balmy fall afternoon, waving at my former neighbours.

There's only one place I can go—to the house in Encino where I grew up and where my mother still lives. I drive down the tree-lined street and park in the drive of my mother's fake colonial. Keys in hand, I get out and walk up the path and try the brass knob. It isn't locked.

'Mom?'

Footsteps. Johanna Kohlmeyer Morrison appears at the top of the stairs. 'Wyn, honey, what is it?'

To say that my mother and I are dissimilar is to wallow in understatement. She's everything I'm not—perfectly groomed, efficient, organised, tactful, reserved to the point of being stoic, and most importantly, she is that nebulous, hard-to-define entity, a Lady, with a capital L. She always knows the proper dress, behaviour, etiquette for any occasion.

In spite of our differences, she can usually take one look at my face and know when something's wrong. By the time I finish explaining what's happened, I've worked myself into a frenzy. She perches on the edge of her sewing chair, silent, hands in her lap, while I pick up the phone and dial David's work extension.

'David Franklin's office, this is Andrea Wells.'

I try to keep my voice low and calm. 'This is Wyn. Is David there?'

'Hi, Wyn. He's here, but he's in with Hank. Can I take a message?'

'I need to speak with him. It's an emergency.'

She hesitates. 'He told me not to disturb them for any—'

'I bet he did. Tell him to get his ass out there and pick up the phone.'

Her voice becomes anonymous. 'One moment, please.'

It's actually less than a moment till he says, 'David Franklin speaking.' Like he has no idea.

'David, what the hell do you think you're doing locking me out of my own house?'

'In the first place, it's not your house.' His voice is icy. 'In the second place, you left me, so I had every right to—'

'Left you?' I shriek. 'I went to visit my best friend for ten days.'

'I didn't expect you to come back.' His voice has the exact tonal modulation of Darth Vader's.

'You knew damn well I was coming back. I called last night and left a message on the answering machine.'

'I never got the message.'

'Bullshit. What you did is illegal.'

'I assure you, it is not illegal. You have your things. The house is mine. I bought it before we were married.'

Tears of rage are beginning to choke me. 'You bought it for us to live in. Or that's what you said.'

'Yes. I did.' Impatience snaps the ends off his words. 'But we never added your name to the title, so the house is legally mine. Listen, I'm in the middle of something important. We'll talk about this later.' Click.

I stare at the receiver until the off-the-hook noise prompts me to hang up. I walk into the den and my mother's eyes lock on mine.

'Honey,' she says. 'Oh, Wyn, I'm so sorry.'

IT'S AFTER DINNER when I finally catch up with CM's friend Jill Trimble and get the phone number for her attorney, Elizabeth Gooden. When I call her office on Wednesday morning, her secretary puts me through to her immediately. 'Jill told me to expect your call. Tell me what's happened up to this point.' Her voice is low and there's a clipped formality about her speech that suggests schooling in New England.

I give her the broad overview, conscious of how much like soap opera this sounds. She says, 'I can check and see if the house is in his name only. If it is, then he's right, you probably can't get back in. We can get an order for him to let you in to get your things, however. It sounds like your husband wants to play hardball. If I were you I should sit down and make a list of everything that's jointly owned.'

'Oh God. This is insane.' I say it to myself, almost inaudibly.

'Mrs Franklin, divorce is about money. We don't know if your husband has already begun the paperwork for a divorce, but my advice to you would be to get ready to file as soon as possible. If he has, the more time we have to prepare, the better off you'll emerge.'

'It's just that this is all so weird. I can't believe he'd—I suppose you hear this all the time.'

'Unfortunately, I do.'

I sigh. 'Can you tell me your rates?'

'One hundred and seventy-five dollars an hour. I can send you a copy of my fee agreement. I generally ask for a twelve- to fifteen-hundred-dollar retainer to start. But, of course, I won't bill you for this call.'

I know I'm supposed to be grateful. I gnaw at the inside of my cheek. What if I hire this woman and then David realises he's being stupid? Maybe he was upset about something at work.

'Mrs Franklin?'

'Yes. I'm sorry. Listen, Elizabeth, I really appreciate your time. But I just can't . . . I need to think. I'm sorry.'

'I understand. I'll check on the title to the house and get back to you tomorrow. In the meantime, please consider what I've said. Time is of the essence. Oh—and it's best not to have a lot of dialogue with your husband. You need to get used to thinking of him as the enemy.'

My mother was born in San Francisco to parents of German descent. These two factors, when combined, have been known to produce a free-floating superiority complex and an innate assurance of correctness in matters of taste. Living in LA for thirty-odd years has only reinforced her notion that she is not overdressed; everyone else is underdressed.

So on Thursday morning, when I come downstairs, it's not a complete surprise to see her wearing her black linen suit with the imitation Chanel jacket, a white blouse and her pearls. She takes a plate out of the warming oven—cheese omelette, two strips of bacon, two pieces of cinnamon toast.

'Mom, this is really very nice, but I don't eat like this. I'll weigh two hundred pounds by next Friday. All I want is some yoghurt and fruit.'

'Wyn, you need to keep your strength up. You can't afford to get sick on top of everything else. Now just sit down.' She points to the table where my breakfast waits, attended by a rose in a bud vase, and the *LA Times*. 'I have a job interview at ten thirty, but I want you to have a nice quiet morning and eat every bite of your breakfast.'

'A job interview?' It hasn't even been a year since she retired from Hubble Middle School, where she worked as school secretary.

'I couldn't stand retirement. How many times can you clean a house?' I sit down. 'So what job are you interviewing for?'

'Office manager for a big architectural firm in Santa Monica, very busy, gorgeous offices. There's a lot going on.'

'How do you know?'

'I went on a little reconnaissance mission yesterday. They've got a lot of pretty young girls floating around, arranging their hair and inspecting their nails while the phones ring off the hook and people stand around waiting for things. They need someone to take charge.'

I take a bite of omelette. 'They'll never know what hit 'em.'

Thirty minutes later, she's out of the door looking like organisation personified. Why can't I see life the way she does, as a challenging puzzle that requires only logic and hard work to be put in order?

I spend the morning wandering aimlessly through the house and after lunch I dial David's number.

'Hi,' he says. His voice is warm, almost affectionate. 'I'm sorry I couldn't talk when you called the other day. I didn't want to discuss things in front of Andrea and everyone.'

He seems oblivious to my confusion.

'David, tell me what's going on. Why did you lock me out?'

'Wyn, I can't talk now. I'm at work and—'

'So close your door. I want some answers.'

'Look, I . . . care about you. Very much.' Meticulous word choice.

'Then let me come home.'

Long sigh. 'I don't think it's a good idea.'

'A good idea? We're talking about our marriage. If you still—if you care about it, about me, we need to talk—'

'Things have to be different for a while.' He cuts in smoothly. 'Till I get—till I figure out what I need to do. I can't be living in the same house with you. You wouldn't move, so I had to do something.' His tone suggests that locking me out was perfectly reasonable.

'I've talked to a lawyer.' Ungrateful shrew that I am.

'Oh, Wyn.' Surprised and hurt. 'Are you going to divorce me?'

That word hangs in the air. He says it so easily. My throat closes up every time I try.

Another dejected sigh. 'I know I can't expect you to be patient for ever. If you feel you need to make a clean break, I understand.'

How did this suddenly become something I'm doing to him?

'David, we need to talk. We need to sit down face to face and—'

'We could have a drink one night. I'll call you in the next couple of days. I promise. OK?'

'I don't think—'

'Oops, I've got a call waiting. I'll talk to you soon.'

Before my mother says a word, I know that the job is hers.

'I see congratulations are in order. Let's get Takee Outee for dinner. To celebrate your job.'

She takes off her jacket and hangs it in the hall closet instead of draping it over a chair, like I would have. 'Oh, honey, I wish I could. I've got garden-club board dinner tonight. I'm sorry, it's too late to change the meeting; otherwise I—'

'No, it's fine. Some other time.'

After she leaves for the garden-club board dinner the phone rings and I grab it.

'Mrs Franklin, it's Elizabeth Gooden. Sorry to call you so late. I was in court all day. The title to the house on Woodrow is listed in the name of David Franklin only.'

'Oh,' is all that comes out.

'Have you had a chance to make a list of community property?'

'Um . . . no. Not yet.'

'Then there's really nothing else to be done at this point. I'll wait to hear from you.'

At four o'clock on Monday morning, I'm lying awake in the dark. I hear every creak of the still house, every sigh of wind, every barking dog. I sat around all weekend pretending to read, trying to watch TV, waiting for David to call. My mother finally talked me into going to the El Torito Grill on Sunday night, but I was a wreck all during dinner. When we got home, I went straight to the answering machine. Nothing.

At 6.15am, the Ventura Freeway is already jammed. I get off and take Sepulveda south, zigzag over the Santa Monica Mountains on Laurel Canyon, then drive east on Santa Monica to Highland and south into Hancock Park. I stop at the kerb, half a block from where I used to live. The gold Lexus sitting in the drive isn't really a surprise.

At 7.20 the front door opens and Kelley steps out, stunning in a red mini-skirted suit, checking her watch. My husband follows, checking his watch. Like they're synchronising for some planned battle. While I sit there staring, he kisses her—not some impassioned embrace, but sort of a married people kiss, casually affectionate—which is even worse. His eyes follow her as she walks to her car and that's when he sees my little red Mazda sitting down the street.

I have to hand it to him. He's cool. He smiles, waves at her as she drives away. When she's out of sight he walks in my direction, calmly, purposefully, no longer smiling.

I turn my face as he bends down to the window. There's a smudge of red lipstick at the corner of his mouth. 'Early-morning meeting?'

He looks stern. 'Wyn, this kind of behaviour doesn't help anyone.'

I swear to God, if I hadn't just seen him kissing his girlfriend, I'd burst out laughing. As it is, I feel like if I don't keep a tight rein on things, any expression of emotion could escalate into full-blown hysteria. I fumble in my bag for a tissue and hand it to him.

'Better get rid of the lipstick. It's not a good colour for you.'

He sighs audibly, wipes his mouth. 'It's not what you think.'

The scene through the windshield goes suddenly wavy, like an El Greco canvas—the gentle curve of the street, the overarching pepper trees, the precise lawns. 'Wyn,' he says, 'why don't we have a cup of—'

I miss the end of the sentence as I pull away.

The drive back to Encino is a bit of a blur. There's a note from my mother that Tim and Georgia Graebel are coming to dinner and she's gone to shop for the meal. I pour a cup of coffee and sit down at the kitchen table, where my mother's well-thumbed copy of *Mastering the Art of French Cooking* sits open at page 263. Coq au vin.

I stare at the page. It says that in France, this dish is usually accompanied only by parsleyed potatoes, so that's undoubtedly what we'll be having. In my mother's house, Julia Child's word is law. I drink my coffee, while my brain slips into neutral and memory engages.

I was half excited, half terrified when the plane landed in Paris. For a kid who'd never been anywhere more exotic than Rosarito Beach, France could just as well have been Mars. I'd had four years of French in high school and two at UCLA, but the instant the Air France jet's wheels met the tarmac at Orly, it all vanished from my brain.

Sylvie Guillaume was there to meet me, and to take me back to Toulouse on the train. The Guillaumes were my host family and I would be working for her brother, Jean-Marc.

Sylvie was a college student like me, but she didn't look like anybody back in LA. Small and finely made with dark eyes and black hair cut in a sleek bob, she projected effortless chic. Yes, she wore jeans and a T-shirt, but she wore a long lavender and green scarf tossed round her neck. Her face just looked French—something about the way they hold their lips when they talk, as if they're perpetually expecting a kiss.

As soon as we were settled in the train compartment, she produced a slim gold cigarette case from her bag. And she puffed with such aplomb that I didn't even mind inhaling her secondhand smoke. She ran through the entire supply between Paris and Toulouse, all the while telling me about her family and their bakery.

Even though it was late afternoon when we arrived in Toulouse, she insisted on going to the bakery—*La Boulangerie du Pont*—as soon as I was installed in my bedroom on the second floor of their house. The whole town was built around the Garonne River, and the *boulangerie* was on a narrow, curving lane that radiated out from the circular park called Place President Wilson.

I looked through the front window and fell in love—first with Jean-Marc and then with the *boulangerie*.

Inside was a man several inches shorter than me, built precisely to the specs of a French baker—barrel-chested, muscular. In the dim light of late afternoon, his face was an artist's melancholy sketch, with dark hair and eyes only suggested by thick charcoal strokes. He was deep in conversation with a customer, so Sylvie showed me round while we waited for her brother to finish.

My fingers brushed the raised design of the old brass cash register, the fine grain of the walnut cabinets, the cool marble countertop. A huge wrought-iron rack behind the counter displayed the day's remaining loaves like works of art.

When the customer finally left, Jean-Marc embraced Sylvie and shook my hand solemnly. His eyes were so dark I couldn't tell pupil from iris. 'Welcome to Toulouse, Mademoiselle Morrison. You are ready to learn much, work hard, *n'est-ce pas?*'

By the time I met Jean-Marc Guillaume, he was in his thirties, and totally obsessed with bread. He'd been through the arduous *Compagnons Boulanger du Devoir*, the traditional apprenticeship programme for French bread bakers. Beginning at the age of fifteen, he worked for seven years in different regions of France learning to make the different regional breads in every type of establishment, from a tiny shop in a remote village of the Camargue, where a lone baker tended a wood-burning brick oven, to a huge Parisian *boulangerie* with stainless-steel ovens watched over by numerous apprentices and *maîtres*. Apparently to his mother's consternation, he had yet to show any inclination to marry; his only outside interest seemed to be the Toulouse rugby team.

When I finally laid my head on my soft, square pillow that first night, my dreams were full of a French film CM and I saw once, called *La Femme du Boulanger*—The Baker's Wife.

I'm making a half-hearted attempt at presentability when the doorbell rings at seven o'clock. I dip the end of my little finger into the pot of clear lip gloss, give my mouth a quick pass, and walk downstairs.

My mother and the Graebels are sitting in the den and I know they're talking about me because conversation dies when I come bounding in. Georgia gets up to kiss me and Tim hands me a glass of red wine.

'You get prettier every time I see you,' he says. Tim was a corporate attorney at Andersen Development, where my father was finance vice-president, and I grew up with his and Georgia's two kids. He retired at forty-five and took up competitive sailing. He's silver-haired, tanned all year round, and women suddenly seem to find him very attractive. I feel sorry for Georgia, but I don't think she's noticed.

'It's great to see both of you.'

When my mother goes to check on the coq au vin, Georgia turns to me and says, 'We're so sorry to hear about you and David.'

I have to remind myself to breathe. 'Thanks. I was kind of sorry to hear about it myself.'

'If there's anything we can do . . .' she says.

'I appreciate it. I guess it's just one of those things you have to wade through.' Mercifully, my mother calls us to the dining room.

She tells the Graebels all about her new job. Georgia talks about her work at Project Literacy. Tim regales us with stories of breaking in his new crew in time for the Trans Pac Race. I nod and smile a lot. We eat coq au vin with parsleyed new potatoes, then it's back to the den with the rest of the wine. I take charge of the music while they reminisce about old times and gossip about people they know. Inevitably Tim and Georgia start waxing nostalgic and talking about my father. 'Do you think he would've stayed with Andersen?' Georgia asks my mother.

She smiles wistfully. 'I don't know. Probably not.'

'I think he would've gone on his own, don't you, Wyn? He was a risk-taker at heart.' Tim looks directly into my eyes, and it's disconcerting.

I shrug and look away. 'It's hard to know what someone would do. People change, I guess.' That's when I go out to the kitchen to take care of dessert and coffee.

I'm standing there watching the coffee drip into the pot when Tim announces cheerfully that he's come to be my assistant.

He puts the cups and saucers on a tray, carries it into the dining room while I cut the Tarte Tatin that my mother laboured over and dollop crème fraîche on each piece.

'I've always been pretty handy in the kitchen,' he says, reappearing. 'Do you remember?'

'I remember you as the charcoal king,' I tell him.

He laughs with exaggerated heartiness and then he says, 'Wynter, I can't believe you're all grown up. I still think of you, Jim and Terry running around our yard like a bunch of little Indians.'

'Well, that's what happens when you're not looking. Little Indians grow up.'

'But they don't all grow up as lovely as you.'

'Thanks.' I take a step towards the dining room.

'Wynter.' I look at him. 'I know this is a difficult time for you. I'm sure you're lonely. I just want you to know that if you ever need anything. A friend. Or advice or anything at all, I hope you won't hesitate to call me.' Not us. Me. He holds out his card. 'I have a little office at Marina del Rey. You can usually reach me there.'

I want to tear it into shreds and stuff it down his throat. 'Thanks, Tim. But I'm sure my mom has your home phone number.'

Tuesday morning and we're sitting in the kitchen with sun streaming in through the double windows over the sink. My mother is upset because I only eat one piece of French toast.

'You're not going to catch one of those eating disorders, are you?'

'Mother, you don't catch an eating disorder.'

'I know, but I mean, it's a psychological thing. It's a control issue, and I know you must be feeling very out of control right now.'

'I'm not feeling out of control, I'm feeling fat. I've got a long way to go before anorexia sets in.'

She pushes some hair off my face. 'You're not fat, Wyn. You look wonderful. Tim was mentioning last night how pretty you are.'

I set down my fork. 'Tim Graebel is a son of a bitch. He was hitting on me out in the kitchen while his sweet little wife was sitting in there drinking coffee, totally unsuspecting.'

My mother laughs.

'He was,' I insist. 'You should have heard him, telling me he knew how lonely I must be. How I should call him if I needed a friend.'

She laughs again. 'Ah, the old I'll-help-you-in-the-kitchen routine.

Quite a number of friends' husbands have tried that one on me. Including Tim. Make no mistake, Georgia's not so unsuspecting. She just ignores it.'

I shake my head. 'Why do women put up with that bullshit?'

'You know, your language has become quite vulgar.'

'I can't believe this. You're more upset about me using a four-letter word than you are about your friend's husband making a pass at me.'

She takes a sip of her coffee and sets the cup back in the saucer with a delicate clink. 'Men can't help themselves, dear. They really are the weaker sex. And women have either forgotten their moral authority or they've become afraid to use it.'

'Mother, please.'

'All right, I won't go on. Your mind is obviously closed.'

After my mother has gone off to work, I call Elizabeth Gooden's office and leave a message with her answering service.

Elizabeth's office is in a building on Ventura Boulevard. Elizabeth is shorter than I am, but then most women are. Old-fashioned combs hold the dark hair back away from clear grey eyes that telegraph detached friendliness. She wears a navy-blue suit, and her scarf could pass for a man's tie. She shakes my hand firmly, shows me a chair and sits down at her desk, where a file folder with my name on it sits on top of a stack.

'So you've been married to David Franklin for seven years.' She opens the folder. 'How would you characterise the marriage? Would you say that it's been a happy or an unhappy one, overall?'

'Happy,' I blurt out. 'Well, at least until the last year or so.'

'OK.' She rubs the tip of her nose with a pen. 'Suppose you tell me about it, starting from where you first realised all was not well.'

I try to condense everything, to leave out the extraneous details. When I get to the lockout scene, she interrupts me.

'Some of the questions I'm going to ask you may seem more personal than professional, but these things are relevant to how we proceed with the case. This friend you were visiting in Seattle, is it a female friend?'

'Of course.'

'And she is simply a close friend. There's no other kind of relationship between you?'

'Absolutely not. CM's been my best friend since the third grade. That's all we've ever been.'

She scribbles on a piece of paper. 'How would you describe relations between yourself and David since the day he changed the locks?'

'Practically non-existent. I've talked to him once or twice. Once I went over to the house and that's when I saw him with his girlfriend.'

She purses her mouth. 'So you haven't had sexual relations with him since he locked you out?'

I can't help laughing. 'It's been a bit longer than that.'

'How long?'

'God, I don't know. Months.'

'Do you have any idea how long he's been seeing this woman?'

My stomach knots. 'No. But I have a feeling it's been a while.'

She cocks her head to one side like a curious little bird.

'It sounds silly,' I say, 'but it was the way he kissed her. Kind of casually. Not the way you kiss someone when things are brand-new.'

'Good observation.' She nods. 'Do you have any financial records in your possession?'

'No. I . . . all that was at the house.' I pull a skimpy, handwritten list out of my bag and hand it across the desk. She looks at it silently, not giving anything away. 'I guess I haven't been very smart,' I say.

'Don't beat yourself up over it. It's a lot more common than you probably think. It makes things a bit more difficult, but certainly not impossible. We would simply have to rely on discovery to ferret out any concealed assets.' At the look on my face, she volunteers, 'Yes, it does mean more money up-front. But you stand to gain substantially. Do you want to go ahead and prepare to file? That way we'll put him on the—'

'Not yet.' Tears pool in my eyes. She must think I'm either an idiot or a masochist. 'I'm not ready.'

She smiles. 'Then I suggest that we file for some maintenance for you. And we get an investigator to start nosing around. Generally speaking, if you turn over enough dirt, you're bound to dig up a worm.'

MORNINGS ARE THE WORST. You have to drag yourself out of the comfortable black hole of sleep and face it all over again. Yes, it's true. He's with someone else. Probably at this very moment. Doing all those warm, sweet, morning things.

The only remedy is to eliminate morning. So I sleep all day. My mother says it's a symptom of clinical depression. She comes home after work, pulls me out of bed, shoves food at me. I sit at the table in my old pink chenille bathrobe, glassy-eyed, while she tells me about her job. Nothing registers. I belong at the Cryogenics Institute—frozen in liquid nitrogen till a cure can be discovered for divorce.

She hammers relentlessly at me about seeing a shrink. I promise to think about it, and I do. I turn it over and over in my mind. At night it sounds like a good idea, but in the morning, taking action seems overwhelming. The one thing I do with a certain amount of energy every day is strip the bed and wash the sheets. I'm addicted to the smell of fresh sheets, their icy smoothness against my skin.

My mother says it's pathological.

Maybe clean sheets are important to me because I'm awake all night, reading until my eyes ache. I have to keep feeding my brain with words, keep it chewing and digesting. The danger comes when I stop. When I close my eyes, the words are replaced by images of David. The way he smiles. The comical way he lifts his eyebrows in time to music.

So I plough methodically through the two boxes of books that I brought from the house. I don't read them from beginning to end, I skim a few chapters of one, then pick up another. One night, I pick up the first edition of Elizabeth David's *English Bread and Yeast Cookery* that CM gave me when I went to France.

Two hours later I'm still reading, seduced by the elegant prose. This isn't just the history of bread, it's the story of the world, how the growing and milling of grain and making of bread shaped all of civilisation. By the time I've worked my way through thirty centuries of the wheat grain's progress from Kurdistan into Europe, I'm exhausted. And we haven't even got round to milling the stuff yet.

I turn the book upside-down on the duvet, reach for my eyedrops. Artificial tears, the doctor called them. Ironic, since I've been able to produce plenty of the real McCoy lately. I recoil at the sting, blink rapidly, then close my eyes just for a second, to let the fake tears lube my lids. The next thing I know, sunlight's flooding the room, and my mother's telling me that Elizabeth Gooden's on the phone.

I step into my flip-flops, pull on a T-shirt, pick up the phone.

'Good morning, Wynter. I hope I didn't wake you.' She's probably been up since five, run three miles and had breakfast with a judge.

'No,' I lie, 'I was just in the shower.'

'You'll be getting the paperwork in a day or two, but I wanted to let you know that your husband's been ordered to pay maintenance of five thousand dollars a month. He'll be making the first deposit in your account on the 31st of the month. Are you going to be OK in the interim?'

'Yes . . .'

'I was shooting for more, but they were ready to fight, and it would have involved more time and paperwork.'

'No, really. That's fine. Thanks for taking care of it.'

'Wynter, are you doing anything? I mean, getting out, seeing friends, going to movies, exercising?'

'Well . . .'

'That's what I thought. You need to be in motion. Even if you don't feel like it, you'll be better off over the long haul if you stay active.'

'I will. I'm just—'

'But no dating, OK? And don't get a job, at least not a serious one. If you start making good money, he may try to reduce your maintenance.'

'I don't think there's much danger of that.'

'Good. Now remember what I said. Stay active. I'll be in touch.'

After my mother disappears in a cloud of Guerlain, I get dressed and drive to the health-food store, returning with several different kinds of organic flour, seeds, honey, raisins and yeast. I flip through my battered notebook to a recipe for basic wholewheat bread.

> 1 Tbsp yeast
> 3 Cups lukewarm water
> ¼ Cup honey or molasses
> 1 Cup powdered milk
> 6–7 Cups whole wheat flour
> ¼ Cup oil or butter
> 1–2 Cups flour for kneading
> 1 Tbsp salt

I open the new jar of yeast, stir it round with my little finger. I know that yeast is an organism, a single-celled plant. I know it reproduces by budding, producing a whole new generation about every five hours. I understand the chemistry, how it feeds on sugar and starch, breaking them down into alcohol and carbon dioxide. Yet it's still impossible to dismiss the magic of the process. In the merrye olde England of Geoffrey Chaucer, one of the names for yeast was 'goddisgoode', because it was considered a gift of heaven. But until I went to France, I always thought of yeast as something you got in a jar or an envelope at the grocery store.

My very first morning at the *boulangerie*, Sylvie volunteered to walk with me, even though I had to be there at five o'clock. The river breeze was cool and fresh as we turned into the narrow alley behind the bakery. Jean-Marc stood just outside the rear door, leaning against the ancient brick wall, smoking the first Gauloise of the day.

When he saw us, he threw down his cigarette and ground it out under one heavy brown boot. 'You are late,' he frowned. 'The day is nearly finished.' I started to apologise, but Sylvie laughed and I noticed the slight twitching of the corners of his mouth, which was sometimes the only sign that he was making a joke. 'Come, I show you the *fournil*—the baking room.' We stepped through the door and the heat became a tangible presence. 'It takes one hour for the oven to be hot.'

We passed a small storage area filled with huge sacks of flour, and entered a long, narrow room with a stainless-steel oven, six feet tall, at the back. The cooling racks lining the side walls were already full of crackling hot, hissing loaves in different shapes and sizes and I thought I would faint with pleasure at their smell. Two men in front of the oven were using a long rack with a canvas stretcher on rollers to load dozens of baguettes into the oven.

Jean-Marc then led us into a room filled with refrigerators and proofing cabinets and kneading machines with blades the size of aeroplane propellers. One of the men we'd seen loading baguettes into the oven was pushing a wheeled rack full of bread up to the front of the shop. As he passed by the door, Jean-Marc took a small, warm, crusty loaf off the rack and handed it to me.

'Pain au levain,' he said. 'You want to taste it.' It was a command, not an invitation. I ripped off a chunk.

The crust was thick and golden brown, the crumb pale grey with an irregular texture. I took a bite. Sweet but with a slightly sour aftertaste. The interior was dense, moist, chewy; the crust crisp and nutty.

I stopped eating it long enough to say, 'This is wonderful. What is it? How do you make it?'

His little half-smile did something funny to my stomach that had nothing to do with bread. '*Levain* is like your sourdough. We put the wholegrain flour with the white. To make it more strong. The *levain*, it makes the bread less sour. The *levain* that is . . .' He rubbed his fingertips together, searching for the right word.

'Wet?' I suggested.

'*Oui, bien sur,* the wet *levain* make a more sour bread. Like your San Francisco bread.'

That loaf of *pain au levain* was the best bread I ever tasted.

Bearing in mind the gospel according to Jean-Marc, I cut the yeast in half, eliminate the powdered milk and oil, reduce the honey to an eighth of a cup and throw in some toasted walnuts.

I mix the ingredients together in the food blender. Any urgency I feel is about getting it out on the counter and into my hands. Kneading is what you miss with a bread machine. You forget what it is to get lost in the rhythmic fusion, the way you can tell by touch the exact moment when the dough comes alive, when it's ready to rise up and grow.

I leave the dough to proof in the cool air of the laundry room and go upstairs to strip the bed.

The loaves have perfumed the whole house by the time they emerge from the oven. I set them on cooling racks, feeling like a sculptor with a new work on display. Awash in goodwill, I can't wait till my mother gets home. I want to tell her the worst is over. That I know I've been a pain in the ass, but I'm going to make it, the healing has begun.

The phone interrupts my thoughts. My stomach balls up. *Wyn, it's me.* He sounds sad, lonely. *Look, I know I've been acting weird.* Try pond scum, David. He sighs. *It's true. I've been acting like pond scum. I must've been crazy to—Wyn, I love you. Do you think you could . . .*

'Wyn? Hi, honey.' It's my mother. 'How are you feeling?'

'Fine. I'm . . . better. I've been up and I—'

'Oh, I'm so glad. Listen, honey, I'm going to go have a drink with some people from the office, and we might go out to dinner, so don't wait for me, OK? There's some of that lasagne in the fridge for you and there's salad in the bin.'

'OK.'

'What did you do today? Besides wash the sheets.' Her voice is bright. She's trying to be funny, to cheer me up. I want to scream.

'Nothing exciting. I made some bread.'

'Oh, did you? I'll have to try some when I get home.'

'You don't *have* to. It's always optional.' I hate myself.

She sighs. 'OK, Wynter. I'll see you later.'

I hang up the phone, try to ignore the mass of tears that's pushing on my sinuses. It wasn't David; it's never going to be David. Get used to it. My mother has a life. She's going out with friends. I should be happy for her. If I weren't up to my neck in shit, I'd be ecstatic.

I pour a glass of milk and rip a corner off one of the still-warm loaves. I stand at the kitchen sink, eating and crying noisily. When the street-lights start to glow, I go upstairs, remake the bed, take all my clothes off, and crawl between the sheets with Holmes and Dr Watson.

I'm asleep when my mother comes home, and she doesn't wake me up when she leaves in the morning. I can't really blame her. I wouldn't want to have much to do with me either.

I'm curled up on the couch reading *Middlemarch* when she walks in with soup and salad from the supermarket the next evening. She studies me intently, apparently deciding it would be best not to say what she wants to say. She hangs her coat in the hall closet, and says, 'Why don't you put some of your bread in the oven and we can have it with dinner?'

While we eat, she chats, keeping her tone carefully upbeat. 'This bread is wonderful. I sneaked some when I came in last night.'

'I'm glad you like it.' I take a big gulp of wine and poke at my salad.

She sets down her fork and looks at me. Here it comes. 'Wyn, you can't go on like this. I'm concerned about you.'

'I'm concerned about me, too.' I try to smile. 'I was having a good day yesterday. When I made the bread. I felt somewhat functional.'

She frowns. 'So what happened?'

'You called. I mean, when you called to tell me you weren't coming home for dinner, I just felt . . . I don't know. Deflated. I wanted to show you my bread.' I can't believe the way my voice is cracking. 'Like a little kid, you know. It's . . . really stupid. And . . .' I inhale deeply. 'And, when the phone rang, I thought it might be . . .'

'David,' she finishes. 'I know. I used to think that about your dad. After he died, I used to imagine that I'd pick up the phone and he'd say, "Hey, Jo. Put the roast back in the freezer. Let's go out for dinner."'

Now we're both sitting there crying in our salads.

'But he was dead,' I blurt out. 'He didn't dump you for some fucking bimbo.' Suddenly I realise I've just said the F word to my mother. I start to laugh. Then she laughs, too.

'Oh, Wyn.' She gets up and pulls two tissues out of the box on the counter. 'Don't let that Barbie doll run you off. Fight for what you want.'

I drink some more wine. 'I don't know what I want any more.'

She takes the glass from my hand. 'You're too quick to let go. David's acting like a jerk, but most men do at some point. He's also gorgeous and smart and talented. And I think he'll come round.'

'Mother, I believe he's made his choice.'

She sighs, closes her eyes in the expression of frustration I know so well. 'I realise you think I don't know anything about anything, but I'm telling you, wait it out. Don't make any sudden moves. The odds are all in your favour. And if he persists in being an idiot, you'll still end up a very wealthy young woman.'

Next morning I wake up at 6.50, and I know from the stillness of the house that my mother's already left for work. I snuggle down, savouring the familiar smells of my room, the dry scent of the wool blanket, lemon-oil furniture polish and even a trace of Blue Grass cologne. It was my teenage favourite, and the gallons of it that I sprayed into the air must have eventually seeped into the walls and rugs and furniture.

On top of the bookcase, in a silver frame, is my favourite picture of my father. He's wearing Lacoste tennis whites and holding the new racket I gave him for his birthday. I hated baby-sitting for the brats in the neighbourhood, but I did it for a whole year at least once a weekend to buy him this new titanium racket that he wanted.

I pull the covers up under my chin and hold them tight. My bed, my desk, my books, everything just as it was, and me, safe in the middle. Suspended, like some prehistoric insect in a drop of amber.

Tim, the scumbag, was right about one thing. My father was a risk-taker. I wanted to be like him, but I was always torn between wanting to please him and following my own, more cautious instincts.

I reach over and pick up the phone. Within an hour I've talked to Ellen at the McGraw Street Bakery, Elizabeth Gooden, CM, Alaska Airlines. Then I lie back in bed and indulge myself in a moment of smugness. I've daringly changed the whole direction of my life before 8.30am. Without even getting out of bed.

There's just one more thing I have to do.

I'm sitting on the porch when David's car pulls into the drive. He digs his briefcase out of the back seat and walks slowly, head down, to the front door. He can't see me because it's dark, but I can see him in the yellow glow of the streetlight, and my heart breaks. He looks exhausted.

'David.'

At the sound of my voice his head jerks up. Caught off guard, he can't hide the tiny beginnings of a smile.

'Wyn. What are you doing here?'

'I used to live here,' I say softly.

He looks away, fumbles for his key, inserts it into the lock, but doesn't open the door.

'Can I come in?' I say.

Reflexively, he looks over his shoulder, like maybe my lawyer put me up to this and it's being captured on film.

'You never called me.' I keep my voice low, try not to let it tremble. 'We never got to talk.'

'I know. I'm sorry. I—this isn't a good time, Wyn. I'm tired—'

'I'm tired too, and there's never going to be a good time. Is there?'

He turns abruptly, pushes the door open, stands aside while I go in. He flips the switches, flooding the front of the house with light. I look around—the living room, back to the dining room, down the hall towards the kitchen. The rooms seem only vaguely familiar.

I follow him into the living room.

'Could I have a brandy, please?'

He takes off his coat, drapes it carefully over the back of the couch. 'Of course.' His footsteps clack on the slate floor and I hear him rummaging through the liquor cabinet in the kitchen. Soon, he appears with two crystal brandy glasses.

'Thank you,' I say when he hands me one. That's all I trust myself to say until the brandy is burning the back of my throat.

'What would you like to talk about?' He sets his drink on the glass-topped table as we both sit down.

What would I like to talk about? I want to scream at him, throw my glass at his perfect face, but I manage not to do either. I promised myself I'd be dignified, not lose my cool.

'I thought we could talk about us, David.' I like the way it comes out. Very low-key.

'OK.' He loosens his tie and leans back in his chair, waiting expectantly as I place my glass opposite his on the table.

'I'm going back to Seattle for a while.' Is it my imagination or does he look relieved? 'And I was wondering if you've given any more thought to . . . the situation.'

He shakes his head gravely. 'No, I haven't. I've been so busy—'

'If something's important enough, you make time to think about it.'

He leans forward, elbows on knees. 'Wyn, I'm sorry. I can only do what I can do. Maybe the problem is you expect too much of me.'

'Is it expecting too much after everything that's happened, that we might sit and talk about our marriage? Or do you just not care? Can't you just tell me how you feel?'

He looks straight at me for the first time since he stumbled over me on the porch. His face is drawn and there are dark circles under his eyes. 'I can't tell you because I don't know. You deserve more . . . but I just don't know.' His voice is dull. It's clear that this is the wrong night to force the issue. I stand up and walk over to him. He looks up at me.

'I love you, David.'

He takes my hand and holds it briefly against his cheek.

'I'm leaving Sunday. If you get a chance before then, call me.'

'I will,' he says, but we both know better.

'You're doing this because I told you not to.' My mother leans in the doorway, watching me plait my hair.

I try to keep it light. 'You didn't tell me not to go to Seattle.'

'I said you shouldn't make any sudden moves.' Her grey eyes meet mine in the mirror. 'Wyn, you're cutting off your nose to spite your face.'

I drop my carefully subdued hair and it escapes from the plait. 'Mother, you may find it hard to believe, but this is not about you.'

'You're letting this creature just walk in and take over your husband. You're running away. Giving up without a fight. What are you going to do in Seattle, anyway? Cry on CM's shoulder every night?'

'As a matter of fact, I've been offered a job. Making bread.'

'Oh, Wyn.' Her tone drips disappointment. 'Honestly, I don't mean to be critical . . .'

'But . . .' I supply helpfully.

'But how can you make any money working in a bakery?'

'I don't need a lot of money. I've got my allowance from David.'

'That's chicken feed. Especially considering what you're used to. And you have a teaching certificate, for heaven's sake. Why do you want to do manual labour?'

'Because I like it.' We're facing each other now, like gladiators.

'This is utter nonsense.' Her eyes cloud with frustration. 'If you insist on baking bread, at least you can do it here.'

'I don't want to do it here. I've already got a job there.'

'You're as pig-headed as your father.' That's her concession speech.

I take it as a compliment.

ELLEN WANTS ME TO START yesterday, but I tell her I need a week to get settled. CM says I can stay with her, but the idea of having my own place has taken root. Someone at the bakery gives me the number of a leasing agent named Daisy Wardwell. She's a breezy blonde with perfect make-up. When I explain what I'm looking for and how much rent I want to pay, she looks at me like I'm crazy, but says she'll see what's 'out there'.

The very next day she calls, gives me an address on 4th, tells me to meet her at 10.30am. Standing in the street, I stare at the huge creaking Victorian house in the process of being restored, and worry that Daisy has given me the wrong address.

Sidestepping the rotted planks, I pick my way up the steps and round the porch. I peer through one of the tall front windows, but all I can make out is a massive piece of furniture sitting in the middle of the room, covered with dustsheets.

Daisy's black Jeep Cherokee screeches to a stop, bumping the kerb, and she jumps out, breathless. 'Hey, kiddo. Sorry I'm late.'

'Tell me this isn't the place.'

She laughs. 'You're about half right. Come with me.' I follow her up the gravel drive at the left of the house, past a screen of hemlocks to a small, new clapboard cottage with a garage at the rear of the property.

'They were building this last spring,' she says. 'It's never been used. Of course, it needs cleaning up, but it's kind of cute, don't you think?'

The living room is small, but there's a wood-burning stove, a basic kitchen. The bedroom has one decent wardrobe, but no shelves or cupboards. There's a skylight in the bathroom and the square bathtub still has the manufacturer's sticker on it. I wander back out to the covered front porch where I envision myself sitting in the mornings with a cup of espresso. 'What's the catch?' I say.

Daisy smiles. 'The catch is it's month-to-month. I'm not sure how long it's going to be available. The woman who lived in the big house passed away. Her will is in probate; her only son and his wife were restoring it, but she's just filed for divorce . . . It's kind of a mess.'

'Sounds like my life.' There's an empty terracotta flowerpot sitting next to the screen door; I picture it full of red geraniums.

'The only problem I can see is that with no one living in the big house you're kind of isolated back here. There are neighbours all around but no one can see the house from their porch.' She looks at me appraisingly. 'This is a pretty quiet neighbourhood, but it's something to consider if you . . .' Her voice trails off.

Standing there in the warm autumn sun, it's hard to picture burglars or homicidal maniacs slinking around. What I see is a hummingbird feeder, me curled up in a rattan chair with a good book, a Vivaldi violin concerto wafting out through the open door. 'I think it suits me,' I say.

'OK, then. Let's go back to the office and do the details. I can have it ready for you this weekend.'

Linda LaGardia, the McGraw Street bread baker, has got an attitude the size of the Yukon Territory. When Ellen introduces us a few days before

I'm to start work, she checks me out the way my grandmother used to inspect a rib roast, then snorts, 'We'll see how long this one lasts.'

I watch her carry two lidded buckets of flour back to the storeroom, her biceps bulging.

'Are you sure she wants an assistant?' I ask.

'Actually, I'm sure she doesn't.' Ellen pats my arm. 'But don't worry, she's all bark, no bite.'

I tell myself that I can quit any time.

On Saturday my boxes of clothes and books are delivered at CM's, and the next afternoon we cart them over to the cottage to join the odd collection of furniture I've managed to acquire in the last two days. She sets down a small but weighty carton and looks around, hands on hips. There's a green paisley wing chair and a gold and brown, very ugly plaid club chair in front of the wood-burning stove, courtesy of the Salvation Army thrift shop; a small round table sits between them. At a junk shop on Capitol Hill I snapped up a writing desk with a broken leg, now mended with Super Glue. The ladder-back chair and a tarnished bronze lamp caught my eye yesterday at a neighbourhood car-boot sale.

'Wyn, are you going to be all right here? It's so . . .' CM gropes for a polite description. 'Spartan.'

'I'll fix it up,' I tell her, with more confidence than I feel. 'It'll be fine.'

She laughs. 'I think you've just articulated your philosophy of life. Well, you know you can always come back to my place if it gets to be too much like camping. I still don't see why you won't stay there at least till I get back.' CM was starting a masterclass series on Monday, and would be away for three weeks.

'I just want to be on my own.'

'If I'm not there, you can hardly be more on your own.' She looks at me. 'Oh, never mind. You're wearing your pig-headed look.' She hands me keys to her apartment and car. 'Just in case.'

As the light fades, the temperature drops and I look around for the thermostat. Then I skim the information sheet that Daisy gave me until I see the word 'Boiler'. On the opposite column is the word 'None'. I need to get some wood for the wood-burning stove.

I sit down in front of the cold, silent stove. I look around the room at my few sticks of furniture, the basket of dishes and glasses I scavenged from CM. What the hell am I trying to prove?

I order a pizza and eat it sitting at my writing desk. I try to read, but I'm too cold. At 8.30, I pull on tights, jeans, sweatpants, a sweatshirt and sweater. Seat cushions from the two chairs are my makeshift mattress, and I pull up the three blankets I borrowed from CM and try to sleep. Tomorrow I'll order a futon from Bon Marché.

Monday morning I huddle, shivering, under my blankets and reach for the rental file. Daisy included a sheet with names of outfits that deliver firewood. 'The ones that are starred will stack it for you,' she said.

I call the one whose name makes me smile—Norwegian Woods. The guy tells me that for a wood-burning stove I need hardwood, gives me the price for half a cord. 'When do you want it delivered?' he says.

'Now,' I say. He says tomorrow morning is the soonest he can deliver it. 'I need it now. I'm freezing.'

'Sorry. It's that time of year. Everybody wants their wood yesterday.'

'Forget it then. I'll find somebody who can bring it today.'

'Good luck to you,' he says politely, and hangs up.

I call all the other names on the list. The soonest I can get wood from anyone else is Thursday. I crawl back onto my makeshift mattress, pull up the covers and cry hot tears of frustration.

When the tears run out, I pick up the phone, call Norwegian Woods again. The same guy answers.

'Can I get a half cord of hardwood delivered tomorrow?' I say, hoping he won't recognise my voice.

'Sure,' he says. 'Over on 4th Street, right? I'll be there around three.'

It's pitch-black and freezing when my alarm goes off at 11.30 on Monday night. I peel off the sweats, step out of the jeans just long enough to remove the tights. It's the first time I've ever got undressed to go to work. I brush my hair, pull on a jacket.

Soon I'm walking down the alley behind the bakery. I knock on the back door. When Linda opens it, I smile. 'Hi.'

She doesn't say anything, just steps back with a grunt to let me in. She goes to the storage room, comes back with two buckets of flour, walks out again. I get an apron off the pile of clean ones, slip it on. She comes back with two more buckets, glares at me, walks out again.

'Can I help?' I say, following her. By the time I get to the narrow passageway, she's roaring back out like a locomotive, with more buckets, and I have to flatten myself against the wall to keep from being run over.

'That's what you're here for,' she throws over her shoulder.

The storage room is floor-to-ceiling shelves, housing a mind-boggling array of buckets, sacks, tins and boxes. She slaps a wrinkled piece of paper into my hand. 'Get those things and bring 'em out.'

It takes a few minutes to figure out the storage system, but eventually I find everything on the list and stack it in the centre of the floor. She's standing there, hands on hips. 'Well, that didn't take long,' she says.

'Sorry. It was a little difficult to find things. Maybe we should get a dolly.'

'A what?'

'One of those little platform things with wheels. It would be faster to get everything out of the . . .' She stares at me like I've just arrived from Venus. I dust my hands. 'Now what?'

'Are you gonna be askin' me that every five minutes?'

'You're going to have to give me some kind of clues about what you expect.'

Her eyes narrow, giving her the look of an angry sow. 'What I expect is for you to watch and learn. And don't get in my way.'

She takes a black loose-leaf binder down from a shelf over the sink and hands it to me. 'We're doing wholewheat walnut and white sand-wich first.' She points to a stack of huge stainless-steel bowls. 'Weigh out the flours on that scale and put them on the worktable.'

While I'm working, I notice dozens of books on baking on the shelves next to Ellen's desk. 'Do you ever use those bread books?' I ask.

'Nope.'

'I've got some good ones at home. Maybe we could find a different kind of bread to try some time?'

'Don't do to be messing around with different things all the time. If it ain't broke, don't fix it.'

Every attempt I make at conversation is rebuffed, so I quit trying and just do what she tells me. I'm wetting the worktable and scraping the dough off with a bench scraper when Ellen arrives at 6.00am.

'Morning, ladies,' she sings out, as she bustles around out front, turn-ing on the espresso machine, wiping the counters, putting money in the cash register. 'How'd it go?' she asks.

'At least she knows how to clean up,' Linda says grudgingly.

I smile sweetly. 'Fine. Had a busy night.'

I walk back to the cottage and take a hot shower. Just as I'm reaching for the towel, I hear someone pounding on the front door.

Dripping wet and shivering, I dive into my robe, twist my hair into the towel and run for the door. I open it a crack. A man is just stepping off the porch. 'Yes?' I venture.

He turns round. 'Where do you want the wood?' It's an effort not to shrink back. He looks like he was sent over by Central Casting to play

the psycho-killer-handyman. His next shave should have been yesterday. Brown hair hangs to his shoulders under a baseball cap pulled low
on his forehead, so his eyes are barely visible. I have the impression of a
wolf peering out of a cave.

'Over there.' I point to the garage.

I finish drying, pull on sweats and a raincoat, run out into the grey
drizzle, the towel still wrapped round my head. He's laying out four-by-
fours next to the garage and he stands up when he hears me.

'They said three o'clock.'

'We had a cancellation and you were in such a hurry, I thought you'd
be glad if I came early. You have a tarp?'

'Do I need one?'

'Unless you want to try burning wet wood. I've got a few in the truck
if you want to buy one. Twelve dollars.'

'For a piece of plastic?'

'It's not plastic. It's waterproofed canvas. It'll last for ever.'

I want to tell him that nothing lasts that long, but instead I tell him,
'Oh, all right, bring me a tarp.'

Every few minutes I set down the hair dryer, pull back the curtain to
watch him push wheelbarrows of wood up the drive, stack it neatly
against the garage. When I hear boots clomping on the porch, I go to
the door, cheque in hand.

In spite of the cold, sweat runs down his face. 'I put some of it up
here.' He points to a small stack by the door. 'So you don't have to keep
running out to the garage.'

'Thanks,' I mumble. 'Where's the tarp?'

'On the wood.' He looks at me like I'm an idiot. 'It's ninety-four total.'
I fill out the cheque and hand it to him. He hands it back. 'Sorry, I can't
take an out-of-state cheque.'

'That's all I have.'

'I'll have to have cash then.'

'I don't have that much stuffed in my cookie jar,' I say indignantly.

He takes off the cap, pushes the hair back with one hand, replaces the
cap. 'How much have you got?'

'I'll have to look.' I'm replaying Daisy's warning about the isolation of
this house, the fact that no neighbours can see the front door. As if he
can read my thoughts, he steps back, lounges against the porch rail
while I raid my wallet. 'All I have is forty-five dollars.'

He holds out his hand. 'I'll make up the difference for Rick and you
can pay me tomorrow.'

'Is that OK?' I ask.

'It'll have to be.' He folds the bills, stuffs them into the pocket of his grungy wool shirt. 'I'm sure not going to load it back up and cart it out. I'll see you tomorrow, then. About ten.'

I wait till I hear the truck drive away before bringing in some wood.

I've been reluctant to open a bank account here. As if it would commit me to something more permanent than an extended vacation. And when the account services rep at Washington Mutual finds out I've been gainfully employed for only one week, she shares my unease. But she opens the account anyway and sends me off with my temporary cheques and $100 in cash.

In the linen department at the Bon Marché, where I've gone to choose a duvet, I discover that David has cancelled my MasterCard. I write him one of my new cheques, and when I get home I sit in my ugly plaid chair and dial David's work number. 'It's me. Can you talk?'

'Of course. I've been trying to reach you all week.'

'You have?' My stomach lurches.

'I've decided to sell the house. Do you want any of the furniture?'

My knees are wet cement. 'So . . . does this mean you want—'

'No, Wyn, it doesn't mean I want a divorce.' It's the talking-to-a-retarded-child voice. 'I just think that while we're living apart, it's best not to have the expense of a big house, particularly when I'm n—hardly ever there. I hope that's all right with you.'

'Fine.' Then I remember the reason I called him. 'Why did you cancel my MasterCard?'

'Because you started piling up huge charges.'

'What huge charges?'

'Some place called the Bon Marché for five hundred dollars.'

'Five hundred dollars isn't huge. I bought a futon and a frame. And some kitchen stuff.'

'What the hell for?'

'Because I have my own place now. I got a job.'

'Doing what?'

'Baking bread.'

'Baking bread?' He says it slowly, incredulously. 'Wyn, for goodness' sake. What are you trying to prove?'

'Not a damn thing. And I'll be paying my own bills, so what difference does it make to you how much I spend?'

'I don't want my credit involved with yours. In case you default. Look, Wyn, I'm late for a meeting. We'll have to talk about this later.'

'When, David?' I'm practically shouting, but he's already gone.

I want to rip the phone out of the wall and heave it through the window, but I think that would be counterproductive.

A pounding noise wakes me. I don't even know where I am at first. I stagger to the door and look bleary-eyed at a lanky, crewcut guy in baggy denim overalls and a filthy sweater. 'Yes?'

He says, 'Hi, I'm Rick. Norwegian Woods. You got money for me?'

'Oh.' I turn quickly, take the forty-nine dollars out of my wallet. He counts it before shoving it down into his pocket.

'Brought you some cedar.' He smiles, revealing a couple of missing teeth. 'Cedar's perfect for kindling. Smells great, too. Like a campfire.'

'Oh. Thanks. Thank you very much.'

He hands me a business card that looks like it's been run over by a truck. 'If you need anything else, give us a call.'

I watch him limp down the driveway, wondering what happened to the psycho-killer-handyman.

Linda notwithstanding, I love my job. I love getting off work at seven in the morning, walking home as the city's just starting to hum.

I've started going to bed right after breakfast. With a down duvet to keep me warm, my new futon opened up in front of the wood stove, and blackout curtains at the windows, I'm having my best sleep in years.

If it's not raining when I wake up, I walk the neighbourhood. I begin to recognise neighbours at work in their gardens, mothers with their prams, kids with their dogs. We smile, say hi or nice day or think we'll get some rain tonight? I discover a tiny park with a bench that has a view of the Sound and the Olympic Mountains.

Sometimes I read, sometimes I just sit there, lost in the way the sun glints off the water like handfuls of diamonds. Sometimes I manage to forget the reason I'm here. That I'm waiting for David to figure out what he wants. Whether the package includes me. I sit on my bench and have imaginary conversations with him. He tells me he loves me, that it's been a terrible mistake, he can't live without me. I smile sadly and murmur that I'm just not sure if it can ever be the same with us.

His voice cracks as he says, 'Believe me, Wyn, I understand, but if you let me make it up to you, I swear you'll never be sorry.'

Laundry has never been an issue for me. For the last seven years, Hildy, our housekeeper, took care of it. Sheets, towels, clothes magically appeared in drawers, in closets—washed and ironed.

Now it's a logistical thing. I have no washer, no dryer. So when I run out of things to wear, I stuff all my dirty clothes in a laundry bag and drag it down to the Queen Anne Launderland on McGraw.

It's a colossal waste of time. You have to sit there while your clothes go through the whole fill, wash, spin, fill, rinse, spin. Yes, you can read. But if you get engrossed in a book and you don't jump up and get your clothes the second the machine stops, you run the risk of some guy waving your black miracle bra overhead and yelling, 'Whose 38B?'

After two forays into this alien culture, I finally figure out that the best time to go is early in the morning. I take my laundry bag to work with me and hit Launderland on my way home. Seven thirty is too early for anyone else to be there except for one or two retired couples drinking their early-bird half-price coffee, and some guy in a baseball cap who never even looks up from the notebook he's scribbling in.

Payday is every Friday. Since I'm not completely comfortable with the reliability of David's monthly deposits, I've got into the habit of picking up my paycheque on Friday afternoons and taking it over to the Washington Mutual branch on Queen Anne Avenue. When I unlock the back door one misty November afternoon, the work area is dark and empty, but I hear water running. Out front Cody bends over the sink, shirtless, pouring blue liquid on her head. 'Hi, Wyn.' She squints at me upside-down, then answers my unspoken question. 'Ellen lets me do my hair here because my dad won't let me do it at home.'

I look at the puddles of blue liquid. 'Does that stain?'

'Sort of. It comes out eventually.' She straightens up, pressing her head with a blue-stained towel. 'So what are you doing here?'

'I just came to pick up my paycheque.'

'And how're you getting along with the lovely Linda LaGardia?'

'Let's just say we're getting used to one other.' I perch on the edge of a tall stool next to the counter and watch her fluffing her hair in the towel. As she pulls on a black T-shirt, I notice one of the tables is covered with paper. Watercolours. Scenes of Seattle in the rain. A dish of water, a box of paints and some brushes sit on the counter.

'Are these pictures yours?'

'Midterm projects,' she says. 'They're all due on Monday.'

'They're beautiful. They remind me of the Impressionist pictures of Paris in the rain.'

She grimaces. 'That's what they're supposed to remind you of. But my teacher says they're too derivative.'

I laugh. 'I think they're beautiful. Do you like doing watercolours?'

389

She gives an offhand shrug. 'I've gotta do something. I'm too dumb for college.'

'You're not dumb. You're just non-linear.'

She laughs, flinging her blue-fringed head forward then back. 'Non-linear. Cool. I like it.' She disappears into the bathroom. A few seconds later I hear the whine of a hair dryer. I study the watercolours, imagining how one might look in a frame on the wall of my living room.

Cody emerges from the bathroom sporting a halo of blue fuzz.

'Done?' I ask.

'Almost. Gotta do the spikes.' She opens the door of the fridge, grabs an egg and deftly separates it, stashing the yolk in an espresso cup. She beats the white with a few drops of water and heads for the bathroom again. 'I'm going to the U2 concert tonight.'

'Have fun.'

I tuck my cheque into the inside pocket of my coat and let myself out. For one minute I wish I was going to the U2 concert, never mind that I don't even like them. I think of CM and me at Cody's age, running wild in the Valley with a pack of girlfriends. Going to the Sepulveda Drive-In Movie in my ancient black Chevy with red baby-moon hubcaps and no back seat.

The bank guard locks the glass door behind me. It's four o'clock and mist halos the streetlights in the early darkness. Trendy places like Starbucks and Häagen-Dazs are popping up seemingly overnight on Queen Anne Avenue, but the old-timers still dominate the street. Arch Plumbing Supply, with its windows full of tools and parts; Fancy Fabrics, where you can barely squeeze between tables piled with bolts of chintz and worsted wools; Thriftway, and a couple of bars.

One of the bars is Bailey's. I've passed by it plenty of times. It looks like a neighbourhood pub—low-key, non-threatening. The kind of place where a single woman could go and have a glass of wine and read without being pestered. I'm not used to going out alone, particularly not to bars. But the mist has turned to rain now, and walking in it isn't quite as much fun. I hesitate for a minute with my hand on the door.

No. Not yet.

Just before Thanksgiving, the weather goes from bleak to abysmal: grey, wet, bone-chilling, every day for a week. Ellen laughs at my whining. 'Honey, you ain't seen nothin' yet. Wait till February when it's been raining nonstop for two months.'

One evening, in an attempt to regain my rapidly loosening grip on sanity, I call my mother. The machine answers. It's 9.15, no, almost 9.30. Where is she? I don't leave a message.

Just as I settle the receiver back in its cradle, it rings and I jump.

'So you haven't drowned.'

'CM! Are you home? How did it go?'

'Great. We got lots of good video, but I'm beat.'

'Are you going to LA for Thanksgiving?' I ask.

'I'm not going near an airport for a long time. What are you doing?'

'The bakery's closed for the whole weekend.'

'Come over here and we can make turkey on Thursday?'

I call her on Tuesday, to see what she wants me to bring. She still sounds tired, but she says she's taking the rest of the week off and she's positive she'll be fine by Thanksgiving Day. She calls me on Wednesday night, and I know as soon as I hear her voice that she's not fine. 'I hate to wimp out on you,' she says, 'But I've got some kind of bug.'

'Oh, damn.' I stare at the blackness outside my window. 'What can I do? You need anything from the drugstore? Groceries?'

'I'm set. The doctor sent out some antibiotics. I've got chicken soup in the fridge. Not that I can eat anything. I'm planning to sleep for the next forty-eight hours.'

'Don't forget to take your medicine. Call me if you need anything. I'll be here all weekend.'

About noon on Thanksgiving Day, I get up and open the blackout curtains, then climb back into my warm burrow. Fog so thick you could squeeze it between your fingers hangs outside the windows. I stare at the textured ceiling. It's not bad, my little house. I've decided the barrenness is oddly restful.

OK, the place is depressing. Cold, stark and empty. I'm sick of the colour—polar-bear-in-a-snowstorm white. As my eyes sweep the blank walls, a bossy voice in my brain says, So, *paint*.

Silly. You can't paint a rental.

Of course you can. You can always paint it white again when you leave.

I sit up, my stomach fluttering with an unlikely excitement. Everything's closed today, but I could get the paint tomorrow morning. How long can it take? Suddenly I'm pulling on my sweats, my socks and shoes, sweater and jacket. An hour later I've returned from the convenience store with an armload of decorating magazines to peruse.

I flip the pages, letting the pictures bombard me with colour. Here's my problem. I've been suffering from acute colour deprivation. I gulp it

greedily. The food colours—dark chocolate, pale salmon and spicy cinnamon. Flower hues—lavender, fern, heliotrope. The earth shades—
clay and teal, pewter. By the second cup of coffee, I've decided on
terracotta for the back room and bathroom, a warm, sunny yellow for
the main room.

On Saturday the clouds part and the sun spills down benevolently. I'll
never take it for granted again. I catch a bus downtown, forgetting that
this weekend is the kickoff of Christmas shopping madness.

The overheated air inside Westlake Mall reeks of stale popcorn and a
dozen different designer fragrances the stores are touting. It's wall-to-
wall bodies and there's a steady drone, like a convention of angry bees. I
push through the glass doors, out into the crisp breeze.

In a junk shop on 2nd Avenue, I buy a 1915 magazine full of botanical prints, and two ornate frames. Then it's down to Cost Plus for some
plaid bedspreads to tie over my ugly chairs and drape over curtain rods;
a fake Tibetan rug to lay in front of the wood-burning stove.

As I wind my way back up to 3rd Avenue, I notice the clouds have
returned, but they're thin and pale and aloof, not the full-bellied, low-
slung kind that promise more rain.

After Thanksgiving the bakery erupts into frenzied activity. Linda and I
are making *panettone* and Ellen's mother's Chanukkah orange bread.
Linda's not thrilled about having her routine disrupted, but I'm glad to
be doing something new.

We all get to make cookies—Diane does gingerbread boys and girls
for every occupation and hobby imaginable; customers fight over the ice-
skaters and skiers. Ellen has the rest of us working on French and Italian
cookies. We make *brutti ma buoni* (ugly but good), bites of almond paste
clogged with candied citrus peel; buttery *baci di dama* (lady's kisses);
zaletti, raisin cornmeal cookies; hazelnut *biscotti* and sesame seed wafers.
The display case looks like a cover shot for *Bon Appétit*. One morning, as
I stand admiring the bounty, a memory of my grandmother Oma's plain
round cookies decorated with coloured sugar, dredges up an old happiness that's more like an ache. The second I'm inside my door, I'm on the
phone to my mother, but she's already left for work.

'Hi, Mom, it's me,' I tell the machine. 'I was just calling to say hi. By
the way, do you have Oma's sugar cookie recipe? I'm going to bed pretty
soon, but I'll be up about three thirty. Could you call me tonight?'

Her voice is all chirpy when she calls back. 'I found Oma's recipe,' she
says. 'Have you got a pen?

'1 Cup granulated sugar
1 Cup cold butter, cut into
   small pieces
2 Eggs
1 Tsp vanilla
3 Cups flour
1 Tsp baking soda
1 Tsp cream of tartar
¼ Tsp salt
Granulated sugar
1 Cup confectioner's sugar
2 Tsp lemon juice

'Cut the butter into the sugar until the mixture resembles oatmeal. Beat in eggs and vanilla. Sift together flour, soda, cream of tartar and salt. Add to butter mixture and beat with wooden spoon till blended.

'Preheat oven to 350°F. Knead dough for 15–20 minutes, then roll into walnut-sized balls and roll balls in granulated sugar to coat completely. Place on lightly greased cookie sheets. Using bottom of a glass dipped in granulated sugar, flatten each ball to about a ¼ inch thickness. Bake for 12–15 minutes until light brown. Glaze with mix of confectioner's sugar and lemon juice.'

'Thanks.' I shake the cramp out of my hand. 'I'd forgotten the kneading part.'

'That's what gives them that great texture.' Her voice goes all dreamy with nostalgia.

I hesitate. 'Thanks for calling me back. How's the job going?'

'It's a lot more challenging than working at Hubble.'

'David used to say challenging was a euphemism for pain in the ass.'

'Actually, I'm enjoying it. How's the baker's life?'

'I like it. Except the woman I have to work with is . . . challenging.' She laughs and then a silence plops down between us like a fat lady in the middle seat on a plane.

'What are your plans for Christmas?' I ask. 'I only have one day off, so I can't go anywhere. I was sort of wondering if you might want to come up here. My place is small, but I think we could—'

'Oh, Wyn, I'd love to, but—I wish you'd asked me sooner. I'm going to Tahoe with some people from the office. We've made deposits.'

'It's OK. I just thought if you weren't doing anything.' I don't want to be pissed off, but I am. She's only been working there since September, and they're chummy enough to go and spend Christmas together? She didn't even bother to find out what I was doing.

'I could see if I can get a refund. I'd hate you to spend Christmas alone.'

'I'm not going to be alone. I've had two people from work invite me for dinner, and if CM's here I'll be with her.'

It isn't a total lie. Cody and Ellen both invited me for Christmas Day dinner. But I envisioned myself making polite conversation with their families and sitting through endless explanations of family rituals, and then I declined as graciously as possible.

December 15—my thirty-second birthday. My mother has sent me a cheque and a card. She calls at 9.00am, forgetting that I sleep in the morning, so she's embarrassed and I'm grouchy. CM calls next, from a seminar in Phoenix.

Last year—where was I? Oh, yes. My mother's house. David had to be at a client meeting in Mexico. But two years ago, on my thirtieth, he took me to Paris for a long weekend, and it was like a second honeymoon. We stayed at the Ritz, sleeping late every morning, waking up to make love and eat perfect croissants dunked in steaming *chocolat chaud*. Every afternoon we walked the boulevards in the winter darkness. My birthday dinner was at Taillevent. I felt like a princess. Is it possible that he's forgotten the day?

I get up, unplug the phone and go back to sleep.

Linda has a black eye. Actually, it's more a hideous purple/green. Her lower lip is twice its normal size.

It's not the sort of thing you can pretend not to notice, so I say, 'What the hell happened to you?'

'My ex-old man, that's what happened to me,' she says, and I remember Ellen telling me that her ex, a sea captain busted for drinking on the job, was still lurking in a corner of the picture.

'I hope you gave as good as you got,' I tell her.

'That I did, missy. That I did.' She cracks a tiny smile. 'Stupid son of a bitch came over drunk. I had to let him in before somebody called the cops. 'Course then he tries to get all lovey-dovey, and when I told him to stick it in a knothole, he slugged me.' She touches her jaw tentatively.

'Are you going to press charges? Get a restraining order . . .'

Her laughter is wheezy, and she flinches from the pain. 'Restraining order my ass. I could paper my walls with 'em.'

Christmas morning I wake up at five o'clock. I turn over. It's still dark, maybe I can go back to sleep. I wish I'd made some plans for today.

At 7.30, I get up, wrap a blanket round me, curl up in front of the glowing remnant of last night's fire. The smell of woodsmoke carries memories of Christmases at Lake Tahoe, the cabin we used to rent. My father loved spending Christmas in the mountains. I think it reminded him of his New England childhood, and there was always the tantalising possibility of snow. I lay in bed every night of the holiday and prayed for a blizzard. I wanted to be stranded in our cabin with my dad building huge blazes in the fireplace and my mother making hot chocolate with little marshmallows bobbing on top.

It's hard to accept that she could traipse off to Tahoe with a bunch of perfect strangers, when it was our place for Christmas with my dad.

Christmastime always turned David into an Armani-wearing, Mercedes-driving ten-year-old boy. Every night when he got home from work we had to sit down together and read all the cards that came in the mail that day. They were mostly from business acquaintances who were artists, designers, writers, so each one was a miniature work of art. We displayed them all over the house, along with miles of garland and shimmery silver ribbon.

He was an extravagant and imaginative Santa. And after the presents were opened, there was always one more, something special, hidden somewhere in the house. One Christmas Eve when we went upstairs to bed, an exquisite gown of yellow silk was draped over my pillow. I can't help wondering what he's giving Kelley today. What she's giving him.

Hopefully something that requires penicillin.

By 9.30 the greyness that passes for winter morning light is spilling into the darkest corners of the room. I stand up, stretch, decide not to spend the day moping. I drag my two unopened presents out of the closet, and open the one from CM first. It looks like two very large blue baked potatoes. On the end of the box it says 'Down Booties, size 10'. I smile. My ever-practical friend remembers that my feet are perpetually freezing. I pull them on, walk around. They make my feet look the size of rowing boats, but within five minutes my toes are warm.

My mother's present is an oatmeal-coloured hand-knitted fisherman's sweater. I wonder which of her Christmas bazaars it came from. Underneath it in the box is a cheque for $100.

Well. That was fun. I put the butter into the freezer to make it easier to cut into pieces. Collect the flour and the sugar and the eggs and the food colouring together on the table. I suppose there are worse ways to spend Christmas Day than making cookies.

Out on the porch in my new down booties, I sip at an espresso. Fog obscures the outline of the big house, and hemlock branches poke out of the mist like the arms of sleepwalkers. I've consumed about half my coffee when I notice the little Douglas fir tree I bought sitting on the bottom step. In the mad whirl of my holiday social activities, I forgot to take Doug inside. He was probably happier out here, anyway. I pick up the pot and bury my nose in his soft green needles, sparkling with droplets of dew. The clean, aromatic scent is simultaneously piercing and calming. I'd thought I was all cried out, but apparently not.

Walking to work is cold, but so many houses have Christmas trees in the windows and those tiny white lights draped all over their shrubs that it's like walking through fairyland. Even if you're lonely it's nearly impossible to be sad in the face of this fantasy.

Linda seems subdued tonight, not so much as a sneer about the cookies I brought her. That's what Christmas does—brings out the vulnerability, even in people who are mostly immune to the ravages of sentiment. Of course, she doesn't thank me either.

'What did you do today?' I ask as we're loading the first batch of bread into the oven.

She shrugs. 'Just another day, far as I'm concerned. Got up at four. Had some soup. My kids came over.'

'I didn't know you had children,' I say.

'Why would you?' She glowers. 'Sometimes I don't even know I have 'em. They only show up on holidays. And only if they think there's somethin' in it for 'em.'

I slide the last two loaves off the peel onto the baking tiles of the top deck. 'What are their names?'

'What difference does it make to you, missy?'

'I was just curious.'

She looks over the tops of her glasses at me. 'Didn't you ever hear what bein' curious done to the cat? Kilt him, that's what.'

'OK, forget it.' I start setting up ingredients for the cinnamon bread.

The bakery's quiet since a lot of people aren't going to work today. After Linda leaves I make myself a decaf espresso and take a table in the front. Ellen comes over to sit with me.

'Post-holiday slump,' she mutters, dropping into the chair. She has circles under her dark eyes. 'Had twenty people for dinner yesterday. And I'm Jewish, for Pete's sake. Lloyd's family. What did you do? Weren't you going to CM's?'

'I was, but she ended up going to LA.'

'So you were alone? I wish you'd called. I could have used the moral support.' Her eyes slide over to me. 'Did you hear from Shithead?'

'No.' I blot my eyes with a napkin. 'Didn't really expect to, though.' She puts her arm round my shoulders for a minute. 'We never expect, but we always hope. That's the bitch of it.'

I'VE NEVER BEEN A BIG celebrant of New Year's Eve. I prefer going to sleep in the old year and waking up with the new one firmly in place and functioning. In high school and college there were the usual drunken orgies, but I never enjoyed them. I don't think CM really did either, although she talked a good game. For us, the best part of any New Year was watching the Rose Parade on TV in the morning while we stuffed ourselves with cold pizza from the night before.

This year, she shows up on my porch at five o'clock on New Year's Eve, carrying bags of food. A wedge of Stilton, vegetables to be made into soup, three bottles of champagne. And a small gold box containing six chocolate truffles for medicinal purposes.

'What smells so good?' She takes off her coat, hangs it on one of the hooks I had pounded into the wall by the door.

I set the bags on my new drop-leaf table. 'You're my guinea pig for a new bread. Yeasted orange poppyseed.'

'Always glad to oblige. Hey . . .' She does a three-sixty. 'This looks fabulous. I can't believe it's the same place.' She wanders into the bedroom, now my office. 'These colours are terrific. Where'd you get these botanical prints? I love it.' Back in the living room, she admires the watercolour I paid Cody twenty-five dollars for, the curtains and slipcovers made of plaid bedspreads. Her shrewd green eyes focus on me. 'Quite a little nest you've made yourself. Or maybe I should say a cocoon.'

I laugh. 'Yeah, I'm going in as a butterfly, coming out as a caterpillar.'

'A reversal of fortune,' she smiles. 'By the way, have you talked to Jerk-off?'

I shake my head. 'I tried to call him last week, but his assistant said he was out of the office. He's probably up at Aspen with Barbarella.'

'Barbarella? Let's see. Would that be the love child of Barbie and Godzilla?'

I laugh again—twice in five minutes is pretty good. 'Something like that. Here.' I hand her a bottle of champagne. 'Stash the other two in the fridge. Open that one. Let the party begin.'

She pours two glasses and we settle in to chop vegetables for our soup.

For a while we work in one of those silences which is only possible between two people who know each other so well that conversation is superfluous. I'm thinking about times past and I know she is too—probably the same ones. After a while she looks up from the carrot she's mutilating. 'Neal called me on Christmas Eve,' she says.

'And?'

Her posture is a study in nonchalance. 'He said he wants to see me. He's in Palo Alto right now, but he's coming up here for a seminar in February. He wants to have dinner. Or something.'

I smile and throw a handful of green beans into the pot. 'It's those "or something's" you have to watch. What did you tell him?'

'I said I'd think about it.'

'I assume you've thought about it by now.' When I stir the onions that are slowly caramelising in olive oil, their sweet musky fragrance fills the room.

Heavy sigh. 'I actually haven't thought about much else in the last week.' She gives me a pleading look. 'Help me out here. Please tell me what to do.'

I hand her the can opener. 'For starters, open these.'

In spite of the fact that she's never been shy about trashing David, I've always been reluctant to criticise Neal. I think it's the old reverse psychology. Whenever my parents criticised some guy I was seeing, I became even more enamoured of him. 'You probably couldn't find anyone less qualified to offer relationship advice.'

'No copping out. When you needed advice, I told you to get a job.'

'You already have a job. Do you want to see him?'

'I must, or why would I be agonising over it?' She pours chicken soup onto the vegetables.

'Problem solved.'

When she shakes her head, her hair flows from side to side, catching the light in its red-gold depths, just like in the shampoo commercials. 'You don't think it's a good idea, do you?' she says.

I rest my chin on my hands. 'It doesn't really matter what I think, if you want to see him again. Maybe it would be good. Maybe you've both learned something. If not, at least you won't have to waste any more time wondering what might have happened.'

'Very sensible indeed.' She finishes chopping the last carrot and throws it into the pot. This is obviously what I was supposed to say.

I dump the sautéed onions into the pot and light the burner. She refills our glasses and we curl up on the futon in the warmth from the wood-burning stove to listen to *Motown's Greatest Hits* and watch the old year die.

Ever since I moved into my first apartment with CM in our junior year in college, my mother and I have had an unspoken agreement. She doesn't call me unless there's a pretty compelling reason. So when my phone rings on the afternoon of January 1, it doesn't occur to me that it might be her. In fact, when I hear her voice, my heart stops.

'Mom, what's wrong?'

Her laugh tinkles up the telephone line. 'Nothing, honey. I just have some news. I'm getting married.'

I slide into the club chair. 'Married?'

'Richard. Richard Travers. The architect. My boss.'

'Mother, who is this guy? I don't even know him.'

'You will.'

'Well. Congratulations.'

'He's a wonderful man. We've been working very closely ever since I started there, and we've been almost inseparable for the last month.'

'Well, don't you think I should get to meet this person before you go running off to get married?'

Now she's laughing so hard I'm afraid she's going to choke.

'What is so funny?'

'Oh, Wyn . . . You . . . if you could hear what you sound like . . .' This is followed by gasping for breath and some little groaning noises. 'I'm sorry, honey, but you sound like my mother.'

'What do you know about him? Maybe he's a con artist who preys on lonely widows. He could have a criminal record or a wife in Toronto . . .'

She's still laughing. 'He's divorced. Trust me, I know what I need to know. Besides, the wedding's not till February 14th—corny, isn't it? That gives me two extra months to discover Dr Jekyll.'

'Mr Hyde. Dr Jekyll was the good guy.'

'Wyn, I want you to be my maid of honour.' Like she's making me a peer of the realm.

'Well . . . OK.'

'OK?' Her voice is rapier sharp.

'What the hell do you expect me to say? I don't even know the guy. Does his family know about it?'

'His son knows, yes.'

'But you didn't tell me?'

'Quite frankly, I didn't think you'd be interested. You never seemed to be when you had David and—'

'What's that supposed to mean?'

'Exactly this. When you were married and had a wonderful exciting life, there wasn't a lot going on between you and me. Now suddenly because you're lonely and unhappy, you want me to confide in you.'

The conversation has become a runaway train, captive of its own momentum. I want to hang up, but I can't. Neither can I make a single word come out of my mouth.

'Wyn? Are you there?'

'I'm here.'

'I'm sorry. I shouldn't have said that. I was so happy and I wanted you to be, too. I'm sorry, honey. Please don't be upset.'

One long exhale. Then I hear myself say, 'I'm not upset. I'm just surprised. Disappointed that you didn't tell me before. That's all.'

The silence winds out till it's about to snap. 'Well . . . I'm sure you have things to do. We'll talk again soon.'

I open my door and stand in the freshening air, goose bumps racing up and down my arms. It's 3.30 in the afternoon and darkness is coming on fast. I need to get out of here before I start breaking windows. I pull on my rain parka and head out the door. By the time I reach Queen Anne Avenue, the rain arrives in earnest. I run from one closed shop to another, sheltering in doorways. It's New Year's Day. Nothing's going to be open. I dash under Bailey's ragged green awning and lean panting against the rough wooden door. It swings inwards. I follow it, shivering and waterlogged, looking around in the dim light. It's a funky joint. One of those places where the floor smells like it's absorbed more beer than the clientele, and right now it's empty.

Then I see the bartender. He has his back to me, drying glasses and putting them away. He turns round, surprised. 'Sorry, we're not open till five.' Then he laughs. 'God, you're soaked.'

'You have a gift for stating the obvious.' I turn back to the door.

'Hey, come on in. You can stay if you want. I just can't serve you till five. Go and sit by the fire and I'll get some towels.' He disappears through the swing doors and I hang my dripping coat on the rack. There's a pool table in the back, a fireplace burning cosily on one wall, four tables, half a dozen booths. I drag a chair up to the fire, sit down.

He hands me two white towels and sets a steaming mug on the table. 'It's just hot tea.' He grins. 'But I accidentally spilled some brandy in it when I reached for the towels.' He puts a bear-shaped plastic bottle of honey down next to it. 'Let me know if you want more.'

'Thanks.' I blot the water out of my hair, which is already kinking like mad. He resumes drying glasses, while I sit watching him. He's tall and his short brown hair lies soft and close to his head, like a child's hair.

I squirt a golden rope of honey into the mug and stir it round. My first sip gets me a noseful of brandy, and starts the heat radiating out from my core. After a few minutes, he must feel my eyes boring into his back, because he turns round. 'You OK?'

'I don't mean to stare, but do I know you from someplace?'

He looks sheepish. 'Launderland. I'm the one with the notebook.'

'Oh, right.' I remember him now, head bent, scribbling furiously. He hovers over the notebook the way you did in school so no one could cheat off your test. 'So what are you writing?'

'Nothing exciting. A journal.' He scoops out a dish of peanuts and brings it over. 'You haven't been here before, have you?'

'No.' I smile. 'I didn't plan on coming here tonight, but I thought if I didn't get out of the house I might start smashing things.'

'Cabin fever.'

'I guess I'm not used to the rain yet.'

'It takes a while. Where're you from?'

'Los Angeles.'

His eyebrows go up, making his dark eyes look huge. 'What brings you up here? Or shouldn't I ask?'

His face is open, pleasantly anonymous. You want to tell him your life story. 'Asking's your job, isn't it? Bartender slash therapist?'

'Not much of a therapist. But I'm a good listener. And very discreet.'

'Sometimes that's all a therapist is.'

'Good point. By the way, I'm Mac McLeod.' He holds out his hand.

'Wyn Fr—Morrison.'

'I better finish getting set up. Come and keep me company at the bar.'

He sets a refill down on a coaster. I sip in silence, letting my eyes wander over the colourful rows of liqueur bottles behind the bar. They remind me of this drink my father liked to make. 'Do you know what a *pousse-café* is?' I ask him.

'Let's see—grenadine and crème de Menthe and chartreuse . . . I forget the others. How do you know about a *pousse-café*?'

'My father. He didn't drink them, but he liked to make them.'

'So what does he drink?'

'Not much. Unless they serve manhattans on the other side.'

'The what?'

'He's dead.'

'Sorry.'

'He liked a dry martini every once in a while, too.'

'Sounds like a man's man.'

'He was an everybody's man. People loved him.'

He slices a lemon with surgical precision. 'Your mother live in LA?'

'She's getting married.' I drink some more tea. It's odd saying it to him, but not uncomfortable. I guess because he doesn't know me.

'Do you like the guy?'

'Never met the guy.'

Two tears surprise me by running down my cheeks. He doesn't say anything. He just sets a clean bar towel in front of me and goes back to slicing.

'How long has your dad been gone?'

I give my face a quick pass with the towel. 'Almost fifteen years.'

'Your mom's been alone all this time?'

'She never even dated much until . . . recently.' He lets that one percolate while he cleans his hands then walks over to push the play button on a dinosaur of a tape player. A piano kicks off some kind of Jazz Lite riff and he looks apologetic. 'I know. It's awful. The owner likes elevator music during the week. But on weekends I play what I like.'

'Which is?'

'Friday night is blues night. Saturday's sort of eclectic—rock plus whatever else talks to me.'

'Does Mozart ever talk to you?'

He shakes his head, laughing. 'Never.'

'Opera?'

'Sure. It's a distant cousin to the blues. Same world view, don't you think? Life sucks.'

The door rattles open and a white-haired man comes in, shakes the rain off his jacket and shuffles over to a chair by the fire.

'Hi, Morey. ESB?'

'No hurry. She's prettier 'n me.'

'Where do you work?' Mac says.

'McGraw Street Bakery.' Before he can ask, I say, 'I make bread.'

'How'd you get into that?'

'It's a long story. Too long for now. I have to get ready for work.'

'Next time, then.' He takes the beer to the white-haired guy.

Outside, the rain has stopped and the air is scoured clean.
OK. Next time.

There were basically two ways to do anything at the *Boulangerie du Pont*: Jean-Marc's way and the wrong way. So I learned his way, one step at a time. The mixing and kneading was all done by machine, but the loaves still had to be shaped by hand.

One morning, Jean-Marc brought me a bucket of dough that had somehow failed to meet his standards for bread. He cut it into chunks and showed me how to form a small round *boule* and a *boulot* or torpedo. I watched as he dragged the dough along the worktable. The bottom stuck to the table, causing the top skin of the dough to tighten, and the mass rounded itself into a perfect dome. Simple enough.

Then I tried it. I pushed too hard and flattened the dough, so I pushed more gently and succeeded only in rolling the ball over so that it looked like an upended turtle. He watched me in silence, and I had the sense that he was biting the inside of his cheek to keep from laughing. After I'd tried unsuccessfully three more times I looked up apprehensively.

His face was impassive.

'You must practise, Wynter,' he said. 'You do not have the . . . the touch. Do not worry. It will come.' He placed his hand on my forearm, and I stared at the dusting of flour that covered the olive skin all the way to the elbow. 'You are very strong. This is good.'

Besides learning to make bread and studying French language and culture, I was hoping to put my virginity to rest on French soil. It had become an embarrassment. It was the seventies, after all. And here I was still walking around *virgo intacta*.

I found no shortage of candidates in my afternoon classes at the university. And Sylvie had a few cute cousins—rugged football-playing boys. The problem was, I was in love with Jean-Marc. I compared them all to him, and they came up looking green and silly. So I set about trying to figure out how and when to seduce him.

As it turned out, the when part was easy. Jean-Marc and Sylvie's *grandmère* lived in a beautiful little village about an hour from Toulouse. Nearly every weekend, the whole family went to stay with her.

The best part of the weekend was Sunday afternoon. After lunch, everyone would embark on a stroll by the river. Everyone, that is, except Jean-Marc, whose work ethic would have shamed the Puritans. So he usually found some work around the house to attend to, while the rest of us headed off for the afternoon constitutional. It occurred to me that this would be the perfect time to make my move.

One Sunday, when everyone was arranged on rocks by the river like an Impressionist painting, napping or watching the rowing boats drift by, I headed back to the house on the pretext of retrieving my book. Sylvie gave me a strange look, but she didn't say anything.

I found him on a ladder, trimming the creeper vines that were threatening to swallow Grand-mère's caretaker's cottage.

'Wynter, what are you doing?'

I gave him my best smile. 'I forgot my book.' I went up to the house and rifled through my suitcase, only then remembering that I hadn't brought a book with me. I walked back to the cottage.

'Have you found it?'

'No, I must have forgotten it.' I leaned against the wall of the house in the shade, and we chatted a little. He kept looking down, probably trying to figure out what the hell I was doing. Or maybe he knew. 'You should go back to the river,' he said gently. 'Where it is cooler.'

'It's so damp down there.' I piled my hair up on my head and leaned back, the better to give him a good view of my neck. I'd seen Raquel Welch do it in a movie.

Finally he finished the job and got down off the ladder. He came over and wiped the pruners with a rag, slowly and deliberately, while my heart fluttered like an injured bird. I took a deep breath. 'Would you like to kiss me?'

I've always been grateful to him for not laughing. He sighed. He raised his heavy eyebrows. '*Bien sûr*, Wynter. What man would not like to kiss you? But then what will happen?'

I had my fantasies, of course, but I wasn't exactly clear on the progression of events.

He tilted his head to look at me. 'Suppose for a moment that I desire to kiss you and we find ourselves in a love affair. Suddenly I have compromised a young woman who I have promised to protect. This is bad.'

'I'm an adult, Jean-Marc. I don't need protection.'

'*Oui*, but then consider what happens.' He ran a hand through his short wiry hair, causing it to stand up adorably. 'I suppose we can marry.' He paused. The look on my face must have made great stories for years to come. 'You will, *bien sûr*, become *catholique*. And we must live in the house with my mother.'

'Well . . .' I stammered.

'You will cook and keep the house and have children. At least four, possibly five or six. My mother will take care of them and you will run the shop while I bake the bread . . . What do you think?'

Mon Dieu. I was thinking Henry Miller and Anaïs Nin; he was talking Ozzie and Harriet. He sighed again, attempted to look sad. 'You see, Wynter, unhappily, I do not think this will work.'

Merde.

I LOVE THE QUEEN ANNE Thriftway. It's less pretentious than the gourmet markets in LA, plus they play great oldies on their sound system. I actually look forward to grocery shopping.

On the Wednesday after New Year's Day I'm tooling up and down the aisles with my mostly empty cart, humming along with the James Taylor/Carly Simon cover of 'Mockingbird'. OK, I'm dancing in front of the dairy cabinet, trying to decide which flavours of yoghurt I want.

'If yogurt makes you feel that good, they're probably not charging enough for it.' I wheel round and see Mac the bartender smiling at me.

'I was just—' Why do I feel compelled to explain myself?

He says, 'I like that song, too. But the Inez Foxx version's better.'

I grab two cartons of yoghurt, no longer caring what flavour they are. 'I don't think I've heard it.'

'Come to Bailey's Saturday night. I'll play it for you.' He rips the top off a plastic bag of pre-cut carrot sticks and pops one in his mouth like a cigar. Then he holds out the bag to me.

'No. Thanks.' I grip the handle of my cart. 'I'm not in the habit of going to bars by myself,' I say. 'Especially not on weekends.'

'Bailey's is a neighbourhood joint. We even have a bunch of grandmothers that come in. You won't get hassled. I promise.' He uses the carrot to cross his heart.

'Well, maybe. I'll have to see what's going on.' *In my extremely busy social life.* My hands are actually sweating on the cart handle.

'I'll save you a place at the bar.'

I love to watch Diane assemble and decorate cakes, especially the wedding cakes, because they're the most elaborate. So when, one dark afternoon, and it's just the two of us in the shop, she enlists my help with a new recipe for orange frosting to go on a chocolate fiftieth anniversary cake, I'm happy to oblige. Standing in front of the stove watching sugar melt and turn brown is normally about as fascinating as watching paint dry, but the risk of experimenting with a cake that's due to be picked up at ten tomorrow morning intrigues me.

'What if it doesn't work?'

'Then I'm here till midnight redoing it. So let's proceed bravely but carefully.' She turns on the burner under a pan of milk.

'If you majored in art at college, how on earth did you get into this?' I ask her. 'Was your mother a baker?'

Her laugh is sharp. 'My mother is the real-estate queen of Baltimore. Or was till she retired. She was never home long enough to bake.'

The sugar is a deep golden brown now, and the mercury in the candy thermometer is nudging 360°F, so I turn off the flame.

'To answer your question, my gran was a fabulous baker. She raised my two sisters and me. Till she died, then I inherited the job.'

'What did your father do?'

'Drank himself into liver failure.' Her voice is flat and free of emotion. She peers over my shoulder into the pot. 'This looks ready. Why don't you start on the meringue.'

I separate the eggs and whip the whites in the small mixer. 'I think that might be why I loved art and sewing and cooking,' she muses. 'All the things my mother didn't seem to care about.'

'It's funny. My mother drove me nuts because she was there all the time doing all that stuff. Trying to teach me piano and sewing. Maybe there's no way they can win.'

Diane stops beating the crème Anglaise and stares into the distance. 'Who knows.' For a second I think she might cry. Instead she sniffs a bit and sets a bowl of crème Anglaise into the larger bowl filled with ice.

'Where are your sisters?'

'In Baltimore. Married with children, the image of domesticity.' She laughs ruefully. 'They made their peace with my mother a long time ago. Now they take her casseroles and she baby-sits the grandkids and it's all very huggy/cosy. Me, I had to run off to West Timbuktu to make it on my own.' Her laugh is tight. 'Guess I showed her, huh?'

'Do you get back there very often?'

'I've never been back. It's almost six years now.' She pushes her hair off her face with her forearm. 'OK, here goes.' She adds first the crème, then the meringue, then vanilla and freshly squeezed orange juice to the butter as the paddle turns steadily in its prescribed arc.

She puts a dab on her tongue. 'Mmmm. Try some.'

I spoon out a little. It's one of those flavours that explodes in your mouth. 'I love it—the burnt sugar taste with the orange and the silkiness . . . I want to rub it all over me.'

'A waste of good buttercream,' she laughs. 'Unless you've got someone in mind to lick it off.'

On the first Friday morning in February, Cody calls in sick with the flu.

Ellen looks pained. 'Wyn, I hate to even ask you, but is there any way you can stay till after the morning rush?'

'I don't have a problem with staying, but I don't know anything about using that machine.'

'Misha and Jen are on early shift. Misha can sling the espresso. You can go out back and do muffins and scones with Jen.'

I take my mocha back to the work area where Jen's wearing the biggest grin I've ever seen on her face.

'What's up?' I ask.

'Nothin'. I'm happy because Misha has to deal with the customers out front and I don't.' Her blue eyes sparkle wickedly.

She pulls the bucket of bran muffin batter out of the fridge, hands me an ice-cream scoop. 'We do three dozen of these. When you're done, the dry ingredients for the cranberry muffins are over there.' She points to the other end of the huge worktable. 'Mix in the wet and then you can scoop those, too.'

Jen sticks a pan of cinnamon rolls in the oven about the time I finish the muffins. I wipe my hands on my apron. 'Can I watch you make scones? I love them, but mine never turn out like these.'

'There's two schools of thought about scones. There's fluffy scones and there's short scones.' She dumps the crumbly mass onto the worktable, patting it into a long rectangle. 'What we make here is sort of a compromise.' She holds up two floury fingers. 'Two things. The butter's gotta be really cold, even frozen's OK. And don't handle the dough any more than absolutely necessary. That makes them tough. You can use a knife or a biscuit cutter or whatever you want, just make sure it's sharp. The sharper it is, the higher they'll rise.' We load the scones onto half-sheet pans and stash them in the freezer to bake off tomorrow.

Ellen insists on driving me home at eleven. After she leaves I curl up in my duvet and fall into an exhausted, dreamless sleep.

'Missed you last night.' Mac greets me as I scoot onto my barstool.

'One of the women at work has the flu, so I worked an extra five hours yesterday. I didn't even roll out of bed till eight.'

I've become a barfly. Sort of. I've taken to spending three or four evenings a week perched on this stool, reading and nursing my one glass of wine. I always felt sorry for people who hung out in bars—like if you had a life, you wouldn't be there—but I've decided there's a lot to recommend it. Of course, you have to choose your bar carefully.

I'd be willing to bet that everyone who comes to Bailey's lives within a three-mile radius of upper Queen Anne. I don't get involved in a lot of conversation, except with Mac and the other bartender, Kenny, who is fifty, short and husky, with a broken nose. He used to box, but now he just coaches kids at the community centre.

These two work well together in the small space behind the bar, never getting in each other's way, never forgetting what they're about, never reaching for something to find it's not there. I like to watch them.

OK, I like to watch him. Mac. He's not racehorse gorgeous like David, but then, who is? Mac has more the look of a hawk, with his long nose and high cheekbones, deep-set grey eyes. I like the way he works. I like it that he gives his full attention to anyone that talks to him, even if the person is obnoxious. The way he gets so caught up in the music that he doesn't even know he's mouthing the words.

He told me one afternoon that he's from New York, that he dropped out of NYU during his sophomore year to wander around. He came through Seattle on his way to Alaska and he was low on money, so he took a job tending bar in Pioneer Square and just never left.

I've heard about his ex-girlfriend Laura, who owns an art gallery in Bellevue. They broke up six months ago after two years of hot-and-cold romance. She told him that he was financially challenged, always would be, and she needed someone with more ambition.

I've told him a little about David. OK, I've told him a lot. It wasn't intentional, but he's so easy to talk to, it just slipped out. Anyway, he said he knew I was married the first time he saw me. When I asked him how he knew, he said, 'You looked sad. I see a lot of it going around.'

On Saturdays I can stay till last call if I want, since I don't have to rush home and eat dinner and go to work. The music's every bit as good as Mac promised. I like the way he puts the tapes together.

Sometimes he starts wild, like Billy Idol, and then drops back into the Platters, then punches it up with the Stones. Other times he'll kick off with something sad and slow like 'That's How Strong My Love Is' by Otis Redding, and gradually work up to Chuck Berry or Eric Clapton.

Saturday night the place is usually packed, but tonight's the finals of the high-school district basketball tournament, so a lot of people are at the game. I'm in the middle of a P.D. James mystery, when Mac raps his knuckles on the bar in front of me. 'Hungry?' he asks.

'Yes, but don't bring me any more peanuts. I'll just eat them.'

'You want to go get Italian with Kenny and me?'

'Where?'

'Lofurno's. Down on 15th. You can either go with us after we close up or we'll stop by your place about one thirty.'

It doesn't occur to me to wonder how he knows where I live until he's at the front door. He's lounging against the porch rail, and when he reaches for the visor of his baseball cap, the picture stops rolling and comes into perfect focus. 'Oh my God.'

'What's wrong?'

'You delivered my firewood. That's why you didn't ask where I lived.'

His eyes crinkle with amusement. 'Took you long enough.'

'Your hair. It was really long.'

'That was the day before my annual shearing.'

'Why didn't you say something before?'

'Well . . .' He sticks his hands down into his jeans pockets. 'I had the distinct impression that you were pretty grossed out that day.'

'Grossed out? I thought you were the psycho-killer-handyman.'

His knees bend when he laughs. Then I'm laughing too, and shortly we're both bent double, wiping tears away. I recover myself, pull the door shut. 'Come on, Kenny probably thinks you got lost.'

We step off the porch and crunch about halfway down the gravel drive before he says, 'Kenny bailed on us. His wife wanted him home tonight.' He brushes a hemlock branch aside for me to pass by.

'I didn't realise he was married.'

A battered white pick-up truck is parked beside the kerb. It looks held together with barbed wire and chewing gum, and the left rear fender is grey with primer. 'Sorry, the Beamer's in the shop this week,' he says.

I climb in. 'What is this thing?'

'An Elky.' When he slams the door, I expect the window to fall out. 'El Camino 454SS,' he says proudly. 'Nineteen seventy-one. This truck and I have been through a lot together.'

The engine hacks and strains and dies. Three times.

'Do you realise what the emissions on this thing must be like? There's probably a hole in the ozone layer with your name on it.'

On the fourth try, it kicks right in. He puts it in drive and we pull away from the kerb. We stop at the corner and he looks over at me. 'You can say whatever you like about me, but don't go badmouthing my truck.'

Lofurno's is another place that you'd never find by accident. Just driving by you wouldn't notice the peeling grey clapboard building on 15th. And if you did notice, you'd probably think that because there are no visible lights, it must be vacant. In a hall just inside the front door a bare light bulb hangs from a black cord. On the right is a flight of stairs.

Mac opens the door into what could be a movie set for a speakeasy. The air is heavy with garlic and cigarette smoke, warmly lit by amber lamps. A black woman in purple chiffon sits at a baby grand piano, sipping a clear liquid that's too viscous to be water. She winks at Mac and takes a drag on her cigarette. Two couples sit at the dark wood bar that runs the length of the room, and one of the guys looks up when we enter.

'Hey, Mac. How's it goin'?' He slides off his stool and they do this shoulder-clasping thing that I've never seen anywhere except in movies about the Mafia. His name is Tony—what else? He picks up two menus and leads us to a booth. In a few minutes a waiter in a black waistcoat and long white apron brings a bottle of Chianti and two glasses.

The waiter pours the wine, and when he leaves I lean forward and whisper, 'Where's the guy in the dark suit and white tie with a Tommy gun in the violin case?'

He laughs. 'This place is sort of a throwback. The food's great, though. And so's Arlene. The singer.'

After we order, Mac gives the waiter a five to put in Arlene's bowl. She smiles and pulls the voice mike around. 'You got it, babe.'

Then she flounces her skirt, flicks cigarette ash off her dress, and plays the intro to 'Every Time We Say Goodbye'.

Now that we're sitting here opposite each other, I suddenly feel the nakedness of my third finger, left hand. Lately I've realised how a wedding ring grants protection to the wearer.

'So do you still work at Norwegian Woods?'

'I just help Rick out during busy times.'

The waiter makes our Caesar salad at our table in a huge wooden bowl that he's smeared with a smushed garlic clove, the way it's supposed to be done. It's one of the best I've ever had—lemon, anchovy, garlic in perfect tension with each other, the coddled egg and olive oil smoothing it out, freshly grated Parmesan, just enough Tabasco for a slight afterburn. I could quit right now and be perfectly happy, but then the waiter brings my tagliatelle bolognese and I'm glad I didn't quit. I've never tasted meat sauce like this, sweet and creamy.

I look up at some point to find Mac smiling at me, and I realise he's been sitting there, keeping my glass filled, and I haven't said a word to him in the last ten minutes.

'I'm sorry I'm being no company at all, but this is so . . . incredibly, unbelievably good.'

'Are you always this intense?'

'Only about food. This place seems very New York. Or New Jersey maybe. Is that why you like it?'

'I like it because it's a great place. I'm not nostalgic for the East Coast.'

'It occurs to me that you know an awful lot about me and I know very little about you.'

He twirls spaghetti around his fork. 'You're free to ask questions.'

'OK. Where have you been? For about the last ten years.'

'After I left school . . .' He looks thoughtful, like he's sifting out what to tell and what to leave unsaid. 'I drove west. Spent three years in Colorado and Utah.'

'What did you do there?'

'A lot of skiing and a little waiting tables.'

'You can't ski in the summer.'

'Then it was rock climbing and construction.'

'Rock climbing? You have a death wish, then.'

'Not really. It's based on learning skills, like any other sport.'

'Yeah. Except your butt's hanging over the abyss. OK. Then what?'

'Then I hitchhiked around New Zealand for a year. Then Italy and Switzerland for another year.'

'That's five.'

'Then I came home. That lasted for about six months and then I started working my way west again. Then, like I told you before, I came here and stayed.'

I rested my elbows on the table. 'You do that very well. Cover a lot of ground and a lot of time without revealing anything substantive.'

He grins. 'There's just nothing very interesting to tell.'

'No brushes with the law? No duels?'

'Nope.'

'Ever been married?'

He hesitates for barely a nanosecond. 'One close call. Gillian. She lived on a sheep station in New Zealand.'

'Can you tell me?'

'Some other time.'

After I've stuffed as much tagliatelle as possible into myself, the waiter comes to ask if we'd like coffee. 'Maybe in a few minutes,' Mac says. Then he looks at me. 'So do you like the place?'

'It's wonderful. Thanks for bringing me here.'

Now Arlene's playing 'Blues in the Night'. Mac smiles. 'She's angling

411

for another tip. By the way, Jimmy Turner's coming to Bailey's next Friday. He's a local blues' artist. You'd like him.'

'I'll have to find out some other time. I'm going to LA on Friday.'

'Too bad.' He waits a second before asking, 'Is this the big day?'

'I'm afraid so.' The glow of the evening has become tarnished.

He sets his glass down. 'Why is this so hard for you? You don't seem like the kind of person who'd begrudge her mother a chance to be happy. Not after ten years or whatever it is.'

'Fifteen.' I shrug. 'It doesn't matter anyway. I'll get through it.'

The waiter brings inky coffee in white cups, and hot milk in a jug.

'Why did you drop out of college?' I ask. Mac doesn't look up from his coffee. 'Didn't you want to get a degree?'

A tolerant smile. 'The purpose of going to college isn't to learn, it's to get a piece of paper. The purpose of the paper is to get you the job so you can keep on doing what's expected.'

'Are you really that cynical?' I take a tentative sip of my coffee.

'I'm not cynical. I'm realistic. I like my life. I don't need anything more.'

'That's fine now. But you're going to get old, Peter Pan. What if . . .'

He laughs. 'I prefer to burn my bridges as I come to them.'

The second we finish our coffee the waiter is there with a refill. When we decline, he presents the bill. It's 4.00am. I reach for my wallet.

'I've got it,' Mac says easily.

'No,' I say. 'This isn't a date. We'll split it down the middle.'

He holds up both hands in surrender. 'OK, give me fifteen bucks.'

We don't talk much on the way home, and when he pulls up at the kerb he says drily, 'Since this isn't a date, I won't walk you to your door. Just blink the light when you get inside.'

THE SUPERSHUTTLE LURCHES to a stop, waking me. Still half asleep, I pay the driver and walk to the porch. Before I can touch the doorknob, the door opens and my mother rushes out to hug me. It's a bit overwhelming. 'Mom, hi. You look great. Your hair and everything.'

Her index finger smoothes the curve of her new chin-length bob.

'Thanks, honey. I'm so glad you're here. Now take your bag upstairs. Your dress is on the bed.' She adds almost shyly, 'I hope you like it.'

I run up the stairs, planning to dump my bag and come right back down, but the dress laid out on my bed stops me in mid step.

'Well?' She stands behind me.

'I love it. It's beautiful.'

'Try it on,' she says. 'I've been dying to see it on you.'

I pull off my cotton sweater and step out of my jeans. Even in my stockinged feet and with my hair in a ponytail, I feel like the dress was made for me. It's the colour of sunrise—a gold panne velvet that feels like water against my skin.

'That colour is gorgeous with your hair.'

'Where did you find it?'

She smiles. 'The same store where I found mine, this little boutique in Santa Monica called The Whole Nine Yards. Richard took me there.' I try not to let my stomach tighten. As I'm wiggling back into my jeans, she says, 'Oh, before I forget, there are two boxes of your things in the den and one in your closet. If you want them, you should take them with you. I'm running out of storage space.'

'I thought you sent me all my stuff.'

'The one up here came out of the cedar chest. The two in the den are . . . David brought them by. He said they were more books and some photographs he thought you might want.'

Hearing her say his name is like walking into a wall of glass.

'Right.' My breath jumps raggedly. I jerk open the zip of my bag, pull our my cosmetic kit, set it on the dresser.

'Has he filed for divorce yet?'

'No. At least I haven't seen any papers. Who knows what'll be waiting for me when I get back.' I take a big breath and paste on a smile. 'Let me see your dress.'

In her bedroom, I pretend not to notice Richard's shaving kit.

'What do you think?' Her wedding dress is a simple, elegant long sheath of silk in an old-fashioned colour that she calls ashes of roses.

'It's beautiful, Mom. It's your colour.' I wish I sounded more whole-heartedly engaged.

She looks at the clock. 'Why don't you lie down for a while. We're going out to dinner about seven thirty.'

'We?'

Her smile dazzles me. 'You and me and Richard. We thought it would be good for the three of us to spend a little time together. So you can get to know him before the wedding.'

A golf-ball-sized lump is lodged in the middle of my chest. How well can I get to know him by tomorrow? 'I'm really pretty tired,' I say. 'I worked last night and I didn't sleep on the plane.'

'Wyn, why are you acting like this?'

'Like I'm tired? Probably because I haven't slept in twenty-four hours.'

She chews on the inside of her lip, always a bad sign. 'OK, do it your way. I was hoping you could forgive me for being happy when you're miserable, but apparently . . .'

'This has nothing to do with . . . David.' I still can't say the word.

'Then would you please tell me what it does have to do with.' She yanks open the top drawer of her chest of drawers and starts rifling through her underwear, pulling out a black lace bra, a half-slip. 'Richard and I are going to dinner at Rex,' she says. 'If you'd like to come, we'd love your company, but the choice is yours.'

The bathroom door closes behind her.

I go down to the kitchen, open a can of chicken soup and a packet of dried pasta. While the soup heats, I chop some carrots and courgettes, pour myself a glass of red wine and take it out to the den. I sit down in my mother's sewing chair and take a sip of wine.

So what *does* it have to do with?

It's been only five months since I was here, and it feels like a stranger's house. It's not just the boxes full of Richard's things that are piling up everywhere. There are other, more subtle, changes—the sofa moved back further from the fireplace, the wing chairs grouped with a new table.

It's stupid. What difference does it make? My father's gone. He's not coming back. I can't get another father, but she can get another husband. And why shouldn't she? She's obviously happy.

The sound of a key in the front door makes me jump. Footsteps. Then, 'Wynter, great to see you.' Richard Travers is standing in front of me, filling the room with his presence. 'Fog's coming in,' he says.

Wow! No wonder my mother grabbed him. He's gorgeous! The prototype for tall, dark, etc. With just a suggestion of silver at the temples. His face is all planes and angles. He takes off his coat, lays it carefully over the back of the couch, and turns his dark eyes back to me. 'How's Seattle? Johanna says you're working in a bakery?'

I gather my composure, hold out my hand, and he grips it. 'Fine. Yes. I'm . . . it's nice to finally meet you.'

He smiles. 'I hope you're planning to join us for dinner.'

My eyes go automatically towards the kitchen. 'Actually, I'm taking a rain check. I'm a little tired.'

'I thought you might be. Did you come straight from work?'

I nod dumbly.

'That's rough.'

My mother chooses that moment to appear in the doorway. Richard walks over and kisses her. In my adult memory, no man has ever kissed my mother like that. Like a lover. I can't watch. I slink off to the kitchen, am giving my soup a stir, when she appears beside me.

'What do you think?' She's fizzing like a candle rocket.

'He's amazing.' I give her the best smile I can muster. 'Totally gorgeous. You'll have a better time without me anyway.'

'Probably,' she says. 'But I wanted you to get to know him.'

'I will, Mom. I promise. I'm just exhausted.'

She kisses my cheek, a little coolly. 'Well, get a good night's sleep. We've got to be up by seven in the morning to get the house ready before the caterer and the florist and the wedding coordinator get here.'

From the hallway, 'Jo?' At the sound of his voice, her face looks like she swallowed a light bulb.

Saturday morning at 6.45, I'm sipping coffee in the kitchen and watching the rain hammer on the window. My mother is scrambling eggs when the back door swings open to admit Richard, dashing in a black trench coat, covered with fine droplets.

He smiles at me, and then turns to my mother. 'I hear rain on your wedding day is good luck.' He kisses her neck.

'We don't need luck,' she stage whispers. 'Ooh, you're all wet.'

I guess I'm going to have to get used to this.

After breakfast, the wedding coordinator shows up. Her name is Amanda Brewer and she is definitely Beverly Hills. Blue-black hair, enough eyeliner and mascara for a raccoon, red silk dress, presumably in honour of Valentine's Day, matching shoes. The three of them huddle and then the furniture gets completely rearranged. I stand around feeling useless, not talking much. My mother asks me if I'm feeling OK.

'I'm fine.'

'Well, you could try contributing a little more to the proceedings,' she says.

'Mother—'

'Oh, the caterer's here. Wyn, can you let them in and get them set up in the kitchen, show them where things are?'

'The caterer' consists of a tall guy with slick black hair who seems to be the boss man, two short guys who don't speak much English and two nubile blondes. They clump together, dripping, in the hall.

'I'm Ron,' says the boss. 'This is Tony and Raul, Heather and Frankie.'
'I guess you need to see the kitchen.'
'The bartender's name is Gary. He'll be along later. I want to wait a while before trying to bring everything in, just to see if the weather breaks.'

He talks nonstop while I show them round the kitchen and dining room, and just as I'm getting rid of him, Stuart, my mother's hairdresser from for ever, shows up with his partner, Jason, who's doing the flowers.

'Wynter, darling! So good to see you.' Air kisses. 'Still wearing the big hair, I see.'

'Don't start on me, Stuart.'

He makes wide eyes. 'Uh-oh. A little pre-ceremony tension, for sure.' Just then my mother wanders in.

'*Here comes the bride*,' Stuart sings. 'Jo, darling!' More air kisses.

'I think the ladies should have a glass of champagne to take to their boudoir,' Ron says smoothly.

The popping cork is a cheering sound. In the kitchen, Ron hands us each a champagne flute and we clink and sip.

My mother looks at her watch. 'Oh my Lord, Wyn, we've got to get dressed. Honey, you'll probably need to dress in my room, since yours is so crowded with stuff.' Suddenly I'm honey again.

As soon as she disappears upstairs, Stuart turns me towards the door. 'Wyn, you run along and help Jo. We'll take care of things down here.'

I'm almost at the stairs when the doorbell rings. I open the front door and find myself looking into golden brown eyes under a shock of thick, brown hair. He says, 'Hi. I'm Gary.'

'They're all out in the kitchen.' I close the door and point over my shoulder. 'Just go on back there.' I turn and run up the stairs.

My mother's already brought my dress and cosmetic bag into her room, and we take turns showering in her bathroom. I spend an inordinate amount of time getting ready, using more make-up in one day than I have in the last four months. As soon as we're decent, Stuart and Jason are admitted to the inner sanctum.

After gushing over our dresses, Stuart starts on my mother's hair and Jason turns to. 'And how are we wearing our hair?' he asks.

'We're wearing our hair in a French plait.' I smile sweetly.

'Let Stuart fix it.'

'I can do my own hair.'

'I'll fix some flowers for him to weave in. You'll look so goddess, Wyn.'

My mother has a sort of pleading look on her face.

I sigh. 'Can't pass up the chance to look so goddess, can I?'

The guys smile conspiratorially at each other. After Stuart finishes with my mother, I take her place in the hot seat. He manages to subdue my mane into a French plait in record time, entwining it with a garland that Jason makes from stephanotis, rosebuds and variegated ivy. He adds a little mascara to my lashes. I'm going to look more Beverly Hills than Amanda. Then he stands back and squints at me with one eye closed. 'As close to perfection as you'll come in this lifetime, darling.'

Perfection? Maybe. What I feel as I stare at myself in the mirror is an overwhelming déjà vu. I can almost picture David standing next to me. This is the way he liked me—all dressed up with someplace to go.

I sweep out of my mother's room just as the bartender is stepping out of my bedroom. When he sees me, he grins, like we're old buddies.

'Can I help you find something?' I use my best Hancock Park talking-to-the-servants voice.

'Sorry. I couldn't find any place else to change.' He gives me an appraising look. 'Nice dress. You must be Wynter.'

'I am.'

'It's nice to meet you. I've heard a lot about you.'

In my brain there's a tiny slot machine, with all the pictures lining up—oranges, flowers, dollar signs. No jackpot. Suddenly Richard appears. 'There you are,' he says to the bartender. 'I wanted to introduce—' He sees me. 'Have you two already met?'

Oh shit. I think I've been ordering my stepbrother-pending around like hired help.

'We were just about to,' says Gary Travers.

'I'm so sorry. I thought you were—I'm really sorry.'

'I figured that out when I didn't see anybody I knew in the kitchen.'

The doorbell rings again. I make my escape, thoroughly mortified.

Field-Marshal Amanda marches us through a quick dress rehearsal of who stands where and who does what to whom. In the intervening fifteen minutes before guests are supposed to begin arriving, I slip off to the kitchen to get a glass of water. Abruptly the glass is lifted from my hand and replaced by a flute full of bubbles. 'Don't drink that stuff, little girl,' Gary says. 'Fish fuck in it.'

I stick my nose over the rim of the glass to inhale the yeast. 'They'd probably fuck in champagne, too, given the chance. I know I would.' Did I really say that? I feel my ears glowing.

His laugh rumbles pleasantly. 'I don't think I've ever seen a woman make herself blush.'

'You obviously haven't been around me enough.'

'Something I'm looking forward to.'

No telling where this might lead, but Ron chooses this moment to insert himself between us to reach for a platter of shrimp puffs. Gary grabs a couple and we devour them. I'm hungrier than I realised.

The service begins promptly at two o'clock in the living room. In spite of my best efforts, I'm reliving my own wedding. Must be those words. *To have and to hold from this day forward. Till death us do part.* Except at my wedding, I insisted on changing it to *As long as we both shall live.* David found it amusing that I was superstitious about mentioning death. He looked at me just the way Richard's now gazing at my mother, as if she were first prize in a random draw and he can't believe his luck.

I'm so absorbed in my own thoughts that I'm startled when my mother turns to hand me her flowers so they can exchange rings. When they've finished the formalities and I give the flowers back to her, I notice Gary watching me, eyes brimming with questions.

Then it's over and everyone's clapping. Champagne corks are popping like antiaircraft fire. I hug my mother and kiss Richard's cheek.

'Take good care of her,' I smile. 'Or I'll break your kneecaps.'

'Oh, Wyn.' My mother laughs nervously.

Richard smiles. 'I don't doubt that you not only would, but could.'

I watch them accept congratulations and listen to the details of the wedding trip to Hawaii. They pose for pictures with Gary and me and just about everyone else. I'm introduced to people and five minutes later I've forgotten their names. I keep downing champagne and whenever I finish a glass, Heather or Frankie is at my elbow with a refill.

I watch Richard and my mother. They have this magnetic field between them. They can be on opposite sides of the room and, as if on cue, they both look up and smile.

I try to be happy with them, but they're as remote as if I were seeing them through the wrong end of a telescope. It occurs to me in a moment of self-revelation that I'm jealous. Love, marriage—OK, I admit it—and financial security. All those things that I had. Now she has them. And I don't. I hate myself for the feeling, but there it is.

The rain's stopped and the clouds are breaking up, but the wind has turned frigid. I wrap myself in an old grey sweater and sneak out into the garden. The air smells of eucalyptus.

My father laid this patio when I was seven. He worked on it for several weekends, laying out the herringbone pattern and border while I tried to help by bringing him one brick at a time. I march up and down like a duck, matching my feet to the angle of the bricks. Eventually my head stops sloshing around. All I want is to go back to Seattle, back to my own little house. I don't want to talk to anyone else about anything. I don't have any more fake smiles left.

Voices are calling my name. 'Wyn, what on earth are you doing out here? You'll catch your death.' It's my mother, frowning.

'It was so stuffy, I needed to get some air.'

'You're shivering. Get inside this minute.' My inner child knows that tone of voice and meekly obeys. Then I notice that she's changed into her travel outfit. 'Run up and fix your face,' she says, more gently. 'We're getting ready to leave.'

Sunday I wake up before dawn, deservedly hung over. The illuminated numbers on my watch say 5.35. I sit up in bed, but my head throbs in protest. I lie down again.

At eight o'clock I get up. It's raining again. I open the door, step cautiously onto the landing. I vaguely recall going berserk last night. Pushing some of Richard's boxes out of my room and down the stairs. I walk along the landing and look down. Three boxes lie tumbled in the hall, flaps jutting out awkwardly like fractured limbs. Papers litter the tiled floor. Hopefully nothing's broken. There's a gap in my memory between the newlyweds' departure and my rampage. There was pizza, I know that. Gary and I ordered a pizza. I remember getting furious because he just opened the refrigerator and got a beer, like he lived here. He reminded me that his father does indeed live here. The rest is fuzzy.

Downstairs the air is thick, the palpable silence that follows the departure of a noisy crowd. I get a glass of orange juice and wander restlessly from room to room, in pursuit of my father's ghost. I've always felt his presence in this house, and it's comforted me. He probably won't hang around after the newlyweds get back. Or maybe he'll terrorise them. Materialise next to Richard in the shower some morning.

I go into the kitchen to brew coffee, dunk pieces of stale cinnamon roll in it for breakfast. When I can't avoid the inevitable any longer, I climb the stairs to my room and slit the tape on the boxes that David brought over.

The first one's full of ticket stubs, programmes from plays and concerts, photos. In a lot of the pictures I look less than wonderful. I'm talking, eating, yawning, looking away from the camera.

A manila envelope bulges with wedding cards and gift tags, a few leftover invitations. A letter. I was at a colloquium at San Francisco State the summer before we married. I pull out the blue notepaper.

Dear Wyn,

God I miss you. I detour by your place every morning on my way to work, just in case you decided to come home early. I don't really expect you to be there, but I'm always disappointed that you're not.

I miss our weekends. I hate waking up on Saturday and Sunday and not seeing you next to me. I love the way you look asleep with your hair curling all over your shoulders. Shit. Now I'm horny.

A bunch of us went to Hank and Marie's for the Fourth and everyone was asking about you. By the way, I have a BIG surprise for you. It has to do with the wedding, but I can't tell you anything else. I think you should chuck the seminar and come home early. I promise you won't have to work very much longer anyway. I plan to take very good care of you. Call me about what time your flight gets in. (And make it soon.)

All my love, David

The BIG surprise was our house—the same one he locked me out of. He took me to see it the day I came home from San Francisco. He made me keep my eyes shut till we got there. When the car stopped and he said I could look, I gasped with what he assumed was surprise and delight. He told me proudly about the architect, how the house had been featured in *Architectural Digest*. Eventually I got used to it, to its stark white walls and chilly steel railings, but I never loved it the way he did.

The doorbell jerks me upright. Maybe somebody with a present for my mother and Richard. I run down the stairs and open the door.

David.

Just to make the weekend a full-blown, unmitigated disaster.

'Can I come in?'

I'm a mess. No make-up, hair like a whirlwind. He steps carefully around the tumbled boxes, giving them only a cursory glance.

Finally I blurt out, 'What do you want?'

'Your mother said you were coming for the wedding. I was hoping you'd still be here.'

'How did you slip your collar?'

'Wyn, please.' He takes my arm and I jerk away reflexively. His fingers leave an imprint on my skin. 'Can't we just talk?'

He follows me into the den. I sit in my mother's sewing chair, staring at the little oval table next to me. It's walnut, with impossibly slender, hand-carved legs. A vase containing two dozen yellow tulips sits on the tabletop.

He paces aimlessly for a few minutes. 'How are you?'

'If you actually gave a shit, you could've called to find out.'

'Wyn, I do give—I do care how you are. I've been in Denver for a while. We got the Coors account. I'm setting up a satellite office to handle it.' He lounges against the fireplace, looking around the room like he's trying to figure out what's different. 'How's Seattle?'

'Fine.'

'You're still at the bakery?'

'Yes.'

'I guess it's kind of relaxing.'

'It's not relaxing. It's damned hard work.'

He sighs and makes his way to the couch. He sits down on the edge of the seat cushion, hands clasped loosely, finally making eye contact with me. 'You know I never wanted to hurt you.'

'Wow. I feel so much better.'

He ignores my sarcasm. This is a well-rehearsed speech, brooking no interruptions. 'I didn't intend to start . . . with Kelley.'

'When was the first time?'

There's some small satisfaction in watching him squirm. 'Wyn—'

'Was it the Christmas party? Last summer?'

'How could you think that? It wasn't till you went to Seattle.'

'How can you look me in the face and lie?' There's a stubborn little knot forming in my throat. 'Could you just tell me why?'

The cobalt eyes shift away from me. 'I don't know. I think we both changed. We grew apart—'

'We didn't grow apart. You just saw someone younger and prettier that you wanted, so you dumped me.'

'I didn't dump you. You're taking this too personally—'

Even he knows how stupid that sounds. 'Wait. You dump me for the bionic blonde and I shouldn't take it personally?'

'That's not what I meant to—'

'So what did you mean?'

He runs a hand through his hair, takes a deep breath. 'What I meant was that our splitting up is not a reflection on you. In any way—'

'David. Let's get one thing straight. We did not split up. Splitting up implies that it was mutual.'

'Well, it should have been mutual.' His face is flushed now, eyes angry. 'We weren't happy, weren't making contact any more. And then, with Kelley, there was this intense . . . communication. She was there in the trenches with me every day. We worked so well together.'

'Shut up!' My hands cover my ears like the little hear-no-evil monkey.

'I'm sorry. I shouldn't have come over.' He scoots forward like he's going to get up.

'Then why the hell did you?' I didn't intend to yell, but I do.

He leans back slightly, as if blown by the force of my anger. 'The only reason . . . I wanted to tell you . . . I'm going to marry Kelley.'

I surprise both of us by bursting into raucous laughter. 'I think bigamy's illegal in California.'

He blinks at me like he can't quite place who I am. 'For God's sake, Wyn. I just wanted to talk to you. To do the right thing—'

'The *right thing*?' When I leap to my feet, suffused with righteous indignation, I inadvertently kick the leg of the delicate antique table. It goes over and the vase full of tulips resting on it gets launched. Water and flowers go flying everywhere.

All those pretty yellow tulips. Now come the tears.

'Wyn . . .' Before I can get a grip on myself, David's got a grip on me, ignoring the broken flowers and sopping carpet. Holding me.

'Wyn, don't. Please, please. I didn't want it to be like this. It's for the best. You weren't happy either. Don't you remember what it was like? Wyn . . .' He's smoothing my hair, wiping tears off my face with a tenderness I haven't seen in months. Did he think I didn't care?

When I turn my face up to him, there are tears in his eyes. It's just him and me. Like it was before. Like none of this other shit ever happened.

He loved me. He still loves me.

He kisses me, and my arms lock round his neck tightly. Then sanity regains the upper hand. I feel it rising in a cold wave. He extricates himself. 'I'm sorry. I shouldn't have done that.' He won't look at me.

Unfortunately he's the only one exhibiting a shred of common sense. I slide my hands up under his sweater, kiss his mouth, graze it with the tip of my tongue. 'Hold me,' I whisper. 'Just for a minute.'

Whoever said love has no pride knew what they were talking about.

'Wyn, stop.' He grips my arms abruptly, thrusts me away. 'You're just making it harder.'

'David, you love me, I can tell you still love me.' I grab his hands and he pulls them away. It's like trying to hold on to a fish.

Now he's back in control, and totally turned off by this vulgar display of emotion. He holds my wrists at my sides. 'I'll always . . . care about you, Wyn. But it's time to get on with our lives. I'm sorry.'

He looks around the room. 'I'll help you clean this up.'

'No.'

He's already kneeling, picking up the vase.

I try to dredge up some dignity. 'I want you to leave. Now.'

He turns the table back upright, sets the vase on it. Then he's out of the door. It shuts decisively, like he's afraid I might sprint after him and tackle him on the lawn.

There's half a bottle of champagne in the refrigerator, so I pour myself an eight-ounce tumblerful. I drop into a chair and take a big swallow, letting the bubbles burn my throat.

It's raining when my flight lands at Seattle airport on Monday after-noon. CM's white Camry is waiting outside baggage claim.

'What have you got in here, barbells?' she complains as she heaves the box into the trunk.

'Old things.' We pile into the front and take off.

'So. How did the wedding go?'

'It was a nightmare. Something out of Eugene O'Neill.'

'You want to tell me?'

I shake my head. 'Later. I'm too tired to do it justice tonight.'

'OK.'

'And then yesterday David came over to tell me he's going to marry Barbarella.'

'Shit.' She pokes her tongue into the side of her cheek. 'Well, you sort of knew it was coming.'

'Did I?' She doesn't say anything, so I rephrase the question. 'Did you ever think, before I told you about her, that he might be involved with someone else?'

She's the picture of intense concentration on the road. 'It crossed my mind once or twice.'

'You're my best friend,' I blurt out. 'Why didn't you say something?'

For a second I think she's going to get us killed as she exits across three lanes of traffic. At the bottom of the ramp, she pulls into a deserted parking lot and stops the car, swivels in her seat to face me. 'For God's sake, I thought you were telling me. You were always talking about how he was never home. How he didn't talk to you. That you hadn't had sex in for ever—'

'That doesn't have to mean someone's screwing around.' I hit the window button and the cold air revives me.

'No,' she says. 'Not always.' She reaches over to squeeze my hand. 'I'm sorry, baby.'

Neither of us says another word till we get to Queen Anne.

'I think you should stay with me tonight,' she says.

'I have to go to work. I'll be fine.'

After we've lugged the box and my bag up from the car and put them in the office, I collapse into the club chair, and she sits down on the futon. 'Look, I'm sorry,' she says. 'Maybe I should have . . .'

'CM, it's OK. Really. I'm sorry I blew a gasket at you.'

423

She looks dubious. 'Are you sure you're all right?'

'Yeah, I'm just exhausted. I should probably try to grab a nap before I go to work.'

We trade hugs. I know if I gave her any opening at all, she'd stay, and I'd end up telling her everything. Maybe I'd feel better. Or maybe I wouldn't. Too much sympathy can be worse than none at all.

Besides, I'm fresh out of openings tonight.

'YOU LOOK LIKE YOU COULD use a boat ride.' Mac McLeod stands on my porch on Sunday morning, smiling with just his eyes.

'What I could use is about three more hours' sleep,' I grumble.

'Sorry. You haven't been to Bailey's all week, so I thought I'd check on you.'

'I didn't get back till Monday night. I've been trying to crawl back into my rut.'

He laughs at my surliness. 'Come on, get dressed. We'll just ride over to Bainbridge and back. Being on the water might improve your attitude. Works for me.'

At the Colman Dock we run for the *Spokane* with a few other passengers, stand by the aft rail as she pulls away. The wind's still kicking up whitecaps, but the clouds have broken and the sun tests the water.

I hang over the rail. 'Tell me a story.'

'About what?' he says.

'Tell me a story about you. Tell me the Gillian story.' A gull flies up and hovers alongside, eyeing us impassively.

'I don't think this is . . .'

'Please. Distract me.'

'OK.' He pulls his cap down lower on his forehead. 'I was hitchhiking from Auckland to Wellington. This guy in a beat-up old Land Rover picked me up. He took one look at me and asked me if I was interested in making a few bucks. I was extremely interested. He owned a sheep station and they were in the middle of the shearing season. Somehow a shearing shed had caught fire and because the family were too busy shearing to rebuild, they were looking for guys to work construction in return for room, board and a few bucks. I was thinking I'd work for a week or two and then move on.

'So that night we're having dinner at this long table—about eight or ten guys—and this young woman comes in to help her mother serve. The daughter of the guy who'd picked me up.'

'What did she look like?'

'Not beautiful. Really not even pretty. Brown hair, blue eyes. Tall. Rangy. She had that body ease that people have when they've grown up doing hard physical work . . .' He smiles. 'If you looked at her, she looked right back. I didn't pay much attention to her at first. She was just there every day, helping her mother. Then one day she didn't come and I realised I was looking for her at every meal. She was gone for a week. She came back the morning I was leaving. In fact I was walking down the drive when this car pulled up and she got out. We just looked at each other there in the drive. She smiled. I turned round and went back into the bunkhouse, ended up staying for six months.'

'My God, how romantic.' I grip the rail. 'So what happened?'

'Nothing. She wanted to get married, have kids, raise sheep. I didn't, so I left.'

We get off at the Winslow Terminal, buy ice cream from a cart. We stand, shivering and laughing because we're cold and eating ice cream anyway, then go back to the ferry. Coming out through the turnstile at Colman Dock, he finally says, 'So how was the wedding?' One lurching sob and the waterworks open.

'That good, huh?'

He puts one arm round me and lets me cry all over the front of his flannel shirt. He rubs my back a little, but gingerly. He hands me his handkerchief. As I'm trying to clean up my face, he takes my elbow and steers me over to the escalator. 'Let's walk back up to the market.'

On the way, I spill my guts. I tell him every gory detail. I tell him about my mother and me sniping at each other, about me getting drunk and being a bitch to Gary and pushing Richard's boxes down the stairs.

I say stuff that I wasn't even conscious of until it pops out of me. Like how I thought it was a slap in the face to my father to have the wedding in the house he and my mother had shared. I tell him about how I tried to seduce David. I tell him about CM and the way we parted company that night. He just walks along beside me, hands in the pockets of his denim jacket, the heels of his cowboy boots making a hollow tap.

By the time I'm through it's almost five, and I ask him if he wants to get a pizza or some Thai food, my treat.

'I'd really like to,' he says, 'but I have something I have to do tonight, so I'll take a rain check.'

Men. Why the hell can't he just say he has a date? And what do I care? I was only offering because he baby-sat me all afternoon.

As soon as I get home, I sit down and call CM. When a man's voice says, 'Hello', I think I've dialled the wrong number. Then I remember. It's Neal. This is the weekend of his seminar.

'Oh hi, Wyn,' he says cheerfully. 'She's right here. Hold on a minute.'

'I forgot this was the big weekend,' I say when she picks up.

'No problem.' Her voice is elaborately casual. 'How are you?'

'I'm fine. I just called to apologise for being so weird the other night, but—'

'It's not a problem,' she insists. 'I'll call you later and we'll talk.'

This has to be the shortest conversation she and I have ever had.

It's there when I pick up my mail on Monday afternoon. The plain white envelope with the return address of a law firm in Beverly Hills.

I rip it open and skim several pages of legal war chant. Looks like the way it works is, if one person says the marriage is broken, it is. Never mind what the other person says. It doesn't seem quite fair. We both had to say *I do* to get married but only one has to say *I don't.*

I think about calling Elizabeth Gooden. But I know that once I do, it's the cannon shot that sets off the avalanche. While I'm still procrastinating, she calls me.

Before I can tell her I've been served with papers, she says, 'Our information specialist has come up with registrations from hotels in Cancún, Mexico, in Scottsdale and San Francisco. I'll give you the dates, and you tell me if you accompanied your husband on any of these trips.'

I bite my lip. 'I haven't been to Mexico in at least three years.'

'Interesting. Cancún's the oldest one. Last December. December 15th to 20th.'

It's like being smacked in the face with a wet towel. My birthday. The important client meeting he had to attend. 'And the registration?'

'Mr and Mrs David Franklin.'

The ache inside me transmutes to a molten rage, expanding to fill every crevice in my body. It's not just that he lied, repeatedly. It's that I believed him. I was stupid.

I tell Elizabeth that I've received papers from David's attorney.

'All right, Wynter, here's what I want you to do. Read over the papers, sign them where it's indicated. Make photocopies of everything, then overnight the originals to me and I'll send you a response form to fill out. The sooner you get things back to me, the sooner I can—'

'How long could the whole process take? Worst-case scenario.'

'Everything depends on how cooperative your husband and his lawyer are. My hope is that we can put it to bed by this time next year.'

'Elizabeth, I want to drag this thing out as long as we can.'

She barely hesitates. 'You know, I think we can have it over fairly quickly, and still mop up the floor with him—financially speaking.'

'It's not about the money. I just want him to have a good long time to decide if she is worth it.'

An audible sigh. 'Very well. But there are limits to what I can do.'

Two weeks and one day after the wedding, my phone rings at nine in the morning and I know before I pick it up that it's my mother.

'Hi, honey, I hope you weren't asleep. I can never remember when you sleep. We got home late last night.'

'No, I wasn't in bed. How was Hawaii?' I assume this is proper etiquette for asking your mother about her honeymoon.

'It was so beautiful. We had the most wonderful time.' She sounds totally blissed out.

'Um, Mom . . . about the boxes . . .'

'I found them. Are you sure you want to throw those pictures away?'

'I'm sure. But I was talking about the other boxes. The ones with Richard's things . . . in the hall.'

'In the hall?' She pauses. 'There aren't any boxes in the hall.'

'Oh. I guess . . . I meant to put the boxes from David down there, but I must have forgotten.'

'You're absolutely certain you want to get rid of all that?'

'Mom, David came over the Sunday after the wedding. He told me he's going to marry Kelley. I got the papers yesterday.'

She sucks in a breath. 'Oh, baby, I'm so sorry. That dirtbag!'

'Mom, don't waste your breath. I've got a good lawyer. I'll do OK.'

'It's not just the money, it's the way he's . . . He'd better hope he never runs into me again. Wait till Barbie finds out she's just the flavour of the month. He'll do the same thing to her, mark my words.'

Phone calls at the bakery between midnight and 6.00am are almost always wrong numbers. So when I answer the phone at about 12.30 that night, I am surprised when a man's voice says, 'Wyn! Gary Travers. I'm at the Edgewater for a few days on business. I was wondering if I could take you to dinner tomorrow night.'

I hesitate, recalling our last and only encounter. Maybe he wants to take me to dinner so he can slip arsenic into my soup.

'Unless you're still mad at me,' he adds.

The room has gone stone silent. Linda is quivering with attention.

'Of course not. Dinner would be nice.'

'Tomorrow night then? About seven?'

'Sure.' I give him directions to my house, hang up and resume oiling pans for cinnamon raisin bread. Linda's about to have a fit.

'Zat your ex?'

'Nope.'

Silence. 'You're not s'posed to take personal calls at work, you know.'

I smile. 'Sorry. Normally I wouldn't, but it was my brother. He's here on business. We haven't seen each other since our parents got married . . .'

'Since your parents got married?'

'So we thought we'd have dinner. Catch up on family news.' I pull out the black binder and pretend to study the recipe for cheese bread.

Canlis is the kind of restaurant my father would have liked. Cantilevered over Lake Union, it simulates being inside a Christmas tree ornament, suspended in the dark, while lights that could as easily be candles or stars as headlights shimmer below. The servers all wear kimonos, seeming to glide rather than walk.

We're early for our reservation, so we sit at the piano bar drinking vodka martinis and observing the sales people and their clients, for Canlis is an old-style expense-account watering hole.

After a few sips, I gather the courage to say, 'Whatever happened to the boxes of your dad's stuff that I jettisoned down the stairs?'

He shrugs. 'I thought it would be easier on everyone if they didn't come home and find a mess, so I put them in the den.'

'That was a really nice thing to do. I guess it's lucky I was too drunk to push them all down. I feel like such an idiot.'

'Don't. I understand why it happened.' That makes him one up on me. He pushes a lock of hair off his forehead and smiles.

At this juncture the hostess comes to seat us. 'So tell me. What are you doing up here?' he asks when we are settled and he's ordered wine.

'Making bread.'

'That's not what I meant.'

I look over the menu at him. 'The short version is, I'm separated and my husband's just filed for divorce. What about you? You live in San Francisco, right?'

'Larkspur. Marin. And don't think I didn't notice that extremely smooth transition. I'm divorced. But we're good friends. We have two kids, so it makes things easier.'

'How old are they?'

'My son is eight. His name's Andrew. My little girl Katie's ten.'

'What do you do?'

'I park cars.'

'Where?'

He grins. 'I have a company. Contract valet-parking for businesses.'

'So what are you doing up here?'

'Growing the business. I've been chasing some clients up here for months. It looks like a couple of them are finally coming round.'

The kimonoed waitress is back to take our order. When she leaves I arrange the silverware, lining it up abutting the edge of the table.

'Wyn.' No choice now but to look at him. 'I'm sorry if I'm making you uncomfortable. That's not my intention at all.' His golden-brown eyes are looking very puppylike.

'You're not. I'm just . . . not used to this. I mean, I'm not even divorced yet. It all feels very strange.'

He touches my hand lightly with two fingers, then withdraws. 'Believe me, I know what you mean. I just went through it myself. At the same time, though, I have to tell you that I'm extremely attracted to you.' A pause. 'I think it was the dominant way you ordered me back to the kitchen that day.'

A lot of the tension dissipates when I laugh. 'That was my Hancock Park mistress-of-the-castle persona.'

'And you wear it well.'

'Not too well, I hope.'

Dinner is good, conversation pleasant, not overly intense, although there's a purposefulness about him that makes me wary. This isn't a man who does anything casually. By the time we're finished, I'm relaxed enough to agree to a brandy at the piano bar.

He tells me about his kids; he and his ex share custody. 'They're with me one week, then with Erica one week,' he says.

'That seems like it would be difficult on them, shuttling back and forth. What about school?'

'They're in private school, so that's not a problem.' I calculate the cost of private school in Marin for two children. 'They have a complete set of clothes at both places to keep it as stress-free as possible for them.'

'What about for you and her?'

The laugh lines etched around his eyes and mouth are plainly not all from laughing. 'We can deal with it easier than they could.'

After dinner, he drives me home and parks by the kerb. We walk slowly up the drive. 'I'm glad you called. I enjoyed seeing you.'

'Did you enjoy it enough to do it again on Friday?'

'Gary . . .'

'Too pushy? That's a bad habit of mine.'

'No. I'm just . . . everything's so tentative with me right now.'

'I understand.'

I fish the key out of my bag and insert it in the lock. I'm hyper aware of him standing right behind me, of the heat radiating off his body. I know if I turn round now, he'll kiss me. I do and he does.

'That wasn't so bad, was it?' He's still holding my face in his hands. His eyes are deep, but gentle. If I drown, it will at least be pleasant.

'I'm not sure. Maybe we should try it again.' The realisation of how long it's been since anyone kissed me like this sharpens my need, breaching my defences like a traitor from the inside.

It's a wrench when I finally pull away. 'I have to get ready for work,' I manage. *Take a cold shower.* 'What time?'

He looks at his watch. 'Ten thirty.'

'I mean Friday. What time should I meet you?'

IT'S BEEN OVER A WEEK and CM hasn't called me back. Either her reunion with Neal was a total disaster and she's too depressed to talk about it, or it was total bliss and he's still there.

When she phones me on Thursday afternoon I can tell by her voice it's the latter. 'Sorry I haven't called. I was thinking I'd stop by there on my way home. If you're not busy.'

'Well . . . let me just look in my daytimer. Oops! Today's the day Harrison Ford's giving me flying lessons.'

'We can talk while you're packing your parachute.'

My latest bread experiment is coming out of the oven—all crusty and golden, and filling the house with its sweet toasted corn smell about the time she walks in. 'God, that smells great. What is it?'

'Cornmeal millet bread. Play your cards right and you get to taste it.'

She hugs me. 'Have you recovered from the wedding?'

'Yes. And just in time, too. I got the divorce papers. Have you recovered from Neal?'

'Oh God.' She's actually blushing. 'I feel bad coming over here like some goosey teenager when you're dealing with divorce papers . . .'

'I'm young, I'll get over it. So tell me.'

'It was incredible. We talked all weekend and he cancelled his flight and stayed till yesterday. I think he did some major soul-searching after he left last fall. He was feeling inadequate about losing that job and he was taking it out on me . . . Anyway, he asked me if I'd be willing to try it again, and I said yes. He's moving back up here in two weeks.'

'Into his own place?'

'Well . . . no. Why would we do that?'

'Maybe to see how it goes?'

'It's going to go fine,' she says firmly. 'His dissertation topic's been accepted by the committee, so all he has to do is write it.'

'Is he going to work?'

'I'm sure he'll find something. Some tutoring, maybe.'

I run my tongue between my teeth and my upper lip to keep from saying anything nasty, but she knows what I'm thinking.

'He's never going to be a Type A overachiever,' she says.

'I just don't like the idea of him living off you.'

'I wouldn't mind supporting him while he writes his dissertation.'

'I know, and I'm sure he wouldn't intentionally take advantage of you, but . . . sometimes . . .'

'Sometimes what?'

'Sometimes nothing. You're smart enough to know what to do. And I'm certainly no one to be giving advice.'

'So tell me what David said. If you want to.'

'The whole thing makes me tired. The gist of it is—we both changed. We weren't communicating. Meanwhile Kelley was there beside him every day. In the trenches, I believe he said.'

She screams with laughter. 'The *trenches*? The closest David's ever been to a trench is when CalTrans had Highland all dug up.'

I laugh till the tears come, which is good, because otherwise it might just be tears. 'But I haven't told you the good news. I had my first date.'

'Really? With who?'

'*Whom*. My new stepbrother. His name's Gary. He lives in Marin. He's just here on business.'

'Good for you. You need a transitional man. To sort of get you back in the swing of things. What's he like?'

431

'Kind of cute. Nice.'

'What else?'

'I'm not sure what else. I'll let you know after Friday.'

That first batch of cornmeal millet tastes great, but it crumbles like baking-powder corn bread when I slice it. Not enough gluten.

I try again, cutting the cornmeal in half, adding another cup of wholewheat flour, and grinding half of the millet in the bakery's hand-crank grain mill. This is more like what I had in mind—chewier, but still with plenty of crunch from the cornmeal and millet.

I take some to Linda, and she grudgingly admits it's good. 'You have fun playing with all these trickity things at home,' she warns me, 'but if you think we're going to be changing anything around here, just get that idea out of your head right now.'

'I wouldn't dream of changing one teaspoon of anything in the sacred black book.'

She's a one-woman stone wall, and I have no intention of inspiring her to even greater heights of antagonism.

Gary and I agreed to meet in the bar at the Edgewater, in case he was running late, but he's sitting at a table near the fireplace, and his face lights up like a birthday cake when he sees me.

When he stands up to kiss my cheek, my stomach gives one little flip of protest and then settles down. This is OK. I can do this.

'What would you like?' he asks.

'Chardonnay, I think.'

After he orders my wine, Gary tells me that his meetings went better than he expected.

I smile. 'That's good.'

'I'll say. It means I can come back in three weeks.'

I think I'm supposed to be enthusiastic at this point. When I don't say anything, his hand moves to cover mine. But gently.

'I was hoping you'd be pleased.'

'I am. Really. I'm just . . . nervous, I guess.'

'Perfectly natural. But I wish I could say something or do something that would make it OK.'

I laugh. 'Men always want to *do* something. Sometimes you just have to sit tight till things work themselves out.'

He says, 'I talked to Andrew and Katie before I came downstairs.'

It's a few seconds till my brain kicks into gear and I realise he's talking about his kids. 'What are they up to?'

'They're at Erica's, my ex-wife. Katie had cheerleading practice this afternoon and Andrew's science project won first prize in the school competition, so now he takes it to the district.'

'You must be very proud of them.'

'I guess it's hard to understand if you don't have kids. I just get such a kick out of every new thing they do. Sometimes I tend to run on about it . . . I don't want to bore you.'

'I'm not bored.' In my head, I hear CM: *'Liar.'*

'Do you ever want children at all?'

'I never have.'

'I think you'd be a great mom. You're such a warm, caring . . .'

'I'm selfish and spoilt. Besides, I don't relate well to kids.'

'You would if you had some. Or if you met . . .'

'Oh no. Don't go there. Not even hypothetically. I've always believed that once you have a child, your own life is pretty much over.'

'Not true. It's really just the beginning.' Gary looks at his watch. 'We'd better get going. We've got a reservation at the Dahlia Lounge.'

The Dahlia's a pretty romantic place, in spite of the fact that it's small, crowded and noisy. The service is efficient but relaxed. I unbend, even taking the liberty of looking into my stepbrother's pretty eyes. He picks up the cue, resting his arm on the back of the banquette so his fingers just touch my shoulder. 'How long were you married to David?' he asks.

'Seven years.'

'What's he like?'

'Oh . . . handsome, charming, bright, successful.'

'Sounds like the ideal husband.'

'My grandmother used to say, "if something sounds too good to be true, it probably is." How long were you and Erica together?'

'Eleven years.' He smiles like a man who's found out more than he ever wanted to know about divorce.

'You miss her, don't you.'

'I miss all of us together. The way it was. After she went back to law school, nothing was ever the same.' He shakes his head. 'I guess I never understood why she wanted to go in the first place. She was making good money as a paralegal.'

'It must have been really important to her,' I tell him gently. 'Studying law isn't a commitment you make lightly.'

'Neither is marriage,' he says.

After dinner, when he asks me if I want to go back to the Edgewater for a drink, I know what he's really asking, and I say yes. In the lobby, neither of us glances at the bar; we head straight for the elevators. We're the only ones in the car and he pulls me into his arms. He tastes like the red wine we drank at dinner, the apple dessert. The first recognisable emotion is relief. It's all coming back to me now—how it feels when a man wants you, how it borders on reluctance, because he's not sure once he's touched you that he can stop himself. It's like a drug, that touch.

With obvious effort, he takes me by the shoulders. 'Wyn . . .' His breathing is ragged. 'I don't want to push you.'

If he only knew how close he is to being jumped in the elevator.

Before the door to room 324 shuts behind us, I'm tugging his shirt-tail out of his slacks. He pulls my jacket down over my shoulders, kisses my neck, my ear, my hair. My jacket drops on the floor and we both step on it in our race to the bed. 'God, I want you,' he murmurs in my ear. 'I just don't want it to be too fast.'

I look into those golden-brown eyes, now chocolate-dark with lust. 'I do. Then we can do it again.'

He pillows his head in my neck and we laugh.

It's too easy, almost familiar. My body seems to remember his from another time; it knows his hands, his mouth. He's intense, methodical, obviously used to being in charge, and I'm happy just to ride the sensations like waves. Every time I expect him to slip inside me, though, he backs off and starts over.

My fingers tangle in his soft, thick hair. 'If you want me to beg, I will.'

He smiles, moving his body over me.

The phone rings—probably once or twice before I hear it.

I whisper, 'Don't answer it.'

I can see the battle raging. 'It might be the kids.'

He's embarrassed, apologetic, torn. But he rolls away from me and picks up the receiver. 'Yes? Erica. What's wrong?' He sighs through his teeth. 'Well, I thought since I talked to them earlier—no, it's OK. Of course I want to say good night to them.'

He chats patiently—no, it's more than patient. He's into it. First Andrew, with the science project. Then it's Katie's turn. The cheerleader princess. His tone is teasing, cajoling. I look at him curled up on his side. The Titan Rocket has become a miniature gherkin, lying meekly on his leg. In one flash of clarity, I see a world comprised of six o'clock Saturday-morning phone calls from Erica reminding him that it's his turn to drive to early soccer practice. Two sweet, freckled, serious little faces, smiling up at me. *You're not my mother. You can't tell me what to do.*

He's off the phone now, and looking miserable. 'I'm sorry.'

'It's OK.' I lean over to kiss his cheek. 'I need to get ready for work.' I pick up my clothes and take them into the shower room.

The wind knifes through my jacket. I scurry down the alley towards the bakery's back door, knock, shift my feet back and forth, try to keep warm. Linda must be in the storeroom or the bathroom. I knock again, louder. Still no answer. I fumble in my rucksack for the bakery key.

Inside, only a few lights are on. None of the flour buckets are out. For that matter, nothing is out. The worktable is clear.

'Linda?' No answer.

I lock the door behind me, take a few steps into the room and then I hear something—a cross between a groan and a grunt. 'Linda, where are you?' I trip over her foot before I see her.

She's propped against the wall next to the ovens, eyes closed, mouth open. Her breathing is noisy, laboured. 'Linda, are you sick?' When I bend down, I smell the bitterness of juniper berry. Linda is drunk as a skunk. An open bottle lies next to her. Looks like I'm making the bread tonight. But what to do with Linda?

In the storeroom I find a couple of canvas tarps. I lay one of them next to her and manage to roll her onto it. By dragging the tarp to the other side of the oven, I eventually get her out of my way, throw her coat over her and get into high gear for breadmaking.

When I've got both mixers heaving dough around and I'm sitting on a stool oiling pans, I hear a noise that sounds like a big Velcro fastener being ripped apart, and I realise that Linda is throwing up. I grab an empty flour bucket, stick it under her head. The stench is overpowering.

When I think she's finished, I wet a towel and toss it at her. She wipes herself, lies back down and drifts back into oblivion. I throw the bucket and the towel into the dumpster, leaving the back door propped open. This is something we never do because of security.

I haul the white bread and wholewheat out of the mixers, into the troughs for their first rise, dump in the ingredients for the raisin bread and cheese bread without stopping to scrape down the mixers.

At 6.00am, I'm removing the cheese bread to the cooling rack when Ellen unlocks the front door. 'Holy shit, it's freezing in here.' Footsteps. 'What is that godawful smell?' Then she's standing there, looking from Linda to me, to the back door, to me. 'What the hell happened?'

'Linda's really sick,' I say, staring into the heat of the top deck, shuffling some loaves from back to front.

Linda starts rolling around on the tarp, moaning.

'We've got to get her out of here and get rid of that smell.' Ellen's eyes narrow as she looks at me. 'Has she been drinking?'

I shrug, look her in the eye. 'Beats me. She was fine when I got here. Then she just sort of collapsed.'

Ellen looks at me hard for a few seconds. 'I'll call her daughter.'

Paige, the daughter, is here in less than thirty minutes, almost like she was waiting for a call. She's surprisingly pretty, in a severe way. I notice that her eyes are red-rimmed, as if she's been crying. She stands over Linda, a mixture of disgust and concern on her smooth features.

'I expect she's been drinking since late afternoon,' she says. She looks at Ellen. 'My father was killed yesterday.'

While Ellen and I scurry around cleaning up the bakery, it occurs to me that Linda's loss, while undeniably sad, presents me with an opportunity. I scrape together a fist-sized lump of dough from one of the mixer bowls, mix it into a cup of water. Throw in two handfuls of flour, and we have a *chef*, the seed of a sourdough starter.

Jean-Marc showed me how when I told him I wanted some *levain* to take home with me.

'First you must make the *chef*, OK? You take the flour . . .' He threw a fistful of white flour into a small bowl. 'And a little wholewheat to make it stronger. Then the water.' He dumped the flour into a mound on the table, made a well in the centre and filled it with water. Then, using two fingers, he began to combine the two, adding just enough flour to make a firm dough. He handed me the walnut-sized lump. 'Knead a little . . .'

When the dough was springy, he produced a small earthenware crock. 'OK. *Ici*.' I dropped the dough in. He took a towel, wet it, and laid it over the top of the crock. 'Now we wait.'

'For how long?'

He shrugged. 'Until it is ready. Two, three days maybe. And you must keep the towel wet. Do not forget this.'

Two days later, when I took the towel off to dampen it, I was disappointed to find that my lump of dough had solidified into a rock. I took it to Jean-Marc. 'What's wrong? What did I do?'

He laughed. He took the ball from me and began to peel it like a hard-boiled egg. Under its crust, the interior was full of tiny bubbles and it smelt sweet. '*Bien*. It is ready for the first refreshment.' He handed it back to me. '*Allons*. I watch you. Two hands of flour this time. That is good. Now in the middle.' He made a circular motion and I made a well in the middle. 'Now put the *chef*. Yes. Now a little water. Yes. No. Do not mix the flour yet. First you . . .' He rubbed his fingers together.

'You smush it?'

'Smush? This is a word?'

'Absolutely. *Bien sûr*.' I squished the dough and water between my fingers until the lump dissolved.

'*Bien*. Now the flour. We wait again. Tomorrow perhaps.' He replaced the towel.

'Don't you know how long it will take?'

He looked at me gravely. 'Wynter, the bread tells you. *Vous comprenez?*'

I don't mind the morning fog. In fact, on this particular morning, it suits me perfectly as I jog home, replaying last night's fiasco in my mind. I push through the hemlocks on the drive, instead of walking round, and a movement draws my eye to the porch. Gary materialises out of the fog. He looks endearing in his jeans and battle-scarred leather jacket. I want to be happy to see him, but something almost like dismay nips at me. At the same time, I'm thinking about his mouth on my breasts, about how that jacket would feel against bare skin—mine, for instance.

He starts to say something, but before he can, I blurt out, 'One more apology and I'll never speak to you again.'

He laughs. 'OK. No apologies.'

Inside, I hold his jacket for a minute before hanging it up. 'I thought you were leaving this morning.'

'I changed my flight to this afternoon.'

'Why?' OK, it's a rhetorical question, but I want to hear his answer.

'Unfinished business.' He holds me gently, resting his cheek on my hair. 'I can't believe how good you smell.'

'The bakery.' I smile. 'Want some coffee?'

He's as tall as I am, so when he pulls back, we're exactly eye-to-eye.

'No,' he says.

By Monday night, when I take the towel off, the *chef* has doubled in volume and the surface is textured with tiny bubbles. The unmistakable odour of fermentation rises from the bowl. I add more flour and water and mix it energetically.

The third time I check the *chef* it's doubled in volume again. It's soupy and roiling with life. It's ready to make *levain*.

I've conveniently forgotten that Linda's coming back until I let myself in the back door on Thursday night, just in time to see her standing over the garbage can with my *chef*.

'What the hell are you doing?' I shout.

She recovers quickly from the shock of seeing me. 'Who told you to make this?'

'Nobody told me to make it. I did it for myself. Ellen said I could let it ferment here. I'm taking it home tonight.'

She looks me in the eye and dumps my *chef* into the garbage. Total disbelief immobilises me. Then I hear myself say, 'You are the sorriest excuse for a human being I've ever met.'

She's grinning, she's so pleased with herself.. 'What did you say?'

'I said, you're a bitch.' I turn and walk out of the back door.

I hear the back door open and she screams, 'You're fired! You know that, don't you? You're fired!'

It's what she wanted all along.

I light the stove, wrap a blanket round me and sit in my chair, drawing my knees to my chest.

OK, now what? Linda's a bitch. She's unreasonable, impossible to work with. She's pathetic and stupid. But I'm unemployed and she's not.

Why did I let her get to me? It's just a *chef*. Worst-case scenario is I make a new one. I reach for my pillow on the futon.

When I open my eyes it's light. I have incredible kinks in my back and neck from sleeping in this weird pretzel position, and someone's banging on the door. I unfold myself, lurch for the door.

'Wyn, I'm so sorry.' Ellen rushes in before I have time to say anything. Then she looks at me. 'Oh, I woke you up. I'm so upset.'

'Sit down.' I point to the chair. 'I must have fallen asleep.' I fill the kettle and put it on. 'What time is it?'

'Seven.'

'Ellen, I'm sorry I lost my temper . . .'

She shakes her head vehemently. 'I'm sorry you had to put up with her. I've already told her she has to apologise to you.' She gives me an ingratiating smile. 'And I told her you're going to be making some new kinds of bread. That is, if you want to, of course.'

I look at her in surprise. 'You still want me to work there?'

'Are you nuts? First of all, you're a great baker. Second, you've lasted with her longer than anyone in the history of the place.'

'Can I ask you a question? Why do you keep her on?'

'I just can't bring myself to fire her. She'd never get another job.' She shoots me a pleading glance. 'You'll stay, won't you?'

'What I don't understand is why she threw my *chef* out, even after I told her it was mine and I was taking it home.'

She runs a hand over her close-cropped dark hair. 'She's just a miserable human being, that's why. Her bitterness poisons everything she does.' Ellen's gaze shifts to the kettle, whistling softly.

'Want some tea?' I ask.

'No, thanks. I've got to get back. I just ran over here to make sure you weren't pulling up stakes and heading for LA.'

I'VE NEVER HAD A MAN friend before. Not one who'll sit with me through two and a half hours of Rocky and Bullwinkle cartoons. I reciprocate by accompanying him to his favourite secondhand bookshops, where we spend hours in search of anything 'interesting'.

I blink as we emerge from yet another bookshop on a narrow street off Pioneer Square, each of us carrying two recycled grocery bags full of books. 'I feel like a pack mule,' I complain.

He laughs. 'Oh, quit complaining.'

'What is this fascination you have with books that have been pawed over by two or three other people?'

Even before I catch the sidelong glance he throws me, I already know I've inserted my silver foot in my mouth.

'I can't afford new books all the time,' he says, without belabouring the point. Most men would have seized the opportunity to remind me that I'm a spoilt brat who's not accustomed to giving much thought to the price of anything.

Mac, however, isn't most men. In fact he isn't much like anyone I can recall knowing. His brain reminds me of a meticulously organised filing cabinet full of interesting but often arcane information. His favourite subject, no contest, is music; and he's maddeningly opinionated.

I asked him one night at the bar why he never plays instrumentals. He said because they sound like something's missing.

I said, 'You think lyrics are more important than the music?'

'Not exactly. It's best when the words and the music work together. Like that Otis Redding song I was telling you about. The way the horns follow every phrase, kind of drawing you in.'

'I don't remember.'

He gave me a disapproving look. 'You need to learn how to listen.'

The one thing we never get around to discussing is his love life. He knows my history, of course, and every once in a while he'll refer to David as the Evil Prince. Gary is 'your brother', but he doesn't expend a lot of breath on either one. I know the basic plot outline with him and Gillian, less about Laura. And if he's seeing anyone, he's not talking. I've tried asking him about it, but he's a master of evasion and diversion. It's probably just as well.

At Steve's Broiler early one Sunday morning we sit in a booth eating feta cheese omelettes and watching the old guys at the counter suck on unfiltered cigarettes and drink coffee.

A young woman comes in with two little boys and they climb into the booth next to us. The rugrats are cute—about seven and five years old—and they could've been made by the same cookie cutter, except the older one has brown hair and his little brother has blond curls. The kids have colouring books and their mother gives them a box of crayons and tells them to share. She sips her coffee and gets engrossed in a magazine. Mac watches them with more than casual interest.

'So tell me about it. You never talk about your childhood. What you did or what it was like. Was it happy? Unhappy?'

He folds his napkin and lays it next to his plate. 'OK, here's the condensed version. My mother was an art student. She met my dad—the original happy wanderer—in a museum. In a few hours they were madly in love. They went to his place and screwed their brains out . . .'

'Mac . . .'

'I've kind of distanced myself from the whole thing. Anyway, she got pregnant. I guess in those days there weren't many options in that situation. They got married. My brother Kevin was born. Things were fine for a while, then my father got restless. He took off for South America working for an oil company. After a year or so, he came home. She took him back. Bingo. I'm in the oven.'

'Didn't they ever hear of birth control?'

He just shrugs. 'And so life went on. He'd be home for a while, then he'd get the blues in the night. When I was twelve he went to Canada to hunt moose or something, and he never came home. His plane went down in the Canadian Rockies and they never found it. For years I was convinced that he was alive. I made up stories about him being taken care of by a hermit. I even wondered if he'd wanted to disappear.'

'Is that what your book's about?'

His eyes lock on mine. 'What makes you think I'm writing a book?'

I start to laugh. 'Oh, come on, Mac. It's the way you're always scribbling in those notebooks.'

'I told you, it's a journal.' He seems somewhat abashed.

'My bullshit indicator is blinking double reds. Why are you so embarrassed about it?'

His eyes are suddenly dark. 'I don't want to be an asshole about it. I'm not a writer. I'm a bartender who writes stuff.'

'As long as you think of yourself that way, that's what you'll be.' I take my last bite of a piece of cinnamon raisin toast.

Sounds of a scuffle draw our attention to the next booth, where the kids are locked in a tug of war over a blue crayon.

'Knock it off or nobody gets to colour,' the woman says, not looking up from the magazine. The kids act like they don't hear her. The older boy manages to get the crayon away from the younger one and starts writing on his napkin. The little one chooses an orange crayon and imitates his older brother's artwork on his own napkin. Then the older kid decides he wants the orange crayon too. He grabs it away from the little guy, who promptly begins to cry.

The mother looks up. 'I told you guys to share.'

'Christopher took mine,' the little one wails.

'Get another one and stop being a baby.' She resumes her reading.

The waitress sets our bill down. Mac hands her a twenty and continues to watch the kids while I watch him. The younger boy pulls out a green crayon. The waitress counts out our change and we scoot out of the booth. There's a sharp slapping sound and a yelp. The older boy now holds the blue, orange and green crayons and the little one's crying again.

'Brian, I told you to shut up,' the mother says. 'If you're gonna sit there and cry like a baby, you can't colour any more.'

Suddenly Mac leans over and pulls two crayons out of the older boy's hand. The mother and both boys stare open-mouthed as he looms over them. He smiles sweetly and says to the kid, 'It's always a good idea to share. Some day he'll have something that you want.' He hands the two crayons to the little brother and we walk out.

Spring and winter are having a tug of war. Some afternoons when I walk up to Parsons Garden in the mild caress of a chinook wind, I think spring is winning. Crocuses push up through the dank black earth, yellow and purple and white. Pale green flowers of hellebore, that my Oma called Lenten Rose, gleam like tiny lamps in the deep shade.

One morning Ellen arrives, her eyes hollow and red-rimmed. She's one of those people who's normally so up in the morning you sometimes want to kick her in the knees, so I start worrying. But after Linda goes home, Ellen says, 'Diane's mother had a stroke last night.'

'Oh shit.' My very first thought is how she'll be drowning in guilt. I would be. 'That's terrible. I'm so sorry. Is she going home?'

'She's on her way to the airport as we speak.'

'Let me help you set up.' I turn on the espresso machine and wring

441

out a cloth in the enamel pail of Chlorox solution to wipe the counters.

After Ellen finishes counting change into the register drawer, she fills the espresso basket, with two quick snaps of the grinder. 'I feel awful for her,' she says, handing me a double shot of decaf. 'And I'm a terrible person for worrying about the bakery at a time like this . . . but we're in a real bind here. We've got all these cake orders.'

No one else can decorate cakes like Diane so Ellen has to call people who have orders for the following week, advising them that Diane is away on a family emergency.

The next time I see Diane, I almost don't recognise her. It's Friday afternoon and I'm making my weekly financial pilgrimage. When I step round the cooling racks, Cody's talking to a woman who's arranging pansies on a small pink-frosted wedding cake. My brain skips to the idea that Ellen's hired a part-timer till Diane comes back. Then they both look up and I see that Diane is back.

'Hey, Wyn.' She smiles at me, but her face is bleak.

'How's your mom doing?'

'Not bad, considering what she's been through.'

'What's the prognosis?'

She pushes her hair back with her forearm. 'It's too early to know for sure. The haemorrhage was on the left side of the brain, so that means it affects the right side of the body. She hasn't got much mobility on that side right now.' She sighs, a sound of utter exhaustion. 'And of course she can't talk very well.'

She blinks and tears glint in her eyes. 'Hell, what am I saying? She can't talk at all. She makes weird noises, and everyone's supposed to know what she wants.'

'I'm so sorry.' I feel the total inadequacy of the words.

'Well . . .' Cody clears her throat. 'It's my turn to cook dinner, so I'm outta here. Later, you guys.' She disappears and I lock the front door after her. 'Should I make us a mocha?' I say.

Diane manages a laugh. 'And blow us all to Hawaii?'

'Hey, I can barmaid with the best of them these days.'

'OK. I could use a jolt to keep me going.'

'You need some help tonight?'

She shakes her head. 'Cody made all the buttercream, thank God. All I have to do is slap it on.' She pulls more pansies out of a white plastic bucket. 'How's Linda?'

I laugh. 'Some things never change.'

I hand her a mocha and she takes a sip. 'This is good.'

She takes another sip, sets the cup down, and I watch helplessly as her face crumples and she begins to sob.

All I can do is put my arms round her and wait.

I lose track of the time till she steps back from me, hiding her red, puffy face in her hands. 'I'm sorry. I am so fucking tired.'

I get a clean towel, wring it out in cold water and hand it to her.

'I've been up and down all night, every night since I left. God, Wyn, she's just impossible. And I would be, too.' She holds the towel to her face, muffling her words. 'This is a woman who ran the most successful real-estate office in Baltimore. She said jump and everyone asked how high on the way up. Now she can't wipe her own ass.'

Diane sits up and drapes the wet towel over her head like a scarf. 'And she's determined to make everyone in the family as abso-fucking-lutely miserable as she is.'

April, everyone agrees, is too late for snow. But the weather gods aren't paying attention to the calendar. Or maybe it's just their idea of an April Fool's joke.

I suppose in New York and Chicago and places where it happens every winter, it's just an inconvenience. Traffic snarls, people have to shovel their drives, salt their porches, drag out the snow tyres. The majority of Seattleites aren't that jaded. People clump together on corners, sipping hot chocolates and scrunching their boots just for the sound of it.

Saturday night at Bailey's, it's like a party. Kenny's made hot buttered rum in a crockpot. Mac's playing sixties tapes and people are doing the twist.

I'm caught up in the festivity in spite of the little pincerlike pain that started last night and has now turned into a pretty decent stomachache. I feel vaguely nauseous. Could I have food poisoning?

I should probably go home and go to bed, but the thought of walking home alone in the snow is somehow daunting. If I just sit here a little longer, maybe I'll feel better.

When Inez and Charlie Foxx start singing 'Mockingbird', Mac comes out from behind the bar and grabs my hand. 'There's your song.' He pulls me off the stool and we manage a few steps before he tries to twirl me under his arm and I double over. 'Hey, what's wrong?'

I straighten up. 'Nothing. I've just got a stomachache. Maybe I'm getting that flu that's going around.'

He frowns. 'You don't look so good.'

'People usually don't when they're getting the flu,' I snap at him.

'You want me to take you home?'

I shake my head. 'I'll just sit here a while and then I'll go home.'

'Let me know if you start to feel worse. The truck's out back.'

By 1.15, most of the crowd has departed for the comfort of their warm beds. I must have the flu. My eyes are hot and my stomach is churning. A ride in Mac's smog-mobile's sounding not half-bad.

'Hey, Mac.'

His grin fades as he focuses on me. 'Jesus, Wyn. Are you OK?' Without waiting for an answer he says, 'Come on, we're going to the walk-in clinic.'

'No, we are not. Just take me home. Please.'

'You look like hell. You need to see a doctor.' He shrugs into his jacket and helps me with my parka, wrapping my scarf around my head.

I yank it off. 'Will you stop?'

'Back in a minute,' he hollers at Kenny. The cold air in the alley feels good, but even the snow can't cover the smell of rotting garbage, and that's all it takes. I'm on my knees puking my guts out.

Mac lifts me from behind and pain rips through my lower abdomen. Pinpoints of light explode in front of me and fade like tiny fireworks. 'Try to breathe shallow. Nice and slow. That's it.'

I must have yelled, because the back door opens and Kenny's head sticks out. 'What's wrong?'

Mac shouts, 'Call 911.' Then he turns to me. 'Where does it hurt?' He grips my arms.

I rest my hand on the tight, warm place under my jacket. Mac looks at his watch.

Finally Kenny opens the door. 'I got through, but they said it'll be at least fifteen to twenty minutes. They're swamped tonight. The snow—'

'By that time . . .' Mac's voice trails off, which is fine with me. I don't think I want to hear this. Kenny helps him fumble me into the truck.

Then Mac slides behind the wheel and turns the key. The truck makes a kind of groaning, grinding noise, and he strokes the dashboard like it's a big old dog. I'd laugh but it would hurt. He turns the key again. This time a hiccup follows the groan, and the truck starts to chug, slowly.

Snow is falling again in big starry flakes. It would be enchanting, except that I feel like I've swallowed a live ferret. The headlights carve out a tunnel of light in the alley and he turns left, then right on Queen Anne Avenue. 'Where the hell are you going?' I ask.

He stops at a light. 'We're going to Virginia Mason.'

His face blurs. My breath pumps out in short white smoke signals of panic. 'Just take me to urgent care, then. I don't need to go to the hospital. Really. I'll be fine.'

'Breathe and swallow.' His voice is calm but he's gripping the wheel so hard that his knuckles look like a white dotted line.

Every nerve-ending in my body is on full battle alert.

'How's your boyfriend?' Mac's voice interrupts my thoughts.

'We had dinner twice. That doesn't make him my boyfriend.'

'Did you make him split the bill?'

'Are you trying to distract me or piss me off?'

'Your choice.' He smiles infuriatingly.

I wince as we take a bump. 'What is it? What's wrong with me?'

'Appendix, I think.'

'No. Shit, no. It can't be. I can't be laid up for a month.'

'I don't think you get to decide. Anyway, you'll like it. You get lots of sympathy and TLC.' He frowns. 'The only problem is . . .'

'What?'

'String bikinis are probably out for a while.'

My head falls back against the seat. 'Fuck you, McLeod.'

'Remember, you have to eat with that mouth.'

'Will you quit laughing at me? I'm scared.'

'It'll be OK. Trust me. I've been there.'

'Show me your scar.' He laughs, and I feel the tyres spin. 'Oh God.'

'Just a little slick patch,' he says. But I can tell by the way the stuff is splatting against the windshield that it's turning to sleet. The truck crunches forward, gaining traction with its sheer weight. 'Recite a poem for me.'

'I can't remember—*ahh*.' I grip the armrest, rock back and forth.

'OK, I'll do one. *I think that I shall never see a poem lovely as your knee*—'

'You've never seen my knee.'

'Sad but true.' He turns left, then right. Downtown is eerily beautiful in the falling snow. I let myself drift, and I am vaguely aware of a tenor singing 'I Only Have Eyes For You' on the car radio.

Abruptly I feel the unmistakable dip of a driveway entrance. Mac leans on the horn as we skid to a halt in front of a red cross and a sign that says 'Emergency'. Mac leans on the horn as we skid to a halt.

'Stop that. I feel like an idiot.'

He's out of the door, leaving me curled up around the hot pain.

There's movement outside and noise, lots of people in green scrubs and white uniforms. I'm on my back on a wheeled contraption.

'When was your last meal?' a nurse demands. I look at her stupidly, then say, 'Breakfast.' She rolls me over on one hip, and I feel the bite of a needle, followed by a wave of warmth. Miraculously, the pain begins to break up and wash away. It's like a silent movie with that fuzzy black border. The border is getting wider and wider till I can't see the picture any more.

I'm throwing up. Or wanting to. But the world's perkiest blonde nurse is smiling at me, saying, 'Don't vomit, honey. You'll feel really bad.'

I shake my head. It would not be possible to feel any worse than I do.

Later I wake up in a different room. As the fog recedes, the first thing in focus is CM's worried face. I smile weakly with relief. She takes my hand in both of hers. 'How are you feeling?'

'Never better.'

She gives a little giggle and presses my hand against her cheek. 'God, I was so worried. How did Mac know how to reach me?'

'Your phone number's in my wallet.'

'He seems like a pretty nice guy.'

'We're just friends.'

'He asked me to call your mom, but I thought I'd better wait till you were conscious . . .'

'Thank you for that,' I sigh. 'I'll call her later. What day is it?'

'Sunday afternoon. The snow's already melting.'

When I try to shift my weight, a quick turn of the screw makes me gasp. 'Shit. I think they left a scalpel inside.'

'It's your incision, dum-dum. You'll be fine as long as you don't cough, sneeze, laugh or breathe.'

The sound of knuckles on metal draws our attention to the doorway, where a young guy with a stethoscope hanging round his blue surgical scrubs stands grinning. 'How's it going?'

'Are you the one who did this to me?'

'Guilty as charged, Your Honour. And it's a pretty bang-up job, all modesty aside. How are you feeling today?'

'Like the magician's assistant who's been sawn in half. When can I go home?'

'Whoa, easy there. You are one fortunate lady. You were about that close . . .' he holds his thumb and index finger together, 'to a ruptured appendix. Your friend got you here just in time.'

'I assure you, I'm grateful to all concerned, but I'd like to go home.'

He gives me a bemused smiled. 'Tuesday. Maybe even tomorrow. As soon as you can pee by yourself. And when you can promise me that you won't lift anything heavier than a sandwich for about six weeks.'

'You must be joking. I'm a baker. Lifting's half the job.'

He shakes his head. 'It's going to be a minimum of six weeks before you can resume a normal routine.'

'Well, fine. You want to come home and wait on me?'

'It's not the worst offer I've had, but I can't spare the time right now.' He gives me a charming smile, but I'm way beyond crabby at the moment. 'Miss Morrison, all kidding aside, your body needs a certain amount of time to heal properly. That's just a fact of life. Do you know what adhesions are?'

When I shake my head, he says, 'Well, if you don't let your body heal properly, you will. And it won't be pleasant.' By the time he finishes describing adhesions, bowel obstruction, abcess, chronic pain and future surgeries in detail, I've reluctantly accepted my new status as an invalid.

When Mac calls on Monday afternoon to see if I want company, I announce that I can pee by myself. I haven't been this proud of going to the john since I was potty trained.

He laughs. 'Does that mean you need a ride home?'

'If you could, I'd appreciate getting out of here a.s.a.p.'

He was right about one thing. It's been a long time since I had this much attention. Of course for the first few days, I'm too drugged out to enjoy it. CM fills my freezer with soup and casseroles and helps me bathe. Cody brings me scones and cookies and a wood-block print of a loaf of bread in warm shades of brown and rust.

'Cody, this is wonderful. This should be hanging in the bakery. Can you make another print of it?'

'Yeah.' She shrugs, looks embarrassed by the fuss. 'By the way, Linda says hi,' she says. 'She totally misses you.'

'Cody, stop. It hurts when I laugh.'

Mac brings me cassettes and books, which he reads aloud when I'm too groggy to focus. One morning he shows up at 9.30 with a white bag and a copy of *The Great Gatsby*.

I crawl back under the covers while he makes coffee. 'If it wasn't for the pain, I could get used to this. Sleeping late, having people bring me food and music. Read to me.'

'Enjoy it while you can. As soon as you're up and about I'm planning to get sick so you can read to me.' He hands me a cup of coffee and tosses the white bag on the bed. Inside is one perfect golden croissant, still warm.

'Oh, Mac, thanks.'

I take a bite of the croissant and the butter-crisp papery layers shatter into toasty shards. 'Oh God, this is so perfect. You want a bite?'

'No, I had one on the premises.' He sits down in the club chair.

'You're out early for a Sunday.'

'Actually I haven't been home yet. Kenny and I went out last night and ended up at a party on Capitol Hill.'

I feel a weird little jab in my stomach. 'Was it fun?' I ease out of bed and creep carefully to the stove for a refill. 'You want any more?'

'You finish it.' Just a breath, then, 'Laura was there.'

'Did you talk?'

'No. She was with somebody.'

'How did that make you feel?'

He leans his head back against the chair and laughs. 'You can take the girl out of California, but you can't—'

'OK, OK. I just thought you wanted to talk about it. If you don't, fine.'

I close my eyes and listen as Mac becomes Nick Carraway, lost in the glittering world of the Buchanans, and I recall hazily that after reading Gatsby for the first time, I wanted to change my name to Jordan.

Eventually he snaps the book shut. 'Sorry. I'm really tired.'

'That's what happens when you stay out all night. Go home and get some sleep. Leave me the book.'

He rubs the back of his neck. 'God, I'm stiff.'

'Come here. My dad always said I gave good neck rubs.'

'Don't go ripping anything.'

'Sit down and shut up.'

He lowers himself to the floor, stretching his long legs out in front of him, and I massage the stiff cords at the base of his skull. Everything's fine until I start thinking about it. Mac and I don't touch each other. It's an unwritten rule with us. Now I remember why.

Because I'm imagining my fingertips on the smooth curve of his back. I'm staring at the hollow where his neck joins the shoulder, wondering how it would feel under my mouth. God, no, this is all wrong. I need a friend, not more complications. 'OK,' I say, too cheerfully. 'That's it. I'm a little sore. I guess everything is connected to your stomach muscles.'

'Thanks.' He doesn't get up or turn round.

When my mother was trying to teach me piano, she explained about the una corda pedal, the one on the left. When you depress that pedal, the entire action and keyboard shift just slightly, nearly invisibly to the right, so that the treble hammers strike only one of the three strings. The pianist continues playing just as before, but the music is different, softer. That's how the world has just shifted.

A knock on the door makes me jump, sending a twinge through my incision. Mac scrambles up.

From my angle, I can't see the porch. I can only see Mac's face, the neutral expression that drops like a curtain after the play. He steps back and Gary walks in, hidden by giant bundles of pale yellow roses.

I find my voice. 'Gary! What are you doing here? I'm sorry. This is my friend, Mac McLeod. Gary Travers.' They exchange some kind of genetically encoded male information at a glance, then shake hands.

Just so nobody misunderstands, Gary bends down to kiss me. I try to make it a short one.

'I better get going.' Mac picks up his denim jacket.

I look round Gary and the roses. 'Mac? I'll talk to you soon.'

After the door shuts behind him, Gary off-loads the roses onto the kitchen table. He hangs up his leather jacket and sits down next to me, taking both my hands. 'Why didn't you call me?'

'There was no need to. I figured I'd be seeing you next week.'

He runs a hand through his hair. 'I'm sorry, Wyn. Maybe I shouldn't have barged in like this, but when I rang and your mother told me you'd had emergency surgery, I panicked.'

'You and my mother.' I smile. 'It was all I could do to keep her from getting on the next plane up here. But I'm fine. It's just a matter of resting until everything finishes getting stuck back together.'

'Then that's exactly what we're going to do. I'll just go out to the car and get my bag.'

My eyes open wide. 'Your what?'

'My bag. My suitcase. I arranged things so I could be up here all week.'

'My place is so small . . .' I feel like my protest is not only feeble, but petty and ungrateful. 'You won't have room to—'

'I'm here to take care of you. I have a few phone calls I have to make tomorrow, but for the most part I'll just be your devoted slave.' He bends down to kiss me. 'By the way, I hope you don't mind, I gave Erica and the kids your phone number. I told them they could reach me here.'

For dinner he heats up some of CM's soup. He brought a loaf of Paisan sourdough with him and two bottles of a Napa Valley cabernet. Afterwards I enjoy watching his butt when he's standing at the sink washing dishes. At some point he turns round with his sleepy-eyed smile.

'What are you laughing at?'

'I'm not laughing, I'm smiling. Enjoying the after-dinner show.'

'You better not talk like that if you can't follow through. Remember the theory of rising expectations.'

When he's finished with the dishes, he takes off his shoes and stretches out next to me. Gary pushes up the sleeve of my sweatshirt and tickles the bend of my elbow.

'God, that feels good.'

'When are you going to be seaworthy again?' he asks, nibbling my ear lobe.

'I don't know. All they said was something about gradually returning to your previous level of sexual activity.'

'Gradually?' His breathing kicks into second gear. 'If we have to work up to it, maybe we should start slowly. How about if I just touch you?'

I smile. 'How about if I just touch you? You're the one with a gun in his pocket.'

His breath catches when I run my hand down the ridge in his trousers. He unbuckles his belt. I ease the zip down and slip my hand inside, freeing up Junior. His Class 5 excitement is a turnon, but his gratitude leaves me vaguely uneasy.

'That was incredible,' he breathes when he's holding me later. 'I wish I could make you feel good.'

'Gary, you are making me feel good. I like the way you hold me. It doesn't always have to be about orgasm, you know.'

Around noon the next day, he showers and gets dressed. 'I have to go to a meeting.' He looks worried. 'Are you going to be all right here by yourself?'

'Of course. I've been mostly by myself since I came home. People wander in and out and leave me food. I eat, sleep, get fat and lazy.'

'Do you feel up to going out tonight?'

'Possibly. Go to your meeting; we'll talk when you get home.'

When he's gone, I'm exhausted. Like I've been on stage or at least on display for the last twenty-four hours. I potter in the kitchen, wash out the coffeepot, make myself a peanut-butter sandwich. I put on a tape Mac gave me. Bo Diddley's 'A Gunslinger', Chuck Berry's 'Sweet Little Sixteen'. Then Jackie Wilson starts winding out 'Doggin' Around'. The way he hits that high *Yeah* and slides down into good man feelin' bad blues gives me goose bumps.

'You must be feeling way better. Sounds like party time.' CM flings open the door.

'I feel pretty—' The word dies in my mouth when she flashes a diamond solitaire under my nose. 'Oh my God.'

There's a cavernous silence. 'Is that all you can say?' She laughs.

I put up my arms for a hug. 'Congrats.' I want to smile but my face is numb. Come on, Wyn. Lie. 'I'm really happy for you.'

'Yeah, I can see you are.'

'I'm just . . . stunned. So when did this happen?'

She holds her hand out and turns it from side to side so the sun shaft coming in the window makes rainbows on the wall. 'Pretty righteous rock, don't you think? Last night.' She flops into the club chair. 'He just came walking in the door with a bottle of Dom Pérignon and some roses and I said what are we celebrating and he said—'

I'm wondering, since he's not working at the moment, where the hell he got the money for a diamond and Dom Pérignon.

'Gee, I hope I'm not boring you.'

I look at her. 'CM, please don't be mad at me. I just can't help wondering—is this what you want?'

'Not really. But I didn't have any classes scheduled for spring, so I though I might as well get married.'

'Sit.' I ease down and pat the space next to me on the futon. She walks over to the window and pretends to be looking at something.

'CM, I want you to sit down and listen.'

She perches on the chair. Right on the edge so she can jump up and throttle me.

'I want you to be happy. You know that.' I pause, hoping she'll agree, but she doesn't. 'Why did he give you a diamond?'

'They must have removed part of your brain when they got the appendix. Why do you think he gave me a diamond? Because he loves me. He wants to marry me. Is that so hard to fathom?'

I should just shut up. We can patch this up now. Except I can't stop myself. 'No, but—he knows you. He knows you don't like diamonds—'

Her eyes narrow. 'What's with you? Does it really matter what kind of ring it is?' She starts walking back and forth in front of me.

'Neal got you a diamond because it's what he wanted to give you, not what you wanted—'

'You!' She points her finger at my nose. 'You are way jealous.'

'Yeah, I am, but it has nothing to do with this.' She's already angry; I might as well go for broke. 'The man can only love you when everything's hunky-dory for him. Don't you remember how we always said if one of us was getting ready to make a bad mistake, the other one should tell them, no matter what? I'm trying to help—'

'The hell you are!' she snaps. 'You're jealous. You didn't want your mom to get married and you don't want me to get married. When did you get to be such a selfish, spoilt . . .'

She doesn't finish, but I can fill in the blank. She slams the door so hard it bounces open again. I struggle to my feet and hobble after her, reaching the hemlocks just in time to see her car pulling away.

I want to vomit, but I know how that would feel, so I pop a warm Coke and take little swallows till the nausea passes.

Doesn't she realise it will never work? As soon as his dissertation hits the skids—and it will—he'll be Mr Moody Blues again. Accusing her of neglecting him, of being self-centred. He'll bitch and moan and make her feel guilty. Then she'll come running to me.

Just like I always go running to her.

Of course, this whole thing will pass, and in a couple of days we'll be talking on the phone and we'll laugh about it.

Except, how could she think I'm jealous? I mean I am, but only in general. How could you not be jealous of someone who sometimes renders you invisible by her very presence? But jealous about her getting married? Not likely.

I need to make bread. I need to and I can't, so I get on the phone to Jen and take down the ingredients for her recipe for 'short' scones.

        3 Cups flour
        ½ Cup sugar
        5 Tsp baking powder
        1 Tsp salt
        1 Cup unsalted butter, chilled, cut in small cubes
        ½ Cup currants or dried cranberries, soaked in orange juice
        1 Egg
        ½ cup milk
        Zest of one orange
        ½ Cup chopped toasted pecans

Gary comes back while I'm taking down the recipe, and paces until I hang up. Then I have to give a report of my activities. I skip the whole CM scene. When I start dragging out flour and sugar and butter, he says, 'What are you doing?'

'Making scones.'

He looks at me like I'm in a delirium. 'Why? Can't we just buy some—'

'Gary, please. It's not the scones I need, it's making them. Why don't you get us a glass of wine and park yourself in that chair and tell me all about your meeting?'

He uncorks the wine and pours two glasses. I confess I'm not listening too closely about the meeting. I'm rubbing the butter into the dry ingredients with my fingertips and thinking about CM.

'Have you thought about tonight?' Gary says.

The way my head snaps up, he probably realises I wasn't listening, but he sits there, hair falling softly on his forehead, smiling like a choirboy. He tries again. 'So, what do you feel like doing?'

I pull out a cookie sheet and arrange the scones on it in orderly rows, lay it in the freezer. I turn round. 'Can I ask you a question?'

He smiles. 'Sure.'

'Did you ever cheat on Erica?'

The smile evaporates like water on a hot griddle. 'No. Why?'

'Did you ever want to?'

'Not really.'

'What does that mean, not really?'

He looks directly at me. 'It means I met someone once that I was attracted to, but I never pursued it. Later I realised it was probably just a revenge fantasy.'

'Revenge for what?'

'Erica had an affair with a friend of ours,' he says quietly.

Batting a thousand today, Wyn. 'I'm sorry. That was a stupid conversational gambit.'

'You obviously had a reason for asking. Is that what happened with David?'

'Sort of. It was a woman in his office. Now they're getting married.'

'I'm sorry.'

'Isn't it weird, us sitting here talking about our exes? Like they were former employees or something. Instead of someone you thought you'd be waking up next to for—You know what I want to do?'

'What?'

'I want to go on a tour of that house out front.'

He rubs the back of his neck. 'I think that's called trespassing.'

'We won't break anything. If nothing's open, we won't go in. Come on. Before it's too dark.'

'This would be the tradesmen's entrance,' Gary says. 'All these big old houses had one. By the kitchen.' The rusted knob is so loose that the door swings open at a gentle push.

We step inside, inhale the damp, stale air. My eyes gradually adjust to the dimness. There's something about a house that's been shut up.

He takes my hand and pulls me into the kitchen. They got as far as gutting it. The bleached shadows of cupboards and appliances are all that's left on the dirty walls, except for stubbed water and gas pipes.

The dining room's obvious by the chandelier hanging over the spot where the table would be. We pass on to the living room where the thing covered with dustsheets turns out to be an ebony grand piano. With one finger I pick out the melody line of 'Moon River', the only song I remember from my abortive piano lessons.

The stairs groan and our footsteps echo off the bare wood. Dust motes dance in the last light of afternoon, spilling through a tall, narrow window. We stop on the wide landing halfway up.

'This is where you make speeches from.' He leans on the railing and jumps back smartly as it bows out.

I laugh. 'And that's what happens when the speeches go on too long.'

The doors leading off the upper landing are closed except for one. I wander in and he follows. No furniture, just moving crates sealed with tape and labelled optimistically 'Master Suite'.

'Look.' He points to a box under the bay window. Sitting on top is a pair of fuzzy bunny-rabbit slippers. Not something you'd buy yourself. Maybe a birthday present. To say I'm sorry. Or I love you.

I can't breathe in here. I turn abruptly, back down the stairs, through the kitchen and out of the side door, as fast as I can without my incision protesting. Gary's right behind me.

How could you leave someone who gave you bunny slippers?

You want some more wine?'

'No, thanks.' He sits down in the club chair while I rinse the glasses out. 'You still haven't told me what you want to do tonight.'

'Well . . .' I reach for the blind on the kitchen window. Then I walk over to the door and lock it.

'I promise I won't run away.' From his silly little grin, I'd say he's picking up the signals OK.

He reaches for my hand. 'Are you going to be all right with this?'

'We'll just do what we can.'

'I like the sound of that.'

When I straddle him, I can feel his erection under me. 'Are you ready already?'

'All I have to do is look at you and I'm ready.'

I'm dissolving against him, sediment falling through still water. Tears stream out of my eyes and when he feels them on his face, he looks up at me. 'Do you hurt?'

'Not physically. It's just been kind of a shitty day.'

His thumbs gently push the tears off my face. 'What can I do?'

I lean over to kiss his mouth. 'This will be just fine.' I stand up and pull the sweatshirt over my head. The rest of the clothes are laid aside and we settle in carefully. His hands cradle my hips and I lower myself, letting him fill me.

'Are you OK?' he whispers.

I smile. 'Better than that.'

He begins to move inside me and I fall thankfully into darkness.

Sunday night. My attempts to function on impulse, without analysis, have always met with limited success. Gary is snoring softly while I lie on my back, brain turning over.

The whole week has been about him taking care of me, pleasing me, helping me. It reminds me of being in a mink-padded cell. And just when I get annoyed, feel like I have to get away, his breath on the back of my neck turns my knees to water and we end up sprawled on the futon.

When I open my eyes on Monday morning, he's lying there propped up on one elbow, smiling at me. Awareness of his imminent departure produces a twinge of regret. It wasn't so bad. In fact, it was nice. He pulls me closer and I snuggle up against him.

'Wyn?'

'Hm?' I rub my cheek drowsily against his chest.

'I want you to come down to San Francisco for a weekend.'

I raise myself too quickly, grimacing at the pain. 'Why?'

He smiles, unperturbed. 'I want you to meet Andrew and Katie. It's time for the three people I care most about to meet each other.'

'I cannot possibly be one of those people. You don't even know me.'

'I know what I need to, Wyn. I know myself. I want you in my life.'

'Gary, for Chrissakes, it's just sex.'

'That's not what it is to me.' The way he says it, slow and very sincere, makes me ashamed of myself. 'I don't think that's all it means to you either, but you're scared. I can understand that. You think if you can diminish it by calling it "just sex", you can avoid getting hurt again.'

There's just enough truth in what he says to make me hesitate. 'My divorce isn't even final. I can't think about . . . stuff like this.'

He sits up, too, facing me. 'I'm not asking you to think about anything. I'm asking you to come to my house, meet my kids.'

'Gary, I'm not comfortable with—this.'

'Why not?' He traces the outer curve of my ear with one finger. 'You know how I feel. I know how you feel. Everything's . . .' He touches my throat with just the tip of his tongue and my body responds without consulting my brain. ' . . . up front and out in the open.' When his thumbs graze my nipples through my T-shirt, they stand up and salute.

He knows he's won this skirmish.

Saturday night is clear. Clear like I've never seen in LA. The stars look like this jacket my mother used have—rhinestones set in black velvet.

Dark silhouettes of gulls float against the jewelled towers of the city. The boat shakes with the efforts of its engines and metal clanks against metal on the car deck below us.

Mac wants to be on the water tonight. He's been sort of preoccupied lately, and I tend to blame his close encounter with Laura at the party on Capitol Hill. Or else he's suffering from writer's block, which, like most writers, he takes out on everyone around him. We hang over the rail of the passenger deck, side by side. Suddenly, I'm aware of him so acutely that my fingers ache. The smell of pine bark that clings to his jacket, smoke from the fireplace at Bailey's. Something grassy—maybe shampoo.

He's staring up into the black sky. 'What is it?' he says.

'I was just—Is that the Big Dipper?'

'Yes.'

'That's the only constellation I know.'

'If you know that one, you actually know two. The Dipper's the tail of Ursa Major, the big bear.' I try to follow his finger tracing the outline of a long-tailed bear.

'So where's the Little Dipper?'

He looks behind us. 'If you follow a straight line from the two stars on the cup of the dipper, you'll see Polaris, the North Star, which is the end of the Little Dipper's handle.'

I look past him. 'Who'd have guessed that the psycho-killer-handy-man would know so much about stars?'

'You can't see that many here,' he says. 'Too much light. This would be a great night to be up in the San Juan Islands.'

Something about the way he says it. I feel hot and cold at the same time, and I know it's too early for menopause.

'I'm probably going up there.'

'Probably?' My voice is faint.

He studies something down on the car deck. 'No. Not probably. I'm going. Next week.' Fortunately he keeps talking, because I know I can't make any sounds. 'I've been in Seattle longer than I've been anywhere since New York. It was a hard decision. Sorry if I've been moody or—'

'What will you do there?' That voice isn't mine. It belongs to one hell of a ventriloquist.

'Write.' He turns his face towards me. 'I got a letter from an agent in LA. I sent him the first three chapters and he wants to see the rest.' He laughs. 'I didn't want to tell him there is no rest, so I told him I was revising and he'd get it by September.'

'Congratulations.'

'I'm not breaking out the champagne yet. There's no promises.'

'There never are.'

He exhales noisily. 'Anyway, Rick—the guy from Norwegian Woods—has a cottage up on Orcas and he said I could use it if I'd do some maintenance on the place. The rest of the time I can write.'

'Sounds like an offer you can't refuse.'

He gives me a little nudge with his elbow. 'I'll probably be back in the fall.'

'Probably?'

'Yeah. Probably.'

The morning air is so thick with spring that it's hard to believe there was a foot of snow on the ground six weeks ago. Everyone on Queen Anne is nuts for window boxes and by now they're spilling over with cascading blue lobelia, white dwarf snapdragons, yellow mimulus.

When I get home from work, Mac's leaning against the Elky's passenger door drinking coffee out of a big white cup.

'You shouldn't drink anything acidic out of a Styrofoam cup,' I tell him. 'The acid dissolves that stuff right into your drink.'

'So that means if I drink it slow enough I don't have to worry about recycling the cup.'

'I'm sorry I missed your going-away party. I promised CM months ago I'd go to this dance thing. She had the tickets . . .'

The truth is, I had dragged CM against her will to some terrible French film. I didn't see how I could possibly stand around Bailey's listening to everyone wish him good luck, knowing that in a couple of days he'd be gone.

'That's OK. I'm on my way out of town. Thought I'd stop by.'

'So . . . good luck with the book.'

'Thanks. I hope your . . . situation turns out OK.'

I smile fixedly. 'Jean-Marc used to say the bread might not always turn out the way you want it, but it always turns out.'

'Take care of yourself.' His mouth brushes my cheek awkwardly. He climbs in the Elky, and the door rattles as he slams it. He rolls the window down as if he just thought of something else. 'Here. I made this for you.' He hands me a cassette.

I turn it over. 'What is it?'

'All the songs and artists are on the card.'

My stomach is making little warning noises. 'Mac, thanks. For every-thing. You've been a great friend.'

He turns the key. Of course it doesn't start. We both laugh and then he looks at me. He's wearing a green T-shirt that says *Eat Water: Raft the Colorado.* It looks good on him. Makes his eyes grey as river water.

He tries the ignition again and this time it catches. I start walking back to the house. Quickly, so I don't have to see him drive away.

IT'S POURING ON THURSDAY afternoon when I wake up. Probably a good day to delve into my time-capsule box that I brought home from the wedding. Getting rid of non-essentials always makes me feel good, sort of clean and strong. Still, I sit at the table long after I've eaten my cheese omelette, wondering if it's raining in the San Juans.

Mac said one time that they actually got less rain than Seattle because they were in the rain shadow of the Olympics. He explained what that means, but I can't remember now. Sometimes I think I'm always paying attention, but not to the right things. There was something with Mac— some tension, a dark shape in my peripheral vision. How else do I explain it? The vague restlessness when I wake up. The nagging sense of missed opportunities.

OK, maybe I was distracted, but it wasn't just that. I mean, what about Laura, the ex-girlfriend? I wasn't interested in setting myself up for another rejection. Then there's Gary. And I'm not even divorced yet. It's all happened too fast. What was it John Lennon said? Something about life being what happens to you while you're busy making plans.

I get up and make space on the floor for myself and a giant plastic bag. I slit the tape on the box and dump the contents on the floor.

Engagement calendars. I open one, flip a few pages. Most of the names and places scribbled in the squares don't sound even vaguely familiar. I toss them all in the bag.

I save my high-school graduation tassel, and my high school and college diplomas in their folders. I throw out all the pamphlets CM and I worked on for the National Organisation for Women. A rolled up T-shirt unfurls like a banner, making me laugh. CM gave it to me when my steady boyfriend dumped me just before the senior prom. It says *A woman needs a man like a fish needs a bicycle*.

There are photographs. Halloween party at Zelma Wallis's house. A Polaroid snapshot of CM and me standing by my old black Chevy, leaving for freshman orientation at UCLA. She looks confident, gorgeous, in a dark paisley shirt, bell-bottomed trousers. I'm smiling, but still manage to look grimly determined. I'm wearing a tie-dyed T-shirt and hip-hugger jeans. Three hours later I'll be in the women's rest room of the administration building, throwing up.

My heart aches and so does my stomach. This is worse than breaking up with a man, sitting around mooning over old pictures and remembering the good times. CM and I have been together almost twenty-five years, longer than a lot of married couples. I used to think we were closer than sisters, but now I'm not sure. Sisters at least know they love each other, so they don't always have to like each other.

I'm grabbing handfuls of stuff and jamming it into the bag when a piece of old-fashioned ivory stationery floats out of the pile like a leaf on the wind and settles on my foot. My grandmother's handwriting. It's a letter to my mother, or part of one, probably mixed in with the papers from her cedar chest. As I start to crumple it up, my name leaps off the page.

'. . . *If he really means to leave you, there is nothing you can do to prevent him. You could make things very unpleasant for him; but I don't believe you have the strength of will to pursue that course. So it behoves you to consider other alternatives. Of course, you and Justine are more than welcome to stay with us until you decide what to do.*

God bless you, my dear child, and comfort you. Justine is behaving well and seems to be enjoying herself.

Lovingly, Mother

As I read and reread it, the wheel of my memory turns easily, gracefully, and pictures click silently into place like slides, enlarged, illuminated and projected onto a screen.

They were an unlikely couple. He was handsome, maybe a little bit wild when he was young—daring, adventurous, self-assured. She was pretty, but sweet, quiet, serious. How long before he realised she wasn't enough for him? How long before she knew?

I reach for the phone book that sits under the little drop-leaf table and flick through the A's till I get to Alaska Airlines.

459

Saturday morning at 11.15, I'm standing in front of my mother's house. I ring the bell. When she opens the door and says, 'Wyn! What a wonderful surprise!', the revulsion I feel at the sound of her voice nearly unhinges me. 'How are you? How long can you stay?'

'I need to talk to you about something. Privately.'

Her tone changes instantly. 'What's the matter?'

By this time we're in the den. I set down my bag, and before she can say anything else, I say, 'I found this.' I take the letter out of my jacket pocket, unfold it and hand it to her. 'In that box I brought home after the wedding.'

I see that she knows what it is. She lowers herself onto the couch. Her face turns pale. 'Oh, baby. I'm so sorry you saw this.'

'Please tell me what happened.'

'Wyn, it was so long ago and it wasn't really—'

'Please.'

She scans the page and then lays it on the coffee table. 'When you were four years old, your father decided he was in love with someone else.' Her voice is calm, matter-of-fact.

'Who?' My voice, by contrast, is more like a squeak.

'No one you'd know. She worked in Andersen's Chicago office. He came home from a trip and told me he was in love with her and he asked me to divorce him.'

I've never been anywhere near a tornado, but this is how I think it must be. The black wind howling around you and the dead calm centre. For a second I'm actually dizzy. 'What did you say?'

'I didn't say much. I just cried and got quietly drunk and passed out.' The idea of my mother drinking enough to pass out is hard to grasp. 'He moved into a hotel that night.'

'Where was I?'

'Thank God you were at Oma and Opa's. That week was a nightmare. Your father came over to the house every night to talk about divorce and who would live where and how we would settle you.'

'And you really had no idea he was? . . .'

'None.' She looks away from me, out of the sliding-glass door to the patio. 'He had an attorney. And a list of attorneys that he thought I might want to call. He'd apparently given it quite a bit of thought.'

I see David, sitting on the couch in our den, telling me about the great condo he'd found me. 'So? . . .'

'I begged him not to leave, not to break up the family, but he was determined. I was desperate. I was ready to try anything that might put my world back together.'

I must look thoroughly confused, because she leans closer, peering into my face. 'It wasn't such an everyday occurrence then, you know. Things had to be pretty bad before you resorted to dumping your husband.' She attempts a laugh. 'Divorcées were women who wore too much make-up and frequented cocktail lounges.'

'So what did you say to him?'

'You have to understand, Wyn . . .' She talks about her desperation, her fear, the pain. She hasn't said anything yet about loving him. In my head I'm screaming, cut to the chase, but I sit listening. 'The next time he came over, I was ready. I started with the house and the car. His salary, insurance, a college fund for you. He was very accommodating.' Her eyes sweep up to mine, 'And then I said, "Oh, and one last thing. You will never contact Justine again once the divorce is final."'

My mouth opens slightly in protest. 'You can't do that.'

'Not now.' She smiles faintly. 'Twenty-five years ago men didn't have many rights as far as child custody went. Particularly under those circumstances. Anyway . . .' She shrugs. 'Two days later, he moved back.'

For an instant I see her the way he must have. Beautiful, yes. Always. But no longer accommodating, pliant. He's underestimated her. She's willing to push it to the limit. Exactly the kind of thing he would have responded to. I can see him falling in love with her all over again.

I should say something now; I just don't know what.

'And that, my dear, is pretty much the story. I'm going to have a glass of sherry.' She stands up. 'Would you like something?'

'No. Thanks.'

'It's very good. Quite dry. Richard's favourite.'

She goes to the walnut cabinet that came from my grandparents' town house. Amber liquid splashes into a small crystal glass. Standing there in her black linen slacks and expensive white cotton sweater and a chunky gold necklace I've never seen before, she's gathered all the pieces together. She's Richard's wife, not someone's washed-out widow, fending off her friends' husbands in the kitchen.

She comes back and sits down next to me, sipping her drink. 'We had twelve wonderful years before he died.'

'Why didn't you ever tell me?'

She appears genuinely surprised. 'Why would I do that?'

'So I'd know the truth. About what kind of man he was.'

'Wyn, you've always known the truth. Your father was a good man who made mistakes. Like everyone else. And he loved you more than anything in the world. When I made him choose, he chose you.'

I get up and push open the sliding door to the garden. I sit down on the chaise longue and lie back, put my feet up. The black walnut tree that's thrived there for twenty years shades the whole garden at this time of year. The shells were so tough I used to put them on the drive before my father came home from work so they'd be crushed open by the weight of the car. He used to say that they only tasted good because you had to work so hard for them.

My mother is standing next to me, although I didn't see her come out. She sits down. 'Did we hurt your feelings a lot?' I say.

She gnaws on the inside of her cheek. 'Sometimes I just wanted to be in on the joke. Wanted you to look at me the way you looked at him. Sometimes I even wanted him to look at me the way he looked at you.' Her face is flushed.

It occurs to me that I have no idea who this lovely stranger is. Haven't had for years. What she thought about, wished for, laughed at, loved.

'After he died, people would always say to me, "At least you have Wyn".' She touches my arm. 'But I didn't. There wasn't much left of you. And what there was, you weren't willing to share with me.'

'Momma . . .' The word cracks my voice.

I'm so much bigger than she is, it's hard for her to hold me while I cry, but somehow she does. This hasn't happened in a very long time.

When I get my mail on Tuesday, there's a fat envelope bearing the postmark of Larkspur, California. I rip the end off and an airline ticket drops into my hands. I'd conveniently forgotten that a week from Saturday is the day Gary and I finally agreed on for me to stand inspection.

I should be happier about this. More excited . . . something. I jam everything back in the envelope and toss it on the kitchen table.

Of course, it wouldn't kill me to go down there. It obviously means a lot to him. The thought of his note sends a pleasant little *frisson* of anticipation down my back. Yes, that part of it will be fine. It'll be better than fine.

Everything's always fine, when he's with me. When I'm looking at him, touching him. But when he leaves, that's fine, too. I don't miss him. It's like he's a convenience, like junk food. Satisfies the craving for something sweet, but without any lasting nutritional value. What's wrong with me? He's a person, not a Snickers bar.

He's Gary. Sweet Gary. Who thinks he wants to take care of me. Make me feel good. He wants to take up where David left off. Same story, different setting. Marin instead of Hancock Park. Same shit, different day. *Why did Erica have to go to law school? She was making decent money as a paralegal.* She had it all, didn't she? You can always find another job. You can always make bread at home. He wants me in his life. But it's *his* life, not mine.

I picture CM, leaning across the table. *Does your life make you happy? Is this what you want to do?*

I decide that my first priority is weaselling my way back into CM's good graces. Bread. Not just any bread, but something special. A *couronne*, the crown-shaped loaf. In fact, a double *couronne*, like interlocking wedding rings, will be my peace offering.

If this doesn't make CM call me, nothing will. It smells like heaven. The presentation is another matter. I don't have a box big enough, so I wrap it carefully in a clean tea towel and carry it over to the bakery.

Ellen and Misha stop what they're doing to admire my handiwork.

'It's sort of an engagement present for CM,' I say. 'I need something to put it in.'

'You can use one of those display baskets if you promise to bring it back,' Ellen says.

I arrange the tea towel in the basket and nestle the bread into the centre. Then I pull out a plain white gift card that I bought and I write *To CM, Love, Wyn* in the middle of the card, then as an afterthought, I scrawl *and Neal* next to her name.

Neither of them is home anyway when I take the bread over there, so I leave it with the building manager after making her promise to deliver it the second they come home. I walk home feeling anxious. Like I've just delivered my first-born child into some dubious day-care centre.

Of course Gary's first question is, 'Is there someone else?'

'No, there's nobody else.'

'Wyn, I don't understand. I thought we had something pretty special. Even if you want to call it just sex, where's the harm in seeing if it turns into something more?' The man is a born negotiator.

'It wasn't just sex. You were right. I was saying that to protect myself. The harm is that it's not going to work and the longer we drag it out, the harder it gets to break up.'

'Why are you so sure it isn't going to work?'

'Because I don't want it to work. We have different priorities. I'm not willing to give mine up again.'

'I'm not asking you to give up anything—'

'You don't have to ask. It just happens. Like quicksand. I sink into your life and disappear without a trace.'

He sighs. 'I don't understand.'

'I know you don't. You're just going to have to trust me.'

The silence goes on so long I think he must have hung up. Then: 'Wyn, you sound so confused. Why don't we talk next week—'

It's my turn to sigh. 'What part of this is giving you trouble?'

I wasn't feeling so unwaveringly positive that he couldn't have changed my mind. For example, if he'd said *I love you and we can work around whatever you want to do.* But what he said was, 'Katie and Andrew are going to be really disappointed.'

'Gary, I'm going to hang up now. Take care of yourself.'

I send the ticket back.

Voices wake me. Raucous male laughter. One thirty, Saturday afternoon. I pull on my sweats and open the door. A guy wearing a baseball cap is standing at the corner of the big house, yelling to a guy on the roof.

I step outside. 'Do you mind? I'm trying to sleep.' That old Hancock Park voice still comes in handy once in a while.

He wheels round, stares at me. 'Who are you?'

'I'm the tenant and I'm trying to sleep. Who are you?'

He walks towards me, offering what I'm sure he hopes is a charming smile. 'Sorry. I didn't know there was a tenant.' He holds out a card. 'Marty Crowley, Arvis Brothers Construction. I'm putting together an estimate for Mr Keeler, the owner of the property.'

'Yes. Well . . . I'd appreciate it if you put your estimate together without shouting. I work nights and I'm trying to sleep.'

'We'll be as quiet as we can. I didn't know anyone lived here.'

I go back to bed, but I know I'm not getting any more sleep today. I've lost David. CM. Mac. And now Gary. My house is next. What else could possibly happen?

My grandmother used to say it was tempting Fate to ask questions like that.

The new bartender's name is Shaun. He looks like a very young Kenny—short and squared off, hair the colour of wet sand, pretty blue eyes. He has an engaging crooked grin and calls all the women 'babe' no matter how old they are, and his musical knowledge could be held comfortably in a teaspoon with room left over for sugar.

That's one reason why I don't go to Bailey's much any more.

Kenny's eyebrows lift when he sees me; a huge grin splits his face. 'Hey, lady, where've you been keeping yourself? What are you drinking? It's on the house.'

I laugh. 'In that case, I'll have a glass of your finest red Bordeaux.'

He sets a glass down on a napkin and scoops out a dish of peanuts for me. 'Château Bathtub for mademoiselle.'

'Have you talked to Mac?' I keep my voice casual and pay closer attention to the peanut I'm working on.

'Couple of days ago. Thursday, I think. He said to say hi. Told him I would if you ever showed your face again.'

'How is he?'

'Mac? Fine.'

'What's he doing?'

'He didn't say. I guess he's working on Bensinger's place, mostly.'

I eat another peanut and drink some more wine before I ask, 'Did he say anything about coming back this fall?'

Kenny shakes his head. 'He won't be back. He's talking about driving up to Alaska in September. He always wanted to go up there, you know.'

I rip off a damp corner of the napkin, roll it into a little crumb. 'Does he have a phone or anything?'

Kenny gives me a smile that skates on the edge of pity. 'Nope. There's an emergency number, but it's just a rental agency. You want it? Or you want me to tell him anything next time he calls?'

I think for a minute. 'No. Just tell him hi from me.'

Even though it's the end of June, it's still cool enough at night to use the wood-burning stove. I light a pile of kindling.

So Mac's finally going to Alaska. I rummage through my tape box in search of the last tape he gave me. I've never played it. I turn it over and read the card and I have to smile. Title, artist, record label and running time painstakingly printed for each song. I lay it back in the box and pull out Mozart's Symphony No. 40 in G minor.

On July 1, I call my mother. Just to say hi. I've been doing that every couple of weeks since I came home, and it makes her so absurdly happy that I have to wonder why I never did it before.

After the usual pleasantries, I ask, 'What are you guys doing for the Fourth?'

'We're going down to Long Beach. We're spending the night on the *Queen Mary*. They shoot fireworks off from the bridge.'

'Sounds like fun.'

'I think it will be. Gary and Erica and the kids are coming down.'

I nearly choke. 'I'm sorry. Did you say Gary and Erica?'

'Yes, we were rather surprised when he told us they wanted to come.'

She pauses. 'I'm not sure what's going on. For a while I thought he was rather enamoured of you. Whatever happened with that?'

'I'll tell you all about it some time.'

'He seems like a very sweet boy.'

'He is. Please tell him hi for me. Make sure you say it in front of Erica.'

She gives it her merry laugh. 'Will do.'

Friday is the Fourth of July and the bakery's closed. I was thinking about going down to the waterfront to watch the fireworks, but Cody convinces me that I should go with her and her friend Barton, a hair-stylist, to Gasworks Park to watch the display over Lake Union.

Barton is a tall, thin guy with an infectious grin and bleached blond hair with black roots. He bats his big dark eyes at me. 'I'm Barton. How do you like my shirt?' The shirt in question is a blue Hawaiian number with ugly red flowers all over it.

I laugh. 'It's a great example of the genre.'

'Very tactfully put.'

'Should we take snacks with us?' I ask on the way to Barton's green Plymouth Valiant.

'Barton packed us a gourmet picnic,' Cody says. 'With a flask of his secret recipe Strip-and-Go-Nakeds.'

'Fat, sugar, alcohol, chocolate, hallucinogenics,' he intones. 'All the major food groups.'

Parking is scarce around Lake Union, so we end up having to carry our rugs, basket and cooler for blocks before we find an unoccupied patch of grass. Barton's first official act as host is to pour drinks out of the flask. The concoction is refreshing and lemony; I gulp it down.

'Careful, baby,' he warns. 'It's got the alcohol content of jet fuel.'

I lie down on the rug, balance the glass on my stomach. 'What's in it? Or is that a trade secret?'

'Basically lemonade, vodka and beer. It'll cure whatever ails you, as my granny used to say.'

I watch the stars appear in the slowly dimming sky, listen to Cody and Barton chatter about people they know.

'Wyn, darling, you're quiet over there in your little corner,' Barton says presently.

'She's in pain,' Cody says. 'A busted marriage, two boyfriends gone missing.'

'They weren't boyfriends. One was my stepbrother. The other was just a friend.'

Barton raises one eyebrow like Vivian Leigh in *Gone With the Wind*. 'My, my, my. I have to say, I admire your style.'

'I just don't seem to be very smart about men.' I take another good swig of my drink.

'Now, there's NO pity like SELF-pity!' He does a great Ethel Merman. 'Barton knows what will make you feel better.' He gets up, comes round behind me. 'Sit up, sit up.' When I do, I feel the effects of my one Strip-and-Go-Naked. Before I know what's happening, he's taking my hair down, combing it out. 'You don't mind if I play with your hair. Strictly on a professional basis, you understand. A new do always makes us feel better.'

So we sit, listening to jazz from somebody's boombox, getting high on Strip-and-Go-Nakeds, while Barton braids my hair into plaits. I probably look like the Medusa, but it does feel good.

Finally, at 9.15, the first salvo goes off from a platform in the middle of the lake. I never tire of watching fireworks. They're utterly useless— just beauty for it's own sake, a life span measured in seconds. After the inevitable gut-busting finale, Cody and Barton start packing up our stuff and talking about going to some club on 1st Avenue.

'You guys go ahead,' I say. 'I don't need anything else to drink tonight. I'll catch a bus home.'

'We can take you home first,' Cody says.

'I want to sit here a while. It's too hot to be inside.'

Barton gives me a hug and they disappear into the crowd. I know I should get up and leave now, but a few more minutes won't hurt. I sit up, hug my knees to my chest, rest my forehead on them.

'Are you all right, miss?'

I look up quickly at a middle-aged couple carrying folding chairs. He has a crew cut and nice eyes. Her eyes are cautious.

'I'm fine, thanks.' I stand up, smile at them. 'I was just trying to muster the energy to go to work.'

'Where do you work at this time of night?' he asks.

'The McGraw Street Bakery. On Queen Anne. I bake the bread.'

She says, 'You're kidding. That's where I get my bread. It's wonderful. Especially that new banana cinnamon stuff. You really make all that?'

I think I'm blushing. 'Thanks. I'm glad you like it.'

'I'm excited to meet you,' she says. 'Maybe we'll see you there some time.'

They wave and move towards the street, but I stand still. Waiting for him to appear out of nowhere, like in the movies. Take off his baseball cap. Smile his great smile and say, 'I figured I'd find you here.'

Finally I turn to follow them. The bus driver has his directional signal blinking, ready to pull out. As I run for it, I catch a reflection in the glass doors of a building—someone else trying to catch the bus—a famous bread baker, plaits bouncing in the wind, yelling at the driver to wait. I slide into a seat and catch my breath.

If I were writing a story about myself, it would begin: 'In her thirty-second year, she discovered her Right Livelihood . . .' Or as CM would say, I've discovered what I am. I've peeled off the outer layers one by one—my father's daughter, David's wife, a divorcée—and I find at the core, a baker of bread. A woman who enjoys living alone, who doesn't own a car or a house. Who's happiest in jeans and a flannel shirt. Who chooses friends for the pleasure of their company, not their usefulness. Who's open to love. Or would be, if she could learn to recognise it.

Saturday morning I'm getting ready to hit the sack when there's a knock at the door. I open it and there's Daisy Wardwell, in yellow warm-ups and a white T-shirt, smiling through her perfect make-up. She says she was in the neighbourhood and wanted to stop by and say hi. 'Oh my God, look what you've done to this place.' I can't tell if she's horrified or impressed. 'This is wonderful. It's so . . . warm and inviting.'

'Listen, Daisy, I have a pretty good idea why you're here.'

She gives me a mock pout. 'Yeah, it looks like Mr Keeler's about ready to take over the property again.'

'When do I have to be out?'

'There's no rush. He can't move back in until the house is ready.'

'I guess I better start looking around anyway. You know of anything off hand?'

'Nope. It's not a real great market right now. But we've got a couple of weeks. I'll get on it and see what I can find. Meanwhile, start getting ready, just in case we have to make a fast jump.'

'Yeah, probably a good idea.'

'Sorry, kiddo.' She fluffs her blonde curls.

'No problem. I knew the deal going in.'

I've accumulated an amazing amount of stuff in an amazingly short time. Clothes, books, *batterie de cuisine*, tapes, furniture, linens. I fill boxes with various non-essentials and stack them against a wall.

Tuesday night I'm packing the contents of my desk. It's warm and I've got the windows open, entertaining the neighbourhood with Van Morrison. One of Mac's all-time favourites, 'Cleaning Windows'.

There's nothing specific—I don't hear a noise or see anything, but I have a sense of someone on the porch. I get up and wander into the living room, push open the screen door. CM's sitting on the rail. I think she's been crying, but it's too dark to see for sure.

I fling myself on her, nearly knocking both of us over the rail onto the ground. In a second she's hugging me back and we're both crying and then we're both laughing.

'I love you,' I say, wiping away tears. 'I missed you. Oh God, CM, I'm so sorry. I was such a bitch. I promise I'll dance at your wedding.'

She wipes her eyes on the sleeve of her sweater. 'Thanks for the offer. Unfortunately there's not going to be one. A wedding.'

'What? Why not? What happened?'

She gives me a crooked smile. 'You were right.'

'No I wasn't. I was petty and bitter. And jealous.'

'Maybe.' She laughs. 'But you were still right.'

I slip my arm through hers, pulling her inside. 'Let's have a glass of wine and debrief you.'

We sit Indian-style on the couch with glasses of wine, and she says, 'Thanks for the bread. It was great.'

'Why didn't you call me when you got it? I thought you hated me.'

She shrugs. 'I'm sorry. By that time I was too embarrassed.'

'So what happened?'

'Exactly what you said would happen. He started having trouble with some of the resources he listed for his dissertation. His adviser claimed they didn't exist. So he was exchanging nasty notes with his adviser and then the whole committee got involved and he went into his Olympic door-slamming routine. From there it was a very short drive to me being selfish and not understanding what he was going through. We were fighting every other night and humping like bunnies in between. I got to the point where I was so wound up I started breaking out in this hideous rash under the ring—a sign from God, no doubt.'

She waggles her reddened, puffy ring finger at me. 'Anyway, I threw it at him last night and told him to get his ass out of my apartment. He stormed out and I haven't see him since.' She stops for a long swallow of wine and a sigh. 'How did you know?'

I shake my head. 'I didn't. I was just being petty. And jealous.'

'You were not. You're not that kind of person,' she says firmly.

Which just proves that a true friend is somebody who believes the best of you, even when faced with evidence to the contrary.

'Tell me what's going on with you. What about the stepbrother?'

'He went back to his ex. He was more enamoured of the family lifestyle than of me specifically. And I was starting to have déjà vu. You know—a second term as executive wife, in Marin instead of Hancock Park.'

'Oh well, he was a good Transition Man.'

I treat her to a Linda-style snort. 'The shortest transition in history.'
'How's Mac?'
'Fine. He's up in the San Juans, writing the great American novel.'
Her X-ray vision burns into my brain. 'Too bad. I liked him.'
'I sort of liked him too. But we never got beyond the platonic.'
'Maybe he'll come back to Seattle.'
I start chipping orange flakes of polish off my big toenail.
'And what about all this? Where are you going?' She nods at the boxes.
'The owner's starting work on the house again. I knew it would
happen eventually, but it's not good timing. The market's stagnant.'
'Wyn, just move into my place. As soon as I can get butt-head out.'
'Don't you think you need some peace and quiet? Time to yourself.'
She grins. 'What I need is to have my blood sister around.'

CM goes home and I skip off to work in a rosy glow, which lasts until
about 5.55 in the morning. At that point, Ellen comes in looking like
Death's blue-plate special.
'Diane's gone to Baltimore again,' she says in reply to my questioning
look. 'They think her mother may have suffered another stroke.'
'That's the way the cookie crumbles,' Linda mutters, before heading
for the door, leaving me to arrange the bread on the shelves.
Ellen's floundering this morning. After filling the register, she sinks
into a chair and lays her head on her arms. At a loss for anything inspi-
rational to say, I crank up the espresso machine and tamp the finely
ground coffee into the brew basket. 'Did Diane say when she'd be back?'
Ellen shakes her head. 'She wants to stay there while things are so
precarious. I guess I have to draft Cody again.' She rambles on, talking
more to herself than to me. 'And call all the cake orders for this week
and tell them Diane's gone again.' She turns abruptly. 'Word's going to
get around, you know. That we can't deliver.'
I hand her a steaming mug. 'It's not that we can't deliver. It's just that
we can't deliver what they've ordered.'
She frowns. 'Duh.'
'I'm just saying maybe there are people out there who are looking for
Cody's style of cakes, too. You know, punks and artists and students get
married too. They probably don't all want a white wedding cake with
violets. I'm just saying we might tap into a whole different market.'
She mulls it over, shifting the mocha from one cheek to the other,
before she swallows. 'You may be onto something,' she says. 'I'll have to
talk to Cody about it.'
By Saturday, CM's apartment has been cleansed of all traces of Neal. I

move in on Sunday. Most of my furniture ends up in storage, but Neal had set up a tiny office in one corner of the living room and CM assigns it to me for all my books, papers and tapes. We sleep in shifts in her queen-sized bed, because I'm getting ready for bed about the time she's getting ready to leave for work. It all seems designed to work as smoothly as a set of well-lubed gears, but I'm too used to the luxury of solitude. I call Daisy and tell her I now have the leisure to be particular, but not to stop looking.

One morning as I'm putting the bread out, I notice a well-dressed woman pacing back and forth in front of the door, clutching a briefcase. At 5.45, Ellen appears, shakes the woman's hand and then a guy in a navy suit comes up and they all shake hands. My stomach gives me a couple of well-placed nudges. When Ellen unlocks the door, they follow her in.

'Hi, Wyn,' she says. She doesn't make any move to introduce me to the yuppies, so I just go about my business while the three of them wander around.

I know what this is, but it's not until Ellen goes to her desk and comes back with her old green ledger book that I give up trying to formulate other explanations.

'Wyn, come here a second,' she says eventually. 'I want you to meet Terry Sullivan. With Great Northwest Bread Company. And this is Donna Baird.' We shake hands. 'This is Wyn Morrison, one of our bread bakers. Wyn studied at a *boulangerie* in Toulouse.'

'That's marvellous,' Donna Baird gushes. 'Of course Great Northwest requires that all bakers go through the Great Northwest programme. Just to ensure uniform quality, of course.'

Franchise? Uniform quality? Ellen's having a nervous breakdown, there's no other explanation. Why else would she want to turn the McGraw Street Bakery into a bread machine?

They're through with me, so I head for the back door.

'Hey, where d'ya think you're goin', missy?'

'Your turn to clean up.' I throw my apron in the basket and make myself scarce, leaving Linda to stare after me.

I jog back to CM's. The apartment is uphill from McGraw Street and by the time I burst through the door, I'm gasping for air and I've got a major stitch in my side. I drink a glass of water while I ransack the little desk for my address book, and finally, I sit down and punch in Elizabeth Gooden's number. I need to start working out again. Even if it's only—

'Elizabeth Gooden, please.'

'Speaking.'

'Oh, Elizabeth,' I pant, 'it's Wyn Morrison. I didn't recognise your voice. Why are you answering the phone?'

'Wynter, hi. I'm the first one here. You sound as if you just ran a race.'

I laugh, breathless. 'You're close. Listen, we need to talk. About the divorce,' I gasp. 'I want it now. I mean as soon as possible.'

A few seconds of silence. Then, 'Are you certain?'

'Yes. I'm even willing to make a few concessions—'

She laughs, a cool dry sound. 'No need to go overboard, Wynter.'

'OK, but I'm serious.' My breath is starting to slow.

'And you're absolutely sure this is what you want?'

'Yes. I'm sure.'

'You don't have to tell me, but I have to ask. Why?'

I look around at the cosy tangle of my things with CM's, out of the window to the sapphire-blue water, the buildings of Seattle, golden in the morning sun, and the day is suddenly full of promise.

'I just have better things to do, I guess.'

'OK. I'm going to overnight your husband's financial declaration to you. Go over it with a fine-tooth comb and let me know if anything's missing. We'll proceed from there. OK?'

'OK. Thanks, Elizabeth.'

'You're welcome, Wynter. And congratulations.'

By three o'clock that afternoon I'm back at the bakery. Ellen clearly doesn't want to talk to me, but I corner her in the storeroom.

'Don't do this. You know you'll regret it for ever. Think of what this place will be like as a franchise of the Great Northwest Bread Company.'

She spins round to face me. 'You think I want this?' Tears pool in her eyes. 'I have no choice.'

'Why?'

'Wyn, believe me, I've tried for months to find an independent baker to buy it, but nobody wants to work this hard any more.'

'Months? How long have you known about this?'

She runs a hand through her hair, leaving a floury trail. 'Well, I suspected a long time ago that this was where things were heading. I started putting out feelers after Diane went home the first time.'

'But why do you have to sell?'

'Because I don't know what else to do.' She pulls out a tissue and blots her eyes. 'Diane's not coming back. She's decided to stay in Baltimore and take care of her mother. Anyway'—she lowers her voice—'our partnership agreement states that if one person leaves, the other has to buy her out. I just don't have the money to do that right now.'

'Well, I do.'

'What?'

'I've been making some phone calls. My mother's loaning me thirty thousand dollars against the divorce settlement.'

She laughs ruefully. 'Oh, bless your heart, Wyn, it's a lot more than thirty thousand dollars.'

'Of course. But there's nothing in the agreement that says you have to pay her the lump sum all at once, is there?'

'No . . .'

'So we negotiate. I think Diane will be amenable, don't you?'

She nods slowly, afraid to put her full weight down on this solution for fear it might collapse under her. 'Why do you want to do this?'

I smile. 'It's sort of about missed chances.'

I hold out my hand to shake on it, but she grabs me in a bear hug. 'Wyn, thank you. Thank you so much.'

'That, and I'm looking forward to being Linda's boss.'

Her sudden laughter bounces off the walls of the storeroom.

CM and I are having a celebration dinner. Halibut with a white wine sauce. Puréed acorn squash. Salad of baby lettuces. Champagne.

CM raises her glass. 'To my best friend—now an official bread expert.'

'Yesterday I couldn't spell entrepreneur; today I am one. You know, I don't think one bottle of this is going to be enough. I'll put another one in the fridge.'

As I grab another bottle of champagne, I recognise the music coming from CM's tape deck. It's the tail end of 'Cleaning Windows' by Van Morrison. 'What tape is that?' I ask.

She shrugs. 'I found it in your box. It's got some great stuff on it.'

She hands me the card. Twelve songs. Title, artist, record label, running time.

'It's the tape Mac gave me when he left.' On the back he scrawled, *Remember to listen.*

'Let me see it.' She pulls it out of my hand and studies it while I fill our glasses.

'I'm starving. Let's get dinner started.' I turn on the fire under the sauté pan, but CM reaches round me and turns off the burner.

'You need to listen to this,' she says. She takes my hand and pulls me over to the futon. 'Don't you see what this is? It's about you.'

'Give me a break.'

'Look at these songs.' She waves the card and reads, "Brown-Eyed Girl". That's you—'

'Right. After all, I *am* the only woman in the world with brown eyes.'

She ignores me. '"Sally Go Round the Roses"—That's about finding your significant other with someone else. "Changing Horses"—about breaking up. "Tangled up in Blue" . . .' She pushes her hair behind her ears and flops down next to me.

'It's just a coincidence. He likes Dylan.'

'You don't believe that. Look at this . . .' She laughs. '"Coldwater Canyon"—obviously Gary. "Cleaning Windows"—that's Mac.'

'You have a vivid imagination.'

'"I Only Have Eyes for You". That's so romantic—'

'It's not romantic, it's just—'

'Just what?'

I stare at the lights of the city framed in her window. 'It's what was on the radio the night he drove me to the hospital in the snow.'

'Wyn, call him.'

'He doesn't have a phone. Besides, even if you're right, which I don't think you are, he made that months ago—'

'No excuses. No, you need to go up there. Take the Camry. It's only about an hour and a half to Anacortes. Then you get on the ferry.'

The last song is playing now. 'The Dimming of the Day' by Richard Thompson.

'CM, don't do this to me. I was just getting used to his being gone.'

She folds her arms and gives me her green-eyed stare. 'If i'm wrong, you'll have plenty of time to get used his being gone. If I'm right . . .'

The ferry glides through a dreamscape of islands that emerge from the fog and then disappear back into it. I've been hearing about the San Juans ever since I moved to Seattle, but this isn't what I imagined—no sandy beaches, no palm trees. Just rocky, conifer-covered mountains thrusting up from the cold blue Pacific.

The ferry's metal ramp clangs down on the Orcas landing, and the Camry bounces cautiously onto the road.

I'm scared. Like riding my two-wheeler for the first time after my father removed the training wheels. I have no plan, no idea what to say to Mac when I see him. I'm just pedalling. God, why did I let CM bulldoze me into this fool's errand? What if he doesn't feel that way any more? What if he never did? I bang my palm on the steering wheel. Goddamn him. This whole mess could have been avoided if he'd just had the balls to say something to me.

Soon I'm cruising along the Horseshoe Highway towards Eastsound. In the village I park outside Jamie Johnson Real Estate.

'I'm Wyn Morrison,' I tell the receptionist, 'Rick Bensinger talked to someone about my getting a map to his cabin.'

'Oh, yes. I'll mark it on the map for you. It's real easy,' she says.

I lay the photocopied map on the passenger seat. Back on the Horseshoe Highway a sign warns potential oyster rustlers to keep off the oyster beds. In a few minutes I start to see tantalising glimpses of water on the left. Half a mile later, a sign announces Madrone Cottage.

I slam on the brakes even though I'm not going that fast, and turn in, bumping up the rutted drive.

A white clapboard bungalow appears suddenly, poised on the edge of a meadow as if preparing to dive in. The Elky sits on a patch of gravel beside the covered porch. He finally got the fender painted.

I park near a clump of trees about twenty yards from the house and get out, closing the door gently. I can smell the sea, but the only visible ocean is the swaying green and gold meadow grass. A squirrel's piercing chatter makes me jump like a guilty trespasser.

Bob Dylan's nasal twang blasts out of the open window. 'Subterranean Homesick Blues'. I'm almost at the porch when the music stops.

'I'm going for a run. You coming?'

Obviously he's not alone. My heart thuds in my ears, less a noise than a vibration. If I circle round into the trees, I can wait and see who he's with. If it's a guy, fine. If it's a woman, I need to decide whether to humiliate myself or just slink back to the ferry landing.

Two steps into the tall grass, my left foot hydroplanes and sinks up to the ankle in thick black mud. Shit! My brand-new cross trainers. I nearly fall down trying to pull it out. Wouldn't that be a great scene. He walks out with—God knows who—and here I am floundering around like a rhinoceros on a wet clay bank.

Before I can decide whether or not to bolt, the door opens and a face looks out. A face with button eyes and a black nose. A scruffy yellow dog. As soon as he catches my scent, he bristles and starts growling.

'You protecting me from a vicious squirrel?' A stranger steps out, dressed in running shorts and a sweatshirt with the sleeves cut off to reveal tanned, muscled arms. His sun-streaked hair is pulled back in a low ponytail and he has a full beard. But his eyes are Mac's.

'Wyn.' His gaze ends up on my feet. 'You're all muddy.'

'You have a gift for stating the obvious.'

Yellow Dog decides I'm OK. He bounds down the steps and starts licking my leg with his warm, sandpapery tongue.

'I don't know quite what to say,' Mac says.

At least he looks pleased.

'Must be a first for you.' I bend down to scratch the dog's ears.

'How did you get here?'

I look over my shoulder at CM's Camry. 'Drove to Anacortes and took the ferry over.' I pause awkwardly, then flounder on. 'This place is so . . . magical. It's not what I expected.'

'It's great, isn't it?' When he smiles, my stomach turns upside-down.

I ease down on the top step and extract my foot from the gooey cross trainer, peel off the filthy sock. 'I'll get something to clean your shoe,' he says. He comes back with a putty knife and a rag, then sits down next to me and takes the shoe.

I rummage around for a clean, unwrinkled smile to wear. 'What have you been working on?'

'Painting. Inside and out. Fixed the roof. Built a storage shed.' While he talks, he cleans the muck off my shoes. 'I think you're going to have to scrub this one down.'

His expression I remember from the first time I met him. Open, direct. But no longer anonymous. I know certain telling details now. Like he can't stand his brother and he gets one haircut a year. He likes Raymond Chandler and John Irving. That he loves the blues and songs that tell stories. Riding the ferries just to be on the water.

'Or you could hang out here till the mud dries. Then it'll brush off.'

I want to run a finger down the muscle in his arm that contracts when he grips my shoe. 'I don't want to keep you from your run.'

He stands up. 'I can always run. Come on in. I want to show you something.'

He pushes the door open, and I step past him into the pleasantly musty interior. Bookshelves overflow with books and board games. An old maroon couch. Rag rug. Brick fireplace.

'It's cosy. Like a grandma's house.'

For a minute I almost think he might take my hand, but he turns and walks into the next room. 'In here.'

The kitchen floor slants crazily away from the rest of the house. There's a vintage Wedgewood gas stove, a refrigerator, a battered wooden table and three chairs. In the centre of the table is a cardboard manuscript box. He's looking at the box, not at me, so I reach over and lift the lid.

Accident of Birth
A novel by
Matthew Spencer McLeod

He's trying to look modest and self-effacing, but without success.

I smile, momentarily forgetting that I'm pissed off at him. 'Oh my God, Mac. You must have worked your butt off.'

'I kept thinking about what you said—that if I thought of myself as a bartender who wrote stuff, that's what I'd be. So I decided to try thinking of myself as a writer who needed a day job.' He gives me his little wry grin. 'Well, are you going to tell me why you came all the way up here? Or am I supposed to guess?'

'Why not? You made me guess.' My voice breaks embarrassingly, like a kid entering puberty. 'In fact, I'm really pissed off at you.'

He looks puzzled. 'Why?'

'How dare you give me that tape then skip town like a fugitive? Why didn't you say something?'

'I could have, but I didn't. You weren't listening anyway. You were too busy fooling around with your brother.'

'He's my stepbrother. Quit trying to make it sound like incest.'

'You could have said something, too, you know.'

'What would I say? Stop mooning around about Laura and try—'

'Laura?' He stares at me.

'Yes, Laura. You were wrecked after you saw her at that party with somebody else.'

'I wasn't wrecked. I was half asleep from staying up all night, and then just when things started to get interesting, your brother—your stepbrother—showed up with the whole flower mart in his arms.'

'But you were all depressed and grouchy for days after that—'

He shakes his head. 'God, I was grouchy because I was getting so involved with you, and you obviously had other fish to fry. I just figured it would be better if I got out of town for a while.' He eyes me accusingly. 'You didn't have to wait all summer to get in touch with me.'

'I just heard the tape yester—a few days ago.'

'Why did you wait so long?'

'I couldn't listen to it because I missed you,' I say crossly.

'I missed you,' he says, and the feeling I've been holding under house arrest all summer suddenly escapes, flaring up in my chest.

'Kenny said you were going up to pollute Alaska.'

'That's the plan.' I look out of the window again, and he makes the three feet between us disappear. 'Why don't you come with me?'

'McLeod, you make me cry and you're roadkill.'

He laughs right before he kisses me. His mouth is warm and smells of freshly cut pine and woodsmoke and meadow grass.

I put a hand up to touch the beard.

'Too scratchy?' he says.

I try rubbing it in different directions. 'I can see how it might work.'

'Come to Alaska with me. It would be so—'

'Can't.' This is where I nearly lose it.

'Why not?'

I press my lips together. 'You're looking at the proud half-owner of the McGraw Street Bakery.'

'So the divorce is? . . .'

'Practically a *fait accompli*.'

He smiles. 'Is that anything like a done deal?'

The second kiss is longer, more interesting. Mac holds me against him in a way that leaves very little doubt as to his intentions.

When we break for air, he says, 'On the other hand, fall's probably not the best time to go to Alaska.'

'Maybe you should play it by ear,' I suggest. 'At least until spring.'

There's a pause, no more than a space between heartbeats. I feel as if he's about to make some monumental pronouncement, but he just winds a strand of my hair around his finger and says,

'At least.'

JUDI HENDRICKS

It will come as no surprise to anyone reading *Bread Alone* that its author, Judi Hendricks, is just as passionate about breadmaking as her heroine, Wyn. She has always been an enthusiastic baker and after a course at cookery school in Seattle, she worked for a short time as a professional cook at a gourmet takeout. This was followed by a longer stint at the McGraw Street Bakery, a small neighbourhood bakery near her house in Seattle. She quickly became fascinated by breadmaking and did a lot of experimenting at home. 'I cook almost all my own bread. I usually bake a huge batch and put it in the freezer. I like variety, so I have to keep trying different things.'

Judi Hendricks is a woman with many interests, and, as well as her recent job as a baker, has worked in a number of different areas. 'I have a very short attention span,' she says. 'I think that's why I love writing fiction, because if you get bored you just start writing about something else.' After gaining a degree in journalism, she began her working life on a newspaper in New Orleans, but over the years she has also worked in the travel industry, running her own travel agency for a while as well as working for Delta Airlines in various capacities. As an employee of Delta she was able to indulge one of her other great pleasures: travel. She took advantage of the cheap fares avail-

able to staff and travelled abroad as often as she could. She was a frequent visitor to Europe, particularly to France and the United Kingdom. She says that nowadays she is less interested in trying to cram everything in when she travels. 'We still love going to Europe but now we are more inclined to stay in one place and explore the environs.'

Judi Hendricks always wanted to be a writer but found the demands of everyday living meant that she never got down to writing creatively. Then a serious operation to remove a benign brain tumour led her to re-evaluate her life. 'I came out of surgery and figured that, if I wanted to write, I should get going.' *Bread Alone* took four years and six re-writes before it was finished. 'I think that was due to the fact that I'd never written anything longer than thirty pages before then. *Bread Alone* was my self-taught course in fiction writing.' After her training as a journalist she finds the freedom of fiction exciting. 'It's so much more fun to be able to make up stories instead of recording exactly what you see.' She even enjoys re-writing. 'That's like decorating the cake once it's baked. That's the fun part. You get to do all the embellishments and shave off the unnecessary things.' She is currently hard at work on her second novel, which she describes as being very different from *Bread Alone* and much darker. But fans of her mouth-watering descriptions of bread will be pleased to know that it *will* feature food.

Sally Cummings

Printed and bound by Maury Imprimeur SA, Malesherbes, France

601-013-1